COURT OF SHADOWS

BLADE AND ROSE SERIES BOOK 3

MIRANDA HONFLEUR

Cover art by Mirela Barbu

Proofreading by Patrycja Pakula at Holabird Editing

Paperback ISBN: 978-0-9994854-5-3

First Edition: February 2018

http://www.mirandahonfleur.com/

ALSO BY MIRANDA HONFLEUR

Blade and Rose Series

"Winter Wren" (available on www.mirandahonfleur.com)

Blade & Rose (Book 1)

By Dark Deeds (Book 2)

Court of Shadows (Book 3)

Queen of the Shining Sea (Book 4)* *Available October 2018*

Enclave Boxed Sets

*Of Beasts and Beauties** *Available April 2018*

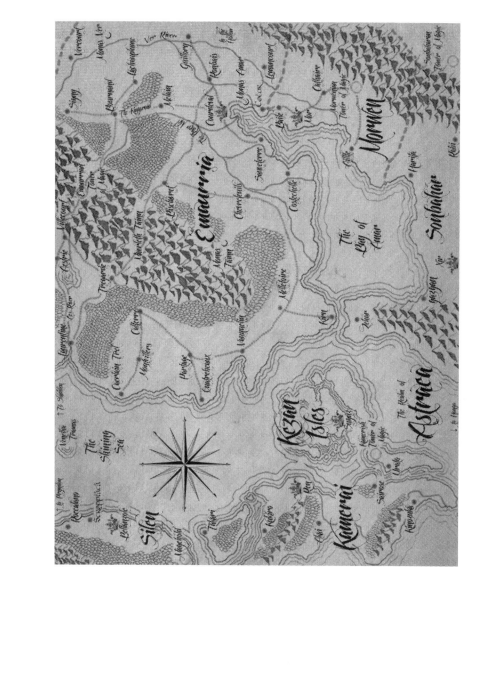

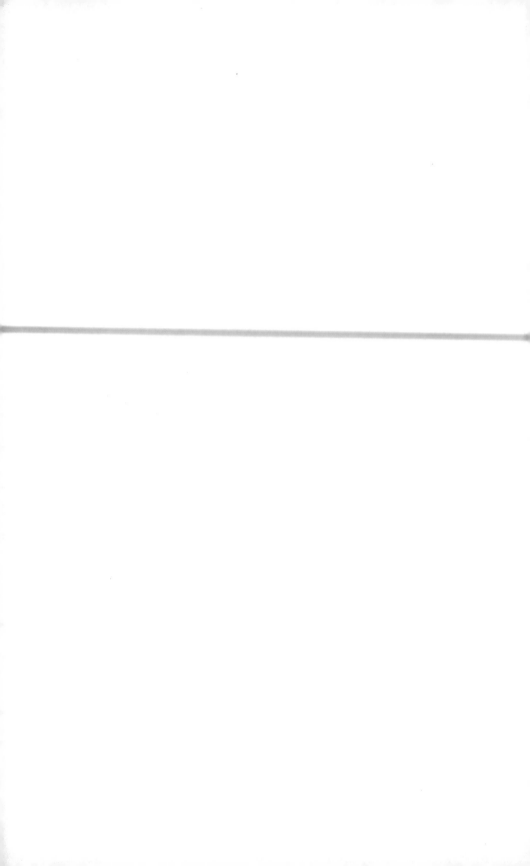

CHAPTER 1

*I*f dirty looks were daggers, she'd be a pincushion.

Forcing a smile, Rielle reached for her wine goblet. She sipped the full-bodied red, glancing away from Duchess Caterine's cold smile to Nora's piercing glare across the gleaming purple-heartwood table.

Warmth rested on her knee, Brennan's palm, even as he remained still and entirely at ease next to her.

Just get through dinner. Get through dinner. Just dinner.

His youngest sisters, Caitlyn and Una, were better, at least. Their looks weren't pointy, or at least pointed *elsewhere*. Twirling a curly lock of dark hair, Caitlyn feigned interest in her wild-mushroom soup, her perfectly shaped eyebrows raised. Her tight-laced teal gown, much like Nora's, cinched in a tiny waist, so feigning interest in food was likely an everyday practice.

Una wore a mischievous grin as her gaze slid from the duchess to Nora to Brennan. Other than those Marcel hazel eyes and her beautiful face, she couldn't have been more different than her sisters, her hair pulled back in a tight bun at the nape of her neck and her clothes the height of fashion— men's fashion, just like Brennan. At least she'd left her sword behind for dinner.

All three Marcel sisters had done little more than scrutinize her, although she'd done nothing more than the same herself. But since she'd arrived, it had been nothing but cold glares, whispered gossip, and bitter silence from everyone, even the help. She sighed inwardly.

"An autumn wedding," Duchess Caterine declared, her full smile in no way matching her bitter green glare. Her face was cold and unblemished like ice, with but the finest of lines daring to mark her classic beauty. She exhaled a light breath and waved a jewel-encrusted hand. "It's been a very, very, *very* lengthy engagement, hasn't it?"

Nora huffed a half-laugh, staring Rielle down across the table. Somehow she made even such an ugly expression effortlessly beautiful. "Some length was needed to allow for distractions, wasn't it?"

Brennan's eyelids lazily hooded his eyes as he exhaled slowly, sprawled in his high-backed chair like a jungle cat. A tall, well-muscled, criminally handsome jungle cat. "Nora..."

A grin. "I didn't mean *yours*, dear brother. Although that list is lengthy, too, isn't it, Bren?"

More wine. Definitely more wine. Rielle tipped the goblet and eyed the half-empty decanter. Her lifeline from this torture was quickly diminishing as the meal dragged on.

Two weeks ago, Brennan had been the one with the fever, and yet she'd been the one to suggest complete madness. *Maerleth Tainn, home of the Marcels. Why not? What could possibly go wrong?*

"Are you enjoying the wine, Favrielle?" Duchess Caterine asked. "Should you be drinking so much of it while with child?"

Coughing, Rielle set down the goblet and drew the napkin across her mouth. *Divine's flaming fire—*

"What poise," Nora mumbled, while Una chuckled under her breath.

"W-with child?" Rielle cleared her throat. "Your Grace, I am—"

"A wedding—my *son's* wedding—in but a few months," Duchess Caterine said matter-of-factly with a pleased sniff. "There's no doubt—"

"She's not with child, Mother." Leaning back in his chair, Brennan swirled his brandy slowly, then took a drink. His voice was dismissive, apathetic, although he blinked slowly, staring into his glass, wistfully almost.

Castle Tainn's great hall was massive, its twelve-foot-high double doors far, far from this dinner table. And the harpist was either hard of hearing or well practiced in letting no reaction show on his face. Did he ever consider tossing aside the harp and running as far and as fast away as his slippered feet could carry him? Rielle swallowed. If he did, she might follow.

"Not with child? Why not?" Nora crossed her slender arms over her chest and raked her with a disdainful once-over. "Are you barren?"

A fireball. No, an ice spike—

"It comes as a complete surprise," Brennan said with a yawn, "that no suitors are fighting one another for the honor of courting you, Nora. Especially when you're so well mannered."

Nora slid another smug look Rielle's way. "I'm still feeling quite contented by my *last* suitor, thanks."

He didn't seem to feel the same way about you.

But Rielle bit her tongue before the words could leave her

mouth. Jon wasn't hers to fight over. Not anymore. Some other woman no doubt claimed him now, as well as all the jealousy that went hand in hand with loving a king. These barbs didn't matter, and if Nora and Jon so chose, they could "content" each other all they wanted.

Rielle folded her arms in her lap and turned to Duchess Caterine with a smile. "We want to marry this autumn because, as you said, Your Grace, it's been a lengthy engagement, and we don't want to wait longer than is necessary." Before the duchess could reply, she continued, "I realize it's an inconvenience, and I beg your pardon. But I ask for your sympathy in this," she said, glancing at Brennan. At his soft hazel eyes. His long, dark lashes. His warm, subtle smile. His strong, loving arms.

She wasn't doing this for Duchess Caterine, or Brennan's beautiful sister with the personality of a lemon. She was doing this for *him*, for herself, for their future.

She turned back to the duchess. "Your son is an honest, loyal, honorable man. Strong and supportive. Loving and kind. And I don't wish to delay the moment I become his wife. Not a month longer than necessary. Not a day."

Duchess Caterine's eyes widened, their ice fading to warmth as a corner of her mouth turned up.

Brennan cleared his throat. "You forgot charming."

Rielle pursed her lips.

"And devastatingly handsome." A completely straight face.

She narrowed her eyes at him even as a grin fought its way out. "Of course, yes, I did forget *some*thing... *Humble*. How silly of me."

He shrugged, his face schooled to the merest fraction of amusement as he took another drink of his brandy. "Next time you'll remember, won't you? For the sake of thoroughness, of course."

"You two," Una said with a slow shake of her head and a twist of her thin lips. "You'll make my dinner return for a visit right here at the table."

Caitlyn's shoulders rippled girlishly with silent laughter, but she didn't look up from her wild-mushroom soup. She was either a fungophile or practiced restraint along with the harpist... Yet not nearly the expert he was, however.

Duchess Caterine sighed and set down her napkin. "On *that* pleasant note, perhaps it's best we retire."

No more sought-after words had ever been spoken.

"And Favrielle"—the duchess eyed her softly—"planning a Marcel wedding in but a few months is a nightmare—"

Rielle winced.

"—but I'm pleased that you two are eager to begin your life together. Perhaps you'll consider joining us when we summer in Silen, so that we might all get to know one another better." With that, she stood, as did everyone, and she left the table, gliding elegantly toward the doors and out.

Summer in Silen... This was a small step, but a *step*, nonetheless, in the right direction. And she wouldn't miss it.

To go, she'd have to report to the Tower of Magic first and put in for time off.

Time off—

Nora gave her a sharp look, turned on her heel, and stormed off. Caitlyn sketched a curtsy, and she, too, departed, her so-very-interesting soup uneaten.

Una, tall and lean, adjusted her doublet over her trousers in a crisp pull, and bowed. "If you can give as good as you get, Favrielle, we'll make a Marcel of you yet." She offered a friendly smile.

The first she'd gotten from any of the other Marcels here. Rielle returned the expression. "I'm open to tips."

Una winked. "Here's one... Always remember there's nothing in this world our mother loves more than *her precious son.*"

Brennan shot her a sardonic grimace.

"But you seem to have mastered *that* tip already," Una finished with a lilt, then bowed and, with a confident stride, followed Caitlyn out.

Una's bit of warmth was promising; maybe fitting in with Brennan's family wouldn't be so impossible after all. Even as they traded barbs and cold glares, they were loyal to one another when it mattered, they loved one another, they cared for their own. They never forgot their shared blood, and it was a note of an older song she'd heard around the dinner table with Mama and Papa, Liam, Dominique, Viviane, and Dorian, one she hadn't heard in ages and now longed to hear again.

As the servants began to clear the massive table, Brennan's warm hand closed around hers. Around the one wearing a ring with a garnet the size of her eye—a jewel that had been in his family for centuries. An engagement gift.

"She likes you," he murmured, with a playful half-laugh.

"Well, one Marcel is progress."

A slow grin. "*I* like you, too. Or have you forgotten?"

As a big, dumb smile claimed her face, she looked away and shook her head. He was impossible. Completely, utterly, wonderfully impossible.

"Oh, you have?" His voice was a low, seductive rumble. "I'll have to... remind you."

The rumble rolled through her, slow, throbbing under her skin, warm and warmer until the heat made her want to fan herself.

Not that she *would*. At least not in front of him.

His thumb stroked her knuckles in slow, delicious circles

that melted away her composure. Why did he tease her like this? Her heartbeat pulsed against her chest, so loudly he would hear even if he weren't a werewolf. Divine, she was making a fool of herself.

He tucked her hand around his arm. "How about some air?"

Swallowing, she nodded. Where had her voice gone? He walked her out of the great hall and toward the courtyard at a leisurely stroll.

It had been a couple of weeks since they'd left Stroppiata. Since she'd told him about refusing the papers to dissolve their betrothal. All this talk of weddings, events, and so on, and they hadn't even *kissed* yet.

And as for their future, everyone seemed to expect she'd retire to Laurentine or Tregarde, stay in the castle, bear one heir after another. Some time off from the Tower was one thing, but give up field operations? Give up on using her magic to help others altogether?

It wasn't in her to sit on her hands when they had the power to help someone somewhere. As a mage, she had a responsibility to use her gift for the greater good. Brennan knew that. He wouldn't expect what everyone else did.

And as for heirs—

She crumpled. After losing Sylvie, even thinking about having another child right now was out of the question. She'd told him that and he'd agreed, but—

Footmen opened a set of doors, and then she and Brennan were out in the spring evening, heading toward the circle of nine Emaurrian hazel trees that had stood for over a thousand years. One had been planted for each Marcellan king before the Farallan dynasty had come to power. Although the Lothaires had never had such strong claims to royalty, Mama had planted a Suguz pine to mark the birth of each one of her children. After the fire, only one remained.

And at the center of the Emaurrian hazels was a pool, a serene surface over a powerful Vein of anima deep below, reflecting a glittering tapestry of a million stars above.

Tiny white blooms dotted their path. Jasmine. She inhaled their sweet scent as Brennan covered her hand with his.

They'd both agreed to take things slow, but nevertheless, she brushed her fingertips along her lonely lips. *Still there.*

Since Stroppiata, she and Brennan had been inseparable, spending nearly every waking minute together, even sleeping side by side, but... he hadn't kissed her. Not even once. Hadn't pushed for more. No, he'd driven her mad with longing, anxiety, and pathetic, girlish angst.

A part of her still remembered that patience was a virtue. Barely.

When they made it to the circle of hazels, he stopped, turned her to face him, then walked her back under a tree's canopy until she collided lightly with a trunk. He planted his palms against the pale gray-buff bark on both sides of her face and leaned in. Close.

His eyes searched hers beneath dark, drawn brows, the scent of cinnamon spice, cypress, and *him* strong, heady, delightful, and she breathed him in, deeper, fighting her needy fingers that longed to touch him, to keep touching him, to never stop.

"Has it been long enough?" he whispered, his voice an octave deeper than his usual low baritone.

Her pulse quickened. "What?"

"Being so close to you every day, every night, sleeping next to you, all the while denying everything I wish to do to you"—he shook his head, his muscular chest heaving beneath his fitted black-brocade doublet—"that's asking much. But you expect me to watch your fingers brush these lips"—his voice dropped, and his gaze lowered to her mouth—"coy, teasing, provocative... and not take you right here in this garden, hard upon the grass?"

She didn't breathe. Didn't move. Kept her eyes locked on the intensity of his.

"You wanted to take things slow. That's what you said in Stroppiata." Tension kept his body as rigid as the hazel she pressed against.

A breeze rustled the leaves, made her shiver.

"Has it been long enough?"

The need charging her fingers—she let it have its way, let them stroke up his firm chest to the warm skin of his neck, up over the bristly stubble of his jaw to cup his face in her hands. The intensity in his eyes turned amber, wild, werewolf, but she didn't fear him; she only feared not touching him, not continuing to touch him until her fingers forgot themselves and she could no longer tell her own flesh from his.

"Far too long," she whispered, and she'd barely spoken the last word before his mouth covered hers, seared her lips like a hot brand.

She embraced him as his hard body pressed into hers, as his hands held her to him, their touch firm as they planed up her body, turning her so his own back crashed against the bark.

His fingers buried into her hair, a large palm cradling her head as he deepened the kiss, as his tongue sought hers, devouring her with a fury that made her lower body throb; the need spread to her belly, where she leaned into him, against his hardness, against everything she wanted and shouldn't yet want and would take with all the greed that had coiled in her body these many nights.

"Tell me you love me," he hissed against her lips, and it was all she could do to moan into his mouth. "*Tell* me." He growled, deep in his throat, and rolled his hips against her, and Divine's flaming fire, she could weep for the long, long way to their bedchamber—

"My lord," a timid voice called from a distance.

"*Not. Now*," he growled around her mouth, his voice more beast than human, but she broke away. He stared down at her, heaving breath after heavy breath, amber eyes bright, intense.

She couldn't agree more.

"I beg your p-pardon, my lord, but it's an urgent—"

"*What*," he snarled, those irises glancing the man's way and fading to his human hazel.

"—message for Her Ladyship, from Laurentine."

From home? Frowning, Rielle smoothed her skirt and approached the man, who closed the distance to her and handed her a wax-sealed note as he bowed deeply.

The bright fist—Olivia's seal of the Archmage.

"Thank you," she said, and cracked it open.

"You are welcome, Your Ladyship. Please f-forgive the intrusion."

She nodded and gestured a candlelight spell above her as she unfolded the parchment.

Pirates raiding the coast of Laurentine at dawn of 21 Germinal. Jon has turned the Emaurrian Army north there from the surrounding villages after defeating the basilisks.

"That's today," she whispered.

At *home*.

Her home.

How many were dead? How many injured? How was the defense faring? How long would it take her to get there?

The fire of ten years ago burned in her mind anew, but she blinked it away. She wasn't that scared little girl anymore, or the fractured woman of months ago. Not anymore.

Her people counted on her to keep them safe, and if the pirates got past Laurentine's knights and city guard, then she needed to be there to protect them, no matter what.

She looked over her shoulder at Brennan, who pushed off from the tree, buttoning his doublet.

"What is it?" he grunted.

She handed him the message. "I need to leave tonight. Now."

He lowered his chin and frowned. "Why? Can't the army and—"

"No," she shot back. "I'm not leaving anything to chance."

A sigh. "I'll order our horses saddled. Gather what you need, and we'll leave as soon as you're ready."

CHAPTER 2

With his sabaton, Jon rolled a man over on the beach and peered at him. Arrow through the chest. Dead. He heaved a sigh.

"Tell me at least one is alive," he called to Olivia, who crouched beside another pirate.

The wind battered past them and the squad of Emaurrian soldiers and paladins in the sand. She tucked a stray lock of blood-red hair behind her ear, its color matching the spatter on her face—no doubt his own was just as gory.

She looked up at him and shook her head. "Afraid not."

He grimaced. The day before, they'd routed the invading force, repelling them from the castle city and decimating their rear guard as the bulk of the invaders took boats back to their ships. A fleeting victory, but time to shore up defenses.

Off the coast, a fleet of pirate ships lay in wait—two carracks, a twenty-gun brig, and half a dozen schooners and sloops. Raiders that had been brazenly pillaging Emaurria's western coast.

A number of small parties had returned in the night, only to be destroyed by Laurentinian archers from the cliffs. His officers hadn't coordinated well enough with Laurentine's Captain Dufresne to ensure there was at least *a* survivor to question.

Olivia approached, dusting off her brown-leather mage coat and staring out at the ships bobbing on the rough waters. "Scouting parties," she declared.

He nodded. "They want to know our numbers, determine how many I'll leave behind so they can wait us out in *greater* numbers... while they send the remaining ships up and down the coast to raid the villages." It was a poorly kept secret that the Royal Emaurrian Navy currently had very few ships to its name —among them the carrack HMS *Isabelle*, currently stationed in the Bay of Amar, and that Emaurria had no strong ties to any country that would send naval forces to assist.

Least of all Silen, after Aless had left.

And he wasn't about to split his forces so the pirates could sack Laurentine. Especially as it was Emaurria's primary ship-building hub.

But neither could he allow them to raid the nearby villages.

A plan. Terra help him, he needed a plan. Now. Either that, or at least double his current army. Triple would be even better.

If he could just use his Earthbound powers, this would be over in an instant.

He closed his eyes, picturing himself and Olivia on the beach, the sand, the surf, the waves coming into shore—

"Don't even think about it," Olivia snapped. "I told you, after what you did with Stonehaven, it's too much strain on your heart. You've gotten worse each time."

Strain or no strain, if he ran out of options, he would use his Earthbound powers. He wasn't about to let an entire city fall for an extra day or two of his own life.

"They'll send another scouting party." Olivia passed him by and headed for the gates of Laurentine.

He followed. "Another scouting party we'll defeat," he called to her. "But we need at least one of theirs alive."

She slowed down, and he caught up with her. Together with his squad of Royal Guard, they made their way into the city and back to the command post set up within the castle's high-ground inner bailey. With a clear view of all surroundings, it was the perfect vantage point.

Through the bustling activity in the camp, he and Olivia approached the command tent and entered. The map was just where he'd left it, and just as impossible as he'd left it. He leaned over the table, scouring it for any new revelations, and moved aside a spyglass.

Miraculously, no new insights fought for priority.

Since negotiating the terms of Stonehaven's surrender, it had been one thing after another. Minotaurs in Villecourt. Gorgons in Aestrie. Basilisks north of Caerlain Trel. And now pirates in Laurentine. Olivia had joined him in Caerlain Trel with a company of fresh troops and a plea that he not miss his own coronation next week.

Which was highly probable unless they devised a plan to handle these pirates. He raked his fingers through his hair.

"We can't stay here indefinitely," Olivia said. "And you need to sleep. You've barely rested since you left Vervewood." She looked him over with the worried frown that said *Because of your heart problem* without speaking a word at all. After she'd joined him, she hadn't left his side, quartering in adjoining rooms or having her tent pitched right next to his, an ear perked in case he should start screaming his dying throes and need healing. And that same worried frown more often than not.

He wasn't dead *yet*. "I'm not leaving until they do."

Captain Dufresne led the city's forces, including the long-bowmen stationed on the cliffs. As useful as they were, there was still no way to effectively reach the pirates.

And no amount of staring at the map would change that. "We need mages," he said, his voice low.

"I sent for Ella and Cédric, but they're still—"

"Fighting the wyverns. I know."

"And Pons—"

"Managing Courdeval."

"And the Order of Sages—"

"Assisting the paladins with the harpy invasion outside of Melain." The Order of Sages was small and fledgling to begin with, and they had their hands full. He pinched the bridge of his nose and exhaled. She well knew he wasn't referring to individual mages, but the entire Emaurrian Tower. "Olivia—"

"I know," she bit out, and moved to stand next to him. "I can't in good faith advise you to break international law. We haven't exhausted all diplomatic options with the Div—"

"What options?" He indicated the map with a sweep of his hand. "I've sent for more mages. Offered the Grand Divinus any price."

Olivia bowed her head and cleaned her nails. "We need to—"

"Your Majesty," a man's voice interrupted from outside the tent.

Jon straightened. "Enter."

The tent flap opened, and a squire came in. "Riders, Your Majesty, up on the cliffs. Orders?"

Enemy scouts taking a new route? Jon grabbed the spyglass and left the tent, rushing for the wall. He took the stairs two at a time until he reached the battlements, then panned the spyglass to the cliffs south of the city walls.

"Is it her?" Heavy breaths next to him came from Olivia.

"Her?" He focused on two figures on horseback. Long, straw-blond hair in a braid. Rielle with a dark-haired man riding alongside. Brennan. *Terra's troth.* He clenched his teeth. "I told you not to disturb her."

"With all due respect, to hell with that."

He looked away from the spyglass to shoot her a scowl.

She shrugged. "These are her lands. It is her right to know."

He focused back on the cliff.

"Orders, sire?" the squire asked from behind him.

"It's the marquise. Hold fire."

"Yes, sire." With that, his footsteps departed.

Olivia was right; of course she was right. And yet, a dark mood settled on him like a heavy shroud. He'd wanted to handle this on his own. *For* Rielle. *Without* Rielle. Especially after their last night together in Courdeval nearly a month ago.

A comfort, handling this alone. An *immature* comfort. One Olivia was too wise to allow him. She gave him as much space as a vise, but sometimes good friendship was pushy... as much as it irked.

In the distance, Rielle dismounted her horse, her turquoise cloak trailing, and stalked to the cliff's edge. Facing the coast, she raised her hands.

Out on the Shining Sea, the waters behind the ships churned, roiled, and a wall of water rose like a mountain from the depths, high, high up, veiling the sky. For a moment, a kaleidoscope of colors filtered through its iridescence before its primal crash against the ships.

Raging waves pushed and shoved in unnatural movement, forcing the ships to their whim.

Rielle's hands moved, molded like a master sculptor, and overpowering waters shoved the ships to the beach north of

Laurentine, delivering them on wave after rolling wave. When the surf receded, the ships remained upon the sand, like prisoners left stranded.

Above them, the skies darkened, clouds graying until they blackened, blotting out the morning sun, rumbling and sparking.

A white bolt split the heavens, shooting down to the deck of a ship, the sky's judgment come down in bright-hot lightning. Another. Another. Fires sparked and smoked, with shouts and screams in their wake.

"Forcing them out," he whispered. *Perfect.*

"Jon?" Olivia prompted.

"Tell Captain Perrault to advance but keep a safe distance from the aeromancy. The pirates will disembark and surrender."

Olivia shouted his orders on while he remained, watching through the spyglass as Rielle glared out at the ships, and as Brennan's arm wrapped around her shoulders.

RIELLE SCOWLED down at the sliver of beach at the bottom of the cliff, and curled her index and middle fingers.

An updraft—it held. "I'll meet you below," she said to Brennan over her shoulder, then leaped before he could reply.

The aeromancy pushed up against her as she descended, a wind that eased her descent and held her just above the ground.

She uncurled her fingers, dispelling the updraft, and clad herself in a flame cloak as she strode to the beached ships, fire wreathing her body from head to toe in protection. Her magic would force every last one of them from their ships. Every. Last. One.

Beneath her lightning storm, some pirates had dropped boats from the ships and were fleeing to them.

She dropped the lightning storm and instead spelled up a wall of sand between the ships and the sea, then enclosed them almost entirely, with the only open side being hers.

All faces turned to her, most paralyzed, some backing up, others taking up ready stances.

That's right. Come here.

One pirate readied a bow, then as she gestured a spell, her flame cloak dispelled and he disappeared in a pillar of flame. A bit of pyromancy she'd read about in Xir. It dimmed her anima a bit more, but... *Worth it.*

She raised the flame cloak once more.

Soldiers surged down ahead of her from the gates of Laurentine. A platoon—two—a small company. Royal blue and white. The Emaurrian Army. They surrounded the pirate forces, who dropped their weapons.

But it wasn't all of them. The ships remained, with some holdouts inside. Not for long.

Indigo sails. Crossed cutlasses.

Those colors. She *knew* those colors. Kezani pirates. Perhaps even—

The *Siren.*

She dispelled her flame cloak and sparked the sails on the beached ships—a controlled burn that spread downward, billowed great clouds of smoke.

More men climbed down the rigging, gathered on the beach. She kept it up as the numbers reduced to a trickle, as at last, a small party emerged. A tall, bearded man with a wide-brimmed, decorated black hat.

Sincuore.

Every single muscle in her body hardened to painful rigidity.

Even surrendering, he held his head high, carried himself with all the self-importance he'd believed he'd built over these years.

She dispelled the flames from the sails and stalked toward him. *A red stain.* It was what she'd promised herself.

Blood for blood. And you dare to judge me? Shadow's words.

She shook her head as she closed the distance. Emaurrian soldiers apprehended him and kicked him to his knees.

"You'll release me if you want to survive the summer," he shouted to the troops gathered around him. "I'm the king of the pirates."

"And I'm the queen of the Shining Sea," she called back bitterly, tongue in cheek. All eyes turned to her. "No one will care a whit whether you live or die."

His gaze lifted to hers—all narrowed defiance—but then his unruly eyebrows rose. That flicker of recognition.

He had once kicked her face to the ship's deck. Starved her. Left her thirsty. Drugged her. Thrown her in his ship's brig, left her half-conscious and half-mad, delirious and terrified. And then he'd sold her to the Harifan slave souk.

Holding his unwavering gaze, she approached him and, with a flick of her finger, popped off his large hat.

His tangled, greasy dark hair flapped in the wind. He was just a man. And now the tables had turned.

She cocked her head. "The Divine is not without a sense of irony."

Those dark eyes narrowed once more. "How pathetic you were, shackled to the deck. Weak. Trembling."

No. She hardened her expression. "Why are you here?"

"Eyes wild, like a hunted and starved quarry, desperately gaping at any drink."

I won't let you. "Did anyone send you? Are you working for anyone?"

Those dark eyebrows drew together, then he smiled. "What was it you said when my crew changed your clothes? *'No, please, don't,'* I think it was."

A flash of dark metal, then blood and teeth shot from his mouth as he hit the sand. Flinches and winces rippled through the pirates.

Next to her, Jon flexed his bloodied, armored hand. "Arrest them," he commanded.

Immediate movement as soldiers and paladins rushed to action. He glanced at her. "Leave me your questions for him, and I'll see that they're answered."

"I only have one question for him—how does he want to die?" she replied, tracing Sincuore with narrowed eyes as the paladins dragged him away.

Shadow had accused her of being the *same*, twisted up in vengeance, but Sincuore had committed countless atrocities, and he would face *justice*. And she trusted Jon to make sure of it.

Unmoving, she faced him while activity swirled around them. It had been about a month since she'd last seen him—that terrible, beautiful, horrible night—but he looked like it had been years. Red stained his armor and skin in trails and spatters, and dark circles shadowed beneath his eyes. If he'd slept in the past month, it hadn't been much.

Those Shining Sea eyes took her in beneath drawn brows, down to the garnet ring on her left hand, then rose back to her face. He exhaled slowly as his expression softened, a glimmer of her Jon sparking in his gaze. Fleeting, then it faded. "It's good to see you."

His deep voice, gentle with her, took her back to that night. Veris. His arms around her, her tears streaming down her face—or his tears, maybe both together. That broken question. *Have I lost you, Rielle?*

For a moment, she couldn't move, couldn't speak, couldn't think. A ghost of an embrace clutched her shoulders, weighed into her flesh, her bones, her memory.

She blinked, trying to break away, and if only she could remember those age-old words every Lothaire kept ready for their liege... Something she could say to him besides all the thoughts that had torn through her mind since then.

She bowed, her parents' words coming back to her. "As Marquise of Laurentine, I bid you welcome, Your Majesty. All doors in Laurentine are open to you. All that is mine is yours."

The slightest frown creased his brow for a fraction of a second, then the kingly mask was in place. This wasn't her Jon.

It was King Jonathan Dominic Armel Faralle of Emaurria.

"It is my honor to be here, Marquise Laurentine," he declared, "and I gratefully accept your hospitality." When she raised her gaze to his countenance once more, he glanced subtly about their audience. He hadn't expected the tonal shift, then.

"You came to the defense of my people, my home." She took a step closer. "I can't tell you how much that means to me. Thank you, Jon," she whispered.

The corners of his mouth lifted in an expression too somber to be called a smile. He nodded. "It's my duty."

"It's *my* duty."

He rested his hand on his sword's pommel. Faithkeeper—the sword he'd had the night he'd invaded the Tower grounds. It seemed a lifetime ago. "And you carried it out in ways I've never before seen."

The magic? She clasped her hands behind her back. "I was only able to because you held them at bay."

"We work well together." A muscle flexed in his jaw. A restrained smile. "We're a world away from you caging me in geomancy to fight Flame."

Her mouth fell open. That spell? Not one of her better moments. "I—That, um, never happened?"

His lips twitched. "Right."

As he fought back a smile, the past several weeks and weariness fell away from his face; he lit up and, for a moment, looked like he had in Bournand, in Melain, before any of this had ever—

"I see you got my note." Olivia's voice carried from just outside the gates.

"Olivia!" She raced through the sand and flung her arms around Olivia, who hugged her back.

"I'm glad you're all right," Olivia said, with a relieved breath. "I received your letters from Stroppiata."

Letters about defeating Shadow. About cryptic threats. About Brennan recovering in an inn, and then... their recommitment to each other.

Rielle took a step back to look Olivia over. Not as worn down as Jon looked, but Olivia was in battlemage leathers again. Just like old times. Far from *Lady Archmage* and more like her partner on many a mission from the Tower. "Well, well, did you step out of last year, or was palace life getting too dull for you?"

A grin lit Olivia's face. "Even the Archmage must flex her muscles now and then."

"She saved my skin at least once," Jon added from next to her, the deep rumble of his voice all too familiar and comforting.

Olivia grinned at him, then sniffed. "I wouldn't have to if you didn't insist on fighting *every* Immortal in the land yourself."

"I can hardly sit around while—"

"No," Olivia cut in, "instead you insist on getting whipped across the battlefield by a basilisk's tail."

He crossed his arms. "I wasn't petrified, though, was I?"

"Ah, yes. Being alive absolves you of your recklessness."

"That's all I needed to hear," he teased.

They bantered like the best of friends. She looked from him to Olivia and back again as they went at it; they'd gotten close since Spiritseve, and only closer since fighting alongside each other these past weeks.

Behind Olivia, Brennan approached, jerking his head toward the ships and raising a brow. Not what he had expected, then. Well, he'd just have to reacquaint himself with what she was capable of.

He must've run the long way—well, every other way was *the long way* compared to jumping off the cliff—but he'd barely broken a sweat.

"Took you long enough," she called over to him.

Smiling mischievously, he joined them. "Cliff jumping isn't for everyone." He inclined his head to Olivia and bowed to Jon. "Lady Archmage, Your Majesty."

They greeted him in return.

"An updraft spell is safe," Olivia said, wrinkling her nose. "You could have followed."

He couldn't have; as a werewolf, the magic wouldn't affect him. He'd have plummeted to the ground. But that was a secret, even from Olivia.

"Well—" Rielle began.

"I wanted me to make sure no flanking force had invaded the city." He nodded to her. "All clear, by the way."

Quick thinking. "Thank you." She made to step around, but Olivia grabbed her hand.

"Oh no you don't." Olivia raised Rielle's hand. "I'm taking a closer look at that ring."

Jon went rigid next to her.

Would Olivia mention the wedding?

Divine, not like this. She'd wanted to write to Jon, to tell him herself, make sure he didn't find out about the wedding date only when he got the invitation—

Olivia turned her hand this way and that, letting the multi-faceted garnet catch the sunlight. "Was the entire *mine* unavailable to wear as a ring?" she asked over her shoulder.

Brennan smirked and came around to Rielle's side, pressing a quick kiss to her cheek. "It's been in my family for... eight hundred years? Something like that."

"It's stunning," Olivia said, with a disbelieving shake of her head. "When's the—"

"Let's go inside, shall we?" Rielle blurted, nodding up toward the castle. "We rode straight here, and I, for one, wouldn't say no to food. I'm sure you both could do with a hot meal and some rest." Laurentine made the *best* custard tarts, and cutting through the awkwardness would be a great bonus.

Jon looked up from her hand, managed a quick smile, and nodded. Olivia's brow furrowed, but she nodded, too.

Good. And she didn't need an inward glance to know what else she needed. "After all that, I'll need resonance. Would you mind?"

CHAPTER 3

 rennan brought up the rear with Jon while Rielle and Olivia took off for the castle. Fortunately, Rielle's *friend* was here to oblige her with resonance; he'd have to look into retaining a mage at Tregarde once they were married. A healer, maybe. A woman, preferably.

He'd see to that when they returned to Maerleth Tainn. Rielle wanted to review Laurentine's defenses and household— or at least she was saying so to Olivia—and hire a hydromancer for the city guard. It had been some time since she'd conducted a review, and this incident had revealed her steward's incompetence.

And Nox's black breath, he'd forgotten the stench of coastal cities in the spring. Salt and the briny stink of the sea, the pungency of decaying fish and unwashed peasants, assaulted him, along with the tang of blood and burnt flesh. The last two were almost preferable. He flared his nostrils and exhaled sharply.

There was one scent—Sincuore's—that he'd make certain

would disappear from the face of the earth. Arrest or no, trial or no, he *would* see Sincuore dead.

Fingernails bit into his palms, and he uncurled them slowly. Best not to think of Sincuore now.

"How have you been, sire?" he asked Jon, just making conversation. The sooner they entered the lesser stink of the castle, the sooner he could breathe freely again. "Better than you look, I hope."

Jon huffed, but smiled. "Is bloodied armor not in fashion?"

"This spring, it seems to be the horse-collar-tied cravat."

"Right," Jon said with an indulgent nod. "I must have left mine next to my hairbrush and cologne."

"You've had a lot on your mind, so this solitary oversight can be forgiven."

Jon side-eyed him.

He wasn't just here because pirates had attacked. There had been attacks on Costechelle and Sauveterre, down south—where even Princess Sandrine had invaded, challenging Jon's claim. Yet he'd allowed his generals to handle that, and here he was. Because it was *Laurentine*. Rielle's home. He couldn't help but come, perhaps some part of him holding out desperate hope she'd return.

But any hope of that would soon be destroyed.

The streets of Laurentine were lined with its residents—shipbuilders, fishermen, sailors, netters, and others, who cheered as their lady greeted them, took their hands, asked after their health, gave coins to children, the elderly, and the infirm. The children laughed and played, tugging at their parents' clothes and gleefully pointing out their lady.

Her gaze lingered on a golden-haired little girl with two long braids, smiling in a blue frock. He couldn't help but grin, too. Someday, he'd love to raise a little girl just like her, with

Rielle, and teach her about the world, watch her grow and become a strong woman, just like her, just like the women in his family.

But Rielle's gaze dulled, and her happy face slipped for just a moment before she returned to greeting her people. Not ready. Her thoughts must have still been with the child she'd lost.

Many of the townspeople reached out for Jon and wished him well, some just brushing fingertips in contact. Others thanked him for his help and generosity—he must have already given them coin when he'd arrived.

Well loved by the people. It had to have been some time since an Emaurrian king had raised a sword in defense of his subjects here.

If Father's plans to take the throne hadn't yet fallen apart, then they soon would. And it would save everyone the hardship.

But once Rielle became a Marcel, as Marquis of Laurentine he'd make sure *he* had the people's loyalty. He had the sums to spare. The years he'd spent managing Tregarde and Calterre had taught him everything he needed to know to win the hearts of the people. Feed them, treat them fairly, and share his bounty —and they'd fight to keep him and his line in power.

As they ascended the road to the castle, the crowds thinned. Rielle and Olivia discussed the dark-elves and Shadow, and plans for a long night in. It sounded like she'd be spending tonight with Olivia instead of in his arms...

And they had yet to finish what they'd started in Maerleth Tainn's gardens. He'd been waiting until he could be certain she loved only him, until she wanted only him. But how much longer would that be? And it didn't help that her former lover was skulking about.

"How long will you be staying?" he asked Jon.

"Only long enough to resupply and rest up before returning to Courdeval. It's been a long month."

"You haven't been to the palace in a month?" Brennan raised his eyebrows. Perfect time to mention the wedding. "You might not have received it yet, then."

A slight grin ghosted on Jon's lips. "No, I did. I received the wedding invitation a couple days ago."

Brennan suppressed the frown before it could etch his face. Jon had received the wedding invitation? His heart beat steadily, and his breathing was even. Almost entirely unaffected?

He'd given up, then? Good.

"Congratulations." The word was low, quiet, yet cordial. Not bitter.

"Thank you. I must say, I wasn't expecting you to—"

"There's no sense in dredging up the past. What's done is done." Jon hung his head a moment as they entered the castle's outer bailey. "Just honor her, respect her, *love* her—"

What right did Jon have to make threats?

"—or you'll lose her. Some unsolicited advice."

Not a threat after all. "With all due respect, I don't need your advice."

Another huff. "Then let useless words cast no shadow on your superior wisdom."

With a slight grin and a nod, Jon moved on ahead. He grazed Rielle's arm, informed her he would be along soon, then headed for the command tent. Olivia joined him.

As Jon walked toward the command tent, Brennan traced his path, narrowing his eyes. The Wolf snarled his displeasure but, with a glance at Rielle, calmed.

She was with *him*, and she would stay. The wedding was five months away, and not even the damned pirates would have missed the way she'd looked at Jon as he'd jested with Olivia—like a wildfire at an untouched grove just ahead.

But Rielle was *his*. He had every advantage, and he'd use them all to elicit those three words from her. And then once she was in bed beneath him, she'd forget Jon had even existed.

Rielle glanced away from Jon and Olivia's direction to him, wrinkling her nose. "What's with that face? He came to Laurentine's aid when it was sorely needed. Be *nice*, Brennan. Please."

He offered her his hand, and she took it. "Nice? What's that?"

She sighed, then rolled her eyes. "It's that way you never are. You should give it a try."

He fought back a grin. "I have. Not for me."

"Well, you'll have another chance to get it right at dinner. *Try*, please. For me." She held his gaze until he heaved a sigh and nodded his surrender.

"All right. I'll be 'nice' at dinner," he murmured. "But I won't like it."

Smiling, she leaned her head against his arm and nuzzled it as they made their way to the castle. "Charming... handsome..."

He shook his head. "Humble." It was less a joke and more like a prayer this time.

One night. He could be civil with her former lover for one night. Couldn't he?

After reviewing a stack of papers from Captain Dufresne, Rielle sat on a bench in the courtyard. She needed to resolve her status with the Tower, get back on track to magister, but Laurentine was a mess. She wasn't leaving until that was rectified.

Above her, the single Suguz pine, tall, slim, tilted heavily to one side, as if bowing to a fierce wind, but its foliage remained still, unruffled, caught in time.

It was the only one of Mama's trees to have survived the fire. *Her* tree, really, planted the day of her birth.

She clutched the locket on her chest that bore the mermaid scale, passing her fingers over the warming gold.

Nearly everything in the castle had been rebuilt, but it had really been in this courtyard where everyone had *lived*, where Mama had turned a garden into a magical wonderland, lined with trees, bursting with color, attracting butterflies and bees and songbirds. In the dreamy haze of memory, sunlight always glittered on leaves and petals, and laughter always carried on the air, and Mama always danced in a circle with her and Dominique and Viviane, hand in hand in hand...

A throat cleared, and she started, jerked her head to glance over her shoulder.

Dressed simply in one of his white shirts tucked into brown trousers, Jon towered next to Hugues Naudé, Laurentine's rotund steward, who wore an extravagant overcoat of chartreuse velvet trimmed in gold and embroidered with pearls in a vine pattern. The pearl buttons strained over a rounded belly, which contrasted sharply next to Jon's tall, sculpted warrior's form. The two men couldn't look more different if they'd tried. What were they doing together?

Two Royal Guards had taken up posts at the entrance to the courtyard, their watchful eyes on Jon.

"Good afternoon, my lady," Hugues said with an elaborate bow. All the elaborate bows in the land weren't going to make up for how he'd underfunded the city guard. "Pardon the intrusion, but—"

"Forgive me," Jon said, inclining his head. "I asked for a tour of the grounds. I didn't mean to interrupt."

Shaking her head, she stood. "No, no. Not at all. You're welcome to go wherever you please in Laurentine, J—Your Majesty." No need to provide Hugues with fodder for rumors. The man was worse than a Proctor's wife. "Join me, if you like." She gestured to the seat on the bench next to her.

Hands clasped behind his back, Jon nodded, turned to Hugues and offered his thanks, then approached her as Hugues departed. She'd speak to Hugues later—about a great many wrongs he needed to right.

Jon loosened the collar of his shirt before he sat down, exposing further glimpses of his pyromancy sigils. Beneath his shirt, they scrolled down to his collarbone, then winded into geomancy sigils. Her fingers twitched, recalling the pattern, and she clamped them on the bench and breathed deep. How could someone feel so familiar and yet be worlds apart?

Jon seated himself on the other end of the bench, as far as he could, really, just on its edge. He glanced above, at the Suguz pine. "Your tree appears to be... falling over."

She laughed. "This is a Suguz pine, native to the Kezan Isles. My mother had a whole courtyard of them, here, before the fire. One planted for each of us the day we were born." The line of pines used to shade half a dozen benches. "They all tilt toward the center of the world... So, down far south, they tilt toward us, and up here, they tilt toward the south. She used to say they remind us that there's something beyond ourselves."

Jon's gaze traced its trunk, from root to crown, and he looked out toward the sky. "That's a worthy thought."

This tree had joined her at the Tower, and when other novices and even her doyens had told her it was a waste of time, she'd spent the better part of a year healing its burn damage. The rough, gray, resinous bark flaked a bit in strips, with a black burn scar she hadn't been able to heal, but it was otherwise healthy. It had lost every last one of its mates, but it still lived, still grew, despite its scar.

"You tilt toward innocent people," Jon said, "always wanting to help, whenever you can."

She smiled. "So do you."

"It's my responsibility." He eyed the burn scar. "It's from... before."

She nodded. "This tree, outside of my people, is the most important thing to me in Laurentine."

"It didn't survive on its own," he guessed. "Someone tended it well. Loved it. Helped it."

"An entire year." A faint smile claimed her lips.

"And here it is, like a living memory."

A living memory... That was exactly what it was to her. Hopefully it would live on for future Lothaires to enjoy, along with the trees planted for their births.

Their daughter would have had a Suguz pine. Sylvie's tree would have been planted at the end of Messidoir in the summer, when she would have been born. If only...

Golden hair in braids and a bright blue frock, a happy, smiling face... That little girl could have been her. Or Sylvie as she might have been. Would her hair have been blond like hers, or brown like Jon's? Would her eyes have been light-blue or his sea-blue? Whose laugh would she have had? Whose nose?

Did he ever think about her, too?

Jon leaned back, his gaze resting a moment on her hand atop the bench before climbing to her face. "So, where's Brennan?"

The question broke into her thoughts. Probably for the best.

She exhaled a sigh. Brennan's commitment to Sincuore's execution was nothing short of exacting. "Sincuore has 'escaped' prisons before. He wanted to oversee the jailing of the pirates himself to ensure that doesn't happen."

Jon's lips pressed together grimly as he dipped his head. "It won't. My own Royal Guard secured him in the dungeon. Only I have the key."

Then Sincuore wouldn't have a chance. But Brennan didn't share her trust. She shrugged.

"Right." He cracked his knuckles. His large hands were callused as ever, and up from his wrist was a long scratch, scabbed over.

"What's that?" She tipped her head toward it.

"Oh, this?" He lifted his wrist. "Boar hunting, while we were camped outside Caerlain Trel."

Ever since she'd left Courdeval, he'd been doing battle, risking his life. "Jon, you can't keep taking risks like this."

"What, boar hunting?" He raised an eyebrow. "This was hardly worth bothering Olivia with."

"Not the hunting, and you know it." As a paladin, he'd risked his life daily, but it had been different. A *paladin's* risks. Criminals trying to escape justice. Thugs trying to steal arcanir. Now, he lived a king's life and faced a king's risks. Assassins and enemy nations. Everything and everyone standing in opposition to anyone in the kingdom. He took it all on, the kingdom's bulwark, taking every attack and every beating until one day... he could take no more.

He stiffened. "I'm the king. I can't hide behind armies while my own people die."

And if you're the one to die? But she couldn't bring herself to ask it. "They couldn't bear to lose you. You can't just—"

"I have to."

"So, what? You're just going to burn out?"

He sighed, cloaked in the heavy weariness of an ancient who'd wandered the earth too long. But he was only twenty-seven. "You can't change my mind, Rielle. Not about this."

He'd clearly forgotten that she could be just as stubborn as he could. But for now, under the warm afternoon sun and in the gentle spring breeze, she could let it lie. It was a beautiful day, far too beautiful for arguing, and for the blood that had already been shed.

He looked her over, an inquisitive frown creasing his features, but although he opened his mouth, he paused. His hand reached for his ring finger, where the Sodalis ring had once been. The Sodalis ring he'd given her.

"What is it?"

"Rielle, are you... happy?" The question washed in like a wave coming to shore, slow and gentle. There was a tenderness there, but over something great and dark, whose depths went farther than she wanted to fathom.

She blinked, probably more times than she should, then forced a smile. "Shadow is gone for good. Sincuore is locked up. I have yet to face the Divinity after everything, but for once, it's a quiet moment."

Those depths lingered, waited, but she'd only touched the surface. He'd been asking about more than that.

Yes, I'm happy with Brennan, she wanted to say, but was that what he expected? Barely a month after their parting, would the truth be a balm or a dagger?

Why was he asking?

No, she wouldn't turn back now, even if that's what he wanted. She did love Brennan, wanted to marry him, spend their lives together, be part of his *family*. And life as a mistress was no life at all, even if—even if...

"I *am* happy," she said at last. "Brennan is... wonderful. He's kind, supportive, loving. Patient," she added, while Jon nodded to each word. "He's changed since Melain, I promise."

"I know," he said, bowing his head. "I just—" He glanced at

her briefly. "I'm glad to hear it." He rose, rolling the kinks out of his shoulder as he looked toward his two guards. "I'll leave you to your thoughts, Rielle." As he inclined his head to her, she stood, too.

"I'll see you at dinner."

CHAPTER 4

Olivia drank deeply of her wine in Laurentine's great hall from her seat next to Rielle, who indeed looked the part of the marquise in a stunning sapphire-blue gown. Across from them, Brennan eyed Jon, who sat at the head and recounted the string of battles against the Immortals and the pirates since Vervewood.

Custom dictated Rielle sit on the opposite end, but with a table seating thirty, it would have made for a night of shouting.

And they had important things to discuss. Perhaps Rielle or Brennan would have an idea on how to keep Emaurria's people alive *without* betraying the world's greatest power. Trying to lure the Emaurrian Tower to break with the Divinity would only invite complete isolation from the Divinity and its allies— at best—and outright war at worst.

Or this would end with Jon and Brennan wrestling each other on the floor until someone threw a bucket of cold water onto them.

Laurentine's steward, Hugues Naudé, who'd managed the

march in Rielle's absence and while she was under the Divinity's contract, hovered in the periphery. All pleasantries, of course.

Tonight, the household had served up six courses of thirteen dishes, six of which were hors d'oeuvres. Extravagant. The meal opened with a pair of soups and a quarter of veal, followed with glazed eels in a Sileni sauce, and among other entrees and hors d'oeuvres, a ragout of larks with truffles, wild mushrooms, and foie gras, moistened with veal stock and bound with cream and eggs. The soups were replaced with a turbot and salmon, with the second course repeating the pattern of the first. Hams, cakes, sweetbreads, duck tongues, and eggs with a pork sauce—

It was an overwhelming meal, and overwhelmingly expensive. The food matched the grandeur and luxury of Trèstellan Palace, and clearly had been purchased while its marquise hadn't even been in residence. Laurentine's steward had a costly appetite and, it seemed, no shame.

Even deep in conversation, Rielle cast a critical eye over the vast opulence of the table from time to time; she'd never been fond of such ostentatious spending. Hugues was in for a rough morning tomorrow.

"You can't just wear yourself out going to every battle personally," Rielle said to Jon, scrunching the fabric of her richly embroidered gown under the table.

She gave his stubbornness too little credit.

Raising his eyebrows, Jon leaned into the high-backed chair and shrugged, his leather overcoat catching the shimmer of candlelight. "If I don't go, who will?"

"The army—"

"Overburdened."

Rielle frowned. "The Order—"

"Spread thin."

"The light-elves," she snapped.

"Rebuilding."

She glanced at Olivia, then back. "The Divinity?"

Brennan scoffed across from her. "Only if there's something in it for them."

Rielle scowled at him.

"I agree," Jon said. "Coin—a vast sum—seems to be insufficient."

So they were supposed to ignore international law and try to integrate the Emaurrian Tower under the Crown? The Divinity would certainly take note, and not at all in the way Jon desired.

"The Grand Divinus can be vain," Brennan offered with a sigh, then took a long swig of his brandy. "Or so Father says. Perhaps she expects you to appear in person and bend the knee."

Jon shook his head and breathed deeply.

"He barely has time to sleep," Olivia chimed in, "let alone take a lengthy voyage just for appearances." It was something a queen could do, but Jon had refused to even consider marriage, whether Rielle loved him or not. And judging by that massive ring on Rielle's finger, everything was on track for her wedding to Brennan.

Jon needed to either take note and move on, or tell Rielle how he still felt.

"I could help," Rielle said, while Brennan winced. She shot him a sour look, and he shrugged and plastered on a smile. "After Khar'shil, it's not as though we're doing anything, and—"

"Another unsanctioned mission?" Jon grinned. "Would this be... number three?"

"I'm sure I could convince the new Proctor to sanction it, whoever it is. And besides, I need to go to the Tower anyway."

The Proctor? Kieran. Rielle's rival and worst enemy in the Tower now held its supreme position of power.

Olivia took Rielle's arm. "Don't be so sure."

"What? Why not?" Rielle asked with a tilt of her head.

"It's Kieran Atterley."

Rielle stopped breathing, swallowed, looked away. "He, um, in Bournand, I—"

"He's the interim Proctor," Jon interrupted.

Brennan slammed down his brandy. "That grasping, insolent milksop?" His eyes almost—they almost seemed to turn golden for a moment? A trick of the light, perhaps.

"He... He's alive?" Rielle whispered.

"Unfortunately." Olivia heaved a sigh. "Wait—why wouldn't he be?"

Rielle licked her lips and raised a shoulder. "Around Vindemia, Leigh... confessed to killing him."

"What?" Olivia remembered to breathe.

"Sloppy work," Brennan grunted.

A servant topped off her wine. "In any case, just write to the Tower. Don't go in person."

"I—I—" Rielle chewed her lip. Why was she so nervous? "He'll never approve of all I've done. If it's up to him, my career with the Divinity is finished. I'll have to go over his head."

Career with the Divinity finished... like a heretic. A heretic outside the Divinity...

The Covens. Something she'd discuss with Jon later.

Rielle raised her gaze to Jon's. "I'll state my case to Magehold, but in the meantime, I *can* help. Just tell me where to go and what to do."

"No," Jon replied, pushing away his plate. "You've done enough. And I'm very grateful for the ships." She'd given him the pirate ships she'd captured today.

"What else am I going to do? Until Magehold gets back to me—"

"*No.*" He glared at her, and Brennan slid a look between them.

"Why not?"

Jon didn't waver. "You have a wedding to plan."

An incredulous sound escaped Rielle's throat.

"These aren't your problems. Go be happy. Live a good, long life. You've more than earned it." His tone was matter-of-fact, but every insecurity he'd ever spoken about his terminal condition, every heartfelt word of love for Rielle, every sadness he'd ever voiced about losing her brimmed in the intensity of his sea-blue eyes. He would not be swayed.

He didn't want her nearby. Didn't trust himself not to confess his feelings to her?

Rielle's gaze meandered to Brennan, who seemed unable to restrain a smile. He shrugged. "You heard the man." He cleared his throat in a smooth sound, clearly well practiced. "And you, Your Majesty? Are we to have a queen soon?"

Jon grimaced, crossing his arms with a creak of leather sleeves over biceps.

"No rush to commit to just *one* woman, right?" Brennan shot him a lopsided grin.

"You're *really* going to waste my skills when the kingdom clearly needs them?" Rielle hissed.

Jon didn't look at her, holding Brennan's gaze.

Brennan's grin widened. "No doubt there will be many awaiting your courting pleasure at Courdeval. Perhaps our future queen among them."

Rielle took her wine and drained half the goblet, then straightened and fixed Jon with a fiery glare.

"I'm here," Rielle said to him, her voice bitter, almost mocking. "Trained, capable, and I've been fighting for half my life. Use me. Relying on your skills alone... is... is willfully crippling yourself—"

Jon's eyes widened for a moment before his eyebrows lowered once more. He held up a hand.

Rielle scowled. "Or does it only mean something when *you* say it?"

"No, and we'll not speak of it again." He swabbed his mouth with a napkin, set it down, and rose. "Thank you for your hospitality," he said with an abrupt bow, "but I think it's time I retire." He glanced at Olivia, cocked his head toward the double doors, and she nodded.

Rielle had just given them the solution to their mage problem. The Covens. They had much to discuss.

Olivia stood from her chair—Brennan rose as she did—and touched Rielle's shoulder. "I'll meet you in my quarters shortly?"

Unclenching a fist, Rielle looked up at her. "You'd better." She grinned.

"Wouldn't miss it." At that, she caught Jon's grave look and followed him out of the great hall. The idea was radical, but surely he could set aside his paladin past and work with some heretics?

As RIELLE ROSE, Brennan held out a hand to her. Blowing out a breath, she took it and let her nerves cool as he wrapped her arm around his and led her out of the enormous white double doors of the great hall.

The sconce-lit corridor was empty; Jon and Olivia must have already gone to each of their quarters upstairs, or outside.

And dinner... It had been eye opening. Hugues had been burning through Laurentine's coin like an inferno through paper. When next she spoke to him, it wouldn't be about righting wrongs, but about packing his bags. She had always been willing to give second chances, but when people abused those chances, her sympathy wasn't limitless.

And after detailing how thoroughly the Immortals and the pirates were trouncing Emaurria, Jon had refused her help. He'd seen on the coast today what she could do. He *knew* her capabilities, and yet—

"He's being a stubborn ass," she hissed through pinched lips.

Brennan rumbled a deep laugh next to her as they strolled past portraits of past Lothaires and toward the dark stairwell. "Great Wolf save any man who dares stand in your way."

She shook her head. "Why won't he let me help? He has no legitimate reason." When he grinned and opened his mouth, she added, "And don't say 'wedding planning.'"

He sighed, and soon all traces of levity faded from his countenance. He paused on the landing and swept her into the corner, then waited attentively. In Tregarde, years ago, he'd pinned her just so, sharing intimate breaths in close quarters and a kiss that sometimes still stalked her dreams, despite the disaster that had happened that night.

"When a man who spends day and night dreaming of you can't have you," he said, clearly satisfied no one was listening, "do you suppose he wants to be anywhere *near* you?"

Her mouth dropped open.

"It would be easy, you know, to ask you to go *here* or stay *there*, run into you *coincidentally*, and torture himself with your presence when he can't have you. He knows it. And he'll try his hardest to avoid it," Brennan answered.

She lowered her gaze, staring into the black velvet covering Brennan's chest.

Jon wanted to *avoid* her. Maybe... maybe he was trying to be with someone else. Maybe he wanted to marry. Maybe he needed one fewer complication in his life. "But I repeat, he has no *legitimate* reason."

Just because their history was messy didn't mean he should turn down her help for the kingdom.

"Kings don't need legitimate reasons," Brennan said. "And *you*..." He raised her chin, forced her to meet his eyes. "Why are you forcing yourself into his circle? Don't you have any mercy for a man pining after you?"

"This is bigger than my *mercy*, Brennan. This is about the kingdom, and it's falling to ruin. And *I* can help defend it."

"The *kingdom* is the *king's* responsibility, and his queen's. You're a marquise. Worry about your march, like you did today. Defend Laurentine, Tregarde, Calterre. Defend your *piece* of the kingdom. That's how you can help."

She crossed her arms and leaned against the cool stone wall.

As a mage, she had a responsibility to use her magic for the greater good. Jon couldn't stop her from fighting the Immortals and the pirates, even if the Divinity excommunicated her.

Which was what she needed to handle next—settling her status with the Tower. With Kieran. Tomorrow, she'd write him a letter and find out what fate held for her. If he decided to stand in her way, she'd step right over him and see what Magehold had to say. For nearly a decade, she'd worked tirelessly toward the magister's mantle, and some idiot as interim Proctor wouldn't stop her now.

She grimaced. "Fine. You win. He wins. You both win. For now."

The moonlight cast a gleaming reflection on Brennan's dark

hair as he leaned in, his mouth curving in a roguish grin. "Oh, *I* definitely win."

Shaking her head, she rolled her eyes, but she couldn't keep the stupid smile from her face. With him so close, the air was all cinnamon spice and cypress, and it heated her blood, stoked that heat pooling in her lower body.

He cupped her cheek with a big, warm hand and raised her mouth to his. His lips were hot against hers, blazing hot, and as he leaned into her, pressed her against the stone, the whole of his perfect, hard body blazed just as hot against her.

As he deepened the kiss, his tongue seeking hers, a moan escaped her—or a whimper; she couldn't tell, and she didn't care. Her arms curled around him of their own volition, fingers clawing into his back, pulling him closer, urging him deeper, and Divine, it was *cruel*, completely and utterly *cruel*, that his tongue was a virtuoso, and his body a master, and *he* was doing all this to her when she had plans with Olivia tonight.

Brennan paused a moment before booted footsteps ascended the stairs—one, two, three, *four* sets—then abruptly stopped.

She broke away to glance around Brennan's bicep.

Jon's hardened expression met her squarely as he stood perfectly still, his arms at his sides. He held her gaze a moment with a piercing intensity, an immobilizing grip that froze her completely.

He was angry. Divine, he was angry. He and Olivia must have taken a moment outside after all. Brennan was right. It really was difficult for Jon to be around her, especially like this.

He blinked, clasped his hands behind his back, and a cordial smile appeared that didn't reach his eyes. He inclined his head, slowly and carefully. "Goodnight."

Without waiting for a reply, he proceeded up the stairs. Behind him, Olivia followed with an arched eyebrow, a gaping mouth, and a look that said *We are definitely talking about this later.* Two members of the Royal Guard—the one with the scar across his face, and the other with the short, thick curls—trailed after them.

After their footsteps faded from earshot, she looked up at Brennan, who didn't move an inch but to eye her, his lips pressed tight.

With his werewolf senses, he would have detected their approach.

"You *knew*," she grumbled. After all that talk about Jon keeping his distance because of his remaining feelings, Brennan had knowingly done this? "You said you'd be nice."

"I said I'd be nice at *dinner.*" He touched his nose to her temple, brushed it lightly into her hair, and breathed in deeply, slowly, the momentary chill tracing a shiver down her spine. "And it is now most *definitely* dessert."

She shifted her hips, but the throb between them only intensified. Divine's flaming fire, she wanted to scold him and scream at him for using her like that, tackle him right here in this stairwell... tear his clothes open, shove him onto the stairs, and—

His mouth closed over hers once more, and before she could seize him and have her way, he parted. "Goodnight, Rielle. Have fun catching up with Olivia."

Grinning wolfishly, he took a step back, and then another, and another.

"That's it? You think you can just—You're not going to—We won't even—" Her mind seemed only able to churn out parts of thoughts, and couldn't decide between dressing him down or aching for his touch.

"Oh, I *will*," he said, his voice a low rasp. "But not tonight." With a tip of his head, he ascended the stairs.

She stood there, staring, long after he'd gone. What had that been all about? Showing off to Jon? Marking his territory?

And what had she become? A pathetic, desperate pool of *want*, unable to even form a coherent sentence, too seduced to even be properly angry?

Closing her eyes, she leaned her head back against the cool stone. Divine, Brennan had become a spell of some kind, inhabiting every corner of her body and pulsing it to life whenever he chose, moving her to his liking, leaving her mesmerized, enchanted, spellbound.

And all they'd done was *kiss*.

He already knew her so well that he could rip the life out of all her anger with just a kiss.

She curled a fist and lightly tapped it against the stone. Nothing would happen tonight. And this possessive behavior would end once Jon was in Courdeval again.

Gathering what motes of composure she could, she exhaled a lengthy breath and headed upstairs to meet with Olivia.

CHAPTER 5

Olivia followed in silence as Jon strode down the dark, echoing hallway, tension brimming in the rigid set of his shoulders. It would never be easy for him to see Rielle with another man, especially if he refused to let her go in his heart, refused to marry, refused to move on.

He had to face reality. Everyone walked on eggshells around him, trying not to say Rielle's name or mention the wedding, but that wasn't what he needed. Truth had to cut deep, take root, and remain. That was the only way.

For his part, however, he'd managed to appear somewhat composed today. After that night of the Veris Ball a month ago, that was an accomplishment.

Perhaps once he cooled down, he'd be amenable to listen to her solution to all their problems: the Covens.

He approached the quarters Rielle had provided—the lord's suite of rooms, her very own, as the unmarried marquise of the castle—and the two Royal Guards stood aside. Raoul and

Florian entered first, swept the quarters, then stood at attention as Jon went in.

He passed through the candlelit antechamber with the door to the adjoining quarters—her own—and through a small study to the bedchamber. A fire burned in the large stone hearth, where three cushioned armchairs sat around a circular, low wooden table. Upon it lay a small block of wood, a knife, and some wood shavings—Jon must have taken to carving something.

Despite the luxurious curtained, canopied bed and the fine crimson-and-silver rug, the bedchamber had a comfortable, rustic quality—exposed stone walls, massive timbers overhead, a wrought-iron chandelier of candles formed in a simple, large circle. The window was open to the Shining Sea, glittering under the moonlight, and Jon breathed deeply as he stood in its rectangle of evening glow.

The sea air was bracing, fresh, and reminded her of days spent walking the beaches of Caerlain Trel, collecting seashells, far from the fish market, of course.

He rested his big palms on the stone sill, fingers scraping into the grain.

Denying Rielle's request had to weigh on him, too. But agreeing could have led to diplomatic problems with the Divinity—Rielle still contracted with the Divinity, after all, and without permission to fight for the Crown, it would be an unsanctioned mission.

There had been no word from Magehold about Jon establishing the Order of Sages, but there was no compelling reason to exacerbate any problems with the Grand Divinus. "It's best that you said no," Olivia said gently.

"She's amazing in battle, but it would only complicate matters," he murmured.

Did he mean matters with the Divinity, or matters with him? Perhaps both.

"She's going to find a way to fight the Immortals whether it's at *your* side or not. That is simply who she is." Smiling, she joined him at the window.

He eyed her, his mouth restraining a knowing grin as the candles cast a golden glow on the planes of his clean-shaven face. Somehow, he looked more like a paladin now than ever.

"But you mentioned other means." She cocked her head toward the armchairs and headed there, with him in her wake. When they were seated, she leaned back and clasped her hands. "All the talk at dinner about Kieran trying to cast her out of the Divinity sparked a thought."

He raised his eyebrows expectantly.

"The Covens."

Those eyebrows lowered, drew together. He glanced at the fire, stared, cracking his knuckles. "The Covens," he repeated, quietly, pensively. He glanced back at her. "Are you out of your mind?"

Laughter bubbled from her throat. "You're an Earthbound king, werewolves stalk the land, dragons rule the skies. If I'm out of my mind, then the world has taken me there."

"You know the only thing heretics hate more than the Divinity is the Order, right?" He rested his ankle on the opposite knee. "They'd sooner kill me than help me."

"And if you're on the same side? They want to take down the Divinity, remember?"

He grunted. "And since when do you support that?"

"*Magehold* has denied you aid. Denied *Emaurria* aid. We can't handle the Divinity as an enemy, but if it's not going to be an ally, we must sway the court of public opinion—not just here, but in the region—to our favor. And *that's* how we'll get our mages, one way or another."

"Olivia, you have that look on your face like you're about to take over the world," he said with a grin. "Terra have mercy"— he heaved a sigh—"but tell me how."

She wasn't going to take over the world, but together, *they* would. Oh, yes. She steepled her fingers beneath her chin. "The Grand Divinus has ignored your petitions, and the privacy of that has been in her favor. How can the public condemn the Divinity for a failing they don't know about?"

"We must bring it into the light."

"But mere word will not be enough."

His eyes lit up. "Bend the knee," he whispered.

"Bend the knee." If he went to Magehold in person and requested aid, the Grand Divinus's response—or lack thereof— would spread far and wide, and with it, approval or condemnation.

"If she agrees, we get mages from the Divinity," he said, eyeing the fire ruminatively. "If she doesn't, the public turns against the Divinity, both here and elsewhere. The situation is dire. We'd have grounds to treat with the Covens. Then we'd have the *might* to turn the Tower."

"Precisely." Many skilled mages had abandoned the Divinity, but even more had never been a part of it. The Tremblays, the Forgerons, the Beaufoys. They and their Covens, if they could be swayed, would bring enough might to topple a single Tower, as long as the public and the king were on their side.

A slow smile flashed across Jon's face.

"All we have to do is drag your dignity through the mud to do it." A king bending the knee was no small humbling.

He shook his head. "It's not my dignity I'm concerned with.

Publicly bowing to another power and asking for aid makes Emaurria look weak—"

And ready for the taking.

"—but if it's a formality before we build up our strength, then it's a risk we must take." The grim line of his mouth obeyed the gravity of his eyes. "But we must be ready. As soon as aid is denied, we must be ready for the Divinity—and any other opportunist."

She nodded. The true problem would be winning over the heretics if the Grand Divinus rejected their request. They'd have no reason to trust her word, since she'd been a Divinity mage prior to her appointment to Archmage of Emaurria. But that was a problem for tomorrow.

"Let's plan a trip to Magehold, then."

She rose with a smile. "I knew you'd see reason."

That knowing grin again. "Good ideas make it easy."

Fortunately, he hadn't proceeded blindly to the Tower to sway Kieran to break it from the Divinity. These days, time loomed larger and larger over Jon as the days of his life moved toward an inevitable and impending end. But the inevitability he believed so ironclad was only another challenge for her to defeat.

I'm going to save you. I'll find a way.

"So you're catching up with Rielle tonight?" He stood, leaning over the hearth with a certain effortless grace. He had a measured way about him, his movements always thoughtful, certain, as if he did nothing without true intention. It lent him a very masculine elegance that oft reminded her of James.

"We're overdue," she said as she headed for the door. "But we'll be in the adjoining quarters, so if you need me, I'm nearby."

He hadn't suffered an episode since Courdeval, but things

would only get worse as his heart condition deteriorated. If she couldn't find a solution in time, she'd *have* to tell Rielle, whether Jon agreed or not. Otherwise she'd never forgive herself.

And although Rielle was engaged to Brennan, perhaps her feelings for Jon yet lingered? Maybe she could set Rielle off that course, so both she *and* Jon could move on.

If a cure couldn't be found in time, he'd only have a couple of years to live at most, and spending them pining after a woman who was marrying another man would be a miserable rest of his life. Moving on would help them *both*.

"I'll be fine," he said, glancing at the block of carving wood before waving her off. "Have fun, and goodnight."

"Goodnight, Jon," she answered, leaving him to his thoughts and the fire as she unlocked the adjoining door and entered her quarters, where she'd find the strength to turn her best friend's heart.

IN THE LADY'S APARTMENT, Rielle stood in her nightgown and robe as a maid rolled in a cart of pastries, confections, and wine. Custard tarts, sugared almonds, chocolates, cakes, and port: the makings of a perfect night. Nothing would get in the way of fun tonight.

It had been too long since she and Olivia had enjoyed one of their fabulous nights in.

Olivia had lost a lover and gone through a horrific ordeal in the dungeon, but her strength had carried her through—and she appeared as composed as ever. Now that she was Archmage, what new challenge had she set her mind on? And was there someone new in her life, in her heart?

Rielle popped a sugared almond in her mouth and looked

around the rebuilt suite of rooms. The lady's apartment didn't look vastly different from when Mama had been alive, and yet... it was entirely different. The parlor had two sofas and an armchair, as it used to, but that armchair, although beautifully upholstered and crafted of fine cherry wood, didn't have that one worn spot on the armrest where Mama used to rub her palm when reading a good book.

The intricate sky-blue-and-white rug was gorgeous, but it was missing the stain where Dominique had spilled ink while penning her latest tale of Dame Marie the Brave. The bookshelf had all the wrong books, and none of their favorites. And the study didn't have the desk Mama had brought from Aestrie, where she and her mama had carved flowers into the underside.

The rooms were empty, and yet somehow even emptier than they seemed. Everywhere she looked was something that wasn't where it used to be. Someone who wasn't where she used to be.

She rested her hand on her belly. Sylvie would never know any of these things, nor those that were, nor Mama, Dominique, any of them. If she'd lived, these rooms might have been filled with laughter again. Flowers carved on the underside of this new desk. New favorite books on the shelves. Another ink spill. Another worn armrest. It would have been a difficult life, a different life, but a good one with Sylvie.

Voices carried from the lord's apartment, where she'd invited Jon to stay.

Since when had Jon and Olivia started requesting adjoining rooms? Did he worry about her, want to be near? Did they discuss the kingdom's affairs long into the night?

It... didn't really matter, did it? It didn't matter what the reason was. It shouldn't.

The adjoining door opened into the parlor. She walked back to find Olivia eyeing the decanter of port on the cart.

"I had the necessities brought up," she said brightly to Olivia.

" 'Necessities' is right," Olivia agreed as she nibbled a praline. She grabbed the cart and pushed it toward the bedchamber. "We're going to need these supplies nearby."

"Couldn't agree more," Rielle said with a grin as she followed.

Once in the bedchamber, Olivia shuffled about, grabbing various items. The bedchamber wasn't the same as when Mama had been alive, but it was warm, inviting—Gran had made sure of that when she'd overseen Laurentine's rebuilding. The delicate double doors opened into an airy room with white-paneled walls adorned with portraits, while a periwinkle rug trimmed in lily white and decorated with lily-white scrolls cushioned the shining parquet floor. The four-poster bed was curtained in red velvet trimmed in gold fringe, its twining posts romantic and pleasing to the eye. Two enormous windows leading out onto a balcony added a final touch of grandeur to an already opulent room.

Home.

She'd claimed the lord's apartment as her own, but someday, when she'd marry, these would be her rooms when she stayed at Laurentine. Someday soon, when she and Brennan were wed, finally committed to a life together for the rest of their lives. And a wedding night.

"So tell me everything," she said as Olivia moved behind a privacy screen with a handful of clothes.

"Everything?" Olivia's tired voice carried as her arms stuck out above the screen. "Where to even begin?"

"How were your first days as Archmage?" Rielle

approached the fire and warmed her hands. The white-marble fireplace was small but intricately carved with mermaids—the same one that had always been here. Restored, it seemed.

"So *everything* everything, then," Olivia replied with a laugh. "About how you'd expect. King Marcus's Grands were skeptical of my worth—"

More the fools they.

"—but the former Archmage had recommended me highly, and King Marcus seemed to take a liking to me. I probably worked harder than all of them combined, and maybe they were beginning to respect me."

Beginning to? "Until the regicide happened?"

Olivia cleared her throat. "Until James took a liking to me."

Nothing quite stole respect like a superior's love. That was an achingly familiar insight.

Raising her eyebrows, Rielle sat on the bed with a sympathetic sigh. Olivia seemed to have loved him, and... everyone knew the fate of Prince James. "I saw a note from him in your rooms in Trèstellan. He seemed... good."

"He was. Dashing, wise, romantic, handsome. After he and his wife became estranged, he became known as somewhat of a rake at court. Witty, carefree, irresistible. An accomplished lover, by rumor. That alone had me falling at his feet."

"You, falling at a man's feet?" She laughed. "There's a first for everything, I suppose?"

"Well, naturally, *he* pursued *me*. I only fell at his feet when he caught me. Does that count?"

"I see." She rose and moved to pour herself a goblet of port. "And did rumor deliver?"

"Oh yes it did."

She sat on a deep-blue sofa before the bed, with golden

wood armrests, set before a low table with a small bouquet of wildflowers.

James had seemed a wonderful match for Olivia, but they both knew how that story had sadly ended.

Something inside of her twisted. Who was in Olivia's life now? "And... since James?"

A heavy sigh. From behind a privacy screen, Olivia emerged in her nightgown and robe, lengthy white linen under forest-green brocade. Her emerald eyes took on a dull cast.

"There was... potential." Olivia's voice had an uneven lilt to it that broke.

She moved past a card table near the large wall bearing a massive portrait of Mama in her youth and one of Papa from her uncle's barony, among others, then poured herself a goblet of port, a lengthy pour, as if it were lifeblood. She sat next to Rielle on the sofa.

"Torrance?" Rielle asked. He and Olivia had gone to the Veris ball together.

Olivia drank deeply of her port. "Wasn't who I thought he was."

"Well, not *every* man can be Olivia Sabeyon's match."

"Quite right." Smiling, she nodded perkily.

Brennan's uncle hadn't measured up, but there would be other men. "Besides, I don't think I could've called you 'Aunt Olivia' with a straight face."

Olivia laughed, spitting port back into her goblet. "I can't say I'd thought of that." A mischievous grin slowly appeared on her face. "Speaking of which... how's *Marquis Tregarde*?" She waggled her eyebrows. "Also can't say I ever thought I'd see the day."

Neither could she. Not until Sonbahar. "He's—We—"

Divine, he was infuriating, amazing, maddening, *wonderful*. "I think I'm in love with him."

"You *think*?" Olivia cleared her throat and straightened. "That's the kind of thing you want to *know* before you marry, isn't it?"

Know. When Brennan looked at her, she melted. His voice stroked something deep within her, made her want to curl up against him. When he held her, she could close her eyes and surrender to sleep without worrying about overseers, masters, hisaad... He'd supported her, helped her, and in the first time in years, been honest, loyal, honorable, kind. He was perfect. "I *do* love him, Olivia."

Olivia arched a brow and reached toward the cart for a handful of pralines. She offered some, and Rielle picked one. "These things can take time. It's been a month, right? You'll only grow closer."

"That's my hope," she said with a lengthy sigh, thinking back to the stairwell. The dark, hot, tight, *wanting* stairwell.

"Oh? So then you haven't—"

"No!" she blurted. "And we sleep together *every* night, and tonight, he... It's like he's teasing me." No doubt that was *exactly* what he'd been doing, especially when he knew her impulses better than she did.

"Maybe he is," Olivia said with a fleeting grin, then hid behind her port. "Maybe you should let him. Maybe it might be fun."

"Mm, *not* letting him would definitely be more fun. Infinitely more fun. Every night, just fun, fun, fun, *fun*—"

Olivia spat chunks of a praline back into her palm. "You're awful! And impatient."

"You're one to talk."

Olivia rolled her eyes and nodded, then shoved the praline

back in her mouth, chewing loudly. Nights like this had been far too few and far between this past year. "So do you ever... think about Jon?"

She froze.

No.

Yes.

Not really...

All the time.

Not in that *way.*

She rubbed her forehead. What a strange question. Olivia knew what had happened upon her return to Courdeval, Veris, everything. She knew about Brennan. So why...? "I... Things are over between us."

Olivia had stilled completely, staring into nothing very intently. Only her fingertips moved, scrunching the white linen of her nightgown.

"There's no point in thinking about him."

"Do you think..." Olivia began. "Do you still love him?"

Thinking about the question just pulled everything out of her, emptied her chest, like a great big blade had carved a hole there and scraped out everything inside. "He shattered my heart into a thousand pieces. I... I'm not sure I've found them all. Or if I ever will."

Olivia wrapped an arm around her and rested her head against Rielle's, the soft lavender smell of her a familiar comfort. "I'm sorry."

She blinked away tears she'd already shed a hundred times.

Olivia rubbed her upper arm gently. "You'll be the Marquise of Tregarde soon. A whole new life. A legion of women would love to be you."

She smiled, wiping at her eyes. This new man that Brennan was—she hadn't expected him or deserved him, and yet he'd appeared in the darkness of her life like a flame in the night.

Was that why Olivia had asked, or was it—

"So after you deal with the Tower," Olivia began, "what will you do?"

Gran would have wanted her to manage their lands and households, maybe someday think about having another child... It was an idyllic life. And maybe even entirely wonderful.

But she could never live a life just for herself and her family. Magic came with duty, and she had work to do. "Move out of the Tower, but still take missions. Work on joining the Magisterium." She glanced at Olivia. "What's next for you?"

Olivia stiffened. "A bit of a research project, actually."

Was she nervous? "Researching what?"

"Oh, it's... some of the new... healing possibilities the Immortals can offer."

Healing? That was Olivia's forte, but... she was hiding something. "Anything in particular?"

"I'll let you know when I find it," she said with a smile.

Her lips were sealed. What was the big secret? Olivia had never hesitated to share the details of her research. More and more, it felt like Olivia was keeping things to herself, asking more than sharing, something that hadn't happened in the nearly ten years of their friendship. "So, a big, secret project. Anything else? Dueling other mages? Fighting more basilisks? Magicking every idiot that looks at you wrong?"

Olivia laughed. "Saving Jon from himself. He needs to do every single thing personally, fight every battle with his own hands, and he'll work himself to death unless you stop him, you know?"

Rielle shivered. A twist of a smile emerged on her face, she could feel it, and a hollow laugh, but it wasn't a reaction she recognized. Being told who he was, it just—it was as though she weren't quite in her body, as if she floated above it and listened from afar.

And yet, Olivia knew him, had spent more time with him than *she* had, knew him better, enough to explain to her who he was.

The feeling of it possessed her body like a ghost, one that displaced her completely.

But Olivia was right. That sounded like him, and he needed Olivia to keep him balanced. He was lucky to have her friendship, although the longer they spoke, the less like friendship it seemed. Olivia kept turning the conversation to Jon, and her thoughts couldn't be too far from him, then.

Something more. Something more was happening between them, or would, and although she felt a pang in her stomach, that wasn't her place anymore, *couldn't* be her place anymore. Just as she had moved on, so would Jon. And if it were with Olivia, he'd be a fortunate man.

"I'm glad he has you." She nudged Olivia. "And I'm glad you were here to save my people."

"All in a day's work," Olivia said with a laugh. "And have you heard about Leigh's light-elven lover?"

CHAPTER 6

*G*reat Wolf, she was hard to walk away from.

Letting his breathing even out, Brennan lay in the massive bed, his gaze fixed on the waxing gibbous moon through the open window, ebbing its ghostly light into the darkness.

For months, she'd been setting him ablaze, and he'd burned and burned and burned. A couple nights ago, the burning had become an inferno, and tonight—well, it should have been a challenge to ascend the stairs when his body was no more than ash upon the floor.

He tucked an arm behind his head on the pillow and sighed. She wanted him. He could see it, he could smell it, he could feel it in his bones. She wanted him to take her, take her hard, claim her, and make her scream. And oh yes, he could do that. He *wanted* to. Badly.

But while once he may have been content just to have her in his bed, that alone wasn't enough. Not anymore. She'd agreed to marry him, and she wanted him, but was she in love with him?

She'd come to care for him. She did love him, but was it as a friend? A friend she wanted to bed?

It wasn't a promise or a good swiving that would make her stay—it had to be *love*. And nothing he did would keep her hand in his unless he had that.

He was good, *very* good, but even he couldn't fuck a woman into falling in love with him.

She'd been shaken tonight at dinner. Jon still got under her skin, and it was more than his stubbornness.

With a grunt, he rolled over. Her love with Jon had just fallen to pieces a month ago, and what she needed was support. Patience. Definitely a good swiving, but that would have to wait. She might still be in love with Jon, but if either of them had risked screwing this up, it was *he*.

Brennan sighed. There were things he'd done, horrible things, terrible things she could never discover. Their life now, idyllic as it was, had been built upon a single pillar, the one remaining chance he had with her. A thin and vulnerable chance. One that would not withstand the harsh truths he should confess to her.

What he'd done before the night of Veris...

What Father had done...

How he'd covered it up...

But as long as that single, vulnerable pillar held, they'd be married and he would spend the rest of his days living for one purpose: her happiness. And nothing would stand in the way of that, not truths, not Jon, not that pirate captain in the dungeon.

Father had told him after Spiritseve that he didn't know where Rielle was, and his body had shown no signs of lying. Yet someone—with deeper pockets and greater worth than that shadowmancer bitch—had paid for Rielle's abduction, had allowed Shadow to arrange it all.

Father had hired Gilles, and Gilles had hired Shadow, but someone else had directed Shadow to hire Sincuore. At least one more player who'd wanted Rielle off the board.

And answers could be found in the dungeon. He'd seen to the jailing—making sure the guards were loyal and trustworthy, but he'd done no more.

No waiting until Jon decided to question Sincuore, or until his inquisitors attended to the matter. Brennan sat up. No, this had to be handled personally. Tonight.

He got out of bed, cleaned up, and dressed, his usual finery, but deepest black. All the better for obscuring red stains.

He gathered his weapons belt—which he'd need for once—and made sure his dagger and rapier, Bite, were clipped to it. Far better if he didn't need to expose his claws tonight and have to kill innocent guards to keep his secret.

A couple hours after midnight, the castle was quiet, filled only with soft breaths, the distant steps of patrolling guards, and the occasional crackle of sconces, torches, or hearths. He strode to the east wing stairwell that smelled of damp, and it led all the way down to the dungeon.

A single Laurentine guard stood at the entrance, and the young man blinked to attention, meeting him squarely as he approached. "Your Lordship," he greeted with a bow.

Brennan nodded his acknowledgement. "Stand aside."

The young man's gaze darted away for a moment. "His Majesty's orders were to—"

"His Majesty is leaving tomorrow," Brennan answered matter-of-factly. "In a few months, I will be your lord and master. Choose wisely."

The guard stared into space for a moment, his pulse racing in Brennan's ears, before he stood aside. "My lord."

"Keys," Brennan demanded.

"I don't have them. His Majesty does," the young man replied with a tremor in his voice.

"I was never here," Brennan said as he swung open the heavy, iron-wrapped door and crossed the threshold.

"Yes, my lord."

The proper response. The guard shut the door behind him, leaving him among the sparse torchlight. A variety of stenches lay thick upon the air, unwashed flesh, mold, old blood, piss, shit, infection. He held his sleeve to his nose, for all the good it would do, and scented Sincuore deep in the cell block.

Behind the iron bars, Sincuore had been stripped of his finery, left merely in his dirty and bloodied white shirt and his breeches. Not even boots. Half his face was swollen and dark— Jon's doing—and made Brennan smile.

He wouldn't need the keys to the cell.

A rat scurried by, and Brennan tapped it farther along the mildewy stone with his boot, making the thing screech and hurry. "How far the mighty have fallen," he taunted. *Come and get me.*

"I am a *captain*, boy. Mind yourself," Sincuore spat, with a slight lisp. Half his face being swollen probably complicated speech just a bit.

"Captain," Brennan mused aloud. "Captain of this cell? Captain of your pisspot? Captain of the rats?" He grinned.

Sincuore launched himself from the stone for the bars, and with inhuman speed, Brennan grabbed his neck and yanked him against the iron.

"How dare I talk about your rat crew like that?" Brennan tsked.

Sincuore's human hands clawed his arm. Pathetic. Weak. He could break them with barely any effort.

"What are you?" Sincuore grunted. His throat bobbed as he tried to swallow.

"The man with your life in his hands. An interested party. Your executioner." He laughed quietly in his throat, tightening his grip ever so slightly, and a slight tremor began in Sincuore's hands. "The answer depends on you."

JON SAT BEFORE THE FIRE, well into the night, with a piece of linden wood and his knife. When he'd been just a boy, Derric would whittle all manner of figures for him—paladins, horses, dogs, hawks, boats. It hadn't been long before he'd begged Derric for a knife of his own, and to carve together. When they'd sat by the fire before bed, Derric would tell him stories as they'd carved, and as he'd grown older, it had become a meditative activity, something to keep his hands busy when his mind had gone places he hadn't wanted it to go.

As a paladin, he'd vowed to give up all but the very basic essentials allowed his order, and it was only on rare occasions that he'd whittle a horse or a knight and give it away.

For the past month, that rarity had become ritual. Every night before he went to bed, he found himself before the fire with his knife and piece of linden wood, making straightaway rough cuts while his mind went elsewhere.

If he'd acted as he should have, Sylvie would have been about six months along now, big and growing in Rielle's womb. He could see it in his mind's eye, taking Rielle's hand while the midwife checked on her, and building Sylvie's crib with his own hands, holding Rielle close every night, whispering to her belly in the morning and every chance he could, talking to Sylvie, letting her know he was here for her, waiting for her, and that he loved her.

He rubbed his hand with the grain of the linden, but it wasn't the grain he felt, but warm, smooth skin, happiness and the world as it should have been beneath his touch, a world where Sylvie would have lived, where he'd never betrayed Rielle, where his heart would never fail him. Where they'd have spent their lives in joy and sunlight, alive. Together.

A world that existed only in dreams and fantasies.

He set down the knife and wiped his hand against the fabric of his braies, then rubbed his eyes. *Most Holy Terra, Great Mother, please keep my daughter in the joy of your light until we meet again.*

He opened his eyes, staring at the piece of linden. It looked nothing like the plump little bird it would become, but slowly, day by day, it was closer to becoming what it had always been destined to be.

With a sigh, he set it down. His hands felt too light, too empty, as if they knew they'd never feel the weight of Sylvie the day she'd have been born. As if they knew they'd already lost that future.

He'd lost too much to ever be whole again, and downstairs in this castle, deep in the dungeon, was a man who'd helped rip it all away.

His hands curled into fists, and his gaze rested on Faith-keeper, sheathed upon the table. He couldn't kill the man, not until Sincuore stood trial, but Terra have mercy, did he want to. The emptiness of his hands could never be filled, but for one shining moment, they might almost be, and there would be some measure of justice for Sylvie, or some measure of relief to lessen the pain of her loss.

Perhaps it was time to pay Sincuore a visit, ask him what it had all been for. Have answers and names to hate in those low moments, and blood to balm the grief.

Before he could talk himself out of it, he pulled on his trousers and boots, threw on the leather overcoat, strapped on his weapons belt, and headed for the antechamber. Through the adjoining door, soft voices and laughter trickled in, unintelligible but happy. Good. Rielle deserved a night of happiness, and so did Olivia.

Nights he'd spent laughing with Rielle still lived in him, brightened and kept him warm on grim days. He'd never have those with her again, would go to his grave never knowing that joy again, but she'd have it—with Olivia, with Brennan, with her children someday. He'd do all in his power to see such halcyon days renewed, bring peace back to these shores. Anything and everything.

With a last wistful look at the adjoining door, he headed for the hall.

"Your Majesty?" Raoul asked gruffly from his post.

"Midnight snack?" Florian joked.

Jon grimaced. "Something like that. Up for some interrogation?"

Florian's stance loosened. "Just like old times. Not going to let that asshole have a good night's sleep, are we?"

"Not until we get some answers," Jon replied. "And even then."

"Beats standing around here," Florian said.

"Lead the way, Your Majesty," Raoul added in his usual monotone.

Two new guards took up the posts as Jon led them to the stairwell and down. He trusted Raoul and Florian with his life. Against the dark-elves, Raoul had almost died for him. No matter what, that made him a brother.

When they got down to the dungeon, the young guard straightened, his pockmarked face creasing. "Your Majesty," he greeted with a bow, but didn't move to open the door.

"Open this door."

The young guard moved to comply, wincing. "Your Majesty, it's just that—"

"Someone's been down here?"

"Marquis Tregarde."

Terra have mercy. Sincuore might already be dead. "Open this door. Now."

The young guard immediately did so, and at the end of the block, Brennan stood, his arm out, clenching Sincuore's neck through the bars.

"...drugged her. Did anyone hurt her while she was aboard?"

The question froze Jon to the spot.

"*Hurt.*" Sincuore scoffed.

Brennan moved him away from the bars only to slam him back into them. "Answer."

"Do you think I could captain a ship if my entire crew spent all day and night lining up for their turn with the prisoner? Of course not. Everyone waits for shore leave."

Brennan searched the man's face, then shoved him to his knees. "What brings you to the dungeon on this fine evening, Your Majesty?"

Jon rested his hand on Faithkeeper's pommel as the torchlight reflected off Sincuore's sweaty face. "The same thing that brought you." He approached, feeling the weight of the cell key in his trouser pocket. "Who hired you?" he asked Sincuore.

The man laughed. "Maybe the world did."

"Lying won't get you anywhere," Jon replied. The key in his pocket was the freedom to throw open this cell door and slide

Faithkeeper through Sincuore's throat. "Maybe if you tell the truth, we'll let you go."

"Now who's lying?" Sincuore's dark eyes gleamed.

With another yank, Brennan slammed him against the bars, opening a cut on Sincuore's forehead. "'Now who's lying, *Your Majesty?*'" Brennan corrected.

Jon rolled his eyes. As long as it helped elicit some answers.

"If I tell you who hired me, I'll have *no* hope of freedom," Sincuore murmured.

Olivia had learned a great many things from Tor, who'd claimed to have been dissuading his brother from further treason. Tor, who'd been like a father to him. *Tor.* He still couldn't believe it, but at least Tor's plotting had given them some answers.

"You were hired by Shadow, who was sent by Faolan Auvray Marcel," Jon offered, and both Sincuore and Brennan's faces jerked to his. "Who worked with Faolan?"

"You *know?*" Brennan asked.

"Princess Sandrine Elise Faralle El-Amin?"

Sincuore looked away.

Jon drew Faithkeeper and leveled the tip at Sincuore's throat. "Yes or no."

Brennan pulled Sincuore closer until the blade's tip just pierced the skin.

Sincuore's throat bobbed. "No."

"Prince Raadi El-Amin?"

"No."

Jon grimaced. "Was your employer working alone?"

"No."

Brennan cocked his head. "The Grand Divinus."

Sincuore dropped his gaze.

"Yes or no," Brennan pressed, drawing Sincuore closer and

closer to the blade once more, pressing the tip into his flesh, drawing blood—

Jon pulled Faithkeeper away. *The Grand Divinus.*

Why else hadn't Magehold's army arrived to restore order during the siege? Had it conveniently been "just after" he, Rielle, Brennan, Leigh, the Black Rose, and the Order had already done the job?

Was this why the Grand Divinus refused to send aid now?

But why? What reason would the Grand Divinus have had to wipe out all the Faralles? They'd been nothing but compliant when it came to the Divinity.

Brennan bared his teeth. "You're just going to let him—"

"Leave him be. He'll stand trial in Courdeval." And he had the answers he needed tonight. Or at least enough of them. The key to the cell door could stay in his pocket. For now.

Brennan struck Sincuore into the bars once more, hard, then threw him back upon the stone. "I'll see you dead, Captain of the Rats."

No answer.

Brennan spat upon the stone, then joined Jon on the way out.

"Did he lie about anything?" Jon asked. With his werewolf senses, Brennan could tell the truth from lies, or so Rielle had claimed.

"No," Brennan snapped. "You think it was really the Grand Divinus? Why bother with the Faralles? No offense," Brennan said quietly, just before they reached the door.

They exited, passing the young guard, and entered the stairwell with Raoul and Florian.

"I intend to find out," Jon replied. This single fact could bring down the Divinity entirely, disband the Towers, put mages under the dominion of their respective countries' rulers. "If it's true, our prayers will be answered."

"Good luck proving it." Brennan shrugged, jogging up the stairs. "We should have just killed him."

"We got some answers," Jon said, "but Courdeval's inquisitors have ways of loosening his tongue further."

Brennan eyed him peripherally. "You've changed. I like it."

Like it or not, there were necessities he couldn't turn away from. He wouldn't compromise on the cornerstones of who he was, but he wouldn't cripple the kingdom with immovable rigidity, either. At least not for his remaining time.

He still had to choose a successor.

CHAPTER 7

$\mathcal{I}$t was a strange thing to wake up without Brennan beside her. She'd grown accustomed to the sultry heat of him next to her, like sleeping by the fire, and of his strong arm around her, holding her close, holding her safe. His warm breath on her head, that low, rolling sound he always made as he stirred awake. The way she could wriggle into him, press the whole of her back against his hot, solid body, and make that embrace of his curl tighter.

But this morning it was Olivia, softly snoring even as the sun rose. Olivia had said they were leaving today, and then it would be time to face the Divinity.

There was no way she was giving up being a mage. She'd worked too hard to earn her mastery, thrived on missions too well to turn away now. If Kieran wanted to throw her out of the Tower, he could go right ahead. But that wouldn't be the end of it. Not until she contacted Magehold.

Marko had come to awaken your sister. She would have had her éveil and served the world, served the Most High. On

Khar'shil, Shadow had alleged it had been the *Divinity*, not pirates, who'd planned the attack on Laurentine.

Liam hadn't believed it, and she wasn't sure herself. There would have to be more evidence than the word of a homicidal mercenary mage-captain to prove such a claim against the Divinity.

Until then, she still planned to earn the magister's mantle. The Magisterium was still the most powerful and influential body of mages on earth, where international policy could be set to save thousands. To end piracy on the Shining Sea altogether. And maybe even use the position of magister to investigate Shadow's dubious claims.

A door closed softly in the hallway. Probably Jon heading out to the practice yard, keeping to his routine.

Olivia blinked her eyes half-open sluggishly, inhaled, and chuckled softly. "Are you watching me sleep?" she slurred, closing her eyes once more.

"Mm-hmm. That's what happens when I barely get to see you. I need to work harder to memorize your face."

Another laugh. "Make sure you memorize my good side."

"Which one's that?" Rielle ducked before Olivia could swat her with a pillow.

They got out of bed and prepared for the day while Jon's servants packed up his things and Olivia's.

After writing to Kieran and finishing her review of Laurentine's defenses—and hiring of a new steward, she and Brennan would probably leave in a couple days, too, traveling fast on horseback in a small group.

Outside, in the castle's inner bailey, she held Brennan's hand as the royal host prepared to leave. Olivia gave her a hug, threatened Brennan with a thrashing if he misbehaved, then took to a carriage while the grooms led out Jon's white destrier.

He followed in full armor but for his helm, flexing his fingers and their knuckle-dusters. The shadows under his eyes had faded with a good night's rest, and he looked to be well this morning.

"Thank you," she said to him, bowing, "for saving my people. I am in your debt."

A corner of his mouth turned up, his Shining Sea eyes glimmering as he inclined his head. "There is no debt. Thank you for your hospitality." He mounted his horse and glanced at them once more, pulling the reins tight. "Will I see you both at the coronation?"

She grinned. Of course—

"We'll be there, Your Majesty," Brennan replied, "assuming someone clears the road of beasts for us."

A low laugh rumbled in Jon's throat. "A blade's job is never done." His gaze moved from Brennan to her, and his face softened, dulled, for the briefest of moments before he gave her a final slow nod, smiled politely, and departed.

For a long while, she just stood there, holding Brennan's hand tightly in hers, watching as the last of the soldiers exited with the prison carriages—including Sincuore, for trial—through the gates. Children chased after them cheerily, and Brennan watched them as they laughed and played, his smile wistful... fatherly. He wanted to be chasing after his own laughing children.

She tried to watch with him, but a knot tightened in her belly, and she shuddered. *Not now. Not yet.*

The last sounds of clinking armor and clopping hooves faded. Her feet stayed firmly planted, didn't follow. Wouldn't.

He gave her hand a yank until she fell against him with a yelp, and then he wrapped her in his arms, where she belonged.

She'd missed this last night, how perfectly she fit into him, the flow of familiarity and comfort sweeping through her body like a warm caress. A warm caress that, against his firm muscle, heated.

She tucked her head under his chin, relishing his heat, his hold, him. That hold slid down to her hand, and with a devilish grin, he headed inside with her.

When there was no one in the foyer, she pushed him up against the wall, rose on her tiptoes, and kissed him, claimed his hot lips, sought out his tongue while she pressed into his hard body, inhaling his spice. She hadn't forgotten their moment in the stairwell last night. Far from it.

Laughing between kisses, he held her close, taking her mouth playfully at first, then with a growing hunger that became urgency as he spun her and molded his body to hers. Breathlessly, she leaned into him, against his hardness, his fire —and Divine, it was the strongest, darkest magic that infiltrated her body from his, a rush into her that flowed into every corner of her being with a rising heat, a will that would not be denied, that moved her in ancient, primal ways. He hissed into her mouth, taking hold of her hips, his firm touch sliding to grip her backside before lifting her up, flush against his core.

"Please," she breathed against his lips, locking her legs around him. "Make me yours, Brennan," she whispered.

Something like a frustrated growl vibrated low in his throat. "All in good time, bride."

A snarl rolling in his chest, he set her down, amber eyed, then smoothed her hair in a fluid movement and held her to him, his back to the stairs.

"What—"

He closed his eyes, breathing hard. "So help me Nox, if it's another messenger, I'm going to—"

Hurried steps came to a halt. "My lady—" a maid stammered, then swallowed.

Rielle looked around Brennan, still clutched in his hold, and laid eyes on a pale maidservant, her blue eyes stark against her blanched skin. "Yes?"

The maid inclined her head and held out parchment with a trembling hand. "This just arrived from Magehold, my lady."

Magehold. The word shuddered through her core like a bolt of lightning.

She accepted the message.

"By your leave, my lady." With a bow, the maid departed.

It wasn't until the paper fluttered loudly that she realized her own hand was shaking. Answers. This was it.

With a slow exhale, Brennan cradled her head against his chest. He rubbed her back gently. "Whatever it is, it'll be all right." He kissed the crown of her head. "I promise."

When he promised everything would be all right, it felt like the truth. Like she could close her eyes and breathe deeply and stride into the future of her life without fear, always knowing he was there should she falter, should some shadow attempt to cast its darkness over her. He wouldn't let her down, let her hurt, let her fail.

He pulled away only to raise her chin and kiss her softly. "Come. Let's find out what Magehold wants of you."

Tucking her arm around his, he led her upstairs and to the lord's apartment, where her household had moved her things since Jon had left.

They crossed the antechamber and the study, and in the bedchamber, Brennan led her to one of the armchairs by the fire and lowered her into it. He pulled another nearer and sat, eyeing the message in her hand.

A part of her needed to know—right away—what her fate

would be. But another part, a larger part, wanted *never* to know, and couldn't bear to crack open the Grand Divinus's wax seal.

Divine, the *Grand Divinus* herself had sent it?

She shivered, shook her head, and covering her face, held out the message to Brennan.

This was either the next step in her career, or the end of it.

The paper wisped from between her fingers, and then the telltale crack of wax and crinkle of unfolding paper followed.

"To the distinguished Master Mage Favrielle Amadour Lothaire, Champion of Courdeval," Brennan read in a wooden tone.

Distinguished. It couldn't be so bad if the Grand Divinus used *distinguished.* Unless it was ironically. She winced.

"You have been bestowed the great honor of an invitation to participate in the Magister Trials at Magehold, to begin the 16th of Floreal," Brennan continued. "The victor will be granted the title of Magister and a single boon. I trust we shall see you then. Regards, Eleftheria II."

Divine. She thought she'd spoken the oath aloud, but only a tremulous hiss emerged. "Test for magister."

With a sigh, he tossed the message on the low table before him. "An invitation you can ignore completely."

Ignore? She shook her head and lunged for the message. Could it really be—

But as she read, it only confirmed what she'd heard. "Test for magister..."

Brennan leaned back in the chair and sprawled out. "You don't need the Divinity anymore." When she didn't reply, he continued, "You're about to become the Marquise of Laurentine *and* Tregarde, Baroness of Calterre, and a Marcel. You'll have plenty of power and influence, and more than enough to do. This test is the last thing you need. Refuse the invitation."

She stared at him. He couldn't possibly be serious. "You know this is what I've worked toward for almost ten years."

He shrugged. "And we've been betrothed far longer than that. Trust me, you'll have plenty to do. You won't even have time for the Divinity."

For years, the magister's mantle had been all she'd wanted. Mastery of her magic, membership in the Magisterium, access to the Grand Divinus herself, and a chance to stop the piracy that had killed her family.

A single boon...

She could ask the Grand Divinus to end piracy on the Shining Sea. The Divinity could dedicate more resources to coastal settlements and maybe merchant ships.

Just how stupid are you, Favrielle? Shadow's words rang in her head. *You didn't think it strange that "pirates" attacked and didn't kill anyone? Not even as a show of force?*

She clutched the paper tight in her hand. Shadow had claimed that her husband had come to awaken Dominique, that it had all been the Divinity's scheme.

If that was true, the only people who could confirm would be the Hensarin. If there was any record, it would be in the Archives at Magehold, a place she'd never had access to, never even had an excuse to be *near* to...

The chance to end piracy. Access to the Archives. "I won't refuse."

"Why not? Weren't you staying with the Divinity to keep me from"—he paused, sliding an amused gaze her way—"enforcing the marriage contract?"

Oh, *that*. It seemed like ages ago. She smiled. "Partially, yes. Obviously that doesn't matter anymore." She reached out and stroked his hand lightly, playing softly across his skin. "But that wasn't the only reason, and you know it. I wanted to learn all there was to know about my magic, controlling it, mastering it—"

"You have."

"—so I could use it to help other people. You know pirates invaded Laurentine. I also thought I could work to prevent such attacks, as part of the Magisterium—"

He took her hand, rubbed the garnet ring with his thumb. "You can be far more influential once we're married. And someday the Duchess of Maerleth Tainn."

She blinked slowly. There *was* power in land and title, but that wasn't everything either. "There's also what Shadow told me." She swallowed. "That the Divinity is responsible for what happened to Laurentine."

With a crease etched between his eyebrows, he tapped a finger on his bicep as he stared into the fire. "You want to look into what she told you."

A darkness passed over his face.

After that day on Khar'shil, she'd told Brennan everything. "Why shouldn't I? We have an invitation to go to Magehold, and once we're there, the Archives are just another door. All the secret records will be there, even for black operations, in the Archives."

He glared at her.

If what Shadow had said of the Divinity was true, then its dark dealings had to be brought to light, its power stripped, every victim made whole, or as whole as could be made.

"I want to go for everyone else who *doesn't* know why their loved ones were killed, and for those who might be hunted by the Divinity in the future."

Brennan slapped a palm against the armrest. "They're not your responsibility."

"Yes, they are. If I pass the test, I'll get a boon from the

Grand Divinus. I could end piracy on the Shining Sea. That'll help Laurentine, and every other coastal city, town, and village, and so many more. And once I'm part of the Magisterium, I could fix how the Divinity operates from within."

He heaved a sigh. "And you want to stick your finger in Jon's eye."

After he'd rejected her help? Maybe a little.

"That *would* be a bonus." He exhaled lengthily.

"I'm going," she said. "Are you coming with me or not?"

"What else do I have to stay for?" He held her gaze. "Where you go, I go."

Good. Even if it wasn't what he wanted, at least he'd support her in her choice.

"But you're conveniently forgetting that if you're caught infiltrating the Archives, the Grand Divinus will lock you up."

With the entry to the Divinity's secret Archives being through the tightly guarded Hensar, there had always been rumors about what wonders were inside—priceless treasures, relics, artifacts, private documents and letters between the most powerful people in the world's history.

But the most valuable items in the Archives were also the most mundane: records. Leigh had told her the Archives contained meticulous records of every order ever given—both public and private—by any Grand Divinus. Continuity of history for each new Grand Divinus, with access only to the highest ranks—the elites among the Hensarin, those chosen by the Grand Divinus, and the Grand Divinus herself.

Records like those for a black operation to attack Laurentine and compel Dominique's éveil.

Others had surely tried to infiltrate the Archives... but she had an advantage they wouldn't have had.

She grinned. "If they caught me trying to break in, they'd

lock *me* up, but... Brennan," she asked, turning to face him, "how good a thief are you?"

His eyes widened briefly before he crossed his arms. He'd stolen her from House Hazael. He'd infiltrated Courdeval during the siege. Could he find a way into the Archives?

Could she ask him to?

"Thief?" He arched a brow.

She folded the note. "What if I had a daring werewolf fiancé, who could stealthily move about Magehold in my stead and learn the truth of the matter while I participate in the trials?"

He huffed. "Is that all?"

Her grin widened. He was immune to magic, could turn into a wolf, and was stronger, faster, and more perceptive than a human. If he agreed, they'd have answers.

"Wherever you go, bride, you bring trouble on your arm," he said with a sigh and a smug smile.

"Oh, is that your new nickname?"

"Trying to ply me with your feminine wiles?"

"Why, is it working?"

He laughed. "Not even close," he whispered, and she gasped. "You see, I'd agreed before you even asked." A grin teased his mouth. "I mean, who can resist a good eye-poking?"

"Not you?" she tested.

He let the grin broaden. "Not me." He nodded to the message in her hand. "But it did say 'victor.'"

The Magister Trial was a series of tests, which if the master mage passed, she or he would be granted the magister's mantle.

But the invitation had said the Magister *Trials*. Plural.

"It's a competition," she breathed. There was no telling what would be involved. It could be anything. But the Magister Trial had always been designed to test for three specific qualities all magisters were required to possess—perceptiveness, resourcefulness, and willingness to sacrifice for the greater good. These new trials couldn't deviate too far from that, could they? They'd only be different in that they'd have multiple candidates instead of one at a time.

"You still feel up to this?"

She hadn't been known as one of the Tower's best duelists for nothing. "Magic is my life."

His gaze fixed on the fire, Brennan nodded solemnly, letting the silence settle. "All right, then. It begins in two weeks, so we'll have to leave tomorrow."

"You'll really come with me?" She couldn't imagine doing this without him.

He nodded. "I'm certainly not about to let you go by yourself."

CHAPTER 8

Samara smoothed the book page as she wrote in the last of the heart tonic's ingredients, sunlight dancing a pattern on a page through the window's mashrabiya.

Coriander, karia algae, horned turtle bean...

The pounding of heavy steps came from the hallway, and she lifted her gaze to the door, squinting in the light.

A black-clad guard strode in, willowy and young with a dense beard. "Pack your things."

Pack her things? What? "Taj?"

"Now," he said, gesturing at all her medicines, the myriad shelves that lined the walls with jars. "Pack up everything. Your things, your tools, whatever it is you use. Immediately."

Before she could open her mouth to ask further questions, he turned on his heel and strode out.

Pack up everything. Immediately.

She put a hand to her forehead. Sold. She had to be.

Zahib Imtiyaz had died in the fire, and now there was no certainty of anything. Just over a month ago, right after the fire, a woman had inquired about her purchase, explaining to Zahib Farrad that she sought an apothecary to tend her while she awaited the birth of her first child, but Zahib Farrad had sent her away. Had he changed his mind?

Her hands already worked, packing what few personal belongings she had into a leather satchel. Her house robes and her mother's comb. She packed her mortar and pestle, weights and scales, empty jars, surgical tools, as well as common liniments, potions, and pills. If she was being sold, had he sold the apothecary equipment, too? Did her new zahib not have anything?

By the Divine, let it be the woman needing some midwifery. Not some brutish zahib. But no, it wouldn't be—

A soft rap on the open door. A shadow loomed in the doorway. "I trust Taj told you to pack?"

He looked nothing like a man who'd nearly died in a fire a couple months ago, who'd been deceived and attacked by his enslaved lover. No burns, no scars, just nearly six feet of warrior, and zahib of this house.

"Yes, Zahib," she said sullenly as he entered. Why? Why had he sold her? Hadn't she served this House well her entire life?

But she could ask none of those questions. It wasn't her place.

He simply stood while she continued packing, just standing there, hovering, and the urge to shout all those questions and more at him rose.

"You're free, Samara," Zahib said softly, "but on one condition: you agree to attend a university to further your apothecary studies."

Free?

She dropped the jar of queen's lace in her hand, and it shattered on the floor, shimmering in the sunlight.

Zahib, having watched its fall, merely raised a dark eyebrow.

"Free?" she repeated.

"Yes. I've planned this for years, and now that..." He lowered his gaze, then straightened. "Now I have the power to do it. You're to be packed and ready for travel first, and then I'll make the announcement to the rest of the House. Every single slave is to be freed, given enough araqs to live on for at least a year, and House Hazael is to hire all the help it needs, or any freed slaves who wish to stay on as freemen to work."

This was—She couldn't—"University?" she squeaked.

"Yes. I want you to further your studies, and you can't stay here." He sat on the stool across from her table, hitching his rapier.

"Can't?" she asked before she could think the better of it. *Free* or not, she was still in House Hazael. Until her brand was removed, until she had her documents in hand, until she was far, far away from Xir, *free* was just a word.

He exhaled lengthily. "You're the only one I can trust not to revert to the old ways."

The old ways. Slavery. "The only one?"

He cleared his throat. "The only one of my children."

So *now* she was one of his children? For years, she'd been nothing but property, but *now* he wanted to call her his child? She shook her head. "I don't understand."

"I've made you my heir and left everything I own to you. When I die, everything here will be yours," he said, holding her gaze.

The words had been said, but seemed no more than air. Heavy, stifling, suffocating air.

Figures moved past in the hall. Time went on. But she couldn't believe her ears.

"Zahib, I am in no position to—"

"I'm your Zahib no longer, Samara. 'Ab.'"

Ab? Call him her father? She was still in House Hazael, but the word would never pass her lips. "That is all I have ever known, Zahib. For all my fifteen years."

"It is my hope that you will come to know me for who I truly am, Samara, not who my grandfather forced me to be."

He asked too much. Far too much. Her hands resumed their work, stuffing pouches into her satchel. "You could have left," she dared to murmur.

"I wanted to," he snapped. "And then where would you be? Under Ihsan's thumb. Or worse."

Did he expect her sympathy? As her zahib, she hadn't had a choice but to openly sympathize with him.

He reached into his thiyawb and pulled out some papers, then handed them to her. "Your freedom. The documents have all been signed and recorded."

As she reached for them, her arm trembled, and she could barely feel her fingers, but they closed around the paper. Smooth, with small, occasional bits of grain against her skin. She held them to her chest, the fresh smell her first as a free woman.

It was true. All true.

"But Zahib, your wives will—"

He stood. "They won't," he said firmly. "That's why we need to be far from here as soon as I announce the House's freedom. What happened to your mother will *not* happen to you."

"But when I return—"

"You can't return. Not until I'm dead, and even then, you'd need guards. Trusted guards. But I will accompany you to university and ascertain you're properly settled and well guarded before I travel back here and bring the House to order."

Then that was the rush? He truly was setting everyone free. "If only Thahab had—"

His hand clenched his rapier's hilt. "Do *not* speak that woman's name to me. If ever she crosses my path, I will see her dead."

It was all Samara could do to nod.

Thahab had been with child, had wanted her child to be born in freedom. Didn't he understand that? And it was only her rebellion that had led to Zahib Imtiyaz's death and everyone's freedom.

And if he crossed her path, he'd challenge her to a duel? No doubt she couldn't fight well with a sword, and dueling was law in most countries.

He'd always been the fairest of the Hazaels, but still a zahib. Still a master.

No, she would not sympathize with Farrad abd Nasir abd Imtiyaz Hazael, heir to House Hazael and its old ways, whose rebellious thoughts had amounted to nothing but perfect obedience to Zahib Imtiyaz's wishes until a *slave* had rebelled. No, she would not sympathize with a young lord who had benefited from his House's cruelty, been served by its slaves, taken them to bed when they hadn't felt free to deny him, allowed them to be mistreated and even killed.

Poor rich, powerful, sated young lord.

She stuffed her satchel and fastened its closure.

No, she would not sympathize with Farrad abd Nasir abd Imtiyaz Hazael, no matter what he said or did now.

THE CRIMSON PEAKS of Laurentine's castle just came into view when Leigh brought his horse to a stop behind Ambriel. With any luck, they'd charter a ship tonight or tomorrow to take them searching for Venetha Tramus.

It was just past midday, and he could do with lunch. Well, *Emaurrian* lunch. None of that raw-vegetable light-elven nonsense.

He shut his book on light-elven history and looked up. "I normally don't make the offer, my dear," he began, "but after the atrocity of leaves and grasses that was breakfast, *I* shall make us lunch."

Ambriel shot him a glare over his shoulder, a narrowing of his honey-gold eyes. Even when he was annoyed, those chiseled features were art. "Not lunch, dreshan," he murmured. "We only just ate a few hours ago, and you had that... *that—*"

"Walnut loaf?" If any food gods were listening, they deserved the highest praise for inspiring the Emaurrian Army to bring *baked goods*—precious, precious *baked goods*—from Courdeval when they'd gone to war.

"Yes, 'walnut loaf.' You had some on the way, and now you want lunch, too?" Frowning, Ambriel shook his head. "How did you think we'd make any progress?"

Leigh urged his horse up next to Ambriel and paused, arching a brow. "Does it matter whether we spend another night on the road—or a night on a ship—as long as it's together?"

Ambriel pursed his lips and lowered his eyebrows. Pretending to be impervious to his charms? He'd sing a different tune tonight. A loud, full-throated tune.

"Besides, walnut loaf is part of your mission," Leigh said with a smile. Queen Narenian had agreed to let Ambriel accompany him to Venetha Tramus with the stipulation that Ambriel "witness" modern human civilization, record his observations, and ensure that, if they succeeded in performing the Sundering ritual again, the light-elves be excluded.

"There's a large party approaching," Ambriel said, looking into the distance.

"Mother earth, grant me your sight, / Show through your eyes, reveal all life," Leigh whispered, casting the earthsight spell with an incantation.

Indeed, hundreds of people approached, with two near the front glowing like a sun. He dispelled the earthsight and smiled. "It's His Majesty."

Ambriel's wide eyes blinked once, twice.

Different. Tune. Leigh grinned broadly. "Well, let's go meet with him, shall we?"

Clearing his throat, Ambriel nodded and urged his horse to a trot. It wasn't long before Jon, gleaming in full armor, waved and met them, bringing his cavalcade to a halt. He and a squad of Royal Guard headed off the road and dismounted.

Leigh inclined his head, but arms closed around him. Smiling, he patted Jon's back. "Did you miss me, Your Majesty?"

Jon laughed and pulled away, then clasped Ambriel's arm. "I can't deny things are much easier with a wild mage around."

Weren't they always?

"Leigh!" Olivia gathered her skirts as she ran to him, then kissed his cheek and hugged him. "You've been busy, haven't you?"

It had been over a month since he'd seen her in Courdeval. There was more color in her cheeks, a vitality to her movements—new life in her. Being out of the palace had done her good.

He turned to Ambriel. "Ambriel Sunheart, this is Olivia Sabeyon, the Archmage of Emaurria and my former apprentice."

Olivia bowed gracefully as Ambriel inclined his head. "It is my honor to meet you," she said in Old Emaurrian.

"The honor is all mine," Ambriel said in passable Emaurrian. They'd been practicing in the evenings.

Olivia lit up. "Has Leigh been practicing Emaurrian with you? That's wonderful," she said in Emaurrian. "I'd love to learn Elvish myself."

Ambriel smiled.

"Well, Fabien is working on it," Leigh interrupted. The young man Jon had sent to replace him as Ambassador to Vervewood had arrived with linguists and an impressive work ethic. "He boasts that there will be a text ready in a few months."

Olivia's eyebrows rose.

"It's a blessing we've run into you," Jon said, placing a hand on his shoulder. "How would you like to help us break with the Divinity?"

More welcome words had never been spoken.

It was less than half an hour later when fires had been built, a tent had been pitched, and servants brought out fresh rye bread, butter, goat cheese, grapes, and smoked fish. And wine. Heavenly, delicious, essential *wine*.

He drained a goblet before he sat down and sighed happily as the serving man poured a second. Although Jon did not partake, Olivia joined him for a drink.

Ambriel was "witnessing" the soldiers, although they both knew he was being polite and giving him the space to meet with his king.

"So what is this help you require with the Divinity?" Leigh asked, leaning back in his chair.

Jon and Olivia exchanged a look, and Jon nodded to her.

"Although we've sent for aid and offered exorbitant payment, Magehold has refused to send us the help we need to handle the Immortals and the pirates attacking the west coast. Kieran sent a single pair of mages, as much as his discretion would allow without having to ask the Divinity," she said.

Ella and Cédric. Not nearly enough to address Emaurria's needs. "Clearly a problem. I hope you don't think I hold any sway with Magehold?"

Olivia laughed. "Don't be ridiculous."

"At least *pretend* it's possible," Leigh grumbled.

"The Divinity isn't the only source of mages," Olivia continued.

"The Covens." But essentially an act of war.

"Right. But if we ally with the Covens, we'll be siding with the Divinity's enemies and inviting its wrath," she said. "And the Divinity hasn't *publicly* denied Emaurria aid—"

"So you mean to force the Grand Divinus's hand." Brilliant. "If you request aid publicly and she denies you, then she's abandoned Emaurria first. You're free to pursue assistance from whomever you choose. And if she grants your request, you have your mages."

Jon nodded.

"So what do you need my help with?"

"When Rielle was escorting me from the Tower," Jon began, leaning forward, "we fell into some underground ruins and faced some heretics. They spoke of someone stopping a hydromancer from reaching his destination." He raised his eyebrows at Leigh.

Nina Bousquet and Richard Vallée. Both dead now, courtesy of Rielle and Jon.

"If you have any ties to the Covens, would you use them to win them over to our side?"

Ties—oh, he had ties. Many, and many more than he

should. Ava being one he didn't want to tangle further. And Blaise—

He sighed. "But you don't even know if the Divinity will deny or grant your request."

Jon crossed his arms, a corner of his mouth turning up.

"You *do* know. You think the Grand Divinus will find a way to deny you."

"If she's refused to send help so far, especially considering the vast sums offered, I doubt she has any intention of helping." Leigh sighed. "But the formality must be observed."

"And as soon as it is, we *must* have a force in place," Olivia said, "or the world will know our weakness."

Jon prostrating himself before the Grand Divinus would be a ripple across the region, signaling Emaurria's readiness for conquest.

They had to have a force prepared, and a *show of force* at that, to contradict any such notions.

So they wanted him to negotiate with the Covens and win them over for the Crown.

"The Tremblays, the Forgerons, the Beaufoys—" Olivia began.

Leigh held up a hand. "I understand." The last thing he ever wanted to do was visit Axelle and Adeline—Della—Beaufoy, but if the prize was breaking Emaurria from the Divinity, the proposition was worth hearing. Ava didn't need to know who he was to her, especially if her mother hadn't told her where the money came from each month. It was better that way. Safer. "But what I need to know is... What if the Grand Divinus gives you everything you ask for?"

Jon shook his head. "It would be for a nefarious purpose." He lowered his gaze. "Pons agreed when Derric asked him to send me an escort to Monas Amar. *Pons* did. The Grand

Divinus has never lifted a finger to help me. And she wouldn't start now." He looked at Olivia, who patted his hand supportively. "If she grants my request, it'll only be a waiting game until she turns on me. The Covens are Emaurrian. I *will* unite them under the Crown, whether it's next month, next year, or in a few years. But we need to open a dialogue now."

The Covens had been waiting for a king who didn't kneel at the Divinity's feet, completely under its control. And Jon—a former-paladin king—was their best chance.

Leigh crossed his legs. If he had to sell this to the Covens, it would mean favors. Lots and lots of favors.

And funds... Oh, the funds. "I'll need broad latitude to—"

"You'll have everything you need," Jon said. "You've proven yourself with Vervewood. You're committed to this. That's all I need to know."

Leigh raised his eyebrows. He'd serve the Crown until the end of time if Jon kept talking like *that*.

"Will you do it?" Olivia asked, her green eyes gleaming.

He and Ambriel had been on their way to charter a ship, to search for Venetha Tramus and answers about the Sundering, but... the Divinity had been a problem he'd long needed to solve.

He might be able to coordinate the Covens in a couple of months, and then he and Ambriel could proceed. Would Ambriel be willing to wait? Would he join him on this mission?

Well, it *was* more "witnessing" of modern human civilization, wasn't it?

Either way... It was something he had to do. For himself. For Hana, Takumi, and Yuki. For every mage out there.

He extended an arm to Jon, who clasped it. "I'll do it."

CHAPTER 9

*I*t was almost dusk when Brennan pulled Rielle up behind him on his black destrier. She sneaked open a saddlebag, but he clapped it closed.

She pouted audibly. "Just a peek?"

"Not yet." He took her hand as she sighed and curled it around his waist. She interlaced it with her other, holding tightly to him.

"All right... My hands *are* happy to wait right here." She moaned softly, happily, as she pressed her palms against his abdomen.

He shook his head, fighting a smile. *Touch all you want, snarling little she-wolf.*

She was in a good mood, at least. All day, she'd been a tangled knot of nerves and worry, ruminating over the trials when they knew nothing of them, but when he'd come to her with a *surprise*, she'd perked up. If he could keep her from worrying, even for an evening, it was worth the effort.

"But at least tell me where we're going," she whispered in his ear.

"Not a chance," he said over his shoulder as he urged his horse on. They'd spent the afternoon arranging travel, writing correspondence, and preparing. At her urging, he'd written Kehani again, asking if she'd successfully purchased Samara from House Hazael to free her. He'd even included their travel plans so Kehani could contact them as soon as she'd succeeded. They'd sent their regrets about the coronation to Jon, and she'd sent a message to Liam in Gazgan about the trials. "It's a surprise, since we're leaving tomorrow morning and we're missing Ignis."

No place celebrated Ignis like Maerleth Tainn, which was where he'd planned to celebrate with her before they'd gotten word of the pirate attacks. With such a wealth of land there, the fertility rituals to ensure a bountiful crop each season were critical. The bonfires, the music, the decorations, the *food*—and the dazzling maypoles. But what he'd most looked forward to was the maying, the maidens all running out into the forest with their chosen suitors in pursuit. The thought of Rielle running into the woods, wishing for *his* pursuit, waiting to be caught—

Heat rippled through him. "Before we get on a cramped ship and walk into a death trap, I want us to have at least one evening together, alone, quiet."

She rested her cheek against his back. "No messengers."

"No visitors." He urged his horse faster. There was a spot nearby, a place he used to visit whenever his moonlit runs brought him near Laurentine, and he'd finally share it with her and hear those three words. Tonight.

He would surprise her, impress her, reassure her. A quiet night together. Perfect. Just the two of them. And she'd love only him. She'd say it. Finally.

He shook off a shiver.

When they reached the edge of the woods, he slowed, picking their way through the white-barked aspens to the small hilltop glade, where the clear waters of the Aes River rushed nearby.

He dismounted and helped her down, then tied the horse to a tree.

"Where are we?" she asked, looking around.

He took her hand and led her to the center. "I used to come here on my runs, sometimes to watch the sunrise or the sunset, or just for the quiet." He paused, and the river's hum claimed the moment. "That's the Aes River just below." He took her to the edge of the hill that overlooked the water.

Clear, clean, and only about eight feet at its deepest, it was perfect for drinking, bathing, swimming. The aspens framed it with their happy white trunks, shaded it with feathery canopies. The golden rays of the setting sun poured in, dappling the river water with a dancing shimmer.

"It's beautiful," she whispered, covering her mouth.

All the more with her here. She'd braided her long golden waves over her shoulder, and wore her usual outfit of crisp white shirt, vest, fitted trousers, and riding boots, although today the vest was gray brocade and she'd donned an elegant deep-pink velvet riding coat over it all. Well tailored, it hugged her curves, showing off her round breasts and the swell of her hips and ample bottom; since returning to Emaurria, she'd regained some of the weight she'd lost and was beginning to look like herself again.

"You used to go on runs near Laurentine?" she asked, squeezing his hand.

All the time. "Even when I was being a bastard to you, I think a part of me still wanted to feel close to you in some way."

She laid her head against his bicep and eyed the flowing river pensively. "We wasted so many good years fighting."

"That's why we won't waste even a single day more." He kissed her head, then gently urged her back toward the horse.

No, he'd enjoy every moment they'd have together until the day he died. Although that—that was a problem in and of itself. As a werewolf, he was an Immortal, wasn't he? There would be no dying for him unless she broke the curse. Unless she agreed to have his child, something he wanted very much, for different reasons.

If she didn't... If she didn't, someday he'd have to watch her *die*, watch his life breathe its last breath, and yet keep walking this earth for all time.

He sighed. That was an issue for another night. Nothing had to be resolved *now*. Tonight was about... *far* more pleasant things. After he'd hear her say it.

He built a small campfire that she spelled alight. Grinning, he pulled out a blanket from the saddlebags, spread it near a tree, then removed a large wedge of soft Milun cheese in its white rind, a sliced boule loaf, sausages, oatcakes, green almond compote, quince marmalade, and custard tarts—her favorite. And the all-important bottle of Melletoire red, along with a pair of goblets.

"Brennan, you..."

As he laid it all out, he could feel her eyes on him, hear her pulse quicken. All as intended. A smile curled up the corners of his mouth as he finished. When he finally turned to her, arms spread, she jumped into them.

"All of this," she whispered, her awed voice quivering. "You did all of this for me?"

Tightening his hold, he breathed her in. "Sit before we miss the sunset."

She giggled and did as he bade, a little grin teasing her mouth. "Humble."

"Charming," he replied.

"And devastatingly handsome." She arched a brow and held out her goblet.

"I can't argue with the truth, can I?" he replied as he poured the red. He sat against the tree and spread his arms and knees.

She wriggled into his embrace, resting her back against his chest, and watched the sky change with him.

Golds became pinks and pinks became reds as the daylight began to slumber. They ate and drank, watching the sky's dazzling show of color, letting the quiet's serenity flow into their bones.

As the last rays of sun bid them goodbye, he tightened his hold around her, rested his chin on her shoulder, and breathed her in.

Great Wolf, she smelled like rapture. Her earthy scent, subtle sweetness, that rose note—he wanted to inhale her, drown in that rapture, live in it.

She leaned into him, bared her neck, and he traced his nose along her delicate skin, slowly, gently, the lightest of touches. A shiver rippled tremulous breaths out of her, and she whimpered softly.

Her heartbeat quickening, she wriggled, turning in his embrace to face him on her knees. She captured his face in her gentle palms and leaned in, the fading sun casting a shimmering glow on her golden hair as she brushed his lips with hers. He stroked a hand up her back, brought her closer, and as her tongue demanded his, she shifted, rising to bring her knees around his hips in the grass.

Heat settled on him, and he growled into her mouth, his hold tightening, his kiss deepening. Great Wolf, she drove him mad with hunger, a deep-seated, ever-growing hunger that would not be denied, never be sated until he buried himself in her.

Say it.

Holding her securely, he rose enough to lay her on the blanket, and pinned her. "Rielle—"

"Your next words are 'I want you,'" she whispered, kissing his neck as she unbuttoned her riding coat, shirt, and vest, "or you'll leave me no choice..."

"No choice?" He pressed his lips to the space between her breasts. "No choice but what?"

She laughed under her breath.

As the evening breeze brought the freshness of the grass, the musk of the aspens, he slid his hand down from her waist to her hip, then lightly over her round ass, sweeping soft circles with his palm that grew in firmness.

He gripped that supple flesh, eliciting a sharp exhalation as he pulled her closer. Her eyes locked with his, she nodded, and her breathing shallowed on parted lips. Lips begging to be reclaimed. He bridged the distance, and she met him, her hand gliding up his chest and around to the back of his neck.

Say it.

Fingernails dug through his hair, and she gripped a fistful, keeping him to her as she took his mouth with a growing ardor. Soft wool bunched in his hand as he lowered her trousers until at last his fingers brushed linen and lace. He traced a finger down her hip to her upper thigh, her soft, squirming, upper thigh.

No, as much as he wanted to, he couldn't do this. Not until he knew it for certain. Not until she said it.

"Brennan," she breathed against his lips. "Don't stop."

Closing his eyes, he paused, then drew back. Perhaps they weren't ready after all.

She stood, then bent to remove one boot, and the other. Drew her trousers and socks down and off. Let the unbuttoned coat, vest, and shirt fall off her shoulders until only her corset and lacy underwear remained—baring long, shapely legs. An invitation.

A very *tempting* invitation.

She reached behind her back and loosened her corset, unhooked it in the front until it, too, fell away. Shimmying out of the lace, she finally stood gloriously naked and unbound her hair from its braid.

His eyes wanted to look everywhere at once. At her round, beautiful breasts, the smooth expanse of her stomach, the crux of pleasure between her legs. Her gleaming eyes, her raised chin, her full lips. Like she'd stepped out of one of his dreams, all these years as his friend, his enemy, his everything, when he'd pictured her eyeing him just like this.

"Deny me." She said it like a challenge, daring him to turn away from her as she faced him bare, bold, confident.

He grabbed ahold of her, crushed his mouth against hers, taking everything she had to give. No words, but her love was in her lips teasing his, her soft hair tickling his neck, her hands rushing in their work, unfastening his buttons, pulling at his clothes, ripping, and he helped her, throwing down everything but his overcoat without abandoning her delicious lips for even a moment.

RIELLE KEPT her arms locked around him, the heat of his mouth against hers irresistible, delicious, addictive.

That heat lit a fire that demanded more, and she obeyed,

pillaging his mouth with her tongue, laving fiercely, undeterred by the spring chill, her hands ravenously exploring his body. Every touch, every part of him against her skin filled her up, with heat, with need. With him.

She would know him, every part of him, tonight. Before the voyage, before the trials, before everything.

He knotted a hand in her hair, cradling her head, and pulled her closer still, matching her need with his own. His breaths came faster and harder, and as she leaned into him, she felt his unmistakable arousal—and it stoked the heat between them to blazing.

She inhaled the familiarity of him, cinnamon spice and cypress amid a scent undeniably his, undeniably masculine, that had driven her mad with desire years ago and still did. *Brennan.* Her *Brennan.* Here, under her touch. She'd known the smell of him since her childhood, as she'd cared for him, loved him, hated him, and the need for it had long been a part of her. A part now thriving.

Her palms glided over the hot skin of his back, pressing against the powerful muscle beneath her fingertips, and he kissed her with a passion to match the searing heat of his body. They came together again and again, their gasps for breath the only thing to dare separate them.

With every passing second, she wanted him more, and more, and more, until her desire built to a pressure that ached, a pressure built over a decade of ties and strain. When he broke away, her lips chilled, and she shivered, but he clad his black velvet overcoat around her shoulders.

"Put it on."

She did as he bade, sliding her arms through the too-big sleeves, leaving it open. His eyes flashed, then darkened as he walked her to the tree, pushed her back against it, warmed her chilled lips with the passion of his own. So much like the garden in Maerleth Tainn that night—the one that had been teasing her dreams for the past few days before she slept. He interlaced her fingers with his, then raised her hands above her head, pressed them against the aspen's trunk.

She didn't know where he was taking this, but wherever it was, she wanted to follow.

"Don't move." He kissed his way down her neck, lips brushing over a sensitive spot that made her reach for him—

He paused, intense gaze darting to hers.

Don't move. She returned her hand to its place on the trunk, and he resumed the heaven whispering across her skin. His big hands stroked down her body, firmly gripping her waist, her hips, her backside as he kissed his way down her breasts, down her belly, and he descended to a knee.

His lips brushed below her navel, the sensitive contact making her squirm, before he parted her thighs and tucked one of her legs over and around his shoulder.

Divine, he was going to—

Those hot lips of his teased her inner thigh, close, closer, and closer, as he breathed deep, as he moaned low in his throat, until those lips met her throbbing core.

A choked cry escaped her mouth, sensation pooling irresistibly between her legs, and she wanted to reach for him but only clapped her palm back onto the trunk above her head.

His kiss was light at first, gentle, answering her pulsing need with a blooming warmth and lips that brushed her sensitive skin with the lightest of touches, teasing her flesh awake, aroused, alive. That kiss turned sensual, wet heat firm in long, slow strokes that made her thighs tremble and her eyes squeeze shut.

"Watch me." A low, deep command.

He waited until her eyes found his, their focused intensity, and she gave him a bewildered nod, her belly contracting as it longed for his pleasure.

His tongue found her once more, his slow coaxing building the pressure at her core, concentrating it to a fine point that begged for more, for release, for ecstasy, his eyebrows creased together in determination, determined to take her to the edge and gloriously over, and then—*Divine*—he took her into his mouth.

She hissed, his pleasuring godly and unbearable, forcing panted cries from her lips as he increased the pressure, groaning a deeply masculine sound that vibrated against her core and made her cry and lean her hips into him, tears blinking from her eyes as he stroked, stroked, stroked, warm, firm, wet, pleasing, giving, taking, taking, *taking*—

She screamed as the pressure exploded, as the transcendent pulse pounded between her thighs, rippling warmth and pleasure into her blood, into every corner of her body, waves of sensation that rolled inside of her in that sublime contradiction of too much and not enough. His gaze met hers as he brought her over the edge, pleased, smug, and she wanted to run her fingers through his dark, thick hair, touch him, but she dared not move or look away lest he cease that splendid magic consuming her alive.

Great Divine, every frisson of lust, every moment of desire, every wanting second over the last few weeks, everything that had mounted to maddening pressure inside of her until tonight, he took it all, freed her body of anxious need with his carnal spell.

As the throb ebbed in her blood, his strokes slowed, eased, his touch perfectly attuned to the waves subsiding within her. He lavished her tender skin with kisses, softer and softer as her breathing leveled, and nuzzled her inner thigh with his cheek, brushing the barest coarseness of his face against her.

She gasped, arms shaking above her; they begged for reprieve, but she dared not move them.

Carefully holding her steady, he stood and relieved her hands of their post.

"Brennan, you—" Her breath caught. She wanted to tell him everything at once, about the pleasure, how he made her feel, how—

"You have no idea how long I've wanted to do that." He dipped down and rested his forehead against hers, breathing deeply and unmoving but for the heaving of his chest. His sultry breaths mingled with her own in the close space between their lips, but that short gap threatened to destroy her if it wasn't bridged at once.

"Rielle," he said, his voice raw, deep. If not for his hold, she'd be a collapsed heap upon the grass. He took a step closer, leaned into her, and his hardness pressed against her, ready, demanding.

Divine, she could barely feel her legs, and she wanted nothing on this earth more than Brennan Karandis Marcel inside her. A lustful shiver began in her core and shook through her body.

She rubbed her damp forehead against his, rested her hand against his chest, feeling the fast and powerful beating of his heart. She had never needed anything more than she needed him right now. "Please," she whispered.

He covered her hand with his own, then raised it to his lips, pressing a kiss to it before guiding her arms around his neck. His palms glided their way down and over her backside, cupping her gently until he scooped her up. She clenched her bare legs around his waist, and as he lowered to his knees, she leaned in to kiss him, closing her eyes to isolate the feel of his lips against hers, his tongue against hers, his warm breath and hot skin against hers.

Their lips locked, he removed the overcoat from her shoulders and laid her down upon the blanket, propped up on an elbow next to her. His warm palm cupped her cheek, feathered down her neck, teased her breasts.

Over the years, questions of this had surfaced in her dreams, in her daydreams, what it would be like to give herself to him, to be taken by him, questions that had so long remained unanswered, that had chilled in the face of their enmity and strain. Questions that had blossomed back to life in the past few months, that now received warm, bright answer.

His lips were soft against hers, his tongue delicate in its playful probing. They kissed for what felt like hours, and she just enjoyed the simple pleasure, the desire simmering in every part of her body as his tantalizing hands explored further and further. Her hips lightly rocked against him, and when he finally reached down and touched her where she ached for him, she gasped, pulling the air from his mouth.

"I need you inside me," she pleaded, tightening her hold, wriggling closer to him. "Please." She reached down between them, her fingers brushing against him. In all the years she'd seen his nakedness, it had only ever been like this once, in Xir, powerful, magnetic, and it had never quit her mind.

"Not yet." He teased her tender flesh, made her shiver, made pleasure softly bloom and little moans tremble from her lips between kisses. She tried to angle her hips against his hand impatiently, but he smiled against her mouth and took his time, intensified her need, built it to intolerable height, made anxious tears well in her eyes. "Not. Yet."

"You're too cruel, Brennan Karandis Marcel," she whispered.

A quiet half-laugh rumbled in his throat as he gazed down at her, his eyes hooded and serene, a corner of his mouth turned up.

"Am I?" he asked, at last drawing his fingertips where she wanted him, his touch silken and firming, perfect, making her back arch as she leaned into him and moaned: the man knew what he was doing.

The immense pressure rose and rose and rose, the exquisite ache unendurable, making her weep, making her writhe, twist, scream—"Now," he said—and then it broke, overflowing in powerful quakes, pounding through her like ancient music, possessing every inch of her consumed body with living, breathing heat that only demanded, demanded, demanded as her hips bucked against his touch.

"Tell me how it feels when I touch you," he rasped in her ear. "Tell me." His voice turned rougher, deeper.

"Like dying," she whimpered, as shudders of pleasure rocked through her, "and being... reborn—"

His mouth devoured her next words, seducing her tongue in slow, soft kisses that deepened, mounting in urgency. She moved, pushing against him, but to no avail.

A wicked laugh vibrated into her mouth, and she had time only to gasp when he lunged to loop his arm under her leg, hoisting it over his shoulder, her backside in his lap.

Through her dreamy haze, she watched him on his knees and absorbed every inch. His body appeared designed for pleasure, rippling muscle, broad shoulders, and large, skillful hands... Her gaze traveled lower, over gleaming dark skin, his sculpted abdomen, and—her head swam at the prospect of becoming one with him.

An amused huff directed her gaze up to his face, refined strength, powerful lines with sinful curves; and his eyes, Great Divine, his eyes were sex personified, passionate hazel darkened with desire, laughing at her, teasing her, with a predatory gleam.

"Brennan," she heard herself say again, a short-winded whine, exhausted but craving.

"Again," he said, his blazing heat pressed against her, just there, close, so close—

"*Brennan,*" she whimpered, breaking off into a gasp as he drove into her at last, slow and deep, a ripple of pleasure cascading through her body, leaving her gaping, reluctant to even breathe for fear of diluting the feel.

His eyes flashed amber, but he blinked it away. A low hiss fell from his lips, and holding her gaze, he rolled his hips against her, a deep grind that made her belly contract.

A shaky exhalation was all she could manage. This was what it meant to be his lover, his fiancée, his soon-to-be bride. This was what it meant to belong to him.

It was the promise of that sultry night in House Hazael, never lingering too far in her memory, at long last fulfilled.

His gaze never left hers as he thrust a slow, powerful rhythm, using his hold on her hip to guide her to him each time. Need contracted her body, rattled her, his every movement making her quiver, and with a raging intensity, he watched her, tautness walling his body, holding something at bay, something that threatened to escape, and to dominate.

She reached up, shaky palms worshipping his damp, hard abdomen, the solid muscle of his chest—

Still kneeling, he captured her other thigh, positioned them both against his abdomen, her backside still on his lap as he stroked her legs up to her ankles on either side of his head. He kissed her calf before seizing her wrists and, leaning forward, locking her hands down on either side of her.

His thrusts turned deep, hard, forcing moans from her open mouth, and they only became deeper, harder as he grabbed her hands and pinned them behind her head, his body bearing down on her, the pressure mounting, heat flooding her core.

Unable to move, she'd been given the ultimate freedom. No thought but this, no feeling but this, and her body could do anything, move in any way, and she could give herself over to pleasure entirely, knowing he would keep her from going too far, keep her grounded, keep her safe.

He anchored her wrists in the grip of one palm, and his rhythm merciless and controlled, he covered her moaning mouth with the other.

She closed her eyes and gave herself over to the ceaseless sensations, screamed into his hand, let the pleasure tear from her throat, as loud as it needed, but the sound muffled into his palm, bottled within her.

He huffed a quavering breath, his eyes rolling to the back of his head as he thrust faster, rougher, and she lost herself in his rhythm, writhing on the blanket as the throbbing in her lower body intensified, built and built, its pulse pounding deeper, heavier, harder, until his palm released her and the pleasure fled her mouth in tremulous breaths.

She looked at him through a blurry haze; amber burned in his eyes, a warm glow in the dark, otherworldly and yet familiar. Brennan.

Brennan, who Changed with the moon. Brennan, who'd saved her more times than she could count. Brennan, who loved her. "Brennan," she breathed, more of a sob than a word as she squeezed her eyes shut and ground her hips against his. "I love you."

With a blink, he drew away, and her backside met the blanket, her thighs a sprawled, exhausted, quivering heap.

His mouth crashed against hers, and when he finally took her anew, she exhaled sharply, her hands climbing his rigid arms, traveling his taut back, greedy for every part of him with a need that only wanted and wanted, despite the satisfaction and pleasant ache of her spent body. She could spend hours like this, days like this, weeks, and it would never be enough, never be enough of him.

With an eager tongue, he plundered her mouth as the throbbing in her core mounted again, making her breathe shakily between his hungry kisses.

She locked her arms around his neck, breathing raggedly as she slid a trembling hand along his back, fanned out her fingers to firmly press them into his flesh, wrapping her legs around him. His mouth broke away only to descend to her neck, the feel of his lips, his tongue making her close her eyes and pull him closer.

His teeth grazed her tender skin, a soft bite, the shivery caress a rippling drop on the surface of her overflowing pleasure, veering dangerously into too much sensation until he pulled back, moving one of her legs before him to roll her onto her belly.

"On your knees," he whispered.

Great Divine, *yes.* Her palms found the blanket, and her head spinning, she attempted to comply, but her legs didn't feel like her legs anymore. He snaked an arm under her belly and raised her backside to his level.

She pushed against him, arched her spine, and he grabbed her hips, then took her mercilessly, powerfully, pulling her toward him with every thrust, maddened, wild, rough, one palm leaving her hip only to seize a thick fistful of her hair at the base of her neck. His every breath scintillated her ears, forceful exhalations that lengthened, deepened, crescendoed. He dragged her closer, tighter, lengthening and deepening his thrusts. He was about to—

With a gasp, she spasmed, contracting as pleasure pounded inside her, weeping and panting and screaming, tears warming down her face to her chin.

Raw moans tore through him as he shuddered; she rotated her hips, her mouth falling open at the sensation until she found her pleasure again, whimpering. He curled over her, the heat of his full body pressed against her back, his chest to her shoulder blades, his face to her neck, and he held her through the shaking, whispered soft words in her ear she couldn't discern, and kissed her neck until the pulsing in her blood subsided.

Blissful quiet claimed the glade, only his breaths and hers marking the silence, his hold the only thing keeping her together as his strong body rested against her back, the press of an inhale, the release of an exhale, his hair feathering against her neck, a soft kiss on her bare skin.

His hold on her loosened, and he moved only to lay down on the blanket and pull her to him, thread an arm under her neck, and nestle her against his chest in a close embrace. She rested her cheek on him, listening to his breath slow, enjoying the soft play of his fingers against her upper arm. Her nose itched, but too exhausted to move, she let it itch. As a yawn approached, she closed her eyes and let them stay closed.

Brennan kissed her head, a soft press of his lips—once, twice, a third time, and then he lingered. "You said you love me." A quiet rasp.

She nodded. "I did."

He nuzzled her hair, breathing in deeply. "And now?" A grin rode his question.

"I still love you." A little laugh escaped her. "Maybe a little more, even, after *that* performance."

Nose buried in her hair, he inhaled lengthily, deeply several times. What was he doing?

She blushed. "Are you—?"

"If I suffocated and died in this intoxicating scent, it would be a good death."

She tried to wriggle away, but he held her tight. "Did you inhale all your other lovers?"

"You're not '*other lovers*.' With you, it's—I'm not sure if it's the bond or my love for you or both, but... you're like breath itself to me." He moved away and rolled onto his side. When she opened her eyes, he smiled, gazing at her with warm hazel affection. He brushed a curl away from her face, cupped her cheek, leaned in and kissed her gently, stroking her shoulder and arm in that hypnotic back-and-forth motion she'd grown used to. "Was it all right?" he asked delicately between kisses.

She moaned softly, happily. Certain things he'd done, demanded, had been new and unusual to her, but some part of her had expected the unexpected with him. He'd always had a need to control, a sensitivity to power, and yet an uncommon generosity that somehow all made sense tonight. And she'd loved every second. "More than all right."

"Nothing was too much?" Those fingertips of his lulled her into deeper relaxation.

"It was perfect." *He* was perfect.

"I've waited for you all my life, Rielle," he whispered, his fingers playing softly in her hair. He lowered his gaze for a moment. "There are things I can never give you—magic, resonance—but I want you to know that for the rest of our lives, I will gladly give and give and give until you are unable to take any more."

He'd already made good on that promise tonight.

She reached for his face and urged him down to hers. His kiss, soft at first, slowly deepened as he stroked her with a gentle hand, gliding over her skin, cupping her breast, and whispering over her navel before grasping her hip and pulling her to him anew.

She huffed against his lips, but couldn't resist wrapping a leg around him anyway. "You're not sleepy?"

A laugh rumbled in his throat, low and rolling. "You shouldn't plan on sleeping tonight, Rielle. Or any time soon. Or doing much during the day. As a matter of fact, just clear your schedule entirely."

Her face heated. "But aboard the ship—"

"I will take you."

"And in close quarters—"

"Every night."

"With hardly any privacy—"

"Hard."

She grinned up at him, at the sinful gleam in his eyes.

"Does that please you?"

She threaded her fingers through his hair and urged his mouth down to hers. It pleased her. It pleased her very much.

CHAPTER 10

*J*on opened his eyes to Derric's nudging at his shoulder. The earliest glow of dawn filtered into the Trèstellan chapel.

"It's time, my son," Derric said softly, flanked by a group of Terran priests.

Jon rubbed his eyes. The morning of the coronation. He'd observed a night of vigil before the Sacre, spent in prayer, and it was finally time.

They escorted him to his quarters, where after he washed and shaved, they assisted in dressing him. The vigil had been a night of reflection and prayer, and he'd spent the night thinking about his dreams. As a boy, he'd wanted nothing more than to be a paladin and serve others. He'd never wanted anything for himself, really, until *her*.

After they'd left the Tower together, he'd slowly allowed himself to want a future. And then, once they'd reached Melain, to hope for it. A life lived together, honest with her, sharing an unbreakable trust, making her happy for as long as he lived, saving the world together. Having children if she wanted them, watching them grow up. Growing old with her. Dying hand in hand, surrounded by family and love, having lived well and long.

Dreams, idyllic as they were, could be cruel when they were unattainable. Like dreams of water to a sun-parched man who would die of thirst.

He'd decided that, when the time came to open his eyes from his vigil, he'd open his eyes from his dreams.

And he'd opened them. Once he was crowned, he wouldn't go back to dreaming of water, even as he died of thirst. He'd lost Rielle, and he needed to let go of his dreams of the life he'd wanted with her—a life that now could never be. His time with her had been about what he'd wanted, but now he needed to return to service over self.

He could still be who he'd always been: the paladin, but made king. Emaurria's blade. Terra's justice. And champion of right.

That he could do.

While they put on his coronation robes, he chose who would participate in the coronation.

It was a formality, nothing more, as the nobles had all been chosen already.

The Duke of Maerleth Tainn and Brennan's father, Faolan Auvray Marcel, despite his duplicity, was to carry the royal crown, gird him with Faithkeeper, and give him the order of chivalry. The Duchess of Melain, Rielle's great-grandmother, would carry the first square banner, and her son, the Marquis of Sauveterre, Marquis Sébastien Duclos Auvray, would carry the second square banner.

The duchess's brother, Marquis Auguste Vignon Duclos of Montvilliers would carry the spurs, while Marquis Jean Vignon

Armel of Quatrebeaux would carry Faithkeeper. It would be his first time meeting the late queen's—his mother's—father. *My grandfather.*

And finally, Marquis Perceval Auvray Amadour of Villecourt, Rielle's great uncle, would carry the banner of war.

Olivia would bear the Sacred Ampoule, containing the myrrh that had been mixed with the anointing oil used during the coronation of the first Farallan king, and the Sacred Chalice.

When he was finally dressed, he had a moment to himself. In the mirror, the sapphire-blue coronation robe had a six-foot train and was completely lined in white satin, trimmed in a half a foot of ermine fur around the entire perimeter, with a large foot-and-a-half ermine caplet about his shoulders. Two dragons' heads anchor medallions secured a heavy, golden closure chain.

Beneath, he wore well-tailored white trousers, black riding boots, and a fitted military coat of the finest black wool, adorned with the king's sash. He fingered a shiny gold button, perfectly matched to the rest, all in a straight, neat line. Here he stood, in royal finery, in the royal apartment. The extravagance was appalling, but it was tradition. Inarguably.

With this, he'd be sworn. He'd quell all threats to the succession. While he'd been fighting in the heartland, Princess Sandrine had sent a covert force to Emaurria that had gotten as far as Costechelle before the paladins had routed them. After his coronation, her odds of success would plummet.

Just before the doors to the hallway, he rested a palm on the upholstered wall—he'd pressed Rielle against this wall the night of Veris. His fingers brushed the corded silk where her head had rested, then her cheek.

It was a dream.

He turned back and crossed the dining room, where he'd carried her, through and to the study, to his desk, where he'd laid her on the purple-heartwood surface. He braced over it, heaving a deep breath. She'd whispered in his ear, *Please. I need you, Jon. Now.* A fluttering plea. And he'd kissed her, made love to her, right here.

No more than a dream.

He scrubbed a hand over his face, slowly straightened, and headed back to the bedchamber. He could leave all that behind. He could. When these moments came upon him, he didn't have to give in to them.

His hands on his hips, he stood in the doorway. The bed, and everything in the center of the room, had burned, and new furniture and textiles took their place. How long had that bed kept kings and queens before he, Rielle, and Shadow had destroyed it?

But this new one—a purple-heartwood four-poster canopied bed—would be a symbol, a sign of a change in the line.

The end of the line, a wayward thought stabbed.

After this, he was expected to wed, to produce heirs, to secure the line. None of them expectations he intended to meet. Even if he could bring himself to do what needed to be done, leaving a queen and a child unprotected was cruel. If Faolan wished to usurp *him,* with the Order of Terra at his back, what would he do to a child with a dead father?

For a year or two, he'd ignore talk of marriage and heirs due to his constant travel, protecting the kingdom with his forces, and then a successor would have to take over. Someone the people would accept, the nobles would accept, the *world* would accept. And the Farallan tree had withered.

A successor from another family.

Service over self. It wasn't about his line, but about Emaurria and his people. He leaned against the wall.

A knock came from the hallway. "Enter," he called.

Light, quick steps. Eloi. He entered, pausing wide-eyed before he bowed his curly-haired head, and approached with a neatly tied stack of folded parchment. "Your correspondence, Your Majesty. The Grands have handled any official matters, but..."

Personal correspondence. He accepted the bundle. "Thank you, Eloi."

Eloi bowed again. "My pleasure, sire. By your leave?" When Jon nodded, he departed.

At the very top of the stack in his lap was a note bearing Tregarde's seal. *Brennan's* seal.

It is with the utmost joy that we celebrate your coronation, Your Majesty. We are honored and privileged to serve at your pleasure.

The coronation will be a historic, monumental occasion, and it is our wish to see you crowned and to celebrate at your side. Unfortunately, Rielle and I will be unable to attend and must regretfully decline...

Well wishes and regards, and Brennan's signature and seal.

So be it. He folded up the message.

Another knock, and when he allowed entry, a maid came in. Not Manon. He'd had her transferred to Olivia's household before Veris.

"The carriage is ready, Your Majesty," Clarice said with a bow, her face wan.

"Thank you." He headed for the bedchamber door, but glanced at Rielle's portrait one last time. It was still here, hanging above the fireplace, where he could see her every night before he slept and every morning when he first awoke.

It was time.

Clarice bowed again. "By your leave—"

"Wait," he said, and she straightened, her eyes wide. "Before I go, tell the Lord Chamberlain to have this portrait sent back with the Duchess of Melain, along with my thanks."

Service over self.

Another knock—Eloi. "Your Majesty—"

"What?" he grunted.

"There's been an attack. Basilisks have destroyed Rouzenac."

LEIGH STOOD at the front of the nave with Ambriel, while the entire crowd waited for the coronation to begin. The choir had been singing The First Hour since dawn. Where was Jon?

There had been murmurs of an entire village being destroyed by basilisks, this time near Costechelle, so he had to be in talks with his generals and the Paladin Grand Cordon, planning military operations.

The loss was neverending, and until Emaurria was secure—until the *world* was secure, safe from the Immortal beasts—Leigh wouldn't rest.

Ambriel squeezed his hand, and Leigh gave him a faint smile. Together, they'd help fix this.

As soon as the coronation was over, he could begin dealing with the Tremblays, empowered by a crowned king. Gustave Tremblay, Archon of a Coven of battle mages, was known for his strict observance of protocol... and teaching any disrespectful visitors the meaning of pain.

Time to test protocol.

The singing continued, the same as it had for the last hour, and Leigh sighed.

"The end is upon us!" a voice cried from outside.

"If only," Leigh murmured under his breath. The singing was growing tiresome.

The madman was escorted away.

"What *is* the plan to defeat the Immortal beasts? At least before we can learn more about the Sundering?" Ambriel asked quietly next to him, dressed in Emaurrian finery from head to toe. He was quite a picture in a navy velvet overcoat, tailored brown trousers and riding boots—his six-foot height and sleek, powerful frame begged to be touched. Oh, and it would be. Later.

"*I* am the plan," Leigh replied, tugging at his white shirt cuffs. The tailor had outfitted him well, too—Edouard always did, the man was a sewing genius—in a violet samite doublet lined in smooth cendal, and white trousers. The dyaspin shirt was worth wearing for its subtle sheen, as long as the weather remained cool and comfortable.

Ambriel gave him a sardonic eyebrow raise. "I know what you're capable of, dreshan, but—"

A grin. "Oh, my dear, you've only seen the very tip of what I'm capable of. And this will require finesse, which I happen to possess in large quantity."

"Finesse?" Ambriel's lips twitched. Holding back a smile. "And here I thought overwhelming *might* was more your style."

"If finesse doesn't work, explosions are a good contingency plan." And infinitely more fun.

Voices shouted orders outside, and horns blared. The clopping of hooves on the cobbles drew to a stop, and everyone in the nave turned to the door.

Jon had arrived. Good timing, too, as nearly an hour of standing was becoming tiresome. And the singing. The blasted singing.

"Keep an eye out," Leigh hissed in Old Emaurrian. "These things sometimes turn into bloodbaths." Although anyone seeking to bathe in the new king's blood would have *him* to deal with. He hadn't waited so long for a free-thinking monarch only to lose him to something so gauche as a coronation massacre.

Ambriel scanned the crowd. He wouldn't find any visible malcontents here among the nouveau riche and the nobility. Outside, they were obvious enough, but here, everyone wore their dissatisfaction on the *inside*.

The choir stopped—praise any and all gods—and Jon entered, his broad shoulders wrapped in ermine, a massive coronation cloak trailing him. Beneath, what looked to be a royal military uniform clad his figure, and his booted steps echoed in the abbey as he strode down the aisle, gaze fixed on the large golden throne far ahead, and the altar behind it bearing the crown. Everyone bowed reverently as he passed before them, a line of nobles following behind him.

"The man just behind him," Leigh whispered in Old Emaurrian. Duke Faolan Auvray Marcel, master rake and courtier, decked out in finery that rivaled that of the king, strode behind him, a certain ever-present gleam in his eye. Tall, fit, and handsome, he clearly had lent his good looks to his son, and had aged like a fine wine. "If anyone is making a move, it's him."

Ambriel traced Faolan's walk to the front with a sharp gaze.

Derric Lazare began a prayer, and then there was more blasted singing. Olivia, wearing ceremonial golden Archmage robes, stood at the base of the altar's dais, waiting, watching her king approach attentively. *Very* attentively.

The abbot and monks followed Jon and the nobles in a procession, with the white-clad abbot bearing the Sacred Ampoule in its reliquary about his neck, and every head stayed bowed as he passed.

Jon knelt at the fore, while the abbot and his procession approached Olivia, who swore to return the Sacred Ampoule after the coronation. Then she, the abbot, and monks proceeded to the altar.

Faolan eyed the sword held by the Marquis of Quatrebeaux, then slid that gaze to Jon. Was there a noble in the abbey who didn't know what that look meant?

Derric began the petition that the traditional rights of the Order and the Divinity be maintained so long as they respected Emaurria's sovereignty and all agreements.

"I so swear," Jon replied.

Next was the coronation oath on the Terran scripture.

"What are they saying?" Ambriel whispered.

"He's promising to maintain the rights of the Emaurrian Crown," Leigh replied, "protecting it against all other claims."

Derric, Olivia, the abbot, priests, and monks recognized Jon's oath, the choir sang a song, followed by a prayer—

Leigh yawned.

A great roar shook the very foundations of the abbey.

Screams rang outside.

Gasps rippled through the crowd, and Jon dropped his head back to fix his gaze on the ceiling as powdery debris rained down.

"My sword," Jon said to Quatrebeaux, who brought it to him. Jon grabbed the hilt, touching the arcanir of the crossguard.

A force of winds beat against the roof, then another roar, more distant.

"A dragon," Ambriel murmured, frowning. "It just seems to be passing through."

No one moved for a long moment, until the silence had gone on too long, and Derric cleared his throat and nodded toward the nobles. Jon slid his blade back into its scabbard, and Quatrebeaux backed away.

The Marquis of Montvilliers shifted on his feet, then placed the spurs on Jon's boots. Quatrebeaux handed Jon's sword to Faolan, who eyed it a long moment before girding Jon with it. "Accept this sword from our hands," he said firmly.

Olivia approached with the Sacred Ampoule bearing the myrrh oil used to anoint the first king of his line. It was ancient, no more than a drop used for the coronation of each subsequent king.

Jon unfastened the chain clasp of his coronation cloak and let it fall, then removed his overcoat and unbuttoned his silk shirt to expose his tattooed chest, upper back, shoulders, and biceps.

The priests chanted a prayer while Derric placed a paten upon the altar with anointing oil. Olivia opened the Sacred Ampoule and with a small golden stylus, removed a single drop and carefully mixed it into the contents of the paten.

The chanting stopped only for Derric to say a prayer of consecration, and then he asked Terra's blessings for the new king. When he finished, Olivia anointed Jon with oil in the form of a moon on the top of his head, holding his gaze. "I anoint you with the holy oil in the name of the Maiden, the Mother, the Crone."

"Terra's blessings upon him," Leigh and the rest of the assembly responded.

Then on the center of his chest, between his shoulder blades, on each of his shoulders and on the joints of both of his arms, each time repeating the words and getting the same reply from everyone. She held Jon's gaze as if he were the only one in the room.

He sighed inwardly. This would not end well.

"May the king live forever," Olivia shouted, and the assembly repeated.

After yet another lengthy prayer, Olivia, Derric, and the assisting priests and monks readjusted Jon's garments.

Jon rose, and once standing, they replaced the coronation cloak on his shoulders and fastened the chain. They gloved his hands in white, then placed the Ring of the King on his fifth finger. The scepter was placed in his right hand, the sign of kingly power, and then the staff with the Hand of Justice in his left, the sign of virtue and equity.

Derric removed the crown from the altar. "Terra crown you with glory."

He set it upon Jon's head, while the nobles touched it with their right hands. Derric led them in blessings, and then they all stepped away, knelt in two aisles between which Jon stood, turned, and faced the assembly as he sat upon the throne.

He looked out over everyone assembled, his eyes searching but his hands steady.

Finally, a king not bound to crawl at the whim of a power that *killed* mages' families to steal their talents. A king who would see mages refuse the chains thrust upon them, let them be mere citizens, not heretics or hedge witches, but just Emaurrian mages. A king who would help dissolve that corrupt power.

A king he would gladly serve. *Finally.*

"May the king live forever," Derric cried out, and his cry was taken up by the nobles, Leigh, and everyone present, acknowledging Jon as the duly anointed, crowned, and enthroned king.

There was a Terran service, an hour long and dull, and then the Oriflamme banner was blessed.

Finally, at its end, Jon stood, descended, and strode out of the abbey to the blessings and cheers of everyone, meeting Leigh's eyes as he passed and giving him a slight nod.

Good. It was time.

Outside, cheers rose up and a parade toward the palace began.

"A feast," Ambriel said. "And there wasn't even a bloodbath."

"With our luck, it's been saved for us," Leigh grumbled. "We have a meeting with the most powerful man in Courdeval," he murmured, filing out into the aisle.

"The king?"

"Gustave Tremblay."

CHAPTER 11

*L*eigh leaned back in his chair. "I'm offering you the chance for status. Likely the only chance you'll get in your lifetime."

Ambriel had elected to keep watch at the upstairs entrance to the apothecary, while *he* was sharing ale in a cellar, of all places. Two grim-faced witches flanked their Archon, staring a hole through Leigh's face—one a tall, rake-thin man, and the other a large-set woman.

"And why should I care that one suffocating power will let another collapse? We protect our Coven. That's what matters." Gustave Tremblay, of the Tremblay line of Archons that controlled an influential Emaurrian Coven, folded his hands together and regarded Leigh squarely. In his forties, Gustave still bore the remnants of his youth's good looks—thick, blond hair; piercing blue eyes; a well-kept beard; and sun-touched skin. He looked nothing like an ordinary apothecary, but then, an Archon was anything but.

Leigh smiled, running his fingers casually through the

candle flame before him. "I thought we were far beyond
pretense, Gustave. Power is not something you ignore." At the
table, the candle illuminated no more than their faces and the
space between them. "Which power lands on top matters. It
could either be the Crown, which is offering you influence, or
the Divinity, which wants to end you. Which is better for you
and your Coven? Oh, and do remember that no matter who
wins, there are dragons, wyverns, and all manner of Immortal
beasties to deal with."

Scratching his beard, Gustave looked away. "Sure of yourself, aren't you, Galvan?"

"As sure as the sun."

"If the Crown stands in the Divinity's way, doesn't that help
your cause?" Gustave narrowed his penetrating eyes. "Why not
let one hand wash the other?"

"Because one set of those hands is indelibly unclean." Leigh
fixed Gustave with a stare. The Tremblay line would join their
cause or face the wrath of the Forgerons and the Beaufoys.
Gustave's reluctance was a losing game.

"I don't disagree," Gustave said, with an abundance of
caution, "but I have my hands full here just taking care of my
people. What could I possibly contribute to such grand plans?"

Finally, the man had come to the bargaining table. "If the
Divinity is to atone for its crimes, to be brought to its knees, we
need to wage war within and without. For that, we need the
Divinity to fail in its responsibilities, for the people to lose faith
in its power. His Majesty will handle the first step. You and
your people are needed to rally your Coven, the commoners,
and nobles in this region against the Divinity and for the
Crown. We have some forces, but we need mages ready to
fight... against the Immortals or the Divinity."

Gustave shook his head. "You want me to ask my people to

fight the Divinity? Are you mad? The Emaurrian Tower alone is too big a threat."

The rake-thin witch, his face contorted, moved to take a step forward, but his companion gave him a grim nod. Opinionated, for a lackey.

"The Tower, too, will bend," Leigh replied, his voice measured.

The candle flame flickered, shrouding the cellar in darkness for a moment. In the face of Gustave's silence, he continued, "How much longer are you willing to hide in the shadows to keep your freedom as a mage? How many more atrocities are you willing to let our people suffer? How many mage families need to be wiped out to satisfy the Divinity's lust for power? Make no mistake, the Divinity has been centralizing magic and power for centuries; its head has grown so large, the beast itself is unwieldy. Now is the time to support the Crown, break away from the Divinity, cripple the beast. Lead your Coven into the light, into power. No more hiding."

For a long while, Gustave breathed deeply, tugging at his beard in consideration. "And you will take the first step?"

"Yes." The Divinity had taken everything from him and others like him, and if it was allowed to continue, the world would soon bend the knee to Magehold and its chosen leaders.

"What about your former apprentice? The Archmage. Will she be a problem?"

"No. Olivia's loyalty is to the king, not the Divinity." *That* had been more than evident during the coronation... like smoke gently rising over a city. About to burn down.

The Covens didn't trust easily; it had taken him years to earn their trust. But perhaps his word would be enough for them to give Olivia a chance. "Now, what will it take for you and your Coven to pledge allegiance to the Crown, help fight the Immortals, and help destroy the Divinity when the time comes?"

When Gustave didn't answer right away, Leigh held his pose, shifting not an inch until he had his answer.

"We... have a problem with a den of heretics," Gustave said cautiously. "They call themselves the 'Trien Coven.' We've attempted to... handle them before, but there's a Forgeron among them."

So he needed a third party to wipe out the heretic rebels without harming the Forgeron.

Luckily, killing and abduction were great talents of his. "Done."

The rake-thin witch stepped forward. "Archon, I could—"

Gustave raised his hand, and the witch apologized and took a step back. Opinionated *and* bold for a lackey. Gustave slowly extended his hand, and Leigh shook it.

"By Most Holy Terra, Coven, and Archon," Gustave swore.

Leigh smiled. All the pieces were at last in place. The Divinity of Magic had long held a veil before the people's eyes, making them believe it was integral to their protection when, in truth, it hadn't lifted a finger to help against the Immortals.

Once he did what Gustave wanted and won over the Forgerons and the Beaufoys, that veil would come down.

He stood. "Now, then. Ambriel and I have some work to do. Before we go, do you know where we can get some walnut loaf?"

WHILE TOR TRIED to get his attention, Jon left the council chamber with Olivia and strode toward the Treasury, deep in the heart of Trèstellan.

While he and Olivia would be in Magehold, someone would have to remain as regent. He'd been unable to leave Tor in charge—for obvious reasons—and Pons would be a negative sign to the Covens, as would Derric. And Leigh *needed* to succeed with them.

So he'd left Auguste in charge. His cousin and the Secretary of State for Foreign Affairs. They often disagreed in council meetings, but Auguste had pledged to enforce Jon's will, and the Grands had agreed he'd be the best choice.

If Auguste mismanaged the kingdom, he'd answer for that later.

He'd spoken with his grandfather, Jean Vignon Armel, after the coronation, who'd offered to provide honest counsel should he ever have need of it. Perhaps he'd welcome Jean to Courdeval when he returned from Magehold.

Pons had briefed them on the strained situation, with the Emaurrian army, the paladins, and their allies barely holding the line against the Immortal beasts. Especially after Rouzenac, a village near Costechelle, had been massacred by basilisks the night before the coronation. One hundred and thirty-one lives lost.

Captain Perrault would see to the hunt, joined by a light-elf unit from Vervewood.

As for Magehold, they'd presented Olivia's idea and gotten agreement, with advice.

"We need to bring a gift," he grunted under his breath.

"An extravagant, impressive gift," Olivia added.

Because bowing and begging aid wouldn't be enough as a sign of good faith. No, in order for the world to believe Emaurria blameless when the Divinity didn't agree to send help, he had to come bearing a priceless tribute for the Grand Divinus.

The feasting had gone on long into the night, but after that dragon had flown over the abbey, he'd only been able to think about Rouzenac and securing the kingdom once and for all.

Once his travel was announced, he'd have to leave immediately, to give the Grand Divinus the least amount of time to prepare should her spies give her notice.

"What will you bring her?" Olivia asked while they approached the Treasury's guards. They opened the doors and stood aside.

"Something valuable that means nothing to me." He strode through each set of doors as they opened, until they reached the inner sanctum, where he had to use his key.

The guards opened those doors, too, and he and Olivia entered the glittering center of the Treasury.

All the Crown Jewels were here, and the most famed treasures in the kingdom. Olivia gasped, her fingers hovering over a display, perhaps the single most valuable collection in all the kingdom. A golden hair comb, enameled with a dragon at its center and jeweled with diamonds, chalcedony, lapis lazuli, and sapphires, lay amid a parure of five other pieces of jewelry—a tiara, a necklace, ring, brooch, and a pair of earrings, all set with the Faralle royal collection of sapphires, diamonds, and pearls. The most perfect in existence.

A betrothal gift fit for a queen.

He approached and stood next to Olivia, reaching out to brush the fine enamel of the comb. "The Farallan parure."

"I-It's beautiful," she whispered. "I've read that the kings of old would adorn their queens in jewels, to show the kingdom all was well, that the monarchy was healthy. And so was the kingdom."

Next to the parure lay a small blade, a rapier.

"The Queen's Blade," Olivia said. "King Tristan Armand Marcel Faralle commissioned it for his queen."

The subtle sage shimmer was arcanir. While the parure signaled a healthy monarchy—flush with coin—the Queen's Blade symbolized something deeper. A fighter. A warrior queen. A partner who protected the kingdom along with her king. He extended an arm towards it, hovering over the ornate hilt.

"This," he said.

Olivia cocked her head. "You want to give the Grand Divinus a sword?"

"With it, she can either help us fight the Immortals," he said, "or sever the bond between our kingdom and the Divinity." The symbolism wouldn't be lost on a calculating person like the Grand Divinus.

"Jon, are you sure this is what you—"

"We have a ship to catch." He grabbed the sword and handed it to Olivia. "And would you have Tor summoned here?"

This blade would serve as his gesture of good faith in dealing with the Grand Divinus. He would stand by her word one way or another—there was no dishonor—but she was too committed to turn back now. She'd already withheld her troops when Courdeval had been under siege. She'd already perhaps participated in the regicide. And she'd refused to help against the Immortals.

The Grand Divinus couldn't call his bluff. She wouldn't.

Olivia accepted the sword hesitantly. "Tor? You're finally going to speak to him?"

It might be his last chance to. "Yes. Have the Guard escort him here."

She knitted her eyebrows together as she bowed and left, but things weren't as they used to be; Tor had made his move, chosen his side, and if he ever wanted to be trusted again, he would have to prove his loyalty.

Nearby, his crown from the coronation sat on display, gold inlaid with sapphires and engraved with dragons. The Faralles had claimed to be descended from an ancient line of dragon hunters, and although he might have doubted that a few months ago, it now seemed entirely possible.

"The Lord Constable," Raoul announced.

"Leave us," Jon replied, without turning to look at Tor.

"Majesty," Raoul acknowledged, with two sets of departing footsteps. When the door shut, the silence settled.

Tor had grown a beard for the past month, something he hadn't done in all his years as a paladin of the Order. The dark circles under his eyes had remained, and deep lines in his face had joined them. He'd aged beyond his forty-four years. Treason could do that to a man. But he still dressed well, still kept up appearances, despite being watched by the Royal Guard at all times.

"I'm not sure how much you've heard—"

"Do you accuse Olivia of lying?" Jon faced him and leaned against the display.

Tor took a deep breath and clasped his hands behind his back.

No matter his reasons, Tor had kept Faolan's treason secret for months, had *known* of his intention to commit further crimes, and yet had said nothing. All in the name of playing both sides.

That stung, but it—it wasn't what grated the most.

Tor shook his head. "I thought—"

"You thought you could single-handedly prevent *another* regicide, while allowing your brother to evade justice for murdering my entire family," Jon said coldly.

"And you believe my word alone is enough to condemn him?" Tor asked, taking a step closer. "That if he knew I'd turned on him, he wouldn't have you killed immediately?"

Jon huffed. "So being complicit to treason, you were saving my life?"

"That is exactly what I was doing. Delaying him. Keeping *you* alive. Keeping my family alive. Giving myself room to think, to continue dissuading him—"

He advanced on Tor. "It wasn't your decision."

Tor bowed his head, resting his hands on his hips.

"You think I would have let your entire family be executed?" Did Tor know him at all?

"You wouldn't have had a choice. Punishment of treason must be swift, severe, and absolute, or—"

Jon held up a hand. "I spent the last several months believing I had no choice. That everything I did *had to be done.*" A lie that had paved the path to his own destruction. "No, it was *expected* to be done. But I had a choice. There's always a choice."

He'd made mistakes—terrible mistakes—believing he'd been inadequate to lead the kingdom, and he'd sacrificed all of his ideals to become a cloud of expectations. But a man could only ever be a man, and he could only ever be himself. He'd spent his life putting fists to faces and bending wrong to right as a paladin, and that would be his leadership—the only kind he could ever provide.

Frowning, Tor blinked. "But you would have been perceived as weak if you didn't—"

"Is mercy weak?" Jon asked. "You don't think it's easier to just erase what makes you hurt, to remove it from your sight and pretend it doesn't exist?" He rested a palm on his chest for a moment. "It takes strength to face what hurts, to be honest with yourself, to live unfettered by expectation."

Tor met his gaze, his face going slack. "That is why I am still here." He said it more like a question.

"Arresting you and executing Faolan and everyone even remotely involved would be fear," Jon said. But he and Tor had built a bond over a decade and more, and killing him was unthinkable.

Faolan *would* pay for his crimes. They had the courier in custody and were assembling all the correspondence he'd sent to Tor, along with establishing funding connections. Faolan *would* ultimately be executed. He'd committed atrocities—willfully—too vile and malicious to forgive.

Tor had made a stupid decision out of a desire to save lives, and a hasty arrest would only alert Faolan to their knowledge. More than that, Tor hadn't hurt anyone. He hadn't even *intended* to hurt anyone. He had wrongs to right, but none of them would be solved by his death. His atonement, and his continued life, could do great good.

And Tor hadn't been entirely wrong to try to make peace between the Faralles and the Marcels. The Marcels had been a dynasty of kings before his own, and many looked to them for protection and wisdom when conditions turned dire. Without even revealing his identity, Faolan had rent the kingdom with the regicide and the siege, and if he'd come forth, there would have been a civil war, no question.

Jon lowered his gaze. When he appointed a successor, whether Faolan was alive or dead, would the *kingdom* accept anyone other than a Faralle or a Marcel? There were no choices among the Faralles—all had conflicts of interest or were too remote to be suitable.

For the sake of his people, could he name a Marcel as his

successor? Not Faolan—a man given over to violence and ambi-tion—but... his son? Brennan?

Perhaps the hope for his kingdom could still be found in Rielle as its queen and her heirs. If Terra chose to allow the irony.

"Can you forgive me?" Tor asked.

"I already have," he replied solemnly. The succession was a matter for another time. "But things aren't what they were." They might never again be. "Prove your loyalty. While I'm abroad, develop a plan to take down Faolan and bring him to justice, just as we would've done as paladins."

CHAPTER 12

Samara smoothed her fingers over the fine brushed cotton of her thiyawb as she rode through the predawn streets of Gazgan, from the more luxurious larger buildings to the smaller, modest district of the poor. Zahib kept a watchful eye, his hand on his blade's hilt, as they made their way to the runist, who would remove her slave brand and make her untraceable forever.

She now wore the thiyawb of a freewoman. No more of the neutral-toned two-piece house-slave robes. Zahib had presented her with a thiyawb and halla dyed an impressive indigo, worn by some shafi and nawi, and suitable for the legitimized daughter of a Hazael.

The past several days journeying across the desert had given her freedom a tactile quality. Camel reins in her hands, sand in which she could bed down wherever she chose, oases with water that was hers to drink if she wanted, ingredients she could gather along the way. The other travelers in the caravan had spoken to her sometimes, asked her about her family and her destination.

Family. Zahib wasn't family, no matter that his blood ran through her veins. A true father raised his daughter, loved her, taught her, spent *time* with her. Zahib had merely been saddled with her, an unexpected result from an affair with a slave. Sand in his boots. Something he'd had to bear but certainly hadn't wished for, nor loved. Just used, as his slave. She wouldn't fool herself into believing he'd changed—he'd simply found a new use for her as his heir.

Perhaps he *had* been an idealist, and she a means to an end. A way to keep his other heirs from killing one another or killing him to restore the old ways. She was sand he needed to throw in their faces and spite them.

No, Zahib was *Zahib,* and no matter that he no longer owned her, she would always know him as *Zahib* to remember that he *had* owned her, for all the fifteen years of her life.

If she had any family, it had been the other slaves. She'd only gotten to hear the words freeing them before Zahib had swept her away. Shenaz, who was her age, talked faster than a falcon could fly —at least when it came to boys, and styled the dancers' hair. Naima, whose loving arms always held an embrace for those who needed it, who smiled all the way to her soft, loving eyes as she slipped leftover werqa to the hungry. Even Thahab, for the months she'd spent in the House, who'd chatted with her about spells and spoken High Nad'i like a noble. Her need to protect her baby hadn't killed Zahib, but it had killed his grandfather. And it had set her free—and hopefully, somewhere far from Xir, she had found the father of her child and planned for a joyous birth in a few months.

And as for her destination? She ducked beneath a tattered fabric canopy as they neared the runist's shop.

A girl whose life belonged to a master hadn't the reason to dream of destinations. Or goals. What did she want to do with her life?

Umi had taught her about medicines before she'd disappeared, enough to help others, but was that what she wanted to do? Follow in the footsteps of her mother?

And even if she wanted to be an apothecary, did she *want* to go to a university? Or maybe become an apprentice? Or open her own shop? Travel, maybe, and sell whatever medicines she crafted as she journeyed—see all the places she'd never even dreamed of, where people spoke in foreign tongues and wore foreign garb and lived such vastly different lives than—

"We're here." Zahib dismounted from his camel and handed the reins to a boy, then approached her and offered her his hand.

Ignoring him, she climbed off on her own, sliding along the camel's side to land heavily upon the ground. The camel brayed, and she fell back, hoping to avoid a bite.

Zahib remained still, expressionless, as she gathered her composure, and then he jerked his head toward the runist's door. Beneath his watchful gaze, she entered.

Inside was pleasant enough, with sitting rugs and tapestries, but only two people were inside. A young man huddled in a corner, his black hair a matted mess and his clothes in shreds, hastily eating flatbread and cheese, and an old woman sitting on a chair, half-asleep.

It took merely a moment of Zahib's facade of charm with the old woman, and a couple of gold araqs, before a large man—who loomed even over Zahib—emerged, a row of gold hoops adorning his ears, shining like his clean-shaven head. He had the enormous arms of a blacksmith, and wore only the vest and baggy trousers of the Hongo hill tribes. His eyes were the darkest brown and pleasant, soft, kind.

"Msizi?" Zahib asked, spine ramrod straight as he regarded the man. So he didn't know him, and wasn't even remotely at ease.

Those darkest-brown eyes hardened as Msizi crossed his massive blacksmith arms. "Your kind isn't welcome here, Hazael. I do not brand."

Zahib, with the slightest cordial smile, glanced in her direction. "It is not my kind that requires your services, but she. Remove her brand. She is free."

Msizi's hard gaze slid to her, and as she shrank back, it softened. He relaxed his arms to his sides. "Do not fear me, young one. To you, I am ever a helping hand."

He was a stranger to her, but she'd seen those soft eyes before. Naima's eyes. Kind eyes. Loving eyes.

He stood aside from the doorway, parted its blue strung beads, and nodded toward it. "After you."

A runist that doesn't brand. He didn't help masters; he helped slaves seeking their freedom.

Carefully, she stepped toward the door and through, followed by Msizi.

The small room, full of shelves lined with jars ringing a narrow bed covered with a crisp, freshly washed sheet and a small table next to it, was inviting and almost familiar. Msizi handed her a warm cup filled with liquid, whose spice she could already smell.

"For the pain," he said.

The tart sweetness of cherry and the spicy heat of chili already wafted from its surface; he wasn't lying. She nodded and took a sip. Spice and heat burst on her tongue. "Cherry, chili," she began, "white willow bark... birch leaf, and..."

"Devil's claw extract," he supplied, with a warm smile.

Ah, yes. The hooked desert fruit. She'd never tasted it herself, but now she'd remember.

"You know your herbs," he said brightly, shuffling about the room. He gathered a long needle, gauze, and other supplies.

"I'm an apothecary," she said, finishing the pain-relieving tea. "And my mother was an apothecary. I've been learning all my life."

"There are many who could use your help." He gestured toward the bed, and she removed her thiyawb and halla, handed them and the empty cup to him, and pulled her chemise up above the hips of her trousers before lying face-down on the bed.

He pulled up the chemise to expose her lower back, then gently brushed an herbal oil over her brand. It was hot at first, then cooled, and finally numbed her skin there.

A sharp prick pierced her flesh, and she winced, but the sensation was dulled. He chanted an incantation, removed the needle, then repeated the process.

"My father was a runist," he said to her between repetitions of the incantation. "So was his father, and his, in a long line of my family."

"They taught you?" she asked quietly, flinching. It was a painstakingly slow process—piercing, incantation, removal, and repetition. But not as unpleasant as branding often was. New slaves did not receive a pain-relieving tea or herbal balm.

"They did," he replied. "My tribe had done runes for wealthy patrons, and I grew up studying my brothers' work, but when I was a little older, my father took me with him as an apprentice, to the Harifan slave souk."

The Harifan slave souk collected hundreds or thousands of slaves, selling them individually daily, and auctioning them off monthly. Men, women, and children from all around the world were sold there.

"I tried to please my father, but I didn't have his... distance. One day, he ordered me to brand a little child, perhaps four years old, and I did it."

Samara's vision blurred. Such young children rarely survived the transport, let alone the slave souk, but if they did, they were widely sought-after, some as playmates to House children, if they were fortunate.

"That night, I was so ashamed and so overcome that I fled. I ran to Gazgan, where Bisar found me, and she helped me use what I'd learned to help others."

Bisar... Was she the old woman in the chair? "Do you ever think about your family?"

"Sometimes," he said, then pierced her skin anew and began another bout of the incantation. "But fleeing was the ultimate dishonor. I am nameless to them."

"What about the little child?" she asked.

He breathed deeply. "She is every slave whose brand I remove."

The rest of the removal passed in silence, her occasional gasps and his incantations the only sounds. Msizi had defied his father's expectations and done what he'd felt was right.

Zahib wanted her to go to university, but she already knew enough to help others. She wanted to save lives, ease suffering. And she didn't need to leave Sonbahar to do it. Maybe she could even help here, with Msizi and Bisar.

"Your brand is removed." He helped her up, and she adjusted her clothes and put on her thiyawb. "There will be some lingering pain for a couple of weeks," he said, and handed her a small jar. "Apply this nightly, and it should ease."

She held it up to her nose, and the hot spice was similar to the oil he'd used on her back. "Thank you."

He smiled and held open the strung beads for her. "Live your life, young one. Yours."

When she exited, Zahib was waiting for her, his hands on his hips, body angled toward the huddled boy. He didn't trust him, it seemed, and as a Hazael, he could never trust anyone who might have been a slave. Many would want to kill him for who he'd been, for what he stood for, and perhaps they weren't even wrong. Old, dark deeds released like horses into the plains, who'd always find their way home.

He lifted his gaze to her, nodded to Bisar, then guided Samara out into the street. The boy already had their camels ready, and despite Zahib's offered hand, she struggled on her own to mount. The sun had already risen, but it was only early morning.

Zahib rode ahead, leading them toward the docks. "We'll arrive just in time."

Just in time to board a ship. "What if I don't want to go?"

He didn't turn to look at her. "There is no question that you're going. The only question is whether you will go willingly, or whether I will make you go."

She scowled at the back of his head, at his shoulder-length black waves. "I am a free woman. I don't have to go."

This time he did look over his shoulder at her, his eyes icy. "You are still my *daughter*. And you will go where I tell you."

When he faced forward again, her hands trembled as they gripped the reins. "Where are we even going? I don't speak any other languages. I won't know anyone. If I stay here, I can help. I can—"

Zahib slowed his camel until he was alongside her. "And you'll end up *just* like Amaya."

Like Umi.

"In Sonbahar, you're not beyond the reach of the family, do you understand? Just because you're my heir, just because you're *Amaya's* daughter and free, they could choose to have you killed at any time." He blew out a sharp breath through his nose. "I can't be by your side at all times, and I can't protect you. So I must take you to someone who can."

Umi hadn't run away.

Zahibi Nazira, Zahib's first wife, had ordered Umi to accompany her to the marketplace. When she'd returned, she'd said Umi had run away. "My mother didn't run away. I knew. She would never have run away."

"Of course not," Zahib said, dismounting at the docks, as did Samara. He stepped around to face her, less than a foot between them. "Amaya loved you, Samara. She would have never left you." The words were broken, raw, as if they hurt him to speak.

He didn't believe Umi would have left *him* either.

"I loved her, too, Samara," he said softly.

"How could you—"

"Don't believe me if you don't wish to. It makes no difference. But Amaya was my first love, and if I had been free to, I would have married her." He held her gaze. "It was what had infuriated Nazira so much. She wanted to be my true wife, but what she got was the remnants of a man already in love." He sighed, a pained frown creasing his brow. "It was my affection that made Amaya a target. Thirty lashes wasn't enough."

When Nazira had returned without Umi, she had received thirty lashes for losing Zahib Imtiyaz's property. Zahib was right about one thing—it hadn't been enough. "If you loved her," she said coldly, "you should have *begged* Zahib Imtiyaz to free her. You should have married her, run away with her, *protected* her—"

He grabbed her shoulders. "You think I didn't try? I did everything I could."

She turned her face away, and he released her.

"I tried everything I could. But if I'd run away, *Ihsan* would rule the House now, and neither you, nor any of them would be free. As much as I hated it, I *had* to stay," he snapped, while sailors loaded their packs onto a ship.

She crossed her arms and looked away. "You didn't seem to hate it so much with your pick of lovers from the slave quarter," she grumbled.

"Each one agreed," he snarled.

She stepped into his space and looked up directly into his face. "Could they refuse their zahib?"

He held her gaze for a burning few seconds, then averted his. "I'm not perfect, Samara. But I did my best."

"Your *best*," she said, tears welling in her eyes, "was not good enough." Not good enough to save Umi. Not good enough to free *her*. Not good enough to free everyone, until now, when it had become convenient.

A sailor waited behind him, their packs already loaded and their camels taken.

"Board the ship," Zahib said coldly.

"No!" she snapped, her face already tear streaked. He'd made a target of Umi, failed to protect her, allowed House Hazael to own slaves for his entire life, taken lover after lover from among them, and he expected her sympathy? Her obedience? Her daughterly affection?

"Board. The. Ship." He turned on her, but she shook her head.

"No!" she shouted into his face while he grabbed her by the arm. "Stop—I don't want to go! You can't make me—" He threw her up the gangplank and shoved her aboard the ship. "Let go!"

She kept repeating *no* the whole way, and it wasn't because she disagreed that it was her best chance to survive, or that she had to take this voyage for her own sake.

It was because she could *refuse* him, and it felt good. She'd never said *no* to him her entire life, but now she could say it as many times as she wanted, and she'd get no lashes. No punishment. She wouldn't have to worry about being maimed or killed.

No. As many times as she wanted, for any reason, or no reason at all.

When at last he pushed her into a small ship cabin, she narrowed her eyes at him. "I *hate* you."

He didn't look away, but faced her like a lion, undaunted and bold. "Hate me all you wish, Samara. It changes nothing. I loved Amaya, I am your father, and no matter how much you hate me, I love you and will always do my best for you." He jerked his head toward one of the two berths in the cabin. "Now lie down and get some rest. We have a long voyage ahead of us across the Shining Sea to Magehold."

"No." She said it slowly, deliberately, firmly, and moved toward the berth. She sat on the hard deck next to it.

It was unforgiving, rough, and uncomfortable, but it was her choice. And that felt better than a soft bed and following orders any day.

CHAPTER 13

*R*ielle hurried to keep up with Brennan as he led her back to their cabin aboard the *Mariposa*. She'd spent all morning buried in books on the eleven schools of accepted magic, practicing spells, counter-spells, and anti-defense spells. When it came to dueling, she always entered a more primal state, and the magic just *came*, but it helped to practice patterns.

The Magister Trials might not even involve duels. They could be oral examinations, or demonstrations, or even combat.

But she'd still worked on her pillar of flame gesture on the weather deck, over the sea, trying to get it just right so it dimmed her anima the least she could get it to. "Do you think the trials will—"

As she opened the door, Brennan gave her a push, and she tumbled into their cabin as he slammed the door shut and captured her in his embrace from behind, his grasp at her throat as he plied her neck with kisses. She leaned into him, unbuckling her belt as his other hand slid into her trousers, his fingers reaching their mark.

Divine. Throwing her head back onto his shoulder, she gasped and angled against his touch, savoring his ragged breaths in her ear.

"Tell me how it feels," he hissed, and she complied, broken words quivering from her lips as he took her to the edge, then abruptly withdrew his touch, leaving her aching, wanting, incomplete. "On the table."

Aside from their berths, they had only a lacquered table and two chairs in here, and she heeded him, hopping onto it. He dragged off her boots and her trousers, then grasped her face in his hands, taking her mouth with a vigor that promised so much more.

True to his word two weeks ago, he'd taken her at all hours of the day and night, until she didn't remember what it had been like before the constant ache and need. Aside from feeding him her blood this month, these past days had been nothing but magic practice and lovemaking—and that was more than fine with her.

She reached between them, unbuckling his belt, unfastening his trousers, taking hold of him, making him groan into her mouth. The feel of him was power, as much as he allowed her to have. He still hadn't permitted her to pleasure him as he did her—perhaps a type of power he didn't want to give her yet.

He secured her legs around him and moved her arms around his neck before grabbing her waist and dragging her to the edge of the table, where he took her, rasping panted breaths in her ear with each rough stroke.

"Divine," she breathed, meeting his movements.

"The Divine isn't taking you right now," he said, his voice that deep, low authority. "Tell me who is." His movements roughened.

"*Brennan,*" she rasped, as he lifted her off the table and

carried her to the door, pressed her back against it. She raised her arms above her, bracing her palms against the ceiling as he took her.

"Tell me who's taking you."

Between moans, she breathed his name, squeezing her eyes shut to isolate the pulse pounding at her core.

"Keep telling me," he bit out, and as she began to repeat his name, he clamped a palm over her mouth, taking her harder, faster, bringing her to the edge, right up against it, right there, there, there, and gloriously over, *Brennan*, spilling over, making her scream his name again and again and again into his hand, weep, cry, and lock her legs tighter around him as he hissed, finding his own release, grinding against her, deep, deeper, until he was utterly spent.

He uncovered her mouth and buried his face between her breasts, nuzzling her as his breathing evened. Her heart pounded like a drum, pleasure spreading like music to every corner of her body, its notes lulling her muscles to rest, to melt into him. She circled his neck with her arms, kissed the top of his head as her racing heartbeat slowed.

His hands secure around her backside, he took her to the bottom berth and gently lowered her to the bed. She moved aside, made room for him, and he dropped into it, collapsed onto his back, holding his arm open for her. With a smile, she wriggled close and nestled against his chest, as was their ritual. His gaze fixed on the berth above them as he relaxed.

"What are you thinking about?" she whispered, resting a hand on his abdomen.

He interlaced his fingers with hers. "Taking you again in five minutes."

She barked a laugh. "I'm beginning to wonder whether one woman is enough for you."

He sighed and cracked a grin. "Now you know the problem I've suffered for so much of my life. Tragic, isn't it?"

She moved to smack his arm, but his fingers only intertwined tighter with hers. "Smug, aren't you?"

He nudged her hair with his nose. "With every reason to be."

There was no arguing that.

"You're all I want, Rielle," he whispered, all traces of levity gone. "All I need. Believe me."

"Really?" She wriggled closer.

"There's been no one since... before Melain. I've only been able to think of *you*. Want *you*. Love *you*." He rested his head on hers. "I've wanted you for so long that I don't think I'll ever take you enough."

She smiled. "Then we'll have a splendid time discovering how much could ever be 'enough.' "

"Mmm. I like that." He leaned back and breathed deeply. "Have I ever told you how *perfect* you are for me?"

She mounted a leg over him and rolled on top, hands braced on his abdomen. "I promise I won't get tired of hearing it."

He seized her waist in his grip, let his palms drag to her hips, and to her backside, where he squeezed her firmly. "Perfect. *So* perfect."

"Mm-hmm." Now she knew exactly what he defined as *perfection*. She drew her other leg over him and dismounted, finding shaky footing on the deck. Her queen's lace was in their packs, and she wouldn't miss a dose, not even while cuddled up to him in dreamy comfort.

Once she found it, she uncorked their bottle of wine, poured herself a full goblet, and dosed it. He propped up on an arm, watching her contemplatively.

"The preventive," he said, and she nodded. He lowered his

gaze, letting the silence pervade a moment as the *Mariposa* bobbed and voices carried from elsewhere on the ship. "Do you ever think about... not taking it?"

She dropped into the nearby chair.

Sometimes when they'd been around children, she'd caught the way Brennan looked at them with that certain wistfulness. It wasn't about breaking the curse anymore, not for him. He wanted to be a father, wanted a family of his own, and Divine, he was wonderful with his nephews.

But as soon as those thoughts appeared in her mind, her hand would drift to her empty womb, where Sylvie would now have been just over six months along. At the thought, an ache would form in her chest, hollow and yet painful, bleeding memories she'd never make, visions of a little girl who'd never see the world, of a family that'd never be. And never far from those thoughts was Jon, who—if things had gone a little differently—would have been at her side, expecting their first child together.

Pressure formed behind her eyes, and she turned away, sipping her wine. That future—all of it—had shattered. Unforgettably.

"I do," she whispered, draining the goblet, "but I can't." Her composure recovering, she faced him, that lowered gaze, that sullen look. "I know you want children. I know that. But I'm not sure when, if ever, I'll be ready. I love you, Brennan, so much, and I'm so happy with you, but... I don't want to hurt you. It's still not too late for you to—"

He glared at her, sharp, hard. "Nox help me, Rielle," he swore, his voice raw, coarse. "Not another word. Not. Another. Word." His entire body had gone rigid, so taut that waves of tension practically rolled off him.

They had the perfect relationship now, and despite their

different plans for the future, he'd promised her it would be all right. But that promise wouldn't end well unless one of them bent toward the other. If they didn't discuss it, he'd assume *she* would... and she'd assume *he* would. And they'd both end up unhappy.

But as if he'd sealed her mouth shut, the words wouldn't pass.

At last, he exhaled. "I do want children—a whole house of them, Rielle," he said, and her heart broke. "But I want them with *you*. If that doesn't happen, then... it doesn't happen. I love *you*. I want *you*. No one else." He stood from the bunk and approached her, knelt at her feet, took her hand in his. "Don't ever think you're not enough. Ever."

He meant it now. She believed him. But if she didn't change her mind, would he still mean it in five years? Ten? Or would he regret it, wish he'd chosen someone else?

Some distant calls came from the upper decks, and Brennan paused attentively, then handed her trousers and boots to her.

"Get dressed," he said, rising and buckling his belt. "You're going to want to see this."

See what? But she scrambled into her trousers and tugged on her boots, buckling her belt as they darted out of the cabin. He took her hand, leading her down the passageway and up the ladder to the weather deck.

A number of passengers and sailors gathered at the starboard railing, and Brennan wedged them between the crowd to find a spot, positioned behind her, his hands on either side of hers on the railing, keeping her from all others.

Out in the crystalline turquoise waters of the Shining Sea, just beneath the surface, iridescent scales mirrored the afternoon sunlight, and dazzling glowing eyes surveyed them.

"Mermaids," she whispered, her hand going to the golden

locket hanging from her neck, enshrining the scale she'd been honored with on their way across the Bay of Amar. A pod of mer-people swam alongside the ship, gazes darting about the faces of the sailors and passengers, vocalizing musically to one another beneath the waves.

The world had changed. Immortals, both peaceful and not, had returned. This new reality was often terrifying—the krakens, wyverns, basilisks, dragons, and so on made sure of that—but sometimes, it was beautiful and full of wonder, like now, when she was blessed with hearing this lovely song, a sound she'd have never heard if not for the Rift.

"What do you think they're saying?" she mused aloud.

Brennan leaned in, his embrace closing from behind as he rested the side of his face against her head. "If I had to guess, 'Look at that attractive couple. They look like they belong together.' Or something like that."

Rolling her eyes, she tried to look over her shoulder at him, but his hold was uncompromising. She sighed. "Yes, I'm sure that's it," she deadpanned, even as a reluctant smile stole her mouth.

"Like a flash of lightning," he whispered in her ear. "They can't help but look, catching a glimpse while they can."

BRENNAN OFFERED Rielle a hand and helped her into the carriage to Magehold, out of the rain, eyeing her garnet ring with a smile. He'd arranged to have some of the Marcel villa's staff in Magehold meet them here. Once they arrived, she could finally set aside the books on magic for once, relax for a week, and focus on *them*.

Perhaps after this, these trials, once she'd won the rank of magister, she could pull back from all of this Divinity work, from this obsession with magic and missions. All of that only got her into trouble, and the future duchess of Maerleth Tainn couldn't be risking her life regularly.

Mother was one of the strongest women he knew, and aside from the broken relationship with Father, perhaps Rielle would find her life an inspiration. Flawlessly running Maerleth Tainn and all the lesser holdings, supporting Father, raising the next generation of Marcels to be strong, intelligent, clever.

Blinded by the trials, Rielle didn't see the appeal of that life now, but she enjoyed her time with him, and taking her place as the future duchess would only mean more time spent together, enjoying each other, taking care of their lands, their people, and someday soon, their own family. She'd come to realize it before they returned to Emaurria. He'd make certain of it.

He hopped in after her, taking the seat across from her, and looked her over as she rearranged her turquoise overcoat, hitting him with a breeze of her intoxicating scent, mingled gloriously with his. She smelled like him, thoroughly claimed, and wore his marks on her skin—the violet of his kiss on the side of her neck and, beneath her clothes, on her breasts and just above the crease of her thigh. And on her hips, the dawn-colored imprints of his hold in the heat of passion. It was just as well that she couldn't heal them, since he would have forbidden it anyway. She'd given him her blood earlier, as she did monthly to help him control his Change, and he still had the taste of it on his tongue.

And on her finger, the ring of a Marcel bride—the future duchess. Any man, ignorant or doubtful, had only to look there to know to whom this beautiful, deadly woman belonged. In just a few short months, they'd be married—bound to one another in law.

And she wasn't ready yet, but someday she'd be full with his heir, his woman in every way possible. Someday.

She crossed her legs and raised an eyebrow. "I'm no mentalist, but with that look on your face, even I can tell what your thoughts are."

"And do they please you?"

A little smile. "*You* will." Even as she held his gaze, boldly, irresistibly, she squirmed, straightening in her seat.

"That's a given, bride."

Her cheeks reddened as she grinned and looked away, out the carriage window at the rain pounding the grass. "How long before your family gets here?"

When he'd sent word to Mother about their trip to Magehold, she'd made some hasty new arrangements. Although they usually summered in Bellanzole, this year Mother, Nora, the boys, Una, and Caitlyn would meet them here in Magehold at the villa.

It seemed Father had extended his stay with Marie de Brignac in Courdeval, or gone on to Xir to see Kehani.

Although Father had always kept mistresses, as the years wore on, he did so with increasing openness, and Mother had always been a proud woman. Too proud to wilt in Maerleth Tainn alone while her husband openly chose his mistresses over her.

"A couple weeks," he replied. "Mother had some business to handle before the voyage."

She nodded. "Is there anything we can do for them? Maybe order this season's gowns, or arrange for some entertainment—"

He could have laughed, but suppressed it. Only just. After

the past few weeks of wild lovemaking on the ship, wearing the Marcel ring on her finger, having sent invitations to their *wedding*, she worried about their family accepting her? "It'll be fine, Rielle."

Her cheeks reddened. "I—I just want your family to... I want them to be..."

He leaned back, sprawling out on the seat. "You want them to like you."

She looked away. "You say that like it's ridiculous."

It was. What did it matter whether she ordered gowns or entertainment? He'd brought her *home*. He'd preferred to take his conquests elsewhere, and here, he'd kept a room in a nearby inn—it was Silen, after all, with a beauty in sight every fifty feet —but Rielle was different. They *knew* she was different.

He leaned forward and rested a hand on her knee. "Trust me. You're my bride, not just some woman."

A fleeting smile, and she nodded. The Marcels rarely liked each other, but if the need arose, they *killed* for each other. He leaned back again.

Fidgeting in her lap, she watched out the window as the rain came down harder. "So you think they'll eventually like me?"

"It doesn't matter," he replied, because he was marrying her regardless. "But I think they already do. And considering the trials, they'll only be all the more impressed when you win."

She rolled her eyes.

And as for him, he hadn't exactly won over her brother, but her great-grandmother approved. That counted for something— to her, maybe. And he wouldn't have to deal with her ship-captain brother for some time, praise the Great Wolf.

"I think the trials will involve combat." Her voice dropped.

"Has to be. 'Victor' means multiple candidates, and I don't suppose they'd just grade exams against one another. Not when there's a banquet and fanfare."

It did no good to speculate when the Grand Divinus had clearly thrown tradition out the window; there was no way for Rielle to plan the trials. The only way she could prepare was to gather her confidence, calm her nerves, go into this knowing she had all the knowledge and skill she would need—and if she faced any true danger, he could take care of it as soon as she pulled on the bond. "Whatever they are, you'll beat them."

She exhaled sharply through her nose. "Magic is my life. Whatever's coming, I'll be ready." She crossed her arms. "What about infiltrating the Archives?" she whispered, her gaze unfocused. Worried. "Are you sure you want to risk that? Do you think you'll find the records we need?"

"Leave it to me," he replied. "I want to do this."

"I don't want you to get hurt," she said softly.

"Being immune to magic helps. Don't worry. I'll be fine. It's the Divine Guard you want to save your sympathies for," he said with a smile, and she mirrored his expression.

The answer to who'd killed her family was important, but after questioning Sincuore, he needed answers, too—that Rielle knew nothing about. And telling her would mean admitting Father's treason, and his own role in covering it up. Someday, perhaps, but not yet. Not until they were married.

Had Father been working with the Grand Divinus? Why would she back him? What could have motivated the regicide, the siege, so much scheming?

And was Father in too deep to extricate the rest of the family? He wouldn't let Mother, his sisters, or Rielle fall over Father's all-consuming ambition. This had to end.

While Rielle participated in the trials, he'd work behind the scenes to break into the Archives. If he found proof of a conspiracy between the Grand Divinus and Father, he'd destroy it... and anyone else involved. For the family.

If he found evidence that the Grand Divinus had ordered the attack on Laurentine that had killed Rielle's family, then she would have it. And use it to burn down the Divinity if she wanted to, with him at her side.

The rest of the way, she fell into a contemplative silence as the sky stormed, raindrops pattering the carriage's roof, and they were at the Marcel villa just before dark.

The grounds were well kept, and inside, the style was old-world Emaurrian, with touches of Sileni antiques and a purple palette of colors. Mother's style, as expected.

Once the chamberlain showed them to quarters, Rielle immediately headed for the desk, hastily sitting down and scrambling about for writing supplies. No doubt writing a note to Magehold about her arrival.

With a relaxed exhalation, he approached her from behind, his hands finding her shoulders. He rubbed them gently at first, slowly increasing the pressure to sensual rhythm. The quill in her hand struggled at its task before abandoning it entirely. No more magic—nor all the distractions that went with it—tonight.

He untied her braid and glided a hand up her neck, his fingers threading through her hair to massage her head as he bent to her ear, nudged her tresses aside.

"We've arrived in time for the welcome banquet next week," he whispered, then kissed her cheek. "They'll know we're here."

"I just—" She moaned as he kissed down her neck.

Worrying too much, again.

"Once I send this, it'll be out of my head. But right now, it's just—"

He locked his lips with hers, kissed her deeply, as his fingers unfastened her overcoat. "My bride," he whispered against her lips, low and deep, "there are much better things to fill your head with."

As she gasped, he claimed her mouth once more, and with needy arms, she reached for him. Only him.

CHAPTER 14

$\mathcal{M}$arfa shivered in the darkness, against the slick stone of the cell. It wasn't the cold that made the fine hairs on her skin stand on end, nor the damp air, nor even the dark. The reek of old magic flooded the air heavily, suffocatingly, but that wasn't it either.

It was the great void, the quiet, the echoes of echoes with not a soul in sight. It was the arcanir bars and the small cell, the growls, snarls, and scratchings of beasts all around her, the vast nothing of this place.

She had been accompanying Lisandra at the river, not far from the pack, when it had happened. On the bank, she'd watched Lisandra spasm and cry out, even as she'd spasmed and cried out herself. The last thing she remembered was trying to rise, trying to get to the water and to Lisandra, and then she'd awoken in a vast, dark chamber, shuddering violently on the ground, while a Coven of witches—no, many Covens, all together—had dragged her and the others and beasts of all kinds here. To these cramped, dark spaces. To this... prison.

Where was the river? The pack? Lisandra? What had happened to her? Why wasn't she here?

She always felt Lisandra nearby, and the pack, like a distant song just past the trees, but now... Now there was nothing.

How had she gotten here, to this chamber? Why had the witches taken them prisoner? Why had the Dragonlords allowed it?

These witches had taken away her clothes, cut fur from her body, beaten her, stabbed her, starved her for months. So many witches, all wearing the same uniform, the blue overcoats with gold buttons. When she was in human form, they gave her a little more food perhaps, a little more water, although never enough.

And even with her heat, it was cold here, and she hadn't even a blanket nor a shirt to stave off the chill.

The way the witches looked at her, like an unwanted dog, sent shivers down her spine. Humans didn't keep dogs that had no use, that couldn't herd, couldn't watch, couldn't guard. What use did they want of her? And if she didn't serve...

Why were they keeping her here? For how long?

Where was the pack?

She dropped her head in her hands, palming back matted, greasy hair, then drew in her knees, rested her chin on them. There were eight others here, not pack, although none seemed to speak the common tongue or, if they did, none desired to respond.

She was alone. Completely, maddeningly, unendingly alone.

And where did that leave Lisandra, somewhere out there in this new, human-run world? They had only each other and the pack, and Lisandra was a gentle soul, a kind soul, and would never survive alone among the humans. Not for long.

Marfa chewed her chapped lower lip and rocked herself. The witches were keeping her for a reason. They'd expect her to serve sometime, and when they did, she would have her chance. If they didn't control her with sangremancy, she'd try to escape, maybe fight, whatever it took, but she'd get out of here alive, and she'd find Lisandra.

As NIGHT FELL, Leigh entered the mixed-oak forest outside of Courdeval, with Ambriel behind him, his bow at the ready.

Gustave had passed along intelligence that the heretics were meeting in the woods tonight, some ritual. Dancing under the moon, whatever. Leigh shrugged. If this group was hoping to usurp the Tremblay Coven, then it stood to reason that they would try to practice some of that Dark Age of Magic nonsense.

"I hear them," Ambriel whispered, "chanting. There are... many."

"It'll be worth it." The Tremblays were known for their battle magic, and they were essential to any force standing against the Divinity. Along with the Forgerons—known for their magical smithing—and the Beaufoys, with their forbidden magic and daring eyes and long, flowing locks and swaying hips and—

"There's something else," Ambriel said quietly. "The trees, they're—"

Leigh looked over his shoulder as Ambriel shook his head. The chanting was loud enough that he could hear it, and flashes of firelight filtered through the tree trunks. Torches amid dancing bodies, surrounding an oak—

No, at the center, entangled among the wood, was a *woman.* Her body was claimed by oak tendrils that gave way, gave way, gave way. Her face was beautiful, the most beautiful thing he'd ever seen, eyes with long lashes closed.

"A dryad," Ambriel hissed. "The fools are waking a dryad."

He'd read myths of the dryads, how they spoke to trees, could take on the form of a tree themselves, and sometimes did, forgetting themselves for centuries or all time. How they despised fire above all things, and humans nearly as much. How they could turn seeds into towering oaks in the blink of an eye, and an entire forest against any enemy.

"They are waking her in the dark, amid fire," Ambriel said, taking a step back. "She will kill them all. It'll be a massacre."

A massacre, and a Forgeron potentially killed on Tremblay territory. "We need to find the Forgeron mage. Fast. Most of them are red haired, so—"

"Don't look directly at the dryad. She'll—"

The last bit of wood keeping the dryad extended her outward, placing her gently upon the grass, which greened vividly at her feet. Her ghostly white skin took on a greenish hue, growing from her toes up her legs, over her limber naked body, and up to her hair, which sprouted thick and massive, moss green and growing leaves like ornaments.

Her eyes opened, and it was like staring into a wellspring of life, bright white and pure, immaculate. He would live for her. He would die for her. He would do all her bidding.

The circle of dancers all froze, mesmerized, and she reached out a slender arm to hold the chin of a torchbearer, who smiled and relaxed in her touch.

His head wrenched off.

He dropped the torch, his blood spurting to douse the fire.

Oaks twisted and curled as if made of clay, growing and grabbing the dancers.

"Dreshan," Ambriel hissed in his ear, but the dryad's eyes were stunning.

Hands covered his eyes, and he shuddered, the tang of blood in his nostrils, and when Ambriel uncovered him, he raised a hand to cast.

Ambriel grabbed it. "No. If you kill her, the entire forest dies."

She stood at the center as trees captured all the dancers.

Heart pounding, he scanned all the captive dancers, those who were yet alive. Who looked most like Joel Forgeron? Like Helene?

Shining red hair in a high bun. High cheekbones—Joel's daughter, barely old enough to leave home, high in the canopy.

"Katia," he whispered, circling around the creaking oaks to the one that held her. When he was just below, he spelled a cut right through the branch binding her, severing it, and she plummeted as the dryad shrieked an otherworldly howl.

Katia fell into his arms, and he set her down, backing away and looking down as she fixed her glowing white eyes on him. His repulsion shield sprang up in a bubble around him, Ambriel, and Katia, as the winding trees slammed into it from every side, but it held, it would hold, it *had* to hold until they were out, and then he could destabilize it and destroy every—

Singing—strange, hymnal singing—began. Elvish tree-singing. Ambriel.

The branches didn't renew their assault, but stayed still, waiting. Listening? The dryad followed them with slow steps, her head tilted.

"Ambriel," he warned, but the singing only loudened. Trees bent and curved over them.

She closed, and the grass beneath their feet grew taller, and his feet began to tangle in it.

"*Ambriel*," he warned again.

A few steps more, and no more grass pulled up around his ankles. They were beyond the forest's edge, and the dryad paused, her gaze fixed on Ambriel as he kept up the song, bowed to her. Trees and branches crowded the edge of the forest, filled out every empty space, a dense wall of oaks that grew and grew and grew.

The dryad leaned against the edge, pushed.

Ambriel grabbed Leigh's shoulder, turning him around.

"Don't look," Ambriel said at last in Old Emaurrian, hurrying him along while Katia kept pace.

He held the shield in place, maintaining his focus, while Ambriel sang scattered notes.

"We—we thought she would protect us," Katia stammered, "protect the forest from the beasts—"

"Don't look," Ambriel repeated.

Otherworldly shrieking and howling rang out through the night, wooden creaking and groaning spreading through a thousand awoken trees.

He didn't turn, didn't stop, just grabbed Katia's hand and ran after Ambriel.

THE VIOLETTE DISTRICT was quiet when they returned to the city, some windows glowing with candlelight. Few passersby walked the cobblestone streets at this hour, but even fewer guards—the beauty of middling Violette: rich enough that the average riffraff didn't fit in, but not so rich that it was teeming with guards.

"Is she all right?" Ambriel asked in Old Emaurrian, glancing toward Katia.

Leigh shrugged. Katia walked at his side, quiet but for the

rare gasp as she found some new spot of blood to rub from her skin and clothes.

As soon as he presented her to Gustave, he'd have the favor of the Tremblay Coven.

"What did you sing to her?" he asked Ambriel in Old Emaurrian. "To the dryad?"

"I sang to her of Vervewood, of the dryad I'd met there in my youth. Of the trees I knew, and what they had told me."

The dryad had been intrigued—enough to reach the edge of the forest, where she could not cross. "You saved us," Leigh said.

Ambriel dipped his head. "I know you could have destroyed the forest and destroyed her—"

He could have. Once they'd gotten Katia, it had been instinct to destroy everything.

"—but I'm so glad you didn't."

Ambriel had been teaching him about the forests, and the trees, and their spirits, and perhaps he wouldn't have cared a few months ago, but he cared now.

"I didn't expect her to be so angry," Katia said in Old Emaurrian. "We expected her to be more like the forest, serene, but with a depth of blackness. Power."

Leigh quirked a brow. "You speak Old Emaurrian?"

"Most of my family does." She kicked a pebble in the street. "How else would you read the old texts?"

Well, the Covens certainly weren't as strict with knowledge as the Divinity was. "What were you thinking?"

She shrugged, eyeing the domed crown of a nearby horse-chestnut tree. "My family are all smiths—transmutors, and actual blacksmiths—and I'm a geomancer. Is it so terrible that I wanted to find greater meaning in the natural world? I know everyone is afraid of the Rift, but when I heard about it, all I could think about were all of the wondrous possibilities that had become reality. When I heard rumors of what this new Trien Coven was trying to do—I... I mean, who could imagine a dryad? A real dryad? Talking to the heart of a forest?"

"So it was curiosity, then?" Curiosity could be dangerous enough *without* the addition of magic. "And it didn't occur to you that your precious dryad might be like one of the countless horrors that Emaurria has faced since the Rift?"

She lowered her gaze and wrapped her brown cloak about herself.

"Dryads are the forest's power incarnate," Ambriel said quietly. "If they slumber, let them slumber. They wake when they are needed."

She nodded solemnly. "I know that now. But it's too late. Everyone is dead. All of them."

As a geomancer, she had felt out of place with her family of smiths all her life. She looked for meaning in life where there was none. And how many more curious, naïve witches would repeat her idiocy?

He'd had his own bout, acting on blind determination instead of knowledge, and now the world suffered the Rift. So many horrors had emerged from it, and how many more witches and mages would proceed blindly and only wreak greater havoc?

"Where are you taking me, anyway?" she asked.

If she'd grown up in a Coven, she knew the answer to that. He had to take her to the local Coven's Archon.

"You know where I'm taking you," Leigh said.

"The Archon will just send me back to my father, won't he?" The question was lifeless, dejected.

What had she expected? To flout Gustave Tremblay and, with her fellow rebels, usurp his Coven? And when she failed, to get away with it? To be embraced?

"You are alive," Leigh said. "Don't ignore that gift. Find another purpose. A *better* purpose. And don't shit on the Tremblays' territory unless you want to start an inter-Coven war."

Her shoulders curled inward.

Her older brother, Blaise, didn't have a slumping bone in his body. Leigh exhaled slowly, warmth flowing through him at the memory. A couple of years ago, he'd met with Joel Forgeron to discuss subversion strategies, and who had been at Joel's side but his eldest son and heir to the Coven leadership, twenty-nine-year-old, stone-faced, gray-eyed, red-haired, marble-sculpture-made-flesh Blaise? Stiff-lipped, Blaise had said nothing during the meeting, simply taking in his father's process, but Divine's tits did he have a mouth on him later that night.

Blaise didn't have a slumping bone in his body, but Katia had *left behind* the safety and status of her family, the support of her Coven—all to pursue her own dreams. That took courage, something she shared with her brother. Courage would take her to high, powerful places, but only if she learned measure first. Maybe tonight's bloodbath would be the first of many lighter lessons to take her there.

Finally, they arrived at Tremblay's home, an upscale mansion among more modest homes, guarded by two witches.

"Why are we not meeting him at the apothecary?" Ambriel whispered in his ear.

"Because that would mean waiting until tomorrow, and I'm not keen on babysitting all night—are you?"

Katia shot him a scowl, while Ambriel fought a smile and looked away.

"This is not a man you approach unannounced," Ambriel said.

"Don't worry," Leigh said, waving at the witches. "They'll announce me."

One of the witches, a young blond man, approached. "What business do you have here, mage?"

Leigh cleared his throat. "Gustave knows what business. Fetch him."

The witch looked him, Ambriel, and Katia over with narrowing eyes. "*He* does not come when *you* call."

"Do you know who I am?" With a whirl of his fingers, Leigh spelled a force ball in his hand, dense and translucent, which he spun nonchalantly, while the witch stiffened. "It's dark, so you might not."

The witch blinked, giving him a once-over that stopped at his hair. His platinum-white, wild-mage hair. "L-leigh Galvan."

Leigh grinned. He'd worked very hard to make sure his reputation preceded him. His reputation for impatience, importance, and violence. Extreme violence. "He will come when *I* call. Now run along, lackey."

The witch's face contorted in a snarl, and he looked back to his partner, the tall, rake-thin one from the cellar, who nodded.

Well, well. Stupidity *was* treatable after all.

The blond witch clenched a fist.

He would do as bidden. Any further posturing would lead somewhere unfortunate. Unfortunate for the lackey. And the other lackey. And the District.

The blond witch backed up, jogged up the drive, and entered the mansion.

"You are well-known in this city," Ambriel observed.

"My dear, I am well-known in this *kingdom*. Make sure you write that down in your witness diary." Although *well-known* wouldn't precisely be the term he'd use. *Notorious*, perhaps. *Infamous*, maybe.

"Witness diary?" Ambriel repeated, arching a brow, and Leigh shrugged.

"You can even jot down our names and draw a heart around them. It's this human practice—"

"Dreshan, if you don't want that second 'walnut loaf' you bought to mysteriously get lost, you'll stop now."

Was Ambriel blushing? It was too dark to tell. Maybe with a little more prodding... But he didn't want to risk the walnut loaf.

"You two have walnut loaf?" Katia whispered. "Can I have some?"

That was a definite *no*.

Within moments, two figures exited the mansion, one of which was a very frowny Gustave Tremblay in an unbuttoned overcoat. Hastily thrown on, probably. He walked halfway down the drive, then beckoned.

Good enough. Leigh strode to meet him, Ambriel and Katia in his wake, gravel crunching beneath their feet. His own home, in Ren, had only ever had a dirt road—all he'd been able to afford as a farmer with a family; he'd refused to ask his father for money.

"So that's a no, then," Katia said from behind him.

Leigh cleared his throat. "I would have sprung for cobblestone," he called to Gustave.

"I try not to garner too much attention," Gustave grumbled.

Leigh smirked. "That explains the mansion and guards."

With a grimace, Gustave led them into the grass, walking the grounds. "Report."

Leigh cleared his throat. "Well, as you can see, I have one gray-eyed, red-haired Forgeron in tow."

With a glance at Katia, Gustave paused and inclined his head. "A pleasure. If only we'd met under better circumstances, Mademoiselle."

Katia shrank deeper into her cloak and inclined her head—lower. "The fault is all mine, Archon Tremblay. I searched for a sense of belonging in the wrong place, and I apologize. I beg your forgiveness."

Well said. She was a proper Forgeron after all.

A lengthy pause lingered before Gustave nodded. "My Coven has shared a long alliance with the Forgerons that should remain intact."

Mercy, and a subtle warning. As expected. "Wonderful," Leigh said, stepping out in front of Gustave. "Now, the upstarts are all dead, you have a dryad in your forest, Katia is—as you can see—quite alive, so I believe that concludes my part of the bargain?"

Gustave bit his thumb and held out his hand in the vowing clasp—sangremancy the Covens still used. "As long as you safely return Katia to her Coven, I pledge my loyalty and that of my Coven to the Crown."

Leigh cocked his head. "Returning the girl wasn't part of the bargain."

"It is now," Gustave said, eyeing the girl. "I'm not about to trust her return, given what's now out there, to anyone else."

Leigh heaved a sigh. So much for not babysitting tonight. He glanced at Ambriel and raised an inquisitive brow.

Ambriel hesitated, then nodded.

Leigh bit his thumb and clasped Gustave's arm, each imprinting blood on the other's skin. *"As we agree, so let it be,"* he said in unison with Gustave three times, and the imprints seared into their skin.

Exactly what he wanted. A damn thumbprint branded on his arm. He sighed.

"That concludes our dealings. Goodnight, Galvan." Gustave nodded to him, Katia, and Ambriel before turning back to his mansion.

"He could've invited us to stay for the night," Leigh grumbled.

"Well," Katia ventured, "he *did* say he was trying not to garner attention. And, well, you're *you*."

There had been something he'd liked about this girl since the moment he'd met her. "Good point."

A night at the palace before heading out on the road again would serve just fine.

CHAPTER 15

On the *Aurora*'s weather deck, Jon gripped the railing, watching the chop of the Shining Sea's turquoise waves in the late-afternoon sun. They'd been sailing for nearly two weeks, but it felt like forever. In all his twenty-seven years, he'd never passed beyond the borders of Emaurria, except maybe in some skirmishes with Skaddish warbands in the North.

Now, here he was, on a ship, crossing the sea. It had been quiet so far. Captain Bittencourt had kept them clear of pirates, and other than wayward Immortals, that was the only concern on these waters. The fact that they'd had to hire a Broadsteel warship instead of taking an Emaurrian Royal Navy ship would have been laughable if it weren't so grave. Any ship "suitably secure to transport a king," as the Grands had put it, was still months from being completed.

He didn't need a special ship, but the replenishment of Emaurria's navy was yet another deficit he had to shore up.

He closed his eyes. Out here, he didn't feel the same. The

constant familiarity at his back—the land—was fading. On shore, if he wished, he could melt into it easily, tap into that connection. The *Aurora* had kept within sight of the Emaurrian shore whenever possible, but the farther they sailed, the more remote that constant familiarity became.

"What are you thinking about?" Olivia's voice. She rested her hands on the railing next to his, shrugging in her brown leather coat.

A sword hung at her side. The Queen's Blade.

"You're wearing it?"

She glanced down at the hilt, then up at him and smiled a little. "Why not? You're giving it away to the Grand Divinus. I just... thought I'd see what it felt like."

What it felt like... to wear a sword? Or what it felt like... to be queen?

He'd been catching glimpses of it lately in her gaze—lingering a little longer, resting on him more often than not—and he'd seen it his fair share as a paladin. Women who'd looked, who'd liked what they saw. Women he'd been able to dismiss, because he'd had his duties and been sworn to the Sacred Vows, and they'd been strangers.

He was king and she was one of his Grands. They both had their duties, but Olivia was no stranger. No woman he could pass by and ignore. In truth, she'd become his closest friend, his most trusted adviser, and the guiding star he turned to when the woods of his life became too dark and deep.

She was beautiful—gorgeous, even, and he could understand why many men's gazes swept to her, why they pursued her, courted her. But from the moment he'd met her, he'd seen her as someone else. A beautiful woman, yes, but a friend. A friend and no more.

Perhaps he'd been too open, too close, and had given her

some sign of his romantic interest. It was completely possible he'd erred in some way.

If she was attracted to him, he had to do his best not to give her the wrong signals, not to lead her on and disrespect her.

"If you want me to, I'll take it off," she said, taking a step back.

He'd been staring. Intensely.

He cleared his throat and looked back out to sea. It shouldn't disturb him. He'd never have a queen, but if he could have...

He'd made a promise once, on the bank of the Propré River, that he'd go somewhere with *her*, just the two of them, to a winter cottage, where they'd enjoy each other's company, where he'd teach her the sword, where she'd teach him magic, and they'd make love until they forgot their names—

No.

He slammed a palm against the railing, clenched so hard the wood bit into his palm. Just another dream. And he was done with those.

He had an entire kingdom to set right.

If all went well in Magehold, he'd soon bring the Tower into the Crown's fold. And then the Order of Terra in Emaurria. With both powers firmly in hand, he'd strengthen the kingdom. Emaurria would finally have the tools it needed to survive the Rift.

He'd do it.

He'd do it, or he'd die trying. And it'd be worth it.

"Jon?" Olivia nudged his hand.

Less than a cable length away, something burst from the water, massive, blacking out the sun—a serpent.

The ship rocked, teetering erratically. Jon clenched the

railing tight with one hand, thrust out his arm and swept Olivia behind him as she locked her arms around his waist.

Crewmen slid across the deck while Olivia chanted a hydromancy incantation.

He gestured a repulsion shield before him while shouted orders rang out, and slowly, with Olivia's chanting, the waters stabilized.

Its massive maw open and gleaming with spine-like sharp teeth, an enormous serpent leaped from the water, arcing over them from port to starboard as it plunged into the water. Blinding sunlight glinted off its lengthy serpentine body scaled in iridescent light blue.

Jon moved the repulsion shield along, keeping it between the serpent and him and Olivia.

Royal Guards and Broadsteel mercenaries drew bows—the guards had arcanir arrows.

A large, fin-like tail passed over them and into the water on the starboard side. Olivia kept up the incantation.

"What was that?" he hissed.

"Water dragon," she blurted between incantations.

He and Olivia were the only mages aboard. How would a healer, a novice enforcer, and bows defeat a serpent this size?

His gaze darted around them. Nothing but open sea. And far on the horizon, another ship. On an intercept course.

It, too, would fall prey.

The constant hum. The Earthbinding. "How far into the sea does Emaurria extend?"

"I don't know," she shouted. "Twelve nautical miles? Why?"

"Hold the incantation, Olivia." Jon closed his eyes, took a deep breath, pictured Olivia with her arms locked around him, his hand on the railing, the deck, the ship, the Shining Sea around them... Shimmering waves like shifting glass, reflecting the bright sunlight across a neverending surface. There was a flow there, brilliant with life, wind blowing across an incalculable vastness, pushing water into waves, and as he focused harder, his consciousness tapped into it, pushed, pushed, harnessed that energy, collected it, flowed into a massive force.

Distant shouts disturbed the water, and something massive broke the surface, less than a cable length away—the water dragon—sending energy swelling against his and breaking, falling apart.

His consciousness crashed against the water dragon with the force of a thousand waves, crushing it against the shifting sea—

Lightning broke through him like a blade, and the water twisted. His consciousness fell back across the surface of the water, across the flow and the mirrored sunlight on turquoise waves to the prow of the schooner, and railing, and Olivia's arms, and he opened his eyes.

Pain needled his chest as his heart thudded wildly. His head pulsed as he stared through a blurry white haze, doubling over as another searing bolt ripped through him.

He reached for his heart, and a hand was on his chest, Olivia's hand, glowing white and warm while she chanted, keeping the water stable, and cold streaked over his lips, down his neck, and into his shirt, and dripped on the deck.

Blood. He reached around for support and grabbed a handle —a hilt—and there was a soft swish...

He blinked as the blurry haze grew, and he hit the deck.

SAMARA LEANED AGAINST THE WALL, observing as the ship's

physician treated a boy perhaps a couple of years older than she, maybe seventeen or eighteen. He had a thief's build—compact but muscular, a few inches under six feet, and wore an eye patch over his left eye, his long, back hair secured in a tail. She'd watched for his type in the souk all her life, wary of those sticky fingers that could earn her lashes.

But perhaps he wasn't here to steal anything. He'd claimed to be the carpenter's apprentice, and the physician, a balding man with a skeptical gaze, didn't question him.

"Undress to the waist, Zero," the physician said.

The boy—Zero—smirked as he untied his shirt and slipped it off his shoulders. "There's a lady present, Doc. Have a care for her virgin eyes, eh?"

Virgin eyes? She'd grown up in a pleasure house. Her eyes had seen things he'd only dreamed of. And then some.

The physician grabbed Zero by the shoulders. "That *lady* is an apothecary. Her interest is academic."

Zero slid a look her way from beneath a stray lock of thick, black hair falling over his eyes. "What's your name, academic?"

"Shh," Doc chided, then gently shook Zero by the shoulders, while applying his ear directly to Zero's chest. "I'm attempting to determine the presence of thoracic empyema."

"What's that?" Zero asked, coughing.

Doc pulled away with a grimace. "A chest infection."

Zero straightened and gaped while Doc turned to his medicines and filled a pouch. He approached Samara and held it up to her nose.

"Ingredients?"

She breathed in deeply. "Horseradish root, anise..."

He nodded. "Good."

"Something else I can't name."

"Sea lavender," he said with a grin. "I gather what ingredients I can, given our circumstances."

Of course—a law every apothecary lived by.

"If I start smelling fancy, the crew might get ideas," Zero said, scowling at the pouch as he righted his shirt.

Doc rested a hand on his shoulder and thrust the pouch into Zero's palm. "Brew it as a tea. Thrice daily until you finish the entire thing."

Finally dressed, Zero hopped off the examination table and turned over the small pouch in his hand. "Thanks, Doc," he said, giving her one last look over his shoulder. "I'll catch you later, academic." The words were low, honeyed.

Any boy who spoke with that voice only wanted one thing.

Oh no you won't.

"I think not." Zahib, arms crossed, stood on the other side of the doorway, watching Zero through slitted eyes.

Suddenly Zero was a small measure attractive.

He smirked and passed by, while Zahib's gaze bored a hole in his back. As soon as Zero had ascended the ladder, Zahib rounded on her and grabbed her arm.

"Come." He led her back toward their cabin.

"Ah," she grunted, resisting his pull. "I won't stay in the cabin all day, every day. I need to breathe. See something. Learn something. Work."

He finally dragged her to their cabin and shoved her inside. "You're mingling with the wrong sort on this ship."

"They might disagree on who *the wrong sort* is," she snapped back at him. Zahib had gone by an alias aboard the *Liberté*, Sayid Berrada. The ship had already been transporting other passengers from Sonbahar, so they'd blended in well among them, especially considering the son of a *prince* was here —Tariq al-Rhamani, son of Prince Raadi El-Amin abd Hassan abd Ahmad of Sonbahar. His entourage was large and impressive, and his skill as an elementalist was renowned in Sonbahar, so the passengers flocked just to meet him. He was traveling to some magic competition, from what she'd overheard.

Zahib put a hand to his forehead and sighed. "These men have spent years chasing slave ships. But Samara, you are my heir. You will have to accept that responsibility, and rise to your proper caste."

Zahib had freed her from slavery, but now he sought to bind her in yet another kind of obligation. She was *free*, but not free to do as she willed.

"This... university," she said slowly. "It's not for medicine, is it?"

He sighed. "Samara, a woman of your stature needs to know many things. About magic, runes, sigils, history, language—"

Pressure pushed behind her eyes.

"—and these potions and powders are a fine hobby, but a Hazael cannot practice medicine in the city like some commoner. These are the constraints every Hazael has lived by."

"Slave-owning was a constraint every Hazael lived by." She faced him squarely.

"Samara—"

She clenched fists. "Why did you even bother to free me, when you never intended for me to have a choice in anything?"

His dark eyes bored into hers, intense, fierce, terrifying as his whole body brimmed with tension. "You will be *safe* at university, you will have the education you should have had, and you can make all the *choices* you wish once I am dead. Until then, I am still your father."

"You conceived me," she said, trembling inside but praying her voice was firm, "but that does *not* make you my father."

She marched to her berth and threw herself onto it, curling on her side away from him and shutting him out—along with everything else.

No matter what he said, she would never give up on helping other people. Ever. No matter what he—or anyone else—said.

CHAPTER 16

*J*on blinked his eyes open. A wooden ceiling above him, with shadows cast against the glow of candlelight. A small bed—his feet reached past the foot of it—and a goblet rolled on a floor that shifted and bobbed.

His hand was warm, and he glanced over to see a creased porcelain brow, and teary emerald eyes. Her hair long and unbound, Olivia sat on the edge of the berth in her floor-length white linen nightgown and green brocade robe, holding his hand with a soft glow.

"Jon," she rasped, a soft smile lighting her face. "You're awake."

Still at sea. He blinked sluggishly. "What day is it?"

"15 Floreal. You've been asleep for two days," she said, giving his hand a squeeze.

He frowned. The last thing he remembered was hitting the deck. And a dragon—

"The water dragon," he blurted, trying to sit up, but Olivia leaned over and urged him back down onto the pillow. "Did it—?"

"It's gone." That should have been a relief, but there was still a crease on her brow.

"What is it?"

She toyed with his thumb, the healing warmth still seeping into him. "It's just that..."

"What?"

She raised her eyebrows and shrugged. "It's ridiculous."

He clasped her hand in his. "Tell me."

With a deep breath, she met his eyes. "It's just... I think the dragon was after you."

He jerked his head back. That *was* ridiculous. "You think that dragon was... after me?" That made no sense, and yet... a dragon had approached the abbey, where *he* had been, and now had attacked the *Aurora*, of all ships, with him aboard. It could be a coincidence, but Olivia's theory seemed likelier. "Does the crew know?"

"Bad idea," a low, masculine voice answered from a corner of the cabin.

Jon jerked up, reaching for Faithkeeper that wasn't there, despite Olivia's reassuring palm on his chest.

"It's all right," she said. "He came to our aid. Helped us gather the men who'd fallen overboard, and he's been keeping my anima bright so I can keep up your healing."

The man stood from his chair and walked into Jon's field of vision.

A six-foot-tall muscle-bound man faced him, with straw-blond hair tied back, a rapier at his belt, and a long, brown over-coat hanging open.

As he came into the light, his eyes—it couldn't be. He was

seeing *her* everywhere he looked, even in a stranger's face. Sky-blue eyes, bright like summer, in a man's face.

"This is Captain Verib," Olivia said, and the man bowed mockingly.

"The one and only." Those sky-blue eyes flashed, and the resemblance was uncanny.

Jon frowned, propping up against the headboard. "Do you know you look—"

"I've said he must be an Amadour at least, with those features, but he only replies with 'Verib,'" Olivia said, scowling at the man.

Verib shrugged sheepishly and poured himself some wine. "Let it go, Liv."

He could have sworn Olivia shivered.

"You should keep this between us," Verib said. "If the crew sniffs out so much as a suspicion that you're bad luck, king or not, you're going for a swim."

Olivia rolled her eyes. "We're less than a day from port. I think we'll make it." Smiling, she turned back to Jon. "You're doing much better, but *don't* do that again. I mean it."

It was either that or die. Better him alone than an entire crew of innocent sailors, guards, and Olivia.

"Thank you for your assistance," he said to Verib. "I am in your debt."

"I didn't do it for you." Verib took a swig of wine. "I did it for *her*." He cocked his head toward Olivia.

Somehow, even while unconscious, he'd already offended this stranger. "All the same, you have my thanks."

Verib shrugged, then slammed the goblet onto the table. "I'll see you at Il Serpente, Liv?"

She nodded, and without another word, Verib exited the cabin.

They'd arranged to go somewhere together. "How well do you know that man?"

"I've met him before." She moved to sit closer. "Actually, he brought Rielle back from Sonbahar on his ship. I met him in Courdeval at her inn, after she came to the palace that night and you—"

He held up a hand. "Got it." If he never recalled *that* night again, it would be too soon.

Olivia winced. "In any case, if Rielle trusts him, then I do, too. At least enough to let him help us."

He could agree with that.

"Jon," Olivia said softly, "I told you not to use your Earthbound powers."

He shook his head. "We had no choice. I wasn't about to let everyone die."

She dropped her gaze. "Every time you exert yourself like this, to the extreme, and have an episode, you're causing more damage. I can treat the episode, but I can't heal the lasting effects."

He was making it worse.

"You're shortening your life each time, and if you do something like this and I'm not there—"

"Dead." He exhaled sharply. "Got it."

"Have you really?" she asked, holding his hand, intertwined with hers, up to her chest, and sniffling back tears. "Because I want you to live. As long as possible."

She'd taken great care of him, and without her, he would already have been dead, several times over.

But he had these Earthbound powers, and he couldn't ignore them when others needed help, especially those he loved. No more than he could ignore his skill as a swordsman.

He wanted to live long enough to stabilize the kingdom and ensure a peaceful succession, but to protect someone he loved, he would die if he had to.

But Olivia... the way she was holding his hand, the way she was looking at him... and next to him, there was another pillow and a second depression in the bed—she'd *stayed* with him. Slept by his side as she'd taken care of him.

This went far beyond friendship. Beyond attraction, even.

She might have romantic feelings for him.

Terra have mercy, he couldn't imagine life without her. But if he asked her about this, shared his own truth of the matter, would she leave? Would he lose her?

"All of our things are ready for tomorrow," Olivia said, nodding toward some finery hanging nearby and a small stack of boxes. She'd chosen their attire for the Grand Divinus's masquerade.

The welcome banquet to this year's trials for magister. "Is there always such pomp for the magister trials?" he asked, changing the subject for now.

Olivia shook her head gravely. "No, this is entirely different. They're not separate exams. The Magister Trials are something new, a series of trials pitting multiple candidates against one another, with a single victor."

"What about the rest of them?"

She shrugged, pulling up his blanket higher.

If the Divinity had made such a production of this, the Magister Trials would have an element of entertainment, too, no doubt. But what would be at stake? Promotions... or lives?

His own trial would come before any of theirs would even begin, with all of Emaurria at stake.

~

MARFA LICKED the wound on her arm carefully. It was healing, but slowly, very slowly, and the witches weren't giving her enough food or water to keep her strength up.

The beatings had become more frequent, more *violent*, with a different witch returning each time, bearing *her own* patch of fur. Her *own* fur. Taunting her. Recently, as soon as she smelled it, she would brace herself, and her Wolf would raise its hackles.

But there was one witch. He—

She'd learn *his* name. She'd learn his name and end him.

After him, she always Changed for them now, since her human form was so vulnerable, and that only elicited worse torture.

Some days, she wished for anything to end it. *Anything.* She'd even pledge herself to a maestru if only one seemed of a disposition to help. But there was no help, ever, only cruelty. Only pain.

A distant whine—a door opening—and she inhaled deeply. Her own scent, and *his*. He strolled slowly down the dungeon corridor, and loud banging followed—the giant and the griffin. Sharp, ear-splitting hisses and cries—the wyvern, the hydra, and the dreaded basilisk. The basilisk had already killed one of the witches, so at least it was drawing blood in this torment, but they were careful now. *Far* more careful.

Lend me your strength. She welcomed the Wolf and Changed, her pale skin giving way to black fur, and she stood on her hind legs, beholden to the collar.

The witch, taking his time, arrived at her cell at last and set down her tray of bread and water—always befouled. No one befouled it, of all the other brutal witches, but he did. Always, and with a smile. He peered at her in her cell, her neck collared in arcanir, chains binding her to every corner, and stroked his black beard slowly, thoughtfully.

He crooned something to her, and she recoiled. His honeyed tone was a deception, a mask over his cruelty, and she'd been naive enough to trust it once. Only once.

Her fur adorned his belt like a trophy, and he stroked it softly before holding up a small case of bottles. Even sealed, she could smell their contents. The burn of lye and the metallic tang of silver. It was something different every day, like some madman's experiment.

He picked up the first bottle and unsealed it, the strong odor singeing her nostrils.

I will kill you.

She yanked at the chains, threw her body weight to one side, to no avail. As he threw the liquid at her, she squeezed her eyes shut, but the burn ate through her eyelids, her fur, the skin of her face, neck and body, lye stinging its way in. The sharp, shrill noise in her ears was her own crying and whimpering, but he didn't give her a minute of mercy.

I will kill you.

The silver followed, flakes tossed at her that pricked like blazing-hot needles impaling her skin, and he threw fistful after fistful at her, laughing and grinning as she cried and whimpered.

Her hind legs wouldn't hold her up much longer, and her body was collapsing upon itself, hanging her from the collar.

"Erardo!" a female witch yelled, and he took a step back, blowing a handful of silver flakes in parting.

They hit her chest, and she bucked, throwing her head from side to side, but the collar and chains were unforgiving. Through the dizzying spin of her vision, she stared at him as he kicked the tray to her, picked up the case of bottles, and strolled back the way he had come to the cacophony of loud banging and the sharp, ear-splitting hisses and cries of other Immortals.

Erardo. The female witch had called him that. It had to be his name.

By moon and pack, I swear I will have your head. Erardo of the mad Coven.

CHAPTER 17

*a*s their carriage pulled up the drive to Divinity Castle, the clang of metal on metal made Rielle draw open the black velvet curtain. The clang repeated, again and again, and in a small square, two men dueled with blades. One with a rapier and a buckler and the other with a long sword.

"A duel," Brennan said in a bored monotone. "It's how many matters are resolved here, more so even than Emaurria. Silen—even Magehold—resolves things *in style.*"

She shook her head. "Won't one of them die?"

He leaned in next to her. "The one with the long sword. His footwork leaves much to be desired."

"I mean... it's senseless death."

"Not to them. They're fighting for something worth it, clearly." He shrugged and relaxed back onto the seat.

"What if someone challenges you, and you don't know how to use a sword?"

Brennan scoffed. "Not a problem I have."

She looked away from the carriage window. It was a

problem *she* had. But the Magister Trials probably wouldn't involve swords.

"Don't worry, bride. If anyone so much as looks at you wrong, I'll be your champion in any duel."

Despite his joking tone, she believed every word.

Shimmering dark-teal brocade and blackest-black tiretaine showcased his strong, lean frame, and a silver mask covered the upper half of his face, metallic tentacles sprawled across it. Not long ago, she'd seen a *real* kraken's tentacles entirely too close, been constricted in them all too tightly.

They'd barely strayed from bed for three days, but even now, on her way to the Grand Divinus's welcome banquet, some part of her wanted to rip his clothes off. Some part of her that would get its due later.

"All in good time, bride," he drawled, his sultry gaze fixed on her.

She cleared her throat. "I don't know what you mean."

A corner of his mouth turned up in a devilish grin. "Yes, you do."

He knew her too well.

They pulled up to the entrance and exited the carriage to enter through two vast doors manned by Divine Guards, who collected any and all weapons. Would the Grand Divinus explain the trials? Offer some clue of what she'd face?

As she walked in, the questions disappeared. The splendor of the Grand Divinus's court had been rumored within the Tower and beyond, but as Rielle set foot inside the Most High's palace, her jaw dropped.

The domed, intricately frescoed ceiling was at least thirty feet high, and the white-marble walls were inlaid with gold over shining, sculpted reliefs of mythological beings and mages— Magisters and Grand Divinii. The gleaming floor tiles were intricately patterned, immaculate white with gold and bright colors. It seemed a grave sin to even set foot upon them.

The inner sanctum—including the great hall—was entirely encased in arcanir, supposedly. Although she'd never heard of anyone testing just how much of the great hall was made of arcanir. How much had been required to build and fortify the great hall and its adjacent chambers was unfathomable, but with it, the Grand Divinus would be protected from outside magic.

She adjusted her phoenix mask and smoothed the voluminous feathered crimson taffeta she'd been clad in tonight.

"You'll be the most beautiful woman in the room," Brennan said next to her matter-of-factly, covering her hand on his arm. "Raise your chin," he said in his low, deep bedroom voice, and she obeyed. "Pull back your shoulders."

Her body did as he bade with unwavering obedience, and she was convinced that as long as he commanded her in *that* particular tone of voice, she'd do just about anything.

He leaned in. "Watch me later," he whispered.

Watch him...? Her gaze met his, and he held it, dark, intense, locked.

A phantom night breeze teased her shoulders, and she was back in the glade outside Laurentine. *Watch me,* he'd said to her, and then she might have died of pleasure.

Did he mean—

Her breath caught.

Smiling, he dropped his gaze to her chest. "Yes, bride," he drawled. "Yes."

The great hall was a sea of masked faces and expensive fabrics in deep, rich colors, and in true masquerade fashion, no herald announced them. Dinner tables, lengthy and elegant, filled half the massive space before a head table, where presumably the Grand Divinus and any magisters in attendance would be seated. High above them were glittering chandeliers, enormous and replete with crystal, and the grand walls were adorned with detailed tapestries, great feats of magic, momentous events in the Divinity's history.

Her slippered heels clicked on the stone floor—arcanir infused, if she wasn't mistaken—as Brennan led her into the throng of fancy guests swarming the tables.

Lightning, hot and electrifying, shot up from her hand, where another had brushed it. She glanced back over her shoulder, at who had passed by.

A tall, well-built man in a black dragon mask looked back at her, with a gorgeous woman in teal taffeta on his arm. His lips, his jaw, his gait, and there, on his neck, it was—

"Jon's here," Brennan hissed, brushing her ear with his nose.

Divine, he was exactly the same. As always. Exactly the same. Same build, same face, same gait. She could pick him out of any crowd. Feel him nearby. She shivered.

And the gorgeous woman was none other than Olivia.

Why were they here? What did they have to do with the Magister Trials?

Brennan led her through the guests, closer to the raised head table, where a woman dressed in swaths of golden silk stood, arms out. The Grand Divinus.

It was *her*. It was actually *her*.

The Grand Divinus hadn't always been Eleftheria II, but had once been known as Magister Samanta Vota, a Sileni enforcer known for mastery of her power. She'd written manuals even *Leigh* had studied. Before his time, the Grand Divinus had once stayed at the Emaurrian Tower as a magister, fighting the Skaddish warbands during King Marcus's youth.

Her heroism was legend, and what every young novice with stars in her eyes aimed to become.

And here she was. In the flesh.

"Welcome to Magehold, treasured guests," the Grand Divinus declared, as the entire hall stilled and quieted. She had an elegance about her, an ever-placid face that was as pleasant as her pulled back onyx-and-ash hair was severe. "If you are here, you are among the elite few invited to celebrate this year's Magister Trials."

The Magister Trials had never been such a... spectacle. This... was something different.

"Ever since the Rift, the world as we knew it changed." The Grand Divinus's voice dropped. "Where there was once certainty, there is risk. Where there was once safety, there is danger. Where there were once rules, there are none."

Nods and murmurs rippled through the crowd.

"Today's magisters must not only fulfill the requirements of the world we knew, but the requirements of the world we now live in. It is with this reality that the Magister Trials have evolved. To win, there is only one objective: be the last to survive the trials. No certainty, no safety, no rules."

Her heart raced, and as her hold on Brennan's arm tightened, he rubbed her hand softly.

Survive? Then there would be death, and with no rules, killing. Any of the masked faces in the room could hide killers... or victims.

What kind of trials would force mortal stakes? The Grand Divinus could explain it any way she liked, but these trials weren't just about a promotion, but something ulterior, something nefarious. Gladiators in Sonbahar fought to the death, but this was the Divinity of Magic, and its own mages. Even for a boon, it was a lot to risk—both dying *and* killing.

Would she have to kill for this? She shook her head, looking over the crowd for the other candidates.

The black dragon mask faced hers from across the room. Jon, rigid as stone, staring her down. She knew that look, that posture, the way his hands were at his sides, open, ready.

Run, that look said. *It's too dangerous.*

"The first trial begins here on the 20th of Floreal, with the second three days later, and the third and final trial three days after that. Until then, let's celebrate having survived the Rift." The Grand Divinus gestured to the musicians, who began to play as the household started dinner service.

Celebrate? They were going to celebrate with death?

Brennan seated her, then sat down himself.

"No rules," she whispered to him. But there was so much at stake—securing help against the pirates, the truth about Laurentine, learning whether the Divinity was friend or foe.

Too much at stake to turn back, and magic was her life.

As Jon GRIPPED THE GOBLET, Olivia cleared her throat, then after a moment, tapped his thigh. He glanced at her.

"You're going to break it," she said quietly, rearranging the napkin in her lap.

His knuckles around the silver goblet were white. He loosened his grip and set it down.

No safety, no certainty, no rules? What did this woman have planned? If Rielle was here, it could only be for one reason: she had been invited to the Magister Trials.

She'd offered her help against the Immortals and the pirates, and wanting to keep her from risking her life, he'd refused it. And now, here she was, risking her life anyway.

Closing his eyes, he sighed, then turned to Olivia. "You were right."

She smiled beneath her cat half-mask. "I often am. This time...?"

"I should've just... let her help."

Olivia took a sip of wine, set it down, then shook her head. "Maybe so. But if she'd gotten this invitation, she would have come here anyway, and you know it."

Rielle had long wanted to become a magister, and this was her dream coming true—only was it as she'd expected?

After he and Brennan had questioned Sincuore, it seemed likely the Grand Divinus had been involved in the regicide. How far could that possible involvement have extended? To sending Flame, Phantom, and Shadow after him and Rielle? To abducting her and having her sold into slavery?

This invitation might have been sent to her in bad faith. The Grand Divinus could be luring her here to *kill* her.

Hadn't Brennan tried to convince her not to? Wouldn't he have told her about what Sincuore had said?

I have to try.

His gaze found her again. In that bright, bold red dress, she had doubtless drawn every eye in the room. With a glittering phoenix half-mask on her face and an elegant strapless red ball gown wrapping her body, she was stunning. Her arms, half her back, and her shoulders were bare, shoulders he had kissed hundreds of times before, soft caresses that had made her shiver, little moans falling from quivering lips—

Stop it.

With a lengthy exhale, he picked up his goblet and drained its water.

He was here to ask for aid, be denied, and return to an

alliance with the Covens. What Rielle chose to do was her choice, but she deserved to be warned.

Across the hall, on the raised dais, the Grand Divinus sat on a massive throne of gold and jewels. Tonight, he would submit to her before everyone in attendance here and ask her help. He hadn't even been allowed to bring in the Queen's Blade he'd brought as tribute—the Divine Guard had taken it at the entrance for holding and suggested scheduling a private audience to give it to her.

Which wouldn't be tonight.

The most demeaning moment of his life, probably, and it would ripple across the world, but no choice. Everything hinged on this moment—the fate of his kingdom, of his people. No turning back, even if he had to prostrate himself entirely. If it earned the support of the Covens, it would be worth it.

"You want to persuade her to go home," Olivia said between dinner courses.

"Don't you?" he asked her. "Especially after that opening address?"

Olivia readjusted her Ring of the Archmage. "After dinner. We'll approach her."

A minute or two of conversation, and then he could focus on what he'd come here to do. Reasonable enough.

The rest of the dinner was a blur, and although the food was elaborate, it was all the same to him. Extravagant.

Soon the musicians began the dance suite, and he took to the floor with an insistent Olivia while Brennan did with Rielle, the kraken and the phoenix, sea and sky mingling with otherworldly grace. They were a perfect pair, elegant, twirling skillfully about the crowd.

"I'm going to find a way to save you," Olivia said to him as he turned her.

"I don't need saving." He pulled her close. "The kingdom does."

Olivia frowned as she twirled away once more. Her determination knew no bounds; she wouldn't give up on her goal.

Neither would he on his. There was work to be done.

When the musicians struck up a volta, Olivia wouldn't quit the floor, so he danced with her. Other men had requested her, but she'd refused them, refused to leave his side, as though she believed he might drop dead at any moment unless she was present to save him.

Or she'd chosen to stay with him because she fancied him. And he'd have to broach that subject with her soon.

"I don't know how I earned your friendship"—he lifted her—"but I praise Terra for it, Olivia."

She grinned. "Just remember you said that, won't you?"

He spun them, catching a glimpse of that phoenix half-mask, facing him—Rielle, looking right at him.

She quickly turned away, and as the volta finished, she and Brennan left the dance floor toward a set of doors. Were they leaving?

"Wine," Olivia said, and he escorted her to one of the heaping trestle tables along the walls. A servant poured her a goblet full, and she sipped it, catching her breath. "She won't want to withdraw from the trials, even if you do warn her."

No certainty, no safety, no rules? "We have to try."

Olivia nodded, and they made their way to the doors Brennan and Rielle had disappeared through.

The hallway was dark, empty, with nary a sconce lit against the shadows. Olivia's arm wrapped around his, they slowly made their way deeper, toward a corner, but Olivia came to a stop, her fingers digging into his bicep.

Panted breaths, whisper-soft, that had graced his ear countless times. Little moans, an octave higher than her usual voice, and the swish of fabric.

He froze, gaze fixed on the end of the hallway, the wall, the dead end.

A groan, deep and masculine, rolled low, eager, and around this corner had to be—

The pull on his arm was Olivia, taking a step back. Swallowing, he remembered how to move again, and took a step back with her, and another, and another.

His chest was pounding, and he was breathing hard, blood spiking through his veins like ice, its coldness piercing him to his core.

An awestruck gasp, and another, and another, Terra have mercy, that he'd heard so many times before—

And now with someone else. Not him. With *Brennan*.

Brennan, who had superhuman senses and could probably hear him here, and Olivia, right now. Brennan, who was taking Rielle right around that corner.

Olivia dragged him now, dragged him away down the dark hallway, through the doors, into the light and myriad reflections from crystal chandeliers and gold, amid chatter and laughter and dancing, and he blinked, blinked again, staring at those doors, where his mind still stood, fixating on that dead end, listening to the sound of his heart breaking.

This was—

Two betrothed lovers, doing nothing wrong.

But his pulse pounded in his ears, and he couldn't look away.

Olivia, her grip tight, urged him back toward the trestle table, saying something to him, but he couldn't hear her, could only hear those breaths, those moans, those gasps—

He stood there, breaths heaving, unable to look away—

Olivia swept in front of him, into his field of vision, and blocked the doors. She pressed her palms against his chest, pushed him back. "I won't let you do this to yourself. I won't."

When he wouldn't meet her eyes, she took his face in her hands.

She rose up on her toes and pressed her lips to his.

CHAPTER 18

*R*ielle glanced up at Brennan as he guided her back down the hall, his palm at the small of her back. Her heart was still racing, hammering in her chest like a wild thing, pleasure singing in her blood, and his smug smile only made her want to tear off his clothes and do the same to him, but he'd denied her.

"Why won't you let me—"

A low laugh rumbled in his throat. "Soon, my bride. Soon."

That was what he always said when *she* wanted to pleasure *him*. When it came to making love, nothing happened until he allowed it. Although it wasn't something she'd been accustomed to, Brennan was worth the change. His happiness had become so important to her that there was little she wouldn't do for his sake. But this wasn't about happiness. There was an uneasiness there, a fear even, and it had to be about that night at Tregarde nearly four years ago.

Was that it? Despite all she'd said to him, did he still think her unwilling, deep down? Wary?

She trusted him, through and through, enough to submit to him entirely. He wouldn't lie to her, he wouldn't harm her, and she knew it. If he had any doubt of that, she'd have to relieve him of it. Soon.

She stopped in the hallway, and before he could say anything, she urged him against the wall and kissed him. That laugh again—but he wrapped his arms around her, ran his palms up her bare back, met her kiss with his eager tongue.

He pulled away and swept a lock of her hair off her mask. In the dark, he stroked her cheek with the back of his fingers, the smooth sensation making her close her eyes and shiver. "Care for a dance?"

A smile stole onto her face. "Once I can feel my legs again, yes."

A half-laugh. "We'll have to work on your stamina."

"Perhaps all night."

"Brazen words," he said, tracing her lips with a finger. "Will they deliver?"

She pressed a kiss to his fingertip and held it. "With pleasure."

His grin broadened a moment, then he looked away, curled her arm around his, and led her to the doors. "Show me what those lovely, unfeeling legs can manage."

They'd continue this at the villa, but for now she did as he wished.

With Brennan leading, any woman would be hard pressed to fail in the dance, but then again, her failures were legendary.

"Catch me when I fall," she whispered.

"One of my many skills." He opened one of the doors and led her through.

Off to the side, not far from them, stood Jon in his dragon half-mask, with Olivia's hands on his face, his arms around her waist, gaze locked with hers; she rose on her toes and kissed him.

"Well," Brennan whispered in her ear, "that explains why he's in no rush to wed."

She grinned, grinned so broadly her face hurt, laughed a little, even, a hollow sound she didn't recognize.

That night in Laurentine, Olivia had asked her if she ever thought about Jon... Was this why? Had she wanted... permission?

Olivia was highly capable, witty, intelligent, beautiful. And Jon...

A new movement in the dance suite began, the gigue, and Brennan led her into it. Her shoulders melted in Brennan's hold, but he led her through the dance without error.

It didn't matter if Jon and Olivia were together. It was none of her concern. She was marrying Brennan, and he—and *Jon* was none of her concern. None.

She met Brennan's eyes, their hazel gaze spearing her, and a shudder tore up her spine. Her foot missed a step, but Brennan caught her and expertly transitioned her into the next.

"Almost there," he whispered, turning her. "We'll leave shortly. Just endure a little more."

Endure? Her face went cold.

He *knew*. He *knew* how she felt about this? Of course he did. Of course. Pressure pushed behind her eyes, tears, but she wouldn't let them through. Not now.

"I'm sorry," she said softly as the dance ended.

Brennan pulled her in, gently stroked her arm in that lulling back-and-forth motion. "It's not your fault, bride."

Soon these last traces of whatever she'd had with Jon would disappear, and she could be the woman Brennan deserved. She *would* be.

The crowd parted, and through them walked Jon, unmasked, Olivia by his side, toward the dais and the Grand Divinus.

The Grand Divinus motioned to her Hensarin, who stood down. Jon handed his mask to Olivia, and she stopped at the edge of the crowd as Jon proceeded to the Grand Divinus.

"Good evening to you, Most High." He bowed, with all the carefully controlled elegance of a lifelong courtier. "My name is Jonathan Dominic Armel Faralle, King of Emaurria, and I have come here to beg Your Excellency for aid, to spare my people the ravaging of the Immortals."

As he lowered to a knee, gasps wove through the crowd. Her own breath caught in her throat.

"And for your magnanimity," he declared, his voice loud and deep, "I would gladly pledge my fealty." His head bowed, he remained on his knee, holding the position, an exercise in patience and humility.

He'd submitted himself—wholly and without pride—to ask help for his people's sake. The king of her realm had just humbled himself completely to another power.

The entire hall of guests stood with bated breath until the Grand Divinus opened her arms. "You are welcome at my court, King Jonathan. Please rise."

He stood with perfect control, his lone, powerful figure regal as he raised his chin and met the Grand Divinus's gaze, every bit a monarch. "Thank you for your hospitality, Most High."

The Grand Divinus gave the slightest of nods. "As for your request, you are aware the Magister Trials are about to begin in four days?"

"I was among those honored to hear your introduction, Most High."

"It is our tradition that a magister may ask a boon," she said. "Our resources are not infinite. This year's candidates will have chosen various boons to ask should they emerge victorious."

The Grand Divinus paused—an opportunity to argue, to plead, but Jon simply stood, tight-lipped.

Surely the Grand Divinus wouldn't turn him away? Deny all of Emaurria the aid she was bound by treaty to deliver?

"Our treaty ensures aid against invasions by foreign powers, but the Immortals, as we understand the Rift, are domestic. As much as we are sympathetic to your cause, we cannot act, lest we violate the treaty's terms." The Grand Divinus rested her chin on her hand.

Jon kept his gaze fixed on the floor.

That answer was unacceptable! The Immortals had come *through the Veil* to ravage the land and its people. That wasn't foreign? And the treaty's drafters might not have conceived of such an invasive force, but the spirit of what they'd written had been to bind the Divinity to grant aid to countries suffering invasions, which this surely was, even if it wasn't by a human power.

The Grand Divinus wanted to abuse that elasticity to let a party to the treaty be destroyed? Fall to ruin?

She took a step forward, but Brennan's hold on her arm kept her from advancing.

"However... You are familiar with Emaurria's candidate, are you not?" the Grand Divinus asked Jon.

"If she has not chosen to withdraw."

Withdraw? Rielle straightened.

"Master Mage Favrielle Amadour Lothaire," the Grand Divinus called, her voice echoing throughout the hall.

With a deep breath, she stepped forward, removed her

phoenix half-mask, and bowed. "You have asked for me, Most High?"

"Have you chosen to withdraw from the Magister Trials, Magos?"

"I have not, Most High," she answered, rising, "nor do I have any such intention."

The Grand Divinus turned back to Jon. "Are you confident in Emaurria's candidate, King Jonathan? Do you believe she will emerge victorious?"

He stepped forward, meeting her eyes for a moment before looking back to the Grand Divinus. "With all my heart."

"Then hereinafter, your fates are tied," the Grand Divinus declared. "If she does emerge victorious, you will have your aid. If she fails, you will not."

What? She moved forward, but Brennan caught her before she could go anywhere and hushed her.

Why? The Grand Divinus was being ridiculous. How could she tie a competition for a promotion to the fate of millions of people?

If the Magister Trials even *were* about promotion anymore.

For a long moment, Jon didn't move, then he swept a bow. "My thanks, Most High."

"Enjoy the trials, King Jonathan, and all Magehold has to offer." With that, the Grand Divinus gestured to the musicians, who immediately began a tune.

Jon took three receding steps, turned on his heel, and strode across the hall, offering his arm to Olivia as he passed her by. Together, they headed for the doors, past her and Brennan.

"Wait," she called after them, and Olivia looked over her shoulder, but Jon didn't stop.

He'd agreed to hinge the fate of the *entire* kingdom on her performance at the trials. Trials they knew nothing about.

Couldn't he have fought more? Refused the offer? Made an argument?

She was skilled at magic, but there were eight other candidates competing who were the best of the best.

If she failed... there would be no aid for Emaurria. The Grand Divinus would grant nothing. And the world had just watched Emaurria's *king* kneel before another power and beg for aid.

If he didn't receive it, the kingdom would fall. To Immortals, to other powers, to lawlessness. So many innocent people would die. *So many.*

If she failed, there might be wide scale devastation. If she withdrew, there *certainly* would be.

He had to have a contingency plan. He *had* to.

"Let's go," she snapped to Brennan, and he nodded, leading her after them.

JON STORMED out of the castle's great hall and through a grand corridor toward the exit with Olivia on his arm. He passed painting after painting, sculpture after sculpture, and looked at none of it, would stop for none of it. There was no way he could face Rielle after what he'd heard, and no way he *should* face Brennan.

"That could've gone better," Olivia said, trotting to keep up.

It wasn't her fault. With a deep breath, he slowed down. He kept breathing slowly, mindfully.

He'd just asked the Grand Divinus for aid, been rejected—and then had been maneuvered into tying the kingdom's fate to Rielle's performance in the trials.

If she won, he'd have the Divinity's dubious support but collapse the alliance Leigh was building with the Covens.

If she lost, he'd have the alliance with the Covens, but what would happen to *her*?

"The Grand Divinus interpreted *foreign powers* in the treaty to exclude the Immortals," he thought aloud to Olivia. "By accepting her unconventional deal, did I agree with that interpretation publicly?"

She let out an exasperated breath. "It could mean that allying with... others," she said quietly, waggling her eyebrows at him, "would still be considered first breach of the treaty, by *Emaurria*, and not the Divinity."

"But to remain in compliance, then," he hissed, "I'd have no recourse but to forego magical help entirely... and allow the kingdom to fall to ruin. Unpopular publicly, for obvious reasons."

"Between a choice of lawful-but-unpopular compliance and ruin, or unlawful-but-popular non-compliance and salvation, there's a clear winner," Olivia whispered.

He couldn't agree more. Even in the worst case, their course was set.

Footsteps clicked behind them in rapid succession. Terra have mercy, the last thing he wanted was to speak to Rielle after she and Brennan had done... whatever they'd done in that hallway.

Terra help him, but he couldn't face her. Not yet.

"Your Majesty," Brennan's voice boomed from behind them.

Brennan, intentional and vindictive *Brennan*.

His knuckles cracked—he'd clenched a fist too tight. This was the last thing he needed right now, but there was no evading Brennan and Rielle.

He froze, that tautness weaving up his arms from his fists. Taking deep, slow breaths, he forced a placid smile and glanced at Olivia, who nodded to him. Together, they turned.

Once again, that voluminous, bold red dress, drawing in to her hourglass waist, leaving her shoulders and arms bare but for the golden ringlets cascading from her elaborately pinned hair. She had removed her phoenix half-mask, revealing her beautiful face—those sky-blue eyes that locked with his in memories and dreams, and long, dense blond lashes framing their power. Provocatively painted red lips, full, slightly kiss-smudged. And there, just beneath her jaw, the violet mark of a love bite. Brennan's.

Brennan covered her hand on his arm, claiming her, possessing her, gaze locked on his.

He knew what it meant. He needed no reminder.

Brennan and Rielle bowed, and Jon inclined his head in turn.

"What a surprise to see you here, Your Majesty," Brennan said sardonically, by way of greeting.

They both knew that Brennan was never surprised by anyone. But Jon held that placid smile in place.

"Equal to mine," he replied, his gaze sliding to Rielle, who stared at him with all the ferocity of a tigress.

"You might have told your best friend you were competing," Olivia interjected, releasing his arm to approach Rielle.

"I didn't know until you'd left Laurentine." Rielle shook her head while Olivia mouthed something to her.

"May we speak?" Rielle bit out to him.

"We're speaking now," he said, straightening and clearing his throat.

"In private," she said, enunciating each word through clenched teeth.

She glanced at Brennan, who released her and gestured her forward with a jutted chin.

"Hope you're wearing armor under there," Brennan murmured to him, then turned away to chat with a frowning Olivia.

Rielle strode past him to a door, opened it, and stormed inside. With a defeated sigh, he followed, entering what appeared to be a small library, utterly dark but for the ambient light of the evening pouring in through the open drapes.

As soon as he shut the door, she turned on him, hands on her hips. "What were you thinking?"

"About what?"

She closed her eyes, biting her lip as she took slow, deep breaths.

"*About what*," she repeated under her breath. When she opened her eyes, she charged up to him and crossed her arms, so close that her rose scent embraced him. "You're betting the fate of the kingdom on me? Tell me you have a contingency plan."

He took a cursory glance around the library, then leaned in close to her ear.

"This isn't our only hope," he whispered, breathing her in for a fleeting moment. "Your conscience is clear."

And he never would have humiliated her by withholding his faith. He didn't want her to lay her life on the line, but she was strong, capable, and he'd swear it with the world watching.

As he drew away, her eyes slowly opened, and she gazed at him with slightly parted lips and heavy-lidded eyes that blinked wider, wider.

Terra have mercy, his mind was playing tricks on him, showing things as he wished they were, not as they truly were. False. A dream. He needed to get out of this room. Now.

And yet, his feet wouldn't move as he looked her over, his

eyes taking far greater liberties than they were allowed. Her breasts swelled over the neckline of her gown, heaving, and she looked him over, too, with wide, intense eyes that took him back to Courdeval and the night of Veris.

Her fingertips brushed the brocade of his overcoat, and he realized he was holding her arm. He let her go, and she took a step back and cleared her throat.

"Rielle," he said quietly, "it's not Emaurria you should be worried about."

She wrapped her arms around herself, looking everywhere but at him, those bare shoulders curled inward.

"We questioned Sincuore in Laurentine," he whispered, "and he suggested the Grand Divinus was involved in the regicide. Given everything with the Crag Company and... Shadow... this invitation could be a trap."

Her eyebrows rose. "What?"

So she hadn't known. Brennan hadn't told her.

And it seemed not only had he not told her about the Grand Divinus's possible complicity, but he'd also neglected to mention questioning Sincuore altogether.

Her gaze slowly dropped, and she worried her lower lip, her brow creasing. "Motive?" she whispered.

He shrugged.

"And who's 'we'?"

The *we* he'd mentioned questioning Sincuore? He cleared his throat. "My guards were there."

As much as he hated to lie to her and omit Brennan's involvement, he wasn't about to cause trouble between them. Not over something like this. Let Brennan figure it out with her.

She blew out a breath through her nose with an air of finality. "It doesn't matter. I'm still doing this."

Becoming a magister had been important to her for as long

as he'd known her. If, despite everything, she still wanted to pursue that, then at least she was pursuing it with her eyes open. And he would do his all to support her. "Tell me how to help."

Her features softened, relaxed. She reached for his hand, then covered it with her other, her heat flowing into him, her skin smooth against his.

"Thank you," she whispered, smiling up at him warmly for a moment, her misty eyes taking him back weeks, months. "I'll come to you when I need your help."

Whenever she had need, he wanted to be there for her. Help her.

She gave his hand a gentle squeeze, then slowly let it go, and watching her pull back was the slow twist of a knife in his heart.

He couldn't be there for her, and this was why. This would always be why. This... *whatever this was* between them, this lost dream, this unwanted echo, when she was in love with another man. *Marrying* another man.

He'd promised himself he'd leave her alone, but when she was around, his body didn't know how to do it. His heart didn't know how to do it.

He'd stay away from her. He'd have to try.

"I..." she began softly, resting her hand on the table next to her. "I'm sorry we missed your coronation. I really wanted to be there, but this..."

He pressed his palm to the same table. "I realize that now. I got Brennan's note, but now I understand why you couldn't come."

She frowned. "He didn't mention why?"

No trouble. Not on his account. "Perhaps he did. It's been a busy month."

Her head flinched back slightly, but she finally nodded. "Things are getting worse at home, aren't they?"

Worse. Bad enough to warrant begging the Grand Divinus for assistance, she meant?

Not here, he mouthed to her, and she looked around the library, rubbing her arm, and nodded.

"I'll call on you at the Marcels' villa." Presumably where she was staying.

At last, she nodded and moved to walk past him.

"Rielle," he said, taking her hand and turning to her, and she looked over her shoulder, a world of unspoken words shadowed in her eyes. Everything inside of him fought for freedom, to tell her he was dying, that he still loved her and always would, that he thought of her and Sylvie every day, and if she but said the word, he would do anything, give anything, destroy anything for her.

"Congratulations," was what he allowed himself to say, "on your wedding."

The smile didn't reach her eyes as she glanced down to their joined hands, the garnet engagement ring catching a glimmer of moonlight.

He let her go.

CHAPTER 19

Brennan escorted Rielle out of the castle in silence, only nodding or smiling cordially as expected, and helped her into the carriage. He sat next to her and took her in his arms, holding her close, and still he didn't speak. Not out of anger or umbrage or hurt, but because he didn't know which of the things he wanted to say he should choose, and if he did choose one, he didn't trust his voice to remain as cordial as his actions.

Since that night in Laurentine, he and Rielle had only grown closer. She'd confessed her love for him, taken down her walls, and hungered for him daily and nightly with a vigor only outmatched by his own. Her heart hadn't been whole yet, but isolated here, just the two of them, it had been well on its way.

He might have even been able to confess some of his sins to her—covering up Father's schemes, planting Nora's negligee in Jon's bed the night of Veris... All the things that once might have hardened her heart to him, but with her love, could have allowed them to be wholly honest with each other.

And then tonight had arrived. And Jon.

The moment he'd caught Jon's scent, he'd stood straighter, raised his chin higher, the unexpected meeting only coaxing the swell of victory inside him. Rielle loved *him*, was on *his* arm, in *his* bed every day and night, wearing *his* ring and marrying *him*. *His*, wholly and utterly. In such complete possession of her, coming by Jon again would have only been the crown on an already glowing accomplishment.

And then her heart had skipped a beat. Raced. Her breathing had turned erratic. Nervousness, suffering, longing, all tangled together, as her gaze had followed her former lover.

She'd tried to resist, of course. Restraint had been visible in her rigid bearing, her calculated movements, her attempted air of nonchalance as she'd pretended to be unaffected. For her sake? For his? For Jon's? For them all?

Her hand had tightened on his, and as he'd swept her away into that secluded corridor, in full view of Jon and Olivia, her kisses had only been all the more passionate, her focus on him all the more intense as he'd brought her to pleasure—and then again. And again.

When he'd heard the footsteps, he'd smelled the two of them—Jon and Olivia, in that doorway at the end of the corridor, Jon witnessing the extent to which Rielle gave herself to *him*, wanted *him*, loved *him*.

How the man's heart had raced, how his blood had coursed —Brennan suppressed a grin—and the retreating footsteps had completed the victory. Jon had witnessed its decisiveness and quit the field in utter defeat.

That hope, that pathetic hope on the beach at Laurentine, had been snuffed out.

But then, after that dramatic plea to the Grand Divinus, stopping him in the hallway, meeting his gaze and that serene mask over a heart beating too irregularly to still be called a heart, that victory had swelled.

For a moment.

He'd stood there, making idle chatter with Olivia, until Rielle had left that room, left Jon, her eyes downcast, frowning, as if she'd left a piece of herself behind.

Perhaps she had.

There was no claiming her, not entirely, while Jon still held influence over her, while he still appeared before her eyes. Perhaps in time, far from him, that influence would fade, but like this? Never. He sighed. Maybe it was time for him to take matters into his own hands.

The salt of her tears filled the carriage, and he swept them away with gentle fingers, holding her closer. He should be furious. He should confront her, shout at her, demand she choose, once and for all. He should challenge Jon, duel him, demand he abandon pursuit of her utterly and forever when he lost. He should do all those things, and yet, he wiped her tears and tightened his embrace.

None of those things he should do would elicit more than empty words, no matter how badly he wanted to do them. In her heart, Rielle would feel the same anyway, and *that* was what he truly needed to move. Hearts did not move with confrontation, shouting, and demands, but with love, patience, and compassion, all mysterious to him and risky, and yet here he was.

The carriage came to a stop outside the villa, and he walked her up the cobblestone drive and inside, helped her up the stairs and to their rooms.

He dismissed the maids and undressed her himself, unpinned her hair, helped her wash her face. She watched him in the mirror, sitting uneasily like a caged animal, her gaze uncertain as if she expected him to rebuke her.

Never.

He took her in his arms, and she rested her cheek against his chest, nuzzled it with a slow stroke, as if she savored every second. And then the salty scent of her tears renewed.

He cradled her head to his heart.

I'm here, and he isn't. I'll never abandon you, betray you, or let you suffer. I will protect you, from everything and everyone. I will love you with all my heart, whether you love me with all of yours or not.

These were the vows he made to her tonight, and would make to her when they wed. Vows he would keep, for all of time.

And once they'd wed, their bond would be sealed. He'd spend his life arduously working all trace of anyone else from her heart, with all he could give her—love, devotion, a family. He'd fill her up, fill her heart, until she did become utterly, completely his.

He smoothed her hair away from her face and lifted her chin, met her teary gaze as she searched his. Even when she cried, she was beautiful.

He pressed a kiss to her forehead, and a quavering breath left her mouth. When she raised her head, he pressed another soft kiss to her lips, stroked a delicate line down her tear-streaked cheek, down her smooth neck. She leaned into him, whimpering low in her throat, and his arms could do nothing but envelop her, hold her, keep her close as she gave herself over to him completely.

They bared each other to the dim candlelit luminance of the night, and tonight, there would be no restraints, no commands, no words, none of the things he needed. No, tonight there would only be the one thing she needed above all others: love.

Silently, he lifted her and took her to bed.

SAMARA KNELT in the lush grass, still within sight of the copious olive trees just off the coast. Here, prairial wort was in full bloom, bunches of bright yellow five-petaled flowers with their conspicuous black dots crowning the soft grasses with sunlight. Past the horizon of flowers and grass were cypress trees, and the walled city in the shadow of misty black mountains.

She plucked the yellow flowers and carefully packaged handfuls of them in paper.

"So many?" Zahib practiced with his blade as he did every day, patterns of movements and lunges.

"These flowers make a red oil called prairial liniment," she said, folding another package, "and you can use it to treat severe burns, along with bruises and other skin conditions. Just this flower can help a lot of people." When they'd docked, she'd fully expected for him to take her directly to university and leave as soon as he could. "You didn't have to do this."

He finished a pattern and sheathed his blade. "I wanted to."

With a slow breath, she plucked some nearby salvia. An ingredient in four thieves vinegar, it would be good to have on hand in case of the return of plague.

He knelt next to her and plucked some prairial wort to add to her pile. "You think I look down on what you do, Samara. Nothing could be further from the truth. I am very proud of you."

Pausing, she averted her gaze. *Proud.* He didn't have the right to be proud of her. He hadn't earned it.

"How many lives would you save over a lifetime of being an apothecary?" he asked, his voice gentler than she'd ever heard it. Perched next to her, he rested his hands on his knees.

Even saving one life was worth everything. Most people came with simple—not life-threatening—matters, but even so, many went to an apothecary instead of a physician or a healer because of the cost. For little more than the price of her herbs, an apothecary could give them a remedy. "Hundreds, perhaps."

"And that is important to you?"

"Of course it is," she snapped. All her life she'd done it, first with Umi and then on her own for anyone in House Hazael, and sometimes for friends of friends of slaves who had no one else to turn to.

"If one of my other children takes over our House when I die," he said, "there is no doubt it will return to the old ways. Grandfather's influence, and their mothers', was strong. Too strong for me to sway."

Was it any wonder? He'd been complacent for so long that his actions would have betrayed any such words.

"By being my heir, you will save 813 lives, Samara. You will keep them free."

813. The number of slaves House Hazael had kept. She crumpled.

"I know it is a lot I ask of you, and when I die, you'll have the power to do what you wish," he said, pushing off from the ground. "But I've watched you help others all my life, doing what I only *wished* to do, and there is no one who can do this but you."

He stood and drew his blade once more, returning to his training.

There had been a time when she was very young, four perhaps, when she'd seen Zahib and called him *Ab*. All the other children had called their fathers that, and she'd heard Zahib's own children call him that.

Umi had snatched her away, her grip unrelenting, to a far, empty room, and taken her over her knee. *Zahib*, Umi had said, and with tears in her eyes, had hit her bottom. *Zahib*, Umi had repeated, and hit her again. And hit her and hit her and hit her. Samara had cried, but it hadn't been until she, too, had repeated *Zahib* that Umi had stopped, taken her shoulders, and forced eye contact. *You have no ab*, she'd said. *Zahib. To you, Samara, there will only ever be Zahib. Remember this, for your life and for mine.*

After that, it had been some time before she could sit. The lesson had lingered, and so had Umi's words.

She'd seen other girls with their fathers, and when she'd had Umi, seeing that didn't matter. Most of the time. But every once in a while, she imagined what it would be like to be held by an *ab*, to smile with him, to tell him what she'd learned and feel the rush of his pride, to confess her problems to him and feel the reassuring stroke of his hand on her head and firm commitment to help her. To know that no matter what threatened her or Umi, her *ab* would keep them both safe.

Grabbing a stem, she broke off another salvia.

She didn't mourn the loss of Zahib as her *ab*. But sometimes, she did mourn never having one.

Zahib had opened himself up to her more, shared his thoughts and his hopes, and he was right about saving 813 lives. She would need to know many things to manage the House competently—things she didn't know. University wasn't the only place to learn them, but he wasn't wrong about this.

If only she didn't have to give up her dream.

She packed up her ingredients and stood. "I'm ready."

Zahib eyed her as he finished his pattern. "Good. We will find lodging, I will set up your accounts here, and purchase everything you need. In a few days, I will see you settled, then take my leave of you."

She nodded.

He wasn't wrong, and he had opened up to her.

But he was still Zahib opening up, and only ever Zahib.

For her life and for Umi's.

THE CITY GUARDS at the gates to Bournand already knew Leigh and admitted him on sight. On the wall, there weren't only the yellow tabards of the guard, but also stern-faced people in plain clothes. Witches.

"Things have changed since my last visit here," he said to the graying guard escorting them in.

"The world has changed," the guard replied gruffly and bowed to Katia before returning to his post. Katia waved at a few of the witches posted on the wall, and they nodded their acknowledgment, eyeing him and Ambriel.

If Joel Forgeron had formally taken a role in the city's defense, the Divinity's influence was already waning here. But so were the Coven's resources.

At the center of the city, the domed roof of the Temple of the Divine loomed like a mountain over everything else. The world hadn't changed that much.

With a bounce in her step, Katia led the way uptown, past the market stalls closing up at twilight. Ambriel eyed the various offerings and slowed every so often to inspect a bolt of cloth, cookies, spices, clothing.

"You know, last time I was here, I made certain to purpose-fully ignore the wonders of this market," Leigh said to Ambriel.

"Why?" Ambriel held up a pair of specs, looking through one side of them.

"Showing off a bit, back when the king didn't have two argents to rub together." Leigh grinned. Jon had followed him wide-eyed, eyeing silk and saffron, and now he had more gold to his name than the Grand bloody Divinus.

Forgeron's shingle came into view, a fist clenched around a hammer. Archons were prickly as a bunch, but Joel Forgeron especially required a certain amount of mettle to face, even in the comparatively less bloody battlefield of conversation.

The last time he'd seen Joel, he'd come through Bournand during Ignis, and a roll in the hay with Blaise had ended with massive, brawny Joel demanding he keep himself and his trou-bles far from Blaise. Although he generally laughed in the face of such demands, something about the protruding vein in Joel's forehead—and the Coven ready to do their Archon's bidding—persuaded him to comply.

They could hardly be called friends, but—he shrugged—no one had died.

After opening the gate, Katia led the way around back, and Leigh followed, slowly down the narrow walk between the smithy and the stable to a small, twilit courtyard, quaint, like the tall-but-cramped house the Forgerons lived in.

Their modesty belied their power, and anyone who believed them as common as their circumstances would leave an alterca-tion with an overly enchanted sword shoved where the sun doesn't shine, probably shooting rainbows and singing "The Maid in the Hay" until his eardrums exploded. Leigh frowned. Or just dead. Leaving the altercation just dead was also fairly likely.

A stout older man, with a full gray beard and long matching hair tied back, sat by a table with a book under a crabapple tree. He sat with an unmistakable patriarchal air about him and hadn't moved a muscle at their entrance.

Katia's steps lightened. "Papa—"

Joel held up a thick index finger. He seemed to finish a page in the book before slamming it shut and placing it on the table. "In the house."

She frowned. "But Papa—"

"In. The. House. Katia."

Heaving an exaggerated sigh, she stomped a foot and stormed off into the townhouse next to the smithy. She slammed the door, and a crabapple fell from the bough above Forgeron.

With a gesture like a snap, it poofed into glittering dust that feathered softly onto the tabletop and, with a gentle breeze, blew away, shimmering. Diamond dust.

Leisurely, Joel lifted his gaze. "Galvan," he said, his brown eyes narrowing.

"Forgeron," he greeted, with the widest, brightest smile he could muster. Hopefully, the man's memory was as short as his hair was long. "This is Ambriel Sunheart of Vervewood."

Ambriel inclined his head, his long, fair hair slipping forward in strands that reflected the sunset.

Joel nodded to the chairs across from him. With a polite nod, Leigh seated himself, leaning back into the wrought-iron chair and finding it strangely comfortable. Much like himself, it brimmed with magic. "You were expecting us?"

"Made it myself," Joel said in Old Emaurrian, ignoring his question, and watched his expression. Indeed, the work of a master transmutor was impressive.

With an appreciative nod, Leigh ran his finger along the edge of the seat. "How have you been, old man?"

Huffing a laugh, Joel shot him a critical look. "Better since you've been away."

So he was going to let the seduction of his heir slide. Leigh chirped a laugh. "So, I would love to know: how did you foresee our arrival?"

Joel looked out at the courtyard's sparse vegetable garden. "You know," he began slowly, "when my youngest daughter was born, I was happy to meet her."

Leigh rolled his eyes. Great. A story.

Joel turned to him with a glower. "Just listen, Galvan."

Leigh flashed a brief but huge grin until Joel sighed and looked away—the man was too powerful to insult a second time, after all. "Katia was trouble, even in her infancy, but the girl had fire. She would be a smith among smiths. A virtuoso. She practiced every day, never left my side, or Marie's, or Helene's when we were at the smithy. She prepared and prepared and prepared for her magic." Joel grinned nostalgically. "When she had her éveil, imagine her surprise when she discovered she wasn't a transmutor but a geomancer."

The transmutor line was usually dominant, so the fact that Forgeron's transmutor wife had given birth to a geomancer was unusual.

Forgeron nodded without looking at him. "A blessing. Fresh magic in the family, magic that could bend the world to our purpose. But she didn't see it that way." The old blacksmith bowed his head. "She had to find herself. Run away to Courdeval and start running with a local gang of troublemakers that called themselves a 'Coven.'" He scoffed. "Gustave would have to find an outside solution or risk stepping on old, established lines between Covens, even though Katia stepped first. When I heard that 'Coven' had been wiped out—but no word of my dear Katia's death—there was only one answer. A man who could survive what wiped out an entire Coven, and saved my Katia? And not one of Gustave's, or he'd have written."

Leigh grinned brightly. "You're welcome."

Ambriel gave him a slight shake of his head as Joel blew out a breath.

"I trust your gratitude extends to helping the Crown break with the Divinity?" he asked hopefully. "Swear fealty to the new king, and he will break with the Divinity and bring the Covens into the light."

Ambriel gaped at him. Too much?

Folding his hands together and resting them on the table, Joel turned in his chair. "Tell me, Galvan, are you a man of tradition?"

It was exactly what he'd hoped to hear. The Dark Age of Magic. The Archons. The Covens. No Divinity. No Grand Divinus. His eyes locking onto Joel's, he replied, "Yes."

"Then we have much to discuss."

Much indeed. Leigh cracked a smile. "Before all that, how's Blaise?"

CHAPTER 20

Olivia directed their carriage to Il Serpente, Magehold's poorer bazaar district, full of narrow, winding roads and the entrance to Il Mercato Sotterraneo. Verib had said anything could be found at the Mercato, and she needed answers. If this black market had any forbidden books about dragons and other Immortals, she'd buy them.

Dragons were drawn to him. After the coronation and the *Aurora*, it was too strange to be coincidence. He was sigiled against nearly all magic, so it had to be something else... something forbidden.

Sangremancy.

Rielle had written to her from Stroppiata about Shadow and Khar'shil, and the possibility of sangremancy. Had Shadow somehow commanded dragons to hunt him? But then, if that was so, why weren't more coming? Why hadn't they come immediately?

And then there was the other problem: extending his life.

If there were any solutions to harnessing the Immortals' longevity, they would be for sale at Il Mercato Sotterraneo.

Verib had said to look for the black arch after the masquerade.

"Where are we going?" Jon asked.

"If I tell you, you won't want to go."

He scowled at her. "I already don't want to go."

After the evening he'd had, she couldn't blame him, but... "See?" She smiled at him. "I'd better not push my luck."

"All right. Let's see this surprise." He shook his head and glanced away, out the sliver between the drapes where evening revelry spilled out onto the streets. Here, the people were having their own masquerade, celebrating in the streets with a vigor Divinity Castle's great hall couldn't match.

Tonight hadn't gone well, not nearly as well as they'd hoped. The Grand Divinus surely did not intend to grant aid—which meant she didn't intend for Rielle to win the trials.

The Grand Divinus wouldn't leave things to chance. With some of the world's most capable mages in the Divine Guard and the Hensarin, she'd *ensure* the result she wanted.

She took a slow breath. That couldn't happen. If only Leigh were here... He'd keep a close eye on how the trials unfolded, and if there were something amiss, the upheaval he'd stir in the magical community would shake the Divinity to its core. He was well known, powerful, had once been a magister. Other mages would trust his perspective, and—

That's it.

A trustworthy mage, someone with good standing in the Divinity but not unconditionally servile. Someone important who knew Rielle.

Magister Daturian Trey.

He was the world's most famous conjurer, and a wild mage.

Even the Grand Divinus would think twice before giving him reason to protest. Despite his power and undeniable charm, the Grand Divinus hadn't invited him to the court of Magehold, nor to the trials, it seemed.

But I can.

Last she'd heard, he'd been in Bellanzole, visiting with Crown Prince Lorenzo, one of his best friends and Princess Alessandra's older brother. Perhaps he was still there—she'd write to him, invite him to come witness the Magister Trials. His presence would keep the Grand Divinus in line, and if it didn't, Daturian would shake the magical community to its core.

If he arrived.

With fairer conditions, Rielle would be fine. She hadn't come so far without being strong, capable, and choosing well when it counted. And she had friends—herself, Jon, Brennan—to turn to if she needed help in preparing for the trials.

Jon had made progress away from Rielle, had slowly begun to accept severing the withered limb that was his past with her. But then the minute he'd seen her again, that flash of vivid red, blood had flowed through it anew. And his devastation in that hallway had been—

She shifted the Queen's Blade on her lap. They'd need to schedule a private audience with the Grand Divinus to even give it to her, and the symbolism would be lost publicly. She stroked the hilt, eyeing him as he caught glimpses of the streets.

She'd *kissed* him.

Great Divine, she'd *kissed* him, and he hadn't said a thing about it.

Biting her lip, she lowered her gaze. She'd been his father's lover—that made kissing Jon all manner of *wrong*, and then there was her friendship with Rielle, who'd loved him, and perhaps still did. Olivia sighed.

She was a friend to him, the Archmage, an adviser, and he'd never looked at her with that hunger in his sea-blue eyes.

Hunger. She rubbed her face, finding the cat mask still in place. These were not the thoughts to have about her *king,* her *lord,* her *friend,* her best friend's former love... Forbidden.

"Jon," she said, and he met her eyes, making her squirm, "about that kiss—"

He took a deep breath. "I've been wanting to talk to you about that, about us—"

"It was just to distract you," she blurted. Great Divine, he'd been about to let her down gently, hadn't he? She didn't need to hear it, didn't *want* to hear it.

"To distract me," he repeated cautiously.

She nodded. "There were more important matters, and I just needed something to bring you back to what we'd come to do."

"Something." His eyebrows drew together, his face hard, contemplative. That strong jaw clenched, flexed, and the planes of his face were unforgiving. She'd give anything to know what thoughts simmered behind that bulwark.

"It worked, didn't it?" She straightened a bit, crossing her legs.

"It did," he said, lowering his gaze, "but Olivia..."

She peeked out the window into the night, watching the shabby storefronts and shacks of Il Serpente go by, until a black stone arch marked a dark corridor.

"Stop," she ordered the coachman, who did as bidden. Whatever Jon wanted to tell her, he could say when they *weren't* trapped in a carriage together.

He grabbed the seat and raised an eyebrow, planting his boots firmly on the carriage floor. "Where are we?"

Lively fiddle music played outside, accompanied by clapping.

She handed him his black dragon mask. "Put it on. You'll need it where we're going."

He sighed, holding the mask, and a corner of his mouth turned up in a dimpled half-smile. "Is this where you kill me?" He nodded toward the street. "And then long reign Queen Olivia?"

"There's a thought," she joked back. "But no. Now hurry up and put it on."

He fastened the mask's leather ties and then spread out his arms, sprawled on the seat across from her. "And now?"

Her heart beat a little faster, and she became very aware of the tight carriage, the shadows and slivers of firelight, and the way that black brocade overcoat showcased his powerful figure to perfection. She wanted to run her finger up the curve of his bicep, glide her palm over his strong shoulders and across that sculpted chest, and down over the—

He said something, and although she watched his lips move, the words eluded her.

"Hm?" she asked, trying very hard to listen.

He laughed under his breath. "I said that's quite a grip." He nodded to her lap, where she clenched the Queen's Blade white-knuckled.

Something like a titter escaped her lips as she set the blade aside. Divine, could he tell where her thoughts had gone? "We're going to an underground market."

He rested his ankle on his opposite knee and leaned back. "Olivia, if there's something you want, just ask," he said. "I'll have it bought for you."

When he spoke like that, it only made her want to kiss him

again, bridge this short distance between them in the carriage, and—

She cleared her throat. "I... It's... There are things here that cannot be found elsewhere, and I thought it would be fun."

He sighed. "Or... you thought I can't leave your sight and had no choice but to bring me along."

There was that, too. She hesitated, then reached for his hand. "Come on. Are you afraid you'll enjoy yourself?"

"After tonight, I'm in no danger of that," he said, sobering as he glanced down at the contact.

She squeezed his hand.

A moment passed, then he heaved a breath and clapped the door. "Let's go."

She checked for the pouch of gems tucked into her cleavage —still there—then let him help her out of the carriage.

The Royal Guard, cloaked and hooded in black, were in formation around them as she approached the archway. A man waited there, leaning against the wall with a half-full bottle of wine, wearing a black cloth half-mask. Lean duelist's body, a knot of unruly straw-blond hair, and a rapier at his belt...

"Liv," he greeted with a bow.

Jon and the guards stiffened.

"Verib?" she asked, and Jon motioned the guards to stand down.

"I'd hoped you'd come," he said, taking her hand and kissing it. "You didn't have to get so dressed up just for me," he said with a wink, looking her up and down, "although I'm not complaining. You're a sight to remember on lonely days at sea."

She laughed, and Jon cleared his throat.

Verib's gaze slid to him. "You're here, too. Huzzah," he deadpanned.

Jon heaved an exasperated sigh. She'd have to rush him in before he could change his mind.

There was a break in the fiddle music and dancing nearby, and Verib beckoned them forward to a door in the street, and he pulled it open. A stone staircase led down. "Best not stand around in an alley, unless you want a knife between the ribs and your coin purse taken."

"Olivia..." Jon warned.

"Enjoy yourself," she said firmly, and headed in.

With a deep breath, he followed suit, and they descended underground, where she'd finally get her hands on something forbidden.

JON HEADED OFF OLIVIA, his hand on Faithkeeper's hilt and his guards around them in the shadows. This was a new place he knew nothing about, and especially with Olivia here, he wasn't about to let his guard down until he could determine how safe it was.

Verib cast a candlelight spell that lit the way through the cramped corridor, and Jon hunched to avoid hitting his head on the uneven stone above them.

Laughter, chatter, and music filtered in, echoing from the distance, and loudened as they kept walking. Those were the last things he wanted to hear after the evening he'd had.

"Il Mercato Sotterraneo," Verib provided, strutting next to him with a swagger. "You can find anything here."

Anything.

Jon shook his head. Then that's why they were here. Olivia was still trying to find some miracle that would save his life.

"You can't find what doesn't exist," he said to Olivia.

She nudged his arm. "You won't know it exists unless you look for it." She said it in that lofty way, positive, cheerful even.

He wouldn't waste what time he had looking for *more* time. Especially when there was work to be done.

But there was no dissuading her.

Firelight glowed at the end of the corridor, a lot of it, and they came upon the edge of a staircase winding down into a massive cavern, brimming with tents and people, bartering, laughing, singing, dancing, eating, fighting. There was an entire bazaar down here.

There seemed to be a few exits spaced in the cavern walls, with people lazily entering and leaving. The merchants were cramped together, but not so much so there wasn't room to maneuver.

A bard with a lute sang a rowdy tune in Sileni, her voice rousing the drunks to sing along, and a man approached them holding various bottles, peddling wine. Verib bargained over a bottle of Melletoire red.

One tent—black canvas—was full of books and scrolls sold by a dark-elf man in a black leather hood. The Immortals in Silen had mingled with human society more, then.

Olivia gaped and hurried in, practically skipping, and flitted from book to book. Jon accompanied her, eyes on the strangers around them, as she thrust three large tomes in his arms, then stacked another, then carefully placed a number of scrolls on top.

He couldn't help but grin.

Among the bustle around them, he glanced over the topmost scroll. "Olivia, do you really need all—"

She placed two more scrolls on top of that one, then reached into her bodice and pulled out a pouch.

A laugh rumbled in his throat, and the stack was unwieldy,

but he wouldn't deny her anything. She looked as happy as a paladin at the sacred blacksmith's.

"Well," she said, finally out of the tent, "I just spent the bulk of what I'd brought on these, but they're all in Old Sileni, which isn't actually all that different from Sileni, so I think I can—"

He laughed. She was talking with her hands, and that meant he'd already lost her to whatever subject had struck her fancy.

"There are two on sangremancy and that giant one is a compendium of Immortal beasts, and then—"

He cleared his throat, and Florian offered to take the stack from him. *Terra be praised.* She passed by another tent, where two rangy men offered pelts, leather, claws, and all manner of things derived from Immortals.

She reached into her bodice, but he gave her his own hefty coin purse. Smiling brightly, she darted into the tent.

As he watched her shop, Verib returned and held up a bottle of wine.

"No, thank you," Jon said.

"I wasn't offering. Just showing off my prize." Verib clamped his teeth on the cork and pulled it free, spat it out, then drank some with a loud moan. "I've missed it."

"You don't like me," Jon said, watching Olivia run wary fingers over a large fur that looked suspiciously like a griffin pelt.

"Whatever else they say about you, you're definitely not dumb," Verib took another swig.

Bristling, he quirked a brow. "What do they say?"

Verib shrugged, watching Olivia. "They said you were a paladin before this, and that you fell for a woman. That she disappeared for months, and you betrayed her. Took mistress after mistress. That she came back and forgave you, but discovered another of your betrayals and left."

Jon gripped Faithkeeper's pommel. Tight. Rumor wasn't too far from the truth, except for that last betrayal. And he deserved every word.

"How can a man who can't keep a single woman keep an entire kingdom?" Verib asked, a challenge riding his voice.

"How can a man judge a king's leadership by his private affairs?" Jon asked quietly, fighting the rigidity coiling in his arms. He didn't need another man to tell him how egregiously he'd erred.

" 'Affairs' is the right word," Verib grumbled, narrowing his eyes. His sky-blue eyes.

His Amadour eyes?

His Lothaire eyes?

Jon looked him over. Something wasn't adding up. "Why are you so interested in what I—"

"Because you crushed her heart," Verib bit out, "like it was nothing." He soon took a step back and drank again.

Sky-blue eyes, straw-blond hair, that pale complexion with golden undertones but sun tanned. Even a slight resemblance in the nose... Could it be possible? There was no way this man was her *cousin*.

He was her *brother*.

Jon stopped, watching as Verib swaggered a couple steps more. "Liam Amadour Lothaire."

The swagger stopped. Frozen to the spot, Verib looked over his shoulder, scowled. "What did you just call me?"

"Rielle's brother," Jon said firmly. "How is it possible?"

Verib turned around. "You don't know what you're—"

Jon advanced a step. "What did you say about me?" he asked, his voice low. " 'Whatever else they say about you, you're definitely not dumb'?"

With a slow exhale, Liam crossed his arms and tapped the

wine bottle with a finger, then hung his head a moment. "Only one other person knows about me."

Terra have mercy, it *was* Rielle's brother. "She knows," he guessed.

Liam nodded.

"Since when?"

"A couple months."

Then Rielle had found her brother when she'd escaped Xir. Found her long-thought-dead brother, and hadn't told him. He hadn't earned her trust. He hadn't deserved it.

Rubbing the back of his neck, he eyed the ground before looking back up to Liam. "We never had this conversation."

Liam squinted those sky-blue eyes, then nodded. "What conversation?"

Exactly. If Liam didn't want the world to know he lived and Rielle hadn't fought him on that, then *he* certainly had no reason to.

"You're not going to lecture me on my 'duties'?" Liam asked skeptically, taking another swig.

Jon half-laughed under his breath. He should be the last person to ever lecture anyone on their duties. Coming into his duties as king had been nothing short of a complete failure.

The next tent had a variety of toys—dolls.

"No lecture." Side by side with Verib, he followed Olivia as she moved on to the next shop. "Especially from me... I made the worst mistakes of my life, and I'll spend the rest of it trying to make them right. I'll never be able to"—they'd lost too much for that—"but I still need to do what I can."

Liam assessed him peripherally, then gave a slow nod, looking away to Olivia while she gathered a few items from the hunters' shop and presented them to one of the rangy men.

"Are you and her together?" Liam asked, nodding toward Olivia.

He exhaled lengthily, crossing his arms. Olivia had kissed him tonight.

Distraction or not, that had changed things. He'd wanted to talk to her about it, clear the air, tell her how much she meant to him, how he wouldn't be here or *alive* if it weren't for her, but she'd—

"It's a simple question, man," Liam prodded.

"No, we're not involved," he murmured, although it wasn't that simple when she was definitely interested. The way she'd pressed into him, and the passion in her kiss, had made that very clear. She'd silenced him in the carriage, but he couldn't keep quiet about this for much longer, no matter how difficult the discussion would be. They needed to have it, and he needed to pray she'd still want to be his friend, and his adviser. Emaurria needed her, and so did he.

Face bright, Liam watched her with a meandering gaze. It wasn't the vulgar look he'd expected, but something softer, warmer. Affection.

Olivia seemed to like Liam enough—or, rather, *Verib*. The man would have to know she'd have no part in the kind of roving, sea-faring lifestyle he led. For as long as he'd known her, Olivia clearly valued stability.

She charged out of another book tent with her hands full.

"Jon, you won't believe all the things I bought," she said, as he accepted the armful of bags. "There's a book about sangremancy rituals in Old Sileni, and this one all about Immortals, including dragons, and then there was this old translated tome on healing that the merchant said had to be from before the Sundering, translated multiple times, he said, with medicines and such, too, and I think it will—" She clipped her words and glanced at Liam, who stared back at her with an amused grin and sparkling eyes. Hooking her arm around Jon's, she added, "I'll tell you all about them when we return to the villa."

Sangremancy rituals. She hoped to decode what Shadow had done on Khar'shil. Maybe it had to do with the dragons?

And there would no doubt be concoctions of many kinds in his future, experimentation the likes of which he'd bear if it'd make her happy. And if they worked, well, he wouldn't complain about living longer. More time to put fists to faces in the battle against the Immortals.

In addition to the books, he could already see all manner of claw, bone, fur, and scale, when what he most wanted was blessed *sleep* before calling on Rielle at the Marcels' villa tomorrow, as he'd promised.

Not something he looked forward to. He'd have to explain to her his plan with the Covens, and she'd take it to mean he wanted her to lose.

Yes, he would gain with her loss, but winning would also earn them an inroad to the Divinity, with Rielle's membership in the Magisterium. If Sincuore had been speaking the truth and the Grand Divinus had been involved in the regicide, then there would be some evidence of it somewhere—records in the secret Archives, Hensarin who'd taken part, *some*thing. If Rielle agreed, they could use her membership to investigate, and to bargain with the Covens. The Archons wouldn't turn away an asset high in the Divinity's hierarchy.

If she agreed.

"Aren't you going to buy anything?" Olivia asked. "Something to remember this voyage?"

As if he could forget it? The water dragon and being outmaneuvered by the Grand Divinus were memorable enough. That latter memory would sting for years. And that torture in the hallway.

Still, he glanced at the next tent's offerings, smooth stones engraved with all manner of designs. One was a deep blue, with a sea turtle's shape carved into it.

"For longevity and endurance," the wizened old woman behind the counter said. When he raised a brow, she added, "It's enchanted."

He suppressed a laugh. Terra was having him on today, it seemed.

There was no way this stone would give him another day of life, or help him endure anything. At least not through its supposed enchantment.

But he picked up the stone, running his thumb over the engraved turtle, and he couldn't help but smile at the memory of the forest pool and diving to free Rielle from her turtle captor. Just running his skin over the grooves was enough to take him back to that night, how he'd known in that instant under the moon what she'd meant to him...

He gripped Faithkeeper's pommel. How determined he'd been to help—and to stay true to his Sacred Vows.

Endure. Yes, a reminder wouldn't hurt.

"This," he said to Olivia.

She looked over the turtle stone. "That simple?"

He nodded.

Tomorrow wouldn't be nearly as simple. Sharing plans to break away from an international power never was, but—he thumbed the turtle stone with a smile—he now had hope of enduring it.

CHAPTER 21

*M*orning birdsong chirped outside the windows when Rielle turned the page in *A History of Magisters*, scrawling a note about the early magister trials involving demonstrations, trying to keep her parchment in the sliver of light between the drapes she'd spread.

She had to learn all she could about what the trials might be.

Despite her skill and her commitment to magic and the Divinity, it seemed unlikely she'd be invited to test for magister, especially when there had been no word of her unsanctioned mission breaking the siege in Courdeval, freeing Olivia, or committing to defend Jon from Shadow the night of Veris. All the while in the Divinity's employ, she'd taken steps that would warrant at least inquiry, but likely reprimand.

She'd received neither.

And then discovering these trials had no rules? The Grand Divinus had said it was suited to the circumstances of a post-Rift world, but mages were precious resources. Why risk them with *no rules?* Anyone could kill anyone, during the trials, outside of them, in any way. How would that prove anything other than dishonor and underhandedness?

Just how stupid are you, Favrielle? Shadow's words echoed in her head anew. *You didn't think it strange that "pirates" attacked and didn't kill anyone? Not even as a show of force?*

Setting down her quill, she leaned back in her chair.

What if Shadow was right? What if the Divinity had attacked Laurentine? A black operation meant to compel an éveil...

What if there had been many more of these attacks?

If the Divinity would deceive, attack, and kill for nefarious purposes like that, where would its ethical boundaries lie? Would it be party to a regicide, as Jon had said Sincuore asserted?

If that were true, perhaps she'd gotten too close, learned too much, for the Divinity to let alone. Perhaps these trials would be a trap intended to kill her, something easily explained, instead of some shadowy assassination that would raise more questions.

If Sincuore was lying, perhaps this was something else... She'd ignored the Divinity for the sake of her unsanctioned missions. She'd interfered with the siege, with Olivia, with Shadow instead of asking the Divinity's orders.

Was this her "inquiry"? Thrown into a whirlwind with other delinquents, with death or serious injury as "reprimand"?

Somehow, she'd become an undesirable, and no matter the reason, there was a very real possibility these Magister Trials were her dance with death.

But there was no turning back now, not after last night. She'd prepare, she'd win, and the Grand Divinus would have to deliver mages to Jon or publicly renege and lose face.

No matter the Divinity's ethics, the average mage had to be good, or good enough to help protect innocent people from Immortals and pirates. That's who would be sent—people like her, Leigh, Olivia. Like Rainier and Berny. She hadn't been well liked at the Tower, but the mages there weren't bad.

Other than its current interim Proctor. She sighed.

Focus on the trials. One thing at a time.

Even if the Grand Divinus wanted her dead, many others had wanted the same before. And they now slept in the dirt. This was just another mission, and once she completed it, she'd begin the next: setting right all that was wrong with the Divinity, from the inside—from the Magisterium.

With a nod to herself, she reached over and opened the drapes just a bit more, trying to cast a little more sunlight over her book.

A groan came from the bed, then a shuffling of sheets. Brennan held a pillow over his face. "Rielle," he croaked, "why in Nox's name are you awake before the damned birds are?"

She grinned. "I have work to do. The Magister Trials aren't going to research themselves."

A lengthy sigh. "Come here," he whispered, and she could hear the smile in his muffled voice. "I'll tell you something about the trials."

He was in a playful mood, then. Last night, he'd been different, unlike himself, his touch so gentle, so affectionate, *accepting*. She'd had a strange reaction to seeing Jon, and Brennan... he'd been kind. He could have been angry, but he hadn't. He hadn't said a thing at all.

He loved her, forgave her, and she loved him all the more for it.

She padded across the rug to the bed and leaned in. "Something good, I h—"

An arm hooked her waist and threw her onto the mattress, and he pinned her, looking down at her with gleaming, predatory eyes. "Oh, it'll be good. I promise."

He kissed her neck and made his way lower, untying her nightgown's closure.

"What about breakfast?" she argued. "Aren't you hungry?"

"Hunger can wait." Seductive eyes met hers from between her breasts. "At least that kind."

The heat of his lips on her skin was shiver-inducing pleasure, but she squirmed. "I only have three more days, Brennan, and then—"

"And then the trials won't matter," he said, around a mouthful of her breast as he lavished it with attention. "Win or lose, you'll be one of the most powerful women alive, bride."

His hands explored lower, gathering her nightgown. Divine, there was something she'd wanted to say, but what was—

The pressure of his tongue made her moan.

"Win or lose...?" she panted.

"You'll be a Marcel," he said, exhaling cool air on her sensitive skin, making her writhe.

A Marcel...

Her back arched at his touch. She wanted to be a Marcel, now more than ever, but the trials weren't meaningless.

If she won—

His touch firmed, and she gasped as he repositioned her.

If she won... Emaurria would get its mages... and she'd be a member of the Magisterium... change things from... within...

"I want to win," she whispered, as he pinned back her arms against the pillows, then took her. "I want to—"

He covered her mouth as she moaned her pleasure. "This is what you want right now, bride," he told her. "This."

As Jon ENTERED THE VILLA, the household was unusually flustered—whispering, rushing around, opening and closing doors. The interior was lined with luxury, full of Emaurrian furniture and textiles, much like the palace, but the air was nervous.

"Perhaps we arrived at an inconvenient time?" Olivia asked the chamberlain.

"No, no, not at all, Your Majesty, Your Ladyship," he insisted, glancing at each of them and bowing with the grace lent by half a century of practice. Despite his words, the rest of the household scrambled behind him.

The chamberlain took their cloaks and led them from the foyer, down a hallway, and past a dining chamber—

Two sets of footsteps hastily pounded down stairs, doors creaked open, then closed.

It was almost noon. Surely Rielle and Brennan would be awake by—

Shutting his eyes briefly, he stiffened. This couldn't get any more awkward.

Olivia looked at him inquisitively, but he shook his head and simply followed.

At last the chamberlain brought them to a parlor, where Rielle sat upon a sofa, reading a book and breathing hard, while Brennan leaned over the fire with his back to them. As if they always spent their leisure time as such.

Somehow, it had gotten more awkward.

Rielle glanced up from her book, eyes wide, and stood, straightening her sky-blue dress.

"Jon, Olivia," she said, glancing between them. She hurried to Olivia and wrapped her tight.

Brennan turned and bowed, lingering in his bent posture. "Your Majesty, Lady Archmage, welcome to my family's home."

The words were forced, but cordial.

Jon inclined his head. They'd intruded, but he'd keep the intrusion as short as possible and leave them to their peace.

Rielle bowed to him as well.

He cleared his throat. "I told you at the castle that I'd call on you."

Brennan gestured them to seats, and he and Rielle sat across from them on the sofa.

"How was your voyage?" Brennan asked, sprawling out on the sofa like a cat, his hand covering Rielle's. There was no mistaking his true meaning: *This is my domain, and my woman.*

"Quick," Jon replied, "other than the water dragon that attacked our ship."

Rielle bolted up. "What happened?"

"We were on the weather deck, and it attacked in open daylight."

"How did you defeat it?" she asked, looking him over, as if she somehow expecting him to still be broken and bleeding... despite seeing him yesterday.

He suppressed a laugh.

"While I used a hydromancy incantation to keep the water stable," Olivia said, "Jon held a repulsion shield—"

"Your—your magic?" Rielle asked him.

He nodded, his mouth twitching. If he could show her his progress, she'd be proud... or tease him for having learned as much as a teenage novice just after an éveil. "Olivia's been giving me lessons, but I'm not that good. Still, when the dragon appeared, I—" He glanced at Olivia, and she smiled warmly for just a moment. *Too* warmly. He cleared his throat and looked away. "We were near enough to Emaurria that I used my Earthbound powers and managed a wave to discourage it."

Brennan's eyebrows rose as Rielle's mouth fell open.

She blanched. "Jon, that's... You did something truly amazing."

"And just about died to do it," Olivia said, elbowing him. "Luckily, we—"

Jon coughed. The less that was said about *dying*, the better. "Olivia healed me. After that, it was smooth sailing."

Rielle's gaze darted between them. Her throat bobbed, her posture and smiling face so taut she looked paralyzed.

"And you? You're... in the Magister Trials." He looked her over. The next few weeks wouldn't be easy on her.

Her smile faded.

"We received the correspondence just after you left Laurentine," Brennan answered. "Rielle wanted to accept, so here we are." He took her hand and they shared a smile, then she faced them once more.

"On Khar'shil, Shadow insinuated that the *Divinity* had sent her husband to Laurentine all those years ago, to awaken my sister Dominique. If that's true, then it's possible all the tragedies surrounding certain éveils and mages joining the Towers may very well have been orchestrated by the Divinity itself. We're here to find that out." She glanced at Brennan once more, and he gave her the slightest nod.

She suspected the Divinity of killing for power? *If she didn't before, she is now.*

Rielle perked up. "We're going to try to find evidence by—"

"Your speech last night," Brennan said to him, straight to the point. "What was that about?"

It was why he'd come here. He leaned forward. "I didn't want to discuss it at the castle, but... all of that was supposed to be a mere formality. I was supposed to request aid, the Grand Divinus was supposed to decline for one reason or another, and we could return to Emaurria, vindicated to seek out other options, no matter what the Grand Divinus thought of them."

"But she surprised us by tying our request to your performance in the trials," Olivia added.

Rielle frowned. "Other options? What's happening at home?"

"It's... not good," he said, meeting her intense eyes. "You already know our forces were spread thin dealing with the Immortals. But the piracy has made that strain worse," he said as she nodded, lowering her gaze, "and although Vervewood and Stonehaven are helping take the pressure off in the heartland, the Immortals are only growing bolder elsewhere. Without more mages—mages the Divinity has been refusing to provide— it's only a matter of time before our resources are spent and there's no way left to defend our people."

"I won't let that happen," Rielle said. "I'll win. She'll have to provide the mages then."

Even if the Grand Divinus had constructed the trials as a web of deception, Rielle would be strong enough to navigate it. And he'd help her any way he could.

"You don't have to," Brennan said to her with a shrug. "You can just withdraw if the trials become too dangerous, can't you? He has another plan. A better plan, even."

She scowled at him. "A *backup* plan, Brennan. And even if I 'withdraw,' there are no rules. The other candidates don't have to accept my withdrawal. They could pursue me anyway."

He held her gaze. "Then they'll die," he slowly enunciated, keeping as still as she did.

"The silence has been working against us," Olivia interrupted... thankfully. "No one knows why we don't have

Divinity mages to help. Some rumors say the Grand Divinus doesn't support Jon. Others say that as a former paladin, Jon rejects magical help. So we came here to make it clear to the world: it is the Divinity that has allowed Emaurrians to suffer."

"And once you have?" Rielle asked, scrunching the fabric of her gown in a fist.

"Emaurria is free to ally with the Covens," Brennan said, reaching for her hand again.

"Not exactly," Jon interrupted with a crestfallen sigh. "The Grand Divinus revealed her interpretation of the treaty publicly... that the Immortals aren't 'foreign powers,' which would obligate the Divinity to act. She could deny us aid and *still* declare us to be breaking the treaty first if we seek aid elsewhere, although I didn't exactly agree with her interpretation."

"She can't expect everyone to just *die* to the Immortals," Rielle said. "There would be a public outcry."

He nodded—she understood perfectly. "That's our hope. Survival is definitely more popular, and compliance with the treaty's terms, as interpreted by the Grand Divinus, would be unconscionable."

"Unconscionable... Then even if the Divinity disapproves," Rielle said slowly, intertwining her fingers with his, "its refusal to assist the kingdom puts the public and the international community on your side... A good plan."

"And the Tower," Jon said quietly, before he could lose his nerve. "If the divide between Emaurria and the Divinity is deep enough, we could find the space to bring the Emaurrian Tower under the Crown."

Rielle covered her mouth, her gaze searching his until at last she raised her eyebrows and nodded.

If he held dominion over the Tower and the Order in Emaurria—while uniting peaceable Immortals as allies—the kingdom would have all the strength it needed. It was only a matter of breaking their chains. A nigh impossible matter.

But he wouldn't give up.

"So that's what you intend," Brennan said, with a rictus grin. "Sever the external Divinity ties that tangle in Emaurria, and make it stronger. A brilliant, if risky, strategy. And I'm dying to see whether this works out."

So was he.

Rielle kept her gaze low, looking into nothing, or at the rug. He might've guessed she preferred he leave, but that wasn't quite it. Something weighed on her mind. Heavily. Perhaps the trials? Mysterious, deadly, and beginning in three short days.

Only tell me, and I'll see it remedied.

But it wasn't his place anymore. And for her sake, he couldn't interfere.

"You need me to lose, don't you?" Rielle asked hollowly. She folded her hands together. "So the Grand Divinus could turn down sending aid, and the public outcry can happen."

"No, Rielle. I want you to win." He watched her until she met his gaze. "When you do, we'll find another time to bring the Covens into the fold. I won't turn away help, no matter who provides it. Not anymore."

She smiled a little, that grave shadow fading from her face.

"If you become a member of the Magisterium and you agree our claims against the Divinity are true, would you be willing to work with the Covens to prove it from within?" he asked her cautiously.

Her eyebrows knitted together a moment, then she nodded gravely. "If the Divinity is doing wrong, then I'll do everything in my power to prove it. And if I win, I won't rest until I burn out every ounce of infection from the Magisterium and the

Divinity as a whole. I'll make the Divinity what it was always meant to be, or I'll die trying."

Good. Then they had a plan for if she won. Hopefully Leigh could sell it to the Archons.

Olivia set down her tea. "But Rielle, you should know... If the Grand Divinus never intended to send aid to Emaurria, then she likely wouldn't have changed her mind last night. I think she plans for you to lose."

These Magister Trials could be nothing more than a way to dispose of inconveniences to the Divinity. Worse—encouraging them to dispose of each other.

Or perhaps even an elaborately planned murder, if each trial was tailored to a particular candidate's weaknesses.

"The Grand Divinus may be trying to kill you," he said quietly.

Rielle tightened her clasped hands and lifted her chin. "I know. But she wouldn't be the first, and she won't be the last." She met his gaze unequivocally. "And if she makes a mistake, the world will be watching."

"Do you have a plan?" Olivia asked.

"I've been researching," Rielle replied. "But I have something the other candidates won't—all of you. Your help and advice."

He would do everything in his power to support her during the trials.

Brennan curled an arm around her, and she leaned into him.

He rose, and so did Olivia. "That's everything. We won't keep you any longer."

"I'm always happy to see you both," Rielle said as she and Brennan stood. Her stance firm, she said, "I'll win. For Emaurria, and for myself." The sky-blue of her dress brought out the endless summer of her eyes, and the thundercloud of her ferocity in them.

Jon held her gaze. "Magic is your life. If anyone can win, it's you."

That thundercloud stormed a moment before he turned toward the exit.

In three days, he'd see her at the castle again. Fighting for her life.

CHAPTER 22

R ielle watched the carriage depart, Brennan at her side, holding her hand. The breeze ruffled her dress and hair, but it didn't matter—she had a lengthy day ahead of her, poring over books about the trials.

So Jon had been planning on the Grand Divinus refusing to help. *And my participation in the trials ruined everything.*

Even at the expense of his plan, he'd told her to win, and that was what she would do.

Another carriage pulled up the drive, just as opulent—a coach and six, with carts behind it bearing luggage. "Is that—?"

"Mother, my sisters, and the boys," Brennan said, squeezing her hand. He cracked a grin. "And Nora is yelling at the boys for"—he sighed—"making fish 'sounds' at each other?"

"What kind of sound does a fish make?"

He shook his head, but his mouth twitched as he dipped his chin, paused attentively, and then a laugh bubbled in his throat. He had to be listening in, the look on his face so mirthful that he seemed like he could listen to a lifetime of it.

As soon as the carriage drew to a halt, Nora threw herself out and slammed the door. "Just wait until I tell your grandfather!" she screamed at the carriage. "You won't be able to sit for a week!"

Rielle arched an eyebrow at Brennan. "She's going to have your father discipline them?"

He shrugged. "My brother-in-law parented them most of the time before he died. Nora had... other interests."

Her hair askew and her fuchsia gown wrinkled, his sister stomped up the drive, waved off the servants, then fixed her and Brennan both with a scowl.

"Was that one of your *lovers* who just left, *sister*?" Nora asked, tilting her head as she smirked. "Tell me, which one are you marrying again?"

"Oh, they should be easy for you to tell apart," Rielle said sweetly. "The one in whose bed you'd never leave your negligee."

That had been particularly mean-spirited. She raised her head and glared at Nora, whose eyebrows drew together as she tilted her head.

"My... black silk negligee?" Nora asked, her voice uneven. "I lost it when—"

Rielle frowned. Lost?

But then Nora's gaze darted toward Brennan. As if—as if *he'd*—

Heart pounding, breathing fast, Rielle turned her head to him as the blood drained from his livid face.

He...

He had done it?

He had planted Nora's negligee in Jon's bed?

He had let her think it had been—that Jon had—

"I can explain." Brennan held her gaze evenly.

Pulse thudding in her ears, she spun and strode back inside toward the stairs.

"Rielle," he called, his voice booming. His footsteps pounded behind her, and he grabbed her arm, but she yanked it away and ran up the stairs.

No, no, no. They were *not* going to have this conversation in front of his sister, in front of his *mother* as she came in. *No.*

"Would you stop?" he called after her, but she didn't even slow until she was in his rooms.

Divine, *his* rooms, *his* family's villa—*his* territory. She couldn't even rightly go anywhere in this building to be alone.

The balcony doors were shut, but she could throw them open, then an updraft spell, and—

He came in and shut the door behind him, then rested his back against it, watching her. His face had gone slack, his eyes dull, and she couldn't even look at him anymore.

Her feet wouldn't stop moving, and she paced the room, walking a tight circuit as the night of Veris roiled in her afresh. Finding that silk, that betrayal, while in Jon's arms, while together, it had been like a blade through her heart, sharpness that had destroyed everything going in and ripped it all through going out. All her restraint had broken, and she'd screamed her loss, her grief at Jon, turned away from him and left.

And all of that—the anguish of that night—had been sparked by *Brennan?* Jon hadn't betrayed her again, hadn't done what she'd accused him of, and... Brennan had let her think otherwise, let her cry, let her suffer, all the while having done *this.*

"How could you?" she hissed, voice breaking.

He closed his eyes and let a loose fist thump against the door behind him.

"Do you have any idea how much that hurt? The pain of that night?" She swallowed against the hoarseness.

He tightened his closed eyes and breathed deep. "Do *you*?"

What could he possibly—? She paused her circuit, shaking her head and shrugging.

"Do *you* have any idea how much that hurt?" he asked, voice low, raw. He opened his eyes, overbright and gleaming, intense. "After watching him shatter you, having to stand by and watch you just fall for his manipulations, make all the wrong choices?"

"They were *my* choices to make!" she screamed at him. "And don't you *dare* talk to me about 'manipulations,' Brennan. Don't you *dare*."

He gaped at her. "What was I *supposed* to do?" he shouted back at her, striding right up to her face. "Just watch you go back to him, after all he'd done to you? After he'd treated you like *nothing*, like *less than nothing*, letting you rot in Sonbahar, letting you be abused, your child *die*, while he fucked his way through the court?"

Her mouth fell open, but she clicked it closed, crossed her arms, scowling at the volume of his booming voice. "Don't you dare bring Sylvie into this."

He exhaled lengthily. "Tell me, Rielle," he said, gentler this time, his voice dropping. "Is that what I should have done? Just stood by and watched you go back to a man who didn't value you, never *could*, and just watch you walk right out of my life?"

That love, it... it had lingered, there was no denying that, but the reasons she and Jon couldn't be together hadn't changed. No matter how much she loved him, that would have been a difficult decision.

But Brennan hadn't allowed it, had made that decision *for* them. For *her*.

"You just couldn't wait, could you?" she croaked in a tear-stricken voice. "Things with him never would have worked out —you know that. But you couldn't wait. You *had* to force it, then and there, didn't you?"

Brennan anchored a hand on his hip as he rubbed his forehead. "How long should I have waited, Rielle? Until you became his official mistress? Until he married some princess instead of you? Until he put another child in you? Is that how long I should have waited? Until the weight of that life crushed you into only the rubble of the woman you are now? Would that have been the right time? Would it?"

Tears streamed down her face, and she covered her mouth. The bleak future he painted *hurt*, but not because he had said it. Because it could have been *true*.

But no matter the outcome, it had been her choice... Stolen.

"I'm sorry I caused you hurt, and I'm sorry I lied about it," Brennan murmured. "But I'm *not* sorry I did it. I'd rather you hate me and punish me than spend years of your life suffering for a man who doesn't deserve you, who could never put you first. So hate me if you must. Punish me if you must."

She glared at him.

He'd manipulated her, stolen her power of meaningful choice, had altered the course of her *life* in one moment, and he wasn't even truly sorry?

"Do you not even understand the gravity of taking someone's choices away?" she croaked.

He stared her down. "If you're too blinded to see that there's a wrong choice and a right choice, then I'm *saving* you by helping you choose."

"*Helping?*" she shot back, then ran a hand over her hair, dragging it tight. "How often have you 'helped' me by keeping information from me, by *lying* to me?"

He opened his mouth, but no words emerged.

"Are you struggling to remember, or trying to decide which to mention first?" she bit out.

"You're being impossible," he snarled, his voice booming.

Impossible? "Impossible to be honest with, or...?"

His face contorted, he advanced on her. "Would you just—"

"No," she snapped back at him, striding to the balcony. "I won't *just*. You'd rather I hate you and punish you?" She kicked the balcony doors open. "Done."

Eyes wide, he lunged for her.

She cast an updraft spell and jumped.

BRENNAN STARED down from the balcony as she ran, out of the courtyard and toward the drive, her sky-blue dress billowing behind her.

His grip on the balustrade tightened, crushing into the stone.

She'd run from him. She'd *run*.

Quick footsteps pounded up the stairs, and the door flew open. He looked back past the flowing gauze curtains and across the bedchamber.

Una stood in the doorway, eyes wide and breathing hard, her gray doublet and black trousers wrinkled. Her usually pristine dark bun had wayward wisps. "What's happening up here? I heard yelling." Her sharp eyes searched the chamber.

He glared at her. "It's private. Don't—"

"Don't tell me that, Bren. You've never been 'private' about your relationships before." She entered the room, looking about, then headed toward the balcony. "Where's Favrielle?" She walked out onto it and peered over the edge. "Did she cast a spell or something and jump off?"

She leaned a hip against the balustrade as she crossed her slender arms.

"I'm not Father," he bit out to her.

She nudged him. "I know that," she said. "And you'll never be. But that doesn't mean you are about to botch this completely."

If it had been anyone else but one of his sisters or Mother, he would have thrown them out, but Una was special to him. She'd been around for so many of Mother and Father's fights, and he'd spent them playing with her, distracting her, making her laugh and smile while raised voices had echoed throughout the castle. He'd taken care of her while Nora had been chasing boys and Caitlyn had still been with her nanny. He'd practically raised Una, and the bond he had with her was stronger than with any of his sisters.

But Rielle would not *run* from him before they settled this, not if he could help it. He couldn't chase her off the balcony with Una here, so he strode toward the door.

"You're going after her?" Una asked as she followed him.

As he stormed down the stairs, she kept pace, mumbling pardons to the household staff he shoved aside.

"If she jumped off a balcony to leave, she's probably too angry to talk. And you want to chase her down like this? Bad idea, Bren."

Bad idea?

Letting Rielle *stew* in her anger was a bad idea. A *worse* idea.

Mother's voice and Caitlyn's carried from the front of the villa, so he changed course to the back exit. The last thing he needed was Mother asking if everything was all right... when it most certainly wasn't.

As he strode down the halls, Una followed him. "Wouldn't you rather give her time to cool off? And maybe take some yourself?"

He shook his head. "She said I don't let her make her own choices."

"Hm." Una blew out a soft breath. "And you want to chase her down and bring her back? You'd kind of be proving her right." She hurried to round him and head him off. "Think about what you're doing for one second," she said, holding up a palm, but he walked right into it, pushing against it with his sternum.

He glowered down at her hand, hissed a sigh, and paused, taking a deep breath. Una wasn't going to let this go.

When she said he hadn't kept his other relationships private, she'd been right. She'd always seemed to be rooting for him to finally settle down and have children, but he'd had a penchant for starting relationships quickly and ending them even more quickly. Una was very attached to him—her investment in his happiness was endearing, but also incredibly irritating sometimes. Like now.

"Do you have a plan to win her over?" she asked.

Other than finding Rielle and bringing her back, he didn't have much of a plan. He'd boxed Rielle in before, and the tighter quarters he gave her, the more she tried to run.

But what was he supposed to do? Sit on his hands and wait for her to return? She could run right to Jon, and in the heat of the moment, they might find comfort in each other. All of this, over one argument? By tonight, Jon could be the one holding her—

"You're going to make things worse," Una said, her brows

drawn together.

The longer he waited, the worse things would become. That was certain.

"I can't just leave her be," he muttered.

"Maybe you *should* go after her," Una said, lowering her hand and righting her gray doublet. "But don't go to her just to drag her back. Come to her with choices, ones she can easily see herself, and don't try to force anything."

Choices? What choices? She would return to *him*, and that was the end of that. He'd say whatever she needed to hear.

Una steered him back toward the stairs. "Take her cloak, take her coin purse, go to her with options. Give her a little time, a little space to collect her thoughts. People say things in the heat of the moment that they don't mean."

He grimaced. He'd already made that last part a reality.

"Go to her with her things," she encouraged gently, "make no demands, and she can return with you or be alone or do whatever she wants. If she wants you to leave, leave. Let her return to you on her own terms. And then I think she'll come around."

And if she doesn't want to?

He shook his head. No, Una was right. If he wanted to smooth this over, he'd have to go to Rielle without trying to force her into anything else.

"Fine," he said, facing Una's encouraging smile and letting out an exasperated sigh as Una hugged him tight. He'd bring Rielle her cloak and her coin purse, and let her decide.

But Rielle had accused him of lying, and she was right— although she had no idea how right.

She'd make her own choice all right, but he'd offer her an inducement to come home that she wouldn't be able to turn away. The truth.

CHAPTER 23

*R*ielle walked down the cobblestone street, weaving between passersby as she headed toward a market district.

She'd been walking for what felt like half an hour, without so much as a cloak or a cuivre, in a constricting gown. And in slippers meant for rugs and parquet floors. Her feet understood that now. Very thoroughly.

The crowd thickened the farther she went, churning like a roiling pot, and she lost herself in the churn. It didn't matter where she was going. All that mattered was that she was beneath the open sky, out in the fresh air, with the earth under her feet, and not in *his* room, under *his* roof, in *his* territory. Blocking the door, he'd left her no choice.

She huffed a breath. *No choice.* That was the root of the problem between them, circled by a carousel of lies.

That evening at the Tower nearly ten years ago came rushing back, vivid and tangible. *Me or this place.* Bright hazel eyes boring into her with unshakeable focus, closing in, pushing, pressing—

She shivered. She'd run that evening, too, but in a different way. He'd given her a choice, but she'd chosen magic. And had kept choosing it for a decade.

Rubbing her bare arms, she ducked into a small garden beside a temple. Bright violet and lavender pansies winked at her, so cheery she couldn't face them. She sank onto the low stone wall edging the flowerbed, her fingertip absently stroking a petal.

She loved him—that was undeniable—but had that love and their entire relationship right now been built on that lie the night of Veris?

What if Brennan hadn't done what he had the night of Veris? What would her life look like now?

She shook her head. It would do no good to think about what might have been. Jon and Olivia were together now. And whatever his faults, she loved Brennan, who—despite her own faults—loved her, too.

But there could be no moving forward, not unless he understood that taking away her power to choose was unacceptable. Even when he thought she was making the wrong choice, he had to accept it was *her* choice.

A chill wove up her spine, and bracing on the rough stone, she looked around.

People milled about in the crowd, going about their business in merchant stalls and shops, myriad Sileni voices rising and mingling, but there was an alleyway shadowed under an awning... She squinted, staring into it, her breaths coming faster.

Someone was watching her.

If she cast earthsight, her gesture would give her away, but she could close her eyes and cast it behind her—

"Bonny little flower," a man's low voice said in a lilting Morwenian accent.

She spun, caught in the shadow of a massive, muscled man, his arms crossed, with a square jaw, short copper hair, and the most eerily vivid green eyes she'd ever seen. In an elaborate brocade overcoat and trousers of the deepest black, he nodded toward the flowerbed, at the pansy she'd been stroking.

Her gaze meandered back to his, which looked her up and down, sizing her up with a sportive smile. "Are you lost, bonny little flower? Looking for something?" Those eerily vivid green eyes glinted. "Or someone?"

A shudder trickled down her spine. There was something behind those eyes, something terrible.

Hands ready at her sides, she rose. "Looking for some solitude to clear my head," she answered, staring up into his face. "But thank you for your concern." *Now be on your way.*

"My, my, that's quite a sting," he said, voice thick like honey. Anchoring a large hand on his hip, he chuckled under his breath and ran his big fingers through his hair. "It's a fine day, bonny little flower. You should smile, brighten up that—"

"You forgot your cloak, bride."

Behind her, Brennan's deep voice, a warning tone, and his hot grip was on her wrist, tugging her into his arms, against the solid, firm heat of his chest. The cloak was about her shoulders instantly, and she breathed deep in his embrace, cypress and spice and her Brennan, and looked over his black-cloaked arm at the large man.

Oh, if he so much as *touched* her or Brennan now, he would *burn.*

"Are you lost, sirrah?" The rumble of Brennan's imperious voice rippled into her as the large man's mouth curved in a crooked smile. Brennan tossed a gold corona at him, which hit the man in the chest before he caught it. "Go buy yourself a drink." He swept her back toward the way she'd come, and with a distrustful look over his shoulder, guided her forward by the small of her back.

A thump, and the clink of metal on stone cobbles. The man had thrown the coin at Brennan's back.

Brennan huffed a half-laugh. "Pray our paths don't cross again," he bit out, deathly still.

"I hope they do," the man taunted back.

With a rictus grin, Brennan escorted her along into the crowd. "So do I," he hissed back, before they entered the churn and bustle.

His hand at her back, he pushed her uptown from where she'd come, his mouth a grim line. He hadn't needed to do that— any of that. She'd had everything completely under control.

She struggled to keep up, her sore feet aching at his pace. "Brennan—"

He pushed her along faster, cutting a path through the crowd with his arm, elbowing people aside.

"Brennan," she protested, wincing. "My feet are—"

He circled her waist and hefted her over his shoulder, making her yelp.

Faces in the crowd turned to ogle her, whispering, and she thrashed in his hold. "What are you—"

"Don't ever run from me again, Rielle," he bit out, and she struggled, trying to clamber out of his grip.

"Don't tell me what to do," she snapped back. "I was completely fine. I didn't need *you* to—"

He scoffed.

"Put me down, Brennan."

Nothing.

"Put me down!"

He came to an abrupt stop and set her down, scowling at her as she pushed herself away. The crowd had thinned here, and they were close to the villa. Other than there, she didn't even have a place to go.

After rearranging her cloak, she crossed her arms, looking back toward the villa and away.

"Come home," Brennan said to her.

Home. It didn't feel like home, not without a place of her own, but all her things were there.

"I'll tell you everything," he said quietly. "Just come home."

"Everything?" Every lie he'd ever told her—would he now reveal the truth?

"Yes," he grunted.

What else had he lied about? What else had he hidden?

He kept the silence and distance between them, shifting his weight, gaze darting toward dark corners. "Someone is following you," he whispered. "A mage."

The chill she'd felt—

"Get back to the villa."

Why would anyone follow her?

But with a wary look about the alleyways, she nodded, turning toward the villa and letting him escort her there.

Brennan mentally girded himself as he opened the door to the villa and took Rielle's hand—hopefully she wouldn't yank it away. She didn't. It only took a moment before Mother arrived in the foyer, wrapped him in her embrace, followed by Caitlyn.

"My son, I've missed you," Mother said softly, kissing his cheek. "Where were you?" Her gaze meandered to Rielle, whom she greeted with a kiss on each cheek and looked over with approval while Caitlyn hugged him close. "The dress suits you, Daughter."

Rielle smiled brightly and inclined her head politely. "Thank you, Your Grace. It's lovely to see you again. How was your voyage?"

"Lengthy," Mother replied with a sigh. "And the boys caught cold, so we'll be tending them for a few days."

"Why so stiff, Bren?" Caitlyn asked with an impish grin, poking him between the ribs with a finger. "Did the tailor delay this season's wardrobe again?"

He grimaced. Libretti would have let him look like a fool in the previous year's wardrobe when they'd last summered in Stroppiata, and he'd lost himself a king's ransom in gold for it—but luckily Father had sent his things over ahead of his own arrival, and had nearly the same measurements. "Just could use a rest, that's all."

Mother's lips twitched, failing to restrain a knowing smile as she glanced from him to Rielle and back. "Well, we'll let you rest, then. Come, Caitlyn. We have invitations to respond to."

Caitlyn poked him again for good measure, stuck out her tongue, then trotted off behind Mother.

He held a palm to his side—she was getting strong, especially for a sixteen-year-old.

Holding Rielle's hand, he led her up the stairs while she blushed furiously. "Are you embarrassed?" he asked at full volume.

"*Shh*," she hissed, and raised a hand to cover her mouth. "Your mother thinks—"

"She normally wouldn't be wrong, would she?" he asked, giving her a once-over.

She looked away. "She is *today*."

With an inward sigh, he opened the door to their quarters

and guided her in before shutting the door behind them. At least Rielle had maintained appearances in front of Mother and Caitlyn. She could have done otherwise, and utterly humiliated him, but she'd supported him instead. That boded well for the conversation they were about to have.

She thought he'd stolen her choices, but it wasn't about that. He'd wanted to spare her the hurt, save her from a future that would have left her trapped. One she might have dove into far too deeply, blinded by love, only to drown in its depths.

Across from the bed, she dropped into the desk's chair, in front of her books. Her magic books. She ran a palm over them, sighed with relief, as if she'd expected not to find them here when she returned.

She crossed her arms and looked up at him with unyielding eyes. "You said you would tell me everything."

"Everything," he repeated. He grabbed a chair from the nearby table and dragged it across their quarters to the desk while she winced. She'd sat so far from the bed, in the solitary chair at the desk, hoping for space, hadn't she? His nearness made it more difficult for her to be angry, didn't it?

Once the chair was directly in front of her, he threw off his cloak and seated himself. Within arm's reach.

She straightened. "If there's anything more you haven't told me, any lies or omissions, now is the time. I'd like us to be honest with each other."

For a moment, he didn't move, just let her stew in her thoughts. "Are you certain you want to know? What's past has passed."

"It's past for you, but if I don't know about it, the pain of finding out, for me, is fresh. I don't want to have this wounded trust that keeps bleeding anew. So tell me now, while I'm prepared, while I can listen and be of a mind to rebuild our trust."

He heaved a lengthy sigh. "I found out my father hired Gilles."

She shot up off the chair and bolted, pacing in short strides. "Your *father?*" she squeaked. "*Your father* hired Gilles?" She gaped at him and resumed pacing. "Ordered... ordered the regicide, the assassinations, the siege?" She shook her head. "Your *father* had tried to kill—"

Jon?

But she stiffened, bit her lip, chewed it. "The ship. Did he order the—"

He straightened, his eyes wide. "No." He blinked, frowning. "I don't..." He blew out a breath. "I asked him in Courdeval, before I went after you, whether he knew where you were, or where you were being taken. He said he didn't, and his pulse was even, no sign that he was lying. I believed him." He held her gaze.

No matter his other dark deeds, Father hadn't lied about that. He'd made certain of it.

"Your father... In Melain, we found that sen'a distribution map with several places all over Emaurria linked with black thread, Maerleth Tainn among them."

He remembered well.

"We found a letter that said advance payment had been sent to silence dissent until 'they' could nominate and confirm a candidate of 'their' choosing," she said, pacing. "It had to have been composed by some members of Parliament... led by your father."

He nodded. That sounded right.

"So how did he hire Gilles, orchestrate the regicide, but not know where Sincuore was taking me?" she asked, pinning him with her intense blue gaze.

Sincuore had mentioned the Grand Divinus possibly being complicit in the regicide, and he hadn't told her because it implicated his own father, his own family, even *him*, insofar as he'd covered it up.

"He had a partner," she whispered. "The Grand Divinus," she said, eyes widening.

She was putting things together herself. Maybe he wouldn't have to tell her about questioning Sincuore and expose yet another instance he'd lied... They would number many in her mind after tonight.

"Has to be. Jon told me he questioned Sincuore the night of his capture, and Sincuore didn't deny her involvement. It couldn't have just been Shadow. Sincuore had refused to bargain with me. Your father is powerful, but not so powerful that a pirate wouldn't betray him for all the gold in Emaurria. It has to be the Grand Divinus."

Brennen said nothing. Jon had told her about the questioning, but hadn't exposed *his* involvement. Why not? Jon could've seized the opportunity to reveal him as a liar to Rielle, make himself look better. Why hadn't he?

"The sen'a hub where we fought Phantom, where we found the distribution map and the letter—it was the eastern sen'a distribution hub for all of eastern Emaurria *and* housed the assassins working against the Faralles... All because King Marcus threatened a ban on sen'a over a decade ago," she said, musing. "Their interests had aligned. King Marcus was assassinated over the sen'a trade."

Maerleth Tainn had been on the distribution map, among other lands—Father had to be aware of the trade, had to have profited from it. Something he'd kept from the family.

"It's all connected," she whispered. "Your father, the sen'a distribution, the Grand Divinus, Gilles, King Marcus." With an awed gasp, she leaned against the wall, her hand scrambling for purchase on the wainscoting. "I—I think the Grand Divinus might be the source of the sen'a."

What? "But the Tower dismisses mages for abusing it, for peddling it, right?"

She nodded, spearing him with a stunned gaze. "A cover. The farther the sen'a is kept from the Divinity, the less likely the Divinity seems to be a source of it."

"But why?"

She shook her head. "Why else? Power."

After Shadow, Rielle had suspected the Divinity might be gathering mages, willing or not, through black operations. And now, the Divinity could be selling sen'a, gathering unthinkable sums of coin.

For power.

Why else did an organization need the world's strongest weapons and bottomless treasuries?

"There's a war coming," Rielle said, throwing off her cloak and grabbing a sheet of parchment. "The Grand Divinus wanted to wage it quietly, with sympathetic rulers, but with Jon on the throne, she has no puppet in Emaurria."

The Grand Divinus was planning to take over—Emaurria, and possibly more.

She grabbed her quill, dipped it in the inkwell, and curled over the desk to write.

"What are you doing?" he asked, raising an eyebrow.

"We have to write to Jon and Olivia," she said, scribbling. "The Grand Divinus may not want me to lose," she whispered. "She may have hoped the Immortals would kill him, but they haven't. When he asked for help, she might have wanted to *appear* reluctant... but the odds may be stacked so that I win... So that he gets those mages, and maybe an assassin among them."

He grabbed her hand. She was getting ahead of herself.

"So she either wants to kill you and let Emaurria fall to ruin... ripe for the taking... or she wants you to win so she can get an army of mages into the kingdom," he said. "There's no clear course of action. Even if you tell them, what is there to do?"

She frowned. "I could withdraw—"

"And if you do, or you lose, then when Emaurria allies with the Covens, Emaurria will have broken the treaty first, and the Grand Divinus wins." He sighed. "And if you win... an army of possibly hostile mages quarters in Emaurria, lying in wait."

"But they have to know," she said.

He plucked the quill from her hand. "They will. I'll look for the Archives during your first trial. Let me do some digging first, see what I find, and when we bring this to Jon and Olivia, we might have more than hunches and guesses."

"And if we do?" she asked, straightening. "If we find out the Grand Divinus and your father were working together? Whose side will you be on?"

He shook his head and stood from the chair, rubbing his jaw as he approached the window to the courtyard.

That was a lot to take in. Father's ambitions had led him to assassinating a king, trying to overthrow an entire dynasty, to bringing a country to its knees, and he'd almost destroyed Emaurria.

Brennan eyed the vast expanse of green in the quiet courtyard. He didn't support any of that, nor did he want his family on the throne. And this couldn't go on.

But standing against Father? Watching his arrest, his execution? Casting the family into the shadow of treason?

He didn't have an answer right now.

With a deep sigh, he looked back at her over his shoulder. "I don't support my father's ambitions," he said softly, "but you asked me for honesty. When I found out, I did help cover them up, Rielle."

She blinked, giving him the slightest shake of her head.

What he'd done—he didn't want her to know, but she'd asked him to tell her everything, and if it would earn back her trust, he would. "Before Spiritseve, that night on the Mor Bluffs," he said quietly, "our prisoner—I killed him."

She stepped away from him. "Anton? Why?"

"He... He said someone had wanted you taken alive. At the time, I thought my father would have given that order, knowing that I..." He looked away. "To make sure you and I could marry. So I killed the prisoner. But when I asked my father, I knew it couldn't have been him who'd wanted you taken." He'd killed the prisoner and lied about it for nothing. "I'm sorry."

Rielle shook her head. "It isn't me you should apologize to." When he frowned, she added, "Olivia cared for him."

She did? When had that happened?

It didn't matter... The prisoner had meant something to Rielle's closest friend, who meant the world to Rielle. His mouth opened, and he glanced away.

After a while, he nodded, crossed the room to her, and took her hand. "I promise you: one day I will tell her his fate, and ask her forgiveness."

She eyed him doubtfully.

"I will. I want to make all this right."

Before she could answer, he led her to the bed and urged her to sit. "One more truth, Rielle."

Settling onto it, she wrapped her arms around herself, but she needn't worry. She'd like this truth. He was certain of it.

In fact, he staked the course of this evening on it.

All of this would be over, and things would return to normal, without answering the question about his father, without promising to let her make terrible choices. Those were things they simply wouldn't agree on. But she'd agree with this. Without a doubt.

He knelt, holding her hand in his lap. "When Kieran Atterley pushed you down the stairs in the Tower, my spies told me."

She raised an eyebrow. "You had spies?"

The Wolf brushed up against his control, snarling at the memory.

He knows now. He'll never touch her again. We've made sure of that.

The Wolf receded, and he nodded to Rielle. "He dared touch you. He could have *killed* you, in a stairwell like some commoner." He clenched his free hand tight, imagining the ponce's neck in his grip. "I vowed to myself that he would never touch you again," he said, giving her hand a gentle squeeze, "so one night, when he left the Tower, I followed him to a tavern. His magic wouldn't work on me, as everyone knows I'm 'sig-iled,'" he said, eyeing her with a mischievous grin. It was well known he was immune to magic, but the rumor was that it was because of sigils, which he'd never denied. He could never, of course, confess to being a werewolf. "I set upon him and beat him to within an inch of his life. And I told him if he ever touched you again, I'd return for that remaining inch."

She blinked, her fingers closing around his, her lips parting.

Pinning her lower lip with her teeth, she rose from the bed, and he stood with her, giving her space. She took a few steps, rearranging her braid over her shoulder. A course of emotions passed over her face, and she swallowed, knitting her eyebrows together.

She came to an abrupt stop and turned to him, gazed up into his eyes with a disbelieving shake of her head.

Placing her hands on his chest, she forced him back, and holding her gaze, he retreated, let her push him, let her press him down onto the bed.

He watched her hooded eyes, dark with lust, and grinned up at her devilishly. "My punishment?"

Like a vicious wolf, she climbed onto him, and then she locked his lips with hers.

CHAPTER 24

"The forest," Leigh grumbled under his breath. "Why does it always have to be the forest?" He rubbed his face, eyeing the broken path ahead between his fingers.

Ambriel stepped up beside him, silent as death, and breathed deep, his brow creasing as if he could see the farthest flowers and know how the trees felt. Maybe he could. Or maybe he had a fantastic imagination.

Joel's idea of *tradition* involved finding the local Immortals and asking them to establish a trade for ironwood. After the people of Bournand had attacked them. And Coven emissaries had returned with arrows lodged in their limbs.

"Your limbs are safe with me, dreshan," Ambriel said with a faint smile, glancing at him over his shoulder. "Ferelen knows me and will welcome us." He picked a path through the brush, only the occasional creak of his human-crafted boots making a sound.

With a sigh, Leigh followed, trudging through the undergrowth. Ambriel had said this forest was known as White-

Weald to his people, and a small queendom of light-elves protected it, led by a warrior-queen named Ferelen Brightbark. Queen Narenian had sent a messenger to Ferelen after the dark-elves had attacked, and re-established contact with a Vervewood elf who lived in the White-Weald queendom.

"So this contact," Leigh said, kicking a fallen branch aside. "Who is she?"

Ambriel dipped his head, then another glance back. "It's Ashta, my youngest," he replied. "Narenian life-bonded her to Ferelen's son, Ruvel."

Leigh paused. Ambriel's youngest daughter. In Vervewood, he'd said he had *thirteen* of them. So his thirteenth was Ashta. "What's she like?"

"Ferelen?"

"Ashta."

"Young," Ambriel said softly. "She'd intended to save the world single-handedly—always trailing me and our scouts with her bow." He laughed under his breath. "She was only fifty-seven when Narenian sent her away. Barely out of her juvenile years. But Ruvel had come of age, she had as well, and it was time." His voice faded to silence.

He missed her. Of course he missed her. And the light-elves lived a difficult life, attempting to stay isolated.

"I hope I meet her," Leigh said, catching up to him.

Ambriel's lip twitched. "She's very possessive, dreshan. Be prepared."

Possessive of her father? At fifty-seven? Leigh smirked.

Once they reached the Beaufoys, Ambriel would be meeting *his* daughter, too. And so would *he*. And there was no telling what—

"We're not alone," Ambriel whispered, barely audible. He

drew his bow, had an arrow nocked and pointed at an aspen behind them in the blink of an eye.

Leigh spun, ready to cast a repulsion shield if need be. "Show yourself. Unless you want to be a pincushion."

A hand poked out from behind the trunk first, then a leg. A short one, wearing a fashionable feminine boot with golden spurs. Then a red-haired head and a sheepish smile.

He covered his forehead with his hand. "Katia…"

Joel would kill him. Or rather, shout very, very loudly. Or worse, tell another *story*.

"What are you doing here? Your father is going to lock you up until the end of time," he hissed, stalking over to her.

She stepped out from behind the tree with her hands clasped behind her back. "He's going to lock me up whether I go with you or not. And besides, Ambriel said you'd be welcomed, so…"

"And how did we not hear you?" Ambriel called from behind him.

She lifted a leg and wiggled her foot, the golden spur catching the filtering sunlight. "I *may* have borrowed these enchanted spurs from the Coven's armory," she said in Old Emaurrian. "*Maybe.*"

With a frustrated groan, Leigh took her by the arm and started heading back southeast toward Bournand. "Come on. You and your stolen goods are going home."

"*Borrowed* goods," she snapped, yipping and wincing to keep up. "Leigh, don't be such a grumpy old man!"

"*Old?*" He scowled at her.

Determined gray eyes bored into his. "I… I have a great reason for being here," she said. "You're trying to establish trade between the Coven and the light-elves, but then you're leaving us, aren't you? So… *someone* from the Coven should be here to know what's happening and make sure the transition is smooth, right?"

He sighed. "When have *you* made anything smoother?"

Her gaze meandered the forest, then met his anew, with another sheepish smile. "Here's my big chance?"

They'd lose *an entire day* taking her home, but if they didn't, they'd have an indignant Archon to face when they returned.

Ambriel rested a hand on his shoulder. "Dreshan, she'll be safe with us."

"That won't matter. Her father—"

"Would rather she be safe with us," Ambriel said, rounding to face him, "than finding her way home in the dark."

"But if we bring her back—"

"We'll bring her back regardless," Ambriel said, his golden gaze resting on Katia for a moment, who practically bounced on her toes. "The only question is whether we'll be bringing her back empty-handed, or with an agreement from Ferelen."

"And—and I can tell Ambriel all about Bournand and human things and Coven stuff," Katia offered hopefully.

Leigh sighed and finally nodded to Ambriel. Why was he right so criminally often?

THE DAYLIGHT SUN was darkening to burnt gold when Ambriel held up a hand and stopped them. "Arms at your sides," he said to them, "and don't move."

"*Brashan, shto rabish s timi lyudimi?*" A deep voice, masculine, from high up in the trees. Speaking Elvish, probably.

"*Dolashimo u miru u shushret s Kralyishom Ferelen,*" Ambriel called back.

There was a silence, interrupted only by the breeze rustling the trees.

"*Tata?*" a high, girlish voice called down.

"Ashta," Ambriel answered, his voice quavering, and advanced a few steps.

"*Ashta, zoshtavi!*" the deep masculine voice protested. On edge.

"*Ne,*" she snapped back, "*to ye miy tata.*" And before long, a sleek form dropped from branch to branch until she jumped to the ground.

Tall and slender, her long flaxen hair was pulled back from her alabaster face and twisted in two braids. Her eyes were bright, honey golden like Ambriel's, and she was clad in neutral-toned linen from head to toe, a wrap shirt tucked into loose breeches, secured with a sash. A bow strapped across her body and linen wrapped her legs and feet, with naught but woven soles for shoes.

Ambriel ran to meet her and threw his arms around her. "Ashta, *dushan, propustio sam te.*" His words were like relief rippling from tense shoulders.

"*Tata,*" she said softly, hugging him tightly.

That was her—Ambriel's daughter, whom he hadn't seen since before the Sundering. He whispered quiet questions to her that she answered, rocking gently in his embrace. He pressed a soft kiss to her head as other light-elves dropped down from the canopy—three, all with bows.

A man of about Ambriel's size, with broad shoulders, clear eyes, and platinum-blond hair cut very close, walked up to Ashta, waited a moment, then grasped her shoulder. She shook off his touch and held Ambriel tighter. "Ashta—"

"*Ne,* Ruvel. *To ye miy tata,*" she pleaded.

Two women flanked Ruvel, their hair and eyes matching his, all wearing the same linen clothes, and followed his gaze to Katia and him.

"*Tko su oni?*" Ruvel jerked his head toward them. He hadn't let his guard down at all. Had the people of Bournand done so much damage, or was there some other threat in the area?

"Ashta, Ruvel," Ambriel said, prying himself away from her tight embrace, just a little, "*ovo ye Leigh Galvan, miy ... lyushan.*"

Lyushan... What did that mean? Leigh inclined his head.

"*A ovo ye Katia Forgeron, priyashan. Govoren Stari Emaurri.*"

Katia bowed, smiling brightly.

Ashta eyed them around Ambriel's shoulder, her pale eyebrows drawn. "Your love?" she asked Ambriel in Old Emaurrian. *Incredulous* Old Emaurrian. "A human."

Ambriel urged her to accompany him, and reluctantly, she gave in, clinging tightly to his arm. "Leigh, this is my daughter, Ashta Windsong."

Windsong? Like the Priestess of Vervewood, stone-faced Aiolian? But he smiled warmly. "A pleasure, Ashta."

She frowned. "What's your interest in my father?"

Romantic but extremely physical?

"Ashta," Ambriel scolded.

Leigh cleared his throat. "Quite honorable?"

Ambriel cocked his head and flashed him a knowing smile. To Ashta, he said, "Entirely reciprocated."

She pressed her lips together and sighed through her nose.

Well, he'd certainly have his work cut out for him earning *her* approval.

"And you?" Ashta asked Katia, who bowed again.

"My name is Katia Forgeron, daughter of the Archon of the Forgeron Coven," she said firmly. "I come peacefully, in the hopes of fostering a relationship between our peoples."

Ruvel approached, a hand on his hip, and huffed. "We already experienced your people's concept of *peace* and have had enough."

A grimace from one of the other two light-elves. "We have our hands full with witches' troubles already, on both—"

"Merian, *zoshtavi*," Ruvel hissed, and Merian lowered her gaze.

"Witches' troubles," Ambriel repeated, raising Ashta's chin with a finger.

Her face went slack. "*Tata*, there is an—"

"Ashta!" Ruvel stepped toward her, shaking his head. "Don't—"

"Ferelen will tell him anyway," she snapped back. Clearly theirs was a love match made by the gods. She returned her gaze to Ambriel. "An army of undead from the northwest, from the mountains."

Undead.

"A necromancer," Leigh said. Just north of here was the Beaufoy Coven's territory, and their witches dealt in all manner of forbidden magic, including necromancy. Had one of them gone into fureur? If it was still ongoing, that meant a mage of incredibly bright anima. Limitless, even.

He shuddered.

Ava. Was she in danger?

No, Della and Axelle would keep her safe. They always had and always would. But—

"I am a wild mage," Leigh said, "or as Ambriel called me once... prophet. I will help your queendom in any way I can. Now tell me everything you know."

～

Olivia feathered the quill under her chin, staring at the drawing of the dragon in the massive *Compendium of the Immortals* in Old Sileni. The villa's library had a dictionary of Old Sileni to modern Sileni translation, of which she had a basic working proficiency, but the process of translating each to the next and accounting for dialect and style was tedious.

The book called them the *Dragon Lords*, the first and most powerful of the Immortals, and capable of miraculous feats. All of them harnessing anima from the earth, able to use all magic with mere *intention*, able to shift into any form. Some of the Dragon Lords were written to have shifted in a form and remained in it so long as to have forgotten their original forms. Some shifted into humans, some into wolves, birds, bears, and changing others to join them.

It was written that all Immortals had been either created or descended from the Dragon Lords. Offspring that self-selected over hundreds of thousands of years or more to become what they became. Elves. Werewolves. Dryads. Unicorns.

She wrinkled her nose at her notes.

A Dragon Lord may be killed but cannot die.

That couldn't be right. She'd bungled the translation somehow.

In any case, after two days of research, she still had no leads on Immortal medicine.

Whisper-soft footsteps traversed the small library, and a maid set a steaming cup of tea nearby, in the light of a ray of warm afternoon sunshine coming in from the window. A petite frame, gleaming braided hair, and big, chestnut-brown eyes.

Manon.

Jon had transferred the maid to *her* household—probably too awkward having his pagan ritual lover serving him.

That night, in the glow of the torches, he'd stood before her, naked, powerful. Dirt darkening his skin, covering nearly every inch of his big, hard body, his intense gaze had fixed on her. The chanting had been dense on the air, beating like a heart pumping blood, rhythmic, primal, and that intense gaze had darkened to rhythmic, primal purpose.

"My lady?" Manon's small voice intruded.

Straightening, Olivia swallowed. "You're still here?"

Manon reddened, folding into herself. "I beg your pardon, my lady, but I wondered if I might trouble you for just a moment—"

"What is it?" Olivia set the quill down and turned to her, crossing her legs.

"Well, it's—" Manon's hands fidgeted. "The girls have been talking about you being a powerful healer, and well, Clarice in His Majesty's household is with child and has the childbearing sickness. We thought—we were wondering, if it wouldn't be too much trouble, if—"

Smiling, Olivia held up a hand. "Say no more. If she's feeling ill, she may come to me at any time, and I can heal her," she said. "But unfortunately, healing magic isn't a long-term solution. An apothecary might be better suited for that."

Not that they *had* a Court Apothecary. Not yet, anyway. Many court positions still remained unfilled.

"Thank you, my lady." Manon curtsied and took her leave.

As she left, Jon sidled by through the doorway, and they exchanged a look. It was fleeting, so very fleeting, but there was a knowledge there between them that—in recent months—she envied, more and more.

He begged Manon's pardon and let her pass, then clearing his throat, entered the library. Away from the palace, he dressed simply, in just a white shirt and trousers, and yet it suited him so well. Gifted with natural good looks, he'd never needed embellishment.

"Are you all right?"

She glanced up at his face. "Yes. Why wouldn't I be?"

"You were frowning." He approached the table, tracing a finger over the dragon illustration, the woodsy smell of him near and heady.

Frowning... She shrugged. "Just a healing question. One of the maids is with child."

Jon spun, his head snapping to Manon's wake, and Olivia gasped, reaching for his hand.

"*Not* her," she blurted, and his taut bearing slowly relaxed, until he heaved a sigh and rubbed a hand over his face. "Clarice."

"Terra have mercy, Olivia, you do *not* simply say things like that and—"

She laughed, unable to keep it in.

He eyed her, lips pressed in a line, then looked back to the book. "Find anything interesting?"

"Interesting, yes. Useful? No. Unfortunately," she said with a grimace, sliding her notes over to him.

He licked his thumb and paged through them, his eyebrows creased together with focus as he read, curled over the table, shoulders taut—

No.

Divine, what was wrong with her? Everything about this was wrong, but whenever he was near her, more and more, her mind just went somewhere else. Somewhere... rhythmic. And primal.

She swallowed and reached for the notes. "Don't worry. No concoctions just yet."

He grinned, and Divine help her, she wanted to kiss that dimple. "So I shouldn't be worried about changing into a dragon or something?"

She laughed, louder than she'd intended, and shook her head. "Not just yet. At least not until I start experimenting."

Changing into a dragon. She chuckled under her breath as he arched an eyebrow.

"Olivia, I was wondering if you'd like to take a walk in the garden? Maybe we could talk a—"

"I—" she began. *Talk about how I'm losing my mind.* "I'd love to... but I have a lot of work I want to get done today. Another time?"

He frowned contemplatively, but nodded. "Of course. Another time." Sliding her tea closer, he smiled, but it didn't reach his eyes. "Don't forget to rest now and then, Olivia."

"I won't," she replied brightly as he took his leave.

Then she let herself crumple onto the table, resting her head on the page facing the dragon illustration.

Divine, she was making a fool of herself.

No matter what thoughts broke into her mind, he was her *king.* James's *son.* Rielle's former *lover.* It would only be the most awkward match ever, even if he did feel the same.

Which he didn't.

That gentle tone he took with her when he invited her to *talk*—oh, she knew it. She'd used it herself with colleagues who'd looked at her that certain way, and he'd say the same thing she always said to them. *I'm flattered, but I don't want to complicate our relationship. Can we still be friends?*

She heaved a sigh, and the illustrated page fluttered.

It was inevitable, but maybe once he finally said it, she'd be able to put all this behind her.

She eyed the tea, its surface still moving from when he'd slid it closer. He hadn't been with a woman in months, and it didn't seem like he intended to, at least not anytime soon. But maybe... maybe someday he'd look at her that certain way, hungrily, just once.

And maybe once would be all it took to answer that curiosity, to know what it felt like to be with him, just once, and dispel the alluring mystery that stalked her daydreams and left her no peace.

He'd had casual lovers before, or at least he had with Nora Marcel Vignon, but he wasn't that man anymore. But this could be different, couldn't it? Two friends taking solace in each other? He was in love with a woman he couldn't have, and she... she was right here. Would that be so bad?

She inhaled a deep breath, closing her eyes. *Face reality.*

They'd have that *talk* inevitably. And there was as much chance of *taking solace* as there was of him changing into a dragon.

"Changing into..."

She sat up, staring at the illustration, a thought blooming in her mind, unfurling, with the *Compendium of the Immortals* before her.

Immortal medicine... had been the wrong path.

Immortal.

There were countless tales—Immortals turning humans, the rare few who survived, into vampires, werewolves, all manner of monsters...

Immortal monsters.

If she couldn't find a cure or treatment for Jon's heart, could she find a way to change her king into an Immortal?

CHAPTER 25

*R*ielle pulled on her boots, hastily reading through her notes on Divinity Castle. If the trials were on the castle grounds, then there had to be some specialized area where they could take place.

The arena has been part of Divinity Castle since its establishment as headquarters of the—

Brennan slammed the book shut.

"Hey!"

He handed her a white mage coat and gave her a light push toward the door. "If you don't know it by now, then last-minute studying isn't going to do anything."

She grimaced but accepted the coat and dragged it on, then grabbed a small pouch from the desk. A small pouch containing the Sodalis ring Jon had given her.

Although she hadn't worn it in almost two months, its

arcanir could be a distinct advantage if any other mage attacked her. *No rules.*

"Come on," he said. "You don't want to be late. We have work to do."

Tucking the pouch away, she followed him downstairs, where the duchess, Caitlyn, and the boys—sniffling and coughing—wished her luck, while Una promised to be there soon with two friends.

Beneath a dark, stormy sky, Brennan swept her away and into the carriage, and they headed to the castle. From the seat across, he stared at her, and she stared right back.

He still hadn't promised not to manipulate her. The night of their argument, he'd told her about thrashing Kieran, and she'd had a momentary... lapse in judgment and had fallen into bed with him. But since then, she'd made it very clear what she expected, and he'd made it very clear she shouldn't hold her breath.

That was just fine. It had been two days since they'd last been together, and she could hold out longer than he could.

Probably.

She'd spent the last two days poring over her books, looking for anything that could help with the first trial. It was at the castle, so that was something, at least. It would likely be in the arena, or maybe in the great hall or the courtyard, depending on what would be required. Somewhere that could showcase the spectacle—

"How much longer will this go on?" he murmured, with a slow, bored blink.

"Until you see reason." She made a show of looking out the carriage window as thunder rumbled.

He huffed an amused breath. "I could say the same."

She rolled her eyes.

"In a few short months, I'm going to vow to protect you as long as I live," he said evenly. "Sometimes that'll mean withholding things."

She grunted.

"Actually, by telling you what I did, I've made you a principal to high treason," he said. "If you're revealed, the king could have you executed just for knowing what you do and not immediately confessing."

"Then maybe I should tell him," she bit out.

"And condemn our family?" Brennan crossed his arms, biceps bulging against his overcoat's sleeves. "Besides, somehow I doubt Jon will execute *you*."

She sighed. "Then why bring it up?"

"Because if he were anyone else, I would have been signing your death warrant. All in the name of 'truth.' I'd rather you be safe."

"And blissfully ignorant?" she blurted, scowling. "Brennan, I don't want to be some possession for you to keep safe. I want to be your partner, and share in everything you do, good and bad."

"What I do is dangerous."

She held out her arms. Did he not know her life? She didn't spend it petting kittens and picking wildflowers. "All right, then. Suppose the tables are turned, and *I* want to keep *you* safe. Should I hide things from you and lie to you?"

He scoffed, shaking his head as he looked away. "I'm indestructible, bride."

Indestructible. Of course.

How could he even say those words when she'd lain for hours in the desert next to his dead body?

He let out a breath. "Can we just... start over?"

Starting over, putting all of this behind them—yes, it would be wonderful. "But nothing's changed."

Closing his eyes a moment, he said, "I'll... try."

The carriage hurtled over a rough patch of road, and she jostled along with it. *Try.* That was change, wasn't it? "No more secrets, no more omissions, no more lies or manipulations—"

"I said I'd try," he repeated. "What else do you want from me, Rielle?" He scrubbed a hand over his face.

They were on their way to Divinity Castle, where he was about to search for the Archives and attempt to infiltrate them, a deadly transgression that could get him killed.

Where she was about to compete in a trial that could claim her life.

The last thing she wanted was for either of them to go on tonight still at odds with each other.

She rubbed her sweaty palms on her knees. "I don't want us to fight anymore."

He reached across the carriage and covered her hand with his. "Neither do I."

As the rain came down, Brennan walked Rielle across the causeway to the castle, eyeing the members of the Divine Guard in blue overcoats, stationed in key locations. In all of Magehold, they numbered about a small company, with the majority—some hundred or so—concentrated inside the castle, of course.

Tonight, while Rielle competed in whatever trial the Grand Divinus had devised, he would locate the Archives of Mage-hold. The primary entrance was through the tightly guarded Hensar, the headquarters of the Divinity's elite agents, but there had to be another way in.

The castle was rumored to have all manner of hidden doors

and passages—and while all eyes were fixed on the trial, he would find his route.

Better that Mother and Caitlyn were staying home, taking care of the boys. Nora had made her excuses and left the villa in style. Una was arriving separately. At least there would be fewer questions about where he was disappearing to.

Holding his hand, Rielle was impeccable in her white mage coat, her hair braided tight. Her pulse and breathing were even, and she stared down the entrance with a glare that could kill. Good. Perhaps tonight, she'd have to.

No matter what Jon said to her, she saw this as fighting for Laurentine, and all of Emaurria, and she'd never been one to step away from a challenge.

As they entered, he swept the shadowy corners with a careful gaze, scented the air for changes indicating concealed doors and passages. Nothing yet.

In the great hall, a number of master mages, marked by the four-bar chevron on their double-breasted overcoats, already awaited, some with small chattering entourages or sullen partners and friends, others wholly alone. Jon and Olivia stood off to the side, enshrined among members of Jon's Royal Guard, impossible to miss.

Although no crown graced his head, Jon's finery was unmistakably royal—a timelier tailor than Libretti, then. He wore a fitted crimson velvet overcoat trimmed in gold, and beneath it, a shirt of the brightest white, over white trousers tucked into gleaming black riding boots. Like his Royal Guard, Jon wore his weapons belt tonight, bearing both his arcanir long sword and a dagger, a privilege the Grand Divinus must have afforded him as a monarch. The trials would be dangerous, then.

Next to him, Olivia was an emerald jewel, dressed in a fine brocade gown with long, fluttering sleeves edged in silver, her shining hair coiled intricately about her head. If anyone wondered whether she belonged to the king, the pair they made here would remove all doubt.

As soon as Olivia's gaze met his, she glanced at Rielle, and set off at a brisk pace across the marble floor, her slippered feet clicking an echoing staccato.

Rielle turned her head to the sound. "Olivia," she breathed, and rushed to meet her. They embraced. "I'm so glad you're here."

"As if I'd miss this?" Olivia grinned. "These other mages won't know what hit them."

"I wonder if this is all of them," Rielle said, her narrowed gaze meandering from one master mage to the next. "I count eight."

As Jon walked up, Rielle bowed, her heartbeat quickening—just for a moment. So he still had that effect on her.

"A pleasure to see you again so soon, Your Majesty," he said, as cordially as he could muster, bowing. Even across the Shining Sea, Jon was inescapable.

With an uneasy smile, Jon inclined his head to them. "Good evening to you both," he greeted, his gaze sliding to Rielle. "I think we have yet to see the final candidate here—actually, he arrived on Captain Verib's ship."

So her brother had shown up after all.

Rielle's pulse raced as the blood drained from her face. He took her hand.

"Verib is here?" she asked. "Where is he staying?"

Jon arched a brow, eyeing her carefully. "How do you know him?"

She blinked. "He—Brennan and I sailed home aboard his ship from Sonbahar."

"Who's the candidate?" Brennan asked.

Olivia shrugged. "I'm not sure. But he set out from Gazgan, so maybe a Sonbaharan mage."

Rielle stiffened.

"I doubt it's anyone who'd recognize you," he whispered in her ear, and kissed her cheek. "And if it is, he'll be leaving here in pieces."

It was no easy thing letting her compete here, alone, while he infiltrated the Archives. But each of these other mages knew to whom she belonged, and knew that a Marcel's vengeance was never done. That would offer her some measure of protection.

And if it didn't, she had but to pull on the bond, and Archives or not, Divine Guard or not, he'd be at her side, ripping apart anyone who so much as looked at her wrong.

Breathing deeply, she nodded. "No rules," she murmured icily. "If anyone recognizes me and starts trouble, I'm not in arcanir chains here. It'll be the last thing he does."

Jon watched them gravely, and when Olivia took his arm, he visibly relaxed, although he turned over a small, smooth blue stone in his hand.

"I see no Sonbaharan master here," Olivia said, "but I recognize many of these by reputation." She nodded to a short, dark-haired Sileni young woman with silvery eyes. "That's Ariana Orsa, a gifted lucent. She's become well known recently for beginning work on a translation and update of a compendium of Immortal peoples—a highly anticipated work. Yesterday, Jon and I picked up the original she's working from."

Picked up? She spoke as though they spent their evenings on the town.

Olivia glanced at a tall, lanky man with shoulder-length wavy black hair pulled back well above his nape. "That's Luca Iagar, the famous healer. I'll have to catch him sometime."

She looked over the crowd. "And there"—the copper-haired

giant who'd accosted Rielle—"that's Riordan Mac Carra, probably your biggest competition. There are rumors he can conjure not just *inanimate* magical constructs, but *beings*."

Animate magical constructs? That was magic the likes of which only one other mage in existence was known to perform. A magister, no less.

Had he known Rielle was competing? Was that why he'd accosted her? And next to him stood a dark-haired rail-thin man, also in a master's coat, faded black, his green gaze scanning the great hall. Picking apart scents, he recognized this one—from the day Rielle had gone to the temple garden. He might have been lurking in the shadows, following her, but why?

"It's *him*," she snarled. She looked Mac Carra's way with hard eyes, and the Morwenian copperhead actually had the audacity to *wink* at her and broaden his grin. She blew him a kiss, then swiped a finger across her throat while winking back.

That's my snarling little she-wolf. He grinned smugly, drawing her in a little closer.

Jon stiffened next to him. "You know him?" An edge rode his voice, suspicious, alert.

"We met. Briefly," Rielle answered for him, icy eyes narrowed. She shrugged a shoulder. "So he can conjure animate magical constructs," she said evenly. "I've defeated Flame, Phantom, and Shadow. I'll defeat anything he sends my way."

Jon's eyes gleamed as he crossed his arms, watching her with unmistakable pride. "Any candidate that underestimates your resolve is in for a surprise. You're in your element."

She met his gaze with a wry grin. "Luckily there are no turtles here."

Jon dipped his head, grinning wryly as he lowered his gaze.

Turtles? What were they on about?

Olivia's eyebrows knitted together, then her mouth fell open. Did she know something about it?

A tall, dark man walked in through the doors to the great hall, with his long, sable hair in a bun at the nape of his neck, flanked by a woman covered in a teal thiyawb and halla. He wore the master mage's four-bar chevron on his black overcoat.

"Tariq al-Rhamani," Olivia whispered. "So *that's* who arrived aboard the *Liberté*."

Rielle glanced her way, but it was Jon who leaned in. "He's the bastard son of Prince Raadi El-Amin abd Hassan abd Ahmad of Sonbahar, Princess Sandrine's husband."

Princess Sandrine, who rallied factions against Jon, who mobilized forces to invade Emaurria and install herself as its ruler.

The Magister Trials were tangled enough without regional politics knotting them up further.

Another late arrival—Una, by her scent. She walked in, wearing a golden overcoat sashed with red, along with two friends. With a quick look about the hall, her eyes settled on him, and he cocked his head toward Rielle.

"You made it," Rielle said with a smile as Una approached.

"No way I'd miss this," she said, clasping her hands behind her back. "It's not every day a Marcel trounces mages of international renown."

Rielle met her grin with a blush, and Una shot him a knowing smile. She didn't have to say it—she was pleased they'd made up.

So was he.

A turn of footsteps echoed from the raised dais, and the entire hall quieted.

At the front, the Grand Divinus stood in glittering, golden

regalia, her face dusted with a shimmery powder that softened her harsh lines.

She raised her arms. "Welcome to the first of the Magister Trials," the Grand Divinus declared, gesturing to the entire hall. "Tonight's survivors will move on to the second trial three days from now."

Survivors? He pulled Rielle closer, and she leaned in to him.

The Grand Divinus looked out at the crowd with a smug smile. "But first, I'll introduce to you the best of the best, who have been chosen to take part in this year's trials.

A mage next to her gestured above him, and a massive translucent plane hovered above him, like a mirror, and showed a young woman's heart-shaped face.

"From Silen, Master Ariana Orsa."

Orsa stepped forward among the crowd, the same woman as in the illusion.

The face in the illusion changed to a man's.

"From Pryndon, Master Cadan Bexley." A slight man with spectacles and short, brown curls bowed. Bexley? His ability to transmute anything into anything was world renowned.

Faces in the spell shifted from each to the next. "From Kamerai, Master Sen Taneie. From the Kezan Isles, Master Luca Iagar. From Ferrante, Master Telva Cerdán. From Morwen, Master Riordan Mac Carra. From Sonbahar, Master Tariq al-Rhamani. From Hongo, Master Nandi Sinethemba."

Each candidate stepped forward at their name.

"And from Emaurria, Master Favrielle Amadour Lothaire."

And so did Rielle, eyeing the massive magical display of her nervous face, and schooling it to a lukewarm smile.

"From among these nine, only one will become a magister

after this year's third trial, proving him or herself capable of excellence in these new, harsh times."

With a gesture, the Grand Divinus spelled aside a banner, where a sconce was hidden, unlit. She gestured again, and the sconce clicked, lowering.

The center of the great hall rumbled.

Beneath the floor, a barely audible whirring and clinking passed.

All those gathered receded as the marble-tiled floor split in quarters and opened to a descending stair.

"Not the arena," Rielle murmured under her breath.

"Below, a labyrinth awaits, and it is designed to test for the perceptiveness all magisters must possess. At its end are the keys to your next trial. Be the first, and choose your key." The Grand Divinus motioned to the stairs.

Rielle squeezed his hand and turned to him with a resolute nod.

This was *her* choice. If it were up to him, he'd have her loaded up in a carriage right now and safely at home.

But here they were. He'd be sneaking out of the great hall shortly to infiltrate the never-before-infiltrated Archives, and she'd be going underground with eight other mages who'd gladly see her fail, or worse.

She'd emerge safely. She had to.

He cupped her cheek, and she covered his hand, closed her eyes, and kissed it. "If you need me, you know what to do," he whispered. Just a pull of the bond, and he'd be there.

She nodded. "I know."

A moment of her warmth, her love, then she leaned in and pressed her lips to his, before looking upon him one last time, releasing his hand, and descending into the dark.

CHAPTER 26

*R*ielle followed the steps with the other eight candidates, leaving Brennan, Jon, Olivia, and Una behind. She looked back over her shoulder once more to see their faces.

Survivors, the Grand Divinus had said.

She clenched a fist. If the Grand Divinus planned to kill her, she wouldn't go quietly. Or without burning a raging inferno right in the middle of this castle.

The stairwell leading below was sparsely lit with torches, but a candlelight spell preceded them downward through the tight, dusty stone corridor. A look beside her, and it was al-Rhamani who'd cast it.

A pyromancer, then, unless he was a binary, ternary, or quaternary elementalist. Any elemental magic, and she'd know who to watch for.

The Grand Divinus brought up the rear with her Divine Guard, her presence driving them to a fork in the path, where it split in three. Each carved-stone tunnel led into blackness, mysterious and deep. "You may choose any path and begin at any time—there are no rules."

Just like that.

The rightmost path felt best, and as she moved toward its entrance, al-Rhamani and the Ferrante master, Telva Cerdán, a middle-aged woman with a thick bun of black hair and dense, dark lashes rimming her keen brown eyes, moved with her. They all stopped, glancing at one another.

Bexley, Orsa, and Sinethemba took the center, and Mac Carra, Iagar, and Taneie took the left.

There was no telling what awaited down the corridors. Being the first to go could either be an advantage or an assured death.

No thanks.

She'd been invited to the Magister Trials and was participating—she had nothing more to prove. There was no reason to charge ahead and bear the brunt of the risk.

Al-Rhamani unbuttoned his black master mage coat, swept it back, and proceeded first down the rightmost passage.

This was it. The first step of the first trial.

I hope you're safe, Brennan. He had his own trial ahead of him, as dangerous as this, if not more.

Rielle exchanged a look with Telva, whose brown eyes searched hers, and they followed as the other two groups proceeded.

The others' footsteps, audible at first, slowly faded the deeper she and Telva progressed down the corridor, behind al-Rhamani's sure-footed strides.

She kept her hand ready to cast, a second away from a flame cloak, in case al-Rhamani, Telva, or anyone else decided to cut the competition by one elementalist.

Here, corralled with two other mages, Rielle removed the

pouch containing Jon's Sodalis ring from her coat. Tonight she had eight rivals, all of whom used magic as their weapon, with no rules to bind them but their honor.

She knew none of them, nor what honor meant to any of them. But if they tried to cast anything on her, she'd not only have her magic, but arcanir to dispel it.

She emptied the pouch and placed the ring on her thumb, where it had once been before Shadow had abducted her all those months ago.

Accept it, with my love, he'd once said, and he'd swept her up, held her close, tipped her chin up to his mouth. She'd opened to him, come home in his arms, like a wave flowing in to shore.

Their love had broken, but he'd still given her this ring once more in Courdeval.

"It is very dear to you," Telva said softly, in heavily accented Emaurrian.

"Once." Rielle forced a smile.

"It still is." Telva stared into nothing ahead of her with an intensity most people rarely achieved in their lifetime. An augur, maybe? "And always will be."

She wore a different man's ring on each of her hands—the Sodalis ring on her right thumb, and the engagement ring on her left ring finger. One she'd keep close for the rest of her life, and the other—just a memory.

She followed Telva's gaze to her own undulating fingers. Just nerves, nothing more. She fisted her hands and looked ahead.

"It is no small defense you carry," Telva whispered, "but the feel of it on your hand, its solace, has immeasurable value, too." She fingered a beaded bracelet circling her wrist. "From my daughter," she added with a smile, and Rielle couldn't help but mirror the expression.

Telva had loved ones at home, too.

Remembering that—others supporting her and wishing her well—was a strength, too. She wasn't the only one counting on her success and survival. Brennan, Jon, and Olivia did, too, as complicated as this tie between her performance and Emaurria was.

Laurentine's people, and all those up and down the coast along the Shining Sea, needed her help.

All of Emaurria—to get the Divinity's mages for Jon— needed her help.

And if Shadow's allegations were true, many potential novices and their families counted on her as well.

So many relied on her, and she wouldn't let them down. Not a chance.

Telva had the same, no doubt. Each one of them did.

"Good luck to you," she said to Telva, and meant it.

"And to you."

Al-Rhamani turned on his heel. "This is a *competition*," he said in perfect Emaurrian, narrowing his eyes at each of them. "Each of you would do well to remember that. And keep quiet."

"You can win a competition by your own merit," Rielle shot back. "Or are you so unsure of your own skills?"

He scoffed, walking backward, when his step depressed a tile in the corridor.

Teetering, he reached for them as a clicking came from the walls.

She grabbed his arm and yanked him back, and they both tumbled to the floor as bolts shot from the walls ahead.

He rolled off her and gaped at the needle-sharp projectiles

littering the area before them. "You—" He turned and gawked at her. "You saved my life."

Breathing hard, she struggled to look away from the death trap. "I—"

She shrugged. It hadn't occurred to her not to.

Telva knelt before the trap and picked up one of the bolts, then held it to the light of al-Rhamani's candlelight spell. Light reflected off its razor-sharp, coated edge. Poison?

Al-Rhamani rose and offered her a hand.

"Thanks," he bit out. As he pulled her to her feet, he added, "But it was incredibly stupid of you. Without lifting a finger, you could have faced one fewer mage in this competition."

With a sigh, she replied, "You're welcome."

Telva led the way as the corridor took a sharp left turn.

Screams echoed from the distance.

Far ahead of them, Mac Carra leaned against the stone wall, massive arms crossed, looking down, wisps of copper hair in his face.

Below, there was nothing but total darkness—a pit, the ground open to an abyss.

"Help me! Mac Carra!" A man's voice called from below. "I'll withdraw! I'll tell you your future!"

Mac Carra shook his head, grinning.

There—on the edge—two sets of fingers clinging desperately.

One set of fingers disappeared as she ran ahead of Telva, darting for them, and slid onto the gritty ground to catch a wrist with both hands.

The Kamerish master, Sen Taneie, looked up at her with dark eyes so like Leigh's, dangling in a bottomless chasm.

"I've got you," she said, even as her arms trembled.

"Don't let go!" He reached for her wrist, again and again,

trying to catch hold as his arm slipped from her weakening grasp. "I'll withdraw—I swear it—just don't let go!"

"An updraft," she said, gesturing the spell as he slapped her hand in another attempt to grasp it. "Aeromancy. It'll catch you!"

As she gestured the spell again, a grasp on her upper arm pulled her off her feet.

Screams—Sen—

Mac Carra raised her off the floor, slapping her hand as she frantically gestured the updraft.

"No," he said firmly.

The scream faded and stopped.

She winced, a shudder weaving down her spine. Sen had —He was—

She clung to Mac Carra's forearms, trying to pull up some of her weight. His eyes were ice, and after Sen, she—perhaps she was next.

If he let her go, she could cast an updraft, but not if he killed her first.

No, you don't.

Mac Carra moved her over the pit as she gestured a freeze spell up his feet, meeting his eyes evenly as her ice climbed his legs.

His fingers swept a turn, and a *living flame* circled his feet, melting her spell with every step. Shaped vaguely like a human figure, it glided about him, burning bright.

Divine, she'd heard of elementals, but never seen one, *ever*, much less conjured.

But still, her freeze spell climbed his body.

"You're bonny, little flower, but not too bright," he said with a handsome grin, so unfit for this cruelty.

"Put her back," Tariq said behind him, with Telva in a ready stance next to him.

Mac Carra rumbled a laugh, his cold eyes never leaving hers. "None of you are too bright." The laughter in his too-vivid nightshade-green eyes faded. "But"—he looked her up and down, as no one had since Zahib—since *Farrad* had—"if I let you fall to your death now, fancy woman as you are, I'd always regret never having bedded you first."

Let me fall. Just do it, and I'll surprise you, boor. I'll surprise you.

BRENNAN STRODE down the well-lit hall toward the garderobe, passing two stern-faced members of the Divine Guard. If he timed this correctly, they'd change shifts shortly, and he'd—

There. Incoming booted footsteps. As the guards exchanged words, Brennan passed the garderobe and tucked himself into another hall, dark, disused.

He kept to the wall, wrapped in its shadows, and followed his nose to mustier air. Past an alcove, he paused. That's where it was coming from, somehow.

This could be his way in. Some sort of passage to the Archives.

Crouching, he looked for signs of entry. Disturbed dust, old footprints.

Knocking on the wall and listening to the acoustics would reveal more—along with himself, if anyone heard. There were no nearby fresh scents, but when it came to the Divinity, he couldn't rule out trickery.

He straightened, searching the wall for any obvious mechanism, but there were no sconces or fixtures of any kind nearby.

This section of the wall itself was stone, and he ran his palms over it, feeling for any particular piece with give.

Leaning in close, he breathed in deep, casting aside the stone, timber, old dust, slight hint of mold, mouse droppings, to focus on the barest hint of skin oils, human scents, concentrated on—

He pressed a section of stone with a few fingertips marking its scent, and it gave way with a slight click, disarming a locking mechanism of some kind. The wall itself didn't budge.

Spreading his fingers against it, he leaned forward, distributing his weight against different portions in turn until at last, one side pushed inward, stone grating against stone.

With any luck, not loudly enough to garner attention.

He moved it only enough to slip into the dark on the other side, the source of the mustiness he'd detected earlier. A hidden corridor, narrow, tight. No one could learn he'd found it, so he pushed the panel back into place as best he could, wincing as the stone grated once more.

His vision was excellent in the dark, for all the good it did him in such a tight passage. It seemed to wedge between rooms, and as he moved through it, small streams of candlelight occasionally needled through minuscule holes. Made for spies.

The corridor itself was barely wide enough for his frame, far better suited to his Wolf, but then he'd miss anything at his human form's eye level. He suppressed a sigh.

The primary entrance to the Archives was through the Hensar, which meant finding the Hensar would help lead him to the vault's location. From there, he'd find another way in—other than trying to go through the Divinity's most elite agents.

The Hensar was in the northwest wing, so he'd have to make his way up and around as far as these corridors allowed—

and before the first trial was over. Nine candidates would mean considerable time, but more than an hour? Two? Not likely.

With nothing but his nose and sense of direction, he picked his way silently through the dark as quickly as he dared, closing in on the northwest wing. He passed other locking mechanisms, other entry panels with fresher air and less dust, used more recently, perhaps. That could be used at any time.

Finally, around a corner, light flirted with shadow—a torch. And if there was a torch, someone had lit it... for use. Someone was here.

He couldn't afford to be recognized. The next Duke of Maerleth Tainn, caught infiltrating the inner sanctum of the Divinity?

Wolf form. It would have to be wolf form.

He stripped off his overcoat, shirt, belt, trousers, boots, and braies, and left them tucked into a small alcove in the dark, then welcomed the Wolf. Hands became paws and fur spiked from his skin as the agony of the Change rippled through him; he doubled over, his claws striking stone as his human bones transformed to lupine.

The mustiness of dust and mold inundated his nostrils, and old blood stained into ancient stone. Distant voices echoed, muffled, tucked far into the labyrinth of rooms.

Time dwindled, and he had until the end of the first trial to find a way into the Archives. He eyed the illumination dancing on the floor from around the corner and warily approached to peek around.

A wider but empty corridor, lit with a single sconce.

Through the shadows, he crept closer, and that scent of old blood intensified. He slowed, his nose lowered to the floor, where traces of old spatter had set in. A little closer, and the traces became something more, a splatter, scrubbed with soap but not cleaned well enough.

And then before him—there, between the floor tiles, the slightest dip.

A trap door. Someone had met his end here.

Backing up, he sized up the distance, then took off at a run and leaped.

He landed, clear of it, and took to the shadows once more. Wherever these hidden passages led, it had to be somewhere worth going. There was no sense in trapping a path to somewhere unimportant.

Torches became more frequent the farther in he went, and among the grid of paths, there were even small chambers, places where there must have been centuries of secret meetings for all manner of dark schemes, quiet executions. And then—

Approaching voices. Steps. Human scents.

He froze, backed up toward a dark alcove, and tucked himself into its concealment.

Sileni voices, talking about the labyrinth, about only seven candidates being able to emerge victorious—of the nine.

Beneath everything, deep in his core, the bond was still there. *She* was still there. Rielle would be one of the seven; she had to be.

If she ran into serious danger, she'd pull on the bond. She would.

There was no scent of magic to them. Non-mages. They had to have sigils and arcanir—perhaps to guard against mage intruders.

He liked his chances against mages. And he liked his chances against non-mages even more. If this was all the security the Divinity had to offer, he'd be in the Archives tonight, destroy any evidence of conspiracy with his father, and leave with all the proof he needed that the Divinity was made of lies and murder.

They approached. If they saw him, he'd leap for the throat of one, and then tackle the other—with any luck, before he could scream.

The guards passed him and turned a corner. Part of him looked after them wistfully; it had been too long since the Wolf had spilled blood.

But Rielle's kept him sated every month.

The voices continued fading, and he proceeded toward the northwest wing, toward the Hensar. It had to be close; he'd been walking for nearly half an hour.

Deeper in, the corridors were well lit, the air fresher. More frequently used passages. The locking mechanisms appeared often, with their matching entry panels, the floor beneath them clean.

These had to be important rooms, occupied by guests who preferred to keep their comings and goings secret.

Soon he came upon a battened door. Situated between two statues on massive plinths—seven-headed serpents. Hydras. Mythical beasts with venomous breath, so poisonous that even their tracks were deadly.

The door itself was sturdy, ornate, etched with faces— masked, stony, even burning—tormented, grotesque, but... there was that same locking mechanism. From this side, pulled down, it would allow the door to be pulled open.

The floor before him was even. No stench of old blood. Not even any dust—it had to be used, or at least cleaned, regularly.

Distant voices carried down a nearby corridor.

Nox's black breath.

He sized up the lock. Jumping the distance would be simple

enough; he could bite down on the lock, then pull the door open and slip in.

If he was seen, he would be naught more than a wolf, some creature that had wandered in and now desperately searched for exit.

Now or never.

He jumped for the lock, caught it in his teeth—

Needling pain pricked him in a dozen places on his body, and his jaw released.

He dropped to the stone, muzzle and face burning, tingling, and the rest of him was on fire.

Shit.

Backing up on unsteady legs, he looked over his shoulder, wincing through the flame in his flesh, head swimming.

Fine needles protruded from his fur.

Shit, shit, shit.

One of his paws went numb, then quickly another, and his legs gave out under him. Pins and needles tingled in every part of him that hadn't numbed.

But it began to deaden every part of his body.

He couldn't hold the Change. Before his eyes, his paws yielded to his human hands.

He breathed harder—or tried to—but couldn't fill his lungs.

His Change had broken.

The voices drew nearer.

Move, damn it. He willed his limbs to obey, but they refused, even as air became scarce, abandoning him and too stubborn to return. If he was caught here, especially in his human form—

Black spots stained his vision as he blinked sluggishly.

The swish of blades pulled from scabbards—

Booted footsteps closed in, fingers fisting in his hair, and his skin scraped against stone. Dragged. Somewhere.

A torch blurred by, and another.

"...naked... sick bastard..." one of them said.

Move... damn it... He tried to reach the hand fisted in his hair, or for the one looped under his shoulder, but his arm only dragged against the stone floor. Even his fingers wouldn't move.

Dark walls loomed, close together. One of the small chambers.

Quiet executions. He could have laughed, if only his vocal cords would respond. If only he weren't about to be thrashed... or worse.

He was unceremoniously thrown onto his face, seeing the floor coming and unable to do anything about it.

It didn't hurt, and these two guards were going to kill him.

Nox damn everything.

Those fingers clenched through his hair again, yanking his head up, and a blade glinted in the dim torchlight. Arcanir.

It swept under his chin and arced its sharp bite all the way across his neck.

CHAPTER 27

*A*s Mac Carra's flame elemental melted his feet free, he lowered her, his massive arm steady, and took a step back, ice cracking off his trousers. He set her on her knees before him, hard upon the stone floor, holding her still as he peered down at her. "You look rather fine just there."

She gestured a flame cloak in place.

He yanked his hands back as she spelled a gust of aeromancy so strong it threw him onto his backside and extinguished his fire elemental.

Before he landed, she held an ice spike before his chest and grounded geomancy in the tiles beneath him. In a second, she could rip them away and see him fall through the floor.

"Touch me again, *look* at me like that again," she said through clenched teeth, "and you will be a charred, blood-strewn paste."

Tariq held a wind wall behind Mac Carra—he must have put it in place against the gust to protect himself and Telva.

Mac Carra's fingers moved—

She shot the ice spike toward his chest as he conjured a shield to block it; then she raised the tiles into a stone wall between herself and Mac Carra, forcing the flame cloak to dispel.

Leaving him with Tariq and Telva.

Damn it. She stomped her foot.

She should dispel the geomancy, kill the boor, let Tariq and Telva through—

But she hadn't come here to kill. She sighed, sweeping stray hair from her eyes.

They'd either work together and get past her stone wall, or they'd fight and hopefully subdue Mac Carra, and perhaps between Tariq and Telva, they'd figure out a way past it.

A great thud hit the stone wall, and it shuddered. The time to leave was *now*.

Casting earthsight, she searched her surroundings for the others. Most clustered ahead and to the left, so she dispelled it and chose that direction. Perhaps the routes had converged, and they were all near the end.

She spelled a stone path over the pit, crossed, and left it in case Tariq and Telva followed. It was the least she could do to make up for leaving them with the likes of Mac Carra.

The corridors were dark and quiet—all too quiet—as she made her way deeper, taking any turns that took her left or ahead.

Activated traps lingered in some areas—oil, nail-studded rams, pits. Others must have already passed through. It meant the route was safer, but she was behind. And at what cost?

A distant, quiet voice called out.

As she continued, the voice became clearer, louder. A girl's.

"Chao?" Sileni for *hello*.

Ahead lay another pit, this one narrower. No, *narrowing*. It tightened an inch.

"*Che nessuno? Chao?*"

She peered over the edge. Far below, a young woman braced against both walls of the pit with her arms and legs, keeping herself steady. Dark hair in a braided bun. Ariana Orsa.

"Run into some trouble?" Rielle asked.

Ariana looked up, eyes widening. "Ah, you! Um, Gabrielle!"

Rielle arched a brow. "Favrielle."

Ariana winced. "That's it. Oops."

The pit narrowed another inch, and Ariana staggered but caught herself. "You wouldn't, um, be willing to lend a hand, would you?"

With a sigh, Rielle squinted into the darkness.

"Oh! Um... So there's also this rope around my ankle with a weight, courtesy of Bexley, and it's... well, pulling me down." Ariana puffed a breath and wisped a lock of hair off her nose—for a moment—then grimaced.

Rielle almost wanted to laugh. *Almost.* "That's not good."

"No, it isn't. Not good at all, really." Ariana blew out another breath.

As the pit narrowed yet again, Rielle spelled an updraft inside and jumped in. She thickened the gusting air to catch her just at Ariana's level, and it did, blowing her coat and braid up about her.

It would be costly to maintain for long, but her anima was still bright.

"Hello," Ariana said, her olive cheeks flushing as Rielle examined the rope around her ankle.

She nodded a greeting in reply, then spelled a flame in her free hand. "I don't know what'll happen when I break this rope, so be prepared for a... swift ascent."

Smiling, Ariana nodded half a dozen times. "Ready when you are."

Something hit her in the back from above. A rock.

Up high, Mac Carra waved at her as he jumped over the gap, followed by a wincing Tariq and Telva.

Smug boor.

After hopping across, Telva glanced over the side. "Need any help?"

"I've got this," Rielle called softly. "Get clear of the pit. It's going to get... windy."

Telva nodded. "Good luck to you." And disappeared.

"Friends," Ariana blurted. "It's nice to have, um, friends. I wish my group had been friendlier. Well, friendly enough not to, well, push me in here and leave me to die. Bexley said I'd find my way eventu—"

"Prepare yourself." Rielle burned the rope, and just as it charred through, she flared the updraft, sending them both flying back up into the corridor.

Her palms met the ceiling, and she dispelled the aeromancy, casting a stone slab over the pit as they landed heavily.

Ariana clutched her face, which apparently had hit the ceiling. "Ow," she murmured, then rubbed her backside. "Also *ow.*"

Rielle shook her head and let her laugh free this time.

"Favrielle, um, I think we're the last ones left, and I really hate to do this, but—"

A bright flash of light blinded her field of vision.

Divine's flaming fire—she covered her aching eyes, hissing at the pain, while quick footsteps retreated.

Not too bright, Mac Carra had said. Brennan would tease her for this later.

She struggled to her feet, bracing a hand on the wall, and forged ahead as her vision began to return.

After trudging into a pile of rubble, she scrambled over it to enter a small chamber with a single door. In the center were seven plinths, all empty but for one.

She approached the only one bearing an item, a dark scale of some kind, the size of her palm, and she took it. It was hard as stone, but smooth as a snakeskin.

There was nowhere to go but through the door.

She cast a flame cloak, and when the flames wrapped her entirely, she turned the knob.

On the other side were the other candidates, some dusty and injured, in a circular stone chamber bearing only torches and ascending stairs leading to no exit. The door thudded shut behind her, and she risked only a quick glance backward.

There was no knob. It only opened from the other side.

There were only six of the other candidates before her, which meant two hadn't made it yet. Sen was one... and the other was—

Before her stood Tariq, Telva, Ariana, Bexley, Nandi, and Mac Carra. Which left... the Kezani master, Luca Iagar. What had happened to him? Was he still coming?

There had been no eighth plinth. Maybe only seven were supposed to advance.

Tariq sauntered over to her. "You made it."

"No thanks to you," she remarked, rubbing the scale she held.

He smirked. "Every man for himself. Besides, I knew you'd make it out."

Telva approached with a warm smile. "It was a generous thing you did." Her gaze darted toward Ariana and back, who seemed to be trying very hard to look everywhere *but* at her. "Even if not everyone deserves it."

Finally there was a great sigh, and eyes fixed on the ceiling, Ariana trudged to them.

"I'm... sorry," Ariana murmured, before meeting her gaze and then looking away again. "I really appreciate you saving me and everything, but, um, I came here to pursue something really important, and I had to make sure I passed the first trial, so... I did what I had to do, and it feels really bad, but you understand, don't you? It wasn't like I... *wanted* to do that or anything, I just—I couldn't—"

Rielle raised a hand. "Save it. It was an underhanded thing to do. We're competitors, but we don't have to be *enemies*."

Ariana's cheeks colored, and she lowered her gaze. "I really *am* sorry, and if I could save your life in exchange, I would," she murmured. "But... ah! Um, you got the basilisk scale. Maybe that'll help you."

Basilisk scale? Was that it? She looked at the thing, rubbed it.

"I got the wyvern tooth." Ariana removed a long, narrow incisor from her coat. "For once, the random things I know actually pay off! It should be easier to pass the second trial if you know what you're facing, shouldn't it?"

I'm facing a basilisk. She tightened her hold on the scale. How she'd fight a basilisk, she had no idea. There would be a mountain of research ahead of her.

Telva raised a black feather before Ariana, and Tariq revealed a horn.

Shaking her head, Ariana sighed. "Sorry. I'm only helping the person who saved my life, so, um, maybe you should've done that if you wanted me to help you back."

Tariq rolled his eyes and stuffed the horn back into his dusty coat.

"I would have," Telva said, "if my magic had allowed."

What magic was that, exactly? Telva hadn't revealed it.

Just then, a great rumbling filled the chamber. As the door opened behind her, Rielle looked back.

It flung wide, and Luca Iagar gestured a spell at the nearest mage—the Hongo master, Nandi Sinethemba.

She immediately collapsed in a deep slumber, and Luca crouched, patting her coat, then removed a large—it looked like a toenail? But the size of a person's head.

Rielle gasped, and a couple more rippled through the group.

As Luca pulled it away, the ceiling opened above them, and the Divine Guard stood aside.

Everyone moved to ascend the steps.

"You just—" she stammered as Luca sauntered past her.

"No rules," Luca remarked as he ascended the steps, raking fingers through his shoulder-length black locks.

Shaking her head, she trudged up the steps herself, out to the far side of the great hall.

The Grand Divinus sat on a massive golden chair, legs crossed, surrounded by her Divine Guard. Stone ground against stone behind them, the stairway exit closing. She stood. "Each of you in possession of a key will advance to the next trial," she declared, "where you will fight the Immortal whose part you've chosen."

So Luca, who'd taken the part from Nandi, was advancing.

No rules.

There really was no cheating in these trials—only victory or defeat. And death.

"Stay and enjoy the feast," the Grand Divinus said. "You've earned it."

Feast? After watching Sen Taneie fall to his death, the last thing on her mind was food. Perhaps he'd come with his family or friends, someone she could approach?

She turned to the crowd in the great hall, finding Jon's relieved face and Olivia's grin among them, and Una gave her a proud nod.

Brennan still wasn't here—no doubt still looking for the Archives. Hopefully he was safe and would—

"Thahab!" a thin, high-pitched voice called.

Samara? Rielle followed the sound, where Samara stood, her hand over her mouth, and behind her—

Farrad.

She pulled on the bond.

CHAPTER 28

*J*on's entire body went rigid as Rielle staggered backward in the great hall, paling.

A tall, dark man with hair black as night advanced on her, his hands balled into fists, a young woman pulling on his arm to no avail. He walked as if he owned the place and everyone in it, with a warrior's bearing.

Rielle receded until her back hit the wall. Jon was already halfway across the hall before he knew what he was doing.

As she shot a force of flame from her hands, the man held a bare arm before him, dispelling it. He had a sigil somewhere on his body. This great hall was supposedly made of arcanir—she had run out of options.

Her breaths came rapidly, her eyes widening as she shook her head, flattening against the wall, blocking her face with a raised arm.

"Blood for blood," the man snarled at her in clear but deeply accented Emaurrian.

Over my dead body.

The young woman pleaded with him in a foreign language, but he flung her back. She hit the floor as the man turned back to Rielle, who pressed against the wall, her body tightly compact, trembling as her gaze locked at the man's feet.

Kill him. He would kill him.

"Now I will have justice," the man shouted at her, and she shook. "I challenge you to a duel. Swords. To the death."

The mages around her looked to the Grand Divinus, who merely observed, as if this were a commonplace event in her court.

"What say you?" the Grand Divinus asked, turning to Rielle.

The harsh words echoed through the hall, and Rielle flinched, looking up at her. "I... I..." She lowered her gaze, swallowed, and looked back up. "I... c-can't use a sword."

"If you, or a champion in your stead, do not agree to this man's duel, he wins his grievance against you." The Grand Divinus turned back to the man. "What justice do you seek?"

The young woman wept behind the man and tearfully shouted something that he ignored.

"I am Farrad abd Nasir abd Imtiyaz Hazael, Zahib of House Hazael, Shafi of Xir. This woman is my property and unlawfully escaped," he said, rolling his shoulders, watching Rielle with an unwavering glare as she crumpled to the floor. "I would rightfully take her back to do with as I wish."

Property? Take her back? Every word made Jon's pulse pound louder, his muscles harden.

This man was the master Rielle had told him about in Courdeval. Who'd *owned* her. Who'd *coerced* her into his bed. Who'd *killed* Sylvie.

His knuckles popped; he'd clenched his fists. His heartbeat

thundered in his ears as he crossed the hall. With his bare hands. He'd choke the life out of him with his—

"Very well," the Grand Divinus said, although she glanced at him out in the open, "if you decline to duel him and have no champion—"

Jon stepped between Rielle and Farrad, glared down at the man's face, who took a step back. "I am her champion."

A ripple of gasps and murmurs spread through those gathered—it didn't matter. Brennan's sister broke through the crowd and, her narrowed gaze on Farrad, hurried to Rielle.

This man had taken *everything* from him. Absolutely everything. And the only way he'd leave this room would be in a long pine box. No matter what it took.

Olivia yanked on his arm. "Jon, no. You'll—"

Farrad arched a dark eyebrow, a corner of his mouth turning up. "And you are?"

"Jonathan Dominic Armel Faralle."

A half-laugh. "A singular day. I cannot say I have killed a king before."

Jon narrowed his eyes and met the man's curling smile with a glare.

"Jon, you *can't*," Olivia whispered. "You know that with your cond—"

He snapped that glare in her direction. "Go find Brennan," he commanded.

"But—"

"*Now*."

With a gulp, she nodded, bowed, and hurried away, her slippered feet clicking quickly into the distance.

"I'll get a message to Mother," Una whispered to Rielle, rubbing her arm. "She won't allow him to take you away."

Rielle nodded to her, and with a final sympathetic touch, Una rose, met his eyes gravely, and strode from the hall.

Earthbound and away from Emaurria, he was weaker.

His heart condition meant he could have an episode at any moment.

But he *would* cut the life from this man's body. Terra have mercy, he would do it. Or die trying.

"When do you wish to duel?" the Grand Divinus asked Farrad.

With arms wide, Farrad walked backward, grinning smugly. "As soon as my blades can be brought." He commanded a man in the crowd behind him, who then sprinted from the hall.

Blades. Farrad planned to wield two weapons.

One weapon, two weapons—it didn't matter. His blood would flow. No matter what it would take.

"Jon," Rielle called behind him, and he couldn't stop staring down Farrad, couldn't stop seeing bones break and blood pool, but she called his name again, softer this time, more fragile, and Terra have mercy, but it tore a jagged hole through him.

Breaking away, he turned to her, hitched Faithkeeper at his side, and lowered to a knee to her level.

She trembled on the floor, wrapping her arms around herself, and met his gaze with intense eyes. This man had *done* this to her, traumatized her—

"Jon, you can't," she said. "You can't fight him. *Don't* fight him. *Please.*"

Her voice took on a shrill hoarseness, and Terra have mercy, that shrill hoarseness cleaved his heart in two.

As a tear rolled down her cheek, he took her in his arms, and she embraced him. He shouldn't hold her, he shouldn't comfort her, shouldn't presume, shouldn't do any of this, yet as he held her against him, stroked her hair softly, whispered words of comfort in her ear, nothing had felt so right in months.

"If something goes wrong," she said, her voice breaking, "you—and the kingdom would—"

He pulled away just enough to meet her eyes, and she sniffled. "This is what I should have gone to Sonbahar to do all those months ago."

If only he'd gone then. If he had, maybe Sylvie would still be alive and growing in Rielle's belly, ready to meet them both in just two more months. Maybe Rielle would have been spared all this pain. If only he'd gone.

"He... He has a sigil somewhere on his body, against elemental magic. And—and he's an expert duelist," she stammered. "I heard it many times and saw him kill a man in Xir. He used a rapier."

A rapier. In any duel between a rapier and a long sword, he'd always choose the long sword. Greater precision with two hands, half-swording for thrusts, and greater power. The rapier didn't stand a chance in blocking a crown strike—or any powerful swing. Without a buckler—

"It's too dangerous," she whispered. "Please. There's still time to turn away, and—"

There wasn't, but that didn't matter. He cupped her face, wiping a tear from her cheek. "I'm here. Trained, capable, and I've been fighting for half my life," he repeated to her, old words he'd once given to her, that she'd given back to him in Laurentine.

A flicker of recognition, and then a ghost of a smile shone through her tear-streaked face. She pressed her lips together, shaking her head.

This man had made her cry, and for that alone, he would have rearranged his face.

She covered his hand with hers, his Sodalis ring on her thumb—so she'd taken to wearing it again.

As quick steps echoed from the far side of the hall, he pulled away. *I love you.*

She looked up at him with overbright sky-blue eyes, that world of unspoken words there brimming. Someday, he'd hear them, every last one.

But there was sword work to be done.

Parting from her, he turned to face Farrad Hazael and drew Faithkeeper, staring down the man who'd taken so much from him, who would now pay for it with blood.

CHAPTER 29

Olivia crept down the dark hallway. She'd last seen Brennan entering it, so he had to be here somewhere.

Great Divine, Jon was about to get himself *killed*. What was he thinking, sending *her* away, of all people? The only one who could actually save his life if he had an episode?

She exhaled sharply. He *wasn't* thinking.

The sooner she found Brennan, the sooner he could stop all of this.

A Divine Guard stood near the garderobe, his back to her.

She hit him with a sleep spell, and he collapsed.

No longer a member of the Divinity, she didn't care what the Grand Divinus would have to say about that. After all, the Grand Divinus had let a *slaver* walk into her court and challenge an escaped slave to a duel. Any respect she may have once commanded was forfeit.

Where had Brennan gone? Surely it hadn't been to the garderobe, or he'd have already returned.

She continued past it, scanning the hallway for anything of

interest. Few doors, all closed, and a wall panel—slightly uneven?

With her fingertips, she pried it open. A secret passage.

She'd seen them before—in Trèstellan Palace. *Go, and then flee, mon rêve. Live,* James had once said to her, his last words before he'd disappeared behind a panel just like this.

So Magehold had them, too.

If Brennan was missing, this was where he had gone. She slipped inside, shutting the panel behind her, and whispered the incantation to a candlelight spell.

On the floor, large bootprints headed to the right. Fresh ones. He had to have gone that way. She followed them, rushing down the path they took, through tight, dark corridors with peepholes into castle rooms.

Finally, the tracks... stopped?

She shined the candlelight spell in every corner, and there, bundled in an alcove were... clothes. An overcoat, shirt, trousers —*Brennan's* clothes. Why would he take off his clothes in a secret passage?

Her heart skipped a beat. An affair? He was meeting a lover here while Rielle had been fighting for her life in the trial?

That bastard.

She threw down his clothes into the dust and, clenching her fists, followed the passage around the corner at a run. If he'd been going right, then perhaps the rendezvous for his tryst was nearby in that direction.

Tryst or no tryst, it was still his duty to intercede in any duel for Rielle's sake. At least ones involving swords.

Hold on a little longer, Jon. Divine willing, nothing would aggravate his heart condition, and she could arrive in time with Brennan.

And then *after* the duel, show Brennan what happened to men who betrayed her best friend.

The corridors widened as she rushed through them, and the lighting brightened, so she dispelled her candlelight spell. Floors shone instead of being caked with dust, and there were even little open chambers tucked among the passages, sitting rooms. Divine help her, if she walked in on Brennan with some harlot—

A metallic stench dominated the air. Blood. Strong and thick as smoke.

She slowed, squinting at the dark stain ahead of her. Crimson, shining in the torchlight, pooling in the corridor from an adjacent chamber.

Great Divine.

Someone was hurt, needed help. With a winding gesture of her left hand, she cast a protection spell to heal her next injury instantly.

Her heart thundering, she crept toward the chamber. It widened beneath a pair of feet and a man's bare body, facedown in his own blood. Tall, muscled, deep-bronze skin, dark hair—

"Brennan," she whispered, and darted to him, turned him over with great effort.

His throat had been cut from ear to ear.

She gasped, falling back until her shoulders hit a wall.

He—He was—

Covering her eyes, she looked away, shaking her head. He couldn't be. This couldn't be happening. She'd only just seen him before the trial, and now...

Now he was dead.

If only she'd come sooner, maybe she could've found him in time, but...

She lowered her hand and peered at him. His eyes closed, he would have looked serene but for the blood smeared all over his face and the rest of him. *His* blood.

Who had done this to him? Why?

There was no way she could leave him like this. But in this small chamber, there was nothing... two armchairs, and not even a blanket between them to cover him with.

She approached him again and crouched next to him, brushing his hair away from his face, wiping some of the warm blood off.

Wait, warm...?

Frowning, she pressed her fingertips to the gash beneath his chin. The *closing* gash beneath his chin.

She cast a probe, but nothing happened. Was he sigiled? Poisoned with arcanir?

No, there was no sting. He had to be sigiled. But against healing magic?

The gash continued to close, and his skin... it was warm. Warmer. Hot, even.

Eyes snapped open. Bright amber. He wheezed in a breath and coughed, his hand grabbing her arm so quickly she couldn't fall back in time.

She opened her mouth to scream, but his bloodied hand covered it and he was on his feet before any sound could emerge.

"Olivia," he bit out, those glowing, predatory amber eyes fixed upon her like a wolf's, "I don't want to have to kill you. So when I remove my hand, you're not going to scream." His face was stone, expressionless, cold as death. "Nod if you understand."

She nodded.

He took a deep breath, then another, and another, a slow, silent countdown before he moved his hand away, just a touch.

Very cautiously, she shook her head, willing her pulse to slow.

"I won't scream," she said quietly.

"Good." He pulled away, his cold gaze never leaving her as he straightened to his full height. About six feet three inches tall, he'd always been long and lean with a well-built physique, but she'd never quite realized the chiseled power beneath those layers of silk brocade and court fashion. Not just a warrior, but a *predator*.

No one would want a man like him looking at them the way he was looking at her right now. The question in that inhuman amber gaze was plain as day—whether or not he should kill her.

"You're marrying my best friend," she blurted. "Whatever this is, no one but you, me, and her need to know."

Although *now* wasn't the best time to threaten outing his affair to Rielle.

"She already knows," he replied, his brows lowering as he sniffed the air.

Sniffed the...? Olivia eyed his nudity. "She already knows about your affair and permits it?"

His head jerked back. "Affair?"

"What kind of arrangement is this?" *Am I really asking about his affair right now?* She shook her head, hoping to clear it. "It doesn't matter. Now's not the time to—"

"It's not—" He frowned, then stilled, every muscle aligning to deadly intention. "Follow."

He crept out of the chamber and around the corner, his steps light but quick as he wove through the corridors, keeping to the dark.

Pausing, he looked back at her over his shoulder and held up a finger to his lips, then shook out one hand, extending what looked like—

Claws.

She stifled a gasp as he darted around a corner.

A heave of breath cut off by a gurgle, then the first note of a scream, followed by a squelch.

With uneasy steps and shaking legs, she closed in, warily poking her head around the corner. Brennan tucked a foot under one man's shoulder and rolled him onto his back.

"Good. It was them," he said, presumably to her. His hand—his clawed hand—faded to its human shape as it curled into a fist. Muscles rippling, he turned back to her. "Do you know what I am?"

Werewolf. She'd read about them in the compendium she'd bought from Il Serpente.

The amber eyes, the claws...

The Immortality.

But how? When had he been Changed?

"Why are you here, Olivia?" He walked past her, back toward the direction they'd come from, and she followed in his wake down the tight corridor, suddenly very aware of his nakedness.

"I... It's..." She hushed and gathered her thoughts, looking away from his bare backside. "A man showed up during the trial, a Sonbaharan. When Rielle emerged, he challenged her to a duel. Swords," she explained, watching Brennan's shoulders stiffen as he led them back toward where she'd come from.

When he didn't say anything, she continued, "Rielle froze up, as I'd never seen her do before. But she said she couldn't duel him, and... Jon stepped in as her champion. He sent me to find you."

"He did?" Brennan's pace quickened.

"After the Earthbinding, away from the land, he's... weakened. And there are... other circumstances. I think... I'm not sure he can win."

"Then she'll be..." That quick pace turned into a run, and in no time at all, they were back at the dusty alcove with his clothes. He threw them on as he proceeded.

"Take me there, Olivia," he said, shoving his feet into his boots. "Now."

CHAPTER 30

Jon drew Faithkeeper as Farrad drew his rapier, leaving what looked like a parrying dagger sheathed at his belt, just as Jon left his arcanir dagger sheathed at his own.

The crowd receded, murmuring amongst themselves but giving them plenty of space in the great hall. Good.

"So you were the man too weak to keep her," Farrad bit out, sizing him up. "This will be easy."

If Farrad believed it would be easy, this duel would already be over. But his need to verbally spar implied otherwise.

It was just air. He wasn't here to listen, or to talk, but to fight.

"After her behavior in my possession, are you certain you still want her?"

Farrad's footwork was skillful, sure, responsive. He kept measure well, stepping in and out of distance with a few feints and voids.

Farrad grinned. "It is difficult to resist that face of hers," he said, low, conspiratorial, "the way she squeezes her eyes shut, throws her head back, bares her neck as she comes to pleasure, those sweet little moans, just an octave higher than—"

Jon drove down Faithkeeper, and Farrad parried, just barely, then evaded a cut.

Farrad angled, testing him, but Jon matched every time, adjusting his stance and guard so that Faithkeeper's forte always defended the line between his body and the rapier's tip.

The daggers remained sheathed. Farrad's wouldn't do him much good against Faithkeeper, especially with two-handed strikes. So he left his own dagger sheathed.

Farrad lunged, thrusting for the gut—from middle guard, Jon displaced the thrust as Farrad closed, blades sliding to meet crossguard to crossguard.

There.

With a transitionary step, Jon turned, forcing Faithkeeper over Farrad's rapier, bringing the edge to cut into the side of Farrad's head and swinging it back over one-handed to slice his neck before Farrad could retreat.

One-handed... Not fatal. Not powerful enough to be fatal.

Blood seeped from the wound down into Farrad's shirt as he went back to guard, chuckling under his breath. "A lucky strike."

Jon stayed out of measure, watching him for any hint of movement, keeping perfect guard. With a cut to the head and one to the neck, Farrad would tire over time. Lengthening the duel would end it with less risk.

But the longer he fought, the greater the risk his own weakness would fail him. He had to end Farrad. And soon.

Farrad went on the attack again, a quick series of strikes, and one raked his side. He grabbed Farrad's shoulder and threw him forward, turning to bring Faithkeeper down on his back.

The blade met Farrad's raised parrying dagger as he crouched.

The parrying dagger gave, not strong enough to block him at full power. Faithkeeper bit into a shoulder as Farrad unsheathed Jon's dagger and buried it in his side, between his ribs, and twisted it.

Sharp pain shot through him. Hissing, he pulled away, dragging Faithkeeper free of Farrad's shoulder.

The dagger was buried to the hilt, seeping blood that soaked down his red doublet and into the white of his trousers.

A scream echoed in the great hall—Rielle's.

Coughing, he doubled over, grasping the dagger's handle. If he pulled it free, he might bleed out, but leaving it in—

A thrust of the rapier—he moved to dodge—

A sharpness, pressure.

Agony, and with a groan, he gripped the blade, let it bite into his clenched palm, and peered down.

Run through—run through the stomach.

Screams and shouting filled the great hall, a chaos of sound, and—

He tried to take a step back, but he only dropped to a knee as the rapier slid free of his body, cutting its way out.

Terra help me, but I will kill you...

A grim twist of Farrad's lips. A victorious grin.

...if it's the last thing I do...

As Farrad raised the blade, Jon yanked the arcanir dagger free from his own body and buried it in Farrad's foot, then dropped and rolled to the side, barely avoiding the downward thrust of the rapier.

Farrad howled and bent over the arcanir dagger in his foot, his gaze darting to the crowd. Wide eyed.

The sigil—deactivated—

RIELLE KNEW WHAT IT MEANT. That quick glance—Jon had to have stabbed through Farrad's sigil.

No more. Farrad wouldn't hurt him any more.

Her blood humming, she held Farrad's gaze as she clasped her hands together and lifted them, raising along with them a pillar of flame at Farrad's position.

It shot from just above the arcanir floor and through his body like divine judgment, surging to the ceiling of the great hall, where it blazed through, raining stone, and into the sky, showering the great hall with dust.

An ear-splitting scream shook the hall, deafening and great, ringing with fury, and as agony seized her throat, she realized it was her own.

The pillar of flame flared, brightly burning like an unstoppable, gushing bonfire, piercing the heavens above with its destruction.

A cough on the floor next to it, and her pained gaze fell to Jon, lying in a pool of blood upon the shining marble, clutching his chest, his face creased in agony.

No.

Dispelling the pyromancy, she ran to him, the crowd and his guards parting to let her through, whispering, and she fell to her knees next to him, taking him in her arms, slipping onto her backside in his blood.

His squinted eyes met hers for a fraction of a moment, held her gaze through the crippling pain creasing his face. "Ri..." he rasped.

"I—I can fix this," she said, her wet, red hands running over his wounds, smearing blood, as her tears dripped onto his face, streaking down into the red.

"Sundered flesh and shattered bone, / By Your Divine might, let it be sewn," she blurted, over and over, and his wounds closed, but still he clutched at his chest, his fingertips digging into the flesh as if he tried to rip out his own heart.

What was...? Why wasn't it—?

His face was tight with agony, his eyes squeezed shut, and the healing incantation, it, it wasn't working, and his skin was darkening to blue, and he groaned, a sound so vulnerable it broke her—she'd never heard him so—and it—she shook, trying to hold him as he slipped in her bloodied hands.

He crumpled toward her, resting his head on her lap, and she held him, stroked her fingertips through his thick hair, over and over, over and over, unable to stop, curling over him as he gasped in breaths... slower and shallower, violent, and slower. And shallower.

"Jon?" she asked quietly, but his name was barely more than a cry on her lips, and a spasm seized him, shaking him violently against her. "I don't know what to—Tell me what to do —I don't—"

His eyebrows creased together, forming a deep, pained furrow on his brow, and that agonized groan, vulnerable and breaking, it was... quieter. Weaker.

No. Divine, no, this wasn't—he wasn't—

She tried the incantation again, kept trying it, rocking him on her lap, holding him, and nothing, nothing happened, and he was fading, *fading.*

Pressure pushed at her eyes, and she blinked, watching him through the blur, refusing to look away, and she adjusted her grip, trying to pull him closer to her, but he was so heavy.

"You can't," she whispered, resting her head against his, breathing in the steely scent of his blood, cupping his rough-stubbled cheek, brushing it with her thumb as she had so many times before. "You *can't*, Jon, you *can't*, please—"

A shallow rasp from his blue-tinged lips, lips she'd kissed a thousand times, and the rigidity of his body lessened, weakened, and then a little more. And a little more. His eyes, squeezed shut, opened, just a sliver, and his fading gaze locked with hers. The Shining Sea in a storm, and he...

The hand grasping at his chest released, its grip loosening, and his fingertips inched toward her hand on his arm, steeped in red to her wrists, fingers that had intertwined with hers a thousand times, that she'd once thought would intertwine with hers forevermore.

"No," she pleaded, her voice breaking as she wept over him. "*No*. It's not... You can't..." Her tears trailed through his blood as she shook her head, but she grasped his hand, intertwined her fingers with his. "No, Jon," she rasped, touching her forehead to his, breathing the same air with him as she had so many times before. "You... you're going to live, you hear me? You're going to... You're going..."

That Shining Sea gaze locked on her flashed, just once, like the sun breaking through the clouds, and then he blinked his eyes shut slowly, that light disappearing, his light disappearing, and she wept against him, tightening her hold around him as his faint grasp on her hand went limp.

CHAPTER 31

O livia burst into the great hall with Brennan and Raoul,
who'd found her and led them back with all haste.

In the center of a whispering crowd, Jon lay on the floor
steeped in his own blood, with Rielle curled over him, holding
him, and Olivia was already running before she could think.

Divine, no. Spare him. Please, spare him. Please.

"Clear the hall," Brennan bellowed, his grim gaze meeting
the Grand Divinus's, who nodded to the Divine Guard to do as
bidden. Murmuring and whispering, everyone reluctantly
headed for the exit, guided by the Divine Guard, all the while
gaping.

Olivia slid to the floor next to Jon, ripped open his bloodied
overcoat and shirt, and placed a palm on his chest, glimpsing his
pale skin and blue-tinged lips.

Rielle wept, slurring cried words—

"He's suffocating," Olivia blurted to her. Blood had filled his
lungs, and she spelled it outward, pushing it to flow through the
rest of his body, pushing and pushing, pumping it out, redi-

recting what his heart had overflowed until the episode passed and his heart resumed normal function once more.

His eyes opened wide as he gasped, spasming, his hands wrapping around her arm, and their gazes met. His brows drawn together, he scrutinized her face as if he'd just awoken from a deep slumber, as if he didn't yet know the world around him.

"You're all right, Jon," she whispered to him, taking his big, callused hand in hers. "You're fine. You're alive, and you're all right. I'm here."

Color returned to his face, the redness fading from his eyes as she healed him, as his breathing evened out. "Ri—" he whispered, and coughed.

"I'm here, Jon," Rielle choked out, then covered her mouth. "Great Divine, I thought—" She dragged herself closer with trembling arms, then reached for his shoulder.

He covered her hand with his. "Is he—?"

Rielle's eyes flashed. "We defeated him. He's—"

"Unfortunately," a firm, loud voice rang out—the Grand Divinus, "you've broken the rules of the duel."

Dragging her gaze from Jon, Rielle fixed icy eyes on the Grand Divinus. She braced a hand on the blood-slick floor and struggled to her feet, Brennan helping her up.

Holding the Grand Divinus's gaze, she bowed slowly, in perfect form, steeped in blood, the charred remnants of a body and rubble from the ceiling lying not five feet from her. "With all due respect, Most High, these are the Magister Trials. There *are* no rules."

Perched on her golden throne, the Grand Divinus narrowed her eyes, grinned joylessly, and rested an elbow on the armrest, her head on her hand, her eyes still locked with Rielle's.

Neither of them broke.

"Come on," Brennan whispered gently in Rielle's ear. "Let's go." He wrapped her, held her, but Rielle wouldn't look away.

Tensions were high. The next words could ripple to the world's farthest reaches. Stoke conflicts. Start wars.

Jon tried to sit up, but Olivia pressed him down with her palm.

"Go, Rielle," Olivia whispered, unmoving. She glanced at Brennan, who nodded.

Whispering in Rielle's ear, he dragged her away, out of the hall, those icy eyes of hers never looking away from the Grand Divinus. Open challenge.

Jon growled beneath her palm and pulled it aside. Now was not the time to take sides, not until the trials were over. His brows low over hard eyes, he was not pleased.

Well, neither was she. She sat back on her heels as he propped himself up on an elbow.

Raoul and Florian approached, but he held up a hand and labored to sitting on his own, taking deep, heavy breaths. Bracing himself on his sword, he rose to his feet.

Having bled so much, he wouldn't be able to stand on his own power for long, but he refused his guards. Steeped in blood, he collected his weapons, handed them to Florian, then paused to incline his head to the Grand Divinus, who responded in kind.

Maintaining that posture had to have hurt, had to have been exhausting as he'd lost so much blood and taken so many injuries, but he'd done it anyway. He always pushed himself to the limit, *beyond* the limit, when he set his mind on something.

He pulled one of his guards aside and directed him to personally see to removing every drop of his blood from the great hall, and to send "the young woman" to him if she so agreed.

The young woman—the one who'd arrived with his opponent?

What in the Lone had he been thinking? Challenging that man, taking charge of the young woman who'd arrived with him—?

And did he have any idea the political disaster that had just unfolded here?

The king of Emaurria had agreed to a challenge, and although stepping in to protect one of his subjects had been admirable, duels were bound up in codes of honor. The duel had been ended *for* him. The world would know that Emaurria's subjects didn't respect or trust their king, and that unrest ran deep in the kingdom.

Or they'd know Rielle had intervened for love, and the king's alleged mistress placed her desires above the kingdom's wellbeing. Both he *and* Rielle had made a mess here that would ripple consequences for years, or even decades.

Scowling, she grabbed his hand and, without a word, dragged him out the doors. In the hallway, she caught a doorknob and gestured toward the dark room inside.

She glared at him as she shut the door, facing him, bathed in his own blood and barely standing. "Do you have any idea what you just did?"

He braced himself on the nearby table in what looked like a small library. "One of the most satisfying things I've ever done?"

Frowning, she shook her head. "Jon, you have no idea who he was. That could have caused an international incident that—"

"He introduced himself," Jon said coldly, anchoring a hand on his hip. "I know exactly who he was. A sick bastard slaver that needed to be put down. Hard."

She exhaled a quivering breath. "I know what he cost you.

And it's Rielle. I know," she said. "But you accepted a duel, and one of your subjects interfered in the outcome. Your reputation has been tarnished on the world stage. Do you have any idea—"

"Is he dead?" he asked, voice low, deep.

She gaped at him.

"Then it was worth it."

She scoffed, shaking her head. "Really? Will you think so when no other country wants to treat with you because you have no honor?"

The dim evening light caught his eyes, and their glimmer of amusement. "No country wants to treat with me *now*. It wasn't as though they were lining up to help us with the Immortals."

She took a step back, taking slow, deep breaths. They would have to control the damage, get ahead of the news—

"He held her captive, Olivia," Jon said, barely audible. "Just to survive, she acted on his every wish. Because of him, our daughter is dead. I'm not sorry I fought him, and I'm not sorry she ended him. If that means I have no honor, then as you say... 'to hell with that.'"

He swayed on his feet and braced more of his weight on the table, and she rushed to support him, slinging his heavy arm over her shoulder.

Everything he said made sense, but the world didn't know about Rielle's enslavement, or about the child they'd lost. And she was certain neither of them wanted it known.

"Throwing my own words back at me," she said with a sigh, leading him toward the door. "You just have to say all the right things, don't you?"

"How else can I compete with one of Emauria's most brilliant minds?" he said with a dimpled grin.

"Mm-hmm," she patronized. "We still need to find a way to mitigate this to the rest of the world."

He winced, and she eased him into a chair. She'd have to tell his entourage about the blood here, too. Even a drop could be exploited for sangremancy—not officially *allowed*, of course, but one could never be too cautious.

And he'd have to rest, replenish his blood, and—

"Rielle already gave us the answer," he said, breathing heavily. "Magister Trials. No rules. The Grand Divinus had said it herself."

It could work. It would be seen as an excuse, but what else did they have?

She rested a hand on his shoulder, still sticky with blood. "Our enemies will think the kingdom weak, if a subject stepped in to save her own king. What about that?"

His eyes gleaming in the faint evening luminance from the windows. "The first to test that theory will regret it."

There wasn't an ounce of defeat in him. Good. He was willing to fight for Rielle, for his lost child, for Emaurria.

It was only one step further to get him to fight for himself.

"Jon," she said, waiting until his eyes met hers, "I think I may have found a way to save your life."

CHAPTER 32

*L*eigh followed with Katia and Ambriel as Ruvel picked a path through the forest toward the light-elven camp. The darkening skies obfuscated the deadfall on the ground, and Ambriel guided him aside, around a fallen branch.

"Old *man*," Katia chided in a singsongy voice.

"Katia, *do* shut up," Leigh replied. "I can see well enough. Ambriel just wants to make sure I don't mar this beautiful face by tripping."

Ambriel half-laughed. "Also, I don't want to have to carry you anywhere. You're deceptively heavy."

Katia yelped as she tripped, but caught herself.

"Ha!" Leigh snapped.

Ruvel paused and shushed them, with Ashta, Merian, and the other light-elf slowing. They hefted their bows, eyeing the darkness ahead.

"Something's wrong," Ambriel whispered.

"There should be two scouts here," Ashta hissed back to them, with a sweep of her twisted hair.

Ruvel held up a hand, and everyone went quiet. "Shouted orders in the distance. There's a battle."

"Take us there. Now," Leigh said in Old Emaurrian, then spoke the candlelight spell incantation.

Ruvel led the way, and they rushed through the dense forest. Fallen branches and dead trees blocked the way, and Leigh spelled them aside with Katia as they ran.

Bellows broke from the distance, screams, and guttural hissing, and he sent the candlelight spell ahead. The stench reached him first.

Its illumination glowed over fierce light-elven faces shooting arrows and moving, always moving, as a mass of shambling bodies flooded over the forest floor, breaking like waves through the trunks, trampling over tents and chairs and injured light-elves, stifling their screams. The undead.

"Cover me," Leigh snapped to Katia. He cast a repulsion shield past the farthest light-elf, widening it and widening it.

Loosing an arrow, Ambriel shouted over the cacophony of orders and shrieks, and light-elves pulled into a center that Leigh enclosed in a repulsion dome.

Roots braided up from the ground, capturing the undead in place as the light-elves shot them.

Arrows wouldn't stop them. They needed to be dismembered.

"Blades," Leigh hissed, as bodies pressed against his repulsion dome, piling and pushing. He'd have to destabilize it, push them back.

Ambriel drew his sword and dagger, as did some of the other light-elves who had them, and slaughtered their way through the undead. Katia kept rooting them and hooking them with vines and wood as needed.

"Get ready," Leigh grunted, and fed more and more magic

into the repulsion shield, strengthening it and strengthening it, keeping it compact, feeding it power until it nearly burst, and he pushed it backward, destabilized it, shattered it and the undead against it back several feet in an explosion of limbs and bodies.

Everyone froze, and before the reinforcements could climb over, he spelled an attraction ring in the middle of the pile of bodies, drawing in all the undead on it and around it, holding them there. He kept feeding it power, drawing and drawing, then cast another repulsion shield before himself and the light-elves, matching its power to keep them pushed back as he drew the undead in.

Branches curved toward the attraction ring, pine needles and twigs ripped free and pulled in, and trunks of younger trees leaned in, groaning and creaking as bodies squelched and cracked.

A foul stench suffocated the air, and a sapling burst from the ground and flew into the attraction ring, where a hill-sized mass of decaying flesh and broken bone imploded, forced against itself into a smaller and smaller mass.

"The caves!" Ashta shouted in Old Emaurrian. "Behind them!"

A candlelight spell flew from Katia and past the mass of flesh, over more shambling bodies being drawn into the attraction ring, and then a dark entrance in a cliffside.

Leigh weakened the attraction ring, fisted in his right hand and only strong enough to hold the mass together, then advanced, pushing the repulsion shield with his left. He strengthened it as much as he dared, enough to slowly push the mass and the attraction ring toward the cave.

Step by painstaking step, he pushed and pushed, as Ambriel dismembered stragglers at his right and Katia captured them with winding wood to his left.

Finally, he pushed the mass into the cave, and tapered the power of the attraction ring while compacting the repulsion shield, strengthening it, and directing it inside. "Collapse it, Katia! Now!"

Blades dancing, Ambriel protected her while she wove with her fingers and contracted them. As a great rumble quaked from the cave, Leigh dispelled the attraction ring, pulled the repulsion shield just before them, and a blast of dust puffed across it, breaking across its surface as rock tumbled to the ground, the tremors taking them off their feet.

Leigh held the repulsion shield, keeping the debris and dust from hitting them, until the ruins of the cave settled. He dispelled it at last, watching the collapsed entrance in the darkness.

When silence finally claimed the area, Katia whispered the candlelight incantation once more. Ambriel rose and offered a hand to Leigh, pulled him up, and then helped up Katia. He was bloodied, but unhurt.

Behind them, Ashta, Ruvel, and a stern-faced woman assisted the injured, all of the light-elves numbering about fifty. Ambriel approached his daughter, rested a hand on her shoulder, and scrutinized her for injuries.

With a smile, she took his hand and said something in Elvish. He sighed, nodded, then turned to the stern-faced woman. In the candlelight spell, she had the same platinum-blond hair Ruvel did, only hers was long and tied in thirds down her back, with the sides of her head shorn. Her linen clothes were spattered with blood and stained with dirt. This had to be Ferelen, Ruvel's mother and the queen of White-Weald.

The only indication of her status was her sash—dyed a deep green.

Ferelen clasped Ambriel's arm, then glanced in Leigh's direction before striding toward him.

He bowed, as did Katia. "Your Majesty, we come to—"

"No," she said immediately. "You do not bow."

He straightened, eyeing her carefully. Normally royals enjoyed the bowing.

"Nor you," she said to Katia, who did the same. "You have both helped save my people. *You do not bow.*"

Well, that was certainly a fine welcome. Leigh cleared his throat. "Your Majesty—"

"Ferelen," she corrected, her clear eyes bright in the candlelight flame. She turned back and shouted some instructions to Ruvel in Elvish, who nodded and began delegating. "We are unfit to host you properly, but you are welcome among my people."

He nodded. "Thank you. We have come to establish trade and peaceful relations between your queendom and the Forgeron Coven of witches," he said, gesturing to Katia, who introduced herself.

"We have had some dealings with stupid and cruel humans," Ferelen said, an edge riding her tone, "but you are not they." She held out her arm to Katia, who clasped it. "We will gladly trade with you, as friends."

With a bright nod, Katia thanked her, and Ferelen led them to a small fire her people had built while they bustled around them, treating the injured, building tents, running water from the nearby stream.

"How long have you been facing the undead?" Leigh asked carefully.

Ferelen lowered herself to the ground, sitting cross-legged, and they all sat around the fire. She heaved a sigh, fixing those farseeing eyes on the ruins, a great exhaustion settling in the lines of her ageless face. "Weeks. The groups break off in waves from a larger mass. We travel throughout the forest and traced them here—they emerge from that cave. We're safe now. But there's a witch of great power in the mountains. An uncontrolled witch."

Uncontrolled... In fureur. If there were so many undead, that meant the Beaufoys hadn't dealt with the necromancer, or had been unable to, or worse.

Ava. Was she safe? He shifted.

There would be no more leaving things to chance. No more leaving Ava's safety to Axelle and Della.

"I will handle it," he said. "Tell us what you know."

CHAPTER 33

Rielle sat wordlessly in the carriage as it jostled over the cobblestone streets while Brennan stared at her from the seat opposite.

Brennan leaned his head back against the juddering carriage, and heaved a great, exasperated sigh. A sliver of dried blood arced across his neck and down into his shirt, although its whiteness was untarnished beneath his black overcoat, as if he'd dressed *after* combat.

He'd been hurt...?

She jumped out of her seat to examine his neck, running her fingers along its smooth skin while dried blood crisped away.

He caught her between his thighs as she knelt against the carriage's tremors, his hands bracing her shoulders.

"What—what happened to you?" she asked.

He opened one eye. "Ah, you noticed."

Finally seemed to be the word he left off.

"I think I found a way into the Archives," he said evenly, "but I triggered a trap. Poison."

"Are you all right? How do you feel? Faint in any way, or—?"

"It didn't kill me, obviously, but it was enough to weaken me, break my Change, and members of the Divine Guard decided to... *deal* with me."

She dropped her face against his abdomen. Divine, he could've—if he hadn't been a werewolf, he could've—

His arms closed around her. "It's all right. Olivia found me, and I killed the two guards who'd... done that to me. So don't worry. No one will know it was me. Your mission is safe. You didn't even have to lift a finger to help me."

"That's not what I—" she stammered. "That's not fair," she shot back. "*Farrad* showed up. *Farrad*, Brennan, of all people."

He exhaled lengthily. "I'm sure Jon spilling his guts all over the floor had nothing to do with it. Not one bit."

"Tell me what I should have done, then, Brennan."

She'd pulled on the bond the second she'd faced Farrad, and challenged to a duel, she'd been unable to leave. "Could I have *left* to wander in search of you while someone fought a duel to the *death* in my place?"

"*Someone*," he bit out with a scoff.

"Could I have?" she asked, quiet but firm.

He shook his head. No answer.

That's right, because there *had* been no answer. She couldn't have left even if she'd wanted to, and she hadn't wanted to, not with Jon putting his life on the line for her sake. "Tell me what I should have done, then, in your eyes, to have pleased you, because I don't know where to begin."

He held her gaze a moment, coldly, then looked away.

He was alive, and she was glad for that, beyond glad, but his expectations for her had been impossible. Did he not believe she loved him? Cared for him? How could he think otherwise?

She didn't want to fight anymore.

"Brennan, I..." She wrapped her arms around him. "You know I love you. I *care* what happens to you. And I want you to abandon this stupid mission—"

He straightened. "Rielle—"

"If those guards had chosen to *behead* you, would you... what would I have done without you? None of this is worth losing you, Bre—"

He pulled her up and urged her onto his lap, forcing her gaze to his. "Listen to me. I love you, and that means it's my duty to protect you. If the Divinity attacked your family, I need to know that to better protect you, and us, in the future."

His sincere hazel eyes didn't waver; he meant it. Every single word.

"We love *each other*," she corrected. "That means we protect *each other*. And that starts with me telling you to abandon this mission. It's proving too dangerous."

He huffed a laugh and grinned. "Opinion noted. And may I remind you: I do what I want."

There was no arguing that. Stubborn wolf. "You're unbelievable."

"Thank you." He stole a kiss, but his fading smile turned sad.

He'd almost *died*. It was unthinkable, but it had almost happened.

She covered her mouth, but a coppery tang infiltrated her nostrils. Blood. Jon's blood.

The deep, darkening red of Jon's blood colored her white mage coat, having saturated the fabric, and she couldn't tear her gaze away.

She'd almost lost Brennan today, and Jon.

She'd felt it, in her arms, his life leaving his body. The blood, that look in his eyes as she'd bent over him, holding him—she'd seen it before, been there before, but this had been...

Tears hit her bloodied sleeve, brightening the red for a moment.

Divine, if not for Olivia, he would have died in her arms.

When Farrad had—Divine, *why* had Farrad been here?— challenged her, Jon had intervened, risking his life, and he'd done it without a second thought. Risked *his* life—the life of a king, upon whom so many relied.

He hadn't been himself recently. Something was amiss, but he'd fought anyway. Taken blow after blow, nearly *died*. He'd had an injury she couldn't heal, some blow that must have had lasting and dangerous consequences that Olivia had healed.

It was time she learned to fight her own battles—even when she couldn't use magic. She wouldn't be a liability to Jon, to Brennan, to anyone else, not if she could help it. And if she ever ended up cuffed in arcanir again, she wouldn't be helpless. She'd have to become someone new, someone stronger, someone honest with herself and where she belonged.

Brennan sighed, arms crossed, unmoving. "It should've been me," he said gravely.

"Should've...?"

He scowled, staring into nothing ahead of him. "To kill that zahib bastard."

She rested her head on his shoulder. That night in Xir, she'd thought she'd killed Farrad. When she'd seen him tonight, it had been like seeing a ghost, and everything had come rushing back to her. The constant fear, the arcanir cuffs, the escape that night, always looking behind her... Samara standing up for her...

"Samara!" She straightened in his hold as the carriage jostled over a bump. "She was here. I—We have to go back for her."

"Already taken care of," he said, not releasing her. "At least I think so. As we were leaving, I heard Jon ask one of his guards to have the 'young woman' left in his care."

"Jon did?" She was about to ask why, when it hit her. "He considers himself responsible."

Brennan nodded. "He agreed to a challenge in which her father was killed."

She closed her eyes. Samara would be safe with him, but... "I need to see her," she whispered.

Brennan shrugged and turned away, blinking, before glancing back at her. "What about your brother? Didn't Olivia mention something about him?"

He was trying to change the subject again.

He didn't want her visiting Samara. Visiting Jon.

And if he was changing the subject, he didn't even want to discuss it.

Then it could wait. Much had happened tonight, and too much fighting.

And Olivia *had* mentioned Liam. "It's strange that he didn't write."

Brennan covered his eyes with a hand and sighed.

She shifted in his lap. "What is it?"

"Maybe he did write," Brennan murmured. "Mother checks all the correspondence first."

Brennan's mother might have *withheld* a letter from Liam? She curled a fist, still sticky with blood. "She'd better *pray* she didn't throw it out."

JON PACED the villa's candlelit library, carving his block of linden into something now approximating a bird, pausing every so often to eye Olivia. "You want me to—"

"Yes," she said, with an emphatic nod, sitting before him at the table with her books. "Please."

Terra have mercy, what she suggested—it was antithesis to everything he believed in, everything he'd rededicated himself to after Veris. "You want me to become a... a werewolf?"

"Why not?" She raised her chin. "I've read about it. A bite can transmit the curse, and if you survive, you'll be transformed... in peak health. Immortal." She crossed her legs and shrugged her shoulders as if to say everything would turn out just fine.

Right. Huffing a breath, he looked away and continued pacing. "It's not what you think it is."

Brennan's curse was a special case, from what Rielle had told him and what he'd heard of the werewolves since the Rift.

He faltered and braced a hand on a nearby chair.

She shot up to her feet and rushed to him. "You lost a lot of blood, Jon. Even with healing, you still need to rest. Let me walk you to your quarters."

No. Anywhere but there. "I'm fine," he said, sinking into the chair. He'd eaten just about his own weight in food since returning from the castle, and with a good night's rest, he'd feel better.

But until he and Olivia had that talk, they were going nowhere near his quarters.

Frowning, she plopped back into her chair. "He's a werewolf, and he seems perfectly normal," she said, flinching. "Well, as normal as can be, considering."

"You don't understand," he replied, rubbing his chest over his heart. "You've heard the reports of werewolves in the heartland. They're violent beasts, bound to the whim of their emotions. They have a lesser grasp on their actions than *actual* wolves."

"But he—"

"*He* is different." Jon paused, paring away some linden shavings. "His family was cursed by Rielle's ancestor. She... she gives him her blood every month to help him stay in control."

"Her—?" Olivia's eyes widened, then she looked down, knitting her eyebrows together. After a moment, her face lit up. "Well, can't she give you—"

"No."

"You won't even—"

"No."

Olivia folded her arms and scowled at him. "It's the *least* she could do after—"

"No, Olivia," he snapped. "And that's final." He'd seen all too clearly what the bond between Rielle and Brennan had been last year—brutal, cruel, inescapable. They were on good terms now, and he wouldn't insert himself *permanently* into her life, even if he could bring himself to try becoming a violent Immortal beast.

Besides, the ritual to create that bond... it had been sangremancy. *Deadly* sangremancy, that had claimed a life in its casting. He wouldn't risk Rielle's life, or anyone's, for it.

Olivia threw her hands up and exhaled sharply.

"Her ancestor sacrificed her *life* to cast that sangremancy curse."

"But if *he* is the one to bite you, perhaps you'd be of his line? Maybe she could give you control, too, or someone of her bloodline could?"

This line of thinking was becoming desperate. "We don't know if that would work, and there *is* no one else of her bloodline." Well, there was Liam, but—

Olivia blinked sullenly and hesitated. "When she and Brennan have a—"

He scowled at her, and she quieted. In what world did she think he would ever expect such a thing of a child?

But even so, it didn't matter. "If... If she and Brennan have a child," he said, "that'll break his curse. Even if we went through it all, I'd be human again anyway."

"Then maybe you'd be changed into a healthy—"

He shook his head. "None of this matters anyway. I don't want to be anything but human, but *myself*. When my time comes, it comes. The end." He wouldn't become some monster, immortal, a shade of himself. And if something went wrong? He'd end up a burden to all those who loved him, and to his kingdom. Never. "Death isn't the worst thing that can happen to a man."

Being left behind—

"The girl," he said, thinking back to the young woman from the great hall. She'd lost, too—her father, no matter what kind of man he'd been—because of him. And he had to make that right. "Did she agree to come?"

"She did, but she's gathering her things to move them here. No one in your household speaks more than a few words of Nad'i."

"Is there no one who could translate?"

Olivia cleared her throat. "Brennan and Rielle are fluent."

If the girl was who he thought she was, then Rielle would want to know she was safe, and to see her. "Let them know she's here."

CHAPTER 34

*A*s Rielle entered the villa from the dark outside, light footsteps echoed nearer.

Caitlyn dropped a book on the floor, her large eyes practically round as she scrutinized Rielle from head to toe. Her skin paled almost as far as the blush-pink hue of her gown. "Y-you're *drenched* in blood," she said, her palm meandering to her chest.

She was about to be drenched in more if she didn't get Liam's correspondence.

"Is Mother here?" Brennan bit out, striding into the villa.

Caitlyn blinked slowly and trailed her gaze back to Rielle. "Yes, why?"

"My word." Duchess Caterine's voice came from the hall, flanked by Vietti and a squad of guards, and next to her, Una gasped.

"We were just about to save you," Una said quietly, looking her over. Wisps of hair strayed from her usually perfect bun.

"As you can see," Brennan murmured, "the saving's done."

"Tell the barrister we're fine," the duchess told Una, who

nodded and immediately left. Statuesque in a long, silvery dress with her hair pinned voluminously atop her head, the duchess calmly gave Rielle a once-over, then asked Caitlyn for some privacy.

"Your Grace, I may have had a letter from a Captain Verib," she said carefully, trying to restrain the growl in her voice.

Duchess Caterine raised an eyebrow and made a show of contemplating. "Ah, yes," she said, brightening. "Well, it was from a bordello in Il Serpente. You couldn't *possibly* have business with such riffraff, so I assumed it was trash."

Assumed it was trash. The duchess, chin raised, held her gaze.

She *would* get that letter and see Liam. And then, with only three days before the second trial, begin digging into research on basilisks and—

"Vietti," the duchess said to the chamberlain, "bring the letter from this 'Captain Verib' to my son's quarters."

"Yes, my lady," Vietti said with a deep bow. "I shall fetch the correspondence forthwith." With a final inclination of his head to Rielle, he strode away.

Liam had written her, and *forthwith* wasn't nearly soon enough.

"Brennan, give us a moment. Have Stefania run her a bath." Duchess Caterine approached her, looking her over.

Brennan pressed a kiss to her temple, gave her hand a squeeze, then walked backward toward the stairs, tilting his head toward his mother with a knowing smile before heading up.

Leaving her *alone.* Alone with his mother.

Divine help me.

"Are you all right, child? What happened?" With a gentle hand, Duchess Caterine guided her to a nearby bench and quickly issued instructions to her household—fetch hot water, clean cloths... There was a soft comfort to her words, her touch, and as intimidating as she had been, right this moment, she... wasn't. Or at least didn't *seem* to be. But she'd still hidden Liam's letter.

"I'm sure Una told you," Rielle explained, "but... After the first trial, there was a duel... King Jonathan was gravely injured."

A maid returned with a bowl of steamy water and a washcloth, and the duchess dipped it in the water, then took one of Rielle's hands and rubbed it gently. "Are you hurt?"

Rielle shook her head. "I'm fine... but it was so... there was so much..." The washcloth had turned a deep red.

The duchess curled an arm around her, brought her head to rest against her shoulder, and Rielle closed her eyes, almost let herself take a moment's comfort before the steely smell of blood gave her a start. Red stained the duchess's gown everywhere they were in contact.

She gasped, pulling away. "Your Grace, I'm so—I'm so sorry, your gown—"

The duchess shushed her, rubbing her shoulder before tipping up her chin so their gazes met. "A gown is nothing. *You* matter," she said firmly, her green-eyed gaze uncompromising. "And I think we're past 'Your Grace,' don't you?" She smiled warmly. "Call me Mother."

Rielle's chest tightened, as if the very breath had been stolen from her lungs. *Mother.* Brennan's mother was so much more complicated than the face she wore today, *too* complicated to trust so easily. "I—I—"

A magnanimous smile, and the duchess patted her hand. "It's all right if you're not ready yet, Rielle. When you are..."

"No, no," she said, shaking her head. "I'm—Thank you... Mother."

The duchess paused, beaming, and it reached her soft eyes. Perhaps she was being genuine.

A maid came and whispered in her ear, and the duchess helped her stand. "Your bath is ready, and Vietti left your correspondence in your quarters. Why don't you wash up, let the hot water do its work, and maybe we can have some mulled wine together later? Would you like that?"

That sounded... wonderful. She wanted to see Liam as soon as possible, but she could go to him bright and early tomorrow. She certainly wasn't going anywhere sticky and drenched in blood.

She nodded. "I'd like that."

The duchess enveloped her in a warm embrace, then guided her to the stairs. "Come find me when you're finished, all right? And have Stefania burn some incense for you, something calming."

With a final nod, Rielle rested her hand on the banister and went up to the quarters she shared with Brennan.

His mother had finally accepted her, then. Had it really been as simple as Una had told her—to show their mother how much she loved Brennan?

When she entered their quarters, the large, luxurious bath was already full and steaming, with an array of candles casting their glow nearby. Next to them lay a message from The Red Veil in Il Serpente. She cracked it open and read:

Staying here until the end of the trials. Visit when you can. Verib.

It was dated *four* days ago. For *four days*, she could have been spending time with Liam. And worse, did he think she'd been ignoring him? She'd write him tonight.

And after this first trial, her anima had dimmed, not much...

but enough that she'd want resonance if there was some other mage suitable for it at The Red Veil.

After hastily peeling off her clothes, she scrubbed off the worst of the blood. When she'd cleaned up, she stepped into the tub, submerged her feet, her legs, herself in the hot water. The heat soothed into her, wrapping her in a warm caress, and she sank deeper, letting it clear her mind. So much had happened today—too much—and even a moment's rest would be a luxury before she dove into research... after her mulled wine with the duchess.

A few footsteps, and then came the telltale splash of Brennan entering the bath. They hadn't been together since the night of their argument—the one about Veris.

She opened her eyes.

He settled on the other end of the tub, stretching his legs out on either side of hers. A smug grin flashed across his face as he relaxed and leaned his head back against the rim.

Ah, you noticed, he'd said to her in the carriage.

Did he think she didn't care? When he'd returned to her alive, whole, well, her heart had leapt. Hadn't he heard that? Didn't he know just how much she loved him?

When she'd mentioned wanting to visit Samara—where Jon was staying—he'd changed the subject. To Liam, yes, but changed the subject nonetheless. He didn't want her anywhere near Jon, she knew that, but didn't he trust her? She loved him, and she would never betray him. Ever.

If he didn't know that yet, then she'd have to show him.

He'd nearly died today, nearly been sacrificed for the sake of pursuing the truth. *Her* truth. But when she'd asked him what he'd do with evidence of complicity in the regicide, whose side he'd be on—

He hadn't answered her.

He risked his life going to the Archives for her, but if he found evidence of the Divinity and his father arranging the regicide, he hadn't been able to tell her he'd do the right thing.

To cover up his father's guilt, he might destroy that evidence. Might, in pursuit of his father's interests, end up *helping* the Divinity.

They'd already fought so much, and she didn't have it in her anymore. Not after today.

Earlier today, he'd agreed to *try*, and this could be a fresh start for them both, a way to reset and erase all the lies, manipulations, and distrust between them. And if those certain conflicts came up, they could deal with them later.

The door opened, and Rielle started, but it was only the young maid—Stefania—with incense. She set it nearby, floral and light jasmine, then took her leave.

Quiet blanketed the room and warmth wrapped her, until Brennan took her hand and pulled her across the tub to him. He turned her, bringing her back against his chest, and enclosed her in his arms. Her aching body wanted to argue, but as she tucked her head under his chin, absorbed his heat, melted into his embrace, any inkling of complaint dissolved.

He dipped a small cloth in the water, squeezed it, then brought it to her forehead, softly rubbing at a small spot there— she must have missed some blood. His brows drawn, he moved to her cheek, gliding the cloth bit by bit across her skin, so slowly she could feel the stroke of each individual fiber, so carefully she could have sworn those intense eyes saw nothing else but the mark on her cheek.

His touch was so delicate in its care and softness, and yet brimming with intention, so focused, so thorough, determined. The night of the welcome banquet came back to her, when he'd taken her home and wordlessly held her, kissed her, stroked her... bared her body to the glow of the candle flame, and lain her down. No restraints that night, or commands, or roughness, just his lips on hers, on her skin, his touch soft and careful, his movement slow and affectionate as he'd fitted his body to hers, kept her safe in his embrace as he'd watched her eyes, her mouth while he'd brought her to pleasure. He'd only held her closer then, so tightly she'd felt his heartbeat against her skin, and he hadn't let go until they'd both been spent, both claimed by sleep, just holding her, holding on, with everything he'd had.

That delicate, intent touch brushed across her cheek, and as she blinked, she realized she'd been crying. Divine, why? Why now? About to apologize, she shifted enough to look up at him, but he only cupped a hand to her cheek, tipped her face up to his to slant his mouth over hers.

AFTER SENDING word to Liam with a messenger, Rielle headed to the library, where Stefania had said the duchess was spending her evening.

She smoothed a nervous palm over her robe, a light-blue brocade Brennan had chosen for her, over her long white muslin nightgown. She'd arranged her still-damp hair neatly over her shoulder, and although it was late at night and at home, she still felt underdressed.

You'll be fine, Brennan had assured her, sprawled out on the bed and sipping a brandy. *She just wants to take care of you.*

That was easy for him to say as his mother's son, loved unconditionally. This was entirely different. The duchess could, at any time, find *her* unworthy. Clearly she was already being evaluated, if the duchess passed judgment on her correspondence.

Voices came from the library, and she paused at the door.

"...telling you, Mother, you can't tell the difference. It was perfect. But I lost contact with her," Nora's voice insisted.

"I have some knowledge of these affairs. If the need arises, *I* can help you. Better to keep such things in the family anyway," the duchess replied.

What things? Lost contact with whom?

A maid passed around her with a soft apology, bearing a tray of strawberries and two mugs of mulled wine, and opened the dark wood door.

The duchess faced away, but Rielle straightened, smiling awkwardly as Nora approached. Nora, with every hair in place, her face perfectly powdered, her gown a dream made real, yards of violet silk taffeta draped over a small, shapely figure. Firelight reflected in her shining dark hair as she paused, hands on her hips, and sized her up with a flutter of long, curled lashes. "My, my. *Such* a beauty. Small wonder men fall at the feet of a woman with—what do you call that hairstyle?"

Rielle winced.

"And that makeup! Tell me, who's your beautician?" Nora asked with a smirk.

It was no secret that Nora was a court beauty, always wearing the latest hairstyles and fashions, her face painted to perfection. Everything about her appearance was refined to an ideal, and just about any woman who believed herself in competition with Nora for beauty would end up disappointed.

But she wasn't in competition with Nora. And didn't want to be her enemy.

"I'm marrying your brother," Rielle said softly, her fingers tangling through the ends of her damp hair. "Can't you and I—"

"I think not." Nora stepped up to her, narrowed her sparkling hazel eyes and gave her a disapproving once-over.

"Nora," the duchess warned.

With a smirk, Nora pulled away and left the library.

Becoming a Marcel was going to take more than trading vows with Brennan. Nora might never accept her, ever. And it wasn't disapproval at the root of it.

Reminding herself of that made the barbs sting a bit less.

"Don't mind her at all," the duchess said warmly, glancing over her shoulder. "Come in, Rielle."

With a deep breath, she moved to the sofa and seated herself next to the duchess by the fire. The duchess had changed into a soft gray dress, made of fine tiretaine, well tailored but simple enough to wear at home. Her hair was still pinned elaborately. Beautiful.

Suddenly she did feel underdressed.

With a soft smile, the duchess took a sip of mulled wine and nodded to the other mug. "How are you feeling? You looked refreshed."

"I am." She smiled, taking up the second mug. If she was refreshed, it was Brennan's doing. But she wasn't about to say that to his mother.

"Una told me all about what happened," the duchess said, adding that she have a strawberry. "That had to be terrifying."

"I'm allergic," she explained, before returning to the subject. "It was—"

"I've already sent His Majesty a note," she added, daintily biting into a strawberry. "So fortunate that he was there to step in."

It was, or else... Or else she didn't know where she would be right now, or what would've happened.

There was a momentary lull in the conversation.

"Rielle..." the duchess began. "I wanted you to know that

although you're participating in these trials, winning them isn't the most important thing."

And then her spirits fell, her gaze fixed on the bowl of strawberries, beautiful and, to her, deadly.

"They're extremely dangerous," the duchess said, "and if at any time they become too dangerous for you, there is no shame in withdrawing. An invitation is already honor enough. *You* are more important, your *life* is more important than a victory, a rank."

"My life?" she whispered, looking away from the fruit.

The duchess nodded. "Una said one of the candidates was killed. And then that duel today..." She shook her head. "It's a lot of risk. Unnecessary risk."

Anyone who thought she was only competing for the magister's mantle and the honor might think so. "The victor may ask the Grand Divinus for a boon... I want to ask her to end piracy on the Shining Sea."

The duchess raised her eyebrows. "A worthy goal," she said, "but remember: you are marrying into an influential family. Once you're settled in, perhaps the Marcels will do more business overseas, using Laurentine as a hub. That'll mean more protection for our ships, and deterrence to pirates."

Just like that? If she wished it, the Marcels could *do more business overseas?* "That would be wonderful."

The duchess patted her hand. "You're *family.* Your needs are our needs."

Speechless, she brought the mug to her lips and drank the mulled wine in gulps.

Just like that. Once she and Brennan were married, the Marcels might direct their sizable resources toward her priorities.

But they could never pry the truth from the Divinity, could

they? What Brennan was doing—trying to infiltrate the Archives—the rest of the family would never support, would it?

The truth of what had happened in Laurentine would stay buried, and if the Divinity had done what Shadow had alleged, and had repeated it, killed families to take young mages, then it would... It would never stop.

The Divinity would never pay for the regicide, the attacks, nothing, and would continue taking whatever it wanted, leaving swaths of blood in its wake.

She nodded. "Thank you. That means a lot to me."

The duchess smiled. "Just take care of yourself. Don't risk your health or your life."

She sipped the mulled wine while the duchess plucked another strawberry from the bowl.

The duchess promised much, but what did she expect in exchange? *Once you're settled in,* the duchess had said. What did that mean? *Settled.* Did it mean giving up magic and using it to do some good in this world? Did it mean bowing to the family's interests over the kingdom's interests? Did it mean living the same life the duchess did?

If she wanted to fight the pirates and the Immortals, would Brennan support her in that? The more they discussed the future, the less it seemed their visions matched. She loved him, and he loved her, so it would work out. It had to. But they'd have to discuss exactly what life would look like once they were married. Soon.

But first, Liam. Then Samara.

And using every waking second left in the next three days to learn how to defeat a basilisk.

CHAPTER 35

*S*amara looked up at the palatial villa, with the shadow of Divinity Castle looming in the distance. A stable hand guided the packhorses bearing her medicines, tools, and ingredients away. She nodded her permission and stepped under the roof bridging the main houses and into a small courtyard.

Beneath the starlight, there was a split herb garden and carefully manicured dwarf cypress trees. She walked between them, letting her fingers stroke through soft fronds, textured leaves, abrasive stems.

Zahib had died tonight.

She pulled away a sprig of rosemary and ground it in her hand, letting its fresh scent intensify.

If ever she crosses my path, I will see her dead, he had said to her, before they'd left Xir.

When Thahab had burned down the barracks and nearly killed him, he'd been an unstoppable force, sending mercenary after mercenary to find her and bring her back for judgment.

Zahibi Ihsan had tried to curry favor among the extended family for backing as the stronger choice, but Zahib had had her married off and out of the house in weeks.

Zahib Imtiyaz had died, Zahib Farrad had been soundly defeated, and the slave responsible had escaped. To any zahib, it would have been unthinkable.

But he'd claimed to be *different*. Not beholden to the old ways. How could a forward-thinking man not understand a person's natural desire for freedom? How could he not sympathize?

He'd *tried* to be different, but in the end, he couldn't overcome his name.

He'd freed House Hazael's slaves, but he hadn't freed himself of the Hazael name, or its inbred obsessions. Power, privilege, and above all, pride. It hadn't been justice that had driven him to pursue her, nor vengeance for his grandfather; he'd taken a woman into his bed, believed her toothless, and she had bitten him, made a *fool* of him, and all of Xir had known.

It was for *pride* that he'd pursued her.

The liberating master had met the jilted lover in him; the forward-thinker had come face to face with the noble; and when it came to his reputation, he'd cast off his forward-thinking ideals in an instant.

In that instant, he'd chosen pride, privilege, power, and everything he'd claimed to have left behind over everything he'd claimed to have striven for. In that instant, as she'd screamed and pleaded for him not to, he'd cast her aside and walked backward into a past where nothing he'd said since leaving Xir had ever been said.

A man who didn't want to see the woman he loved returned to chains had stepped forth, and fate had done its part.

Somewhere on the wind there were whispers of a future in

which he'd seen an escaped slave, begged her forgiveness and paid her whatever amount she deemed reasonable in trying to make her whole. In which he'd left his daughter and heir at university but kept in close contact with her and never gave up on trying to build a relationship with her. In which someday, he might have overcome the sins of his past and become someone... more.

A dream of a dream, where ideals lived, not flesh-and-blood people.

She released the crumpled rosemary, and the wind blew past.

On the stairs leading into the courtyard, a red-headed woman stood, regal, exotic, wrapped in finery of the northern style—a voluminous gown, fitted above the waist and flaring below, all the way to the ground. She took a few steps down, said something that sounded like a greeting, and held out her hand.

Zahib—

No.

He wasn't her zahib anymore, and he wasn't her father.

Farrad had warned her that his wives and children would come after her, and she wasn't about to stay in the room he'd rented for them when news got back to Xir of his death.

The *King of Emaurria* had invited her to stay here, from what the Divine Guard had said. She didn't know him, Thahab clearly had. A man who'd been willing to step between her and a drawn blade. Her love, the father of her baby? If Thahab loved him and trusted him, he probably wasn't a bad person. He'd fought honorably... Thahab's interference had been beyond his control.

And he'd kindly offered her shelter, thinking her destitute?

She could trust Thahab's faith in him enough to stay here,

enough to believe he'd protect her if House Hazael sent blades her way.

She didn't know about university at the Divinity, or what tomorrow might hold, but tonight, she took the red-haired woman's hand and followed her to rooms for the night.

She'd write Thahab a letter and ask for it to be delivered wherever she was—surely they'd understand her enough for that—and help anyone here who needed it. And then *she* would decide where her life would take her next.

NEXT TO AMBRIEL, Leigh sat on an old sofa in Joel's home, where nestled within cramped quarters, an entire family gathered, and waited. Where was Katia?

Massive, brawny Joel sat across from them, scratching his beard contemplatively, while nearby, stone-faced Blaise— massive and brawny himself, in his thirties—perched cross-legged on a thick-woven rug before the hearth, with half a dozen small children climbing him and tugging at his red hair. He watched his father intently, unmoving and expressionless, completely oblivious to the dozen sticky little hands on him.

"All of them yours?" Leigh asked.

Blaise fixed gray eyes his way, turned up one corner of his mouth, and grunted before looking back to his father.

Such a chatterbox.

"Don't despair," Ambriel whispered as he patted Leigh's thigh. "I'm certain he remembers you."

"That wasn't—How did you—Are you telepathic?"

A smug smile flashed across Ambriel's pale face. "Katia may have mentioned a thing or two."

So that was where Blaise's power of speech had gone—to his younger sister. For *evil*.

Some delicious, sweet baking scent wafted in from the kitchen, where Marie, Helene, her oldest boy, and the rest of the clan were gathered, talking and laughing and maybe eating that deliciously scented whatever-they-were-baking thing.

The door flew open and Katia burst in, holding up a quiver, her red hair fleeing its braided bun in rebellious locks. "I got them!"

Joel nodded toward Ambriel. "Are you a good shot?" he asked in Old Emaurrian.

"One of the best among my people," Ambriel answered unabashedly, and Katia handed him the quiver containing three arrows.

Three *arcanir* arrows.

"It's gone on too long to be anything but either... deliberate," Joel said with a sigh, "in which case you'll *want* to use these, or a wild mage in fureur... in which case you'll *need* to use these."

There had been no word of a wild mage among the Beaufoys, which meant... a new one. But perhaps Joel's first guess was right—some heretic deliberately wreaking havoc.

Helene strode from the kitchen, dour-faced, and held out a knapsack.

"So good to see you, Helene!" he teased.

With a grimace, she held out the knapsack farther.

Ambriel took it and offered her a warm smile. "Thank you."

Joel stood. "This necromancer is closing in on our territory," he said, "and now that we're allied with Queen Ferelen, we have added responsibilities." He scowled at Katia, who beamed and brimmed with excitement, quivering on her feet. "If the Beaufoys don't handle their business, we will—and we'll be owed a price."

Covens that couldn't keep their territory found their resources dwindling, but the Forgerons stepping in would mean no care to whoever was causing the disturbance, whether their actions were intentional or not. They'd be ruthless about protecting their own territory.

When it came to fureur, the Covens didn't dither.

And if it was someone he knew—Leigh rose, fixing his gaze on Joel. "It won't come to that. I'll take care of it."

"Katia will make sure you do."

"I won't let you down, Papa!" she said, darting to him and throwing her arms around him. He looked a lot like Blaise, enormous, unmoving, expressionless, and oblivious to the sticky hands on him.

"If she comes to harm, Galvan, I'll make good on the promise I made you two years ago," Joel said firmly.

Two years ago, when Joel had walked in on him and Blaise, told him to keep his trouble away from his son, and threatened to craft his jewels into a necklace if he needed a reminder.

Blaise reddened and looked away. That was practically a *riot* from him.

Clearing his throat, Leigh shifted on his feet. "We'll keep her safe."

Joel bit his thumb and held out his massive forearm in the vowing clasp. "If you handle that necromancer, I pledge myself and my Coven to the Crown."

Leigh clasped it, Joel's mark searing his skin, and his own finding space among many others on Joel's arm.

"If His Majesty has need, he may call upon me and mine."

With that, Katia said her goodbyes and they left, mounting their horses.

"This is really important to you," Ambriel said as they headed for the north gate.

Very important. He'd never mentioned Ava to anyone, not even to Rielle, although she'd known he'd sent coin somewhere every month. What she'd assumed, he couldn't say, but it had been a secret not even *she* could be privy to.

Loved ones were a liability to someone like him, someone who could be all powerful, unless he kept them close, protected.

But magic had cost him his entire family, and his protection had meant nothing—he hadn't been able to protect anyone from *himself.*

Ava's greatest protection was her anonymity, and although his heart had ached to see her face, he hadn't seen her in thirteen years, not since he'd made the agreement with Della four days after Ava's birth. The Beaufoys, masters of forbidden magic, would keep her safe, from him and anyone else.

But the Beaufoys had lost control, couldn't even keep their territory safe, let alone the daughter of a wild mage.

His distance might have failed Ava, and once he arrived he'd know... and never fail her again.

"My daughter is among the Beaufoys," he said quietly to Ambriel. "And I don't know if she's safe."

CHAPTER 36

Squinting in the morning sunlight, Rielle fastened her turquoise coat in the mirror as Stefania brought in the correspondence. She'd requested a book from Divinity Castle last night, and it still hadn't arrived. She heaved a sigh. If she wanted to research basilisks, she'd have to go there, or try her luck at the local bookshops.

She snatched up the correspondence. One letter from The Red Veil in Il Serpente, Liam telling her he'd be waiting. And another for her and Brennan, from...

The seal of the Archmage. *Olivia.*

Frowning, Rielle ran her thumb over it while laughter filtered in from outside. She moved to the window, and below, in the courtyard, Brennan wrestled with his nephews in the grass.

With a slow smile, she shook her head, watching as he let them drag him down and pin him, laughing all the while. She'd been rambunctious as a child herself, and no doubt Sylvie would have been, too, climbing all over her and—

She swallowed.

The look on Brennan's face—sheer, perfect joy—was a father's, and here she stood, keeping that from him, depriving him not only of something he wanted but, by the looks of it, something he was meant for.

His gaze met hers in the window, and she turned away, squeezing the letter in her grasp. With a deep breath, she cracked the wax seal and opened the note.

It was short but simple, asking her and Brennan's help in translating between Jon and Samara, and directions to the villa she and Jon were staying at uptown.

Quick footsteps ascended the stairs to the hall. If she told Brennan she wanted to visit Samara, would he just try to change the subject again? Or try to forbid her?

Brennan opened the door, turned to her, and raised his eyebrows, rolling up his sleeves. "You're going now?"

She nodded, and he leaned in and kissed her. "Olivia sent us a note," she said, handing it to him.

As he read, the mirth on his face faded. "Rielle," he said with a deep breath, "I'm not sure this is such a good idea. After everything that happened yesterday, do we really want to have the same argument?"

"We don't have to." She leaned in. "Besides, if anyone has books on basilisks, it's Olivia. I only have two more days before the next trial."

He shook his head.

"What is it that you think I'll do?" she asked. "Don't you trust me?"

He folded up the note and crossed his arms. "I do trust you. It's *him* I don't trust."

She rolled her eyes. The moments she'd spent alone with

Jon since Veris, he'd been perfectly proper, neither said nor done anything untoward. "Do you want to come with me?"

He was silent awhile. "I'd love to, but there's something I want to do here that I've been putting off."

"What?"

He leaned against the doorjamb. "Worship," he murmured.

Quickly, he glanced away; the look on her face must have betrayed her surprise.

The Marcels were well known as Terrans in that they *believed* in the goddess Terra, but it was Nox, god of death in the Eternan pantheon, that they worshipped. Brennan had once told her that the only power able to grant a blessed life was Death. His parents kept a shrine at every property, and she remembered his mother or father disappearing down a set of stairs. Upon return, they'd always exuded the smell of blood.

But she couldn't remember the last time she'd seen Brennan do so.

She placed a palm on his chest, over his heart. "Well, with all due respect, tell Him not to expect you anytime soon. I have big plans for you."

"Oh?" He stroked her cheek with a faint smile.

"Step one," she said, leaning in close to his ear, breathing softly, and placing a kiss on his jaw, "have my way with you later." As she pulled away, his heavy-lidded gaze followed her.

"And step two?" he asked, his voice low, seductive.

"Repeat for the rest of our lives," she said, and pressed her lips to his.

Grinning, she rounded him and stepped out into the hall, but he took her hand. "Take some outriders with you. The first sign of trouble, burn down everything."

～

THE SPRAWLING BAZAAR of Il Serpente was already dense with people when she arrived, peeking out from between the carriage's drapes while the outriders cleared a path. The travel accommodations were lavish, far fancier than she preferred, but if it made Brennan feel more comfortable about her going, then she'd do it to please him. It was too small a concession to fight over.

She stopped at the few bookshops to be found here, but found nothing about Immortals. From what the booksellers said, nothing new had been released, and the antiquarian books that did contain useful information could only be found uptown or on the black market. Her best finds came from a small foreign section that had books in Nad'i, including ones on learning Emaurrian, Sileni, and Morwenian, and then a tome on Sileni herbalism. Samara might like them, something to occupy her mind. *Even if she never wants to speak to me again.*

With a sigh, she let the coachman take her to the entertainment district. The Red Veil was a tall, three-story building wedged between two taverns, with so much raucous noise in the air, she wanted to hold her hands over her ears.

Four of her outriders minded the carriage and horses while the remaining two shouldered their way into The Red Veil. A cozy entryway draped in hanging red silk led into a bustling great room, where all manner of revelry and debauchery unfolded, from drinking and gambling to smoking and flirting, to the many varieties of pleasure this place traded in.

She squinted, blurring her vision and hoping *not* to see Liam among these patrons. Without even knowing their names, she'd seen too much of them already.

"And you are?" a tall woman asked, with the most voluminous red curls she'd ever seen. The madam?

"Visiting Captain Verib," she said quietly, clearing her

throat as a kissing couple bumped into her. The two outriding guards who'd walked in with her directed them along. "He's, um, a friend," she added, hoping to mitigate any rumors.

"They always are," the madam crooned as she rounded the bar and opened a book. She traced a fingertip down a page, then smiled brightly. "He's expecting a visitor. Third floor, second door on the right."

With a nod, she turned to the tight staircase, and the guards moved to follow. "I'll be fine on my own," she said, meeting two stern faces. "You two wait for me here."

They took up posts by the staircase as she ascended. Did they report to Brennan, or to the duchess? What would they say about this?

She sighed. No sense in worrying when there was nothing to do about it. Keeping her eyes to herself, she climbed the stairs all the way to the third floor. At the second door on the right, she knocked, then took a polite step back.

Some shuffling on the other side of the door, a cheery feminine giggle, and then she came face to face with a buxom, gray-eyed blonde with kiss-swollen lips, wrapping a burgundy shawl about her shoulders. With a last look back, the blonde bit her lip and sashayed out of the room and down the stairs.

Bad timing. Very bad timing.

Inside, sprawled out on an armchair, Liam slowly raked his fingers through his tied-back, unruly straw-blond hair, blinking sluggishly, his ankle propped on his knee. Barefoot, he wore only a pair of light-colored linen drawstring pants, the vast sun-tanned expanse of his chest and arms golden against the black velvet upholstery. His sky-blue eyes met hers, and he grinned, with the sunlight streaming in through the window behind him.

"Did I come at a bad time?" she teased, grabbing a gray shirt from a chair and tossing it at him. It hit him in the face and fell to his abdomen.

He smirked. "No, not at all. Perfect time, actually." He rose and threw the shirt on over his head, then wrapped her in a hug.

The sea's fresh salt air and the scent of dry red wine flooded her nostrils, and she breathed him in, the familiarity of him, the reality—even solid and warm in her arms, she could scarcely believe it was really *Liam*. "I've missed you."

Here, in his arms, she felt like she truly *belonged*.

Huffing a half-laugh, he patted her back gently and then pulled away. "I've missed you, too, little bee. It's been too long."

He cocked his head toward an empty chair at the table, and she plopped into it, watching him as he gestured over the teapot until it steamed, spooned some black tea into two cups, then poured. He slid one down toward her.

Such a long way from exploding teapots in Laurentine.

After grabbing an armful of clothes, he disappeared behind the bathing screen. "What took you so long?"

She grimaced, wrapping her hands around the steaming cup. "The Duchess of Maerleth Tainn *curates* the incoming correspondence."

"Can't say I'm surprised." He threw the pants off to the side on the floor. "It's a fancy family you're marrying into."

Fancy was right. "So I would've been here sooner, but I only found out you were here through Olivia."

A pause. "Fine woman, that Olivia."

With a shake of her head, she leaned back, then took a sip of the hot black tea. It was strong, delicious, not sweet at all—just as he'd always liked it.

"Olivia would have *none* of this," she said, glancing about the disheveled room, "so don't waste your time. Besides, wouldn't your companion of five minutes ago be disappointed in how soon your mind turns to another woman?"

A laugh, then the clink of his belt buckle as he stepped out in fitted black trousers, the gray shirt she'd tossed him tucked into it. He fastened his belt. "The best part about paying for companionship is not having to care *what* she thinks."

She sighed. He'd been at this kind of life for quite a while, hadn't he? Living at sea, coming into port for leave once every couple of months, spending a few days in a place like this...

"A woman like her probably wants a marriage," he remarked loftily, dragging on boots.

"And a good one."

"Just another kind of shackle."

She wrinkled her nose.

"One person always secretly wants something from the other. Complete possession. A child. To change you. To keep you stuck somewhere," he listed off, stomping about the room in his big, black boots, upending blankets and pillows. "Not me. I'm not going to let anyone control me."

It was easy for him to speak that way now. "If you love someone enough, you might not see it that way."

"Love?" He raised an eyebrow. "I'm content with what I have," he said, holding up his arms to indicate the room. "At least it's honest. She's upfront with what *she* wants, and so am I." He eyed her doubtfully. "If you think your fiancé is any different, remember who he is. That's a man who does what he wants, *anything* he wants, with no thought to the consequences."

"He's changed," she said, straightening.

Liam pulled a blue doublet out from under a pile of clothes. "I don't trust him."

"You don't *know* him," she snapped back, and Liam

shrugged, then threw on the doublet. "I wish you could spend more time—"

"Well, I can't." He raked his fingers through his hair again, exhaling lengthily. "As soon as I'd set foot in the doorway at the Marcels' villa, or in Divinity Castle, that's it. This life would be over." He held out his hand to her, and she took it, letting him help her up.

"Are we going somewhere?"

"Best place in town." Grinning, he headed past the armchair and threw open the window panes. He climbed out onto the roof, dipping in again to grab a half-full bottle of wine on the window sill, then offered her a hand. "Coming?"

With a smile, she accepted it and stepped out into the great, vast blue, unsteady on the clay roof tiles. Liam helped her to the top, where the beam was wide enough to sit on comfortably. Perched there, he looked out at the sprawl of Magehold, and so did she. Between the rooftops, tiny people moved like the lapping sea, and farther beyond were the villas—the Marcels' among them—and then the enormous shadow of Divinity Castle. Down the other way were smaller, meeker houses, farms, countryside and forests, and then the endless bright turquoise of the Shining Sea, with ships and boats bobbing in the harbor, sails fluttering in the free wind. That color—she could just look at it for days and days and never tire of it. Longer, even. "It's beautiful," she whispered.

He uncorked the bottle, took a swig, and handed it to her. "It's why I always rent this room."

"Nothing to do with your fine companion?"

He smirked. "Vera has her fine points, too." He nodded toward the castle. "Someone put a skylight in last night. Was that you?"

She shrugged. "It was getting stuffy in there. And as it turns out, the ceiling is *not* made of arcanir." A drink of the wine—dry and warm—and she handed it back to him. "It's terrible."

"Don't hate the wine," he scolded, angling the neck of the bottle toward her. The breeze blew straw-blond wisps across his eyes, and he dipped his head. "Rumor says the Emaurrian king fought another man for his lover."

Cheeks warming, she looked away. "This 'lover' is causing him so much trouble. Can't say I approve of her at all."

"Not only that, but she intervened, completely obliterating his opponent to ash."

She bit her lip. "Everyone was thrilled about that, right? Because that might have saved his life?"

"Well, some have said she ended both the duel and his reputation in one fell swoop," he said, and she winced, "but here, the women can't shut up about how romantic it is. He saves her, she saves him, and they'd do anything for each other, right? Reputation and appearances and all that be damned."

She sighed. Put like that, it sounded grand, not like the charged, angry chaos it had actually been. "Only she's not his lover."

"And he's not her fiancé." He fixed narrowed eyes on her. "Where was Brennan?"

Her mouth hung open, but no words would come. Brennan had been helping her, risking his *life* for her. "He was—It wasn't his fault."

Liam cocked his head toward the castle. "What are you really doing there? And don't say competing for magister."

So he'd figured her out, just like that? "Do you ever think about what Shadow told us on Khar'shil that day?"

He spat. "I do my best *not* to think of that bloodthirsty madwoman," he grumbled. "But to be honest, I haven't been able to stop. I think it's true. I keep putting together bits and pieces about the Divinity and pirates, bandits, ruffians, and these attacks and—" He sighed.

"I'm not sure what to believe," she said, "but if there are answers, they're in there." She pointed her chin toward the castle.

He eyed it for a while before snapping his head toward her. "You can't possibly mean—you're trying to break into the Archives?"

She nodded.

"That's suicide."

She pulled out the basilisk scale. "And what do you call this?"

He took it, rubbing fingers over the rocky exterior. "World's worst leather?"

She grimaced. "I'm fighting a basilisk for the second trial, and I don't know the first thing about them."

He half-laughed. "Don't ask me. Mermaids, krakens, water dragons, and selkies I can help with, but land beasts are not my area." He eyed her peripherally, flashing a derisive grin. "I heard your king fought them recently. Can you just bring him? No rules, right?"

The urge to jab him bubbled up to the surface, but she waited until it passed. There had to be some rule about waiting a certain length of time after reuniting with your long-lost brother before you could resume all sisterly activities.

"Joking aside, maybe he knows something that could help you." He returned the scale to her, and she lowered her gaze, catching on the sheath in his boot. The dagger he'd lent her that day on Khar'shil.

Farrad had plunged a dagger into Jon's side, between his ribs, and the look on Jon's face had been—this intensity, this farseeing intensity, as if he'd seen where his life would end, the only path open to him, and had taken the first step.

She couldn't get it out of her head.

"Rielle?" Liam waved the bottle of wine in front of her face, but she swatted it away.

"I'll talk to him."

"You don't sound thrilled."

She shrugged. "Neither is Brennan."

He hadn't fought her on it—much—but she knew he preferred she didn't see Jon.

Liam's sky-blue eyes narrowed on her, and his lips twisted bitterly as he shook his head and glanced away, toward the ships on the Shining Sea. "One person always secretly wants something from the other," he repeated lowly. "Or in this case, not so secretly."

She jerked toward him, grasping the beam as she shifted. "It's not like that."

"This is how it starts, Rielle. First, it'll be 'don't talk to that person' or 'don't go there,' and you'll do it, because you don't want to hurt him," Liam said, narrowing his eyes at the sea. "And then it'll be 'change who you are,' and it'll be a knife in the gut, but you love him, so you'll try. And then it'll be 'do whatever I want you to,' because you've done it already, haven't you, willingly stepped over that line, and what's left of your will on the other side to cling to?"

No. This was—it was ridiculous. It wasn't anything at all like what she and Brennan had. It was some skewed vision Liam had, like looking through sea glass, and he didn't know the first thing about her and Brennan, or perhaps even love.

"That's not... It's not what our love is like," she bit out to him.

"It has nothing to do with love," he argued. "All of us are

capable of feeling love. It's the rest of what's inside of us that's the problem."

Blowing out a breath, she shook her head and looked away. This was ridiculous.

"You're scoffing, but you've already begun to give in." He took another drink. "Some time on the Shining Sea, with no one to lord over you, just you, the wind, and the waves, would do you some good."

"I haven't given in," she said to him.

"Then do what you want to do," he replied. "Trust yourself, and that when it comes to doing the right thing for yourself, you don't need to be told. You'll always find the right answer in one place—inside."

CHAPTER 37

*I*n his robe, Brennan made his way down the longest
stair in the villa, deep into its heart, where the shrine
of Nox awaited.

It had been years since he'd worshipped as he would
tonight. When a man had everything he could ask for, the Great
Wolf clearly favored him already. He always made his offerings,
simple things like fruit and wine, as every Marcel did, but not
the Blood Offering.

Tonight would be different.

He had Rielle, his health, luxury, and pleasure at his every
whim. Yet last night, another man had taken something
belonging to him. In the great hall, her eyes had burned,
gleamed, so intense, so devoted. It was how he wanted her to
look at him, to look when she thought of him. But it hadn't been
him she'd been thinking of.

Perhaps she didn't realize it yet herself, but Great Wolf, *he*
did, like fangs in flesh, like claw against bone, and the closer he

wanted to hold her, the more control he'd try to exert, the more it would push her away.

When she'd wanted to go to see Samara, where she would see Jon, the words on his lips had been, *I forbid it*. But what had he done? Let her go.

She was no fearful hind; she had fangs of her own. And nothing was likelier to make her bare them as trying to restrain her. It would only push her away and into Jon's arms.

Trust her. He had to trust her. That was the only way their marriage could work. She'd do as she pleased, he'd suffer in silence, and she'd stay loyal. Love him. Choose him. Wed him.

With Nox on his side, perhaps she'd even make him a father. When she finally set aside magic, when she finally gave their future a chance, she'd be happy. She would. He'd make sure of it, every day of their life together.

The circular stone chamber was already lit with torches, and a large bull grunted on the platform in the middle, magnificent with white lilies and gold adornment, held in place by chains and two stable hands.

He dismissed them with a wave, and ascended the stair winding the chamber to the platform of planks pierced with fine holes. Beneath it lay a massive circular phiale with Nox's own wolfish image carved around its rim, His maw a hole in its center.

The bull stamped a hoof, bucked against the restraints. On the altar among the candles lay a ceremonial cloth and an aldhammé, which he took in hand before grasping one of the bull's horns.

The bull was strong, but he was stronger. He held the animal in place, and slit its throat.

Fresh blood flowed like wine, left the body in pours as it weakened and gave way.

As the bull collapsed, he cleansed the al-dhammé with the ceremonial cloth and set both back on the altar, inclining his head and whispering his respect to Nox. He descended the spiral stair, casting off his robe as he made his way into the trench beneath the phiale.

Arms spread, he knelt beneath Nox's maw just as the blood poured through.

"*O Nox, Great Wolf, Dark God, Unseen One, Life-Taker, Death-Eater, He-Who-Carries-Away-All, I humbly ask your favor. Make me a father.*"

Wet warmth coated his head, his face, his neck, flowing down his skin utterly and completely, Nox's holy blessing wrapping him entirely.

"*O Nox, Great Wolf, Dark God, Unseen One, Life-Taker, Death-Eater, He-Who-Carries-Away-All, I humbly ask your favor. Make me a father.*"

The metallic tang flooded his nostrils, and he breathed it in, welcomed it, Nox's holy blessing entering him deeply.

"*O Nox, Great Wolf, Dark God, Unseen One, Life-Taker, Death-Eater, He-Who-Carries-Away-All, I humbly ask your favor. Make me a father.*"

The coppery taste seeped onto his tongue, and he savored it, accepted it, Nox's holy blessing becoming part of him. One.

He remained kneeling on the stone, taking every last blessed drop for what felt like hours, repeating his prayer, even as he heard footsteps down the longest stair.

But all he smelled was blood.

It wasn't Rielle. He'd sense her anywhere. He'd already broached the subject of conceiving an heir with her many times, and her mind hadn't changed. Perhaps time, love, and divine favor would sway her when his words didn't. One day, when they had a family, he wouldn't be the only happy one—he would see her smile every day of her life.

"Considering how in love you two are, I never thought you'd need to pray for such a thing," Mother said from behind him. Her voice was soft, careful, matched by her irregular heartbeat. Nervous.

He stood, wiping the blood from his eyes, and headed through the arched doorway to the ceremonial bath. Footsteps and a whisper of fine silk cloth—Mother picking up his robe—and she followed.

"She takes the preventive herbs," he said, descending the shallow steps into the cool water. When he was waist deep, he submerged completely, scrubbing his hair and face before surfacing.

"Perhaps she wishes to wait until after you're wed," Mother said, folding to a kneel at the edge of the bath, tucking her skirts beneath her gracefully. Her face slack, she looked at the center of the bath with sadly serene eyes, like still waters on an autumn evening.

Through the water, he approached her, and covered her hand on the stone with his. "Mother, she lost a child recently. It's been difficult for her, and I think she's healing, but I... I don't know what else to do. Perhaps Nox's wisdom will enlighten me."

Her mouth curved in a fragile smile. "I think her heart would swell to hear you say so."

Would it?

No, he couldn't bring it up with Rielle again. He wouldn't. The more he'd push, the more she'd push back. It had to be patience.

A shadow crossed Mother's face. "Do you... do you think she can carry a child to term? Is she well enough?"

His head jerked back, and he splashed his face with water. It hadn't even occurred to him to wonder. Whether she could or couldn't, he still wanted her for his wife, would still love her. If they couldn't have children together, they'd worry about that later. "That doesn't matter."

Mother's green gaze snapped to his. "My son, it matters a great deal. You must have an heir."

"Mother—"

"No one would judge you for conceiving before the wedding, waiting until the first three months have—"

"No," he bit out. "Didn't you hear a word I said?"

She stood. "Yes, and you must hear the words I have to say. Tenderness matters. Love matters. But so do practical matters. You will be a husband, but you must be the scion of House Marcel first, husband second. In that order. Marriage to you comes with responsibilities. I sympathize with her, but she must meet those responsibilities, or she must find a husband who needs no heir."

His face stung as if she'd slapped him. Was this advice, or did she plan to speak to Father? "And is this my mother speaking, or the duchess of Maerleth Tainn?"

She narrowed her eyes. "Your mother, for now. You must harden your heart and do what must be done." She let his robe drop next to the bath and turned to leave. "If you do not heed me soon, it shall be the duchess."

CHAPTER 38

*J*on offered Olivia his arm as they walked the villa's grounds. "You said you wanted to talk with me?"

She nodded, the rays of the high noon sun catching in her unbound red waves. "I know you've been wanting to, and after yesterday, I think it's unavoidable. Don't you?"

He'd been trying to get a moment alone with her for days, so they could discuss this change between them. After she'd declined a couple times, it had come as a surprise when she'd invited him.

After yesterday... The duel. He tilted his head. "I've... noticed a shift between us. Something different."

A brief smile flashed across her face, but she didn't let him go. "I've felt a... growing attraction," she said.

His heart beat faster, but he fought to stay calm, replying only with a measured nod. "When two people spend time together in close quarters, that can happen."

"Dancing, cramped in a ship's cabin, sleeping in adjoining rooms?" she offered, with a lilting tone.

"It's been the nature of things, especially since..." He rested a hand over his heart. "I can't tell you how thankful I am, for your friendship, your care, your advice. I don't know what I'd do without you, Olivia."

She blinked a pleased acknowledgement, then fixed her gaze on the stables close by. "The more time we spend together, the more I enjoy your company," she said softly, her cheeks reddening. "I know this is... an inconvenience, but..."

He shook his head. "It's not. You're a formidable woman, Olivia. Sharp, witty, intelligent... a force to be reckoned with." He looked her up and down. "And beautiful." He bowed his head, eyeing the grass before them as they came upon the stable. Even if his heart were perfect, it would still belong to someone else. "But I have nothing to offer you. I couldn't give any woman forever, and I can't promise it to you."

She paused as a groom walked a stallion out of the stable into a paddock, her hold on his arm tightening, and urged him beneath the stable's roof. When the groom was out of earshot, she gazed up at him. "I know you can't promise forever," she said, "but how about right now?"

Searching his eyes, she pushed him inside, until his back met a wall, then rose up on her toes and kissed him.

Terra have mercy, he didn't want to push her away and hurt her feelings, but he also didn't want her to—

Her lips pressed to his, and she leaned into him, her body flush against his, as her hand slid from his chest to the nape of his neck. As her tongue met his, everything about this felt wrong, and he grasped her shoulders, held her away, her hands slipping back to his chest.

Her gaze locked with his in expressionless silence, and as

the seconds went by to the soft nickers and whinnies of horses, the chance that he might lose her completely weighed heavier.

"The rest of your life may not be exactly how you imagined it, Jon, but it doesn't have to be joyless or lonely, no matter what promises you may have made to yourself," she said softly. "You have needs like any other person."

"Need and love have become so entwined," he whispered, "that I could never again separate the two. And I wouldn't want to." He'd have neither. He'd lived nearly his entire life that way and had found meaning in serving the greater good, in serving Terra, and so would he do now, and for the rest of his life.

She rested a palm over his heart, pressed firmly there, frowning at it before she met his eyes anew. "You told me once that you'd only ever love one woman."

That hadn't changed. And never would.

"I like to live in the moment," she said, "but someday, I want someone to love me the way you love her." Her tone had a fragile quality, a waver, but she smiled faintly at him. "Maybe that's what draws me to you. What... *drew* me to you. A faraway look in your eyes, a treasured thought."

A thought that lingered no matter how many battles he fought, no matter how much he worked, how much he trained. No matter how many lands and seas and people spanned between them. A thought that had claimed him once in a forest pool and would never abandon him.

"You're my closest friend, Olivia, and I love you like family." He took her hand, kissed it gently. "But friendship is all I have to give. May I have the honor?"

This time, her smile reached her eyes as she nodded. "Friends."

As she bowed her head, he dipped down to meet her eyes, and she laughed.

"Are we... all right?" he asked, grinning.

"Yes," she said, and he wrapped her in a hug. Her arms closed around him, too, and she rested her cheek against his chest. "Don't worry," she teased. "I know this is a friend hug."

He laughed, and she joined him. "Where would I be without you, Olivia?"

"Standing here hugging yourself?" she offered, and only made him laugh more. She pulled away.

They'd accomplished so much together, saved lives and the kingdom many times over, and together, they'd only accomplish more. "Save my life, Olivia."

She started, blinking up at him. "What?"

"We have a lot of work ahead of us, and I'll do what needs to be done to keep our people safe, the only way I can," he said, and folded his arms. "So save my life, Olivia. Let's keep putting things right, for as long as we can."

A wide smile slowly claimed her face. "From dragons, from enemies, and from even death itself." She took his hand and pulled him out of the shade and into the sun's light, footsteps crunching in the lush grass. "I will, Jon. I promise."

She let him go and, with a few steps facing him, then turned and headed toward the villa, pausing only for Rielle, who stood unmoving.

THE SOUND of silence stole the villa's grounds, even the spring breeze that disturbed her coat as Rielle fixed her gaze on him.

Olivia, a dazzling vision of green in her flowing dress against the bright red of her unbound, wind-ruffled hair, rested a hand on her shoulder and smiled warmly. "We're in a good place, Rielle. Don't worry. I'm watching out for him." She looked away and walked to the villa.

Still, Rielle stood there, frozen to the spot, a myriad verdant blades between them.

"Rielle," he greeted softly, a ghost of a smile fading from his lips.

She shivered. Her breath bottled in her chest as he held her still with those Shining Sea eyes, looking at her, beyond her, into her, and he shouldn't see any of those things inside.

On a sunlit Floreal afternoon, in the shade of a stable, two lovers had shared a tryst, had parted with a loving glance, and they'd done nothing wrong, nothing to make her chest tight or her hands tremble or the rest of her so tense she couldn't move.

Divine, take it from me. Cut it out of me and take it.

He lowered his gaze, approached with crossed arms. Closed off. "What can I do for you?"

She clasped her trembling hands behind her back. "Actually, I... I came to see Olivia, about the trials," she said, finding her voice, but her nerves made even her throat tremble. It didn't help that she'd just let Olivia walk by her. "And Samara. The guards said you were here." When he glanced toward the villa, she took a deep breath. "Also, I... Everything happened so fast," she said, taking a step, if only to prove to herself she could. "I didn't get a chance to say thank you last night. I appreciate what you did."

His eyes downcast, he headed toward the villa, giving her a wide berth, and paused just past her. "Don't thank me, Rielle," he said quietly. "Not for that. Not for doing what I should've done." He nodded toward the villa. "I'll walk with you."

Her heart pounding, she turned and fell into step next to him. The villa was grand, larger than the Marcels', a square of brick buildings framing a courtyard inside. It was really only a stone's throw from the Marcels' villa, maybe a half-hour walk.

Jon escorted her, only the crisp sound of their footsteps breaking the silence.

"Are you feeling better?" she asked. "You gave me quite a scare when I wasn't able to fully heal you."

He glanced away, his long lashes hooding his gaze. "Olivia healed my injuries." He cleared his throat. "And you, after the trial?"

"I'm fine," she said, as they neared the herb garden. "Nothing I couldn't heal. I'm more concerned about the second trial, and have about a hundred questions for Olivia."

His mouth twitched as he dipped his chin. "I'm sure she has about two hundred answers for you."

His words were pleasant, but his forbidding posture, his stiffness—something was bothering him.

He was angry with *her*. Had to be. About yesterday, about her intervention, between him and Farrad.

But he had to understand. If she could have dueled Farrad herself, she would have. If anyone should have claimed Farrad's life, it should have been *her*. And it had been.

Was this just about honor? The dishonor of someone interfering in a duel between two parties—

One of whom was *royal*. That changed things. A subject interfering in a duel her king had accepted. It—It implied a lot. That his subjects didn't trust him. That they felt empowered to interfere. That he didn't punish her for it.

That Emaurria didn't keep its word. Didn't trust its king. Didn't behave honorably.

She covered her mouth. Divine's flaming fire, he should have rebuked her publicly. He should have berated her, and she would've deserved it.

"I'm sorry if my intervention caused you trouble," she said as they traversed the garden.

"I don't care about that, Rielle," he replied quietly, evenly.

Don't... care...? Then why was he—

"Yesterday I saw something in you, when... *he* challenged you. Something I never want to see again." His arms flexed, tightened, and he was all hard edges and rigidity.

And for that, he'd face untold political consequences.

"Castigate me publicly. Blame it all on me," she offered. "I was the one who interfered, so if there are any consequences, I should bear them."

He glared at her. "Not your decision to make."

She took a step away. Seeing him now, strong, intense, only summoned the image of his blood pooling beneath his body anew. "You don't owe me anything," she said, with a swallow. "Now the world will assume—"

"You think I care what the world assumes?" he asked, calm, measured.

"You have to. You're the king, and—"

They approached the villa's entryway. "I may be the king, but I'm still a man. There was no part of me that would allow *him* to walk out of there alive."

Neither could she. "I want to fight my own battles, Jon."

He paused before the doorway, finally uncrossing his arms, and looked over his shoulder. "Before you speak to Olivia, there's something I want to give to you."

Give? She tilted her head, but when he ascended the steps, she followed him.

Upstairs, he entered a suite of rooms past two guards posted outside the door.

Inside, the suite was airy and opulent, something she might have imagined in a dream. The sea breeze blew in through open balcony doors, catching gauzy white curtains that fluttered against the parquet floor. A small sitting room led into a bedchamber, where a massive stone hearth and an enormous bed dominated the space.

The fire crackled in the hearth. On the nearby table, his blade sharpening kit sat before an armchair next to a small, plainly sheathed sword. She could picture him sitting there, night after night, maintaining his own blade. Faithkeeper. A king—with servants, squires, pages—and he still tended his own weapons. It should've been surprising, but with Jon, it really wasn't.

Next to it was a carved wood piece, and wood shavings on the rug before the armchair. Something he'd been carving himself? She picked it up, turning it in her hand—still rough, not yet finished. Linden, by its smell. A bird, small enough for a child's hand. A plump little bird, by its general shape, like a—like a winter wren.

It froze her to the spot, sending her pulse thundering. Great Divine, this was—he was—he thought about—

He took it from her, wordlessly, and set it on the mantle.

She frowned, staring at him as he braced over the fire, his shoulders tense. Here, in his quarters, she'd been privy to something inside of him, too, something he hadn't wanted her to see.

He nodded toward the small sword on the table, in the plain brown-leather sheath. "That's yours."

A sword? She picked it up and drew the blade—the arcanir blade. It had to be vastly expensive. "Jon, I—I can't accept—"

"You can and you will." Pausing, he looked over his shoulder at her, a look that softened, and gave a slow shake of his head. "You have your magic, I know that, but sometimes you'll need something... else." He pushed away and crossed his arms again, taking a couple steps back from her before leaning his shoulder against the wall. "Brennan is an accomplished swordsman, from what I've heard. Ask him to teach you."

He wanted to give her an arcanir sword and suggest she take lessons from Brennan?

Since that night of Veris, not only had he never spoken a single word against Brennan, but he'd actually—he'd actually *encouraged* her, just as he was doing now.

It should have been comforting, calming, but something shifted inside of her, rumbled, like a storm breaking.

He lowered his gaze, his face going slack as he turned his head aside. "If you want to learn to fight with a sword, you will. I just... I can't tell you I'll always be there—or that Brennan will always be there."

He was right. Not just that he or Brennan might not always be there, but she... she didn't *want* them to have to fight for her. Maybe it was foolish for a twenty-two-year-old woman to begin learning the sword, but if it meant she never had to watch someone she loved bleeding out for her sake, then she was willing to risk foolishness.

Brennan would laugh at her, but she wouldn't take no for an answer. Maybe it would even be fun, training together every day.

"Olivia should be downstairs, in the library," he said, with an air of finality.

Taking a step back, she nodded. "Thank you for this, Jon."

Unmoving, he looked at her from where he leaned against the wall, his arms crossed, restrained, forbidden, and those Shining Sea eyes of his strained across the distance between them. He glanced away. "You said you wanted to talk to her about the second trial?"

She removed the basilisk's scale from her coat, its texture rough against her skin. "I got this."

"Basilisks," he said, accepting it. "We fought them near

Caerlain Trel. Their eyes are dangerous, of course, but everyone forgets about the tail."

When she only eyed him, he continued. "Its gaze can petrify you—and it eats humans, as we learned—but it also has a twenty-foot-long tail, agile as lightning and strong as stone—that can hit you with the force of twenty men."

She leaned forward. "You were hit?"

He placed a palm on his sternum and glanced down. "The gaze doesn't work on paladins, but that tail certainly does. My armor took the brunt of it, but I'd probably be bandaged from head to toe if not for Olivia."

Jon would have been lying on the field of battle, hurt, and if not for Olivia—

"Watch for the tail. And if all else fails"—he approached her and very slowly raised a hand to her face, and holding her gaze, he pressed his callused thumb under her chin into soft flesh —"they have a soft spot right here."

That whisper of his stroked down the bare skin of her spine like a delicate caress, eliciting a shiver, and she closed her eyes.

It felt good, natural. And *wrong*.

She opened her eyes, slowly, cautiously, as he watched her face with those Shining Sea eyes, soft, warm, honest... as he always had, in the fledgling rays of dawn, in those quiet moments. The serenity of that look was a tender embrace, making her feel safe, loved, wanted—not for a night, but for a lifetime.

He released her, but the warm familiarity of his touch lingered, and he just stood, within arm's reach, looking down into her eyes, searching them.

She couldn't breathe.

He stepped away, back to the mantle, crossed his arms again and leaned against it. "Olivia will be pleased to see you. Ask her about Samara. Last I heard, she was with one of my maids, helping her with morning sickness. Since she arrived, she hasn't stopped finding people to treat."

One of his maids? Was it—

"The maid," he added quickly, "Clarice, is married to my valet, Roger. They're expecting their first."

Of course. Certainly. She glanced away toward the door, her grip tightening on the sword, her breath slowing. "Thank you, for the advice."

He nodded, but wouldn't meet her eyes. "I'll see you at the trial, Rielle."

With that, he pushed off and strode past the gauzy curtains, to the balcony, leaving her alone, and suddenly, she felt cold, like all warmth, all light had abandoned her.

She shivered. This was wrong. *So* wrong, these lingering thoughts, feelings. Brennan *loved* her, and she loved him, and he didn't deserve any of this. Didn't deserve her past still clinging to her, and didn't deserve *her* still clinging to *it*.

With a swallow, she took a step back, and another, and another, and left these quarters, but no matter what she did, leaving him always seemed to feel like leaving a piece of herself behind.

It couldn't go on this way. She wouldn't let it. At the very least, Brennan deserved to know something inside of her was... broken, and no matter how much she loved him, might never mend again. And if he hated her for it, he'd be justified.

She'd tell him tonight. She'd tell him everything, and pray he still loved her.

CHAPTER 39

Olivia turned the page in *Sangremancy Rituals of the Ancient World*, and traced a finger down the lines of Old Erudi text. Unlike Old Sileni, at least she could read it without tedious translation. This section spoke of a bell.

But she was no closer to finding an answer to the dragons coming for Jon.

Divine... Jon... She'd *kissed* him. She'd actually kissed him—with no excuses like the not-so-genius *distraction* she'd cited the night of the welcome banquet.

She covered her mouth. For that first moment, it had felt so right. His sculpted body against hers. The feel of his lips against hers, soft, warm, sensual. Her heart racing so fast it had nearly burst from her chest.

And then it had been cold.

There had been no fire behind it, none of that *hunger*, from his end... nor even really from hers. As a daydream, it had been so intense she'd writhed, ached with need, but as a reality, neither of them had been in the moment.

Her mind had gone to James. To his body against hers, to his lips, to her heart racing in *his* embrace.

And Jon had been in another moment, too. With another person. And she knew that. Had always known that.

Tomorrow, she could find another man. Even tonight, if she so chose. Someone who craved her with the hunger she desired. And someday, she'd find a man who could live a lifetime in the memory of one moment with her. And chose to, over everything and everyone. Someday.

A soft rap on the door to the library, and she glanced back to see Rielle standing there in a coat the color of the Shining Sea, holding a sheathed blade in her hand.

The Queen's Blade.

She sucked in a breath.

"Are you busy, Olivia?" Rielle asked, lingering against the doorjamb.

"Never too busy to talk to you." With a grin, she rose, and she and Rielle embraced. "How are you? How are things with the trials?"

A corner of Rielle's mouth turned up. "One of the reasons I'm here."

Olivia gestured to the chair beside hers, and Rielle sat. "How can I help?"

Rielle rested the Queen's Blade on the table and looked over the open books spread across its surface. "The second trial is in two days, and I'm fighting a basilisk. I think." She removed something from her coat, a scale—definitely a basilisk's—and set it down. "I was wondering if you had any books I could borrow about them... or anything, really, that could help." Drawing her eyebrows together, she smiled sheepishly.

She was in over her head.

Olivia lifted some of the books' front covers until she found *A Compendium of the Immortals*. "How's your Old Sileni?"

Rielle raised a brow. "If it's exactly like normal Sileni, then fantastic."

Olivia heaved a sigh, then sat, rubbing her palms on the skirt of her green batiste dress. "Then it may be slow going."

Rielle grabbed the book and dragged it before her, frowning over its text. "My Old Sileni isn't great, but I can make some sense of this."

Rielle's interests had always skewed to field operations over scholarship, but she'd been raised a Lothaire—educated in multiple languages, and the classics. Even after her parents had died, the Duchess of Melain had insisted on tutoring from the foremost scholars in the Tower.

It had been unconventional, but not even Pons would have been prepared to tell an Auvray—much less the duchess—*no*.

Such was the privilege nobility and rank commanded.

Something I will command someday. She'd already acquired the rank; all that remained was nobility, which an advantageous marriage would grant. A problem for another day.

She sifted through the books, picking out her other finds about the Immortals—the ones she'd already reviewed and made notes of—leaving herself the sangremancy books involving them. Two of the titles could be helpful, so she slid them over. "These, too."

Rielle looked up from a page about dragons. That same one, with the illustration. "Can I borrow them? I'll return them after the trials."

Olivia nodded, staring at the illustration.

"I remember that one I saw overhead, that day on Khar'shil," Rielle said, squinting. "I wish I knew more of what Shadow did there."

"So do I," Olivia said with a lengthy breath. "But she was good at covering her tracks. And the important part is that she's defeated."

Rielle gave a crestfallen nod. "She was just so... obsessed with destroying the man I love," she said with a shake of her head. "And she didn't even realize I'd be marrying Brennan in a few months. Even *I* didn't back then, I suppose. But she got the wrong man."

Did she?

As she'd parted from Jon, left the stable, the look on Rielle's face had been bleak, like her heart had been dismantled to its raw, aching core. Nothing could make a person hurt so terribly, suffer so much, but love.

Rielle had been practically inseparable from Brennan, and the way they were around each other, like they knew one another in every way, looked like love, too, but was it?

She reached for Rielle's hand.

Are you certain you're not making a grave mistake?

The words trembled on the tip of her tongue, and she wanted to tell her all about Jon's heart, about the time he had left if no cure could be found, but... He'd sworn her to secrecy. She couldn't betray his trust.

"Olivia?" Rielle gave her hand a squeeze. "Is everything all right?"

Not in the least.

She mustered a smile and looked back at the page. "Dragons have been drawn to him. There was one at the coronation, that passed overhead. Then on the *Aurora*, the water dragon... It's too uncanny to be coincidence."

Her brows drawn, Rielle reached for the Queen's Blade, fingering the intricate swept hilt. "Is he safe?"

"He'll be safer once we're back in Emaurria. He'll have his

Earthbound powers to fall back on." *Even if he shouldn't use them.*

Rielle nodded. "It may be whatever Shadow did." She chewed her lip, scrutinizing the page. "I wish I could remember more, but the only thing that sticks out is the tower and the bell."

"Bell?" Olivia blurted, sifting through the books again.

"Yes." Rielle frowned. "As we approached Khar'shil, I heard a bell ringing. A massive one."

At last her hands closed on *Sangremancy Rituals of the Ancient World*, and she scanned the page about the bell.

The blood of the caster, the blood of the damned... the water of the sea, the wood of the land...

...beneath the Bell of the Black Tower... thrice summoned and pled, the King of all Lords...

"What is it?" Rielle asked, dragging her chair closer and eyeing the book. "Bell of the Black Tower? Olivia, this could be the same one."

"Lords," Olivia said, thinking aloud.

"Who's the King of all Lords?"

Olivia shook her head. "The Dragon Lords. The King of all Dragon Lords."

Rielle went still. Deathly still. "Are you saying Shadow summoned a dragon king to go after Jon?"

"No," she breathed. "Shadow summoned *the* Dragon King." She shivered. There had been mention in various texts of the Dragon King, a dragon so strong, so powerful, that all the Dragon Lords had bowed to him... until he'd been betrayed by the wild mages he'd helped create.

"Olivia," Rielle rasped, her breathing uneven. "He'll need protection. Mages—"

"I know."

"*Not* from the Divinity," Rielle said. "I think things are worse than we thought. The Grand Divinus may be involved in more than the regicide and the attack on Laurentine... I think the Divinity might be supplying sen'a."

Sen'a? If that was true, then...

Then the Grand Divinus would have had the perfect motive to remove King Marcus and the Faralles, to install a more agreeable king on the throne... Someone like Faolan, if he supported the sen'a trade.

And the Divinity could keep its own mages strong by prohibiting sen'a, all the while peddling it to hedge witches and heretics, keeping them weak and dependent.

"Brennan and I are looking for proof," Rielle said grimly. "We'll let you know if we find anything. He... didn't want me coming to you with all this until we had any, but it's *you*, Olivia. I know you won't do anything rash."

"Of course not." She hesitated. "Are you sure you can trust him?"

Rielle stiffened. "I trust him with my life. He won't lie to me, about this or anything else." Her voice was firm, faithful.

Olivia nodded. Hopefully that faith wasn't misplaced.

In the villa's kitchen, Samara tied closed the bag of the raspberry leaf childbearing-sickness tea blend, and began work on the second blend. A mix of black tea and the tiniest amount of ginger, it could be used for four days at a time to combat severe nausea, with an ample addition of dried fruit to help the taste.

As she laid out her ingredients, Roger—Clarice's young husband—approached, bearing an armful of books. He set them on the table and heaved a breath; for his slight frame, such a load would have been difficult to manage.

"Lady Samara," he greeted amiably, then launched into a string of unintelligible Emaurrian.

She shook her head. "I don't understand," she said in Nad'i, looking over the books.

They were in Nad'i—tomes on learning Emaurrian, Sileni, and Morwenian, as well as *The Sileni Herbal*. She'd been familiar with some of the ingredients before, but with this, she'd be able to add to her stock significantly, and—

Cheeks flushed, Roger indicated the hallway and mentioned *Lady Archmage*. The red-haired woman had a position of importance here, a healer and more, and had been exceedingly kind.

Samara smiled, nodded, and hastily packed up her tools and ingredients, then followed Roger through the hallway, toward the library. He entered, paused, and said a string of words that included her name.

At the table, Lady Archmage sat with—

"Thahab," Samara said, and as Thahab stood from the seat, eyes watering, she rushed to meet her and threw her arms about her.

By the Divine, to see someone she *knew*, a familiar face, a *friend*—it was a great relief, like the cool baths after a scorching summer day. She was warm, but still slight, still—

Thahab pulled away, looked her over with teary eyes. "Samara, I'm so sorry. About yesterday, I—"

Samara lowered her gaze, gently rested a palm on Thahab's

flat belly, and she flinched. *Divine, no. No.* "I had hoped," she said, her eyes stinging, "but it wasn't... It wasn't enough."

Thahab embraced her against her own tears, and that night of fire, haze, and death burned fresh in her mind's eye, the guards bellowing orders and running through House Hazael to the roar of flames and the cacophony of screams.

"I didn't know he would free everyone. I'm so sorry," Thahab whispered.

Samara shook her head. "He was only able to because Zahib Imtiyaz died in the fire."

Because *Thahab* had set it all aflame. The fire had only begun the inferno that had consumed House Hazael as it had been.

"I—I killed him, and for that you must hate me," Thahab said, lowering to a knee and bowing her head. "Tell me what I can do to lessen your grief."

Farrad had tried to right his many wrongs, but ultimately he hadn't set aside his pride, and *that* had killed him.

And Thahab, who'd lost her baby, no doubt that night, if the blood had been any sign, begged forgiveness for his death?

She rested her hand on Thahab's head, who looked up. "I *begged* him not to challenge you, but he wouldn't listen. Everything could have been—"

A shift of paper on wood came from the table.

Her gaze darted past Thahab's shoulder, to Lady Archmage. "Lady Archmage. Forgive me, I should have acknowledged you," she said in Nad'i. Her hands trembling, she bowed.

"Samara," Lady Archmage said, rushing to her. She said something in Emaurrian, crouching, but Samara only glanced up at her before returning to her bow.

"Samara," Thahab said, "we're all friends here. Please, Olivia doesn't want you to bow."

Cautiously, Samara lifted her head and eyed Lady Archmage. She was treated so carefully, so obediently here, and Lady Archmage didn't wish for someone like her to show her deference?

Lady Archmage offered her a smile, sincere and encouraging, but she didn't say anything else, let the quiet flow in.

"Have you liked it here?" Thahab asked. "Earlier... His Majesty said you'd been helping everyone."

His Majesty. The way she said it was stiff, hesitant, and yesterday, she'd called him something else. What Lady Archmage called him. *Jon.*

As Thahab had curled over him in the hall, held him, wept, it hadn't been deference that had claimed her fervent arms, nor obedience that had elicited her trailing tears.

And His Majesty—when he'd stepped between Farrad and Thahab, the look in his eyes hadn't been the duty of a zahib-shada to a nawi or a shafi, but a look that could destroy. A look that could kill. Pure, distilled fury.

The fury of a lover. The fury of a father?

Samara bowed her head, then glanced at Thahab, still kneeling before her. She knelt, too. "He's the father," she whispered, "isn't he?"

Thahab opened her mouth, but no words emerged.

In Xir, Thahab had told her about the father once, about his strength, his loyalty, his conviction. How he'd daydreamed with her about a home, a family, a life together. In that moment, she'd been so far from House Hazael and arcanir cuffs, her eyes starry, full of dreams, *free.*

Thahab nodded. "It is... not well known."

Nor would it ever be on her account. She wrapped her arms around Thahab. "I'm so sorry."

"So am I," Thahab whispered back.

Lady Archmage gathered her skirts and lowered gracefully to the floor, then cleared her throat. She said something to Thahab in Emaurrian.

"Samara," Thahab said, pulling away to sit on the floor, "Olivia wants me to tell you that His Majesty wants to try to alleviate the burden of losing your father."

She blew out a breath. "Does His Majesty know I was Farrad's *slave* for almost my entire life?" She frowned. "He *owned* me. Before that, he owned my *mother*. When he wanted her for a lover, she had no choice." A sudden shiver wracked her. "I am alive and in this world because of him, and I am free by his hand, but no, I do not mourn his loss as a daughter."

Before Rielle could translate to Lady Archmage, Samara grasped her forearm.

"Thahab, I never want to go back there." She raised her chin, her eyes burning. She never again wanted to set foot in House Hazael if she could avoid it. "All I want for myself is to help others, heal them, keep studying medicine. Maybe open my own apothecary shop one day."

"Rielle?" Olivia asked Thahab, who took her hand and squeezed it lightly.

Thahab grinned back at Samara. "How do you feel about Emaurria?"

His Majesty's kingdom? Where every person, rich or poor, was free? It was a dream. She didn't speak the language, but she could try to become an apothecary there, try to make a living, free to do as she chose.

But Lady Archmage would help her? Just like that? She slid a nervous gaze toward Lady Archmage, but Thahab was speaking to her again in Emaurrian.

Lady Archmage evaluated her with a tilt of her head, then smiled and responded to Thahab.

At last, Thahab turned to her with a grin. "Would you want to be the Court Apothecary?"

She gasped.

"We would still have to ask His Majesty, but—" Before Thahab could finish, Samara grinned.

"It would be my honor!"

Thahab said something to Lady Archmage, who smiled and nodded to Samara.

"Whether you become the Court Apothecary or not, we'll get you to Emaurria. You'll have a place in Trèstellan Palace, or with me if you wish, or if you'd prefer to go somewhere yourself, His Majesty will deliver you the blood price."

Blood price. For Farrad.

"Not going back to Xir is good enough for me. I can figure out the rest," she said.

The *rest* would include somehow managing House Hazael, so Farrad's wives and children wouldn't revert to the old ways. That couldn't happen.

I won't let it.

And she'd be coming to court. Emaurrian court.

Thahab beamed at her, then glanced at Lady Archmage, who looked her over with her own pleased smile.

"I have to go," Thahab said, "but if you'd like to write to me, I'm staying at the Marcels' villa. Otherwise, I have the Magister Trials, so I'll be back at Divinity Castle in two days, and then if I pass to the third trial, three days after that."

"You don't stay with His Majesty," she replied. "But—"

Thahab's cheeks reddened. "I—We... When I returned, things..."

Samara's mouth fell open, but she quickly nodded. Many things could change in a few months, and the loss of a child was a lot for a couple to bear. It had happened often enough, even in Xir.

"I'm engaged to my childhood friend, the Marquis of Tregarde," Thahab continued. "He speaks Nad'i, and he—actually, he came for me to Xir. You might have seen him."

Samara inclined her head. "I'll visit you sometime, if I'm welcome."

"You're *always* welcome." Thahab hugged her. "And by the way, I don't think I introduced myself properly. Favrielle Amadour Lothaire—Rielle." She inclined her head.

Samara smiled. Lady Archmage and His Majesty had called her that. "Glad to finally meet the true you, *Rielle*," she said, testing the name on her tongue slowly.

Rielle closed her eyes and breathed deeply, as if a weight had been lifted in finally casting off *Thahab*, and all that had gone with it.

She felt much the same—casting off House Hazael, Xir, and soon starting a new life in the free kingdom of Emaurria.

CHAPTER 40

Seated before the fire in the villa's library, Brennan turned the page of the new treatise on changing practices in dye houses, and rubbed his forehead. Father owned one on the coast of Sonbahar, and if he understood this, he could help raise efficiency. It would all make him a better duke someday, stronger, when he and Rielle finally took over managing Maerleth Tainn with their own children.

Hardly any of it had sunk in—much unlike his usual self—and the scent of the Blood Offering still lingered in his nostrils.

Had Nox granted him favor? Would Rielle be swayed? Where was she now? Could she really be trusted?

Soft steps approached the library, and a quiet knock rapped on the door. Sandalwood, bitter cacao, and gardenia—Nora's warm-weather fragrance. "Bren?"

"Hm?" he asked, without looking up.

She entered, her steps slow, hesitant, her dark-pink skirts swishing.

He took his feet off the sofa so she could sit down.

With a swipe of her hand, she removed any invisible specks of dirt before taking a graceful seat. Typical Nora. "I'm sorry for causing trouble between you and your fiancée. I didn't realize you'd... done that, and I didn't catch on in time."

Done *that*?

Did she mean the negligee on Veris?

Unmoving, he lifted his gaze from his book to eye her. "You? Sorry?" He huffed. "Why are you really here?"

Her mouth twisted, and a crease formed between her eyebrows. "I truly *am* sorry. I would've lied for you, if you'd just told me."

"Thanks?" He waited for what she wanted. It was coming. It was always coming. He just prayed she'd spare him the squeak voice she always used to get her way.

"But," she said, folding her hands together in her lap, "you really did make things worse between Jon and me."

He laughed under his breath. "I *think* manipulating your way into his bed, forcing your son to commit treason, and trying to trap the king into conceiving a lovechild *might* have already done their part."

He lowered his gaze back to the page, rereading a sentence for what had to be the tenth time.

"Well, you certainly didn't *improve* matters."

He snorted. "Oh? Was cleaning up your mess somehow *my* responsibility?"

"I'm your little sister, Bren," she squeaked.

Great Wolf's ass, the *squeak* voice meant she wasn't above using tears for this. He growled in his throat.

She sniffled. "You're *supposed* to watch out for me, take care of me—"

He slammed his book shut. "No crying. What do you want?"

One sniff after another, and then she eyed him. He wasn't surprised this worked on most men, but even on him—when he knew better—it still worked. Perhaps Maerleth Tainn would be better off with *her* as the heir.

"I can't hardly meet anyone, stuffed into some backwater county or cooped up in the mountains at Maerleth Tainn. I want to be invited back to court."

A laugh ripped free of him. "You want—?" He held out an arm, guffawing. "Hold on—" He laughed himself nearly to tears while she only stiffened, her frown deepening, her fist clenching.

"Your fiancée knows the king very *intimately*, and since you're marrying her, you could ask her to put in a good word for me. For *family*."

"Oh my dear Nora, you think citing her past will wound me? I am well aware of whom she fucked and when and for how long. I know where the bodies are buried, and which ghosts may still come back to haunt us... and how to bury them anew. Try again."

A creak of her gritted teeth, and she fixed livid eyes on him. "Look, you don't want me in her hair, do you? And you don't want her thinking about her former lover either? Well, why don't you resolve both situations. Get me back to Courdeval, and maybe I can tempt the king to turn his gaze elsewhere."

He straightened, watching her through heavy-lidded eyes. "Now you're talking sense."

Jon had become a thorn in his paw, and even if the king would have nothing more to do with Nora, her presence would at least keep him preoccupied. Perhaps it would even help douse the old flame still burning in Rielle's heart. He hoped. "I'll have a word with him myself."

Nora's teary expression immediately gave way to a beaming

smile. She threw her arms around him. "I knew I could count on you!"

Anything to stop the *squeak* voice.

She pulled away and eyed him, clasping her hands in her lap once more.

He grunted. "What?"

Her foot tracing a small circle on the rug, she pursed her lips. "Could you... um... keep the boys occupied while I go to Lady Renata's salon tonight? They're becoming much more than Annette can handle, and Mother is coming with me."

There went his usual evening locked in the bedchamber with Rielle. But he never minded the boys. "Have fun."

"You've matured," she said with a smile. "Here you are, reading a book calmly, while your fiancée is visiting her former lover. And you have a knack for this parenting thing. Not at all what I expected."

How did Nora know? Had one of the outriders returned?

With a hug and a kiss in parting, Nora practically skipped out of the library. As complex as his sister was, what made her happy was simple: indulging her selfishness. *That* he could understand. If only it were always as simple as gifting coin, entertainment, or vanity.

Sighing, he lowered his gaze back to the book, and his eleventh read of the same sentence.

It was pointless. He slammed the book shut.

His bride couldn't be seen running into the king's arms. It was the barest modicum of respect. She'd gone to see Samara, but how long had she been there? Had she run into Jon?

The door in the foyer creaked open, letting in a wave of fresh spring air, cypress, pansies, and primroses. The soft alto of Rielle's voice in greeting, but shaky, hollow.

Opening the book anew, he waited.

"His Lordship is in the library, my lady," Vietti said, in the hallway, and she thanked him softly.

When she entered, everything about her slackened—her stance, her expression, even the look in her eye. She was falling apart, right in the doorway. She dropped a sheathed sword to the floor.

He approached her, and all bravado abandoned him as he opened his mouth to ask her what was the matter.

She put a palm to his chest and pushed him back into the library, shutting the door behind her, and kept pushing until they were at the opposite wall. By the time she let him go, tears welled in her eyes.

"I'm sorry," she whispered.

Sorry?

Her palm slid down from his chest, and he caught her wrist, trying to meet her gaze. What had happened at the villa with Jon? Had she—?

"Divine damn you, Brennan, for thinking you could manipulate me," she spat hoarsely—

She knew, then—

"—but you were right. You're a good man. A wonderful man," she whispered between quiet sobs. "And there's something I have to tell you."

This was going somewhere terrible. He reached for her face, but she pulled away from his touch, curling into herself.

He reached for her again, but she stepped away. He lowered his gaze. She didn't have to say the words.

"I keep telling myself to forget him, to move on, but sometimes it's suddenly *there*, like a thorn inside of me, and I can't cut it out," she rasped, drawing a forearm across her face and shaking her head.

She was leaving him. It was over.

"You said my name and said you loved me and said you wanted to marry me," she said, tears streaming down her face, "and I want you, I want all of it with you, so badly, but I"—she sobbed, bending over, and he crouched with her as she lowered to the floor—"I'm so afraid I might be... broken."

He watched her hands trembling in her lap, unclasped, as she submitted all her truth to him, held nothing back.

"I love you," she whispered, "but I don't know what to do. You... You deserve more. You deserve better." Her voice faded with every word until it became nearly inaudible.

So much pain. She held on to so much pain, and yet all he wanted to do was hold her, hold her close, and never let go.

Like a centuries-old tree, she'd been marked by the past, deeply, indelibly, a past she couldn't forget, and those marks had become part of her, scars never to be healed.

But the wounds didn't have to bleed anew. He could make sure of it. He would. He'd hold her, hold her close, and keep her past buried.

He pulled her to him, and she fell against his chest, threw her arms around him, inhaled him like the breath of life, wept against him. "I'm strong enough," he said quietly, "for the both of us."

From the moment he'd agreed to marry her, he'd known. This was her heart, and he didn't hold dominion over it, but merely inhabited a corner. And that was enough, as long as she chose him. He needed no more. He'd give her the whole of his love, more than she could take, and smother out the rest. There would never again be a lack she needed to fill with memories, or with anyone else. That had always been his silent promise to her. And now she knew it.

Whatever had happened when she'd gone to see Jon, he didn't need to know.

He didn't need to know, as long as it never happened again.

"Never see him again," he said, letting his selfishness free, just this one more time. "Never be alone with him again." He could be there for her for the rest of her life, give her everything she needed and wanted and more, but he couldn't win on battlefields she took to alone.

"I won't," she cried. "Never again. I promise you—"

"We'll never speak of this again," he said, his voice breaking as he tightened his embrace, keeping her from looking at his face. Whatever had or hadn't happened between them, he didn't need to know.

As she nodded against him, he breathed deeply, slowly, rigid.

No, she couldn't look. Right at this moment, she couldn't be allowed to look.

He squeezed his eyes shut, tried to fight it, but damn it all, he couldn't stop.

"Brennan," she whispered against his chest, hoarse, soft, and pushed against his embrace to raise her head.

No, she couldn't—

"Brennan," she whispered again, pleaded, and Great Wolf help him, he couldn't deny her anything anymore. With a deep breath, he loosened his hold, and she raised her head, her teary eyes searching his.

"Please," she said softly, her eyelids drawing closed as her lips met his, the salt of her tears on his tongue, their heavy scent filling his nostrils, and the soft press of her mouth was the comfort he needed, the feel of her love against his skin.

She urged his back down to the floor, and he let her do it, let her lips claim his, her tongue meet his, her body brace over his. As she settled over him, her warmth pressing against him, his hands couldn't help but hold her, stroke her, encourage her, and there was a desperation inside of him stronger than he'd ever before felt, this need for her complete embrace, her utter acceptance, union between them that would mean she still wanted to belong to him, still wanted him to belong to her.

Her kiss traveled lower as her fingers unbuttoned his coat, opened his shirt, unbuckled his belt. She'd wanted to pleasure him like this before, but his mind always went back to that shameful night at Tregarde nearly four years ago. It was only a matter of time before her mind would go there, too, and she'd remember him for the selfish, cruel scoundrel he'd been.

He could *never* let her think of that again. Never see him that way again. Ever.

If she ever looked at him that way again, blinked and saw the cruel, selfish boy he'd been four years ago *return*, he would lose her.

She was all he'd ever wanted, and against all odds, in spite of every terrible thing he'd said and done, she was here, in his arms, *his*. It was a miracle that the boy at the Tower ten years ago, rejected by his young fiancée, could have never fathomed. The boy who'd offered her the world, bared his heart to her, and been jilted.

He was offering the world to her now, but he wouldn't bare his heart again, not when it had only blackened since that night ten years ago, only turned uglier in his cruelty and selfishness, an ugliness he couldn't stand her seeing. Couldn't *risk* her seeing.

His heart beat to racing, nearly exploding, and every muscle in his arms quivered. He tensed them against the tremor—she couldn't notice, couldn't realize what he was thinking. Just one glimpse of that ugliness, and it would all be over.

He grasped her chin, urged her to meet his gaze. "Another time, bride," he whispered, trying to sit up.

She blinked, and such a warmth shone in her eyes, a soft-ness, and her mouth curved in an affectionate smile. "You're not that man anymore, Brennan," she whispered, pressing a gentle kiss to his abdomen as she eyed him. "Place your trust in me."

Some part of him feared she'd remember his selfishness, his cruelty, and it would ruin everything. She'd *leave*.

His trust—he'd... withheld it. Because no matter what he offered, what he did, how he changed, there would never be any certainty that she'd *stay*.

"Let me love you," she whispered, and kissed her way lower, lower...

He closed his eyes once more and surrendered to the floor, to anything she wished to do, to any way she wished to love him, to *her*. To soft hands smoothing over his skin, to the loving press of her lips, to her complete embrace and utter acceptance... to the union between them that meant she still wanted to belong to him, still wanted him to belong to her.

To pleasure as she gave, gave, gave, and he gasped, grazing fingers through her hair and sweeping it away from her face as he surrendered everything at last, and trusted her, and she kept that trust, *stayed*.

As the pulse ebbed in his blood, she kissed below his navel and lay next to him, resting her head on his abdomen. He urged her up into the curve of his arm, and she wriggled closer, smiling at him with flushed cheeks.

"You have no idea how long I've wanted to do that," she said to him, those same words, her smile curving wider. But what he heard was *I love you. I trust you. You can trust me.*

He rested a palm over her heart, absorbing its racing beat, and he would never let it go. And as long as he treated her well, she would never take it from him. He knew her boundaries, and he would never cross them. That night in Tregarde that had haunted them for so long had now faded into the past, forgiven.

This was forever.

"Brennan," she said, and his name on her lips felt like a long, slow stroke of her fingers down his spine. She covered his hand with hers, her eyes sparkling. "Is it possible? Have I... have I left you speechless?" She laughed quietly under her breath.

He leaned over her and kissed her, just a brush of his lips over hers at first, then deepening.

Speechless... No, he had much to say. So very much. And he would tell it all to her, here and now, in ways words never could.

CHAPTER 41

*L*eigh slowed his horse as they neared the outskirts of Beaufort. The sun shone through the clouds at mid-morning, and at this time, on a day like this, any town would be bustling with business and movement.

But not Beaufort.

As far as he could see, only the clustered wooden buildings populated the town, with not a single soul on the dirt thorough-fare. A lone chicken waddled before them, pecked at something in the dirt, and continued on its way. He shuddered. Something was wrong.

"Where is everyone?" Katia asked, pursing her lips. "*Hello!*" she called out.

Leigh swatted at her. "Probably lining up to kill you *now*."

She puffed a breath and rolled her eyes.

"Unusual, for a human settlement," Ambriel said quietly, peering into the distance with squinted honey-gold eyes. "No people, but there's the glow of candlelight in the window, there in that large building."

Among the clustered buildings was a three-story house, its steep roof peaking above the town like a guardian. The Beaufoy house.

"That's where we're going," Leigh said, urging his horse on. All of Beaufort seemed deserted, with not a single voice making a sound, not a single candle casting a light but for the Beaufoy house. Axelle was made of fire and steel, and as Archon, she would never abandon her territory, but what about her Coven? What about the town? Had they left? Had they died?

Was Ava in the house?

Della, can you hear me? he thought, concentrating. As a mentalist, she'd listened in often enough, and picked up on intense thoughts. *Della.*

Nothing.

The house loomed over the street, tall and menacing like a gargoyle, and as he dismounted and tethered his horse, a soft glow flickered in a second-story window. Ambriel and Katia tethered their horses out front, too, and followed him up as he ascended the stairs.

Della, I'm here. Can you hear me?

Not a single sound.

Is Ava safe?

"Leigh," a feminine voice called from beyond the door. Della.

He turned the knob, and there she was, standing before him, as waifish as ever, unruly dark-blond curls framing her tear-streaked face.

She dropped her knapsack and ran to him, threw her arms around his neck, and he embraced her. "Leigh, praise Terra, you're *here*," she said in rapid Emaurrian, holding him tight. "What are you doing here?"

"Enlisting support for the Crown, against the Immortals and the Divinity," he whispered. "Where's Ava?"

"Where is everyone?" Katia asked, taking a step into the house.

"Fled," a rasping voice called from another room. A few footsteps, and the Archon of the Beaufoy Coven stood before them, waifish like her daughter, but taller, with gray streaks in her dark-blond curls and the wisest dark-blue eyes he'd ever seen. She crossed her arms over her plain white-cotton shirt, tucked into utilitarian gray breeches.

"Fled? Why?" Katia asked.

"The necromancer—" Della whimpered, pulling away.

"Has taken all the dead in the cemetery, entire battlefields of dead Immortals, and the horde has killed anything living that has remained here," Axelle said, striding to Katia. "We sent our Coven to the outskirts of our territory, and any survivors have fled as far as their feet could carry them. As you should, Forgeron witch."

Katia shook her head. "I'm here to help."

"Where's Ava?" Leigh asked Della again, wiping away the tears from her cheeks as her midnight-blue eyes searched his.

She clenched her teeth as fresh tears rolled down her cheeks. "Leigh, the necromancer... It's Ava."

Stillness seized him, freezing into his core, holding him there, and for a moment, just a moment, he couldn't even move but to breathe.

"Brice, one of our Coven, was with her in the forest. They ran into a dryad, we think, and he must have..." Della shook her head. "He was only a child, like Ava, and she—she had her éveil—"

He'd left Ava here, *abandoned* her to her mother, all to keep her safe, and it hadn't done any good.

"She must have a very bright anima, Leigh," Axelle said. "To be in fureur so long, it must be nearly limitless. Della has tried to get to her, venturing out every couple of days, but Ava's too well insulated. Her horde keeps growing, and no one can get to her."

He hadn't seen Ava, his own flesh and blood, since her birth. Had missed thirteen birthdays. Thirteen Midwinters. Thirteen Midsummers. Her éveil—If only he had been—

A palm, warm and solid, closed on his shoulder, and Ambriel stepped next to him. With a finger, Ambriel stroked his jaw and turned his face.

Those honey-gold eyes fixed on his, calm, loving. "We'll find her together, dreshan. We'll save her together."

They would. They'd find Ava and save her.

He would... if it was the last thing he did.

He nodded, took Ambriel's hand, and turned to Della. "Where did you last see her?"

"What are you going to do?" Della asked, a tremble breaking her voice.

"There's a cave system in the mountains," Axelle supplied.

"What are you going to do?" Della repeated, her voice raw.

"She and the horde usually stay clear of the forest, keeping to the mountain, the caves, clearings, but any living thing that gets too close will draw them."

Della's hands clasped on his arms. "*Leigh,*" she cried, shaking him. "What are you going to do?"

He took her arms. "I'm going to save her, Della."

Ambriel removed an arcanir arrow from the quiver at his back and presented it to Della.

"Arcanir," Axelle said, approaching. "Good," she added in Old Emaurrian. "If you hit her somewhere non-vital, you can break the fureur."

Ambriel nodded, then replaced the arrow in the quiver with a soft swish of his deep-olive wool cloak.

"You're going to shoot our daughter?" Della asked, frantically glancing between them.

"We're going to save her," he repeated. "We're going to destroy the horde, and bring her back safe and sound. I swear it."

Della held his gaze, searching his eyes for a lengthy moment, then gave a solemn nod. "I'm coming with you."

"Della—" he began.

With a deep breath, Axelle wrapped an arm around Della's shoulders. "Della is coming with you. If she can get close enough, she can take control of Ava's mind," she said. "Take anything you need, and bring my granddaughter home."

OUT IN THE COURTYARD, Rielle followed Brennan's movements with the practice sword, trying to do as he did. She swept it behind her back and struck. Then raising it high, she practiced a block.

He paused and moved in, taking her wrist and practice sword to adjust it. "It has to be *here*," he said, holding it up and away, with the middle-to-hilt part before her, "otherwise"—he brought down his hand on the practice sword, and it pressed into her forehead—"you're going to get bloody."

Her cheeks heated, and she nodded. Whenever he fought, he always made it look so easy, but there was so much detail to remember, so many nuances that missing even *one* could get a person killed. He returned to her side and resumed the drill, which she followed, paying closer attention.

When she'd told Brennan she never wanted to be without a blade again, he'd laughed and said she had *him*.

But he couldn't *always* be at her side. There would come a day when another challenge would arrive, and she wouldn't let someone else spill blood for her sake, not when she could learn to fight ably enough herself. Surely not everyone had elemental magic sigils, and well, she had pillars of fire for everyone else.

But the basilisk...

She'd stayed up late, paging through Olivia's books, but there was no certainty she'd be able to use her magic against a basilisk. They seemed to be immune to direct magic, and until she knew the venue for the second trial, there would be no telling whether she'd be able to use the environment.

So, as untrained as she was, learning the sword was her best option, at least enough to get the pointy end into an Immortal beast without maiming herself.

Across the courtyard, Samara sat at a table with a quill, ink, and the Sileni herbalist tome, looking up from time to time to purse her lips contemplatively or watch them practice. She'd arrived in the morning, and had spent the day with them, working.

Rielle breathed deep. It was almost hard to believe that the day after tomorrow, she'd be fighting for her life. After telling him that she'd still had some remaining feelings for Jon, she'd expected... Well, not this. Not soft kisses and warm embraces in their bed, not waking up in his arms, spending the day together practicing. Whatever she'd expected, it hadn't been... love.

But this past year, Brennan had defied her expectations, and he only continued to do so.

Long before he was finished, she already hobbled toward Samara's table, her thighs, arms, and shoulders burning.

"Weak," Brennan taunted after her, and she grimaced as she contorted into a seated position.

"Dead, more like," she remarked to Samara, who giggled.

"I have a salve that'll do wonders for sore muscles," Samara said in Nad'i, setting her quill down.

"Yes, please. I would like to be slathered in salve from head to toe, then wrapped in a blanket and deposited onto the nearest bed until the second trial," Rielle grumbled, letting her head rest on the table next to the arcanir blade Jon had given her. She'd be taking it to the second trial, for better or for worse.

"Do not... worry," Samara said in slow Emaurrian, and it was enough to make Rielle smile and raise her head.

The doors to the courtyard opened.

"You're improving quickly," she said to Samara, eyeing Stefania as she brought refreshments. Finally, some water. As the maid set them down, she grabbed a cup only to find... milk. "This is..."

"Milk," Brennan said from behind her.

"Why is it milk?" She wrinkled her nose.

"Just drink it. After a day of practice, your body craves it."

"And how would *you* know—" No, on second thought, it was not wise at all to ask him how he'd know what her body craved. Especially not in front of others.

She bowed her head, biting her lip against a smile, and Samara laughed.

"It will help you build your strength," Samara offered, although she eyed Brennan curiously. "I'm not sure what I expected," she whispered, "but I had no idea he'd be so..."

"Humble? Charming? Devastatingly handsome?" Rielle offered, and she could just imagine Brennan's smug grin as he heard every word.

"It's just that when I met—"

"Thick as thieves," Brennan said to them as he approached. He grabbed a cup of milk and drank as he sat. "What are you working on?"

Brightening, Samara straightened and nudged the book with the feather of her quill. "I've just identified the gaps in my inventory and cross-referenced them with the available flora listed in *The Sileni Herbal*. I'd like to gather some ingredients locally when there's time."

"Una's been wanting to go for a ride," Brennan offered. "Maybe you might join her and gather what you need?"

"I wouldn't want to impose—"

"She'll be glad for the company." Brennan smiled. "And the opportunity to practice her Nad'i."

Samara nodded and took a deep breath. "I'd love to, but it's... it's just hard to think about when there's this deadly trial looming. Do you have a strategy?" Samara asked her.

Ideally, she'd use geomancy. "It can't be as simple as just fighting the beast in the right environment. My inclination would be geomancy to drop it, then crush it."

"Why can't it be that simple? Surely it would test your skill as a mage?" Samara asked.

"It's not about testing skill." Brennan set down his empty cup, then flipped it over. "No one would have had to die for that."

The first trial had proved that. Master Sen Taneie had been killed for no good reason, and the Grand Divinus had allowed it. The Divinity was supposed to fight for goodness, for justice, to help others.

That was no longer the case. Or maybe it had *never* been.

"There's going to be a twist," she murmured. "Something I don't know and won't be able to prepare for."

Brennan nodded to the arcanir blade. "Be prepared for

anything." He reached for her, stroked her hair from her head down to the end of her braid. "I'll do as much as I can to give you a fallback skill." His hazel eyes were soft, warm, as his slight smile widened. "But always remember that if you need me, I'm there."

The bond. If she was ever under imminent threat of dying, he wanted her to pull on the bond.

He glanced toward the courtyard doors just as they opened.

Vietti approached, wax-sealed note in hand. "From Mage-hold, Your Ladyship." He handed it to her.

She opened it and read, "You have been bestowed the great honor of an invitation to continue in the Magister Trials at the second trial, to be held on the 23rd of Floreal at sunset. Arrive in the dungeon of Divinity Castle, bring your token, and do not be late."

"The dungeon?" Brennan asked, raising a brow. He translated for Samara.

"How am I to fight a basilisk in a dungeon?" she asked. "And what about the other Immortals? Someone else is facing a giant."

Would the dungeon be infused with arcanir? Would she be able to use her magic?

"Maybe you're only *meeting* in the dungeon," Samara suggested.

That could very well be.

Her sword skills weren't even good enough to be called fledgling, so Divine willing, the trial would be held somewhere she'd be able to use her geomancy. She wasn't about to end up as basilisk prey, and withdrawing from the trials was not an option.

Brennan stood and kissed her forehead. "Let's keep practicing for as long as you can handle it. Then I have somewhere I need to be."

CHAPTER 42

In the middle of the night, Brennan strode up the stairs behind the royal valet, who led him past other members of the household, past Royal Guards, and to a small parlor, where Brennan threw himself onto a sofa and sprawled out. Maids flocked about him, preparing his tea and presenting him with petit fours while the valet stoked the fire in the hearth.

He'd promised Nora he'd ask Jon to invite her back to Court, but more than that... Jon had been looming like a ghost in his and Rielle's periphery, haunting them constantly, and it was time to have a word with him and end it. Rielle, exhausted from a day of sword practice, slept soundly, and he'd be back before she woke.

It wasn't long before sure-footed steps strode down the hall, and the Royal Guard opened the doors.

In plain clothes, Jon entered, looking him over with a narrow curiosity, before moving to the drinks cabinet to pour himself a goblet of water from the carafe. "Drink?"

Brennan raised his tea. Besides, he wasn't interested in *water*.

With a nod, Jon took his goblet and sat in the facing armchair, resting his ankle on his opposite knee before leaning back, spreading his arms on the armrests, and watching him evenly. "What brings you here?"

"Besides the tea?" he offered drolly, and set it down.

Jon raised his brows and sketched a smile. The impression of courtesy without actual courteous intention. His tutors had trained him well.

"I've come to collect what I'm owed." Two things.

A drink of water, and Jon peered into his goblet with disinterest. "Owed?"

"I'll get to that in a minute," Brennan said. "First, you interceded on behalf of my soon-to-be bride," he said, resting his shoulders against the button-tufted back of the armchair.

Jon held the silence a moment, and cold eye contact. "You were nowhere to be found."

Never mind that he'd been about Rielle's business. That information was none of Jon's business.

Exhaling lengthily, Jon set his goblet down beside him on a low table, slow, deliberate. "If you want an apology, you'll leave disappointed."

Brennan laughed. "I got all the apology I wanted later that night in bed. That's not why I'm here. If anything, I wanted to thank you for that."

Even that sketch of a smile didn't show now. "Why are you here?"

"You gave her an arcanir blade."

Jon tilted his head, betraying no more of a reaction than a crease between his brows. "I did. When she came here yesterday."

Trying to imply Rielle hadn't mentioned the visit? Not a chance. "Yes, to assist with Samara. We discussed it." Brennan sighed. "You didn't just give her any old blade."

The moment she'd drawn it, he'd known it for what it was. The Queen's Blade.

Jon had given her a royal treasure meant for a queen. A claim.

A corner of Jon's mouth turned up. "Does it matter what blade it was, as long as it's of help to her?"

"It matters."

A slight narrowing of Jon's gaze. "Whatever she needs of me, she shall have. I'll deny her nothing. Ever."

"The list of things she needs from you ends there." His face tight, Brennan scowled at him. "The first thing you owe me," he said, "is allowing my sister to return to court."

Jon scoffed. "All of your sisters are welcome, save for one."

"It is Nora you'll allow to return."

Jon pinched the bridge of his nose. "If I never see her again, it'll be too soon. And that is my answer: never."

"That answer will change," Brennan said, "and here's why. Last year, when Rielle chose you over me, you'd had your chance with her, and she would have stayed with you, even after everything in Sonbahar, but you ruined it all."

Jon lowered his hand and glared at him.

"Among your sins, you fucked my sister." Brennan waved a cavalier hand. "Normally, I wouldn't care, except that she's spent all of her time since then with *us*, and she doesn't waste a single opportunity to flaunt your affair in my fiancée's face."

That glare faded, and Jon lowered his gaze.

"That shouldn't matter, but we both know that it does," Brennan hissed. "Since our engagement, you've been omnipresent. Inescapable, even. And with Nora around, even when Rielle and I are at home, away from your presence, you never truly leave us be."

Jon's chest rose and fell, rose and fell, heavier and heavier.

"You owe it both to *her* and to me—*space* from you and all the pain you caused her. And you can do that by allowing Nora back at court."

The quiet went on too long before Jon nodded.

"And the second thing I'm owed. Stay away from my fiancée. Don't meet with her. Don't write to her. In fact, just avoid being in her general vicinity."

Stormy sea-blue eyes met his.

Brennan didn't waver. "You shattered her when she returned from Xir, repelled her the night of Veris. I did what you couldn't—I made her happy. And now that she's finally happy again, she doesn't need *you* interfering in her life."

Jon inhaled lengthily, lifting the goblet and turning it absentmindedly. "I think we both know who 'repelled' her, as you put it, the night of Veris."

Brennan huffed. So Jon had figured it out and hadn't said a word. "Placing the blame for the flood on the last raindrop?"

"I am to blame," Jon said solemnly, "for everything. If not for my wrongdoing, there would have been nothing for you to exploit." He crossed his arms.

Brennan stood. "So you'll stay away."

A twist of Jon's lips, and then he rose, too, and rounded the table. "You fear me."

"Me? Fear you?" Brennan smirked.

"You fear me, or you wouldn't be here."

That was ridiculous. "You can never marry her."

"That's not it," Jon said, holding his gaze. "It's not her *hand* you fear losing to me."

His stomach turned solid as stone, and the muscles in his

arms quivered, but he only tensed them taut. No, Rielle had given herself to him, and he'd given himself to her, in every way. They loved each other and had planned a future together. He wouldn't lose her to Jon. He wouldn't. "Whatever you have to tell yourself, Your Majesty."

If Jon wouldn't agree, he'd find other ways of keeping her away from him.

Grinning smugly, Brennan inclined his head. "I really must be going—Rielle's waiting for me. You understand." He stepped around Jon and headed for the doors.

"You really shouldn't," Jon called from behind him.

Against his better judgment, he paused. "Shouldn't what?"

"Fear me." Jon looked over his shoulder at him, with a certain dullness in his gaze. Any tautness in the set of his shoulders dissipated. "I want you to marry her, and I want her to love you. And I'm going to tell you why."

Intriguing.

Over the past couple of months, Jon had kept silent when he could have exposed certain lies—questioning Sincuore, Father's guilt, the negligee. He hadn't criticized. In fact, beyond his presence, he hadn't interfered at all.

"Listen," Jon said gravely, approaching him. "Listen closely to my pulse. I know you can tell truth from lies."

He listened. Jon's heart beat evenly.

"There's something wrong with my heart," Jon said, but it continued to beat normally. "Sometimes it doesn't work properly and disrupts the flow of my blood. There's no cure. And unless Olivia discovers a miracle, I'll be dead within two years."

No irregularity. No lie.

Nox's black breath.

He'd heard it—the night of the welcome banquet. Beating too irregularly to be normal.

Dead within two years. "You don't want her to throw in with a dying man."

Jon held his gaze and gave a slow nod. "I haven't given up, but the odds are against me. I plan to use whatever time I have left to set things right in the kingdom. That's all."

Because of this illness, this incurable illness, Jon had backed off completely, had set aside his desires for *her*.

What, as if Jon would have won her love otherwise? After so much irreversible damage, there was no way Rielle would choose Jon over him. "And you think if she knew, she'd come running?" He huffed. "Don't be so sure of yourself."

"Then tell her," Jon said, his voice low, deep. A challenge.

"Why haven't *you*?"

"You know why." Jon walked away and dropped into the armchair. "It's better this way, for everyone." So Jon didn't want him to tell Rielle, perhaps even more than *he* didn't want to tell her.

An eerie silence deafened the parlor, interrupted only by the wind battering the villa.

Jon had revealed this grave secret, and had left it to *him* to decide whether to confess it to Rielle or not?

Rielle had sworn him to the truth—

No, sworn or not, if Jon wanted Rielle to know he was taking the long sleep in a couple of years, he could tell her himself.

"Why tell me?"

Jon looked at him over the rim of his water goblet, then set it down, unaffected. "You came here with demands, worrying that I'm a problem between the two of you—"

Worrying?

"—and now you know I won't be," Jon said expressionlessly,

and glanced at the door. "So, go. Live a life together. Make her happy. And stop dueling shadows."

CHAPTER 43

*I*t was strange having a sword belted to her side. But the day of the second trial, its weight was a comfort. No more challenges catching her unaware. No more loved ones being hurt on her account. Now she could at least defend *herself*, albeit poorly.

It was time. The second trial. The basilisk.

As Rielle entered the carriage, the blade caught on the door, and she stepped back.

"You'll have to unclip it for the ride," Brennan said to her through a smile.

Of course. Grinning sheepishly, she did as he bade and unclipped the sword, then took his offered hand and got into the carriage. He followed and sat across from her while she laid the sword—the rapier—on her lap as the carriage set off.

Altogether, the rapier was about forty-four inches long, with a thirty-seven-inch arcanir blade, long and thin like a thorn. Its swept basket hilt was elegant, and the heavily carved horn grip, wound and inset with a steel wire for better grip, felt made for her hand. The extended ricasso engraved with twining vines was intricate, something she could examine for hours and not quite get the full measure of.

It would take years before she would know how to properly use it.

"Every blade should have a name," Brennan said, nodding to hers. "What's yours called?"

He rarely used his sword, a dueling rapier, but the rumors she'd heard of when he *did* use it never ended well for his challenger.

"What about yours?" she asked.

"Bite." He grinned wolfishly.

Bite. Yes, appropriate for any blade of his.

She peered down at her own, long and thin, sharp. It had been well cared for recently. She ran a fingertip along the leather scabbard and its twisted steel accents, then tapped the point of the tip. "Thorn."

"Thorn," Brennan repeated, looking out the carriage window. "A fitting name."

The rest of the ride passed in silence as visions of what the second trial might entail passed by her mind's eye. She'd never fought a basilisk, of course, but she'd fought a kraken—and won. Olivia's books had given her worthwhile knowledge about the scales: their preternatural hardiness, their susceptibility to arcanir. And Jon had fought these beasts before, and had warned her about its eyes and its tail. For the eyes, she'd brought a hand mirror, which she had tucked in her coat.

If everything went wrong and she got pinned down, Brennan had been teaching her the sword, and although it hadn't been long, some training was better than none.

"If you need me, I'm only a pull of the bond away. So don't worry." Brennan held her gaze evenly, serenely.

"I have my magic," she said, sucking in a nervous breath.

"But should you find yourself cornered, remember that most of them would kill anyone if it meant climbing to success. So we can do the same without any reservations." He flashed a rictus grin.

"I won't kill for this, Brennan." Not if she could avoid it.

"But they will. And you might have to kill to survive."

He wasn't wrong. Mac Carra had proven it. She wouldn't expect mercy from him, or most of the others, for that matter.

The carriage ride took them up the drive to the castle, where footmen escorted them to the ornate double doors. Inside, equerries led them deep into the castle and down a large set of stairs below ground.

She exchanged a look with Brennan. The dungeon. Hopefully it wouldn't be arcanir infused.

Before long, they were in a circular antechamber lit by torches, with only one massive set of doors awaiting. The Grand Divinus sat on a throne-like bench, surrounded by her Divine Guard, holding court before the other six candidates, their entourages, and...

On one end, Una was already with two of her friends. Grinning, she waved and mouthed, *Good luck.*

On the other, Jon stood—tall, regal, in a coat-tailed sapphire brocade jacket trimmed in gold, his hands clasped behind his back, chin raised. Faithkeeper was strapped to his belt, along with his arcanir dagger. So he'd come prepared for any eventuality.

The line of him was strong, elegant, with Olivia next to him in a sleek gray dress, her shining red hair twisted ornately at the nape of her neck. They were always together. Inseparable.

Olivia's smile in the sunlit afternoon came back to her, after she'd parted from Jon in the stable. They were happy together.

Jon turned his head in her direction, looked her over from head to toe in that sweeping once-over of his, his Shining Sea eyes bright sea-blue against the sapphire of his jacket. No smile. A muscle twitched in his jawline, and then he nodded to her, briefly, impersonally, and turned his attention back to the Grand Divinus.

She palmed Thorn's pommel, a comfort, one she'd seen him take countless times with Faithkeeper.

"...and then we will begin," the Grand Divinus finished. Had she been speaking this whole time?

Rielle swallowed, glancing at Brennan next to her. He hadn't moved from his courtly nonchalance, a stylish looseness in his stance. As she looked at him, his gaze didn't waver from the Grand Divinus.

The Grand Divinus turned to a set of doors, and two footmen opened them. She gestured everyone to enter.

A coliseum.

Seats cascaded down into an arena as large as a temple, walled by a blurred transparent wall. Six blue-uniformed members of the Divine Guard ringed the arena from the stands, their hands up. Enforcers holding up a repulsion shield.

From the entrance, stairs led up on both sides into the stands, and one set descended farther. To the arena level.

The arena.

There would be room to maneuver, and perhaps she'd be able to use her geomancy after all.

Ariana Orsa passed by, with a hilt—no blade—strapped to her belt. Next to her stood Mac Carra with a massive two-handed sword—over six feet in length, and the thin master he'd been with before the first trial.

So she wasn't the only one with a blade. Perhaps everyone had been rattled by Farrad's challenge.

No matter.

Before she could enter, Brennan took her hand. She rose on her tiptoes to kiss him.

"For luck?" Mac Carra bit out over his huge shoulder as he passed by. "You'll need it, bonny little flower," he called as he descended into the arena.

"Don't listen to him," Brennan said, eyeing Mac Carra's wake with a glare that could only be called deadly.

Luca Iagar passed by with a smirk, and the last of the candidates descended into the arena.

"I have to go," she whispered, pressing her lips to his one last time before she slipped away and turned into the darkness.

At the bottom of the stairs, she entered a small chamber, where one of the Divine Guard asked to see her wrist. She held it out, and he clasped a tight-fitting cuff around it.

Arcanir cuff.

Brennan left the stands and passed the Divine Guard, and none of them tried to stop him.

Several unusual scents mingled here, many he couldn't identify, except for the scent of a werewolf. It was strong, overpowering, and he was drawn to it in ways the scents around Maerleth Tainn had drawn him.

But he'd known them for what they were then, and he knew now: female werewolf.

One of the candidates would be fighting her today, no doubt, or she'd somehow managed to get into the castle incognito for the trial.

He'd stayed away from them near Maerleth Tainn, and so would he do now. The last thing he needed was to be exposed, and even if he wasn't, there was no telling what might happen when he came face to face with one.

The scents he couldn't identify had to be Immortals. Many of them. *Dangerous* Immortals.

Rielle would pass the second trial. She had to.

He made his way down the echoing, dark halls of the lower level, following the scent of musty, stale air to a padlocked door. After checking for any nearby people, he broke the lock and slipped in.

It was a long, black corridor, tight, carrying the odor of mold, dust, and damp. He shut the door softly behind him and tread the path northwest, stretching the limits of his hearing as he crept along.

Muffled voices faded in and out of audibility above him, through a dense layer of stone. Words of missions and operations, and sure-footed strides.

He was beneath the Hensar.

That meant the Archives were not far. He moved along, palming the uneven stone walls, listening further. The Hensar, as far as he could tell, occupied on the first level, while the Archives delved deep into the lower levels of the castle.

Footsteps neared, and he sidled along the black wall, passing by a door, and kept going around a corner. The footsteps —two sets—approached the door.

"...have the keys, so make sure you bring her the documents she asked for," one voice said, a woman's.

"I will. I'm having them pulled tonight, and I'll pick them up in a few days." The jingle of keys. "Once he gets them, he'll have to fight for the throne, right time or not."

Take the throne. Father.

"That's the plan." A silence. "You'll be meeting her in the

inner courtyard an hour before the third trial, and she'll review the documents before sending them out."

"All right. I'm off to watch the trial."

A laugh. "It'll be a bloodbath."

"Just as planned." A smug lilt.

Brennan suppressed a growl. Rielle's suspicions had been right. The Grand Divinus *was* trying to get rid of her.

I won't let it happen. Even if he had to bodily remove her from the trials, Rielle wouldn't come to harm, not while he drew breath.

The door creaked shut, and the keys jingled before a lock turned, then another door, another lock, and a padlock.

One set of footsteps faded away behind the doors, while the other went back.

The way *he* had come.

This man had keys, keys to the *Archives* by the sound of it, and with one quick swipe, those keys could be in *his* hands. He could be in the Archives tonight, and find evidence of the sen'a trade, the attack on Laurentine ten years ago, the regicide...

The footsteps echoed down the corridor, growing distant.

But the day of the third trial, this man—by what the two had discussed—would be bringing evidence that would compel Father to fight for the throne. Blackmail.

Blackmail I can steal.

The footsteps continued, departed, more and more distant...

If he let this man go, he could stake out the inner courtyard the day of the third trial, catch him as he arrived with the documents, then track down all the originals. Destroy them and anyone who knew about them. Protect Father, and the family, from being compelled to commit further treason.

But the Archives...

No, there were lives on the line. His *family's* lives, soon to include Rielle's. He wouldn't destroy the chance to secure them just to prove the Divinity was as villainous as it seemed.

Besides, even if he took the keys to the Archives, there was no certainty he'd be able to find what he was looking for. There had to be thousands, perhaps *millions* of records to go through. How would he even know where to look?

A faraway door opened, the footsteps faded behind it.

He crept back around the corner to the door, and then found the padlock. Even before his hand closed around it, he knew he wouldn't break it. If he did, the infiltration would be discovered, and these two mages' plan might be changed for the sake of security.

No, he wouldn't be getting into the Archives tonight, or perhaps ever. And he'd tell Rielle. Her good fortune was that she'd get to *live* with it, unlike Father if he was compelled to further treason, and with the lives of Father, Mother, and perhaps even his sisters on the line, Rielle would forgive him. She'd have to.

The day of the third trial, he'd be in the inner courtyard, waiting. And stamp out every last trail of evidence if it was the last thing he did.

For the family.

But the woman had called the trial today a bloodbath. Something was wrong. Very wrong.

Hold on, Rielle. I'm coming.

He headed back to the arena.

CHAPTER 44

*R*ielle shifted on her feet, eyeing the other candidates around her in the small, dusty underground chamber.

"How are we supposed to fight cuffed with arcanir?" Luca demanded, holding up his wrist to the Grand Divinus.

"Why don't you just wait for someone else to do the fighting, then take whatever they win?" Cadan Bexley, the Pryndonian master, remarked, adjusting his specs.

Luca scrunched his face and mocked him.

"Any mage can use his magic to defeat an enemy," the Grand Divinus said, her voice loud, resonant. "But a magister must be *more*. A magister is no mere mage, but the best of all mages. And this trial is designed to test resourcefulness." She met the gaze of each candidate in turn. "If any of you is not up to the task, leave now."

The double doors to the arena were all the more intimidating now, and she palmed Thorn's pommel anxiously.

Ariana spun a dark curl around her finger, while Mac Carra

looked around smugly, tapping his massive blade's crossguard. Had he known about this somehow? Or was it really just a reaction to Farrad's challenge? And Ariana, she had a hilt of some kind, too. What did it do?

Tariq seemed to be mumbling to himself, while Cadan chewed a fingernail. Luca stood with his hands at his sides, at the ready.

It was Telva who stepped forward, tinkering with her thick bun of black hair. "No magic?" She shook her head and looked to the other mages for support. "This is suicide... I have a daughter."

Telva was perhaps the sanest one here.

Can I slay a basilisk without my magic? She touched Thorn's pommel again. An arcanir sword. A hand mirror. An arcanir ring. A mermaid scale in a locket around her neck. And everything but her magic. Could she do it?

For Laurentine. For Emaurria.

She could do this. She could.

The Grand Divinus gestured to the exit, and Telva stood at attention, bowed, and then turned toward the exit. *Good luck,* Telva mouthed, her keen brown eyes intense, on her way to the door.

"Leave Number Three locked," the Grand Divinus said to a Divine Guard, who acknowledged and then passed on her order.

So there would be no third battle. They must have a numerical order, then.

"Anyone else?" the Grand Divinus asked matter-of-factly.

No one else so much as shifted.

The Grand Divinus motioned to the double doors ahead of them, the ones secured closed with an arcanir portcullis and massive bolt. The Divine Guard unbolted them.

"Proceed," the Grand Divinus said, her immaculate face expressionless.

So it was Number One's turn. Rielle lifted her chin. What number would she be?

"All of you."

All? At the same time?

She and the remaining candidates exchanged looks. Surprised looks. So no one had predicted this.

Mac Carra sauntered into the arena, shouldering his blade, and with a deep breath, she followed with everyone else. Someone sidled up next to her, tall and lean—Luca Iagar.

"Are you sure you don't want to quit?" he asked, arching a black brow. "Maybe you want to leave and go back to kissing your man?"

She rolled her eyes. "Perhaps you should focus on yourself."

He smirked. "Just looking out for a lady's wellbeing."

She sighed. "I'll look out for my own wellbeing, thanks."

Once all six of them entered the arena, the doors shut behind them, the portcullis clanked down, and the bolt scraped closed.

"No turning back now," Luca crooned, unbuttoning his long coat. He swept it open, revealing a multitude of throwing knives strapped to his body.

Not just a healer.

The witches of old, during the Dark Age of Magic, had prepared themselves for arcanir, before the Order of Terra had taken such monopolistic control of it. Witches had been trained in martial arts, had carried recondite artifacts like enchanted staves and weapons. They had planned for arcanir and developed their own contingencies.

But few of today's mages did. Few paladins tampered with the Divinity, and few *besides* paladins had arcanir.

These candidates, however, weren't average mages. They'd made it here because they were special, had talents, skills, or knowledge beyond most mages.

Except me.

What was *she* doing here? Did she belong here with Luca, who seemed skilled with knives? Or Mac Carra, who could wield a blade? Ariana, with her... hilt? No doubt Cadan and Tariq had their own skills besides magic.

So why am I here?

Perhaps it really was just to die. Perhaps it really was the Grand Divinus implementing a deadly solution to an unfortunately surviving problem.

She took a deep breath. Regardless of the reason, she had no plans to die. The Grand Divinus would be sorely disappointed.

The walls of the arena rattled, puffing dust.

No, not walls—*doors.*

Doors ringed the entire arena, with numerals over them. She read each one, stopped at three.

Number Three.

The Immortal beasts were to emerge from behind these doors, all at the same time.

Fanfare preceded the Grand Divinus as she raised her arms behind the repulsion shield cast by six Divine Guards. "Welcome to the second of the Magister Trials," she announced. "Tonight's survivors will move on to the third trial three days from now."

The resonance of her voice echoed throughout the arena, and Rielle searched the stands through the spell's blur for Brennan.

No, he would have slipped away to break into the Archives. He, too, risked his life tonight. *Please be safe, my love.*

Perhaps with all the Divine Guard present here, there would be fewer for him to face tonight.

Her look lingered on the stands as she imagined what he'd face tonight, still wishing to see his face now, before this nightmare, for what could be the last time.

Instead, it was the sapphire of Jon's overcoat that she found, his gaze intent upon her, brows drawn together, hand on Faithkeeper's pommel. Her fingers twitched, and his body was rigid beneath her touch months ago, at Donati's resonance den, after he'd thrashed Feliciano, the tautness of violence still holding dominion over him.

It was there now.

His eyes searched the repulsion shield, and his grip firmed on Faithkeeper.

No.

Jon, no. Don't.

Even if her life were at stake, he couldn't do what he seemed to be contemplating now. He'd lose any hope of help for Emaurria, and his reputation.

His head snapped to the side, where Olivia had her arm looped through his. She said something to him, and he shook his head vehemently.

Do what you must, Olivia. Keep him there.

"...Iagar, and Master Ariana Orsa. Each beast has been conditioned to target the candidate bearing its token. All beasts must be defeated to end the trial, and the first three to defeat their beasts will advance to the final trial."

The first three?

Even if they all defeated their beasts, all six of them, only *three* would advance?

"That's not fair," Ariana grumbled under her breath next to her. "Not fair at all."

"...test their resourcefulness, and the speed that is required to act in the moment, when lives hang in the balance..." the Grand Divinus continued. It seemed she could explain away any atrocity and make it sound practical.

"What is that?" Rielle whispered, nodding toward Ariana's hilt.

Ariana beamed, running her fingers over it. "This? This is, um, a spellblade," she said brightly. "If the bearer is a mage, it draws from his or her anima to form a blade. The recondite lets it bypass magic immunity and sigils."

Magic turned into a blade? The hilt had to be recondite. Even with the arcanir cuffs, it would work. "So a pyromancer makes a fire blade, a lucent makes a light blade—"

"Precisely," Ariana said with a grin.

She wrinkled her nose. "What does a healer make?"

"A healing blade."

"A cantor?"

"A singing blade?"

Rielle raised an eyebrow. "Are you asking me or telling me?"

"That was a joke." Ariana bit her lip. "It would make a, um, sound blade. A swing would hit as fast as you can hear something, and it could penetrate, well, anything you can hear through. It's actually quite powerful."

Well, then. Hopefully she'd never run into a cantor with a spellblade.

"...to begin," the Grand Divinus said, facing the arena.

"Good luck," Ariana whispered to her.

"You, too," Rielle whispered back. She stiffened, just like all the other candidates in the arena.

A great rumbling rippled through the ground, and all around the arena, doors lowered slowly.

Giant fingers slipped through the gap of Number Two's door. A thud hit another, then again, and again.

Claws peeked through another gap, and before all the doors were open, a winding serpent with membranous wings poured into the arena, its toothy maw open and large as a man.

A wyvern.

Ariana drew the hilt and pressed a thumb to the crossguard, where blood beaded and flowed—and a massive blade of light emerged, a foot wide and six feet long. She slashed it in the direction of the monster, and a beam of white-hot light flashed across the arena and severed part of its tail before it could dart.

Seven reptilian heads entered through another door—a hydra. And a feathered beast the size of a horse—a griffin.

A giant finally broke through its door, looming a daunting twenty feet tall.

Rielle kept her back to the empty part of the arena, retreating to the safety of the closed door to Number Three.

A black wolf the size of a human sprinted out of Number Six and raced behind the giant. *A werewolf.*

Like—like Brennan.

That's no beast.

But then her eyes found the last doorway, open but shadowed, and what lingered there had not yet emerged. Number One.

Don't look.

She kept her gaze low, on the ground before the door, only occasionally glancing at the chaos unfolding in the arena.

Ariana had severed the wyvern's tail and one wing. It spat a dark liquid that she dodged.

It hit Tariq in the back.

Flames burst from behind him, engulfing his shoulders, and he screamed, throwing off his coat as the griffin swooped down.

And then he was in the air, clutched in its talons, and reaching for one of many bundles on his belt. He threw it toward the griffin's beak.

A powder glittered overhead.

The griffin froze, its wings holding air for a moment before it plummeted to the ground, Tariq in its grasp.

From the shadowy doorway burst a massive, low lizard, launching its sleek body toward her. The basilisk.

With all the numbered bays empty, she ran along the secure edge of the arena, drawing Thorn, while the basilisk sprang after her.

Divine's flaming fire, the thing was fast.

Ariana darted toward Mac Carra as he battled the hydra and tucked a dark-green scale into his belt. He spun, swinging his sword, as she rolled away.

The wyvern leapt for Mac Carra.

Ariana brought down the spellblade, severing its massive head with a beam of light. She swept an exaggerated bow to Mac Carra and, grinning, backed up toward the wall.

Each beast has been conditioned to target the candidate bearing its token.

Quick thinking on Ariana's part.

The basilisk closed in, its spiked tail taunting behind it.

That's how it'll strike.

Rielle ducked as the basilisk's tail thudded into the wall next to her, its spikes buried deep. It pulled them free with difficulty.

One. She rolled away. *Two. Three. Four.*

She faced it, looking just above its head, waiting for the tail again.

Another strike, and she leapt aside as it dug into the wall again.

One. Two. Three.

The basilisk yanked its tail free. Three to four seconds was what she'd have.

She sidled along the wall until the spiked tail targeted her again—

Something sprang from a dark doorway, and heavy liquid hit her arm. *What the—*

With Thorn over her head, she dropped to the ground, one of the spikes burying a corner of her coat in the wall.

With a swing upward, she buried Thorn halfway through the tail. An eerie, sharp cry echoed through the arena.

Thorn was sharp and arcanir cut through basilisk scales, but they were too hardy, and the swing hadn't been strong enough.

For all her yanking, she couldn't pull it out.

The tail shook and drew free—she had to release the blade—and then she was dragged along the dusty ground. By the corner of her coat.

No, no, no. She grabbed at it, but no blade, no magic—

She was up in the air, ten feet, fifteen feet off the ground, when the fabric began to tear—

The ground came rushing back in a painful thud that knocked the wind out of her. The mirror, had it fallen? Was it—

"Favrielle!" a woman shouted, and metal slid toward her face.

She caught it as the basilisk leapt over her. *The soft spot.* Jon's words.

She rolled out from under the claw and beneath its head, her palm around the hilt, her thumb over a sharp point that drew blood—

An inferno burst from the hilt and upward, through the beast's soft hide beneath its jaw and up through its skull. It shrieked, those claws scratching toward her.

Releasing the hilt, she scrambled away, out from under it. Thorn lay a few feet away, and she darted for it while the basilisk screamed. Its tail whipped about frantically, hitting the giant in the back and the griffin, too.

She ducked its trajectory and launched herself at the beast, burying Thorn deep behind one of its front legs, deep enough to pierce its heart, she hoped.

A great cry, rumbling agony, and it fell.

The spellblade lay next to it, and she retrieved it.

Ariana Orsa had saved her life.

She backed up toward the wall, both Thorn and the spellblade in her hands. Up her arm was... silver? It coated her sleeve.

Not far, glass shattered, and the silvery liquid coated the ground where a black-furred wolf had been.

So very like Brennan.

A pained howl, and the werewolf tripped over a silver-speckled leg, and the metallic substance was splattered all over its body, hissing as it smoldered. The wolf didn't rise again.

Ten feet away, Cadan Bexley hefted another glass bottle. "You're not getting away this time."

It's a person. It's a person. It's a person!

"Bexley!" Rielle moved before the werewolf, holding both her weapons as she glanced over her shoulder at it from time to time. "It's a person—stop!"

He adjusted his specs with a finger and glared at her. "Get out of my way!" he snarled.

"It's not a beast, Bexley! It's a person who turns into a wolf. A person with emotions, intellect, *reason.*" Her voice trembled in her throat, but with any luck, it sounded as firm as she needed it to.

Over her shoulder, the werewolf had curled behind her, breathing in deep, tail curled between its legs in submission.

"I don't *care*," Bexley bit out, stomping forward. "Now *move!*" He threw another vial.

She swung the spellblade. Its foot-wide fire flared as the glass burst, the whole of it hissing to ash eaten away by flames. Holding the spellblade before her, she faced him.

Great Divine, what was she doing? She could barely wield a blade. Who knew what Bexley could do?

And this werewolf, would it kill *her* the first chance it got?

"This is my *chance!*" Bexley snarled. "*You—*"

Something hit him from behind, where Luca stood, his arm out as he grinned. He'd thrown something. His token?

An enormous hand closed around Bexley before he could recover, and lifted him high before constricting him, making him scream... until he stopped. The giant brought Bexley to its mouth—

A barrage of blades littered the giant's body from toe to head. One in the eye. It staggered back, sweeping its other arm in front of it, and threw Bexley's crumpled body at Luca, who dodged—only just.

There was no way his throwing knives would win this.

"Luca!" She threw Thorn toward his feet.

Without missing a beat, he grabbed the blade, sprang onto the giant, and buried Thorn in its chest. He pulled it free with a spray of ichor that he leapt away from.

But behind him, Mac Carra already stood, his boot upon a disembodied head next to a dead hydra. As the fourth to kill his beast, Luca had been too late.

A soft yelp, and Rielle turned to face the werewolf, whose gaze met hers.

Slowly, fur became snow-white skin, bare legs, and a human

body—painfully thin, emaciated—and a massive mane of night-black hair. A woman. Hissing, she swept off the silver from her skin, and it burned flesh as it went.

The woman shuddered and knelt upon one knee, her head bowed, the burns slowly fading. *"Agju a ma vita in u vostru servitore, Maestru."*

She raised her hands, shifting a finger to a claw, and slashed it across her opposite palm. As she clenched a fist, blood dripped onto the ground.

Footsteps approached from behind.

Rielle looked back—Ariana. She handed the spellblade back to Ariana, and the flaming blade dematerialized.

"She's swearing herself to your service," Ariana said, her eyes wide as she clipped the hilt to her belt. "Werewolf culture is steeped in codes of honor. I've heard of this from the dark-elves, but I've never seen it. If you accept, you make the blood sacrifice as well."

Rielle shook her head. "No, I want her to be free." She hadn't tried to save this werewolf's life just to enslave her.

Ariana stood next to her. "That's not how it works. She considers herself indebted to you. Until that debt is repaid, she can't live honorably without swearing herself to your service. If you don't accept her pledge, it is a black mark."

Pledge? Rielle sighed. The last thing *anyone* needed was to take on her problems. "What's a black mark?"

"No pack will accept her."

Luca approached from her other side and handed Thorn to her. "Thanks," he said gruffly. "A little too late, but thanks anyway." He rolled his eyes.

Thorn was clean of ichor. Rielle cut her palm near the hilt and, with a deep breath, squeezed out a few drops of blood to mingle with the werewolf's. A sensation like a needle threaded through her, and then it faded.

Divine help you.

The werewolf lifted her head, her deepest-brown gaze softening. She placed a hand on her bare chest. "Marfa," she said.

Rielle did the same. "Rielle."

Marfa shook her head while Luca gave her a once-over with wide eyes. "Maestru."

Rielle elbowed him.

"What?" he shot back.

With a sigh, she removed her coat, tattered as it was, and swept it about Marfa's shoulders, crouching. "You don't owe me anything," she said softly, helping Marfa get her hands into the sleeves. "But I'll be your friend for as long as you want one."

Marfa's black eyebrows drew together, but she wrapped the coat about herself, her mouth curving slightly, and nodded as she rose.

The arena had gone quiet behind them.

Along with the bodies of the basilisk, the wyvern, the giant, and the hydra, the griffin now lay dead, too, and Tariq was barely standing, mangled and bloodied. His powders must have worked.

"That's it, then," Rielle said. "The second trial's over." She looked up to the Grand Divinus, but the repulsion shield was still in place. A moment passed, and lengthened, and still no change. She glanced at Ariana. "What are they waiting for?"

Ariana's eyebrows knitted together as her gaze meandered to Marfa.

"Trial's not over until *all* the beasts are dead," Mac Carra called out as he wiped his enormous blade on the remains of Bexley's coat. He stood and pointed the tip of his sword at Marfa, who started and stepped behind her.

"She's not a *beast*." Rielle planted her feet.

Mac Carra shouldered his sword. "Superhuman strength. Superhuman speed. Superhuman senses. Turns into a wolf," he rattled off. "*Not* like us. A beast." As he sized her up, he tapped the blade against his shoulder.

If he wanted to kill her, he'd do it. Even with Thorn, she stood no chance against him. He was bigger, stronger, more skilled with a blade. It was hopeless.

Ariana stepped up next to her shoulder and drew the spell-blade. Luca stepped up on her other side, sweeping his coat open to reveal his remaining throwing knives.

She arched a brow at him.

"I'm not about to kill an innocent woman, werewolf or no, and I *do* owe you one." A corner of his mouth turned up.

With a shake of her head, she turned back to Mac Carra. Crass as Luca was, his support was still welcome.

Mac Carra eyed the line of them and shrugged a large shoulder. "All lined up in a bonny row." He sneered. "Then how do you plan to leave this arena, great merciful ones?"

The repulsion shield still held.

He had a point.

She looked up at the Grand Divinus again, who simply stared back. There would be no backing down. Marfa had been included deliberately, and the Grand Divinus wouldn't bend, wouldn't risk the appearance of weakness.

They'd be here as long as it took.

Jon stood closer to the shield, his fierce eyes locked on her, his hand still gripping Faithkeeper's pommel. He'd wanted to cut through the shield before, for her sake.

Cut through... She lowered her gaze to Thorn. *Arcanir.* She could cut through the shield, just as Jon had wanted to. Even the arcanir cuffs would let them all through.

But where would that leave them? Even together, all five of them would still be cuffed in arcanir, with only their weapons to fight with. The Divine Guard would make quick work of them. And there was no taking off the cuffs. None of them were strong enough to—

Superhuman strength.

She turned toward Marfa, whose dark eyes widened. Brennan could break an arcanir cuff. Could Marfa?

Rielle dragged up the sleeve of her white shirt and held out her wrist to Marfa, then grabbed the arcanir cuff. "Can you break this?" She squeezed it, pantomiming a break.

Marfa frowned and took hold of it, then met her eyes and raised her eyebrows inquisitively.

Rielle nodded.

Just a flex of Marfa's clenched hands, and the cuff snapped, broken off.

She gestured a candlelight spell, and it flared to life briefly before she dispelled it.

"Me, too! Me, too!" Ariana held hers out, and when Marfa looked for confirmation, Rielle nodded. Luca offered his wrist as well, and even Mac Carra approached, his free hand up, although Marfa's stance was rigid as she broke his.

Not a man to turn your back to.

Marfa wedged herself between them, gaze narrowed on him. Even Ariana and Luca kept watch. Good.

Rielle looked up at the Grand Divinus and faced stony resistance. The repulsion shield remained in place.

It was obvious that all of them could leave the arena at any moment they chose. They could fight the Divine Guard, and as five of the Divinity's strongest mages, they could win. They could fight their way out of Magehold and leave it in shambles.

But they'd be leaving without the Magister Trials' promised

boon, as enemies of the Divinity, and Jon's plea for Emaurria might be denied because of her revolt. And it would look intentional to the regional powers.

The question was, did the Grand Divinus wish to stake her reputation—and the Divinity's—on that? Or would she settle for a reasonable, non-violent, solution?

"Your Excellency," Rielle called out to her with a deep bow. "We have completed the second trial. All beasts have been defeated."

The Grand Divinus slitted her eyes.

"We have proven our resourcefulness, just as the trial demanded, as well as our efficiency and our morality." An olive branch. *Take it, take it, take it.*

"Your *morality?*" the Grand Divinus prompted. "Enlighten all those in attendance."

Enlighten. The Grand Divinus could make the explanation look planned—part of the trial—if she liked it.

"The Magister Trials have had to change to adapt to life after the Rift," Rielle called out. "And the qualities of a new magister have changed, too. We must know how to face the Immortals—how to fight those who wish to do us harm, and how to help those who wish to make peace with us." But how would Bexley have been able to win? She bit her lip. "Master Bexley— Divine rest his soul—could have 'defeated his beast' by making peace with this woman"—she nodded to Marfa—"and acknowledging she's no beast at all, but a person." She glanced toward his body. "In pursuit of the magister's mantle, he made the ultimate sacrifice... and in a way, he had the most difficult challenge of us all today."

The arena went deathly still, and quiet. The Grand Divinus watched her, that cold gaze unbroken. Would it be compromise and settlement, or revolt and ruin?

"And all of you have completed that most difficult challenge, along with your own," the Grand Divinus said at last, nodding to the Divine Guard.

The repulsion shield vanished.

"I declare the second trial complete, and the winners Master Ariana Orsa, Master Favrielle Amadour Lothaire, and Master Riordan Mac Carra, who will proceed to the third and final trial in three days, which will test our candidates for their willingness to sacrifice for the greater good. Join me now in the great hall as we honor the winners, and the passing of Master Cadan Bexley, whose courage in joining the Magister Trials will be remembered."

The doors out of the arena opened.

She'd be going to the third, and final, trial.

CHAPTER 45

*B*rennan watched the arena doors open and the candidates emerge. Groups gathered around to congratulate them, but he shook his head. Her recklessness knew no bounds.

The Wolf snarled its objections, uneasy within.

I know. I'll tell her.

He'd arrived in time to see her take the magical sword, kill the basilisk, and defend the female werewolf—all while cuffed in arcanir. She could have *died*. In the name of winning a useless title, keeping up political appearances, getting help for the Emaurrian coast... help she could get in other ways.

Too far. She'd gone too far.

As soon as Rielle exited, he grabbed her hand as she stepped out, and dragged her to a quiet corner.

"Brennan—what are you—" she began, wide eyed.

He yanked her to meet his gaze and gripped her shoulders. "Are you out of your mind, bride?"

Frowning, she shook her head. "What—"

"The *moment* she wanted to put you in arcanir, you should have *left*." The very second the Grand Divinus had wanted to take away *her ability to defend herself*, Rielle should have quit.

She wriggled a shoulder out of his grip. "But I had a plan, and I had Thorn, and the hand mirror—"

"And you'd be *dead* without the help of that other mage," he snarled. That magical blade. If not for that, she'd be...

"You don't know that," she hissed.

"I was about to watch it happen." His voice dropped. "I was halfway to the repulsion shield before you used that..."

"Spellblade."

"...*spellblade* and survived." It was only the irreversible revelation of his nature that had slowed him at all, made him wait until the last possible minute, or he would have been in the arena and fighting his way to her.

"I'm fine," she whispered, her sky-blue eyes searching his as she rested a hand on his chest. "And... thank you. For teaching me how to use Thorn."

He practically growled at her.

He'd only been teaching her the sword for two days, and she'd used it to fight an Immortal beast *without* the support of her magic. She should have withdrawn.

At least there was only *one* more trial, and then she could put all of this behind her.

Movement from the side pulled his gaze away.

The werewolf woman he'd scented earlier approached to stand next to her, clad in Rielle's torn mage coat, looking from Rielle to him and back again.

Rielle smiled and shook her head. "I'm all right, Marfa."

Marfa. The woman seemed frail, gaunt, but the mage had no doubt starved her while the trials had been prepared. Perhaps even since the Rift. Typical Divinity benevolence.

Keeping her here like a weapon in an armory, waiting to use her for this trial, except without even the regular maintenance a weapon would have gotten.

Marfa faced him squarely, like a guard. Earlier, in the arena, she'd seemed to pledge herself to Rielle, and by the looks of it, Rielle had accepted.

Rielle gently rested a hand on Marfa's arm, smiling and whispering reassurances.

"Do you know what you're doing?" he asked her.

She smiled blithely. "Not even a bit." With a sigh, she added, "But it was the right thing to do. The only thing."

Not unexpected for Rielle to pick up problems.

And this Marfa would come with problems. Ancient ones. And her pledge—was it true? Would she really serve Rielle?

Too risky.

"Tell her to leave," he said, and she frowned.

"I can't do that—Ariana said it would be a... a black mark to refuse her service, and no pack would have her."

Pack? So the werewolves that had awoken with the Rift had packs, and some kind of laws.

Rielle stubbornly stared him down. There would be no reasoning with her. Marfa would be joining them.

"Ariana said it's part of werewolf culture," Rielle whispered, stroking his chest softly.

Werewolf *culture*. They had culture? All he'd heard was howling in the distant woods, but then, he'd never risked venturing nearer. Who knew what they'd do to him?

Nearby, Jon stood at the entrance to the stands, Olivia wrapped around his arm, looking Rielle over with searching, evaluative eyes.

Jon had felt it, too, then—that madness at her recklessness.

He'd moved to the repulsion shield, Olivia dragging him back and muttering reasons not to.

Dying. Jon was dying. He hadn't promised not to see Rielle, but he'd nearly said as much.

Not a threat. Not even remotely.

Rielle grinned at Jon and tapped Thorn's pommel. "Did you see? I did what you said. The soft spot."

"I saw." Approaching, Jon gave her a teasing approving once-over, then that gaze flicked to him for the briefest of moments before settling on Marfa. Hands at his sides, free, ready, Jon sized her up as she did him.

"Nicely done," Olivia said with an encouraging nod. "I would have liked fewer heart attacks, but then again, it *is* you."

Rielle stuck out her tongue and nudged Olivia's shoulder. They shared a smile before Una came over with her two friends, a young man and a young woman about her age. Mother had insisted she socialize while here—Una still had no betrothal, despite being eighteen years of age.

She was unconventional—dressing in men's clothes—but she was amazing. Someday another person would see that, and if deserving of Una's love, would become her partner.

"Congratulations," Una said with a grin. "I especially liked the fire sword. Where can we get one of those?"

Rielle chuckled and inclined her head in thanks. "I wouldn't mind one myself." As Una's gaze turned to Marfa, so did Rielle's.

"This is Marfa. She's with me from now on." Rielle motioned to him, took his hand, and held it up to Marfa, entwined with her own. "Marfa, this is *Brennan*. We're to be *wed*."

Marfa's dark eyes darted to him, and she crossed her arms as she squinted at him.

"Maritu di Maestru?" Marfa tilted her head, tapping the space over her heart. *"Un lupu?"*

"Maritu," Rielle repeated, nodding and bringing their joined hands to her heart. She cleared her throat—then that *lupu* must have bothered her as it did him. "Yes—my *maritu.*"

"A dialect of Old Sileni?" he guessed quietly.

Eyes on Rielle, Marfa cocked her head to Jon. *"E ellu?"*

He pulled Rielle closer. *Ellu?* Why should *ellu* be anything to her?

Rielle shook her head. "My... my king." She bowed to Jon, low, prolonged.

"Vostru maestru." Raising her eyebrows, Marfa turned to Jon and bowed respectfully, a graceful, practiced act. Perhaps *werewolf culture* hadn't been so farfetched a claim. *"Un unore, mo signore."*

With the requisite courtesy, Jon inclined his head in acknowledgment.

If Marfa had only just awoken with the Rift, she was learning quickly, although there was so much more she didn't know. Teaching her the ways of a world far more advanced than she'd remembered would be a hassle. An enormous, tedious hassle.

"Come," Brennan said, nodding to Rielle and Una. "We're leaving. Your Majesty." With a parting bow to Jon, he turned, his hand at the small of Rielle's back, and ushered her away, with Marfa following, their newest problem.

Rielle hadn't yet asked him about the Archives—no doubt their audience had affected that—but he'd have to tell her what he'd decided.

She wouldn't like it, not one bit, but she'd support him in this. She would. He'd chosen their family over the nebulous *good* she wanted to do, and the *truth*, but the choice was self-evident. She'd agree. She had to.

MARFA FOLLOWED Maestru and her husband from the depths of the mad Coven's castle.

Maestru herself was human, of course, but in the fighting circle, her scent had distinguished her from the other humans. A human lover to one of her kind, to a werewolf. Perhaps his mate. Perhaps even mother to cubs.

Perhaps even a potential friend.

Maestru had stood between her and that vile silver witch, as no human would ever do. Saved her life. Earned her service, until such time as her generosity could be repaid.

On the way out, they passed human extravagance so overwhelming, it was almost laughable. Gold shimmering everywhere, frescoes and wall reliefs, tapestries and elaborate rugs, architecture designed to evoke grandeur.

The humans hadn't changed much. Not in this, nor in their cruelty, judging from most of the humans in attendance today. The humans had always believed themselves apart from the Immortals, superior despite their short lives and weakness. They didn't even have the strength of most werewolf cubs.

But Maestru didn't share in that typical human cruelty, and neither, it appeared, did her friends. The other witches in the fighting circle had stood with her, too, inexplicably, in support of her decision to defend an Immortal.

They stepped out into the night, and she paused to inhale the free air, fresh and open, the scents of cypress and grass and earth and imminent rain, and even the innumerable humans. Horse and rabbit, fox and rat, lark and nightingale.

A carriage awaited, but beyond it glittered an entire human city, with countless rooftops fading into the distance, torches and candlelight winking in the night's sable cloak.

Maestru grazed her arm, nodded toward the carriage, and with a smile she hoped was grateful, she boarded.

Inside, Maestru's husband, Brennan, pinned her with a penetrating gaze, every inch of him ready, coiled, prepared to strike. He was large, even for a werewolf, and without a doubt, strong. And, it seemed, young. Born in the last few decades, he had somehow avoided the spasm that had claimed her and Lisandra.

She scented no pack on him. He was alone, but for Maestru, whom he claimed with an arm about her shoulders. His blood relation, the young woman, had elected to depart with her human friends—and she, too, was human.

Perhaps Brennan had been bitten?

Maestru reached across the carriage and rested a hand on her knee, giving it a pat, and said something in the new tongue. Something comforting, affectionate. She would have a home with Maestru. Food. And no more *Erardo*.

She suppressed the thought. No, he wouldn't disturb her here, now, when she was free of that cage and safe with a maestru, but she, most certainly, would disturb *him*. And *soon*.

There was still so much she needed to know besides.

How much time had passed since she'd last seen Lisandra? Where was she? Where was the Ciriaccu pack? Why had the Dragonlords allowed the humans to come to power? Why did no one speak the common tongue any longer?

But therein lay the problem.

Even if Maestru wished to answer those questions, there was no way to ask. It would be some time before they could communicate in anything but the primitive methods.

She'd have to learn... whatever this tongue was that Maestru spoke. But bit by bit, she would. Among the Ciriaccu, she'd always been known for her skill in mingling with the humans— learning their news and their plans, bartering for supplies, even taking a human lover or two from time to time.

She could learn again, and as she caught Maestru's warm smile from across the carriage, she was certain Maestru would help her. And the first thing she'd tell Maestru, as soon as she learned the new tongue, would be all about the mad Coven, their human cruelty, and the *Erardo* she would soon kill.

LEIGH PUNCHED the trunk of a white pine in the twilight, while the others made camp.

They'd been tracking the horde for two days, on the mountainside, in the caverns, in the woods, and although they'd found straggling undead, there was still no sign of Ava. She had to be farther south along the mountain. She was getting closer to the Forgeron Coven's territory, and time was running out.

A firm warmth rested between his shoulder blades, and he glanced back to find Ambriel, unwavering, his eyes soft. "I wouldn't do that, dreshan. A dryad guards this forest."

Just what they'd need. Another *dryad* to wreak havoc.

He stepped away from the tree with a sigh.

"Come," Ambriel said. "I've pitched our tent, and you could use a rest."

Rest. He didn't want to *rest.* Not until they found Ava.

But his entire body was sore from another day of riding, and he was dead on his feet. He nodded and followed Ambriel to the tent. Katia and Della sat by a small fire pit; here, in a clear stretch of land in the shadow of the mountain, Ambriel had assured them they'd be beyond the dryad's reach, as long as they didn't venture into the forest.

Ambriel held aside the tent flap, and Leigh ducked inside, descending to a bedroll with a groan. Nothing was going according to plan. Nothing.

"We'll find her, dreshan. We've been scouring the area for days, and we have leads. It's not as bleak as it seems." Ambriel lowered to the bedroll next to him, sitting cross-legged.

With a sigh, Leigh glanced at him. Ambriel had his own children, but he didn't understand. Not this. Not how every second mattered. "I've... I've lost before. I need to find her, Ambriel. *Yesterday*."

Ambriel curled an arm around him, only the crackling of the fire and the whispers between Della and Katia disrupting the silence. "You're strong, and together, we're stronger. She's your only child, and of course you're worried. But you have to have faith."

Ava wasn't his only child.

"When I was sixteen," he began, "my parents arranged my marriage to a young woman from a neighboring farm. I'm the son of a Pryndonian merchant and a Kamerish mother. Grew up farming in Ren. So it was a perfect match, really."

"You're married?" Ambriel asked softly.

"I was," Leigh said, with a bitter, wistful breath. "We had two children, sons, in short order." His shoulders slumped. "After only two years, Ren was the target of a pirate attack. Every able-bodied man, myself included, was summoned to defend the city, but when we failed, I knew the farms on the outskirts were next. *Our* farm, and my family. Wounded, dying, I staggered to Ren's Temple of the Divine."

The temple in Ren famously housed a Vein, one of the few

places in the world where one could commune with wild magic and become a wild mage.

Where *he* had.

When Ambriel only watched him attentively, he continued. "Of course, when I survived, I helped repel the attack on the farms and made haste for home. You see, my dear, I was a natural enforcer, if rough as a novice." Firelight peeked in from outside. "Mages came from the Kamerish Tower afterward, inviting me to join the Divinity of Magic. I turned them down, even though my family was welcome to come along. I wanted to stay home, keep our farm, our way of life.

"But only a year later, there was a second attack. The pirates had arcanir this time... and they killed my wife. Only minutes before I returned."

Ambriel stiffened, staring at the ground in the dimness. "Dreshan, I... I'm so sorry."

It had been the worst failure of his life. "I went into fureur, killed all my friends and neighbors who had gathered at my home for safety. My own sons." Leigh shook his head slowly, rubbing his eyes with his knuckles, but his shoulders tightened, trembled, and even now, seventeen years later, he felt as raw and broken as he had that day.

Ambriel's embrace tightened.

"I was taken down with an arcanir arrow, and when the Kamerish army defeated the pirates, they surrendered what was left of me to Magehold's judgment," he said. He'd been ready to die that day. He should have. "The Grand Divinus left me in the hands of Magister Shiori Kagami at the Kamerish Tower, and she convinced me not to end my life, but to devote it to preventing such large-scale atrocities from ever happening."

The only thing that had given his life meaning.

Just one mage could save the lives of millions. *He* could. And he had, in the decades since.

Ambriel's eyes watered, and Leigh welcomed him to the warmth of his chest, rubbed the nape of his neck.

"I didn't know," Ambriel whispered. He squeezed his eyes shut, but tears escaped anyway.

"I kept it from you, my dear," he whispered in Ambriel's ear. "I never wanted anyone to see that side of me." He rested his chin lightly on the top of Ambriel's head. He hadn't told anyone —not even Rielle. "But now... Now that Ava is out there, in fureur, struggling... I want to do my all for her. I want to do better for her. Save her from the fate that had claimed Hana, Takumi, and Yuki. And save her from the fate I'd suffered."

Hana. Who'd hummed as she worked. Who'd ridden horses as if she'd been born in the saddle. The wife he'd loved, whose fate had ended at his hands. Takumi, who'd followed his every footstep with a happy smile, and Yuki, who'd only just begun to walk.

His flesh and blood, whose faces were there every time he closed his eyes. Whom he would have died for. Whom he now lived for, hoping to spare others what the pirates and *he* had done to them.

Ambriel crumpled, but Leigh descended with him, his embrace firm. It was too horrible, too terrible for most people to consider. The consequences of fureur. Most would only see him as a monster. Maybe even Ambriel would.

Tremors snaked through Ambriel's hands, and he clasped them.

"All is the Divine," he whispered. "That is what the Divinity says. And as much as I hate them, it's a worthy thought. There was never enough goodness in the world to balance the iniquity mankind has wrought. It is said the Divine has filled us with the violence of our race, has given it to us as magic, and has challenged us few to save mankind." The Divinity had sent those pirates to Ren the day Hana had been killed. He *knew* it. And although the Divinity didn't live up to its worthy stated purpose, he still could. Mages still could. The Covens still could. "We were tested when we weren't prepared, but we are now. And we must sacrifice."

If that was true, he had already sacrificed. Far too much.

But he wouldn't let Ava be sacrificed. He'd find her, save her, if it was the last thing he did.

CHAPTER 46

*W*hile Rielle took Marfa to new quarters—with all the food she could handle, and a whole new wardrobe—Brennan entered the antechamber to their own quarters and shrugged off his overcoat.

It had been a long day, and it would only be a longer night with what he had to tell Rielle about the Archives. She'd understand, wouldn't she?

With a deep breath, he paused at a table. She'd been angry over the lies, and she wouldn't like this, but she'd see it was to save their family. She'd fume, but in the end, she'd support him in this.

A lone envelope lay on the surface. Correspondence. He grabbed it and headed to the desk, where he cracked it open to Kehani's written curls and sworls.

...your father discovered the truth, but he has not cast me aside. He is deciding whether he wishes to raise your son as his own and...

Footsteps, soft but confident, approached—Rielle's. He

swept his hand behind his back, along with the letter, then pulled open the desk drawer.

She burst in right as he slammed it shut, a moment of wide-eyed glancing about the room before she frowned at him. "What are you doing?"

There were a million different things he could say, but not a single one came to mind. *Raise your son.* He'd read that. *Your son.*

His limbs lightened, and heat radiated through his chest. "Brennan?"

Kehani is having my son.

Great Wolf, was that what it had truly said? His fingers drummed against the drawer. He couldn't read it again. Not with her here.

He'd only bedded Kehani *once.* Normally he was careful, but it had been *Kehani.* Father's *mistress.* The last woman who should ever desire to conceive another man's child. She was smart, and she'd want to keep her villa, her household, her income, all courtesy of Father. Why wouldn't she have been careful?

Or maybe months of self-imposed celibacy had dumbed him that night.

Rielle approached, brows drawn together. "What's wrong?"

He straightened. "I... was just about to deal with my correspondence."

The truth. He'd promised to tell her the truth.

Every lie he'd ever told her had been unraveled. And this... He'd *sworn* he hadn't been with anyone since Melain. And he hadn't, not really—Kehani had been a manipulation, nothing more. Not a true lover. Why *would* he have counted her?

But it *had* been a lie. A thoughtless lie. Harmless.

Until now.

If Rielle found out, she'd never believe a word he said again. And fathering a bastard? He'd be lucky if she didn't break off the betrothal and leave him immediately. She'd been all he'd ever wanted for so long, and now he might lose her.

His stomach turned hard as stone.

She glanced around him, squinting at the desk. "What are you hiding?"

Nothing, he wanted to say. But it wasn't true, was it? Not only that, but there was no way to hide this. Kehani would give birth to the child. That was inevitable. And Rielle *would* find out.

And she'd remember this moment. When he'd hidden it from her. When he'd *lied.*

No. She'd hear the truth, and they'd move past this. She'd be angry awhile, perhaps, but they had history, had known each other for seventeen years; he loved her, she knew it, and what more was there? Would she throw it all away over this one little thing? And for what? Jon was dying and had nothing to offer her.

No. She wouldn't leave him. He could tell her. He could.

A tremor quivered in his chest, but he repressed it and lightly grasped her shoulders. "Rielle... will you sit with me a moment?"

Beneath that frown, her eyes searched his, but she nodded. He removed the letter from the drawer and then led her before the fire—to the armchairs—no, the sofa. Close-by. Together. Once she sat, so did he, and took hold of her hand.

Hear me out. Just hear me out.

"We agreed to be honest with each other. I promised you that, and I want to keep my word," he said, and by the second, she hardened next to him, her heart pounding faster.

Only a tight nod was her reply.

Great Wolf, he had to *ease* this, tell her as gently and calmly as he could. "I told you that I haven't been with anyone since Melain, but before I arrived at House Hazael, there was... one night."

She closed her eyes, and her face fell. She pulled her hand free of his to rub her forehead. "Brennan..."

"I didn't mean to lie to you. It just... slipped my mind. Until now. It was one woman, one night, and didn't mean anything. It wasn't for love, or for lust even, but meant to manipulate my father."

She arched a brow. "Your father? How?"

"The woman was his mistress, Kehani."

Her eyes widened, for just a moment, before she pulled back. "Oh."

Just *oh*. A surprised little parting of her lips.

He waited, but she only stared, fell into a silent reverie, a sequence of expressions crossing her face. A confused frown, a contemplative series of blinks, an angry crease of her brow, a deep calming breath—

And finally a slow nod. She swallowed. "Well, that explains some of the looks she gave me," she said, drawing in a sharp breath, then exhaling it slowly, like a hundred years of age and exhaustion. "It was before we were even together. I can hardly be upset you were with a lover before then, even if you didn't tell me."

Hardly can. It didn't mean she *wasn't* upset. She just couldn't justify it. At least she was trying.

There was no way to smooth over what he had to say next. "She and I were only together once," he said carefully, then presented the letter. "And she sent me this." He handed it to her. "Rielle, she's with child."

Her fingers had only just brushed the broken wax seal when she pulled them away. "What?"

It was less a question than a choked cry, pained and shrill like that of a wounded animal.

He could hear her heart begin to race again, her breath quicken, and it was all he could do to stay where he was. "She's going to have a son. My son."

No movement. No reaction. And then her eyes watered, her expression unreadable until she bit her lip, lowered her gaze. For a long while, she just sat, still, staring, tears welling in her eyes.

She wasn't pulling away. She wasn't leaving. She wasn't angry.

Just... still.

The fire crackled in the hearth, and she should've said something, screamed, cried. Looked at him. But she did none of these things, claimed by a deceptive stillness, an eerie stillness, like a quiet wood where unseen wolves lurked deep within, waiting, hungering.

Kehani would be giving him a son, and it wasn't exactly how he'd planned to have a child, but... he would be a father. He would love his son. He would be in his life.

There would be no more talk of Father claiming the boy. He would be brought to Tregarde as soon as he was old enough to leave his mother, and he'd be protected, raised as a Marcel. And Kehani, if she wanted her life to stay as it was, wouldn't fight him on it. He wasn't about to leave the protection of his son to anyone else.

He wasn't just... *him* anymore to Rielle, but *him and his child.*

"I know this changes things," he said carefully.

Her head turned slowly to his, her eyes narrowing, her lips twisting bitterly. She stiffened, clenching her hands into fists.

Now she was angry.

"It changes things," he repeated, "but it doesn't change our relationship, how I feel about you. I love you, want to spend the rest of my life with you. We can still marry, live our lives together, have our own children when we're ready, if you can accept that I'll be in his life. Just don't... walk away from what we have, and what we still could have."

She blew out an exasperated breath and shook her head.

"Isn't there room enough in my life for both of you?"

She closed her eyes, and this time, the tears that had welled there now broke. "You'll raise him."

"Of course."

"And you should. He's your child." She chewed her lip. "But I... By your side, I'll watch a child growing up... But not *my* child. Not Sylvie." She dropped her face in her hands. "I can't even look at other children without seeing her. Not for months. Not now. Maybe not ever."

No, this couldn't—she couldn't—

He wouldn't live without his son, but he couldn't live without *Rielle* either, and she was—what she was saying was—

He couldn't choose between living and breathing.

There had to be some way that they could coexist. There *had* to be, because if there wasn't, he would do anything to make it happen. He would say anything, do anything, swear anything —if she'd only just agree to *try*.

But this... her hurt over losing Sylvie...

If it were him, and *his* daughter, he'd be destroyed, too. He'd mourn the life she'd never have, the daughter whose face he'd never see, the family that would never be the same without her in it.

But Rielle's grief had frozen her, frozen her heart, and if she didn't even attempt to thaw it, even a little, it would remain ice indefinitely. For months, years, maybe even decades, she'd freeze in the arctic wasteland of her grief, always looking back on a past she could never change instead of toward a future that could still hold some happiness for her, and a family that couldn't erase her grief over Sylvie, but still had the power to warm her heart, give her enough joy to keep going. "Rielle, I know your loss was painful, but if you keep dwelling—"

"You think I want to?" She uncovered her face, tear-streaked and red, for an anguished moment. "I loved her, wanted her, but I don't want to have this hurt inside of me, to feel this pain, to look at other children and see only *loss*."

"Then think about moving forward, even taking a little step. Think about the family you could still have, if you want it."

She shot off the sofa, scowling at him, and rubbed her face. "How can you even say that? Haven't you been listening to me at all? I can't—"

He stood and faced her squarely. "You can't just stay frozen in the past forever, stuck in a tragedy you can never fix," he said. "And if you can't even think about moving forward, what do you want me to do, choose between you and my child?"

"No!" She shook her head and squeezed her eyes shut, tears escaping their confines. "I'd never ask you to do that. But *don't tell me* this changes nothing about our relationship. *Don't tell me* everything is going to be fine. And *don't tell me* to just move on and have another child."

She wiped at her face and paced before the fire, shaking her head.

"What, then? How are we going to live a life together if you can't accept this? If I can't even *ask* you to accept this?"

"You can ask me to accept this, Brennan," she said softly,

"but you *can't* ask me to feel nothing about it. And you can't tell me to just 'move forward' and have another child. I'm not ready. I *can't*, not when I'd look at him and just see the one I lost. Don't you understand? I need... I need time."

It had been three months already. "How much time?" He wanted a life with her, a family, but she'd made no steps forward yet, and seemed to have no plans of doing so anytime soon. But he loved his nephews, wanted his own children, more than one... and she couldn't even give him a time frame. "Do you need a year? Two years? Five? Ten? At least tell me so I know what to—"

"I don't know," she whimpered. "I don't know!" Louder this time. "However long it takes. I told you that. I told you that day in Stroppiata that I'd need time. I told you, and you agreed."

He had agreed, but he hadn't agreed to give up. And now that he'd have a firstborn son...

A firstborn son of a firstborn son...

"Circumstances have changed," he said delicately, reaching for her. But she pulled away. "It's not just me anymore, Rielle. An innocent child will be born cursed. I don't need you to tell me this instant, but I do need an answer. *We* need an answer."

Her face went slack. "What...?"

"It's not just about you and me anymore," he said softly. "If you don't have an answer for five years, ten, or more, and then decide you *don't* want children, you'll be allowing an innocent child to suffer for the sake of your grief."

She averted her gaze, curled her fingers into fists, and headed for the door.

RIELLE RUSHED DOWN THE STAIRS, as fast as her feet could take her. He was hot on her heels, but it didn't matter, nothing mattered, nothing but one foot in front of the other, farther and farther from that room, that moment, that conversation, from everything he'd said to her and everything she'd lost and everything he'd wanted to sweep aside as if it were nothing at all.

"Stop," he called after her, boots pounding down the steps. "Talk to me—" He grabbed her arm, but she jerked it away.

No, she'd tried talking to him, but he wasn't interested in what she had to say, but only in what he wanted from her. They needed time, apart from each other, to sort out their feelings.

She loved him, loved him with everything she had, and wanted to make him happy, but not at the price of herself. If *that's* what he wanted, what he expected, and he wouldn't bend, then she couldn't stay here another minute or she'd break.

He raced ahead of her and blocked her path, grabbed her shoulders. "You can't run from this," he said, shaking them. "But that's what you've been doing, ever since Xir."

The solution to every problem wasn't forcing it. "*Grieving* is not running, Brennan. What I've done my entire life, suppressing my emotions, ignoring my grief, *that* was running. No more. I can't live that way."

He glared at her. "It's gone on since—"

"Yes, and it may go on even longer," she snapped back at him, trying to wrest free. But his grip didn't waver. "If I died, would you just replace me? Would you just find a new woman to marry and move on?" She searched his eyes as their intensity faded. "Or would you see my face in every potential love? See happy couples and think only of your loss? Wouldn't you wait until the ice of your heart melted, so it could open again, *welcome* new love?"

"That's not the same," he bit out.

"Isn't it?" She held his gaze until he blinked and shook his head. It wasn't wrong of him to want to know when she'd be ready, but it wasn't wrong of her to not know yet either. "You push me to move on, but is it really for my sake?"

"And my son's sake?"

"I'm a *person*, Brennan! Not just some tool!" She shouted at him, leaning forward, into his space. "I have feelings, too. I can't just make them disappear," she said, while his eyes smoldered. "Your first Change manifested when you were fifteen, Brennan. We have over a decade to spare him the curse. So why are you pushing me so hard *now*? Not for my sake. Not for his." She pushed his hands off her shoulders, and expressionless, he let them fall. "We agreed to be honest with each other, but you need to be honest with yourself first, and ask yourself *why*. What pushes you to hurt me for this, to demand I set aside my grief to fit your timeframe, to try to force me to your will... and against mine?"

Blinking, he shook his head.

No answer. Until he stopped this pushing, until he admitted the truth to himself, there could be no peace between them. And she wouldn't stay here and be told what to feel, how, and when to move on.

She stepped around him and descended the stairs. She'd grabbed her cloak and her coin purse, and she wasn't stuck here. The other candidates were staying at an inn called Staff & Stein. That's where she'd go. That's where she'd stay until he came to his senses.

She'd almost reached the landing when the low grit of his embittered voice called her name.

"You're going to *him*, aren't you?" he spat. "You just can't help yourself, can you? As soon as the opportunity arises, it's back to *him*. Always to *him*. Well, you know what? He doesn't *want* you. He won't *have* you. So *go*. Throw yourself at his feet and cry in his arms. For all the good it will do you."

She froze, a shudder weaving through her like a needle, and when she turned to him, she threw an ice spike just off to the side of his head, buried in the wall.

He flinched, eyed it, and the contorted frown began to fade.

Tears seeped from her eyes. *I wasn't—*

Gathering what little of her composure remained, she glared at him through the veil of tears, at his maddened rigidity that now wavered and unraveled. He caught the railing.

"You are a beast, Brennan Karandis Marcel."

CHAPTER 47

*B*rennan stood on the stairs, frozen, staring at the emptiness where Rielle had been. She was leaving. His hand anchored to his hip.

Why had he said it? He'd known, almost as soon as the words had left his mouth, that they were wrong, that she wasn't going back to Jon, that she *wouldn't*. And yet, he'd said them anyway. She'd glanced over her shoulder, face tight and squinting as if it had hurt to look at him, as if the mere sight had been claws through the heart. She'd looked at him *like that*.

And she was leaving. He couldn't let her leave, not before he apologized, took that back.

Breaking free of his thoughts, he rushed down the stairs, only to run into Marfa on the landing.

She moved into his path, planted her feet squarely, and glared at him, her eyes flashing amber, her fangs emerging as she growled, low and menacing.

He froze, staring her down, but she didn't budge.

A hand hooked his arm. Una's. "Bren," she said gently, gawking at Marfa.

"Let. Me. Go," he snarled, yanking his arm. But she clung tightly.

"If she's leaving, she wants space from you." Una tightened her grip. "Give her that, or you'll both end up saying things you don't mean."

He'd *already* done that.

Cooling, he lowered his arm, then took a step back.

Marfa, her fangs bared, took two steps back before rushing for the front doors, presumably where Rielle had exited.

Una tugged his arm. "What happened?"

"Kehani is having my child," he said, and she gasped. "I just told Rielle it changed nothing between us. I asked her for an heir—while she's still grieving a miscarriage."

Una's lips twisted as she winced. "Oh, Bren..."

He dropped his head in a hand. How he'd said all that, he had no idea. That conversation had gone nothing like he'd planned, other than telling her the truth. That should have been it. He should have told her, assuaged her concerns, then ended the night with her in his arms, comforting her, reminding her she was loved and appreciated.

Una patted his bicep. "Tell me all about it... and I'm sure you could use a drink."

So frayed, he couldn't bring himself to argue when a drink sounded like the best thing in the world right now.

He followed her to the library, where she poured him a snifter of brandy and shooed him toward the sofa by the hearth. While he sipped the warm comfort of his brandy and told her everything save for the curse, she listened attentively and leaned against him, laying her head on his shoulder.

"She told me to ask myself why I pressed her, to be honest," he said, then took a long sip. He'd already told her why—to balm her grief, and to spare his son the curse.

"When she was leaving, you accused her of going to Jon," she said gently. "Is that how you feel? Like she's just waiting for an excuse to go back to him?"

There *was* no going back to Jon. The man would be dead inside of a year or two, and had stated, very clearly, that he had no intention of being with Rielle. That he'd never allow her to suffer with him as he met his end, no matter what it took. There had been no lie in his voice, no lie in his pulse. Just cold conviction.

But... Rielle didn't know that. For all she knew, the situation hadn't changed at all, and maybe she believed that the future she'd thrown away—being a royal mistress for the rest of her life —was still available to her.

Maybe she occasionally weighed discarding a future as *his* wife in order to become Jon's lover, all the while ignorant that she would never again be Jon's lover no matter what she gave up or did.

Maybe he believed she wanted that sometimes.

"Sometimes," he confessed, and Una nodded against his shoulder.

"What do you think holds her back?"

He shook his head. "We're getting married in four months."

Una took a drink. "So, a promise? You think if she wanted to be with *him*, loved *him*, imagined the rest of her life with *him*, that a promise would keep her?"

Not when she said it like *that*. "What are you saying?"

A heavy sigh. "Is it possible, Bren, that there are no nefarious intentions on her part and it is your *insecurity* ruining things between you?"

He scoffed. *Insecurity*. No. Never.

"You act like Nox's gift to women—"

"I *am* Nox's gift to women."

"—but when it comes down to it, you just can't believe your fiancée might actually want to be with *you*, and *only* you, forever."

He frowned. Was that it...? If Jon weren't king, wouldn't she have chosen him? Even after all that had happened in Courdeval, wouldn't she have...?

But he'd had the past months with her. Things were different now. He shook his head. Rielle wanted him—his werewolf senses left no uncertainty. "I know she loves me, but—"

"But you don't know if she loves him *more*. You don't know if she'll stay."

There was still a risk, wasn't there? That she'd leave him? If she found out Jon was dying, she could throw everything away to go be with him in his last couple years, few months, whatever he had left.

But not if she had a child.

Once she gave birth to *his* child, she wouldn't leave. Not Rielle. She couldn't, could she? Never.

He'd wanted a family and he'd wanted her, but asking her to live that future before she was ready would be binding her to him irreversibly. Cruelty to the extreme. That same ugliness taking over.

He dropped his head in his hand and squeezed his eyes shut. Great Wolf, if she *really* loved Jon more, would he *want* to keep her in misery? Would that make anyone happy? Tying her to him if she wanted to leave?

No.

That would be his own special kind of misery. Loving a woman who wanted to leave but couldn't. He rubbed his forehead. He'd wanted to make her happy, had wanted *her*, but somehow those two desires had fallen out of balance.

No—he'd let them. He'd let it happen, and had made a mess of things. Maybe even one he couldn't fix.

His son was a part of his life now, and Rielle had seemed willing to accept that. That part of their argument seemed resolved.

But the other...

He still wanted a family with her, but it had to be when she was certain she could commit to that next step. And not a moment before. She wasn't just some *tool*; their future had to be something they *both* wanted.

"If she loves *you* and wants to be with *you*, all of this is just going to... It'll push her away. It won't be a question of *whether* it'll all go up in flames, but *when*."

He sat still, Una's words sinking in.

How he'd treated her, ignored her feelings, thinking that making her his, forever, would be the answer to everything—she might not forgive him. And maybe she shouldn't. "What should I do?"

"Apologize," Una said, patting his arm. "And mean it. And maybe beg a little."

Beg. He almost wanted to laugh, but—Nox's black breath—he wasn't beyond begging her forgiveness.

He straightened. "Well, thank you."

She grinned. "I like her and want her in our family... but things have to work between the two of you, or it would be for nothing."

He stood, rubbing his forehead. There were no words for how badly he'd ruined everything.

He had a mess to clean up, and didn't even know where to begin.

IN THE DARK, Rielle strode from the Marcel villa's grounds and cast a candlelight spell to light her way.

How *dare* he? How *dare* he accuse her of running to Jon? As if *she* had been the one to *suddenly recall* that she'd bedded someone and would soon have a lovechild.

His ability to hold up a mirror to any issue with him was astounding.

And right on the heels of his revelation, *expecting* her to break the curse? Kehani's son hadn't even been born yet, and he was already demanding *she* break the curse, no matter what she felt.

He would see reason. He'd see it, take back everything he'd demanded, and then they would have peace. Because if he didn't—

She hefted her coin purse, full of gold coronas. If she needed to, she'd stay at Staff & Stein through the remainder of the trials, and book her *own* passage home.

Swift steps crunched in the grass behind her, and blowing out a sharp breath, she looked over her shoulder. "Leave me alone, Brennan, or so help me—"

Marfa held up her hands and slowed, shifting uneasily in her overcoat, made of buttery-soft leather dyed a fashionable forest green. After awakening with nothing, Marfa deserved the finer things. And as her lady, of sorts, it was her responsibility to provide everything Marfa needed. "*Maestru.*"

"Oh, it's you." Heaving a sigh, she beckoned to Marfa to walk with her. "We'll be staying at an inn for..." She shrugged. "For some time."

They made their way from uptown to the market district,

where the temple was, the candlelight spell softly glowing before them.

"*Chì ci hè?*" Marfa asked, her head tilted and her eyebrows creased together.

How to even begin explaining what was wrong? She heaved a sigh, but Marfa tipped her head encouragingly.

"Brennan," she said, and Marfa nodded. But how to explain—?

She pantomimed a curved, pregnant belly, and Marfa lit up. "*Avete avè un zitellu?*"

Zitellu—did that mean *baby*? Rielle gestured to herself, and Marfa nodded.

Not me. Rielle shook her head.

Marfa's eyebrows slowly rose as her face drained of color. "*Brennan hè un zitellu,*" she whispered, with a slow shake of her head, "*micca cun voi?*"

Marfa's incredulous, outraged tone sounded about right. Rielle nodded.

With a narrowing of her eyes, Marfa stomped her foot, then again, and crossed her arms. "*Omi,*" she said with a grunt and a contemptuous frown. "*Tutti... facenu cusì.*" She exhaled a sharp breath through her nostrils. "*Trovu una altra donna.*"

"It's not his fault," she replied. "Well, conceiving the child, maybe. But it was before he and I got together."

Marfa raised an eyebrow.

He had claimed he'd been with no one since Melain. What he'd done hadn't been wrong, but had it really *slipped his mind*? Or had it been easier to lie?

Either way, how was she ever to trust him? Whether he lied or not, the difficulty lay in never being at ease with him, always having to doubt, to question, to wonder. It was an unsteady ground to stand upon, shifting sands that could give way at any time. A lie she could forgive, but this indefinite state of distrust, doubt, unease? That was harder to live with. Not only that, but it made her into a person she didn't want to be, always doubting, always questioning, suspicious—

Marfa grabbed her arm, yanking her to a stop, and breathing in deeply as she scanned their dark surroundings with glowing amber eyes.

Dispelling the candlelight, Rielle cast earthsight, and there, in the tight alleyway between two buildings, a tall, rail-thin mage shone brightly, watching them from the next street over.

She pulled a wind wall up before herself and Marfa. Only days ago, she'd been followed here, too, and that figure, that form—it was the mage who'd accompanied Mac Carra.

If he wanted to take her out of the trials, he could damn well attempt it himself.

"Mac Carra," she bellowed at the figure. "Show yourself. Stop hiding behind your lackeys."

But the figure took off at a run, the bright glow fading with the distance. She stood, watching until it disappeared past her range.

"Coward," she growled under her breath.

He could wait until the final trial and compete with her honorably? Instead he had to send some minion to do his bidding and thin the candidates.

At least the minion was too scared to do anything.

She dispelled the wind wall and her earthsight while Marfa crept along the nearby buildings, pausing attentively from time to time or sniffing the air.

At last, Marfa nodded to her. Apparently satisfied they were safe.

They weren't. Not until the final trial was over, and... not even then.

"*Maestru*," Marfa said with a sigh. "*Avete nimici*." She spat that last word, glaring in the direction the minion had fled.

The number of her enemies only seemed to be multiplying.

"Yes, I have *nimici*. Lots and lots of *nimici*," she replied with a sigh, and they headed toward Staff & Stein. With so many enemies out for her blood, she had to consider—

She wouldn't lose to them. She *wouldn't*. But... but if she did...

Not only would an innocent child suffer, but so would Brennan. He needed her blood every month, and if the unthinkable happened—

She took a deep breath. If only she could ask Olivia...

Wait. I can. Olivia knew about Brennan, and maybe she'd know a way to make sure, just in case...

"*Maestru?*" Marfa asked, with a tilt of her head.

She smiled quickly. "I'm fine. Let's get inside."

CHAPTER 48

In the morning sunlight, Jon parried Florian's riposte and pulled a kick to the abdomen. Hit. Florian grinned, nodded an acknowledgment, and they resumed the sparring.

It was all finally out of his hands.

There was something liberating about it, a sort of peace, knowing there was no more uncertainty. Rielle was marrying Brennan, and Brennan now knew why that marriage would never be under threat. He'd confessed about his condition, the year or two possibly left to him, and his wishes. Brennan had listened to it all, agreed to keep his confidence, and left.

And that had been all.

Strike. He blocked, then stepped offline to avoid a slash from Florian.

With his heart failing, there had never been hope of a future with Rielle. Maybe Olivia could save his life, but he wouldn't bet Rielle's future on it. She deserved more, with the man she'd *chosen*, and now she would get it—and the man to give it to her wouldn't have to worry about him interfering.

Parry. Riposte. Counter-riposte.

He wouldn't interfere—not unless her life depended on it—ever again. He wouldn't meet with her. He wouldn't write to her. He'd leave them be. He'd leave her be, and focus his energies where they belonged: righting all that was wrong in Emaurria.

A series of strikes, parries, lunges, and blocks, and—

His chest tightened.

He staggered backward, sheathed Faithkeeper, and clutched at his chest as his heart pounded, thudding heavily in his chest. He bent, trying to catch his breath.

"Summon Olivia," he forced out between breaths, and Florian called to another guard before bracing Jon, slinging his arm around his shoulders.

"Slow breaths," Florian said, helping him to a chair nearer the doors. "She'll be here soon."

Fighting for breath, he nodded, pain radiating from his chest like needles cutting through him. Terra have mercy, his body—something he'd worked on his entire life—was failing him.

The doors burst open, but it was Samara who ran out, her face contorted.

Florian stopped her, but Jon waved him off.

Throwing her bag down, she grabbed his shoulder and urged him to lean forward in the chair, which helped his breathing a measure. She pulled his shirt open and pressed her ear directly to his chest, completely still.

Olivia burst through the doors. She raced to his side, and as Samara stepped aside, took his hand. The warmth of her healing magic flowed into him, through him.

As his breath evened out, he watched the fine line creasing Olivia's brow, the way her eyes searched his face.

"You won't like this," she said with a shaky breath.

He glanced at his guards and cocked his head toward the doors; they gave him and Olivia some privacy, leaving only Samara, who dug through her bag and pulled out some paper.

"What is it?" he asked Olivia.

Her gaze fell to his belt and Faithkeeper strapped there. "I think you'll need to give up the sword."

His breath caught, filling him up until he could scarcely move. He glared at her. "Out of the question."

"Jon, it's killing you—"

"I'd rather die." Taut, he held her gaze until she bit her lip and looked away, then dropped her gaze to the ground. He would die before abandoning the sword. It was the last thing he had. His final measure of worth. If he couldn't even hold a sword, what was left for him to do?

"There's more." She squeezed his hand. "Anything that would tax your heart. Fighting, training, running—"

He rolled his eyes.

"You'll have to give it up to prolong your life. I fear the duel a few days ago has already exacerbated your condition."

He could feel it. For days, he'd been trying to work past it, continue his regimen, keep up his health, but he couldn't deny the truth of her words. "So... what? I'm dying faster?"

When Olivia's gaze met his, her eyes welled. "I'm sorry."

Closing his eyes, he rubbed his forehead. Nothing that would tax his heart—all the things he lived to do.

Training? Sparring? The sword? Fighting? In the near future, fighting was most of what Emaurria had ahead of it, and was he to sit on the edge, wither and weaken and watch as his kingdom struggled?

"For a man to want his life prolonged... it has to be a life worth living." He covered her hand with his. "I won't become a shell of myself for just a few days more, a couple weeks, a month or two. If I'm to live on, even to tomorrow, it has to be *my* life, Olivia."

She wiped at her eyes and nodded. "I know... just... maybe there's a balance. As long as you have a healer with you, the... episodes could be mitigated. But in public, it won't be long until word gets out that there's something amiss with the king's health." She sighed, softly stroking his thumb. "But in private, well, you could still live your life, as long as a healer is nearby."

As much as he hated to admit it, she had a point. He couldn't be collapsing publicly, or it wouldn't be long before the world would know his secret. But avoiding combat was unthinkable until there would finally be peace.

And he *would* unite both the Tower and the Order under the Crown. He *would* repel the pirates. He *would* quell the Immortals.

A stern crease on her brow, Samara approached and held out a paper to him and Olivia. A quickly sketched heart. She held a piece of charcoal and circled what looked to be a lock of some kind, then tapped it. "This," she said in Emaurrian, glancing between the two of them. "I can help."

Olivia eyed him skeptically. Only those closest to him knew the truth, and they kept it that way. But it seemed Samara had already figured it out.

Rielle had trusted her with her *life*. They were friends, and close at that.

"I trust her," he said, and when Olivia nodded, he looked to Samara. "Help me, Samara. Please."

OLIVIA SIGHED, hunched over the desk in her quarters at midnight. Without a translator, explaining Jon's condition to Samara had been slow going, but they'd labored through it with dictionaries and drawings, and Samara had promised to treat him, with plans for a special diet and an herbal concoction after she could gather some ingredients. Not a cure, but she promised improvement.

Once they were back in Courdeval, Jon had promised to engage an entire team of tutors for Samara, including one in the Emaurrian language, if she so chose. Between her treatments, healing magic, and anything in the texts on Immortals, he would survive this. He had to.

Footsteps sounded past the door adjoining Jon's quarters. Was he all right? Had he recovered from the episode earlier? She rose, knocked on it, and waited.

"Come in," he called softly, and she entered, leaving her door open.

The quarters were dark but for a flickering glow in the bedchamber, and she followed it, finding him already in bed. He sat up against the pillows, but she raised a hand. "Don't stress yourself on my account."

He raised a brow. "The day sitting up in bed becomes 'stressing myself,' it'll be all over for me, Olivia," he teased. His sea-blue eyes gleamed darkly as a corner of his mouth turned up. If he was joking, then he had to already be feeling better.

She sat on the edge of the bed and rested a hand on the covers over his foot. "How are you feeling?"

He gave her a half-smile and shrugged a shoulder. "Optimistic." He sighed. "Anxious to get these trials over with, get our answer, and go home."

Home. Yes, she couldn't wait to get her hands on her books again, research that Bell of the Black Tower, and get some answers. Perhaps the light-elves would know something.

There was a distant knock—from her quarters? She and Jon both answered at the same time, and his valet came through the adjoining door cautiously.

The caution was unwarranted. As impassioned as she'd been that day in the stable, things were different now. But her constant proximity to him, on account of his condition, no doubt stoked rumors among the household anyway.

His valet held out a note to her. "From Marquise Laurentine, Lady Archmage."

Rielle? Olivia grasped it, rubbing the paper softly, and nodded her thanks before the valet departed.

She opened it and read:

Staying at Staff & Stein. Need to see you. Can you preserve blood? If you can, let's do it.
  Rielle

Preserve blood? What the—?

"What is it?" Jon asked, leaning forward a little.

If Rielle was staying at an inn, then that certainly didn't bode well for relations between her and Brennan. "She's staying at an inn. I think she and Brennan had a fight."

He glanced at the note, then quickly looked away and crossed his arms. His eyes dulled and took on a faraway quality. He had asked her to save his life, had committed to reaching for more than he'd been given. So why was he denying his feelings?

To strengthen the kingdom against the Immortals, they planned to bring both the Tower of Magic and the Order of Terra under the yoke of the Crown, and in so doing, Jon would be free of the responsibility to marry outside the kingdom. If he had faith that they could accomplish this, and that she could save him, why wouldn't he pursue the woman he loved?

"I'm going to visit her tomorrow," she said carefully. "Should I tell her anything from you?"

He lowered his gaze, letting the silence settle. "No."

SAMARA WENDED through the shaded grove, scanning the greenery for little white five-petaled flowers. It was a beautiful day, with not a single stray cloud to portend any ill.

"Did you find it?" Una called from behind her in Nad'i, leading their horses into the woods.

They'd left in the morning, and it was nearly noon. Although she hadn't known Una before Brennan had introduced them, she'd been very friendly. Not closed off and mysterious like her older brother, or dramatic and bold like her glamorous older sister. Instead, she spoke with a genuine earnestness, and acted very thoughtfully, as if she strove to be an ideal—or maybe she already was.

"What should I even be looking for?" Una asked, and the crack of wood betrayed her misstep.

"Five-petaled white flowers," Samara said. "They're called hawthorn." She glanced at *The Sileni Herbal* in her hands, and the illustration there. "There's an old myth that they could cure a broken heart."

They did treat the heart, so perhaps that myth had been misconstrued by those hopelessly in love. Or perhaps it did mend *both* types of broken hearts.

"Yes," Una said with a sigh, "but what does it *look* like? Are we looking for a lone flower, or a tree, or what?"

A few pink blooms peeked out between the undergrowth,

and Samara crouched while Una tethered the horses. A squarish stem clad in short hairs, slightly purplish, with bell-shaped pink flowers, with a minty smell. She set down her bag and carefully collected some.

"Is that it?" Una whispered, as if to avoid disturbing the flowers, and crouched next to her.

"This is lion's tail," Samara said, smiling at her. "It can slow a rapid heartbeat, improve the health of your heart, or even just tranquilize the body in times of stress."

"Like valerian?" Una offered quietly.

"In the tranquilizing aspect, yes." It always thrilled her a little when someone knew medicine, like sharing a secret language, even for a bit. And valerian eased the burden of ruling kingdoms, guarding lives, and other stresses too heavy for one set of shoulders to bear.

Una heaved a sigh. "My sister Nora takes it with an over-flowing goblet of wine. She says it's the only way she can handle the boys."

Samara frowned. There was that use, too.

"So this *hawthorn* we're looking for. Will it be growing like this, low to the ground?"

Samara shook her head and held out the book. "They grow on shrubs," she said, as Una stood and proceeded. Just a few more cuts of lion's tail, and she'd resume the search for the hawthorn. "The shrubs can generally be about twenty or thirty feet tall, with spiraling leaves, and thorns—"

"Ow!" Una called out, then hissed. "I... I think I found the thorns."

Jumping to her feet, Samara darted to the large shrub where Una sucked her index finger with a pout.

"This is it!" The shrub was abundant with the five-petaled white flowers, and she cradled one in her hand. Something beautiful among the thorns it had grown from. "Hawthorn."

Immediately, she began gathering the precious flowers. If only she could be here when it bore fruit, too—but perhaps it could be ordered. With this, she would have almost everything she needed to begin preparing a treatment for His Majesty. She would have liked some anjelica, too, but it was abundant in Emaurria, so she'd have to ask that some be purchased here, and then gather more once she arrived in Courdeval.

I'm going to be the Court Apothecary.

Shaking her head, she deposited her collection of hawthorn into her bag, and continued while Una helped. It was still hard to believe she'd gone from being a possession at House Hazael to a free woman honored with a court position.

Because he freed you, a voice nagged. *He didn't have to free you, or any of them. Maybe he did love you.*

She paused a moment, eyeing the blooms in her hand.

Una rose and leaned in next to her, watching them, too. "What is it?"

"Sometimes, I... There's a voice inside of me that wishes things were different. That sees things the way I wish they could have been, and not as they are," she said.

Una placed a gentle hand on her shoulder. "That's all right. It may not be the same, but when I was growing up, that's how I thought for a long time. Wishing my father was..." She gave a small shrug. "Different. Honest. Honorable. Caring. I even pretended not to notice, for a while, when he did wrong."

Perhaps if she let that nagging voice go on, she might want to pretend, too. It was easier, less painful, that way, but... "How did you stop?"

"I... saw my mother cry after an argument one day," she said softly. "And I couldn't pretend anymore. All my wishing, everything I'd hoped he'd be... That's what I decided to become."

Honesty, honor, and care... Yes, she could see Una living those virtues, at least from the brief span she'd gotten to know her.

"What did you wish from your father?" Una asked, leaning toward the hawthorn shrub to gather more flowers. Somehow her distancing herself, even a little, made it easier to consider her question.

"I wish he'd taken a stand when wrong things happened," she began, and the words fell freely. "I wish he'd helped innocent people who needed it... and cared, not just about me, but about everyone who needed caring. I wish... I wish he'd been there, supportive, when Umi and I needed him."

"Maybe those wishes came true, too," Una said, placing the flowers she'd collected in the bag, then dusted her hands off on her overcoat. "You might be living them."

Samara blinked.

If... If that was true, then Farrad hadn't been the father she'd wished for, but despite that deficit, or perhaps because of it, she'd flourished, and had become the person he hadn't been when she'd needed him to be.

"That's... that's a beautiful thought," she whispered to Una, who smiled warmly.

"We could use some, couldn't we? It can't all be Immortals and deadly trials all the time, right?"

The trials... in that place steeped in blood. Rielle was going back there in just two days, and she would—

A shriek pierced the air, ear-splitting and deafening, and both she and Una covered their ears. A great roar rumbled through the ground, and the leaves trembled on their branches.

The horses yanked at their tethers, and Una hefted the bag and urged her to mount.

"We have to get back to Magehold. Now," Una said, after helping her up. She got into the saddle and picked a path through the woods, whispering to the horses.

Every part of her trembled, and she could barely hold the reins, but her horse anxiously followed Una's. They were less than an hour's ride from the city. "What was that?" she asked, her voice quivering.

The look Una cut her way was thin, frayed. "I... I don't know, but we don't want to be here when it comes out."

CHAPTER 49

Running through the clearing at twilight, Leigh blasted the undead body that shambled toward him, and then another. They kept on coming, but he had the limitless anima to take on them all.

"Dreshan, slow down," Ambriel called, beheading an undead dark-elf without a heart. Dozens closed in from the trees —humans, animals, and Immortals, hissing, reaching.

Katia snared them with roots, Della mind-shielded, and Ambriel cut them down.

"We're getting closer," he called back, casting a repulsion shield and blowing it back against a half dozen undead. The scattered stragglers seemed to be coming from a dense force near the mountain. The horde had to be there.

Casting another repulsion shield, he cut through the thickening mass of bodies coming for him, feeding more and more anima into the shield, throwing aside anything that came at him.

He could get to Ava, hit her with his own arcanir ring, and then repel all the undead to get her out.

"Leigh!" Katia's high-pitched voice squealed from the distance.

He spread the shield into a dome, and the undead clustered around him, pushing in until there was a solid wall around him that only grew thicker.

Far behind them, Della grimaced as she held up the mind shield, the translucent force of her consciousness creating a barrier. A small circle had formed, with her, Katia, and Ambriel at the center, and undead pressed up against it, more and more, harder and harder—

"She can't hold it!" Katia screamed, her face pale. Ambriel pressed her behind him as she cast, and he continued cutting a swath around them.

But it was unending.

Ava—

He wanted to keep moving, getting closer, bridging the distance, but—

With a snarl, he destabilized his repulsion dome. It exploded, a blur of force magic throwing all the undead clustered around him at least fifteen feet.

Recasting it, he cleared a path toward Ambriel, Katia, and Della.

"Keep going," Della shouted, but her voice was thin. "Find her. We can handle this—"

"*No, we can't!*" Katia yelped, spelling brambles to pull some of the undead away, but they were breaking through toward the shield. Using her geomancy, she began to drop some of the ground surrounding them, and undead fell over into the pit she'd spelled.

A path still remained from him to them, and he approached, keeping up his repulsion dome until Della let him in, then recasting it over her spell.

"Dispel your mind-shield," he told her, and she blinked wearily, but obeyed. "Catch your breath."

They were losing the daylight, but the rest of them didn't have the anima for this, or the endurance.

Even if he'd accepted Della's reassurances, there was no way he could have left them behind. If something happened to him, Della would have to try taking Ava's mind, and Ambriel's arcanir arrows could reach Ava if he couldn't.

And Katia—well, she was here, too. And at least somewhat useful.

"I'm sorry," she whispered, wincing. "If Papa hadn't sent me with you, maybe you would be—"

"Shut up." He sighed. "We usually work in pairs or teams. Do you know why?"

Looking away, she shrugged. "To watch out for each other?"

"That's right," he replied. "Right now, I'm watching out for you, and I expect you to do the same for me when we reach Ava."

Her eyebrows drew together, but she nodded quickly. "I won't let you down."

Over her head, Ambriel shot him a one-sided smile as he wiped gore off his cheek. He always did know how to impress.

Della slumped against him, her dark-blond head against his arm. He braced her.

"My dear," he said, glancing at Ambriel, "can you—?"

"I've got her." Ambriel sheathed his sword and hoicked her up into his arms.

Holding the repulsion dome to push away the undead, he walked a path into the woods as the last rays of the setting sun faded. He kept the dome powerful enough to force the undead away, and he, Ambriel, and Katia sped up.

After almost an hour of walking, Katia was stumbling over

the undergrowth and Della had completely passed out in Ambriel's arms. Her anima had been reasonably bright last time they'd shared resonance, so in order for her to be so weakened, she must have been venturing out for weeks, alone, struggling, and the failures had to be getting to her.

Beaufort had scattered, and even the Coven had been sent out by Axelle to protect their territory. She'd truly been left all alone to search for Ava.

If only the Tower had worked for the Crown, then other mages could have already come to assist. Other necromancers wouldn't have had to hide what they were, and could have come forward to help bring Ava's horde under control.

But as it was, the Tower would try to take Ava away, if it cared to intervene at all. The Order might kill her, if it wasn't spread so thin, depending on the particular commander in charge of the mission. And the Crown's official stance on the Covens had to be denial in order to comply with its treaty with the Divinity of Magic.

It was so bound up in irrationalities to the point of frustration.

"I hear our horses," Ambriel whispered, and nodded southeast. At least the horses had been smart enough to run from danger.

Another fifteen minutes of walking, and they found their mounts—and their packs.

"I don't hear the horde anymore," Ambriel said.

"Good," he replied, grateful for Ambriel's keen hearing. Perhaps they'd finally gone far enough to make camp. "Katia," he asked, glancing over his shoulders, "lay the wards—"

She swayed on her feet and blinked up at him sluggishly.

With a defeated sigh, he said, "Sit down and rest. Watch over Della while I lay the wards and Ambriel pitches the tents."

He shot Ambriel an inquisitive look, and Ambriel nodded his acquiescence. With a glance back at Katia, Leigh said, "And get that nondescript goo out of your hair."

Her spine bolted straight, and she reached for her pulled-back hair, her palm landing on a glob of some dark-red coagulated *something*, and she cringed. As she walked away, Ambriel leaned in, still holding Della's petite slumbering body.

"Take it slow, dreshan," he said softly. "Your anima may be boundless, but your energy isn't. Don't work yourself to exhaustion."

He wanted to argue, but Ambriel was right. He usually was.

Instead, he pressed his head to Ambriel's, just for a moment, and breathed deep. Divine's tits, Ambriel smelled like spoiled guts, but he was warm, close, and *his*. "I'll take it slow," he whispered.

Ambriel pulled away at that, gave him a warm smile, and set Della gently on a bed of flowers next to Katia, who scrubbed at her hair as if she were trying to rub out its color.

"I think you're just rubbing it in deeper," he teased, but she grimaced and scrubbed faster.

He began laying the ward, weaving his anima thickly into the earth, setting up repulsion on both sides. If anything crossed, the ward would repel everything inside proportionately —and they'd know.

How close had they been to reaching Ava today? How bright was her anima, and how much longer would it last under fureur? She had to be reaching her limit—she was no wild mage.

And what if tomorrow the same thing happened?

"Leigh," Della rasped, curled up on the flowers, her waves unbound and spread around her. She was one of the most powerful mages he'd known, but she looked so beaten down, so fragile there.

As he finished laying the ward, he approached her beneath the glow of a candlelight spell—Katia must have spoken the incantation for it. No fires in the forest. At least not this one. She murmured something to Ambriel as they plucked some food out of a pack.

Della grabbed his coat, and he crouched, pulling up a blanket someone had covered her with. Her eyes, normally a vivid dark blue, were dull, even in the light of the candlelight spell. She had to be exhausted.

"What is it?" he whispered, sweeping a lock of hair off her face.

Her lower lip quivered. "If you ever have to choose between me and Ava again, choose Ava." Tears welled in her eyes, and he sat, then took her hand in both of his.

"Della, it's not a choice. We'll find her *and* you'll stay safe, all right?" he asked, and she shook her head.

"Today, because of me—"

"Because of you, we know where to look," he said softly. "Because you've been out here looking for her constantly."

She lowered her gaze, and tears streamed from her eyes. "You need to get to her, Leigh. Terra only knows how much time she has before—"

"*We* will get to her," he said, rubbing her hand. "Ava needs her mother."

Della's eyebrows creased together, and she curled tighter, fresh tears welling in her eyes. "She needs her father, too," she said, her voice breaking.

He swept a hand over his eyebrows, masking his face, as his own eyes watered.

All these years, he'd been such a fool to think Ava would be safer without him.

After Takumi and Yuki had died because of him—No, had

been *killed* by him—he'd vowed never to have a family of his own ever again. Even just to be with another lover had taken years, and Della—she had secretly wanted a child, desperately, by a mage of great power. Rumor had it that wild mages could pass on their strength, but he'd never believed in such things. But she had, and had wanted Ava so badly that she'd lied to him about taking preventives.

He'd wanted to hate Della just for that, and would have never been a husband to her even if he'd been a proper father. But Ava—she had deserved better. Deserved *more* than a monthly sum of coin as a father.

The years had faded his anger toward Della, but only intensified the hole in his heart for Ava.

"Della," he whispered, "from now on, I will help her in any way I can, in any way she'll let me. I promise."

Della nodded, and as Ambriel called out that her tent was ready, Leigh helped her rise and walked her to it, laid her down on her bedroll and helped her into it.

When she'd finally given in to sleep, he found Ambriel in his own tent, washing up.

Here, in the quiet, in the dark, a part of him just wanted to crumple to the bedroll and think about how terrified Ava had to have been, to watch a dryad kill her friend, Brice. So terrified, so overcome, that it had torn open her anima and released her magic for the first time.

But if he did that, he'd never stop, and only hate himself more for not having been here... and there was time enough for that after she was all right.

Wordlessly, Ambriel unbuttoned his coat, and slipped it off his shoulders, then moved on to his shirt.

"I failed her," Leigh whispered, and Ambriel paused his ministrations to cup his face.

"Today is only one day, dreshan," he said softly, "and tomorrow is a new one. Today isn't the sum of who you are."

"But I failed. She needs me, and I—"

"You're doing all that you can," Ambriel said evenly. "What more could you do? Wander the night alone until exhaustion claimed you?"

He would've wanted to do... exactly that.

But there was sense in what Ambriel said, yet accepting the fact didn't let him feel the way he was *supposed* to feel. The way he *needed* to feel. "If there's nothing I could do, there's nothing to blame this on, and then it feels so... so... unstoppable."

"But you will stop it," Ambriel said, brushing his lips with a kiss. "Tonight, you feel inadequate. But tomorrow, you'll feel confident, and you will do everything you intend to do."

Another kiss, and Ambriel undressed him, held him, made him feel wanted, adored, long into the night... until the hopelessness faded, and the inadequacy faded... and his fears faded... and all that remained was love.

CHAPTER 50

In the large room she'd rented at Staff & Stein, Rielle practice-gestured a flame cloak, then an ice spike, and threw it at Luca, who held up an arm in front of him and practice-gestured a conjured shield.

And a conjured boulder from above.

She rolled, pretending to gesture a fireball, but he pretend-conjured a water bubble, then a stone golem behind her. She practice-pulled up a wind wall behind her as he practice-conjured another boulder above her.

"Dead," he crooned.

Groaning her annoyance, she grimaced and threw herself onto the bed, where Marfa sat, her nose wrinkled as she watched them both and picked at an entire roasted ham.

Sweeping a hand over his pulled-back hair, Luca strolled cavalierly over to her, then planted his hands on his thin hips. "If you actually want to have a hope of winning, you're going to have to get this right."

She groaned louder and covered her face with a pillow.

She'd been poring over books on conjury and light magic, and they'd been at this for a day and a half, when Luca had time. She still didn't know what exactly the final trial would be, but with only three candidates left, dueling seemed likely.

Worse still, she didn't have all the answers when it came to dueling Mac Carra. And the final trial was *tomorrow*.

"Maybe you'll face Orsa," Luca remarked with a hopeful lilt.

"Even better," she said, muffled into the pillow. "She'll just blind me and then obliterate me with a ray of white-hot light." She sighed. "If I don't get chopped by the spellblade while I'm blindly fumbling around."

Marfa nudged her. "*Maestru, ave a fede,*" she said encouragingly.

"I don't know what that means," Rielle replied, "but it sounds good."

She threw the pillow off of herself and against the walnut headboard, staring up at the white ceiling while Luca and Marfa leaned over her with concerned frowns.

With a dismissive wave, she smiled up at them and sighed. "I may not have *all* the answers, but I'll win tomorrow."

Luca raised a skeptical dark eyebrow.

"What?" she breathed. "I'm not great at practice, but when I play it by feel, ideas come to me like instinct."

That skeptical dark eyebrow only rose higher.

She blew out a breath and fumbled with her hand on the open-weave bedspread for Thorn. Her fingers closed around its sheath, and she held it up. "See this? Any construct, one slash and poof," she said.

"And if you're disarmed?"

She held up her thumb with the arcanir ring.

"If you're close enough to a conjured golem to touch a ring

to it, you're probably dead," Luca said, sitting on the edge of the bed.

He had a point.

"Well, if it's Ariana and she blinds me, I have earthsight to see her with, then one spellcasting hand and either the ring or Thorn," she said. "And if it's Mac Carra..." She frowned. "Well, my legs will still work."

"Your grand plan is to run?" Luca asked with a scoff.

"Excuse me," she insisted, "*evade*."

She'd never lost a proper duel in all her time as a mage, but... these trials made it harder to place all her faith in instinct.

"I think the Grand Divinus has it out for you." Luca leaned against the headboard, his whisky-brown eyes deathly serious.

"I know."

"And not just you." He held up a hand. "You publicly humiliated the Divinity by failing to perform the Moonlit Rite —" He lowered a finger.

"That wasn't even *mine* to perform to begin with!" she objected, but he did, annoyingly, have a point. She'd taken it upon herself and failed to complete it in time.

"And then Orsa has been falling all over herself to glean even a tidbit about the Immortals, completely ignoring orders"— he lowered another finger—"and then there's me... When I don't have orders, I'm selling my services to the highest bidder... even the Order."

Yes, that certainly wouldn't win him any points with the Grand Divinus.

"There was talk of Sen marrying into a Kamerish Coven." Another lowered finger. "And Tariq made a political play for Proctor in Sonbahar before the Tower there got orders to cut him down to size." He sighed. "And Telva foretold the fall of the Divinity, and it got out in Ferrante."

Rielle propped up on an elbow. "The fall of the Divinity?"

A loud cracking, and she turned to Marfa gnawing on the ham bone, who continued a while longer before meeting her eyes, smiling, and setting it down on her tray... and taking a bite of the crusty boule that was bigger than her head.

Luca covered his mouth with a palm, his eyes curving into half-moons, and looked away.

At least she had an appetite.

"Don't you think it's odd," Luca began, "that Mac Carra came to the second trial with a blade?"

She shrugged. "So did I. So did you."

"I always carry my knives," he said, "and have since I was a brat in Suguz." He tipped his head to her. "And you—well, you got a basilisk scale, and couldn't use magic on it anyway. And it helps you have a king madly in love with you."

She frowned and looked away. "He is not 'madly in love' with me." Once, yes, but he was with Olivia now, and hadn't said or done anything to suggest he was still interested.

And if he *had*, she'd only have to cut him to size for a wandering eye while he had the attention of her one-in-a-million best friend.

Besides, she loved Brennan, and although they weren't currently on speaking terms, she still wanted to be with him, if they could work out a way they'd both be happy with.

But Luca only pinned her with a knowing look.

"What?" she said with a shrug of her shoulder. "He's not, okay? He's just a close friend."

"A close friend who gives you an expensive sword?" He crossed his arms.

"He happened to have it and wanted me to win the trial, and—"

"And whose ring you wear?"

She held up her thumb. "*This* is strictly for dispelling magic, all right? It's not—"

"Who bet his entire kingdom on your performance at the trials... in front of the whole world?" Luca held her gaze and sighed.

"That—" she stammered, and swallowed. That was far more complicated than just his faith in her. If he'd turned down the Grand Divinus's offer, it would have seemed like he'd only been all too willing to betray the Divinity and ally with the Covens. He had to make a good faith effort for the sake of appearances.

But Luca didn't know that.

Marfa nodded to the door. "Archmage," she said.

A soft knock rapped. "Rielle? Are you in there?"

"Olivia," she said, sitting up. "Come in."

"Not the greatest security at this inn, eh?" Luca remarked, crossing his lanky legs.

The door opened, and Olivia walked in, cloaked in soft pink, a gray brocade dress peeking out from beneath. Her red braided hair was elaborately coiled around her head, with shimmering pearl earrings adorning her ears.

She'd always been glamorous, with a taste for the finer things. With Jon, she'd have them—he'd give and give and give, as long as it made her smile, she was certain of it.

Jon would make Olivia happy, in any way he could.

There was a discordant twinge that came with the acknowledgment of that thought, but she shoved it down. She'd get over it someday. She had to—she had no plans to stop seeing Olivia, who would be closer with Jon as time went on.

Olivia fixed narrowed emerald eyes on Luca. "What are *you* doing here?"

He smiled sweetly. "Oh, me? I was just telling your friend just how *much*—"

Rielle shot up off the bed and blocked Olivia's sight of him. "Just how *much* it'll take to win the trials!" She laughed nervously, getting a peripheral look from Olivia.

The last thing she'd ever want to do would be to tell Olivia about her stupid lingering feelings—*feeling*, singular, really, since it was just one tiny little feeling, not a big, huge, over-whelming bunch or anything—and diminish any of her happi-ness with Jon. They didn't need any of that.

Olivia angled around her. "I really *do* want to talk to my friend in private, Master Iagar," she said. "Although I'd love to talk healing magic with you sometime soon."

With a sigh, he rose. "It would be my pleasure, *Your Majesty*," he said, slanting a look Rielle's way as he headed out the door. Olivia's glare traced his exit.

Well, that was awkward. She cleared her throat.

Olivia glanced at Marfa, who'd eaten through most of the boule.

"Oh, she can stay," Rielle said, and gestured to the bed.

Olivia removed her cloak, set it by the desk on the rickety cane-backed chair, right next to the window that led out to the roof, and then gracefully lowered to the bed with a sprawl of her voluminous gray skirts. She had a small satchel she placed between them as Rielle sat.

"I *can* preserve blood," she said, "but first, what in the Divine's name happened between you and Brennan?"

CHAPTER 51

*R*ielle waited for Olivia to say something, but she only sat collapsed against the pillows and headboard, staring into space.

Only the soft crunching of Marfa eating hazelnuts filled the silence.

It was a lot to take in.

Brennan was generous and kind, passionate, *good*.

And jealous. Hopelessly, endlessly, *suffocatingly* jealous. *You're going to* him, *aren't you?* he'd asked, with the most contemptuous edge she'd ever heard.

She hadn't betrayed him. Hadn't so much as *kissed* another man. Her heart ached that he would think it.

Are you really going to allow an innocent child to suffer so that you can keep indulging your grief? His question needled her heart, and not because it hid a darker motive, but because it wasn't so easily answered. There was time, a decade and a half surely, before it became imperative, but even then... What if she *never* recovered from losing Sylvie? What if the edges remained sharp and jagged for the rest of her life?

She wouldn't let Kehani's child—Brennan's—suffer, but did it have to be *now*? Did it have to be this year, or next year, or some definite time in the near future?

And had he needed to say it right *now*, hot on the heels of this news from Kehani?

Circumstances have changed, he'd said.

Yes, they had. Perhaps he didn't realize it, but this had forced her hand. She no longer could choose a life without trying to have another baby—someday, she'd *have* to. No matter what happened between them, she *wouldn't* let an innocent child suffer.

She'd been willing to accept this news, work out a different vision of the future, but... he'd immediately wanted more. So much more than she'd been prepared to think about now, and without even a thought to what she'd be setting aside.

Taking a deep breath, she shook Olivia's knee lightly. "Well?"

Olivia blinked a while before glancing back at her with a shake of her head. "After telling you he's having a child with another woman, I wouldn't expect his next words to be 'So have my curse-breaking baby soon.' I'd expect maybe... 'I'm sorry' and 'Can we work this out?' but not... *that.*"

Rielle chewed her lip. "It took me by surprise, too."

She hadn't seen him nor heard from him since the day before yesterday, and despite the harsh words they'd exchanged, that hurt. Didn't he care? Didn't he look at the pillow beside him, too, and feel the lack of her there as she did? Didn't he wonder what she was doing, want to tell her all about his day, want to touch her, hold her, just as she wanted to do with him?

That hurt—all of it.

But she could've gone back to the villa, too, and hadn't. Hadn't been able to. Would coming back have been admitting she'd been wrong? Some kind of sign that what he'd demanded had been in any way acceptable?

In this, he'd have to bend first. He'd have to admit he'd been wrong to accuse her of wanting to run to Jon, wrong to try to force her to acquiesce to his demands before she was ready.

Magic was her *life*. Since her éveil, since the attack on Laurentine, it had become an inexorable part of her. It had forged her into the person she was now, strong, but still that girl outside of Laurentine, brought out of fureur by her master and wishing someone had saved her family.

She was that someone. For other families out there, when they needed saving, she had magic, she had training, and she saw her own family in every other one that needed help.

That perspective... wasn't so easily set aside.

She loved Brennan, wanted to spend her life with him, but if it was meant to be, they'd have to compromise. She'd have to agree to eventually acquiesce to his desire for a family, and he... he would have to acquiesce to her desire to use her magic to save others, as she'd once been unable to do for her own family.

Time—she needed time to mourn Sylvie, to come to terms with having another child, and time to devote herself completely to field operations before distancing herself from that guiding star, just enough to make Brennan happy, so she could be happy *with* him.

Five years? Three—?

Perhaps the time apart had been for the best, time to weigh the decision in the back of her mind while she'd researched and trained.

And yesterday... Yesterday, if he'd shown up, she might have screamed at him until her vocal cords exploded.

Marfa had occasionally peered out the window and narrowed her eyes. Maybe he'd come to check up on her, or sent someone. If it had been an enemy, she would have spoken up.

"And you want to preserve your blood?" Olivia asked carefully, pulling the satchel closer.

She nodded. "He depends on it every month. I don't know how it works, or whether it would work if I—" She lowered her gaze. "I'm going to do my all to win, but if I don't—"

Olivia reached out for her, resting a hand on hers. "If you think you might not come out of this—and you have good reason to think so—then maybe you *should* consider withdrawing, Rielle. Is this worth your life?"

"If these trials have proven one thing, it's that the Divinity has lots of power but has lost sight of the greater good," she said firmly. "But it's just a system. People are how it changes. Maybe right now, the wrong people are in positions of power, or making the wrong decisions. If anything's going to change, then it has to start with me, and others willing to do difficult things and take risks for the greater good."

Olivia frowned. "You want to fight to change a system that would destroy you?"

"As things are now, the system invites young talent and ambition, only to abuse it and discard it when expedient. But someone has to get through," she said, curling a fist. "I've come this far, so I have to try."

If it meant preventing needless deaths driven by greed for promising young novices, and stopping bloodthirsty power grabs, and putting a halt to the sen'a trade that claimed so many lives... then someone had to get through. Her family had paid the price, and they deserved justice. As did Jon's, and every other victim of the Divinity's lust for control.

But Luca hadn't been wrong. Perhaps Mac Carra had some assistance, and she couldn't predict what that would be.

It didn't hurt to plan for every eventuality. "So... I don't know if the blood will actually help if things go poorly, but it's *something*. And I can't just leave him with nothing if—"

Olivia nodded and opened the satchel. "I understand."

They moved over the washbasin, and with a cut, a vial, and a healing rune, she had a preserved vial of blood.

As Olivia healed her cut, Rielle asked, "Can I leave it with you?" When Olivia raised a brow, she added, "If things go wrong, you can tell him. But I don't want to give him reason to worry unnecessarily."

Marfa watched from the corner, arms crossed, shaking her head.

"For Brennan," Rielle said, indicating the vial.

Marfa nodded. *"Per controllu di a luna Chjave."*

It sounded close enough to Sileni. "Yes, I think. To control the moon Change."

"Moon Change," Marfa repeated, drawing her black eyebrows together and saying the words over and over. "For Brennan."

With a smile, Rielle nodded. Over the past couple of days, Marfa had picked up some Emaurrian, at least the things they'd been able to connect between the old language and the new.

A cheer rose up from downstairs, and then Luca threw the door open. "You'll never believe who's here."

Brennan? Had he finally come to see her? Maybe he wasn't that angry after all. Maybe he'd come to—

"Do you *knock*?" Olivia demanded, hands on her hips.

Luca huffed an amused breath. "Not when it's important."

He left the door open, then his footsteps pounded down the stairs.

Her finger healed, Rielle beckoned to both Marfa and Olivia. "Let's go see what the fuss is about, and then I'm back to training."

Olivia took her cloak and followed, eyes narrowed. "If it's Brennan saying anything other than 'I'm sorry,' let's make a rug out of him."

"How sweet of you." She nudged Olivia. But as she headed toward the stairs, she really *did* hope it was him. She'd gone too long without seeing his face, hearing his voice, feeling his arms around her... and there had to be a way to live a life together that they both wanted.

But as she set foot on the landing, a black-cloaked man with straight blue-black hair and broad shoulders turned around, and as soon as his bronze eyes met hers, she started.

"Daturian," she breathed, while his arms wrapped her tight, lifting her off the floor while everyone in the tavern gawked and laughed. He smelled of horse and smoke, and must have been traveling for some time.

"Been a while, Spitfire," he teased, and set her down.

He'd called her that since the mission she'd gone on with him, when they'd had to guard Princess Bianca Ermacora on a ship from Courdeval to Bellanzole two years ago. Back then, he'd been practically insufferable, teasing her mercilessly—the entire Divinity knew him for a womanizer.

When she'd met him, he'd felt immediately familiar, and told her his father and Leigh's had been in business together since Pryndon and had moved to Ren together. They'd practically grown up as brothers, except that Daturian was six years younger. Leigh was turning thirty-four in three months, which put Daturian at twenty-seven this year.

"What are you doing here?" she asked, brushing a spike of his blue-black hair from his eyes. He was still wearing the bracelet with the recondite bead that disguised his wild-mage white hair.

"I invited him," Olivia said, stepping next to her. "Thank you for coming to witness the trials, Magister Trey." She held out a hand, and Daturian kissed it.

"How do we not know each other, Archmage Sabeyon?"

With a twist of her lips, Olivia pulled her hand away. "I know you, of course, by reputation."

Daturian's eyes gleamed as his mouth curved in a smile. He looked over at Marfa. "And you are?"

Expressionless, Marfa only stared at him, arms crossed. "Marfa," she said, then narrowed her eyes.

"She doesn't trust mages easily," Rielle offered, with Marfa still unwavering beside her. Eerily.

"She shouldn't," he answered, glancing back at Rielle. "Especially considering what Archmage Sabeyon here wrote to me. Not only did I not know you were competing, I also wasn't aware there *were* Magister Trials right now."

Shouldn't the world know? "How is that possible?"

Perhaps the Grand Divinus hadn't publicized it as much as they'd all assumed. So much of the Magister Trials' circumstances had been kept secret, revealed only with each new trial. What they were, where they were, constraints. No rules. Even *killing* being allowed.

Perhaps fewer neutral and skeptical parties had been allowed to witness them. Intentionally.

Olivia raised an eyebrow, then lowered her gaze and was quiet awhile. "Well, then. Now that you're here, you'll make sure everyone knows, won't you?"

She and Daturian shared a knowing look.

"There won't be a corner of the world that won't know," he said. "Especially if this is worth killing and dying over."

Daturian never could let a wrong transpire without getting involved. Sometimes it got him in trouble, but then, she'd never known him to have a problem handling trouble either.

"Come," she said, nodding to the tables. "I'm sure you've had a long journey. Let's sit." Moreover, since he was a conjurer, she'd have a captive source of strategies for the final trial.

Daturian advised her on Mac Carra over ale and stew while she, Marfa, and Olivia nursed mugs of hot cocoa. It was extravagant, really, considering it came only from a single monastery in Ferrante, and was one of the kingdom's most expensive exports. But today, she didn't care. The final trial was tomorrow, and a long sip of the creamy sweetness soothed her nerves a touch.

"A deep-freeze shield," he said, "keeps any constructs from getting to you, or any other spell, and leaves you free to attack. Why aren't you using it constantly? I hate hydromancers just for *that*."

A deep-freeze shield froze anything entering its perimeter, but its efficacy varied depending on what intruded, so she'd rarely used it—and it dimmed a lot of anima, more than her usual wind wall or flame cloak.

Marfa tapped her palm on the table twice, then tipped her head up toward something behind Rielle.

"Magister Trey, I don't believe we've met," Luca Iagar drawled over Daturian's shoulder as he turned a chair around and straddled it.

Daturian ignored him completely and shoveled stew into his mouth. Typical. And entertaining.

As Luca dropped into the seat, Marfa hissed at him.

He held up a palm to her. "Hello again to you, too, beautiful."

Marfa's eyelids drooped over her eyes as she gave him the deadest look Rielle had ever seen.

She laughed. "I don't think she likes you."

"Tch," he said, smiling and rolling his eyes. "I'm an acquired taste. Like a fine wine."

"Or fermented cabbage," Rielle offered.

"I'm going to stick with 'fine wine.'" He rested his arms atop the chair's back. "So what brings you here?" he asked Daturian.

"Not you." Olivia sipped her hot cocoa and shared an amused look with Marfa.

"The trials, I gather." Luca nodded sagely. "Yes, yes, no doubt you're interested in how they've gone. Well, you've come to the right person."

Olivia laughed, her green eyes twinkling. "When it comes to conversation, it seems a second person is entirely optional for you."

He laid his head on his arms and grinned at her. "Well, it's not all bad. It made you smile, didn't it?"

Olivia glanced away, but her mouth still twitched and her cheeks reddened, just a touch. "You lost... Why are you still in Magehold?"

He shrugged. "Why not? I'll see who wins the trials. My money's on Mac Carra."

Rielle grimaced. "Thanks. Very nice of you."

"No sense in nursing false hopes, yes?"

When she snorted, Daturian slung an arm around her neck. "Don't count out Spitfire. Especially not when she's had my advice."

Completely humble as always. She feigned a smile, but he only stuck out his tongue at her.

"What?" he asked, with a smug look. "Unless you don't want it?"

"No!" she replied, bolting upright and grinning. "I want it. Teach me, oh wise magister."

"That's more like it." A joking nod.

"I'll stay till the trials end," Luca continued to Olivia, unperturbed, "then I'll see who could use a healer that looks as good as he heals." He winked at her.

Marfa scoffed. *"Idiota."* She drained her hot cocoa.

"I'm sure that means 'I completely agree,' " Rielle said with a wink back at Marfa. "I'll let you know if I hear—"

The door to the inn opened, and Brennan ducked inside, black-cloaked and sullen, his gaze sweeping the tavern to land on her... and then on Daturian, and finally on Luca. He grimaced, then jerked his head aside.

"Ah, that's my cue to pretend I was never here," Luca murmured, before kicking his leg over the chair with a flourish and leaving.

Marfa breathed in, then as she looked over her shoulder, a growl rumbled in her throat, and Brennan's gaze locked with hers.

"It's all right, Marfa," she said, and reluctantly, Marfa turned away, mumbling under her breath, then grabbed her empty cocoa mug and stomped away with a toss of her forest-green coat.

"I think I'll have that chat with Iagar about healing magic," Olivia whispered, then followed Luca.

Brennan approached the table, his steps sure as ever, and paused just before her, his imposing form towering over her and Daturian. His hazel eyes were grave in their focus.

He lowered his eyelids, that fraction of displeasure, as his lower lip moved, chewing a choice word or two as he speared Daturian with a glare.

"I'd heard the Marcels were so well bred," Daturian said drolly, around a spoonful of stew. "Guess manners weren't included."

With an irritated sigh, Brennan looked away from him and held out a hand to her. "Let's speak somewhere more private."

BRENNAN FOLLOWED her from the table, where she'd left that mage—the one who'd insulted their family. He could've skinned him for that alone, but the mage had *also* had an arm about her shoulders. A mistake that would have cost him, had it been any other time but now. And Rielle—she was wearing the ring. Jon's ring.

Right now, there was something more important, far more important than skinning loose-lipped mages, or arguing over a ring, or anything else. For two days, he'd taken Una's words to heart, had considered what Rielle might want, what he wanted, and what that would mean in practical terms. Other than checking for her safety from time to time, at a distance, he'd stayed away. Given her space and time to think.

He'd said all the wrong things... and while he didn't expect her to have forgiven him, perhaps the sting of the bite had faded. If only just a little.

She led him upstairs and to a room, and inside, there were maybe a half-dozen scents, chief among them Rielle's blood, its tang making his mouth water, even against his own reluctance. More scents—Marfa, Olivia, other mages. Arcanir. Thorn lay on the bed, next to a tray heaping with a disturbing amount of dirty dishes and bones picked clean. He inhaled deeply—fresh, only from today.

Rielle moved a worn chair from the desk to the window, opened it, and struggled outside, wriggled out onto the roof.

"Where are you going?"

"Trust me," she said, and offered her hand.

He didn't need her help, but he wasn't about to turn away her touch. Careful not to burden her with his weight, he climbed out, and followed her up to a roof beam, where she perched.

"Not very safe up here," he said carefully. He hated to think of her climbing out here, especially alone.

She shrugged. "It is if you know the updraft gesture and have quick fingers."

True enough. He sat next to her and looked out at the market district below. It was still early in the afternoon, and there were families about, shopping, mothers and fathers with their children, talking, laughing.

Rielle's gaze, narrow, intense, was fixed on Divinity Castle.

"Are you worried about tomorrow?"

"Anxious," she said. The breeze caught wisps of her golden hair, blowing them across her face, and she tucked them behind her ear.

"You didn't come back," he said softly.

She shrugged again and didn't look at him. "Should I have?"

No rapid heartbeat, no edge to her voice. She was at ease here, unsettlingly, and had seemed to be having a good time before he'd shown up. Maybe she hadn't returned because she never wanted to, ever again.

His chest tightened, but he only pressed his palm into the roof beam harder, until he could almost imagine the exact detail of the wood's grain against his skin. "I shouldn't have pressed you. I was wrong. You were right."

She raised an eyebrow. "What changed your mind?"

He averted his gaze. It hadn't been easy accepting what Una had suggested, but he had. Still, looking her in the eye when he said it was too far. "For a long time, I've wanted to make you mine, Rielle. And as soon as I had you, all I could think about was losing you."

Her heart beat a little faster, but she didn't say a thing, simply sat, waited. Nox's black breath, this was only making things harder.

"As soon as I began to... worry"—he suppressed a growl —"about that, I wanted to make you mine... *in every way.* Claiming you, marking you, flaunting you... marrying you... having a child with you."

She shivered and looked away. "That's not the only reason."

"No." His knuckles cracked against the beam, and he rested his palms on his lap instead.

"I know you want children," she said quietly. "A whole house of them, you said."

That's where his mind went when he thought about the future, and what it would mean to be happy. Tregarde was quiet, too quiet, missing little laughs, pattering feet, and cheery voices, and the many chairs at the dinner table were all too empty, and he didn't want quiet and empty anymore. He nodded.

"About... making me yours," she said, staring at the castle. "You don't have to *make* me yours when I've already decided to *be* yours. When I *am.*" She looked him over with an uncertain once-over. "And the more you try to *make* me anything, the scarier it feels. Like you want to push me into a smaller and smaller room."

"I don't," he said sincerely. *Not anymore.*

"You did." She looked away again. "I don't want to be *made* to be yours more than I've already willingly given. No flaunting me to anyone. No forbidding me anything. No jealous barbs."

"I know." He hung his head and sighed. "I'm... working on it."

"That's not good enough," she said firmly. "Because while you're 'working on it,' I'll have to be living it, won't I?"

She wasn't wrong, but he couldn't promise to change overnight either. He wanted to be less... restrictive, but that was conscious. What he did in the moment—he could try to change, but promising it would all be different immediately would only be *over*-promising. And lying. "You could call me out on it. I won't push back."

She pressed her lips together and took a deep breath, her brow creased contemplatively. "All right, if we were to agree on the path, what about the destination? What do you see us doing in three years?"

This was dangerous. She'd already made it clear that her vision wasn't as set as his was, or even the same.

"We can't settle this until we both put our answers out there," she said gently.

"You already know," he shot back. Why was she making him say it when she knew? But when she didn't speak, he said, "You and me, hand in hand. Running Tregarde, Laurentine, Calterre. Taking care of our land and our people. Ideally raising a family. Keeping the peace together and living a quiet life in our own corner of the world."

"That's a beautiful life, Brennan," she whispered, and rubbed her shirt sleeves peeking out from her overcoat. "But I'm not sure I can live it."

He took off his cloak and wrapped it about her shoulders, warming her arms up through its wool. No words had ever hurt so keenly as the ones she'd just spoken. He had to look away, take a few breaths, before he would speak again. "Then tell me the life you imagine," he said, and contracted his shoulders against her answer.

"Whether I make it into the Magisterium or not," she began,

"fighting the Immortals in Emaurria, and the pirates... Doing everything I can, using this magic I was given and the skills I've honed, to keep people safe. Even if it means fighting the Divinity, wars, or stopping them. Us together, fighting side by side. Going to Laurentine or Tregarde when there's a lull, spending long days and nights together, wrapped in each other, and not just there, but anywhere we are, anywhere we're needed. Using our strengths to do what we can for those who have none."

She looked out at the Shining Sea, her eyes sparkling in the sunshine. That really was her dream. But while she *was* his dream, he only played a *part* in hers, a single fiber in a tapestry much bigger than him, than her, than any one person. His part in her life was small, claustrophobic, tight, when in his life, she was nearly everything to him.

She didn't want to live a life just for herself—the pirate attack on Laurentine a decade ago had stolen that desire from her. As a child, had she dreamed about someone having saved her family, everyone there, some force of greater good? And now, as an adult, she wanted to *become* it.

No, she'd been living it, and wanted to continue living it.

Her purpose wasn't her own happiness, or his. But being happy *enough* while pursuing something else. Some sort of divine arithmetic, dangerous, and not *her* responsibility.

But that was Rielle. In every innocent person's suffering, she saw her own responsibility. There was a kindness in her, a goodness, that he wanted both to adore and to curse.

When trouble found him, or her, the only thing he wanted to do was get them out of it. He didn't like looking for trouble, and would have never wanted to come here, on his own, to look for it, but Father's treason had made that choice for him. Rielle's need for proof of the Divinity's involvement in her family's death... had also made that choice for him. If he wanted to live *her* life, he would always be running toward trouble, just like her.

But she wasn't his only priority in life, especially not with his son on the way. He couldn't constantly be running toward trouble as a father, endangering himself, and maybe even rippling consequences to a *child*, his child, just to live her life and help her pursue that divine arithmetic. "I'm... not sure I can live that life either."

He loved her, loved her with every fiber of his being, loved her nearly two decades into the past and the rest of their lives into the future, loved her in flowery meadows outside of Laurentine and cramped ship cabins and in castles and sickness and sorrow and celebration, but all his love, all the love in the world, wasn't going to bring her into the life he wished for her to live, and to keep her happy in it.

The salt of her tears carried on the air, and he moved closer, hovered an arm around her before letting himself touch her, hold her. "Can't we... find a life between the two, Rielle?"

She looked at him, with the golden-dappled Shining Sea behind her, those summer eyes watering, tears sparkling on her pale eyelashes, and she touched his face, rested a gentle, loving palm on his cheek, and kissed him.

He pulled her closer, held her tighter, so tight he could feel the swell of her breathing chest against him, and he didn't care to hide anymore, let the tears come as he deepened the kiss, not close enough, not intimate enough, not touching her enough, breathing her in enough, never enough. Caught somewhere between an end and a beginning, he didn't want to leave this moment, this minute with her, right now.

The way she saw responsibility in every innocent person's suffering—it wasn't his way, but because it was hers, he could live it for her. Maybe not all the time, but at least sometimes, enough that they could both agree on, enough that it could fulfill her, and give her that part of her dream for the future that he couldn't. To *complete* her happiness.

"Three years," she said against his lips, voice breaking, between kisses. "Promise you'll give me three years while I set some things right," she breathed, "and then let's try starting a family."

His heart leapt, and he held his breath, just for a moment, as the grin stole onto his face. She'd made him the happiest man alive.

"I promise, Rielle," he whispered, taking her mouth despite the tears between them. "I won't ever ask you to give up magic," he said, "but after those three years, stay with me, on our lands. Stay most of the time, and go only when you're needed. Can you promise me that?"

"Only when I'm needed," she rasped softly, nodding slightly, as if to convince herself.

And whether she was a mage of the Divinity, a witch of the Covens, a heretic, a sage working for Jon—whatever, he'd do his all to stand with her when he could, support her in what she did, because it was *her*.

He'd been ready to die for her before, and although with his son on the way, he couldn't promise *that*, he could promise to stand by her in every other way.

"It's not exactly what you wanted," he said, cupping her face as he pulled away, just to see her eyes. "Will you be happy?"

She covered one of his hands with hers. "It's not exactly what you wanted either," she whispered, stroking his skin gingerly. "But we'll be happy together, *because* we're together, won't we?"

Those summer eyes, intent and watery, begged, pleaded for

something from him, something he couldn't name, couldn't fathom, couldn't give, so he pulled her close. "Come home with me, Rielle. Please."

She nodded against him, and for a while, he just held her, kept her in his arms on a rooftop, living a lifetime in one moment today before they'd each have to put their lives on the line tomorrow.

CHAPTER 52

*I*n the predawn dimness, Brennan held Rielle closer. It was a miracle that she was back in his arms, in his bed, and he wouldn't let her go easily. Never again.

She still breathed the soft rhythm of sleep, and he could lie here listening to it all day, all his life, and planned to.

They'd spent a long night talking through the trials, and although she wasn't sure what format the final trial would take, the Grand Divinus wanted her defeated—and probably dead.

So help him Nox, that wouldn't happen.

In just a few minutes, he would get out of this bed and head to Divinity Castle, where he would hide in the inner courtyard until that mage arrived with those documents to extort Father. He would kill the mage, destroy the documents, and save the family. Right after, he could go to the Archives, look for the records that Rielle sought, and achieve both objectives.

First, he had to tell her.

He pulled her closer, leaned in close to her hair, and breathed her in, deep. Great Wolf, he didn't know what exactly it was about her—maybe it was the bond, or the fact that he drank her blood every month, or that he'd known her for nearly two decades—but he loved her, through and through, and this scent was lifeblood to him.

Her pulse quickened, and she breathed in that first long, slow breath of the morning right before she got up. Today, she covered his arms with hers, stroked his knuckles, and smiled, laughing a little under her breath. "Are you breathing me in, Brennan Karandis Marcel?"

Grinning, he only held her closer. He loved that playful tone of hers.

"Well, breathe me in all you can now, because in five minutes I'm getting up."

Only five minutes? That was a shame. "How about twenty?"

She laughed again, slowly rolled over to face him, and lightly brushed his lips with hers. "I could be convinced."

And... his mouth had made a promise the rest of him wouldn't deliver. At least not today.

"Rielle," he began, gravely, and the laughter on her lips slowly faded. "I didn't get a chance to tell you the night of the second trial, but I could've gotten into the Archives."

Her eyebrows knitted together, and she squinted at him. "You could've?"

He nodded. "I had the chance, but then they mentioned documents that could implicate my father and our family in treason. If I had broken into the Archives that night, I would have missed the chance that I have today... to get those documents and kill that mage and anyone else who'd want to extort our family."

She looked away, and for a minute just stared. There was no expression on her face, no flash or shadow in her eyes, just that blank stare for a moment. She sat up in bed and raked her fingers through her waves of golden hair. "You chose to hide treason... over exposing the *mass murder* of my family?"

If the truth of all Father's dealings came to light, it might only end in more deaths. He couldn't save her family from the fate they'd suffered, but he could still save theirs. Their lives had to come before the *truth*, right?

"I'm not choosing one over the other, Rielle," he said. "But if my father's treason is exposed, Jon will have him executed, and anyone else in our family if they're involved—"

"Your father, maybe, but he would never—" she shot back.

"—and our family will be branded traitors. Do you think anyone wants to associate with traitors? Do business? Fight alongside them?"

She clenched her teeth, but didn't reply.

"I won't take the chance. And my father may be a traitor, but he's still my father."

She glared at him. "A father who knowingly endangered your family with treason."

That was true, but... what was the alternative? Let Father die? Let their family face the consequences of all this? He would never let that happen, and even Rielle had to agree. "I'm going to get those documents first, today before the trial. I still know the way into the Archives. After I get the documents, I'll go to the Archives and I'll get you what you need."

Closing her eyes, she dropped her head into her hand and rubbed her forehead. "It's too risky, Brennan."

She gathered a sheet around herself, stood from the bed, and moved to the wash basin.

"I'll decide if it's too risky." He sat up.

Her shoulders rose and fell in a shrug, and then she turned to face him. "I don't want you risking your life on my account. Especially not for this. If you could've gotten in and out unnoticed, then maybe. But if you take these documents, if you kill someone, then you *will* be noticed. It's too dangerous."

"I'll decide what's too dangerous for me."

She shook her head vehemently. "Brennan, you've missed both of my trials so far. What if that hasn't gone unnoticed? What if this is a trap, and they're waiting for you?"

Not possible. "There was no lie in the mages' voices when they discussed the meeting."

"To *their* knowledge," she emphasized, "the information they were given was genuine, but whoever gave it to them might not have been."

He scoffed. "Would anyone really go so far, not knowing what I am?"

"Who says no one knows?" She held his gaze. "You almost died the first time," she said, a slight tremble in her voice. "I refuse to lose you."

With a snort, he drew up his knees, rested his arms on them, and looked away. What she suggested would require a level of knowledge and scheming he'd never before encountered. Someone would have had to know he was a werewolf, know his abilities, *and* plan accordingly.

But he'd been very careful with his identity, and few, if any, beyond his circle, humans knew what a werewolf could do.

And he'd had *no* indication that anyone knew what he was —no bodily reaction, no looks, *nothing*. The Grand Divinus hated Immortals so much that, if she'd known him for what he was, she would have looked at him with pulse-pounding revulsion, revulsion he would perceive as easily as breathing, and she probably would have had him thrown into the arena for one of the trials.

It was too farfetched.

The real risk lay in successfully handling anyone who'd

notice him today, if that were to happen.

He wasn't so easy to kill, and Rielle knew that. *Indestructible,* he'd told her. When it came to risk, he could make his own decisions in the moment. "Don't worry about me, Rielle."

Soft footsteps padded across the rug, and her shadow blotted out the dim glow coming through the curtains. She leaned in and kissed his head. "I love you. Worrying about you is unavoidable."

That was only an obstacle, and yet the grin stealing onto his face was undeniable. He wrapped an arm around her and threw her onto the bed next to him.

"I have to go," he said. "Will you be all right? Is there anything you need?"

Holding his gaze lovingly, she gave a slow shake of her head. "I still don't really know what I'll face today"—she heaved a sigh—"but I've been researching conjury and light magic ever since the second trial. I've been practicing dueling, and Daturian helped me come up with a strategy for Mac Carra. And—don't be mad—but I got the resonance I needed at Staff & Stein."

He grimaced... but as a mage, she needed resonance, and he would never deny her what she needed.

She took his hand. "I'm ready, Brennan. As ready as I can be."

The woman he loved would be walking directly into danger, willingly, and the only thing that made it even remotely acceptable was that he was always just a pull of the bond away.

"*Don't* let them cuff you in arcanir again. And remember," he said, "if you need me—"

"I know," she insisted. "I'll pull on the bond."

He kissed her, and then with one last look, he rose from the bed and prepared to sneak into Divinity Castle's inner courtyard to clean up Father's mess. Yet again.

CHAPTER 53

*I*n the bedchamber, Rielle buttoned her white mage coat in the mirror and tossed her braid over her shoulder. The mermaid locket was tucked under it, and although she didn't need it, somehow it made her feel better, just it being there.

It was almost noon, and soon the final trial would begin. Today, she, Ariana Orsa, or Riordan Mac Carra would become a magister. Today, she would join the Magisterium, or not, but she would continue fighting for families like her own, against pirates or Immortals or whatever would threaten them, even the Divinity, in any way she could.

I'll do my all. With a confident nod in the mirror to herself, she headed for the door.

She opened it, and Marfa was on the other side in her forest-green overcoat, hands clasped behind her back.

"Are you ready to leave Magehold?" Rielle asked, but Marfa only tilted her head. "Leave... Magehold," she repeated, making a departing gesture with her hand. When Marfa's eyebrows only knitted together, Rielle headed back into Brennan's quarters and then shifted through the books and papers for their maps.

She unrolled one, then pointed to Magehold. Marfa approached and leaned over the table, eyeing the point on the map.

Rielle tapped Magehold and drew her finger across the Shining Sea all the way to Laurentine, and then tapped to the point there. She held up three fingers. "In three days," she said.

Face sullen, Marfa nodded slowly. "Erardo," she said.

Erardo... Is that a person? "Who is that?"

Marfa clenched the edge of the table, her fingernails digging into the wood, spiking to claws, her face contorted in a snarl. "Erardo... Bad. Hurt me," she said in broken Emaurrian, a low growl edging her voice.

"Hurt?" She dipped her head, trying to meet Marfa's gaze, but Marfa would only look at her for a second through her haphazard black locks. And in that second, years of agony and anguish dwelled.

"Who is he?" If this *Erardo* had hurt Marfa, they'd find him together, and show him exactly what happened when someone hurt either of them.

Marfa shook her head. "Kill him," she seethed, laying her palm to her chest. "I kill him."

So Marfa wanted to deal with this Erardo herself.

That was a goal she could understand well... All too well. And she wouldn't deny Marfa the closure she desired.

"All right," she said with a nod that Marfa watched carefully. "Do what you have to do, but please be careful." She met Marfa's deadly gaze with her own, and Marfa nodded. "Come to *me* if you need help"—she slowly reached for Marfa's hand

and then gestured between them—"and we can deal with Erardo together."

Marfa squinted, then lowered her gaze contemplatively.

She let her go. "Just make sure you return in two days," she said, holding up two fingers. She then tapped Magehold on the map again and lightly dragged her finger toward the sea.

Marfa nodded. "Two... days."

Good. Then they understood each other.

Rielle cocked her head toward the door. "Go. Do what you need to do. Find this Erardo, and then find me." She rested her hand on her own chest, and Marfa touched it lightly.

With a nod, Marfa said, "Two days." And with that, she headed out the door and down the stairs in a staccato of booted steps.

Sighing, Rielle rolled up the map and straightened the papers on the desk. She and Brennan weren't the only ones who had business to wrap up in Magehold. Marfa would have only just awoken with the Rift, and already someone had hurt her. Already the Divinity had imprisoned her, tortured her, used her like some weapon. When she found this Erardo, Divinity mage or not, they would deal with him. Marfa had just as much right as anyone to right the wrongs that had been dealt her.

And in an hour, she'd have her *own* demons to deal with. Mac Carra and whatever other traps and surprises the Grand Divinus had laid for her.

But she'd succeed, overcome Mac Carra and any traps the Grand Divinus had prepared, even if she had to duel Ariana. She'd make Ariana withdraw. She'd win.

And then, as a magister, she'd make sure Eleftheria II's days were numbered as Grand Divinus. She'd prove her unworthy, if it was the last thing she did, and do her all to turn the Divinity into what it should always have been: a force of good to protect the world when needed. And one way or another, Jon would have the help he needed to deal with the Immortals and keep their people safe.

But first, the final trial.

After straightening up, she took a deep breath, checked for Thorn on her hip and the Sodalis ring on her thumb, and headed for the stairs herself.

Downstairs, no one was about. Even the household seemed to be occupied elsewhere. Would all of Brennan's family be at the trial? Una had been very supportive, and maybe she would come with Samara; they'd been spending a lot of time together of late, and that was good for both of them—even if they did have to run from roaring Immortals from time to time.

With a deep breath, she stepped outside. The carriage already awaited in the drive, harnessed to the same two black Bellanzanos as always. Pulling on her gloves, she exited, her boots clicking on the cobblestones.

"Good afternoon, Your Ladyship," the coachman said as he pulled open the doors for her, his head bowed.

"Good afternoon," she replied, hitching Thorn on her hip as she entered. She sat in the comfortable darkness of the closed curtains and rested her head.

One hour. Just one hour, and then the trials would be sorted, one way or another.

In wolf form, Brennan crouched in the concealment of the hazel bush in the inner courtyard of Divinity Castle. He'd been here for hours, and even in wolf form, he hated lying in wait anywhere for so long in the daylight. Too risky, like asking to get caught.

But nothing trapped him here. If he wanted to escape, all he would have to do is run. He was immune to magic, and there wasn't a human alive who could catch him when he ran in wolf form.

Mostly the wait had been uneventful. Occasionally, sparrows would chitter, squabbling over something in the carefully manicured flowering trees, or some mice would rustle through the grass, or occasionally, even something so exciting as a cat would pass through.

Although there was a pavilion, no mages had come.

But they would. Of that, he was certain. He listened, pushing the boundaries of his senses' perception, and after the long wait, at last he heard several sets of footsteps. Someone was settling into the pavilion.

He didn't look, but he didn't have to. One set of footsteps stopped, and there was a soft swish as someone came to rest on a stone bench.

The other sets of footsteps shuffled about, purposefully, and then abruptly stopped, too. Guards getting into position.

He inhaled deeply.

It was the Grand Divinus and her Divine Guard.

If she was here, then it was only a matter of time before the mage who'd spoken about the documents in the Archives would come, too.

The rustling of distant steps through the grass sounded in his periphery, and he breathed in. He recognized this sent, a man's, mingled with arcanir, and dust, and damp, and blood, and a woman's scent on him—the mage from the other night. From the entrance to the Archives.

The mage was coming this way.

If he attacked the mage, if he killed him here, it would look like a strange wolf attack. A wild animal had gone into the inner courtyard, and the mage had been killed.

But the documents—

Another scent. A woman's—Marfa's—in her human form.

What was she doing here? Had Rielle sent her?

He chanced a look in her direction and then froze. The mage, with a black beard and a placid smile, carried a set of scrolls toward the pavilion, right past him.

Soft footsteps—Marfa's—edged closer. What was she *doing*? She would ruin everything.

He risked a low growl to her.

Her soft footsteps stopped.

He listened for the pavilion, where the mage's strides echoed off flagstones and then stopped.

"Most High," the mage's honeyed tone greeted, "the documents you requested."

Silence, and then the quiet crumple of papers accepted in a hand's grasp. "Well done, Erardo. I have been most pleased with your work of late."

"You are too generous, Most High," the honeyed tone said again.

A snarl came from Marfa's direction—

What was her *problem*? Did she plan to—

"Come join us, Brennan Karandis Marcel," the Grand Divinus's confident voice called out.

His paws inched out of the bush, raking him against stray twigs and branches, and he didn't want to move—

He didn't *want* to, and yet he emerged from the hazel bush, moved out into the open, still in wolf form.

Completely in sight of all the people at the pavilion.

The Grand Divinus raised her eyebrows, and even from here, he could hear her pulse race.

"Well, you're not what I expected. Not at all." She regarded him with an appraising once-over.

The Divine Guard clustered around her, but she held up her hand. Next to her, Erardo grinned, a rictus grin, an excited grin.

"Change into human form," the Grand Divinus commanded, crossing her legs casually on the stone bench, and clasping her hands in her lap.

His fur gave way to skin, his paws to hands and feet, and the Change *abandoned* him through no intention of his own.

He remained crouched, in the grass, unable to move.

What *was* this? What had she done to him? He was immune to magic, all magic, and the only thing that could affect him was—

"You lost quite a bit of your blood skulking about my castle, Brennan Karandis Marcel," she said, with an amused twist of her thin lips. "We do have an official stance against sangremancy, but surely no son of Faolan Auvray Marcel would be so naive."

Sangremancy—like the bond? The bond between him and Rielle?

The Grand Divinus had done something with his *blood?*

No, not like the bond. *Blood-control.* A sangremancy spell.

A low growl came from Marfa's position. Hate. Unadulterated hate, as strong as any he'd ever heard.

Great Wolf, if he wasn't in control of himself, would the Grand Divinus ask him to kill Marfa? Command him to?

"Is there someone there, Brennan Karandis Marcel?" the Grand Divinus asked.

Yes.

He didn't answer her, but he wanted to, needed to, with

every fiber of his being, a need as strong as the moon's call to his Wolf when Rielle didn't give him her blood.

Rielle—

Find her, Marfa. Tell her. Tell her everything.

The longer his silence continued, the more likely the Grand Divinus would ask him to tell her the answer.

He turned his head in Marfa's direction, and roared, deafening and fierce, clearing every animal in the inner courtyard, echoing off the stone walls, willing through his voice that she run.

A racing heart.

A retreating footstep.

And another.

And another.

Then she ran.

"Stop that this instant," the Grand Divinus commanded, while Marfa's footsteps quickened and retreated, superhumanly fast, into the distance. "Now tell me—is someone there, Brennan Karandis Marcel?"

"No," he said. Someone had *been* there.

"You will never harm me or anyone loyal to me, Brennan Karandis Marcel," the Grand Divinus said. "And the next time you see Favrielle Amadour Lothaire, you will *kill* her."

As fast as her feet could take her, Marfa ran from the inner courtyard.

Erardo had been there, and so had her chance to kill him, but Brennan—

Brennan had been there, too, lying in wait, hunting Erardo.

For a moment, she'd thought he'd wanted to steal the kill, *her* kill, and meant to threaten him, fend him off, but then...

She shook her head, rounding the outside of the castle, and as witches glanced at her, she slowed down. Running would look suspicious, *too* suspicious, and she wasn't about to let the mad Coven throw her back in a cell, not while Erardo drew breath, not while Lisandra was out there, somewhere, waiting for her.

Her paced normalized, but she was still trembling inside.

Something had been *wrong*, very wrong, with Brennan. The mad Coven's Archon had said something in this land's tongue, something in a commanding tone, and he had... he had *obeyed*.

His every muscle had rebelled, but ultimately bent to command.

No one but a Dragonlord or a blood witch could achieve such a thing—or someone casting a blood ritual. The Archon's scent had been too different, a force witch, but that command... the way the Change had abandoned Brennan, it—

A shudder rattled her bones.

And that *roar*—

She rubbed her arms. It was the dying roar of an alpha in battle, a *warning* for the pack to flee, to survive, and never look back. She'd only heard it once before, and she'd thought she'd die rather than hear it ever again, but there it had been.

She had to find Maestru, tell her somehow what had happened, and maybe she'd find a way to break the blood witch's spell. The arcanir sword—if she put it in contact with Brennan, she could break the spell's hold until it could be recast. If she injured the mad Coven's Archon with it, that would break the spell, too.

But if the Archon still had his blood, it would only be a

matter of time before she'd cast it on him again. They'd have to find the blood the Archon had of his, destroy it somehow.

She shook her head, heading to the front drive of the castle. Maestru did not shy away from battle, but such a task, with all of the mad Coven here—it seemed nigh impossible. Yet Maestru loved Brennan, despite all their quarrels, and she would want to know.

I'll find her, and I'll tell her.

Maestru did not shy away from battle, and neither would she.

CHAPTER 54

*J*on scanned the crowd assembled in the castle's great hall. It was full—everyone who'd come to the previous trials was here. He, Olivia, and his guards were here, but so was Brennan's family—his mother, his two younger sisters, one of whom had brought Samara, and... *Nora.* She stared at him with a mischievous smile, even while her boys ran circles around her.

Mac Carra and Orsa had arrived, along with their support-ers, as had many spectators. The two mages answered questions and greeted groups that approached them, those who fawned and admired.

Across the hall, by the Grand Divinus, Brennan stood, unmoving, his hands clasped behind his back, his face utterly expressionless. As his family had walked in, the Grand Divinus had whispered something to him, and he'd nodded to them, smiled, and then turned back to her.

Strange. Was it part of the plan he and Rielle had? Was he distracting the Grand Divinus for her?

The trials were set to begin at noon, and there had to be only minutes left.

Where *was* Rielle?

"She'll be here," Olivia said brightly, patting his arm. "She wouldn't want to miss this for the world."

"It's not her *wanting* to miss this that I'm wary of," he whispered back, leaning in. When Rielle set her heart on something, she became unstoppable, no matter the risk, no matter the threat, no matter the danger. Had she and Brennan changed places? Was she trying to find information about the murder of her family?

But she'd promised to compete in the trials, to do her all, and she was a woman of her word.

She'd be here. She had to be. Any minute now.

A chorus of tittering disturbed the general hum of conversation. Mac Carra stood at the center of a small crowd adoring him, his smug smile in place as he flirted. Orsa was similarly surrounded, bombarded with a hundred questions, every one of which she seemed determined to answer in as many words as possible.

Something wasn't right. "What if there's been an accident?"

Closing her eyes, Olivia sighed and shook her head slowly. "What if she's powdering her nose?"

Powdering her...? "What if something's gone wrong?"

"What if she overslept?" Olivia shot back.

"What if she's been attacked?" he hissed, putting his hands on his hips.

"What if she's in the garderobe?"

He grimaced. But even as he worried, he *knew* if Rielle were in trouble, she'd pull on the bond. Brennan would run to her rescue.

The Grand Divinus stood, and the crowd slowly turned to

her and quieted. Brennan still stood beside her, stiff and expressionless.

"She'll be here," Olivia said, but there was a tremor in her voice. A nervous tremor. "She wouldn't miss this. She wouldn't."

When all eyes had turned to her and all voices had hushed, the Grand Divinus smiled and held out her arms. "Welcome to the third and final trial of this year's Magister Trials. A magister must possess three qualities—perceptiveness, resourcefulness, and willingness to sacrifice for the greater good.

"In the first trial, the winners proved their perceptiveness by avoiding the traps in the labyrinth and finding their tokens. In the second trial, the winners proved their resourcefulness, showing they could still find a way to achieve their goals, even when magic was not available to them. And today, the winner will prove him- or herself willing to sacrifice for the greater good." She paused, looking out over the crowd with dull-eyed gravity. "Sometimes, that greater good requires us to turn on a friend or colleague, or to be willing to risk our *lives*. Today, in the sequence of their victory from the second trial, our three candidates will—"

She paused again, peering through the crowd, and tilted her head. "Master Mac Carra," she called. "Step forward."

Mac Carra raised his square chin, and the crowd parted as he took a hulking step forward.

"Master Orsa," the Grand Divinus called. "Step forward."

With a fuss of whispered pardons and apologies, Orsa picked her way through the attendees and stepped out into the open. "Here," she called out with a grin.

"Master Lothaire," the Grand Divinus called, eyeing the span of the crowd. "Step forward."

Jon's heart thudded in his chest as the silence grew, and he looked to Brennan, who hadn't *moved*, hadn't so much as *blinked*.

Where *was* she? Didn't he care? Wasn't he going to—

"She'll be here shortly, Most High," the Duchess of Maer-leth Tainn declared, bowing her perfectly coiffed head to the Grand Divinus.

The Grand Divinus's brow creased, and she bowed her head contemplatively, breathed deeply, and then looked out at the crowd anew. "The trial begins at noon. Since she is not here, we have no choice but to proceed." She turned her head to him. "Unfortunately, King Jonathan, that also means you have lost our wager."

He met her gaze, held it, every part of him taut to steel. Olivia shook next to him, but stood unwavering, too.

At last, he bowed, executed it to the technical perfection his tutors had taught him in the past months, then straightened, turned to the exit, and nodded to his guards.

They cleared a path through the crowd as he strode to the doors, leaving murmurs and gasps in his wake. Olivia clung to him, her slippered feet taking the quick steps to keep up with him.

As soon as they were past the doors, her grip on his arm tightened. "Jon, what are we going to do? It looks Rielle was purposely late, so once we begin our plan with Leigh, it'll look as though we forfeited here on purpose, and—"

"We have more important concerns," he said without stopping as he strode down the hall.

Rielle was missing, and Brennan didn't seem to care. Something was wrong, and he'd find her. No matter what it took, he'd find her, and if she needed help, he would—

As he stepped outside, Marfa was there, rubbing her arms and striding down the drive.

RIELLE HAD BEEN RIDING in the carriage for almost an hour, or at least it *felt* like an hour. It had to be almost noon, and that was when the final trial would begin. Had the road been so busy?

She was about to draw aside the curtain and call out to one of the coachmen, when the carriage came to a stop. At last they were here.

One of the coachmen opened the door, and hitching Thorn, she stepped out.

They weren't at the castle, but the sea. A sharp, jutting cliff overlooking the wide stretch of gleaming turquoise that was the Shining Sea. The *opposite* direction.

Gesturing a flame cloak, she stepped back and pulled on the bond, a thread of her bright anima, and—but no, there were two—

From behind, a bitter-smelling cloth covered her face as a cuff locked on her wrist—the second coachman.

Her flame cloak instantly dispelled.

Arcanir.

Caught off-guard as she'd emerged, she struggled against him now, trying to draw Thorn. He shoved her sword hand back down, slamming Thorn back into its sheath.

She stomped her heel down on his foot, and he yelped, loosening his hold on her, but not enough for her to break free. She caught a glimpse of his face—that narrow, gaunt face—

Mac Carra's brother. The one who'd accompanied him to the trials, who'd waited with him in the great hall. The one who'd been following her. *Bastard.*

He dragged her back inside the carriage, into its darkness, and the other coachman shoved her in from the front. From the seat onto the floor, they wrestled her arms behind her back.

A cloth tightened over her mouth, tied behind her head, and a hand pressed her face to the floor, grainy dust and rough wood. Abrasive ropes bound up her hands.

She kicked out her legs, throwing the other coachman out of the carriage, but with a smug laugh, he only grabbed at her foot, and then the other, and circled ropes around her ankles.

Divine's flaming fire, there had to be a way out. Some—

"Such a shame," he taunted, tightening the ropes around her ankles until they hurt, "to let a woman like her go to waste. Especially when she's already tied up."

She knew that tone of voice, knew what it meant, and a shudder ripped through her. He would be dead. No matter how she'd do it, he'd be dead if he so much as tried it. She bucked against Mac Carra's brother with renewed force.

He groaned but held her in place, heaving his weight onto her, keeping her pinned so heavily she could hardly breathe. "We don't have time for that. You know our orders."

Mac Carra's orders? Eleftheria's?

Divine, she couldn't breathe—

The other coachman groaned as iridescent white shapes floated across her vision, the edges brightening and brightening...

Thrashing beneath him, she yanked at her bindings to no avail while the white edges of her vision blinded everything and what strength remained in her limbs faded away into nothing.

The other coachman dragged her by her feet out of the carriage while Mac Carra's brother grabbed fistfuls of her mage coat at the shoulders and helped push her out. Someone removed her weapons belt and threw it—and Thorn—into the carriage.

She thudded onto the grassy cliffside and screamed into the cloth covering her mouth, but there was no one here.

Just her, these two men, the carriage, the cliff, and the sea.

They hoisted her up and moved to the ledge.

WALKING down the castle's drive, Jon moved out of the Divine Guard's earshot and toward Marfa, Olivia hot on his heels.

Marfa watched him, but then, like a bolt of lightning, she shot up, clutched her hand to her chest, and turned toward the sea, even taking a few steps in that direction.

"Marfa?" he called out to her. "Where's Rielle?"

Facing away from him, she shook her head, then turned to him, her dark eyebrows creased together, her face contorted in horror.

"*Maestru,*" she said, her voice breaking. "R-Rielle... need..." She hissed, turning her head back to the sea for a minute, then blurted a string of foreign words. "Rielle... *need.*"

"I'm coming with you," he said to her emphatically. Rielle was in need, and that was enough for him. He didn't need to hear any more.

Olivia gripped his arm and yanked him back to face her. "If Rielle is in trouble, then I'm coming with you." The set of her brow brooked no argument.

He put his hands on her shoulders while stable hands brought horses around. "Olivia, I'm going after her, but I need eyes and ears here. Especially if we're wrong and Rielle happens to return."

Frowning, Olivia opened her mouth to argue and then took a breath. With a grimace she nodded. "Make sure she's safe, Jon."

He left four of his guards with her and took Florian and

Raoul with him. "Let's go," he said to them, and got two curt nods.

He took a horse from a stable hand, ignoring his protests, and followed Marfa as she took off at a run towards the sea.

Incredibly fast, she weaved through the crowds in the street, and he picked a path behind her as his guards slowly trickled in behind him on commandeered mounts.

Was this the Grand Divinus's scheming? Had she actually acted against Rielle?

Or was this one of the other candidates, trying to defend the competition?

Either way, he would put an end to it. And whoever was responsible would face justice.

Through the market district, a carriage hurtled toward them. With a hiss, Marfa launched herself from the cobblestones and leaped onto one of the coachmen, burying drawn werewolf claws into his neck as she grabbed the other coachman and threw him down before his own horses.

She rent her claws free of the remaining man, and he tumbled to the street.

Onlookers gasped and fled, but Marfa only climbed around the carriage to grab hold of the carriage's door, and flung it open.

Horses trampled over the second man, and Jon maneuvered his mount to block their path.

He dismounted and stormed to the carriage door.

No sign of Rielle.

Inside, Marfa breathed in deep and held up a sheathed sword. The Queen's Blade. *"Maestru...* here before." She touched a finger to the floor, then held it up. Smudged with red. *Blood.* "Hurt," she said, her voice rumbling eerily.

Rielle had been in this carriage, and—

He turned to the man who'd tumbled to the cobblestones,

who now attempted to scramble to his feet, broken and bleeding.

He grabbed the man by his overcoat and threw him against the coach, drew his arcanir dagger, and pressed it into the man's throat. *"Where* is she?"

The man pressed his lips shut and looked away, shaking.

With the Queen's Blade in her grip, Marfa emerged from the carriage, her claws drawn and bloodied, and her teeth elongated to sharp, wolfish points. She glared at the man with her unsettling amber gaze. *"Where?"*

The man's shaking turned violent, and then he went limp.

Marfa rent him from Jon's grip, her hand clasped around the back of the man's neck, and with the crunch of bone, she threw him into the street.

"Come." She sprinted toward the direction the carriage had come from, and Jon jumped back in the saddle, ignoring his guard's horrified stares.

He urged his horse over the carnage, keeping sight of Marfa as she ran toward the Shining Sea.

The crowd split as people darted aside to let them by, murmurs and gasps rippling in their wake.

He didn't care. Rielle was hurt who-knew-where, and he wouldn't rest until he knew she was safe.

Marfa ran past the outskirts of town and toward the cliffs overlooking the sea, and he stopped breathing as she kept running, all the way to the edge.

He dismounted and looked over the side with her.

Waves crashed against the cliffs at least a hundred feet below, and nothing else was there, just a small stretch of beach about four hundred feet south.

"Maestru," Marfa breathed, and nodded her chin toward the water as she peered down.

She shook her head and yelped, swinging it from side to side, pressing both palms to the sides of her head. "Water.... Can't..." She hissed.

Backing up, he unclipped his sword belt, threw off his overcoat, pulled off his boots.

"Your Majesty," Florian said, reining his horse into a tight circle as Marfa tossed the Queen's Blade to him. "Are you—"

"Meet me on the beach." With a running start, he leaped over the cliff, and Marfa jumped after him.

CHAPTER 55

*A*s she plummeted deeper and deeper into the sea, Rielle struggled against her bonds, chafing her skin against the wet ropes, pulling as hard as she could.

She doubled over, trying to maneuver her bound hands under her feet and in front of herself. As she crumpled, her abdomen strained against the pressure, and she couldn't push herself harder, or she'd inhale water. *Divine's flaming fire—*

She opened her eyes, and as the sting of the seawater wore off, she sank into the darkness, her chest tight.

As her feet met the sea floor, she pushed off, as hard as she could, hoping to buy at least a little more time as her chest ached from holding her breath.

If only she had...

The mermaid scale.

It was right there, right below her chin, and in a locket around her neck. All she'd have to do would be to—sing to it.

Underwater.

She wriggled her head, trying to shift out of the cloth

around her mouth, tugging upward and dipping her chin, straining her head from side to side, until at last the cloth pulled free.

Writhing, she angled to move the locket up against her lips, but—

No choice.

Her chest tightened, so tight she was about to inhale water anyway, and when at last the locket tapped against her face, she *sang*.

Just the first note of "Winter Wren," and water forced its way in, ripping into her, and she coughed, but only more water tore inside.

Inky black dots stained her vision, but she angled up towards the light glowing faintly from the surface, kept struggling toward it, kept struggling, kept...

Little lights twinkled in the darkness, little and glowing against the black, the starry sky, starry, and...

As Jon's feet broke the surface of the water, Marfa was still shouting the entire way down.

He plummeted deep, and let the water take him as deep as it could while he searched the depths for any sign of her.

Above him, Marfa plunged in, too, flailing her arms and legs. She didn't know how to swim.

He'd get her later. But first—

He waded deeper, farther and farther, scouring the sea floor for any sign. In the vast darkness, tiny lights shuttered, winking like stars.

Narrowing his eyes, he swam toward them, faster and faster, pushing himself as much as he could. The tiny lights grew larger, became eyes, mermaids bearing a bubble up to the surface.

Rielle.

Unmoving inside, she lay there, drenched, sopping, her eyes closed.

His chest fit to bursting, he swam alongside her up toward the surface, eyed and surrounded by the mermaids, their long hair floating ethereally, iridescent scales catching snatches of filtered sunshine.

He didn't know how to tell them, what to do, so he just swam, right up alongside her. *Please be all right, please be all right, please—*

Marfa flailed desperately just below, and he swam to her, reached for her. As she locked her arms around his neck, he made for the surface right along with the mermaids and Rielle in her bubble.

It popped in the air above the water.

He caught Rielle, held her, and swam toward the distant beach, with Marfa on his back and Rielle clutched in the grasp of one arm.

Marfa took hold of her, and he let her, able to use both of his arms freely, struggling toward the distant beach.

It wasn't long before shouts echoed across the surface—Raoul and Florian, who'd removed their armor—and they swam toward him.

A born swimmer, Raoul grabbed Rielle, with a hissing Marfa reluctantly handing her over.

They met Florian within the last fifty feet, and as soon as Jon could stand, Marfa dropped off his back to her own feet and he took Rielle from Raoul.

He ran her toward the beach, shoving hair from her face,

leaning his ear close to her nose and mouth, listening for breath, for some sign, for anything—

Nothing.

Terra have mercy, she wasn't breathing.

His heart hammered in his chest as he ran with her, then set her down upon the sand near the sheathed Queen's Blade. As he sank his knees down at her side, Marfa perched on her other side, frantic eyes pinning him.

Rielle would breathe. She had to.

He applied pressure to her abdomen, raised her chin, and respired into her mouth.

She'd been like this once, her lungs full of water and mud, and it had been one of the worst moments of his life.

He respired into her mouth again.

Again.

Again.

Wake up, Rielle. Wake up. Please—

Again.

His racing heart throbbed, tightened, and Terra help him, it would *not* happen, not *here*, not *now*, not while she needed him—

Another breath, and she broke into a cough, spluttering seawater, and he braced her head gently, rolled her over to her side.

He closed his eyes, praised Terra as he heaved a breath of relief. She was all right. She'd be all right.

Marfa dug her fingers into the sand, clutching fistfuls. "*Maestru,*" she shouted, lowered her head to Rielle's eye level, and he couldn't help but grin.

Caked with sand, Rielle curled tighter, coughing, her eyes still closed.

Terra have mercy, that night after she'd dueled Flame came

back to him, vivid and powerful, and the relief that had claimed him when she'd taken that first breath. He'd carried her to camp, taken care of her, watched over her, waited until she'd open her eyes, and Terra help him, but there had been nothing in this life he'd needed more then.

Or now.

He'd agreed to leave her be, not to meddle, and yet... here he was.

Wet ropes bound her ankles and wrists, and his blood boiling, he drew the Queen's Blade and cut them. Someone had *dared* tie her up, had discarded her off a cliff as if she'd meant nothing, had tried to *murder* her—

He resheathed the Queen's Blade.

Rielle groaned. She was coming to, and he couldn't be here when she did.

"Marfa," he said, grasping her shoulders, and she fixed him with an inquisitive stare. "I was never here." He touched his chest, shook his head, and stood while she tilted her head and raised an eyebrow.

"You"—he pointed at her, then the sea, and then Rielle —"brought Rielle back."

She frowned and shook her head.

Armored once more, Raoul and Florian led the horses to them, and Florian held out his boots, his overcoat, and his weapons belt.

"Marfa," he asked, taking her hand in both of his, "swear it. Please. *You* brought Rielle back."

Her fingers wiggled in his grasp as she frowned at him. "*You...*" She pointed at him.

He held her gaze for a moment, searching her hesitant eyes. If she didn't want to agree, he couldn't force her, but he prayed she'd honor his request.

With a sigh, he dragged on his boots, buckled his weapons belt, and threw on his overcoat, leaving it unbuttoned as he hoisted up into the saddle.

"Keep an eye on them from afar," he said to Raoul, "and make sure they're safe. Then report to me."

Raoul placed his right hand over his heart and bowed. "Understood, Your Majesty."

With a last glance back at Rielle—she still coughed, curled up on her side—he nodded to Florian, and they took off toward the city.

Someone in Divinity Castle had tried to murder Rielle. Someone who would answer for it, and never harm anyone ever again.

COUGHING up water on her side, Rielle blinked open her sore eyes, squinting through the blur.

Jon. His face inches from hers, dripping water, a deep frown etched into his brow as he stared down at her with those intense Shining Sea eyes. That frown of his eased as he stroked her wet hair from her face, held her steady as she coughed her lungs clear.

What was he doing here, looming over her? The last thing she remembered was... the scale. Singing to the scale. Inhaling water.

She rolled onto her back, but his gaze remained fixed upon her, still intense, looking her over with merciless scrutiny.

The sea blue in those eyes really did shine, a certain light brightening them from within. She'd spent far too much time in their depths. And not enough. Never enough.

"*Maestru*," a voice said, and a shadow blotted out the blinding sun and bright cerulean of the sky.

Rielle squinted, the blur clearing, but it wasn't Jon over her, but *Marfa*, her voluminous black mane plastered with sand and dripping water onto her face.

Marfa grasped her shoulders and shook her lightly, making her head wobble, and shook her head. "Maestru, you... *live*."

The headache cracking through her skull was a definite sign of that.

With a wince, she sat up, her hands looking for purchase on sand, and around was—a beach. Turquoise waves lapped onto the dark sand, the surf fluttering among rocks, seaweed, and shells. A narrow path wound up a cliff, massive and daunting, at least a hundred feet high.

She took a deep breath and coughed, pain lancing through her ribcage. *Broken*. At least two broken ribs. "*Sundered flesh—*"

She began the healing incantation, but no magic came. Her wrist stung, and as she glanced at it, her spirits fell. Arcanir. *Exactly* like the cuff the Divine Guard had used in the second trial.

"I break," Marfa hissed, then seized the cuff.

Arcanir—

She frowned, closing her eyes. A man had slapped that arcanir cuff onto her wrist, by a carriage—

As Marfa broke the cuff, Rielle craned her neck up to the top of the cliff.

She'd been *thrown* off.

Instead of taking her to the castle, a carriage had taken her *here*, Mac Carra's brother and another man, and they'd put her in arcanir, tied her up, and thrown her off the cliff and into the sea.

They'd *thrown her off a cliff*.

And *into the sea.*

Her pulse pounded as she heaved harsh breaths, as she clenched fistfuls of sand and scrambled to her feet.

Marfa tilted her head. *"Chi ci hè?"*

"Thank you," she said to Marfa, bowing her head and indicating her wrist.

Marfa bobbed her head, and Rielle whispered the healing incantation, wincing as her broken ribs fused back into place.

Marfa had also saved her from drowning, brought her in from the water, severed her rope bonds.

Bond.

When she'd pulled on the bond, there hadn't been a single thread to Brennan as there had always been, but *two.*

One to him, and one to Marfa, one thicker and one thinner.

Brennan.

He'd gone to Magehold, and when she'd pulled on the bond, he hadn't come.

That wasn't like him.

She pulled on the bond again, isolating that thread that had always tied to Brennan, for years and years, and—

He was *there*, she could feel him, but... It was as if he was ignoring her.

Something had to be wrong. *Very* wrong.

She went rigid, clenching a fist as she headed toward the narrow path. Brennan was at Magehold.

And Mac Carra was at Magehold, along with his kidnapping brother, and he'd had *help*. That bastard had kept her from the trial and tried to have her *killed*, with the Grand Divinus's support. Or at least her cuff.

And after that, he wouldn't get to win. He wouldn't even get to draw another breath, not when she was done with him.

"Maestru, where... go?" Marfa asked in broken Emaurrian as she loped alongside her.

Rielle nodded in the castle's direction. "To the castle... where I have lots of *nimici* to kill," she said, borrowing Marfa's word.

"*Nimici*," Marfa repeated, with a deadly glee. "Kill. Yes. *Erardo*."

She nodded. There was a list of kidnapping, murdering bastards she had to kill. Adding an Erardo who'd harmed Marfa?

He had it coming.

"Maestru," Marfa said again, taking her arm, her eyebrows drawn. "Brennan... he..." She hissed, her face contorting angrily. "Magic... blood." Marfa's fervent eyes bored into hers as she squeezed her arm.

Brennan had to be at Magehold, then. Had he killed a mage? Was he in trouble? With a deep breath, she nodded to Marfa. "We're going to him now. If he's in trouble, I'm going to save him."

The Grand Divinus could take from her the chance to become a magister, could try to take from her her life, but she would *not* take another loved one. She would *not* take Brennan.

I won't let her.

CHAPTER 56

"**W**hy does it have to be *me?*" Katia whispered, glancing over her shoulder and wrapping her brown cloak about herself.

Distant growls and hisses echoed from inside the cave, where deep within, the horde was concentrated.

Crossing his arms, Leigh grimaced. "Because you have the most annoying voice. Isn't that obvious?"

Katia's gray eyes turned to steel as she speared him with a glare.

But beside him, both Ambriel and Della waited, too. Katia would find no protests here.

With a groan, she turned back to the cave's inky black opening and approached with slow, hesitant steps. She cupped her hands around her mouth, leaned forward, and shouted, "*Hello!* Hey, horde! Why don't you... come over here and kill us? We're alive and... walking around here, all living and stuff... So come and get us!"

Not the best invitation to come and kill that he'd ever heard, but it would do.

Katia glanced over her shoulder at him, her lips curled in an uncertain grimace.

The distant growls and hisses multiplied, louder, closer and closer.

He cast a repulsion shield around her and then gestured her back toward them with two fingers.

"Well done," he said to her as she approached cautiously. "Not the most convincing plea, but we needed *annoying*, and you delivered." He gave her a bright nod as that steely glare speared him again.

"Can you really do it?" Della asked Ambriel, then bit her lip. Her face was creased with worry, and dark circles ringed her eyes. She'd hardly rested at all.

Of course Ambriel could do it. They wouldn't have hinged the plan on it if he couldn't.

"I have trained as a tree-singer for hundreds of years," Ambriel reassured her. "I know how a dryad is welcomed, and I have welcomed one before."

The forest was behind them, some fifty feet. The horde was attracted to anything that moved, anything that lived. That included them, but once the dryad arrived, it would also include *her*.

And with the entire forest under her command, with her ability to will the trees to move, one hand would wash the other.

"This will work," he said, extending the repulsion shield before all of them as the first shambling bodies trudged out of the cave.

Katia yelped, and as they made for her, she stiffened. He grabbed hold of her sleeve and yanked her back with him toward the tree cover.

The horde flowed out, a sea of moving undead bodies, some with barely any skin or flesh remaining, and yet still animated, moving, by the power of Ava's necromancy.

Hundreds advanced on them, and as they ducked into the forest, Ambriel sang the first few notes welcoming the dryad.

Nothing happened, but he kept singing as they backed up and backed up and backed up—

Katia spelled up roots and brambles from the earth, tangling the approaching horde in the undergrowth, snaring them, but they just rolled over one another like a shifting fleshy wave, advancing and advancing, twisting and groaning, arms outstretched—

"I don't think it's working," Della said as he sang, but Ambriel didn't waver, his song unbroken.

The first wave of undead staggered near, too near, and Leigh reinforced his repulsion shield, repelling them, pushing them back, keeping them at bay.

But this plan relied on *destroying* the entire horde, and he wasn't sure even *he* could achieve that if he had to protect three other people.

If you have to choose between me and Ava, choose Ava. Della had said that to him, but that was no choice at all. He wasn't going to leave her, much less Ambriel and Katia, to all die.

"Ambriel—" he called, hoping Ambriel had a contingency plan.

The singing only grew louder, and then—

An otherworldly white glow in his periphery.

The dryad.

This time, he knew not to look, and they all knew not to look. The tone of Ambriel's singing changed as the horde broke through leaves and branches and twigs, destroyed young saplings, and still tore deeper into the forest.

A howl, like many voices become one, ghostly and anguished, and the trees groaned as they leaned, wrapping branches around bodies, pressing, squeezing, crushing.

Ambriel pushed him in an arc, around the horde and toward the tree line, his singing taking on an insistent tone.

Angling the repulsion shield to keep it between them and the horde, Leigh moved with everyone else toward the forest's edge until they were out and Ambriel's singing stopped, while the forest destroyed anything else that moved. Silently, they crept in the periphery, not daring to speak, hardly daring to breathe.

Squelching, groaning, and cracking continued from the forest, and the flow of undead from the cave seemed endless, pushing and tumbling while they waited.

Necromancers could raise the dead from graves, but some of them had looked newer... and had to have been killed by the horde and collected. Ava's fureur had to have killed at least a couple hundred people, and he well knew that struggle.

Once they brought her out of fureur, she would hate herself.

Not if I can help it.

Finally, the horde trickled down to just a few lines of undead scrambling toward the forest, and soon, there were none, despite the continued noise from the forest.

Even that faded until utter quiet claimed their surroundings.

At last, Leigh stood from his crouch and took a few steps toward the cave. Ava had to be in there, and there was only one way to find out.

Della followed after him, as did Ambriel.

"Are you sure it's safe?" Katia asked, taking a hesitant step.

"Safe is wherever I am," Leigh said. And he'd make it true.

INSIDE, the candlelight spell he'd cast by incantation led them deeper into the network of caves in the mountain.

So far, there hadn't been a single undead straggler, despite at least half an hour of walking. Katia cast earthsight and led them to an aura she claimed to see in the distance, bright, shining, blinding—that had to be Ava.

Katia had *also* ordered him to stay behind her because, as she had put it, while the light in the distance was blinding, he was somehow *even worse*.

That's a wild mage for you.

On one side of him, Ambriel held his bow, ready to draw if the need arose. On the other side, Della chewed her lip, staring in whatever direction Katia did.

The smell in these caves was nauseating, even considering how woefully *disgusting* caves usually smelled. When he closed his eyes, all he could imagine was trudging through a vast ocean of dead bodies, rotting, festering, stinking...

So he kept the blinking to a *minimum*.

Ambriel leaned in. "I hear something. More than one. I'm not sure what, but... whatever it—*they*—are, they're big."

He glanced at Ambriel. Big? The horde had been big, but not the individual undead. Had Ava raised something else? Something... worse?

Katia gasped in a breath, then sneezed.

Grimacing, she cringed as that sneeze echoed, down every inch and every corner of this cave system, for what felt like forever.

When it finally stopped, she dispelled her earthsight and looked back at him. "That wasn't *so* bad, was it?"

"That depends," he answered. "Do you consider *utterly idiotic and potentially disastrous* to be bad?"

There was that uncertain curl of her lips again. She winced.

Snarls echoed through the caves, a number of them, and they sounded like they belonged to... something big.

"Katia," he hissed, "*don't* dispel your earthsight. Not until we have eyes on them."

With an abrupt nod, she recast the spell and turned back in the direction she'd been facing. "The aura's moving, but there's something else... something else coming here."

Something else? "*Mother earth, grant me your sight, / Show through your eyes, reveal all life,*" he said, closing his eyes as he recited the earthsight incantation.

When he opened his eyes again, Ambriel shone faintly, a soothing, glowing white, while Katia shone brighter, and Della even more so.

But in the distance, small though it was, a blinding white-hot aura figured, and he'd only ever seen *one* brighter—Daturian's, a wild mage's. Ava was powerful. Very powerful.

But clustered around her were glowing shapes like phantoms, ghosts, large and hulking. "Corpse golems," he murmured under his breath.

Corpse golems were necrotic minions, controlled by a necromancer just like raised undead, only... they were *constructed* of corpses, dead flesh melded together to form a new creature, massive, strong, loyal. There were tales of necromancers who'd raised *one*, a powerful force in battle. Infamous necromancers.

Ava had at least *four.*

Della took his arm. "Leigh, no, you can't mean—"

"I count four."

She gasped. "That's—not possible. She'd be... she'd be the most powerful necromancer in an age."

Perhaps in *history*.

"Dreshan," Ambriel whispered, taking his hand, "I have faced a corpse golem before." He bowed his head. "It is formidable, a thing of immense power."

Immune to pain, fueled by magic, it could be nigh unstoppable. If a necromancer imbued it with her magic, kept on feeding it, it could stand against nearly any other mage.

Except a wild mage.

Formidable... A thing of immense power...

"So am I," he replied, and stepping free of both Ambriel's grasp and Della's, he forged on ahead, toward the four corpse golems... and Ava.

CHAPTER 57

*S*oaked to the bone and caked with sand, Rielle strode through the town with Marfa beside her. As their boots clicked and sloshed on the cobblestone street, she ignored the horrified gasps and whispers of judgment as the crowds parted for them.

Next to her, Marfa's overcoat was dripping, her hair plastered to her face and hanging in wet tendrils, and she had to look just like her, like some sort of drowned phantom, raised from the sea and stalking the earth. Like an avenging rusalka from cautionary tales told by eerie firelight, instilling fear into men who dared even think to harm maidens.

She didn't care.

She hadn't abducted *herself,* nor bound *herself* in arcanir and ropes, nor thrown *herself* off a cliff into the sea. If there was any judgment to be dealt, it was to those who *had* done all those things, to Mac Carra, and to the Grand Divinus.

And today, she *was* judgment.

They passed an abandoned carriage, *the* carriage that she'd thought had been bearing her to Divinity Castle, ringed by a gawking crowd. Its door hung open, and beside it, a man lay with his neck bent at an impossible angle—the second coachman, who'd tied her ankles.

Beneath the carriage, the only part of Mac Carra's brother—by the resemblance in his face—that wasn't broken and bleeding was his face. He'd been trampled by the carriage's horses, but his neck had multiple puncture wounds that could only have been caused by claws.

She glanced at Marfa, then nodded to the body. "Did you do this?"

Face solemn, Marfa nodded, narrowing her eyes at the body. "They... bad men. Kill them."

"Good," she replied, with an approving nod, earning a conspiratorial grin from Marfa.

Blood for blood, Shadow had once told her, calling her exactly the same, and it had haunted her once.

But as these two men had held her down, bound her, threatened to hurt her and then attempted to murder her, that haunting had dissipated, like scales falling from her eyes.

She didn't harm innocent people, *kill* innocent people, but those who'd done harm to her, had tried to kill her, and countless others. Those who would go on to harm and to kill, to leave swaths of death and pain and grief behind them while they laughed or counted their coin and planned their next bloody excursion.

But not if they were dead.

These were games of variables and equations, and if she removed one murderous variable from the world's equation, perhaps the sum of innocent people would remain living. And taking one murderer's life to save even *one* innocent person—that was a subtraction she could live with.

And once she reached Divinity Castle, Mac Carra would answer to her. The Grand Divinus would answer to her. If it was the *last* thing she did.

The two black Bellanzanos were still harnessed to the carriage, and she approached them, then unfastened their harnesses as one of the horses tossed his head. She handed the reins of one to Marfa as she mounted the other, bareback.

Picking a path through the gawkers, she made for Divinity Castle, with Marfa riding behind her, and pulled on the bond to Brennan again. Still nothing.

When they finally approached the castle's drive, she dismounted, and so did Marfa. There was no one about, only the Divine Guard manning the doors. They let her and Marfa pass toward the doors.

Then one of the two stepped forward. "No one is allowed to enter. The final is currently taking pl—"

While she pulled up a wind wall before herself, Marfa stormed up to him and smashed a left hook to his face, sending him flying. The other spelled a repulsion shield before himself, but Marfa walked through it, immune to magic, and got him with her right hook. With an acknowledging nod, Marfa threw open the door.

Well done.

Marfa had dealt with them before she'd even had to cast a thing.

She walked in with Marfa at her side, and before the Divine Guards could cast, she threw an updraft beneath one, then another, sending them flying up to collide with the ceiling, screaming, before she let them fall with a crack.

They'd live.

Stepping over one, she made for the great hall, spelling

updrafts and gusts while Marfa redefined the meaning of thrashing.

The halls were bare of anyone but the Divine Guard, although clapping and cheering echoed from farther in—the great hall. Someone had won the final trial, become a magister, or the Grand Divinus was giving a speech.

The last Divine Guard spelled a fireball at her, flaming and massive, as he ran for the doors, but she pulled up a wind wall, and it blazed over her, past her, while Marfa grabbed him and threw him against the wall.

Wailing, he covered his head, but she yanked his arm away and punched him in the face until he was quiet, blood gushing from his broken nose. "Shh," Marfa hissed at him.

The clapping behind the doors scattered, and murmurs rippled. The doors loomed, massive, the last gate before she'd face the Grand Divinus, Mac Carra, and the eyes watching the Magister Trials and Emaurrian diplomacy.

She tried to pull one open, but it was locked.

They'd locked her out.

Marfa approached, but she held up a hand, and Marfa stopped.

These were *her* doors to open.

With a deep breath, she gestured a cyclone, holding it before the doors and feeding it magic until they flew open, rent from their hinges, and she spelled a hurricane wind to blast those doors into the great hall.

Screams erupted as one door crashed to the marble, splintering, and then the other, both thudding to the floor.

The crowd scattered, but the Grand Divinus didn't move, holding up a hand to her Divine Guard, eyes narrowed.

And next to her—

Next to her stood *Brennan*, his face turned away, eyes squeezed shut, his posture stiffer than she'd ever seen.

"Master Lothaire," the Grand Divinus called out, her voice echoing, and the crowd stilled. The Grand Divinus looked her up and down with softening eyes, an act—had to be —and then the creased tension of her expression eased. "You seem to have suffered quite an ordeal. You shall have the help you need," she said, and turned to a guard. "Summon the healers."

He bowed. "Yes, Most High."

Before she could stop herself, a laugh bubbled in her throat, and deepened, loudened, continued, echoing into the great hall. "'Seem to have suffered,' you say, *Most High*. But I didn't do any of this to myself."

The Grand Divinus blinked, then glanced at another guard. "Summon the healers, immediately. This deeply troubled young woman requires *immediate* attention," she said loudly.

The crowd shifted as Olivia and Jon filtered to the front, looking her over.

"Rielle," Olivia said, her eyebrows knitted together as she reached out, "are you—"

Daturian stepped out, too, arms crossed.

Rielle held up a hand, and as the duchess, Nora, the boys, Una, Samara, and Caitlyn appeared on her other side, asking questions, she held up a hand to them, too, keeping her eye on the Grand Divinus.

Mac Carra was just below the dais, his black mage coat burned in places, and looked over his shoulder.

"I challenge Riordan Mac Carra to a duel. Magic. Now," she declared, and the murmuring crowd's face all turned at once to the Grand Divinus like flowers to the sun.

"Unfortunately," the Grand Divinus said, clearing her

throat, "the Magister Trials are over, all the candidates save for one have been defeated, and Magister Mac Carra is the victor."

Rielle took a step forward, and the nearby guests flinched. "*I* am still here, and undefeated."

"Master Lothaire, the trial started at noon, and you—"

"No rules," Rielle said, glaring up at her. "That was your decree, was it not?"

Gasps rippled through the hall.

"During the trials, yes, but they are over," the Grand Divinus said, leaning forward.

She didn't waver. "They are not over while I am still standing, undefeated, without withdrawing." She took another step forward, fixing her gaze on Mac Carra and his sickly pale face. "And dueling is law. This man sent his brother to attack me."

He spun to face her. "You *lie*." He stared her down. "You did this to *yourself*."

She held up her wrists, still chafed from the ropes. "Did I tie *myself* up?"

He scoffed.

She pulled the arcanir cuff from her overcoat and threw it on the floor before her. "Did I cuff *myself* with arcanir?"

"You could have taken that from the second trial," he spat.

She gestured to her soaking wet clothes. "Did I throw *myself* from a cliff into the sea?"

Grinning too broadly, he shook his head.

He would face her. No matter what anyone here said, no matter what excuse the Grand Divinus came up with, she would *make* him face her.

"Are you denying me because you really don't believe me, or are you too afraid to face me?" she taunted.

At that, he snarled, stomping up to her, just five feet away, but Marfa stepped up to him, and he froze.

"Your brother and an accomplice abducted me from the Marcels' villa in a carriage, then bound me and had me cast into the sea," Rielle said, and he narrowed his eyes.

"Even if that were true, it wouldn't have anything to do with me," he spat.

"Oh, it *is* true," she said, taking another step. "Because that carriage, and their broken corpses are lying in the streets of Magehold right now."

His eyes widened, and he lunged for her, but Marfa shot out a palm to his sternum and held him back.

"Accept my challenge," Rielle said to him, watching the madness in his eyes.

"I accept," he roared back at her, spittle flying from his lips.

A door in the back of the great hall opened, and several white-uniformed mages entered—healers.

"Erardo," Marfa hissed, narrowing her eyes at one of the healers, a man with a black beard and gleaming eyes.

Erardo—the man who'd hurt her.

"Healers, tend to this girl," the Grand Divinus commanded. "She's been jilted by her fiancé and has become mentally unstable."

Jilted?

Her face contorted in a snarl, Marfa began to traverse the hall toward the black-bearded man.

The healers advanced on Rielle, but she looked up to the dais, where Brennan still stood beside the Grand Divinus, his eyes squeezed shut, his face turned away. What was wrong? Why wouldn't he look at her?

"Brennan," she called out as Daturian stepped into the path of the healers.

"I'm still a member of the Magisterium, and I motion that

we hear her complaint," Daturian declared to the Grand Divinus, who stared him down.

Marfa grabbed that healer, Erardo, by his overcoat, and threw him against the wall. Nearly everyone turned to face the commotion, nearly.

But not Brennan. He just stood, unmoving, tense as she'd never seen him.

"Brennan," she called again, and he flinched—no, *trembled.* She moved toward him, but he shook his head slightly, kept shaking it—

What was wrong? What had the Grand Divinus done to him?

"Brennan," she said again, her voice breaking as she approached the dais.

"Look at her," the Grand Divinus said to him, her voice icy.

His eyebrows creased together, he slowly turned his head and opened his eyes. He locked them on hers, intense as he shouldered his way through the gathered guests, shoving them aside as he strode to her.

Pale, his face was contorted with horror, but his strides were certain—no, aggressive—and she backed up into the crowd.

"Brennan, what—"

"Run," he said, his voice breaking, and advanced on her.

CHAPTER 58

*B*rennan advanced on Rielle, unable to stop himself, violence coursing through his body as he shoved aside guests in the great hall. The Grand Divinus had said the next time he'd *see Rielle*—

Nox's black breath, he couldn't stop himself. He couldn't stop. He couldn't—

A man screamed behind him, one of the healers, as claws—Marfa's—squelched through flesh and the scent of blood filled the air. His screaming soon ended in a gurgle.

"*Run*," he told Rielle, willing her to flee with every ounce of strength in his voice.

"Silence, Brennan Karandis Marcel," the Grand Divinus murmured—barely audible, but enough that he heard, even if no one else would—from behind him on the dais, and even as he wanted to scream more warnings at Rielle, his tongue would not move to speak.

Her sky-blue eyes fixed on him and, as he closed in on her, widened. Her heart beat harder, faster, racing. She extended her hand toward him, fingers reaching out, and something like a choked whimper died in her throat as he didn't stop, didn't even slow, muscles aligned to deadly intention.

Her pulse quickened, and those fingers curled back, that hand lowered, as her feet shuffled backward through the parting crowd toward the open doorway. "Brennan, why are you—"

Great Wolf, run. Run, Rielle, I beg you.

As his hands clenched into fists, something inside of him fractured, broke apart, but his legs kept striding, marching toward her.

Jon stepped into his path, and Brennan shoved him aside, but Jon only grabbed his arm and redirected it. "What are you doing?" Jon hissed, pulling him back, and he wanted to stop but couldn't. "Brennan, what's—"

His eyes still fixed on Rielle, Brennan kept going, throwing off Jon into the crowd, into the arms of his guards. Mother stepped forward—*Nox's black breath, no*—and cried his name, but he only rounded her, just barely, while Una and Caitlyn whimpered questions of concern.

"Brennan, please," Rielle begged, tucking herself around the doorway, "speak to me. What's—"

Run, keep running, and don't look back, please, Rielle —

She kept backing up, stumbling over a fallen guard, but didn't stop. There was no way she could fight him. Not with her magic, that he was immune to. Not with her fledgling sword skills, that he had only begun to teach her. And not hand to hand. Never hand-to-hand.

Her only chance was to run.

"Tell me what to do," she shouted at him, tears welling in her eyes. "Tell me what to do!"

What could she do? Did she even realize it was sangremancy? While the Grand Divinus controlled him with magic, there was nothing—

Magic.

She still had the Queen's Blade strapped to her side. The *arcanir* Queen's Blade... and Jon's Sodalis ring.

He'd only have to touch it—but he couldn't even—his hand wouldn't—

Bloodied claws clamped down on his shoulder. Marfa. Her grip halted him immediately, and as he spun to face her, she threw him to the floor, pinned him, and dug her claws into each of his arms, anchoring them.

Her amber gaze pierced him, and she glanced over her shoulder. "Maestru!" she roared. "Sword!"

Yes, do it, Rielle—

But even as he thought it, his shoulders lifted off the floor, his body sat up, pushed back even against all of Marfa's pressure, her superhuman strength, and his hand closed around her arm. Even as she yanked it back, he threw her into the hallway's wall, her body cracking against a painting frame and a wall relief.

"No!" Rielle screamed. "Don't —"

Breath oomphed out of Marfa's chest, and she thudded to the floor with a groan.

A massive stone golem lumbered toward him from the hall, Daturian Trey standing in the doorway behind it.

The golem swiped, and as soon as Brennan touched it, it dissipated.

Daturian's eyes widened, and he threw gesture after gesture of spelled daggers, each hit disappearing.

"Kill Favrielle. Now." Another barely audible whisper, only just discernible to his werewolf ears, from the Grand Divinus in the great hall, and he could hear her, even here.

Turning, he lunged for Rielle, and tears streaming down her face, she shouted his name as he grabbed her upper arms, the violent grip of his hands too strong—*Nox help me*—too strong—

"Sangremancy," she whispered under her breath.

A bone cracked in his grip, broke, and Rielle's pained shriek rent him in two, hot tears burning his eyes as he shook her against the wall, pounded her into it again and again, and again—

He wept but couldn't stop, and fought it, and tried to fight it—

Racing footsteps from the great hall, and a body collided with him, Jon, who grabbed one of his arms while Marfa grabbed the other as they held him in place, his feet scrambling for balance.

"Arcanir," Jon shouted at her. "Rielle—"

The sword.

But she tackled him, the back of her thumb pressed into his cheek, the Sodalis ring stinging, and red-rimmed eyes searched his frantically. The violence abandoned his body, its tension forfeiting its claim.

"Rielle," he whispered, hoarse. "I'm—"

With a sob, she pressed her lips to his, kissed him, clung to him, her broken arm hanging limp from her shoulder, and that broken thing inside him only fell apart, pieces scattering, and he couldn't put them back, put them together, couldn't bear to kiss her back, to hold her, to even meet her gaze.

A hollow widened in his throat, and he wanted to apologize to her, a hundred times, a thousand times, beg her forgiveness, but they were only words, inadequate words, and his hands had clenched her, had shaken her, had *broken* her—

She pulled away, wiped the tears from his cheek with trembling fingers, and shook her head insistently, a teary smile on her face. "That wasn't *you*, Brennan. It wasn't *you*. It *wasn't*."

The grip on his arms loosened, and both Jon and Marfa stepped away.

With a quivering hand, he reached for hers, and she slipped the Sodalis ring off her thumb and into his palm. "Hold on to this, Brennan. You'll be immune, all right? Just hold on to it."

He could hear her words, but he could only see her mangled arm, hanging, swaying as she moved, and Olivia ran to her, wrapped her in an embrace, staring at him with wide, horrified eyes.

With a gesture, she healed Rielle. "You're going to be fine," she said, hugging her. "It's over now. It's all over. You're going to be fine—"

He couldn't look, couldn't face her, this—

Pulling free of Olivia's hold, Rielle grasped his hand. "Look at me, Brennan."

He shook his head. He couldn't look at her now. Great Wolf, he'd—he'd *hurt* her. His hands had just—so easily, they had—

She darted in front of him, leaned into him, and he stopped, stiff, the press of her against him like ice.

His hands, that had only loved her, had...

"I love you, Brennan," she said hoarsely, wrapping her arms around him, tightly, resting her cheek against his chest.

How could she just—

He'd *broken her arm,* and she just—

He curled around her, his weakness taking over, and these arms had hurt her, but there was nothing he wanted so much as to hold her, renew the way they'd *been,* feel that same way again, and he couldn't stop the boy in him from embracing everything he'd ever wanted when it was now offered.

"She'll pay for this," Rielle whispered, her voice raw as she cried against him.

The Grand Divinus had forced his hand, and he'd been trapped, helpless, a *pawn*. She'd ordered him to kill Rielle, and if not for the way things had gone, he might have. She could have ordered him to kill Mother, to kill his sisters, his nephews, to kill Kehani, to kill his *son*, and he wouldn't have been able to stop. He would have done anything she'd bidden, killed anyone, been a shell with no choice for the rest of his life, or hers. And no one would have known she'd commanded it.

Just like that, one woman had nearly taken away *everything* he cared about.

And for that, she would pay.

RIELLE HAD NEVER SEEN him this way before, trembling, broken, crying... and it clenched at her heart.

But in the great hall was the woman who'd ordered this, who'd hurt Brennan, and there was no way she was getting away with it. There wasn't a person alive who could do this to him and keep breathing.

Who could let mages die like nothing in a competition.

Who could order a *murder*.

Who could kill *her family*.

Eleftheria II would answer, for those crimes, and every other.

She cupped Brennan's face and rose on her tiptoes to kiss him, and although he stiffened, this time he let her, the taut tension in his muscles fading as his arms enveloped her, held her close, the Sodalis ring still clutched in the grasp of one hand.

Great Divine, seeing him so broken, so defeated, crying—it had broken her, too.

She won't do this ever again, to you or to anyone. I'll make sure of it. I'll protect you.

As she pulled away, the duchess took hesitant steps into the hallway, her shocked gaze tracing the cracks in the wall relief, the broken painting frames, and the bloodstains on the floor as she neared them. She paused some five feet away, her mouth falling open, and she took a breath but didn't speak.

Behind her, his sisters entered the hallway, with onlookers gaping, and Una raced right past her mother and threw her arms around Brennan.

He flinched, but then twisted to wrap Una in his embrace, too.

"Are you all right, Bren?" Una cried, glimpsing his face before burying hers in his chest anew. "I've never seen you like that, and—"

"I'm all right," he whispered to her. "I'm all right now." He held them tighter, both her and Una, in his arms.

"What happened?" Una asked. "You looked—"

"He was blood-controlled," Rielle said. Since sangremancy was banned by the Divinity, there was hardly any information about blood-control, which allowed a sangremancer to control a body as completely as a mentalist could control a mind.

The Divinity hunted sangremancers ruthlessly, sending their best agents from the Hensar after them, and kept all knowledge of sangremancy forbidden.

And yet, the head of the Divinity herself had used it against someone. Against *Brennan*.

"Blood-controlled?" the duchess repeated. "Someone tried to *blood-control* my son?"

Within moments, everything about the duchess hardened—her face, her bearing, her fists.

Brennan craned his neck back to look at her. "Mother... Mother, don't—"

As the duchess turned her hard gaze to him, she softened, only for a moment, and then that moment was gone. She was stone. "Nobody hurts my son. Nobody."

The duchess spun on her heel and strode into the great hall.

"Let's finish this," Brennan said to her, taking her hand, and she nodded, trailing after the duchess into the great hall, past his sisters and his nephews, with Jon, Olivia, and Marfa close behind them.

Mac Carra, the Grand Divinus, and the Divinity itself had gone too far to get away with the wrongs they'd done.

And right now, *she* had to stop them.

She'd have to bring charges against the Grand Divinus and pray that both Daturian and the crowd would back her up. And if the Grand Divinus didn't go quietly—

She'd have to be prepared to face the Grand Divinus, who'd been Magister Samanta Vota, and was an immensely powerful enforcer.

"— the meaning of this?" the duchess demanded of the Grand Divinus in the vast great hall.

"These are *lies*," the Grand Divinus shot back, standing from her throne with a pounding of her palms on the armrests.

"They're not lies!" Rielle shouted back at her, her voice echoing. Despite the trembling inside of her, she prayed she'd sound confident, and Brennan's hand in hers gave her comfort.

"I stand by everything Master Lothaire has said," Brennan told them, his sisters standing behind him. He looked out at the crowd. "The Grand Divinus blood-controlled me—"

"A convenient excuse for your actions!" the Grand Divinus interjected dismissively.

"—and ordered me to kill my own fiancée." He opened his hand and revealed the Sodalis ring. "It is only by the power of this arcanir ring that I am able to resist the Grand Divinus's commands." He stared her down.

"The Grand Divinus used sangremancy—forbidden magic —to control him," Rielle added. "This is a crime of the highest degree, and I demand justice."

Mac Carra laughed, his rumbling guffaw trailing. "Everyone knows he chased you out of the Marcels' villa, jilted you, and you were seen for *days* at an inn. You've brought your quarrels here, and now make up wild stories to save face."

His words were designed to make them angry, too stupid to reply coherently.

"Is that *your* defense, *Most High?*" Brennan asked drolly. "You can present it again at an official hearing."

The Grand Divinus scoffed.

"You've led the Divinity of Magic, which is meant to *help* the world, in a direction that is complete antithesis to its purpose," Rielle continued.

Both Jon and Olivia moved to stand beside her and Brennan.

"Magisters are supposed to demonstrate perceptiveness, resourcefulness, and willingness to sacrifice, and that is what they have always been tested for—with exams, demonstrations, duels to first yield."

Murmurs of assent flowed through the crowd.

"But these Magister Trials have twisted those qualities into coldness, cruelty, and eagerness to murder." She glared at Mac Carra, who glanced away. "We were expected to stand by while others suffered, ignore them to fulfill an 'objective.' For what? A mantle? Membership to a legislative body that expects us to kill each other and for innocent people to die? Where is the benevolent Divinity of old? The one every new mage wants to join with stars in her eyes?"

"You know nothing of the strength it takes to thrive in this new world," the Grand Divinus shouted.

"Who would thrive? Not Master Sen Taneie, who your newest 'magister' killed for a body part, to advance in a competition," she yelled back. "Not Master Cadan Bexley, torn apart."

"The world has changed!" the Grand Divinus shot back. "There are Others among us, Immortals"—she jerked a nod at Marfa, whose eyes narrowed—"who prey on us, who don't *belong* in our world, and we must each be prepared to be ruthless. The world *needs* magisters to cleanse this infection."

"We must be strong to fight those who do us harm," Rielle answered. "And that hasn't changed. Before the Rift, there were people who harmed others and people who didn't. And now is exactly the same, except Immortal people are included, too." She took a step forward, narrowing her eyes. "You want to control the world with fear, fear of these 'Others' as you call them, but you don't believe in that fear yourself. You just want to use it to grasp for more power. Because if you did believe in it, you would have granted aid to my king against the Immortals ravaging our people."

The Grand Divinus shook her head. "It is *you* who failed in that regard, by not arriving to this trial in time." She walked off the dais toward the door in the back of the hall. "Enough of this. My guests, I apologize for this embarrassment. The Magister Trials are over," she said, then turned to the healers. "Healers, take her to the infirmary."

Daturian stepped before the healers again and conjured a diamond wall before them that hit the floor and dissipated.

"These charges must be investigated," he declared, his voice booming as he stepped forward. "I motion that the Most High be placed under arrest until the investigation can be completed. Divine Guard, see to your duty."

As some of the Divine Guard moved to action, the Grand Divinus cast a repulsion shield, her gaze darting about the hall.

"These charges are false!" she shot back, flailing an arm as she looked through the open doorway, where some Divine Guard lay from when she and Marfa had broken in. "Master Lothaire attacked my Divine Guard—there they are, in the hallway. It is treason, high treason," she said, but her Divine Guard approached her, and she strengthened her repulsion shield into a repulsion dome, keeping them all at bay. "Mac Carra! Arrest the traitor."

As Mac Carra turned to Rielle, his broad shoulders taut, he held out his hands, ready to cast. "Right away, Most High."

CHAPTER 59

*R*ielle stood in the hushed great hall, across from Mac Carra, as Brennan ushered his mother, sisters, nephews, and Samara out. He argued their myriad protests until they agreed to leave, and take their carriage back to the villa. Others in the hall left, too, shuffling for the exit, leaving only half the crowd.

Good. Whatever happened here would be dangerous. Too dangerous for innocent bystanders to be nearby, especially if they had a choice to leave.

It was time to duel, and it would end in blood. *His.*

She faced Mac Carra as he held his arms out at the ready, and as soon as his fingers moved, she was already casting the deep-freeze spell.

An aura of frost thickened the air around her like mist the density of oil. Mac Carra's floating stone golem charged toward her, but in the ten-foot aura of the deep-freeze spell, it slowed, fractals of ice creeping up its body until it was covered almost entirely.

Mac Carra pulled up a stone wall to fall before him, dispelled the golem, and a shadow cast over her an instant before she shot a pillar of fire over her head and through the boulder he'd conjured. Against the heat of her fire, it was obliterated.

As Mac Carra's stone wall hit the floor of the great hall, it dissipated. She closed on him with her deep-freeze aura, holding the pillar of fire above her as one boulder after another fell—and disintegrated against her pyromancy.

He retreated up the dais, casting a fire elemental toward her, and it floated into her deep-freeze aura, its heat cutting through like a knife through butter.

But she advanced on him, the edge of her aura freezing his feet, and she dispelled her pillar of flame. Cladding her body in a flame cloak, she fed it more and more anima as the fire elemental charged her.

Her heat blazed hotter and hotter, steaming against the deep freeze, and as the fire elemental reached her, it fizzled out like a candle flame plucked between two fingers. As he gestured another boulder, she recast the pillar of flame above her before the boulder even formed, drew Thorn and lunged for Mac Carra.

Thorn's arcanir blade cut through her deep-freeze aura, dispelling it as well as the diamond shield Mac Carra tried to conjure.

Thorn's point anchored in his chest, and she twisted the blade as she pulled it free, and plunged it again lower, into his gut.

She rent it free and darted a step backward, and he immediately began the healing incantation.

No, you don't.

She thrust the tip toward his head.

Angling, he tried to avoid it, but she caught him through the neck.

He lunged for her, but as she leaped back, he only managed to grab the blade, which she pulled through his hand. Holding his bleeding neck, he crumpled to the floor, his only sound choked gasps.

The great hall rumbled.

The walls and floor shook, and she scrambled for balance as dust and debris plummeted from the frescoed ceiling.

The quake took her off her feet, but her back fell against Brennan's chest as he grabbed her and steadied her, looking up at the ceiling. "We're leaving," he bit out.

Leaving? What was going on?

"It doesn't... smell right," he hissed, while chunks of stone broke off from above them, falling to shatter upon the floor to the chaos of screams.

Marfa was at her side. "*Dragomaestru,*" she breathed, staring wide-eyed at the ceiling.

Dragomaestru? A Dragonlord?

"Maestru... all *run.*" The quiver of her voice and the pallor of her face were utter fear.

Sections of the ceiling collapsed, baring the cerulean sky and the darkest shadow of massive, imposing blue wings, membranous and wide, blotting out the sun.

Behind them, a loud crash and screams came from the doorway, where a huge piece of debris now blocked the exit. The Divine Guard closed ranks around the Grand Divinus.

Claws buried into stone above them as a massive head ducked into the great hall, with innumerable pointed white teeth each the size of the biggest sword she'd ever seen.

Walls collapsed and the screaming crowd ran for the edges

as the dragon set one massive foot onto the dais, onto Mac Carra, with a crunch, then carefully stepped onto debris.

Its enormous triangular head swiveled from side to side as it searched the crowd, its rocky blue scales almost the same shade of cerulean as the sky it had descended from.

It opened its maw, and the most deafening choral voice spoke words in something too transcendental to be language.

Images of a black tower, beautiful and magnificent, something that once could have been the ruined Tower of Khar'shil, appeared in her mind, where a massive black dragon perched at the top, overlooking a huge city of gigantic buildings and dragons flying over them. Larger than all the others, the black dragon spread its enormous wings, flapped them with great beats, and took to the air. The entire city burned, and the black dragon's anguish, its anger—was so magnificent and terrifying—

She shuddered, and kept shuddering, and couldn't stop her bones or teeth from rattling, or any part of her from trembling, as massive golden eyes slitted in her mind, searching, scouring —*needing*—and she didn't know what, but if she didn't find it, *she would die.*

The massive cerulean-scaled head prodded people in the great hall, some who shrieked, some who screamed, some who were utterly still and quiet.

And then it turned to Jon and Olivia.

No.

Never.

Not while I draw breath.

Stepping forward, away from Brennan, she cast a flame cloak on herself, then called out to the dragon.

～

BRENNAN BLINKED out of his shock as the love of his life cast a flame cloak on herself and advanced on a dragon.

A *dragon*.

Beside her, Jon drew Faithkeeper and moved in, his stance as wary as the look in his eyes.

Rielle shouted at the dragon.

It turned on her, its massive blue-scaled head large enough to eat her in one bite, and it narrowed pale eyes at her, spoke again in that terrifying harmony, a curt word. Censure that bled pain in his mind.

Unwavering, she stood before it, her flame cloak burning brighter.

Rielle, damn it all—

Opening its maw, it lunged for her.

Leaping, Brennan tackled her out of its path as Jon stepped aside. That maw snapped shut, and the dragon pulled its head up, staring down at them, and roared.

Pulse racing, Brennan completely enveloped Rielle, shielding her with his body, as the gust of the dragon's roar hit them, dowsing her flames, pushing him back like a hurricane. With Rielle clutched in his hold, he slid along the floor with her as everyone in the great hall was pushed up against the fractured back wall.

Praise Nox he'd sent their family home.

The roar—and the gust—stopped, and Rielle fidgeted in his hold, spelling a force of fire at the dragon's head.

Nox's black breath—

A great wind wall instantly rose before the dragon, deflecting the flames, spreading them in every direction.

She gasped. "It's not immune to magic," she whispered.

The dragon roared another gust that rattled the hall, and

Jon stepped before them, his sword up, bracing against the force and dispelling it with his arcanir.

A huge set of claws swiped, and Brennan shoved Jon out of its trajectory as he leaped away with Rielle.

Daturian Trey hovered a diamond shield before himself and conjured a winged air elemental, ethereal, beating its wings to blow strong winds that the dragon shielded with a low rumble in its throat.

"Brennan," she breathed, awestruck. "It's *not* immune to—"

"*We* are not immune to gigantic *claws* or *teeth*," he hissed to her. Was she dead set on getting herself killed, *and* him? Not a chance. He would *not* let her throw her life away, nor stupidly agree that both of them stay and fight. They were getting married in three months, they'd agreed on a compromise, and his *son* would soon be born. They had too much to live for to be running straight into the maw of certain death.

His gaze fixed on a small space between the debris and the top of the doorway. Frantic guests tried to climb it, but it was too steep.

Not for him. He hefted Rielle over his shoulder and clambered up the debris, then nodded to Marfa.

"Brennan—" Rielle protested, wriggling in his grip.

"We are *leaving*," he shot back. Higher than the other climbers, he chanced a look around before shifting his claws to climb up and through. He slid down the stone to the other side, Marfa after him, while Rielle thrashed in his hold.

"*Dragomaestru*," Marfa said, shaking her head and shivering. "Run is good."

"We can't *leave!*" Rielle screamed at him, and he winced at her volume. "Olivia is still in there, and Jon, and—"

"Olivia and Jon can make their own choices." Running to the exit doors, he swung her forward into his arms and pinned her with a glare while the great hall quaked, rippling through the floor. "*That* is a *dragon*, Rielle. A *dragon*."

Scowling, she opened her mouth, but he continued, "It has teeth the size of great swords and claws the size of *me*." He presented his Changed claws to her on his hands. "*This* is what *I* have."

"But magic—" she objected, her face contorted in a snarl.

"I don't care if it's not immune to magic," he snapped. "*We* are not immune to getting crushed, clawed, or eaten. Did you see your new magister, Mac Carra? He is currently in a state of fleshy paste." He would *not* let that happen to her, or to himself.

She shook her head vehemently. "But we can't just—"

"We *are*." They were getting as far away from this place as possible, even if he had to drag her away, kicking and screaming, like a barbarian.

CHAPTER 60

Olivia cast a protection spell on both herself and Jon to heal the next injury, while he stared down the dragon, shoulder to shoulder with Daturian Trey.

The dragon dove into the great hall, scattering the crowd, and both Jon and Daturian had less room to evade physical attacks, even if Jon could dispel the dragon's aeromancy with his sword.

Daturian conjured an ice elemental, an animated icicle, atop a huge chunk of ceiling debris, and it shot a force of frost at the dragon, icing its rocky scales.

Divine, why was it *here?*

Her mind immediately summoned memories of the coronation and the *Aurora,* and her theory—

It's after Jon.

That... vision the dragon had shown, the black tower, it... it was clearly searching for something—someone—that the black dragon had sought. *The Dragon King.*

A dragon so strong, so powerful, that all the Dragon Lords had bowed to him...

Until he'd been betrayed by the wild mages he'd helped create.

Just like *Sangremancy Rituals of the Ancient World* had said. She stifled a gasp.

The dragon raked claws through the ice elemental, dispelling it, while Daturian cast a fire elemental on top of another piece of debris behind it.

Daturian's constructs kept it busy for a time, but didn't do enough damage. With a gesture, he drew a conjured blade larger than himself, wavering white energy that burned in white spirit flames. An anima weapon. With his other hand, he gestured the white energy over every inch of him—an anima skin to protect him.

He and Jon angled for strikes, but they could inflict little more than superficial cuts.

They needed *damage*. And she couldn't cast non-healing magic because it would dim her anima too much, and if Jon needed her, she had to be able to heal him.

Who else is there?

After her duel with Mac Carra, Ariana Orsa was in the infirmary, getting her arm reattached—

Jon buried his sword in the dragon's foot, but as it swept its tail, he rolled away, losing his sword in the fray.

His *arcanir* sword.

In the abbey during the coronation, when Jon had touched the arcanir crossguard of his sword, that dragon had moved on. Then... one had attacked the *Aurora*, of all ships, with him aboard, and once he'd touched the Queen's Blade, the *arcanir* Queen's Blade—the water dragon had lost interest.

Both dragons had left him alone after he'd come into contact with arcanir.

Arcanir disrupted magic... All kinds of magic. Even a dragon's.

"Jon!" she shouted, and he jerked his head back as she ran to him. "Touch arcanir!"

His eyebrows creased together just for a second as he returned his attention to the dragon, then lunged for his sword.

He immediately rested a hand to the blade.

The dragon froze. It stopped moving *completely*, just perched there before them, then looked up and began flapping its gigantic sky-blue wings.

Across the hall, the Grand Divinus dispelled her repulsion dome and ventured forward with confident strides.

An enforcer.

Damage.

Gesturing, she rooted her force magic somewhere in the dragon, then clenched her fist and dragged it off to the side.

The dragon pulled across the floor while the Grand Divinus kept pulling her fist, growling with effort, hauling the dragon up against an enormous chunk of the great hall's dome, and pulling, pulling, *pulling—*

Flesh tore and bone crunched as a giant wing rent free.

A great choral cry pierced the air, ear-splitting and mind-breaking.

With a toss of her hand, the Grand Divinus threw the severed dragon's wing against the back wall, where the crowd scattered. She rooted force magic all around the great hall with one hand, then spelled a repulsion shield as the dragon roared, its gust deflected around her shield.

This was Magister Samanta Vota in the aura of her famed glory.

With a raise of her hand, heavy chunks of the building's debris lifted into the air and, as she brought her fingers together, converged on the dragon.

Olivia gasped.

The discordant cacophony of cries bolted through the air like lightning, blinding-white in her mind, searing, cleaving painfully until it wavered, weakened, and faded.

The Grand Divinus kept her fist raised, tightening and tightening as blood seeped from her force-magic convergence, flooding the hall with black, seeping over every inch of the white marble until it was sleek with dark death.

The convergence compressed and compressed as she kept feeding it her magic, until finally, with a sharply exhaled breath, she let it drop next to the dais.

The Grand Divinus climbed the bloodied steps and settled onto her throne.

"Now," she said, clearing her throat. "As I was saying, the world has changed. There are Others among us, predators, who must be cleansed like an infection." She leaned back with a sated sigh. "Times like this require a firm hand. Mine."

Gaze fixed on the blocked exit, she raised a hand, rooted her force magic in the chunk of debris blocking the doorway, then tossed it aside with a grunt.

HIS GAZE FIXED on Ava's blinding white aura in the distance, Leigh strode through the caverns, with Katia alongside him, and Ambriel and Della close behind.

They'd been walking for hours, and he couldn't tell if it was day or night, or how much time had even really passed, but it didn't matter. The blinding white aura grew and grew in size as they neared, and that was all that mattered.

Wisps of faint white ghosted around that aura, the corpse golems, and he didn't care that there were four—there could be a hundred, a thousand—and it wouldn't change a thing.

As he walked, something jerked him and caught his back— Ambriel—and he blinked to dispel the earthsight.

Under the light of Della's candlelight spell, before him and Katia, darkness lay beyond, deep and stretching—an abyss spanning almost fifty feet between them and the other side of the cavern.

Katia was a geomancer, and normally constructing a bridge made of stone would be a simple thing, but her anima was finite, and his wasn't.

As she raised her hand, he nudged her back. "Save your strength," he said, "because you may need it later."

He could face four corpse golems, but he wasn't sure the rest of them could. As long as they stayed with him, they'd be safe, but...

No, they wouldn't separate from him. They'd stay together.

Gesturing, he rooted his force magic in the stalagmites down below, then with a curl of his fingers pulled them up, his fists tightening to meld them together into a rough stone bridge.

He proceeded across, forging the path before him as he walked, and the others followed him. When they finally made it across, he left the bridge as it was.

They might soon need it again.

He spoke the earthsight incantation again and strode ahead. The path narrowed into a jagged tunnel, its confines tighter and tighter, until he could only just squeeze through, and the others followed, solemnly, the only sign of unease the uncertain curl of Katia's lips. Clearly she wasn't fond of tight spaces.

The corridor let out to a massive cavern, and as gasps sounded behind him, he dispelled his earthsight. Long spikes of stalactites and stalagmites came together like an ancient stone maw, with gaps between its pointed teeth.

Della sent her candlelight spell arcing across the cavern, all the way to the other side.

Beneath its glow, the darkness of the cave was illuminated—and a black pool of water, with massive, bone-spiked monsters prowling on the other side. Each of them was as large as four bears put together, and that very well could've been—they looked like many bodies fused together, melded so tightly to form a new creature.

Corpse golems.

Four of them circled a raised stone platform so like a dais, where on its raised center two small figures lay, both curling toward each other on their sides, eyes fixed on one another in fascination.

One was a boy, no older than fourteen in bracers and leather armor, his dark-brown hair wisping from his face, as if it were wind tousled, revealing a square jaw and intense eyes, far more intense than he'd ever seen, with irises that glowed a magical violet—so vividly that he could see them even from here.

And facing the boy—

Straight black hair fanned out around her, just like his had once been before the Vein had changed him. She was slight, just like her mother, with a heart-shaped face and full lips that reminded him of his own mother. She was beautiful. The most beautiful, precious thing he had ever seen.

Ava.

Next to him, Della gasped, darting a few steps forward, and she clamped her hand over her mouth, tears streaming down her

face. Her brow creased, that familiar determination as she kept
her eyes fixed on Ava, her fingers gesturing.

Mind-control.

If Della could just mind-control Ava long enough, they
could touch her with arcanir—or Della could break through the
fureur.

But almost as soon as that gesturing began, Ava shot up
from her stone dais, turned her head in their direction, and
pointed. The boy rose up to sitting next to her, a little too stiffly,
a little too woodenly, and those vivid violet eyes stared at them
vacantly.

The prowling stone golems ceased their movement, and in
unison, they wound their bone-masked faces in one direction.

In an instant, they launched across the cavern, those
massive bodies belying their speed.

Leigh barely pulled up a repulsion dome in time for the first
of the corpse golems to collide with its translucent force. Over
fifteen feet tall, it dwarfed them all. Pounding a rotting, fleshy,
bone-spiked arm against the repulsion dome.

He fed it power, strengthening the spell as the next corpse
golem crashed into it, and the next, and the next.

Surrounding them, the corpse golems pounded against the
repulsion dome and pounded, the impacts rippling against his
magic, stronger than any force he'd ever had to repel, even
armies.

He kept drawing power from within, feeding the dome,
imbuing it with so much anima that it nearly destabilized—and
it faltered against the impacts, threatening to break even as it
nearly burst.

If he destabilized the dome, it would knock back the four
corpse golems, but then they'd charge right back, and he'd have
to recast the repulsion dome, and they'd be back where they

started. And even if he *did* break them, Ava could just put their flesh back together and form a new corpse golem to attack them.

An endless loop.

Della kept her eyes fixed on Ava, gesturing. Still struggling with her mind-control, then—Ava's will had to be immensely powerful to withstand an invasion from an experienced mentalist like Della.

Katia bobbed her hand at points around the cavern, and as she swept it toward herself with a twist of her fingers, at least a dozen stalactites broke free of their anchors and flew toward the dome.

One plunged into a corpse golem, and then a series hit the dome. He tried to strengthen it as the corpse golems jumped clear, rolling away through the stalagmites.

Snarling, Katia kept pulling stalactites, kept aiming them at corpse golems, but even the one with stone buried deep in its fleshy body still beat against the dome, unperturbed.

Stone debris piled around them, a wreath of ruin ringing the dome.

The other golems renewed their assault, slamming against the dome, completely unaffected.

"It's not working," Katia bit out. "It's like they don't even care—"

"They don't." Under the assault's pressure, he groaned. It wouldn't hold—he couldn't hold it—he'd have to destabilize it—

Next to him, Ambriel drew his bow, nocking an arcanir arrow, and slowly aimed toward Ava.

Something sparked inside of him, a fire, devastating and vast and consuming, and even the thought of that arrow pointing at Ava was—

"Do it, dreshan," Ambriel shouted. "Drop the spell, and I'll save Ava!"

Save.

This would save Ava.

"Prepare yourselves," he warned around pinched lips. "I'm going to destabilize it."

The others stiffened around him, and Ambriel lined up his shot.

Feeding the repulsion dome more and more power—more than he could bear—he pushed past the limits of its stability, and it burst.

An aura of force magic exploded from his location outward, sending the corpse golems flying across the cavern, through stalagmites, crashing into stone walls.

An arrow flew toward Ava's leg, but was beat aside by the boy's bracer. Another shot, but the boy pulled Ava aside.

As the first corpse golem leaped toward them, Leigh brought up the repulsion dome again as Ambriel nocked another arcanir arrow.

"Last one," Ambriel hissed under his breath.

"I can't get through to her," Della breathed, drawing in irregular breaths. "Her will is too strong."

"I'll take care of the boy," Katia said, stepping into a ready stance. She clenched her fist and glanced at Leigh. "Do it again. I'll be ready."

He nodded. Ambriel's aim had been true, and if Katia could deal with the boy, then Ambriel could save Ava.

Katia gestured around the cavern again, rooting her geomancy in the stone.

As the corpse golems threw their massive bodies against the repulsion dome, Leigh overfed it again, destabilizing it, and the blast shot the corpse golems back deep into the cavern.

With a gesture of Katia's hand, narrow stalactites broke off the cavern ceiling like icicles and converged on the boy, while an arcanir arrow shot across the distance to bury in Ava's thigh.

The force threw her back toward the edge of the stone dais, and Leigh cast a repulsion shield beneath her, curling under her, catching her floating in the air.

Charging corpse golems fell apart into lumps of flesh and bone scattered across the cavern floor as he raced toward the stone dais.

He caught Ava in his arms as he dispelled the repulsion field, and Della embraced her while Ambriel took hold of the arrow.

As Ambriel pulled it out, Ava cried out, curling against his chest and his hold, and Della placed a hand to Ava's head and cast a spell.

"She's still so distraught—" Her voice hoarse, Della shook her head sadly. "So much pain—"

"Sundered flesh and shattered bone, / By Your Divine might, let it be sewn," Leigh whispered, the healing spell closing the wound in Ava's thigh.

Katia spelled the stalactites free of the boy, while Ava blinked up at Leigh, and her brow creased together over weary eyes, weary dark-blue eyes, like her mother's.

Smiling tensely, Della leaned in, taking Ava's hand while she stroked her hair, tears trailing from her eyes. "It's okay, baby. You're safe. I'm here."

Ava turned her head weakly to Della, blinking sluggishly. "Mama...?" The light slowly returned to those dark-blue eyes, and they widened as she took deep breaths. Those deep breaths quickened, and she shuddered in his hold. "Mama, where's... Where's Brice? We were carving our names in an old pine, and then there was this—and *she*—and then he—" She sobbed, covering her mouth, and wriggled in his grasp, so he set her down gently.

On shaky legs, she stood, a hand clamped over her mouth, her gaze meandering about the cavern until it landed on the boy, where Katia crouched next to him.

A sob choked through her fingers, and Ava scrambled to him and threw herself down next to his body.

The boy's eyes were open, but he stared into nothing, that vivid, magical violet gone from his irises, replaced with the cloudiness of death.

His body had been mangled and broken by the stalactites, and crying, Katia took off her dark-brown cloak and covered him to his neck.

Ava wept over him, rocking on her knees, keening.

Ava—

As Della ran to her, took her in her arms, he could only look on, his voice paralyzed.

He should say the right words, the perfect thing, but as his daughter cried over her dead friend, he didn't know what that perfect thing was, and he couldn't say a word.

CHAPTER 61

*A*lthough she'd twisted in Brennan's grasp the whole way from the castle, he didn't set her down until they reached the villa, and when she looked back toward Divinity Castle, everything was still. The domed roof was a jagged ruin, but there was no dragon, no magic, nothing but clear, cerulean sky.

She ran back down the drive to the street, drumming her fingers against her thigh, with Marfa at her side.

It seemed to be over, but were Olivia, Jon, and Daturian all right? Had everyone in the great hall survived?

And what about the Grand Divinus? Had she been arrested? Would she face charges?

Glaring at the castle, she clenched her fists. The dragon had threatened everyone, had threatened *people she loved*—and Brennan had—

She snarled. Brennan had hefted her over his shoulder like a sack of flour and dragged her away.

"*Dragomaestru* gone, Maestru," Marfa said with an encouraging smile. A thin smile. Her thick black mane and her overcoat had dried with sand and blood spatter, and her hands were stained red to her elbows. She looked absolutely chilling.

Footsteps strode down the drive behind her. Brennan's surefooted gait. She looked back, and he eyed her evenly.

"It's all over now, Rielle."

All over?

It had only just *begun*.

"What in the Divine's name were you thinking?" She advanced on him.

His eyes narrowed. "I was thinking how nice it would be for you and me to survive."

An awestruck breath escaped her. "And what about Olivia? Jon? Everyone else in the great hall?"

He took a step toward her, his expression a stone wall. "If they were smart, they ran. And in case you didn't notice, Jon took care of himself."

Unbelievable.

He pinned her with his hazel gaze, but she shook her head and flailed an arm out toward the castle. "Didn't you see how badly everyone needed help? The Divine Guard had closed ranks around the Grand Divinus, and there were so few of us to actually—"

"It was a *dragon*, Rielle," he said emphatically, crossing his arms and puffing dust from his sleeves. "The only thing to do was to run."

"*Three years*," she hissed at him. "That's what you promised me. Three years so that I could set some things right. So that I could fight the Immortals that want to kill us, the pirates—"

"But not a dragon, Rielle," he argued, closing in.

She glared up into his eyes. "So is that the promise? That I can be free up until the point you decide I can't?"

He scoffed, rolling his eyes, and planted his hands on his hips. "Free to commit suicide by dragon? That's what you're fighting for?"

"Free to do"—she dragged in a deep breath—"anything I need to. Protect people from dragons and krakens and basilisks, duel murderers, face corrupt world leaders—"

"None of which is your responsibility."

None of—? He didn't understand at all.

To him, everything she did would just be senseless and unnecessary, some sort of hobby, and not the need that it was. "I'm a mage," she began, "one of the few who are born. I'm an elementalist, one of the few types of mages capable of immense power. And I've been training for nearly a decade. If it's not my responsibility, then whose is it?"

Raising his eyebrows, he opened his mouth, but she only stepped closer.

"And what are governments for?" he demanded.

"The government is only as strong as its people, and governments don't act, their *people* do. And if I'm needed, then I'm one of them."

While he fixed her with a judgmental scowl, the duchess approached, her gown a fresh gray frock, but her face wan.

Brennan glanced over his shoulder, and the duchess threw her arms around him, then beckoned to her, too. Rielle joined her embrace—she and Brennan could continue this later.

"Praise Nox you two escaped." The duchess squeezed them both, then pulled away to look at them.

Holding her hand out before Brennan, the duchess opened it and revealed a sage-tinted band. "It's your father's, but I don't think he'll miss it... since he's never here," she added under her breath.

Brennan took the ring, looking over the simple arcanir band between his fingers, and then slowly put it on. Then he turned to her and offered her the Sodalis ring.

As she slipped it back on her thumb, Brennan watched with an intense gaze.

The ring was Jon's.

It had saved his life, and hers. Even if it was Jon's—

"Why don't you come inside?" The duchess glanced at Brennan, her and Marfa, then began walking toward the villa, as if she were fully confident they would follow.

Without even a conscious decision, her feet *did* follow as the duchess, Brennan, and Marfa headed toward the villa. "I've had Vietti send someone to learn all the news. I suspect the Grand Divinus will be charged, and Rielle—after all the work you've done, I think you should be included in the choice of the next Grand Divinus. Wouldn't that be satisfying? Playing a hand in replacing a venomous snake—"

"Actually, Mother, Rielle did win the duel against Mac Carra. Since no one had yet left from the final trial and there were no rules... In theory, Rielle should now be magister."

Divine's flaming fire... *A magister.*

"You won?" The duchess gawked at her.

In the heat of the moment, she'd charged into Divinity Castle and made demands, worthy demands, and yes, she'd dueled Mac Carra and had argued that it was still her right, as a surviving candidate who hadn't withdrawn nor been defeated.

And she'd won.

Was she now a magister? Who would decide? The Grand Divinus had been arrested, so would the Magisterium convene and issue a ruling?

"I did duel Mac Carra, and I did defeat him... But I don't know if I'm a magister." And even as she said it, tension dissipated in her chest, and in its place, there was this... *relief.*

Just how deep did the Divinity's corruption go? The Magisterium had let Eleftheria II remain in power for so long, and perhaps she'd been good, once, but then she'd become something else. If she'd remained in power for so long, then it was due at least in part to some of the Magisterium supporting her.

And one new magister—could *one* new magister change that? Could one new magister ensure that an organization as large as the Divinity could do what it was supposed to do, could fight the Immortals, the pirates, fight for the greater good?

Or... had Leigh been right? Did the Divinity have to be dismantled?

I don't need the Divinity to let me fight for the greater good. I can do that myself, without their backing.

She was Favrielle Amadour Lothaire, Marquise of Laurentine, and a master elementalist. She already had everything she needed in order to fight.

The duchess went on about how wonderful it would be for there to be a magister in the family, when they entered the villa and Samara, along with Brennan's sisters, ran to them.

Samara threw her arms around her while Brennan's sisters embraced him and pulled him toward the library. He looked back over his shoulder at her, an uncertain look beneath low eyebrows.

She didn't follow after him.

After what he'd done today, they had a long, serious discussion ahead of them tonight. And before that, she needed time to think.

"What happened?" Samara asked, as they ascended the stairs with Marfa.

Rielle told her as much as she could, and Samara fidgeted nervously, asking about Jon and Olivia.

Answers that she, too, desperately wanted to know.

She'd change, then escort Samara back to Jon's rented villa, where no doubt he worried about where she was.

In Brennan's quarters, she headed to the drinks cabinet, poured three goblets of wine, and offered two to Samara and Marfa.

Someone rapped on the door, gently, and Stefania came in with a letter from Olivia.

Olivia.

Then she was all right.

Hastily, she cracked open the seal and read.

...Grand Divinus defeated the dragon and reclaimed her throne. Her decision didn't change, and we're sailing back tomorrow on the Aurora. *You are most welcome to join us.*

Reclaimed her throne?

After everything, *the Grand Divinus* had defeated the dragon and snatched back her power?

The breath oomphed out of her lungs.

"What is it?" Samara asked.

"Jon and Olivia are safe." There was that silver lining, at least.

After handing the message to Samara, Rielle moved backward to the vanity, where she dropped into the seat. Her jar of queen's lace sat there, and she dosed her wine.

As Samara approached, Rielle covered the jar again, but Samara's eyebrows knitted together as she eyed it.

"What is that?" Samara took a few steps closer.

Rielle's cheeks warmed as she sipped the wine. "It's queen's lace. I'm sorry, I should've—"

Samara shook her head. "I don't think that's queen's lace."

With a half-laugh under her breath, Rielle opened the jar. "No, it is. I've been using it for a long time, at least six years."

With an inquisitive look, Samara closed her hand around the jar, and Rielle nodded her permission. There was absolutely nothing wrong with it. She'd brought it with her from Emaurria.

Samara held it up, walking into the sunshine, where the soft light hit the powder dully.

"No," Samara said, rotating the jar this way and that, "you see—queen's lace has a very subtle shimmer about it, but this doesn't. There's another plant—wild carrot root—that some tried to use at House Hazael to trick their partners, something I was responsible for catching. Wild carrot root tastes almost exactly the same, and looks very much like it... except for that subtle shimmer."

Marfa drank her wine and slammed her goblet down on the vanity, then sniffed the air, frowning. "Not smell right."

That looks almost exactly the same.

Wild carrot root.

Her queen's lace had been replaced with wild carrot root.

She stared at Samara, who lowered the jar from the light and set it back down on the vanity.

Here in Brennan's quarters, someone had replaced her queen's lace with wild carrot root.

Someone—

She shivered and lowered her gaze.

Everything he'd said to her—had it all been a lie? Had there been even a grain of truth in it? He knew that after Sylvie, she could never take the bitter herbs if she got with child. Never.

He knew that, and—

Her hand went to her belly, where even now there could—
where even now—

A gentle hand rested on her shoulder, and she flinched.
When she looked up to the mirror, she was crying. *Divine's
flaming fire—*

Wiping her face, she forced a smile and stood. "Samara,
could you give me a moment? I—"

"Of course," Samara said, her eyebrows creased together,
and she set Olivia's note down on the vanity table. "If you need
anything, I'll be downstairs."

She padded back to the hallway door and left.

Rielle locked eyes with Marfa in the mirror, and Marfa
tipped up her head inquisitively.

Brennan had promised her three years—of freedom, of
waiting before they tried to start a family.

Then he'd dragged her from the great hall, against her will,
leaving people she cared about behind, and breaking his first
promise.

And now... this. She didn't even know when it had
happened, but for some time, she hadn't been taking queen's
lace at all. He hadn't waited the three years he'd promised at all.

He had broken both promises he'd made to her.

She couldn't stay here. Couldn't stay here another minute.
Not in these quarters, in this villa, in Magehold, in Silen.

Brennan had wrapped her so tight that she couldn't even
breathe, that she gasped for air, struggled just to inhale an ounce
of the future she'd planned for herself. And he would never
loosen that hold. Ever.

*Some time on the Shining Sea, with no one to lord over you,
just you, the wind, and the waves, would do you some good,*
Liam had told her that day on the Red Veil's rooftop, and the

wind, the waves, and hunting slavers had never sounded better.

She rose and turned to Marfa. "We're leaving," she said quietly, changing into her turquoise overcoat.

There was no time to pack. She scrawled a short note to send her things to Laurentine—and that Olivia had something for him. After setting the garnet ring down on top of it, she gathered her cloak and coin purse, and opened the balcony doors.

As SHE AND Marfa walked past Jon's rented villa, the garden was bustling. Stable hands harnessed horses and servants loaded carriages. Jon and Olivia really were all right, and returning to Emaurria. Good.

She hadn't won the Magister Trials, and Jon wouldn't be getting his mages, but surely now, he and Olivia could enact their plan.

After everything, she'd participated in the trials, dueled Mac Carra, and... an argument could be made that she'd won. If the Grand Divinus objected to Jon allying with the Covens, then all she'd have to do would be to announce the winner. And just like that, the Grand Divinus would be able to *stop* the alliance by granting her boon—and sending help.

If not, the public wouldn't forgive her. And would the Magisterium? Daturian was on it, and surely there were other good members like him. After what he'd seen, he wouldn't leave this alone.

The streets on the way to Il Serpente were full of frantic people darting about to load carriages, buy supplies, flee to the docks. Rumor was that the dragon was dead, but if dragons had come to attack Divinity Castle, then it wasn't safe.

Nowhere in the world was safe, not until humans and

Immortals alike came together to defend against the monsters that would harm them.

She rubbed Thorn's pommel, then let her fingers travel down past the hilt, to the arcanir. While she was in contact with arcanir, Brennan wouldn't be able to find her... And right now, she didn't want to be found. Everything he needed to know was on that vanity table.

The Sodalis ring could be in contact with her skin if she put it on her locket's chain, and that's what she did, tucking it back into her shirt, against the skin of her chest.

She and Marfa didn't stop walking until the Red Veil came into view, and as soon as she walked in, Liam embraced her, earning a warning snarl from Marfa.

He eyed Marfa with wary sky-blue eyes.

"It's all right, Marfa," she said. "This is my brother, Liam."

Marfa narrowed her gaze, but nodded.

"Oh, so we're just telling everyone now?" Liam asked, hands on his hips. With his wild hair knotted at the nape of his neck and his clothes wrinkled, he was disheveled as ever, but with a cloak swept over his shoulder, perhaps just slightly less disheveled than usual.

"Marfa's not *everyone*," Rielle said, hooking an arm around Marfa, who glanced at her wide eyed and then at Liam. "She pledged herself to my service after the second trial. She's my friend, a werewolf, and I trust her with my life."

Liam cocked his head, pursing his lips, and rubbed his stubbled jaw. Marfa hmphed and looked away. At least it was a start.

Liam turned a scowl back on her. "I'm not sure where to even begin, little bee," he said, the words whooshing out like a breath. "What happened at the—"

She shook her head. "I'll tell you all about it, I promise. But..."

He had a pack slung over his shoulder. Cloaked, with a pack, here at the door—he was leaving.

"But what?" he asked.

She took a deep breath. "If you're leaving, I'm coming with you."

CHAPTER 62

*B*rennan glanced back over his shoulder toward the entrance of the library as Samara and Una entered. Hopefully after talking to Samara, Rielle had cooled down a bit. He'd only done what he'd done to save her life, and his.

Stefania had told Mother that Olivia had written to Rielle, so clearly Olivia and Jon were all right. That had to go far in assuaging her anger. Perhaps by the time they talked, she'd be calmer.

Tearing himself away from Mother and Caitlyn's questions, he walked up to Samara, who wrung her hands in a violet thiyawb. "How is she doing?"

Samara wouldn't meet his gaze, and instead looked at the floor. "She—I think it's best if you speak with her."

Her pulse was racing, and she slumped her shoulders. Something was wrong. Very wrong.

With a nod to her and one to Una in parting, he headed for the stairs and up to their quarters. Rielle couldn't possibly be angrier, could she? She'd had time to cool off, so what could have made her angrier?

Olivia had written, and—

Olivia.

What if Olivia had been hurt? That would destroy Rielle. Or... what if Jon had—

He ran for the door, and even as he flung it open, he knew she wasn't there. There was no sound of her heartbeat, her breath, no strong scent of her here. He strode inside, searching the surfaces in each room until he found two papers on the vanity table.

He picked up one—from Olivia—and praise Nox, both she and Jon were fine. Not something for Rielle to be angry about, but according to Olivia... Not only had the Grand Divinus defeated the dragon, but she'd also reclaimed her throne.

With a sigh, he dropped his head in his hand.

Great Wolf, now Rielle would never let him forget it, always saying, *If only you'd let me stay and fight, then the Grand Divinus wouldn't have reclaimed her throne. I and the others could've defeated the dragon, deposed the Grand Divinus, and—*

He'd never hear the end of it.

Olivia's note invited them to depart with her and Jon on the *Aurora* tomorrow morning.

The other paper—the garnet engagement ring he'd given Rielle lay on top of it. She—she'd left the ring behind.

It meant—

No, he'd talk to her. They'd straighten this out. He picked up the other paper.

Send my things and Marfa's to Laurentine. Olivia has something for you.
    Rielle

Was that where she'd gone? To Olivia, to give her something for him?

Maybe she just wanted space, to board the ship already, ahead of him. He glanced at the open jar of her queen's lace on the vanity and frowned.

If she'd boarded the ship in haste, she would leave many things behind, but not *this*. She'd take her cloak, her coin purse, and this jar, even if she'd leave everything else behind.

He sealed it, gripped it in the palm of his hand, shoved the ring into his trousers' pocket, and headed downstairs. Samara and Una were cloaked and headed out the door toward the carriage.

"Where you going?"

"Making sure Samara gets back safely," Una said, while Samara rested her gaze on the jar he held, and bit her lip.

"Do you know something about this?" He held the jar out to Samara. She was an apothecary, after all.

She nodded quickly and fidgeted. "I—I noticed that it was wild carrot root and not queen's lace, and I—I told her—"

"It's what?" he blurted, his heart racing.

Samara eyed him, gaping. "It's not queen's lace. It looks like it, but it's actually an imitation. She—"

An imitation? Rielle would've never switched them herself—

He closed his eyes and sighed.

My son, it matters a great deal. You must have an heir, Mother had said.

Mother—

Nox's black breath, of all the things—

Una reached out to him and took his hand. "Bren—"

Taking a deep breath, he took a step toward her and Samara. "If you're going to Jon's, then I'm coming with you."

Doubtless, Rielle would have run into Olivia with this. He'd talk to Mother about boundaries later—and so much more, but he needed to set this right with Rielle. Immediately.

They boarded the carriage, and the ride to Jon's rented villa was short but silent, as if Samara and Una didn't dare speak while he was there. Did he look as angry as he felt? Mother had told him to resolve the situation that night he'd made the blood offering, had told *him* to resolve the situation.

And he had.

Three years. Rielle hadn't known when she'd be ready for a family of their own, but she'd agreed to start trying after three years. But Mother hadn't waited for *him* to resolve the situation at all, and had instead taken the matter into her own hands.

As the carriage rolled to a stop, he threw open the door, greeted the guards, who let him through. He marched into the garden, where the entire household was moving, loading up carriages and tending to horses. Even Jon emerged, carrying a saddle from the stable.

Drawing an arm across his forehead, Jon met his gaze, then set down the saddle on a nearby bench. Dusting off his hands, he approached.

"And what brings you here?" Jon crossed his arms and leaned against the villa's wall.

"Olivia sent a note," Brennan said, then slowly bridged the distance between them until he stood only a few feet away. "I just wanted to talk to Rielle."

Jon tilted his head. "She isn't here."

There was no irregularity in his heartbeat. He wasn't lying.

Then where was she? Had she gone back to Staff & Stein?

"I saw you leave with her," Jon said, his eyebrow raised. "Is there something—"

"I have to go." He didn't wait for Jon's reply before storming out of the villa's garden and into the street. She hadn't come here, so had she left him again for the inn?

He pulled on the bond, but felt nothing. Just like when she'd been cuffed in arcanir.

Had she... used arcanir so he couldn't find her? His strides lengthened.

She was leaving for good.

Nox's black breath—

He ran to Staff & Stein, but she wasn't there, and the only other place he could think of that she would go would be to the Red Veil, where her brother was staying. He went there next.

Il Serpente was dense with people today, and he pushed through them, the Red Veil's steep roof jutting out above the other buildings. He shouldered through patrons filing out onto the stairs and darted inside.

With one hand gripping the bar, he slid a gold corona across to the buxom redhead who seemed to be the madam. "I'm here to see Captain Verib."

She picked up the corona and clamped it between her teeth, then smiled at him. "You just missed him. He checked out about an hour ago."

The bar crunched in his grip, and the redhead gasped.

Liam's ship was departing Magehold.

And the woman I love is on it.

CHAPTER 63

Samara gazed up at the big white sails of the *Aurora* against the backdrop of sea and sky. The last time she had boarded a ship, it had been against her will—with Farrad dragging her aboard. She blinked slowly. If she had gotten her will that day, she would've stayed behind in Sonbahar, where the Hazaels would have sent assassins to kill her.

Her stomach sank.

I'm a Hazael now.

No matter what she felt about him, Farrad had saved her life and given her responsibility over all of House Hazael; she couldn't turn her back on that, or the other Hazaels would only return it to the monstrosity it had been.

That will never happen. Not while I still live. She would find a way to remotely manage House Hazael.

"Are you ready, Samara?" His Majesty stepped next to her, smiling warmly, his hand rested on the pommel of the sword clipped to his side.

She had already begun treating him and had put him on a

special diet—he already seemed much improved. Lady Arch-mage had said that, despite everything that had happened at Divinity Castle, he hadn't suffered another heart episode. That small bit of hope made her cautiously optimistic.

In Courdeval, she'd be an apothecary—helping others, doing what she did best, and *free*. Living in the palace, she would be better protected from any assassins the Hazaels would send after her, and His Majesty had told her that he'd hired tutors for her, so she could pursue her education and learn Emaurrian even while living her dream.

With the crisp nod, she turned to His Majesty. "I'm ready."

"Welcome aboard," he replied, and walked with her up the gangplank.

ABOARD THE *AURORA*, Jon stared out the window at the shifting waves of the Shining Sea. Their objective in Magehold had been completed.

The Grand Divinus had refused to name Rielle a magister, and so, had denied Emaurria the mages he had requested.

Back on the shores of his own land, he'd know whether Leigh had succeeded or not. If Leigh had successfully negoti-ated an alliance with the Covens, then Emaurria stood a chance —against the Immortals, against the pirates, against enemy nations, and perhaps even the Divinity.

And with Samara and her remedies, he felt better than ever, and Emaurria would have a new Court Apothecary.

Olivia entered his cabin and shut the door with a heavy sigh. "If Brennan and his family are here, then he and Rielle must be fighting again."

They'd had some lovers quarrels recently, but he was

reasonably certain that there wasn't a couple alive that didn't quarrel. Once they reunited in Emaurria, Brennan would apologize, or she would, and there would be peace between them again.

Olivia took a few hesitant steps farther into the cabin. "Jon, clearly things aren't perfect between them. And clearly... you still love her."

He continued staring out the window. It was nothing new.

Another few hesitant steps. "Why don't you just tell her? Doesn't she deserve to know? To make her own choice? Instead of this... whatever this is... You choosing to be miserable." She sighed.

Choosing to be miserable?

It certainly felt that way sometimes, but he didn't have time to feel *miserable*. He had one thing ahead of him, and one thing only: doing his all to save his kingdom. And with his answer from the Grand Divinus, he was well on his way to doing just that. If Leigh had done his part, then they'd return to an alliance with the Covens, and all the aid he needed.

"Jon," Olivia said, stepping up next to him. "When I heal your heart, you can spend an entire life happy with her. When you bring the Tower and the Order under the Crown, she doesn't have to be a mistress. She can be your wife. Our queen. So what's holding you back?"

He lowered his gaze to the dust on the sill and ran his fingers through it, disturbed it. "Olivia... I really don't want to talk about this."

"Well, she's my best friend, and I do," Olivia said, jutting out her chin. "I don't like who she's becoming with Brennan. She's... compromising her dreams. And it might work out well, or it might not."

She didn't understand. Brennan would do anything that

was required to make her happy. There was no doubt of that. Rielle was the only thing in his life, the only thing he cared about, the only thing he would kill for, or die for. He'd proven that.

"Olivia, I have faith that you can save my life. I have faith that I can bring the Tower and the Order under the Crown. But this isn't just my life alone anymore. It's hers, too. And I can't risk her life on my faith." He rubbed the dust off his finger. "There's no risk with Brennan. He doesn't have to worry about surviving to be with her, or worrying about moving mountains to marry her. It's easy with him. Simple. And if things don't go well for me, he can give her everything I can't."

She blew out a sharp breath. "He can't give her *you*."

"I'm not irreplaceable, Olivia. If I were, she wouldn't have left with him that night." He'd thought through that night, and thought through it again and again, and again, and that was the one thorn he couldn't remove. He'd caused her pain, immeasurable pain, and he deserved.... all of everything that happened. He knew that, accepted it, deep down. It made sense. Perfect sense.

But no matter how many times he'd told himself that, the ripples of pain from that thorn... that feeling... wouldn't abate.

She'd been angry with him, so angry, disappointed, saddened. She'd ended things with him, and she'd left. That had hurt, but he'd deserved it.

But she'd left... with *Brennan*. She'd walked out of that room, out of that night, out of his love with her... with *Brennan*. And not only had she left, but in the blink of an eye, she and Brennan had gotten together. Were getting married. That thorn in him, buried in his heart, still bled... and she was happy. With another man.

He accepted all of it, but no matter his acceptance, it hurt, that part, and he hadn't been able to reason it into disappearing.

He was replaceable.

That hurt—he would bear it, carry it for as long as he had to. He would go to her wedding, and watch her handfasting to Brennan, and accept that they were sharing the rest of their lives. And he wouldn't interfere.

"I don't believe it," Olivia shot back. "I don't believe it at all."

He looked over at her, at the anguished contortion of her face, and shook his head. It wasn't so long ago that Olivia had been confessing her feelings for him, but here she was, demanding he be honest with Rielle.

Olivia wanted him to be happy, was a true friend, even if her advice was misguided. It didn't matter if she believed it or not, the reality was what it was.

"I don't believe it because... I saw the look in her eyes after I left that stable." Olivia lowered her gaze. "I thought that she was worried about you, but that wasn't it. The look in her eyes, it was... bleak. So bleak. Like the world was falling away from her feet, and all she could do was watch. If she... assumed we'd been together, then that look... It's the look that only a person losing the one they love would have."

He peered at her through squinted eyes and blinked. That wasn't... There was no...

No.

He'd seen that look.

He'd seen that bleakness in her eyes, the world falling away from her feet. But... he'd ignored it, ignored it because of that shifting feeling he'd had in his chest, the one that had been telling him to take her hand and reassure her that he'd always belong to her, and only her, to swear his undying love for her.

He couldn't have. He couldn't have said or done any of that, because it would mean... It would mean...

"You're afraid," she breathed.

He *was* afraid. Afraid that he wouldn't live past two years. Afraid that Rielle would throw away her chance of happiness with Brennan for a man who could never give her anything but suffering and loss. Afraid that even if by some miracle he survived, he wouldn't be able to bring the Tower and the Order under the Crown, that not only would he be unable to give the kingdom the strength it needed, but he'd never be in a position to offer her anything, anything she deserved.

And a life in the shadows—no, she deserved so much more than that.

But he couldn't force Parliament to do anything, and if the kingdom didn't have the strength needed within, the lords would never agree to give up the chance to find that strength from without.

And no responsible person should.

But where would that leave Rielle?

He had faith. He was prepared to do anything and everything to live, to fight, to give the kingdom the strength it needed to survive, and to thrive.

But... if he failed, *if*, then he wasn't going to take her with him. Never.

"Jon," Olivia said, her voice breaking, and she took a step closer. "You don't have to be afraid. I swore to you that I would find a way to—"

"I don't want to discuss this, Olivia." Crossing his arms, he turned back to the windows, shut her out, and stared.

Emaurria had enemies.

And there was sword work to be done.

CHAPTER 64

*W*hen Beaufort finally came into view, Leigh exhaled a relieved breath. The ride back from the mountain had been lengthy and quiet, with Della consoling Ava, and Ambriel and Katia only giving him sympathetic looks.

Beyond some very basic conversation, he hadn't even spoken much to Ava, especially not about being her father, and she'd kept to herself, occasionally crying with Della.

It was clear that Ava had loved Brice. She was only thirteen, but her friend—the boy she'd known since she'd been barely old enough to speak—had been irreplaceable to her. When the dryad had killed him, Ava had fractured.

And even now, free of fureur, she was still fractured.

He knew about that, knew about that hollow ache between the pieces of himself, and how it could never be filled, with anything or with anyone. It would remain there forever, and if he dwelled on it forever, so would he.

Right after Hana, Takumi, and Yuki had died, he'd wanted to dwell on it, had wanted to suffer, as much as possible. Punishment. Penance. The white-hot fire that would burn out every ounce of wrong inside of him until nothing remained but a shell of himself.

But as much as that hurt, it was easy. It was easy to give in, to let the pain destroy him, to feel nothing, to become nothing. What Shiori had taught him was that if he truly wanted to atone, he couldn't surrender. He'd have to devote himself to something greater, become the person he wished could have saved his own family.

True redemption could only ever be difficult.

It had taken him years to truly accept that, and sometimes, he still had the desire to give in to that hollow ache, and let it eat him alive. In each of those times was a struggle, a struggle that he overcame, and here he was, alive, and so were all the people he'd saved over the years.

And so was Ava.

He'd taught Rielle about redemption's difficulty, and soon, Ava would have to learn. It would take time, and it would hurt, but she'd have to accept the loss of Brice and the terrible things she'd done under fureur. And then find the strength to devote herself to something greater, and find true redemption.

Della led the way to the Beaufoys' house, and Axelle ran out, threw her arms around Ava, and kissed her all over, then dragged Della into her embrace, too. She led them all inside, where Katia threw herself down on the softest bed for a nap, and where among tea and conversation, Axelle rested her hands on his shoulders.

"This is Master Leigh Galvan," she said, holding Ava's dull gaze as Della hugged her on the sofa. "He's your father."

Leigh straightened in his seat, tea spilling over the edges of his cup as he coughed. He avoided Ava's gaze while Ambriel patted his back.

"I know," Ava said, rubbing her lips together. "I knew from the moment I looked at him."

Her words were hesitant, matter-of-fact, and he let Ambriel take the cup of tea from him and set it down on the nearby table.

"But if you're my father," she began, blinking those dark-blue eyes of hers, "then why am I only seeing you just now?"

The words were fragile, soft-spoken, but they had a bite that plunged deep, to the bone.

Drawing in a deep breath, he rubbed his palms on his knees. "I... Before you were born, I lost control of my power... and I hurt some people I cared about very much."

Ava pulled her arms in closer to her body, and Della rubbed her shoulder.

"Leigh is the strongest person I've ever known," Della said to her, and Ava swallowed, looked up at her, and then at him. A hesitant gaze evaluated him, and he stayed silent, let her come to her own conclusions about him.

He hadn't been in her life for thirteen years, and now that she was seeing him for the first time, he wasn't about to try to force anything. If she hated him and never wanted to see him again, well, then he'd leave today and come back tomorrow, and get yelled at again, leave again, and repeat it all until she hated him a little bit less.

Ava stood, and Della reluctantly released her as she approached him.

"Thank you," Ava said, "for helping me." She bowed her head to him, then after a moment's silence, left the room before he could say anything else.

He looked over his shoulder after her, but Ambriel took his hand and leaned in.

"Be patient with her, dreshan," Ambriel said softly.

He could be patient. As patient as it would take to become a part of her life.

"Give her time," Della said with a gentle nod. "She's grown up a little more reserved than most children."

Of that he had no doubt. Other children could be merciless to those with a single parent. Another problem he'd caused.

"So what brought you out this way to begin with, Leigh?" Axelle asked, handing him a white cloth. He blotted at his tea-stained coat.

"Ava," he answered, then took a deep breath and thought further back. "Also, King Jonathan wanted me to negotiate an alliance with the Covens, so the kingdom can break away from the Divinity and defeat the Immortals. Gustave and Joel have already agreed." He pulled the sleeve back from his arm, exposing their vowing-clasp thumbprints.

"I've been waiting for a king with the balls to cut ties with Magehold." Axelle bit her thumb and held out her hand.

"Wait," Della said from behind her. She took a deep breath and tucked a stray lock of hair behind her ear before meeting his gaze. "Ava's going to need a master."

Of course she would. Someone to guide her as she learned to control her magic, someone to carefully help her find her strength—

"It has to be you," Della said.

His eyes widened. "*Me?*" His mouth fell open.

Yes, he'd love to be a part of her life, to help her find the strength she needed. But he'd also torn open the Rift and unleashed hell on earth. While he and Ambriel traveled to Venetha Tramus and tried to reseal the Rift—

"Leigh and I are on a mission to reseal the Rift," Ambriel offered in Old Emaurrian. "That may take us to dangerous places, but if he agrees, I will promise to watch over her, too."

"Safe is wherever you are," Della said with a sad smile. "As long as she's with you, I know she'll be safe, both from herself and everything else."

Della didn't believe her magic powerful enough to pull Ava back from the brink again if necessary.

And maybe it wasn't.

His overcoat was practically threadbare from where he'd been rubbing the cloth over his thigh. Clearing his throat, he set it aside. "If you're sure about this, Della, then I can try to—"

Smiling, Axelle held out her hand in the vowing clasp. "As long as you pledge to take Ava with you, keep her safe, and teach her to master her magic, then I pledge my loyalty and that of my Coven to the Crown."

He glanced at Della with a raised eyebrow, and she nodded.

He bit his thumb and clasped Axelle's arm, each imprinting blood on the other's skin.

"As we agree, so let it be," he said in unison with her three times.

The imprints burned into their skin.

He'd allied the Tremblays, the Forgerons, and the Beaufoys with the Crown.

He'd seen Ava for the first time in thirteen years.

And when he left here, she'd be coming with him.

CHAPTER 65

*R*ielle dispelled her earthsight as the *Liberté* sailed over the golden-gleaming turquoise waves. The huge, bright mass of anima had been distant but visible.

"See anything?" Liam called out to her.

"About three nautical miles," she shouted back. They'd been sailing for two days after slavers had raided Takari, and while the Kamerish navy had intervened, two ships had still been able to flee the navy, bearing at least four hundred people.

Those two ships were sailing heavy, and Liam had loaded the *Liberté* light.

They would catch the slavers.

"Those slaver bastards won't know what hit them," Liam yelled out to her with a lilt.

Two elementalists, a werewolf, and a well-rested crew. They were in for a bad day.

Her gaze fixed on the distance, she looked for the tiny specks that were the ships' sails, and breathed in deeply.

Munching on sunflower seeds, Marfa grabbed the rail next

to her, shoving her mass of windswept black hair from her face. "Maestru, happy?"

Happy wasn't something she could think about without wanting to scream into a pillow. Brennan had broken his promises to her, and while that hurt, what had hurt more was knowing that he *hadn't* been willing to compromise on his dream but hadn't been able to tell her. She could never be what he needed, not truly, no matter how much she loved him. And she wouldn't let her love interfere with what he needed to be happy.

She'd keep in touch with Olivia, and if her preserved blood didn't work to grant Brennan control over his Wolf, she'd remove the sting of arcanir from her skin, pull on the bond, and see him before a full month could pass. But if it did work, perhaps they needed this time apart to realize that what they each wanted couldn't be found in each other... or that it had to be.

But for now, she was doing what she did best—working out in the field. She grinned at Marfa and nodded. "Yes, I'm happy. You?"

Marfa narrowed her eyes and sighed, then turned to her, pressing her lips together. "Maestru... My Lisandra... sister..." She pursed her lips for a contemplative moment. "She... lost. We can find?"

Marfa had a sister?

If she'd known Liam had been alive all these years, and hadn't known where he was, she'd have gone mad. If Marfa had a sister, not knowing where that sister was after the Rift had to be painful.

Rielle nodded. "Yes, I'll help you find your sister—I'll do everything I can. I promise."

With a slow grin, Marfa nodded, then looked back out at the

sea, eating another handful of sunflower seeds.

"Hey!" Luca called out to them from the hatchway. "Your ship's new healer suggests you eat something before we catch those bastards!"

"I'm fine," she called back out to him, glancing back to see him pursing his lips at her and Marfa. Shooing him, she turned back to the rough chop of the waves.

She and Brennan still had much to discuss, and maybe more than she wanted to discuss, but for now, this was just fine.

As Jon strode into the palace with his guards while Olivia met with Leigh, a number of uneasy Immortals—a couple of light-elves and a dark-elf—lingered in the palace corridors. He turned over the turtle stone in his palm.

"Who are they?" he asked Eloi, who trotted alongside him with papers grasped in his lanky arms.

"Emissaries, Your Majesty," Eloi said with a nervous tremor in his voice.

"Emissaries?" Their faces had been gaunt and creased, and that didn't bode well. On the High Council's recommendation, he had left the kingdom in the hands of Auguste, his cousin and the Secretary of State for Foreign Affairs, while he'd been in Magehold, to work with their Immortal allies against their shared enemies. "Have they been assisted?"

Eloi swallowed. "Secretary Armel has... prioritized human subjects seeking aid, and Pons was the only voice dissenting, so the council allowed it."

"He's what?" Jon grunted, rubbing his chest. He'd left Auguste in charge with specific instructions, and the man had mismanaged the kingdom.

"He said we had to look to our own," Eloi added.

"Where is he?" Jon bit out.

"In the throne room, sire."

Jon changed course from his quarters to the throne room, clenching his fists. He'd been on a diplomatic mission for months, had told Auguste to provide the help they'd agreed on by *treaty*, ones *he* had signed, and he'd reverted back to this humans-first toxic posture.

Enough was enough.

Two footmen hastily opened the throne-room doors, and he didn't slow as he entered, fixing his gaze on Auguste, who wore an elaborate green brocade doublet and stroked his pointed beard as he laughed with two courtiers.

Auguste looked in his direction, sobered, and bowed. "Your Majesty, you've returned. How was your—"

He grabbed Auguste by his elaborate green brocade doublet and punched him. "I trusted you with my kingdom, and you ruin *everything* the first chance you get?"

The courtiers gasped and took steps back, bowing as they whispered acknowledgments.

Eloi cleared his throat. "Your Majesty, should I call a meeting in the High Council chambers?"

The *High Council* had allowed Auguste to get away with ignoring the needs of their allies. Hissing out a breath, he glanced at the throne's dais.

"No," he said, climbing the twelve steps and planting himself in it. "Call the meeting *here*. I want every member of the High Council brought here within the hour, as well as our former Ambassador to Vervewood and Emissary Ambriel Sunheart. And get me details on Sincuore's trial."

Eloi bowed, but as he departed, Jon called out, "And send

the palace's head gardener to me." He wanted a Suguz pine planted in the palace gardens.

"Yes, Your Majesty," Eloi said as he bowed, and then he departed.

Auguste dabbed at his nose with trembling hands and whimpered.

"You'll live," Jon shouted to him, turning over the turtle stone in his palm.

Auguste had let alliances and responsibilities falter, and the High Council had been too weak to stop it.

Olivia had vowed to save him, and both Samara's treatment and diet was working. He didn't know how much time he had, but he was here now, and no innocent person in Emaurria—human or Immortal—would suffer needlessly while he drew breath.

On the sofa in her parlor, Olivia suppressed a smile as, across from her on the button-tufted armchair, Leigh watched her with an incredulous stare. He sat frozen in an immaculate black master-mage overcoat; he'd been in Courdeval for days.

"She did *what?*" He jerked his head back, blinking pale-white eyelashes.

"She was going to take on the dragon, too, but then Brennan threw her over his shoulder and ran out of there. The Grand Divinus handled the dragon *and* retook her power." She clutched the armrest, tensing. They'd been so close to unseating the Grand Divinus—even the Divine Guard had wavered—but that show of force was indisputably convincing in a world where dragons could burst into castles.

"At least there will be an inquiry," Leigh said with a sigh, crossing his legs. "Daturian won't let it lie. He'll be like a dog with a bone."

"He'll be silenced." In the Magisterium, he'd be outnumbered.

Leigh smiled bitterly. "He's never been one for bureaucracy. I think he'll shake some trees in Kamerai and see what falls out."

Perhaps the Kamerish Tower would break from the Divinity. If multiple Towers rebelled, breaking the Emaurrian Tower away would be easier. And Samara's work would buy enough time to find a way to heal Jon. All of their plans might succeed—other than the Dragon King hunting him.

"You did well, inviting Daturian there." With a gleam in his eye, he shot her a knowing grin.

"My master taught me well." Holding his gaze, she drank her tea smugly. "Now if you could just tell me all about the Dragon King, I'd really appreciate it."

The laugh she expected didn't come.

He jerked his head back, his posture stiffening. "How did you—" He tilted his head. "You know about the Dragon King?"

After that vision in Divinity Castle's great hall, Divine, she couldn't *forget*. That large, golden eye, belonging to the even larger black dragon, its presence terrifying, giving her shivers even now. Compared to that, the dragon in Magehold had been a *lackey*. "There was a book I acquired in Il Serpente about a Black Tower and a Dragon Lord."

Leigh drew in a lengthy breath. "Nyeris," he said, barely audible. "While I was in Vervewood, I learned a bit of history," he said, crossing his arms. The news wasn't going to be good, then. "The Black Tower refers to Khar'shil, which was once the dragons' seat of power."

She'd connected the two with Rielle, and that vision had shown an entire city sprawling around that tower—teeming with dragons, and every Immortal she could name, and even those she yet couldn't.

"The ancient wild mages, in their hubris, decided mankind would no longer bow to the Dragonlords, who were these... benevolent dictators guiding all the races," he said, tilting his chin down as he frowned. "They betrayed Nyeris and used sangremancy to bind him to a recondite bell."

The Bell of Khar'shil.

"Bound as he was, they used him like a tool, summoning him with purpose and banishing him as they desired, using their control over him—and his rule of lesser dragons. They cowed any races opposed to human rule, until finally... the Sundering," he explained. "But when they did summon him, no matter when the bell was rung and the ritual performed, he would be compelled to act, maddened, but he could only emerge at a time of great power, of equal day and night—at Veris."

Veris.

A sudden coldness hit her stomach, and she squeezed her eyes shut. The dragons that had pursued Jon—since Shadow's arrival at Khar'shil—

If the Dragon King had been summoned, maddened by compulsion, but could not yet emerge, had that driven lesser dragons to hunt Jon?

Were more coming? He'd have to be in constant contact with arcanir.

"Leigh, that vision we had at the last trial," she said, her voice quivering, "I think the Dragon King is coming for Jon."

He leaned away, his expression hard as he held her gaze for a long moment, then he swallowed. "Well, if Ambriel, Ava, and I accomplish what we set out to, then this will all be resolved before Veris," he said quietly.

Leigh, his daughter—he actually had a thirteen-year-old

daughter—and his lover planned to go in search of the sky-elves to a place called Venetha Tramus, where the last mage to have performed the Sundering had traveled to after the rite. If there were any clues left behind, perhaps the Immortal beasts could be Sundered once more, and the peaceful Immortal peoples left to survive.

It was a long shot, and in the meantime, she and Jon would have to prepare for Veris—and the Dragon King.

A knock came to the door. "Lady Archmage, Master Galvan —His Majesty has called a council meeting in the throne room."

"In the throne room?" Leigh quirked a pleased eyebrow as he rose with her. "Good. Then he's finally bringing the rest of the council to heel."

While she and Jon had been away, Auguste and most of the council had agreed to *ignore* calls for aid—even from Verve-wood. Unforgivable.

"Now that we have the Covens on our side, it's time to take out the trash... and put things in order," she said with a smile. "Or at least prepare to, before you embark."

"I couldn't agree more," he replied, with a mischievous gleam in his eye. "I couldn't agree more."

CHAPTER 66

Three Months Later

Brennan paced in the hallway, listening to every command, comment, and panted breath, trying to talk himself out of bursting through the door.

After three months meandering on the Shining Sea, he'd only arrived today, and had already been pacing this hallway for four hours. Kehani was in labor.

Tonight, he would see his son's face.

Her voice cried out from the bedchamber again, and with trembling fingers he snatched the knob and threw the door open. Midwives huddled around her, while two healers argued in a corner. A master healer and her apprentice.

"It's as though it's arcanir, or a sigil—" the young man said, shaking his head. "I'm not sure what else we could try, Master."

"We have to keep trying," the master healer replied. "Perhaps after the child is born—"

Kehani cried out again, her voice breaking as it strained. The doctor beckoned to her assistants, and then—

His heart pounded, hammering against his chest like thunder as Kehani brought their son into the world.

"Ranth," she whimpered, reaching her arms out weakly to the doctor holding him. "Give him to me..."

Ranth.

He had a full head of dark hair, and then in the doctor's hold, he cried out, loud and strong, and Brennan couldn't help the smile stretching across his face. He had a son.

He had a son.

Ranth.

The doctor demanded her implements from her assistants, and several people flitted about the room.

Healers cast their magic on Kehani, laying hands on her body.

"It's not working," the apprentice said, pale as he glanced at his master.

The master healer moved to his son, touched him gently. "The healing magic isn't working on him either."

Ranth was of his blood, and the curse remained unbroken. Until then, he would become a werewolf. Immune to all magic but sangremancy.

"She's losing a lot of blood," the doctor said. "I need —"

Kehani was immune to magic. Her blood and Ranth's had mingled. Was she a werewolf?

No, her scent wasn't right. There was a flurry of activity, of healers and apprentices, midwives and doctors and assistants, and as Kehani held out her arms, the light in her eyes fading, he gently accepted Ranth into his arms and held him close, trembling as he pressed his lips to Ranth's forehead.

As he memorized Ranth's face, breathed him in, his vision blurred, but he blinked the tears back. Ranth cooed, and that sound rippled into him like warmth, like a memory he'd only just made but somehow had always remembered.

He would know Ranth's voice anywhere.

There was a bond, an instant bond, and it was stronger than anything he'd ever felt. He would live for Ranth, die for Ranth, do anything to keep him safe.

"Brennan," Kehani whimpered, "bring him to me..."

Slowly, he moved to her, sat on the edge of the bed, and leaned in close enough that she could touch Ranth. Smiling weakly, she took his tiny hand in hers.

Even as his heart leapt, it was breaking.

Something was wrong with Kehani, and none of the so-called knowledgeable people in this room knew the first thing to do about it.

Soon that flurry of activity quieted, and everyone in the room ringed the bed, watching Kehani, watching Ranth, and him, and he held her gaze for a moment as her lower lip quivered.

There was nothing any of these people could do, and she knew her time was running out.

She gave a small nod.

"Clear the room," he said, without looking away from her dark gaze.

"But my lord—" the apprentice stammered, and his master pulled him away.

One by one, they all filtered out of the room, leaving him alone with his family.

He had accidentally turned a werewolf once, a man he'd bit, a man whose blood he'd tasted, who'd tasted his, too. The man had taken fever, and had begun to turn when he'd killed him.

Kehani didn't have time for the fever, but he didn't care. He had to *try*.

Holding Ranth securely in his arms, he took Kehani's hand and turned away from her. "Kehani, this is going to hurt, but it may save you."

"Ranth..." she whispered weakly. She was fading fast, too fast.

Changing his teeth, he gingerly bit into her palm, and she flinched but didn't cry out. He bit into his own and intertwined their fingers, his blood mingling with hers as he turned back to her and hoped.

Ranth fussed in his hold, just a little, and he whispered a soft hush by his ear, listening to Ranth's pulse until he calmed. As Kehani's heartbeat slowed and slowed, she watched Ranth with a thin smile.

Ranth needed his mother, and she was dying.

Bearing the child of a werewolf had made her immune to magic, but not immortal—it had placed her in danger. *He* had placed her in danger.

Kehani's heartbeat slowed to a stop, that thin smile going slack as her eyes glazed over, her head going limp against her dark waves of hair on the pillows.

Brennan tightened the union of their intertwined fingers, hoping against hope that she'd revive, praying, but only silence answered.

And the soft breaths of Ranth in his arms.

He held him close, held him safe. Ranth had only drawn his first breaths, and he'd already lost his mother.

But you'll never lose me. Ever.

END OF BOOK THREE

∾

Ready for the next installment in the Blade and Rose series?
The next book in the series is called *Queen of the Shining Sea*
and will be available later this year!

If you'd like to receive news of my upcoming releases and
exclusive bonus content, please sign up for my mailing list at:
http://www.mirandahonfleur.com/court-bonus/

AUTHOR'S NOTE

Thank you for reading *Court of Shadows*, the third book in the Blade and Rose series. If you'd like to find out about new releases, you can sign up for my newsletter at www.mirandahonfleur.com. As a thank-you gift, you will receive "Winter Wren," a prequel short story to the Blade and Rose series, featuring Rielle's first meeting with a certain paladin.

If you enjoyed this book and would like to see more, please consider leaving a review—it really helps me as a new author to know whether people like my work and want to read more of it.

Rielle's adventure continues in *Queen of the Shining Sea*, the fourth book in the Blade and Rose series, due to be released later this year. If you're on my mailing list, keep an eye out for a sneak peek of the first chapter coming soon!

As always, there are people in my life without whom this book wouldn't have been possible. My husband, Tony, has been a constant font of love and support, without whom I couldn't do any of this. And my mom has been my #1 fan, whose encouragement and excitement has made writing an even greater joy for me.

I'd also like to thank my friends at Enclave—Ryan Muree, Katherine Bennet, and Emily Gorman—you all know this book wouldn't be the same without you. Thank you for your friendship, your support, and your occasional but necessary kick in the pants. Thanks also go to my critiquer, Sue Seabury—I appreciate your thoughtful feedback!

And you, my readers. I couldn't do this without you! I love hearing from you, so please feel free to drop me a line on: www.mirandahonfleur.com, Facebook, Twitter, and miri@mirandahonfleur.com. Thank you for reading!

ABOUT THE AUTHOR

I'm a born-and-raised Chicagoan living in Indianapolis. I grew up on fantasy and science-fiction novels, spending nearly as much time in Valdemar, Pern, Tortall, Narnia, and Middle Earth as in reality. I write speculative fiction starring fierce heroines and daring heroes who make difficult choices along their great adventures and dark intrigues, all with generous doses of romance, action, and drama.

When I'm not snarking, writing, or reading my Kindle, I edit professionally, hang out and watch Netflix with my English-teacher husband, and play board games with my friends.

Reach me at:
www.mirandahonfleur.com
miri@mirandahonfleur.com

24067906R00395

Printed in Poland
by Amazon Fulfillment
Poland Sp. z o.o., Wrocław